Barbara … born in Leeds, and by the … umnist on Fle… nan of *Substa*… nd was follow… *Emma's Secret* … sixty-one million … ghty-nine countries and thirty-nine … lives in New York City with her husband, producer Robert Bradford.

By the same author

A WOMAN OF SUBSTANCE
VOICE OF THE HEART
HOLD THE DREAM
ACT OF WILL
TO BE THE BEST
THE WOMEN IN HIS LIFE
REMEMBER
ANGEL
EVERYTHING TO GAIN
DANGEROUS TO KNOW
LOVE IN ANOTHER TOWN
A SECRET AFFAIR
POWER OF A WOMAN
A SUDDEN CHANGE OF HEART
THE TRIUMPH OF KATIE BYRNE
THREE WEEKS IN PARIS
EMMA'S SECRET

BARBARA TAYLOR BRADFORD

Where You Belong

Her Own Rules

Grafton

HarperCollins*Publishers*
77-85 Fulham Palace Road
Hammersmith, London W6 8JB

www.harpercollins.co.uk

This omnibus edition published in 2004
by HarperCollins*Publishers*

These novels are entirely works of fiction. The names, characters and incidents portrayed in them are the work of the author's imagination. Any resemblance to actual persons, living or dead, is entirely coincidental.

ISBN 0 007 71210 3

Set in Sabon by Palimpsest Book Production Limited,
Polmont, Stirlingshire

Printed and bound in Great Britain by
Mackays of Chatham plc, Chatham, Kent

Where You Belong

TO BOB, AS ALWAYS,

WITH ALL MY LOVE

Contents

Part One

A Matter of Integrity

Chapter One

I
KOSOVO, AUGUST 1998

The three of us sat in a small copse at the far end of the village, taking shelter from the blistering heat in the leafy bower, bosky, cool, on this scorching summer's day.

The jeep was parked out on the road nearby, and I peered towards it, frowning slightly, wondering what had happened to Ajet, our adviser, guide, and driver. He had gone on foot to the village, having several days ago arranged to meet an old school friend there, who in turn would take us to see the leaders of the K.L.A. According to Ajet, the Kosovo Liberation Army had their main training camp near the village, and Ajet had assured us in Peć, and then again on the drive here, that the leaders would be in the camp, and that they would be more than willing to have their photographs taken for transmission to newspapers and magazines around the world. 'Everyone should know the truth, should know about our cause, our just and rightful cause,' Ajet had said to us time and again.

When he had left the copse a short while ago he had been smiling cheerfully, happy at the idea of meeting his old friend, and I had watched him step out jauntily as he had walked down the dusty road in a determined and purposeful manner. But that had been over two hours ago, and he had still not returned, and this disturbed me. I could not help wondering if something unforeseen, something bad, had happened to the friendly young Kosovar who had been so helpful to us.

Rising, I walked through the copse and, shading my eyes with my hand, I stood looking down the dirt road. There was no sign of Ajet; in fact, there was very little activity at all. But I waited for a short while, hoping he would appear at any moment.

My name is Valentine Denning, and I'm a New Yorker born and bred, but now I base myself in Paris, where I work as a photojournalist for Gemstar, a well-known international news-photo agency. With the exception of my grandfather, no one in my family ever thought I would become a photojournalist. Grandfather had spotted my desire to record everything I saw when I was a child, and bought me my first camera. My parents never paid much attention to me, and what I would do when I grew up never seemed to cross their minds. My brother Donald, to whom I was much closer in those days and tended to bully since he was younger, was forever after me to become a model; but I'm not pretty enough. Donald kept pointing out that I was tall, slim, with long legs and an athletic build, as if I didn't know my own body. At least I don't look bad in the pictures Jake and Tony have taken of me. But I'm not much into clothes; I like T-shirts, khaki pants, white cotton shirts and bush jackets, workmanlike clothes that are perfect for the life I lead.

I'm thirty-one years old, constantly travelling, living out of a suitcase, and then there are the crazy hours, the lack of comfort, even the most basic of amenities, when I'm on the front lines, covering wars and other disasters, not to mention the danger I often find myself facing. But I prefer this life to walking down a catwalk showing off Paris couture.

Turning away from the road at last, I went back to rejoin Jake Newberg and Tony Hampton, comrades-in-arms, as Tony calls us. I think of these two men as my family; we've worked together for several years now and we're inseparable. Jake is my best friend, and Tony has graduated from best friend to lover in the past year. The three of us go everywhere together, and we always make sure we are on the same assignments for our news-photo agencies.

I gazed at Tony surreptitiously for a moment, thinking how fit and healthy he looked as he sat on part of a felled tree trunk, loading two of his cameras with rolls of new film. Tony, who is Irish, is ten years older than me. Stocky and muscular, he has inherited his mother's Black Irish good looks, and is a handsome and charismatic man. But it's his masculinity, his potent sexuality that women found most appealing, even overwhelming, and certainly irresistible, as I have discovered.

Considered to be one of the world's great war photographers, of the same ilk as the late Robert Capa, he is something of a risk taker when it comes to getting his pictures. This does not unduly worry me, although I know it gives Jake Newberg cause for concern; he has discussed it with me frequently of late.

I eyed Jake, sitting on the grass with his back to a tree, looking nonchalant as he made notes in the small blue leather notebook he always carried with him. Jake is also an American, 'a Jew from Georgia', is the way he likes to describe himself. At thirty-eight, he is also one of the top war photographers, a prize-winner like Tony. I've won many awards myself but I've never attempted to put myself in their league, although Tony and Jake say I belong there, that I'm just as good as they are.

Jake is tall, lean, with a physical toughness about him that makes him seem indestructible – anyway, that is the way I view him. He's an attractive man, with an expressive face, blondish curly hair and the most vivid blue eyes I've ever seen. Yet despite his puckishness and the mischievous twinkle that often glints in those eyes, I long ago discovered that Jake is the most compassionate of men. And I've come to appreciate his understanding of the complexities of the human heart and the human frailties we are all afflicted with.

Tony glanced up as he became aware of me hovering over him. 'What is it?' he asked, frowning slightly. 'Is something wrong?'

'I hope Ajet's all right, Tony, he's been gone –'

'I'm sure he is,' Tony cut in quickly, with a certain firmness, and then he gave me a reassuring smile. 'It's very quiet, peaceful out there, isn't it?'

I nodded. 'There's hardly any sign of life.'

'Doesn't surprise me. I think the village is probably half-deserted by now. It's more than likely that a lot of locals have already left, are moving south ahead of the Serbian army, crossing the border into Albania as fast as they can.'

'You're probably right.' I sat down on the grass and fell silent, ruminating.

Jake glanced at me and then looked thoughtfully at Tony. He said in a brisk tone, 'Let's abandon this shoot, get the hell out of here, Tony. I've got a bad feeling.'

'But we won't get this chance again,' I felt bound to point out, sitting up straighter, staring at Jake.

Ajet suddenly reappeared. He came wandering in from the road looking as if he had no cares in the world. Not only did he seem unperturbed, he actually looked pleased with himself, almost smug.

'Everything's set up,' he announced in his perfect English, learned during the eight years he had lived and worked in Brooklyn, where his uncle and cousin still lived. 'I saw my guy,' he continued, 'I talked to him at length. We drank coffee. He has just closed his shop, gone out to the farmhouse in the fields at the other side of the village. The farmhouse is the K.L.A.'s headquarters now. He is going to bring the top leaders here –' Ajet broke off, looked at his Rolex watch, a cheap copy of the real thing bought on the streets of Manhattan. He nodded to himself and finished, 'One more hour. Yes, in one hour approximately they will come to the village. We will meet them at the shop. Now we relax, we wait here.'

'Good man!' Tony exclaimed, beaming at the young Kosovar. 'And since we've got an hour to kill we should eat. Let's get the bottled water and the sandwiches from the jeep.' Jumping up, Tony started to walk towards the road.

Ajet exclaimed, 'No, no, Tony, please sit down! *Please*. Do not trouble yourself. I will go for the box of sandwiches and the water.'

I murmured, 'I'm not hungry, but I would love some water.'

'No food for me either,' Jake said. 'Just water, like Val.'

The young man hurried off, and I looked at Tony and then at Jake. 'I might go down the road to the village, mosey around a bit. What do you think?'

Jake nodded but made no comment.

Tony walked over to me, took hold of my hand and pulled me up from the grass. 'I don't like you being out of my sight on a shoot like this, Val, especially since we don't really know the lay of the land around here. But I think it's okay, certainly Ajet doesn't appear to be worried. So go for a walk if you want.'

Slipping his arm around my waist, he brought me closer to him, held me in a loving embrace. Against my hair he murmured, 'I'd like to get back to Belgrade tonight, Vee. There's something about your room at the hotel that I find most appealing.'

'It's because I'm in it,' I answered, laughing, and I kissed his cheek. 'At least, that *better* be the reason.'

'You know it is.' Holding me away from him, he smiled, his black eyes dancing, and then almost immediately his expression turned serious. 'When you get down there keep your eyes peeled and stay on the perimeters of the village. That way you can get back here quickly, should it be necessary.'

I leaned into him. 'Don't worry so much, I'll be fine. By the way, I haven't told you today that I love you, have I? But I do.'

'I love you too, Val.'

Ajet came back carrying the cardboard box. After placing it on the rocks, he opened it with a bit of a flourish, and began to hand out the bottles of water, offered us the wrapped sandwiches from the hotel in Peć. He went on fussing around us and behaving as though he were serving us at a grand banquet, and Tony and Jake exchanged amused, knowing looks and laughed.

I had been loading my camera, and I looked from one to the other and asked, 'Am I missing something? What's the joke?'

'No joke,' Tony said, and blew me a kiss.

II

I focused my Leica 35-mm on the ragtag collection of children ahead of me, a short way down the road. There were about five of them in all, sitting together against a ruined wall. As I peered through the lens, I took in their pallor, their haunted expressions, and the fear clouding their innocent young eyes.

A heartbreaking little band, I thought, so forlorn on this bright sunny day. A day for playing. Not a day for war. I repressed a sigh and began taking pictures.

And then the sound of gunfire was breaking the quietness of the afternoon, and I instantly abandoned the shots of the children.

A flurry of unexpected activity had begun to erupt all around me . . . exploding bombs, mortar fire, the rumble of tanks in the distance. Closer by, I heard terrified screams, the sound of running feet, people scattering, seeking safety. And then more screams filled the air, along with the staccato rat-a-tat of machine guns, and guns not so far away at that.

All of my senses were alerted to danger, and my chest tightened, and I sucked in my breath sharply when I saw Tony rushing out of the copse just behind me. I had left him there only a few minutes ago, sitting on the rocks with Jake, eating a sandwich.

Now he was sprinting towards the line of fire.

I raced after him in his wake. And dimly, in the

distance, I heard Jake behind us, shouting, 'Val! Val! Don't follow him, for God's sake. *It's too dangerous.*'

I paid no attention.

Tony was our leader, and as always he was hell-bent on getting the best pictures, whatever war we were covering and no matter what the cost. Taking risks meant nothing to him. He seemed to thrive on danger, as well I knew. Tony was consistently in harm's way, and so were we because of him, although, as he frequently reminded us, we did have a choice of whether or not to follow him into the fray.

Once again, Jake's voice carried to me above the noise of exploding shells and deafening artillery. 'VAL! STOP! Don't follow Tony.'

I did not stop. Nor did I look back. I was hard on Tony's heels, my camera held tightly in my hands, my mind, my entire being, concentrated on one thing: doing my job as professionally as possible and getting the best pictures for the photo agency I worked for.

Leaping forward, Jake now streaked after me and Tony. I realized his warnings of a moment ago had been pushed to one side, indeed probably forgotten altogether. What he always wanted was to reach me, grab hold of me, and pull me out of danger.

Kalashnikovs were spraying bullets from all sides and the shelling was rapidly growing heavier; the summer air was thick with smoke and dust, the smell of cordite mingling with that of blood. And the stench of death was suddenly all pervasive, numbing, and I wished we had never come here.

We had arrived late that morning to take a few simple photographs of the Kosovo Liberation Army's leaders; now, unexpectedly, we found ourselves in the midst of this violent battle between the K.L.A. and Serbian troops. I couldn't help wondering if this was a deadly ambush, a trap we had walked into with our eyes wide open. And where was Ajet? I hoped the young Kosovar had been smart enough to stay in the copse, and that hopefully he had driven the jeep into the trees for safety.

I knew that Serbian troops had been moving south for days, keeping up the deadliest fighting along the way, brutally driving the Kosovars out of their villages and towns. Thousands of terrified civilians were already on the move, a steady stream of humanity being cruelly driven from their homes and homeland, seeking safety across the borders in Albania and Macedonia.

Unexpectedly, a small boy appeared as if from nowhere, and began to totter forward on his thin little legs, heading directly into the line of fire, oblivious to the fighting and the mêlée spinning around him. I saw him out of the corner of my eye, and reacted instantly. Veering to my right, I sped over to the child and threw myself on top of him, all of my instincts compelling me to protect him no matter what.

Bombs continued to explode, and pieces of shrapnel were swirling like deadly snowflakes, although they were much more lethal. I covered the child with my body, put my arms around him, and held him tightly.

He was shaking, and this did not surprise me one bit. I detested the sound of the guns and bombs myself; they were discordant and frightening, and most especially to a small child.

After a moment, I lifted my head and glanced up.

The sky was a perfect cerulean blue, without cloud, and the sun was shining brilliantly. Summer, I thought; I ought to be on vacation with Tony, not spreadeagled on the ground with my face pressed into the dirt in some obscure village in the Balkans.

Small, rubbery legs and arms began to wriggle, eel-like, under me, and I finally rolled off the child, jumped up and pulled him to his feet.

He gazed up at me soulfully with a faint, perplexed smile; I smiled back and gave him a little push towards a young woman who was rushing towards us, calling out something I did not understand. With a nod to me and the words, 'Thank you,' spoken in carefully pronounced but accented English, the young woman grabbed the boy's arm and dragged him away. It was obvious that she was scolding him as the two of them moved away from the shelling and went behind one of the houses on the side of the road.

I was glad to see the child taken to safety; at least I hoped he was safe. Many of the nearby houses and shops had been bombed, had crumbled into heaps of stones and bricks and there were fires flaring everywhere.

Wondering where Tony and Jake were, I glanced around, suddenly saw their backs disappearing down a narrow side street. Immediately I jogged after them, trying to catch up, not wanting to be left behind.

The shelling had now reached a climax and I knew Tony and Jake were heading right into the maelstrom, their cameras poised. I followed them into the fray, but for once, much to my surprise and consternation, I realized I did so against my better judgement. I had to admit to myself that for the first time in my association with Tony and Jake I had certain misgivings about following Tony's lead. A curious sense of foreboding swept over me and this feeling was so unfamiliar, so unprecedented I was startled, and I stopped in my tracks, discovered that for a split-second I was unable to move forward. I was rooted to the spot.

Then the moment I'd had nightmares about, had forever dreaded, was suddenly and frighteningly upon me. Tony was going down, his camera flying out of his hands as he was struck by a stream of bullets. He was thrown backwards by the impact, lay sprawled on the cobbled street, still and unmoving.

'Tony! Tony!' I screamed and began to run to him.

Jake, who was closer, also shouted his name, and went on, 'I'm coming to you, Tony, hang in there!' But the words had hardly left Jake's mouth when he toppled forward, and fell to the ground, hit by a sniper's bullets.

Without giving any thought to my own safety, I pressed on through the curtain of gunfire and shrapnel, heading towards my friends, knowing I must do something to help them, although I was not certain what I *could* do under these horrific circumstances.

Out of breath and panting, I paused momentarily next to Jake, bent over him and gasped, 'How bad are you?'

'I've been hit in my leg and hip but I'm okay, don't worry about me. It's Tony I'm concerned about.'

'Me too,' I muttered and sprinted away. When I reached Tony I dropped to my knees next to him. 'Darling, it's me.' As I spoke I moved a strand of black hair away from his damp forehead and stared down into his face.

Finally he opened his eyes. 'Go, Val. Find cover. Dangerous here,' he told me in a low, strangled voice.

'I'm not going to leave you,' I answered, looking him over swiftly. I was appalled at his gunshot wounds, and I felt myself filling with dread. He had been hit in his chest, his shoulder and his legs, and other parts of his body as well, as far as I could make out. I was frightened and alarmed by all the blood; he was covered in it, as if he had been riddled with bullets. Oh God, oh God, he might not make it. I swallowed the cry that rose in my throat. It took all my self-control not to break down; I leaned over him, brought my face close to his. 'I'm not leaving you, Tony,' I repeated, endeavouring to keep my voice as steady as possible.

'Go,' he whispered. Summoning all of his strength, he managed to say, 'Get out. For me.' His voice was very shaky.

Realizing that Tony was becoming unduly agitated by my continuing presence, and knowing that I must try to find help for both men, I finally acquiesced. 'All right, I'll go,' I murmured against Tony's face. I stroked his cheek. 'Just stay calm, lie still. I won't be long. I'll be back with help very soon.'

I kissed him lightly and began to crawl away on my hands and knees, keeping low and close to the ground in an effort to dodge the flying bullets. I was making for a small building nearby, one of the few which remained standing, and I had almost reached it when I felt the impact of a bullet slamming into my thigh. I slumped down in a heap, wincing in pain and clutching my Leica to my chest. Then I glanced down at my thigh; blood was already oozing through my khaki pants, and it occurred to me that I wasn't going to be much use to either Tony or Jake.

Turning my head, I glanced over at Jake. 'How're you doing?'

'Okay. Are you hurt very badly, Val?'

'I don't think so,' I replied and hoped this was really the case. Although deep down I was fairly certain it wasn't, I nevertheless had a need to reassure Jake.

He asked over the battery of noise, 'What about Tony?'

'He's not good,' I said, and my voice wobbled. 'He's terribly shot up and in need of medical attention, urgent need of it, and much more than we are. I saw a Red Cross ambulance up on the ridge over there; let's hope the medics get here quickly. Tony's losing masses of blood . . .' I swallowed. 'It's . . . it's touch and go with him . . . I think . . .'

For a moment Jake could not speak. He was obviously distressed by my words. At last he said, 'Tony's going to be all right, Val. He's tough, and don't forget he's always said he has the luck of the Irish.'

'He also says he's blessed by the saints,' I replied tensely. 'I hope he's right.'

Jake called back, 'Just keep cool, hang in there, honey.'

I could hardly hear him. His words were almost but not quite drowned out by the explosions and the thunder of mortar fire, which seemed to be closer than ever. In a few minutes troops were swarming everywhere, both the K.L.A. and the Serbians; they were filling the village, running through the streets, fighting. I wasn't sure who was who. I looked for distinguishing emblems on their uniforms but without success, then remembered that those who wore the black paratrooper berets were the Kosovars. They seemed to be outnumbered. I closed my eyes, hoping I would be taken for dead, and overlooked. I knew there was no longer any possibility of dragging myself over to Tony. My spirit was more than willing, but I was just too weak physically, and the troops were converging now.

So I resigned myself to wait for the Red Cross ambulance I had seen not long ago. Surely it would drive down into the village soon. Putting my hand under my T-shirt I found the gold chain on which I'd hung Tony's ring. He had given it to me only a couple of weeks ago, when we had been in Paris together. Suddenly tears were dangerously close to the surface as memories of those happy days rushed back to flood my mind.

My fingers closed around the ring. I began to pray: Oh God, please let Tony be all right. Please don't let him die. Please, please, let him live. I went on praying silently and the fighting raged on around me unabated.

III

White light, very bright white light, was invading my entire being, or so it seemed to me. I was suffused in the bright white light until I became part of it; I was no longer myself, but the light . . .

I opened my eyes and blinked rapidly. The light was bright, harsh, startling, and I felt disoriented. And for a moment I thought I had not really woken up, but was still in my dream, living the dream. As I blinked again, came slowly awake, I wondered where I was; still somewhat disoriented, I glanced around in puzzlement. The white walls and ceiling and the white tile floor, in combination with the brilliant sunlight flooding through the windows, created a dazzling effect . . . echoing the bright white light that had dominated my strange and haunting dream.

Shifting slightly in the bed, I winced as a sharp pain shot up my thigh, and immediately I remembered everything. Of course, I was in a hospital room. In Belgrade. After the three of us had been shot, we had subsequently been rescued by the Red Cross and patched up by the doctors on a temporary basis, so that we could travel. We had then been taken to Peć, in the ambulance I had seen in the village when the fighting had first started.

Jake and I had not been as seriously injured as Tony, who had been badly shot up and was in critical condition, having lost a lot of blood. Fortunately, the medics in Peć had been able to give him a blood transfusion before the three of us had been flown out.

Details of the flight came back to me as my mind finally began to clear. Tony had been on a stretcher in the transport plane, and I had sat next to him all the way, holding his hand, talking to him, begging him to keep fighting. The medics were hopeful he would pull through; they had told me and Jake that Tony had a better than average chance of making it. He had slept through most of the flight while Jake and I had kept a vigil by his side; our hopes had soared as we had headed towards Belgrade because he was holding his own so well.

But when *was* the flight? Yesterday? The day before? Or even earlier than that?

Glancing at my wrist, expecting to see the time, I discovered I was not wearing my watch. My eyes strayed to the utilitarian metal nightstand, but it was not there either. The top of the stand was entirely empty.

I pushed aside the bedclothes, and, moving gingerly, inched myself into an upright position, and then manoeuvred my body onto the edge of the bed. My bandaged thigh was still quite sore from the gunshot wound but I managed, nevertheless, to stand up, and I was surprised and relieved to discover that I was relatively steady on my feet, and had only the smallest amount of discomfort when I walked.

In the cramped bathroom attached to the hospital room, I ran cold water into the sink and splashed my face with it, patted myself dry with a paper towel and peered into the mirror. My reflection didn't please me. I looked lousy, done in. But then what else could I expect? My pallor was unusual – normally I have such good colour – and there were violet smudges under my eyes.

Moving slowly, I made it back to the bed, where I sat on the edge, fretting about Tony and Jake, and wondering what to do next. My main concern was Tony. Where the hell was he in this hospital? And where was Jake? My clothes had apparently been taken away, and since I was wearing only a skimpy cotton hospital gown, tied at the back, I couldn't very well go wandering around the hospital in search of them. My eyes scanned the room for a phone. There wasn't one.

A sudden loud knocking on the door startled me and I glanced towards it just as it was pushed open, and Jake, heavily bandaged and supporting himself on a pair of crutches, hobbled in. He was unshaven and looked crumpled in hospital-issue pyjamas and an equally creased cotton robe.

'Hi,' he said, and propping the crutches against the wall near the nightstand, he half-hopped, half-limped to the bed, where he sat down next to me. 'How're you doing, Val?'

'Well I'm obviously not going dancing *ce soir*,' I said, glancing down at my bandaged thigh which bulged under the cotton gown and then at him. 'I'll give you a raincheck tomorrow. And you seem to be doing okay with your balancing act on those crutches.'

He nodded.

'How's Tony? Have you seen him yet? Where is he? When can I go and see him?' I asked, my questions urgent, tumbling out of my mouth anxiously.

Jake did not answer me.

I stared at him.

He gazed back at me, still not saying a word.

I saw how pale he was, and haggard-looking, and noticed that his bright blue eyes were clouded, blood-shot, as if he'd been crying. Inside I began to shrivel, scorched by an innate knowledge I dare not admit existed. But it did. *Oh yes.*

Jake cleared his throat and looked at me intently.

My heart dropped. I knew instinctively what he was going to say; an awful sense of dread took me in its stranglehold, and I felt my throat closing. Clasping my hands tightly together, I braced myself for bad news.

'I'm afraid Tony didn't make it, Val darling,' Jake said at last, his tone low, almost inaudible. And final. 'He'd become far too weakened before we arrived here, and he'd lost such a great deal of blood initially –' Jake paused when his voice broke, but eventually he went on, 'It's devastating . . . I never thought it could happen, I –' Very abruptly, he stopped again and, unable to continue, he said nothing more, simply sat there helplessly, gazing at me, shaking his head. His sorrow was reflected in his face, which was grey, bereft.

I was speechless. Finally I opened my mouth to speak but no words came out. There was a long, silent scream echoing through my brain and I snapped my eyes shut, wishing I could block it out, wishing I could steady myself. Instead I fell apart, began to shake uncontrollably as shock engulfed me.

I felt Jake's strong arms encircling me, and I clung to him, sobbed against his shoulder. Jake wept also, and we held onto each other for a long time. And together we mourned the tragic loss of a man we both loved who had died before his time.

Chapter Two

I
PARIS, SEPTEMBER

I have always loved my apartment on the Left Bank where I've lived for the last seven years. It is spacious, light and airy, with six large windows in its three main rooms, all of which are of good proportions. These rooms open onto each other, and this *enfilade* gives it a lovely, flowing feeling which appeals to my sense of order and symmetry, traits inherited from my grandfather, who was an architect.

But ever since my return from Belgrade in August, I've been experiencing an overwhelming feeling of claustrophobia, one which I am still finding hard to dispel. Although I can't quite understand why I should feel this way, every day I have the constant need to flee my apartment as soon as I awaken.

It's not that it holds any heart-wrenching memories of Tony, because it doesn't. Friends for a long time though we were, we did not become emotionally involved with each other until twelve months ago; besides which, he hardly ever spent any time at my place, being constantly on the move for work, or in London where he lived.

I was aware that my urge to get out had more to do with my own innermost feelings of despair than anything else; I've been unnaturally agitated inside and filled with a weird restlessness which propels me into the street, as early as dawn sometimes.

The streets of Paris are my solace, and part of my healing process physically in a very real sense. Firstly, the constant walking every day is therapeutic because it strengthens my damaged leg; secondly, being outside in the open air, amongst crowds of people bustling about their business, somehow soothes my troubled soul, lifts my spirits and helps to diminish my depression.

Today, as usual, I got up early. After coffee and a croissant at my local café on the corner, I set off at a steady pace, taking my long daily walk. It's become a ritual for me, I suppose, something I find so very necessary. At least for the time being. Soon I hope my leg will be completely healed so that I can return to work.

It was a Friday morning in the middle of September, a lovely, mild day. The ancient buildings were already acquiring a burnished sheen in the bright sunlight, and the sky was an iridescent blue above their gleaming rooftops. It was a golden day, filled with crystalline light, and a soft breeze blew across the river Seine. My heart lifted with a little rush of pleasure, and for a moment grief was held at bay.

Paris is the only place I've ever wanted to live, for as long as I can remember; I fell in love with it as a child when I first came on a trip with my grandparents, Cecelia and Andrew Denning. I used to tell Tony that it was absolutely essential to my well being, and if Jake happened to be present he would nod, agreeing, and pointing out that he lived here for the same reason as I did.

I always thought it odd that Tony would merely frown, looking baffled, as if he didn't understand what I meant. Tony was born in London and it was there that he lived all his life. And whenever the three of us would have this discussion about the merits of the two cities, he would laugh and shake his head. 'London is essential to me because it's a man's city,' he would remark, and wink at Jake.

I had supposed he was alluding to those very British private clubs for men filled with old codgers reading *The Times*, the male-dominated pubs, cricket at Lord's, football at Wembley, and Savile Row tailors who appealed to his desire for sartorial elegance when not on the battlefront covering wars. He had never really discussed it in depth, but then he had been like that about a lot of things, an expert at brushing certain matters aside if he didn't want to talk about them.

Thoughts of Tony intruded, swamped me, instantly washing away the mood of a few moments ago, when I had felt almost happy again. I came to a stop abruptly, leaned against the wall of a building, taking deep breaths, willing the sudden surge of anguish to go away. Eventually it became less acute, and taking control of my swimming senses I walked on purposefully.

It struck me as being rather odd, the way I vacillated between bouts of mind-boggling pain at his loss and the most savage attacks of anger.

There were those tear-filled days when I believed I would never recover from his death, which had been so sudden, so tragic, when grief was like an iron mantle weighing me down, bringing me to my knees. At these times it seemed that my sorrow was unendurable.

Miraculously, though, my heartbreak would inexplicably wash away quite unexpectedly, and I would feel easier within myself, in much better spirits altogether, and I was glad of this respite from pain, this return to normality. I was almost like my old self.

It was then that the anger usually kicked in with a vengeance, shaking me with its intensity. I was angry because Tony was dead when he should have been alive, and I blamed him for his terrible recklessness, the risks he had taken in Kosovo, risks which had ultimately cost him his life. Unnecessary risks, in my opinion.

Destiny, I thought, and came to a halt. As I stood there in the middle of the street frowning to myself, I suddenly understood with the most stunning rush of clarity that if character is destiny then it had been Tony's fate to die in the way he had. Because of his character . . . and who and what he was as a man.

II

After crossing the Place Saint-Michel, I made my way towards the Rue de la Huchette, and walked down that narrow street, which long ago had been immortalized in a book by the American writer Elliot Paul, very aptly entitled *A Narrow Street*. After reading the book, I had been drawn to this particular area of Paris, and for the three years I was a student at the Sorbonne I had lived right here in a quaint little hotel called the Mont Blanc.

The hotel came into my line of vision almost immediately, and as I strolled past I glanced up at the room which had been mine, and remembered those days in a swirl of unexpected nostalgia.

Thirteen years ago now. Not so long really. But in certain ways they seemed far, far away, light years away, those youthful days when things had been infinitely simpler in my life.

So much had happened to me in the intervening years; I had lived a lifetime in them, and I had become a woman. A grown-up woman, mature and experienced.

Glancing across the street, I eyed the El Djazier, the North African restaurant which had once been my local hangout . . . what an habitué I had been of that strange little nightspot full of colourful characters.

Sandy Lonsdale, an English writer who had lived in the hotel at the same time as me, had constantly predicted I would disappear one night, never to be seen again, whipped off to some disreputable brothel in Casablanca or Tangier by one of the seedy blokes who lurked in the restaurant most nights.

But of course that had never happened, the seedy blokes being perfectly innocuous in reality, and I had taken enormous pleasure in teasing Sandy about his vivid imagination and its tendency to work overtime. 'You'll make a great novelist,' I used to tell him, and he had merely grinned at me and retorted, 'You'd better be right about that.'

On numerous occasions I had taken Tony and Jake there, and they had enjoyed it as much as me, their taste buds tantalized by the *couscous* and other piquant Moroccan dishes, not to mention the erotic belly dancers in their flimsy costumes and tinkling ankle bracelets.

On these evenings, when we were back in Paris for a bit of relaxation and rest from covering wars, Jake would usually invite us to one of the jazz joints after dinner at the El Djazier. There were several spots on the Rue de la Huchette, where many of the greats of American jazz came to play or listen to others play.

Jake was a jazz aficionado and could happily spend long hours in these smoke-filled places, sipping a cognac and tapping his foot, lost in the music, lost to the world for a short while.

I ambled up the street, and glanced around as I walked. I never tired of wandering around this particular part of Paris, which I knew so well from my student days. It was full of picturesque cobblestone streets, ancient buildings, Greek and North African restaurants, art galleries and small shops selling colourful wares from some of the most exotic places in the world. Aside from anything else, it brought back memories of the time I had attended the Sorbonne, such a happy time for me, perhaps the happiest of my life.

III

My grandfather Andrew Denning had been alive when I decided I wanted to study in Paris. Later, he had often come here to visit me, defying my mother, who had forbidden any contact between us once I had made the decision. My mother was angry with me because I had chosen to study in France, although I never understood her attitude, since she had been indifferent to me from the day I was born. So why did it matter where I studied?

Grandfather Denning didn't have much time for his daughter-in-law; in fact he privately thought she was a cold, unfeeling woman, and he had never paid any attention to what she said. He had reminded her that I was the only daughter of his only son, and his only female grandchild, and he was damned if he would let anyone stand in the way of his visiting me whenever he wished to do so. As an afterthought, he had added in no uncertain terms, that no one told him what to do or how to spend his money, least of all his son's wife. And that had been that apparently. Grandfather had told me all about it later; we kept no secrets from each other. I thought of him as being more like a pal than a grandfather, perhaps because he was so young in appearance and had the most youthful of spirits.

To my mother's great consternation and frustration, she had not been able to influence him one iota, let alone control him, and she had apparently ranted and raved about her father-in-law for months after their original confrontation. This I had heard from my brother, the family gossip, who only reinforced my opinion of him when he became the sidekick to a gossip columnist. According to Donald, my mother had screamed blue murder, but my father had, as was customary, remained totally mute. For years I suspected that this state of being had afflicted Father since the day he entered into so-called wedded bliss with Margot Scott. Until the day he died he hardly ever said a word, perhaps because he couldn't get one in edgewise.

It was my grandfather who supported me financially and morally, once I had decided to study in Paris, and in those days he had been my best friend, my only friend.

My mother had never forgiven him, or me for that

matter. But then I believe my mother has never forgiven me for being born, although I don't know why this should be so. From that day to this she has never shown me any love or given me much thought. It is not that Margot Scott Denning doesn't like children; everyone knows she dotes on my sibling, Donald the Great, as I used to call him when we were children. It is I she has an aversion to, whom she tends to avoid whenever she possibly can.

Grandfather and I were always aware of that, and he had often expressed concern about the situation. I had taught myself not to care. I still don't. He has been dead for five years now, and I still miss him. He gave me the only sense of family I ever had; certainly my parents never managed to induce that sentiment in me. Quite the opposite. I wished Grandfather were here with me now, walking these streets; I always found such comfort in his loving words, his understanding, his kindness and his wisdom. He was the only person, other than Grandma and Tony, who had loved me. Now all three of them were gone.

Was that the reason I had chosen to walk around this particular area today? Because he had been so partial to it, and because it made my happy memories of him and of our time spent together here so vivid in my mind's eye? Perhaps . . .

'Teaching you Paris,' Grandfather used to say as he took me around the different *arrondissements* of the city. Gradually, I had come to learn about many of the great buildings, the architects who had brought them into being, the historical significance of each one, not to mention the many different architectural highlights.

When I reached the top of the Rue de la Huchette, I crossed into the Rue de la Bûcherie, which was more like an open square than a street. It had flower-filled little gardens fronting onto cafés lined up along one side of the square, and overshadowing them was the Cathedral of Notre Dame. This magnificent edifice outlined against the azure September sky stood on the Île de la Cité, one of the islands in the Seine, and on the spur of the moment I decided to go over to the cathedral. I had not visited it in years. In fact, the last time I had been there had been with my grandfather.

Andrew Denning had enjoyed an extremely successful career as an architect in New York, and he had had an extraordinary eye for beautiful buildings, whether modern or ancient. In particular, he had been an admirer of the cathedrals of Europe, forever marvelling at their majesty and grandeur, the soaring power inherent in them and in their design and structure.

And so whenever he came to visit me in Paris he made a point of taking me on excursions to see some of his favourites . . . Rouen and Chartres in France, and, across the English Channel, St Paul's and Winchester; and, up in Yorkshire, Ripon Cathedral and York Minster, the latter being my own favourite. It is from my grandfather that I have inherited my eye which serves me so well as a photographer; that's what I think anyway, and as it happens I've also grown to love cathedrals as much as he did.

Within minutes I was across the bridge and standing in front of the three huge portals that lead into Notre Dame. I chose to enter through the one on the right because the door stood ajar, beckoning to me, I thought.

Once inside I caught my breath and stood perfectly still . . . I was utterly mesmerized. I had forgotten how awe-inspiring this place was, with its beauty and size; and its absolute stillness overwhelmed me.

There were hardly any tourists this morning, the cathedral was practically empty, and as I began to slowly walk down the centre aisle my footsteps echoed hollowly against the stone floor.

Glancing up, I gaped at the apse, that enormous, intricate, domed ceiling, flung so high it seemed to disappear into infinity. 'Soaring up to heaven', Grandfather used to say of it.

He and I had visited many of the smaller churches in Paris and the surrounding countryside, and we had taken part in the services as best we were able. We both spoke enough French to follow the Catholic service; being Protestant, we were not exactly familiar with the rituals, but somehow we managed. We also made trips to other European countries, as well as North Africa and Israel, where we visited mosques and synagogues. Grandfather was fascinated by places of worship whatever the religion being practised in them.

I heard his voice reverberating in my head: 'It doesn't

matter whose house you sit in, Val, as long as you love God,' he had once remarked to me. 'In my Father's house there are many mansions: if it were not so I would have told you. I go to prepare a place for you.' With those words of St John's Gospel ringing in my ears, I continued down the aisle and took a chair, sat staring up at the high altar in front of me.

Sunlight was filtering in through the many windows above the altar. It was a light that subtly changed colour as it seeped in through the stained-glass panes in those breathtaking windows, changing from blue to green to pearl, and then to a soft yellow and a lovely lambent rose.

It was the most tranquil light which seemed to tremble visibly on the air, and dust motes rose up into the shafts of sunlight. The peacefulness was a balm, and how cool it was within these thick and ancient stone walls. Cool, restful, restorative, a welcome refuge, far away from the turbulence and violence of the world I lived in when I was working.

I closed my eyes, let myself fall down into myself, and eventually, as was inevitable in this quiet place of worship, I began to think of Tony, of his death, and of the future. And I asked myself yet again, for the umpteenth time, how I was going to go on without him, how I would manage without him by my side. I had no answers.

It seemed to me that all of my energy ebbed away, leaving me deflated, and I just sat there collapsed in the chair, with my eyes closed, for the longest time. I had no appointments, nowhere to go, no one waiting for me or worrying where I was. Time passed. And after a long while, just sitting there in the silence of the cathedral, I heard my grandfather speaking to me as if from a great distance. His voice was so very clear when he said, 'Always remember this, Val, God never gives us a burden that is too heavy to carry.'

IV

The phone was ringing loudly as I let myself into my apartment an hour later. I snatched it up and exclaimed, 'Hullo?' only to hear the receiver clattering down at the other end.

Too late, I got it on the last ring, and sticking out my good leg I slammed the front door shut with my foot. Swinging around, I went into my tall, narrow kitchen, a place I'd always enjoyed but which I had not occupied very much of late. I like cooking, in fact it's a sort of hobby of mine, a way to be creative, to relax when I'm back from covering wars and the like. But because of my grief and misery I had abandoned the kitchen, having no desire to be in it to cook only for myself.

I had hardly eaten a thing these last few weeks, and I had lost weight. But suddenly, today, I felt really hungry and I opened the refrigerator, frowned at the contents, or rather the lack of them, and swiftly closed the door in frustration. Of course there was nothing worthwhile to eat in there: I hadn't been shopping. I would have to make do with a mug of green tea and a couple of cookies, and later I would go to the corner store and pick up a few things for dinner.

A moment or two after I'd put the kettle on, the phone began to shrill once again, and I lurched towards it, grabbed hold of it before the caller had a chance to hang up. As I spoke I heard Jake's voice at the other end.

'Where've you been all day?' He sounded both put out and worried at the same time.

'Walking. I've been out walking, Jake.'

'Again. I can't believe it. I bet if someone locked you up in an empty room and told you to draw a detailed map of Paris and its environs, you could do so without batting an eyelid. And all from memory.'

'Yes, I guess I could. But you do a lot of walking, too, so why are you picking on me?'

'I'm not. I called to invite you to dinner tonight. I haven't seen you for a week. Too long, Val.'

'True, and I'd love to have dinner. I'll cook for you,' I said. Hearing his voice had instantly cheered me up. I'd missed him whilst he had been in the south; anyway, he was my biggest fan when it came to my culinary skills.

'That's a great offer, but I'd prefer to take you out . . . it's much more relaxing for you.'

'Okay, it's a deal.'

Jake cleared his throat several times and his voice was a bit more subdued when he added, 'I had a call from London today. From Tony's photo agency. About a memorial service for him. They've planned one and they want us to come.'

This news so startled me, so threw me off balance, I was rendered silent, and when I finally did speak all I could manage was a weak, 'Oh.'

'We have to go, Val.'

'I'm not sure . . . I don't think I'm up to it,' I began, and faltered, unable to continue.

'We were his closest friends,' Jake countered. 'His intimates. His comrades-in-arms, he called us.'

'We were, I know, but it's hard for me.'

Jake fell silent, then after a moment or two, he said softly, 'The whole world is aware that we were with him in Kosovo when he was killed . . . that *we* came out alive. How will it look to the world if we don't show?'

I stood there gripping the receiver, utterly mute, as if I'd been struck dumb, shaking like the proverbial leaf as I weighed the odds. Should I risk Jake's disapproval, everyone's disapproval, by not going? Or should I go and expose myself to a large amount of pain and heartache? And could I handle that? I just didn't know. For weeks I had tried very hard to get my turbulent feelings under control, and I was not so sure I could face a memorial service. Not now. It would open up so much and it would just . . . do me in emotionally.

'Are you still there, Val?' Jake asked, cutting into my swirling thoughts.

'Yes.'

'You seem reluctant to go.'

'I'm not . . . I'm just . . . thinking it through.'

He said nothing. I could hear him waiting at the other end of the line, could practically hear him breathing.

Finally, realizing he was waiting for me to say something, I muttered, 'I couldn't bear to hear the world eulogizing him . . . It would be so painful for me, I'd be in floods of tears through the entire service. I'm trying to come to grips with my grief.'

'I understand what you're saying. If you want to know the truth, I'm not so keen to live through it myself. But we don't have a choice. And Tony would want us to be present.'

'I guess he would . . .' My voice trailed off.

'We'll talk about it tonight.'

'All right,' I agreed, my heart sinking.

'Good girl. I'll be there about eight to pick you up. See ya, Kid.'

He had hung up before I could say another word, and for a second or two I stood there clutching the receiver, chastizing myself under my breath. I was so dumb. Absolutely stupid. I ought to have realized that Tony's agency would hold a memorial service for their fallen colleague. One who had been their biggest star. And their hero. If only I'd thought it through properly, and earlier, I would have been far better prepared. But as it was I'd spent the last six weeks grieving for him, feeling sorry for myself, and getting angry at him and the world in general.

I banged the receiver into the cradle and stared at the kettle absently, thinking it was taking a long time to boil. I turned up the gas automatically, and let out a heavy sigh. I'd been caught off guard. And now there was no way out. I would have to go to the memorial service for appearance's sake. And I could easily come face to face with *her*.

That was it, of course. That was at the root of my discomfort and reluctance to go to the memorial. I didn't want to run into Fiona Hampton. Tony's ex-wife. It struck me then that it was unlikely she would be there, in view of their recent divorce and the searing bitterness which had existed between them. Of course she wouldn't go to hear him lovingly eulogized by his friends and colleagues. That would be out of character. She was a hard woman whose contentiousness had driven him away from her and the marriage, and sympathy and compassion did not exist in her makeup.

Remembering how unpleasant things had been between them convinced me I was right, and eased my anxiety about going myself. I made a mug of green tea, took out a packet of cookies and stood at the counter munching on a couple and sipping the tea, suddenly feeling more relaxed.

Of course I had no way of knowing that indeed Fiona would attend the memorial, and that meeting her would change my life irrevocably, and so profoundly it would never be the same again.

Chapter Three

1

After my long morning walks through the streets I always felt tired in the afternoons, and invariably had to rest. Today was no exception; in fact, I felt more fatigued than usual. I went through into my bedroom, took off my cotton trousers and shirt, slipped into a dressing gown and lay down on the bed.

My head had barely touched the pillow when the phone next to my ear shrilled loudly. I reached for it, and pushed myself up on the pillows as I said, 'Hullo?'

'It's me, Val,' Mike Carter announced in his warm, affectionate midwest voice. He was the head of the Paris bureau of Gemstar, one of the founders actually, and a very old, very dear friend. 'How're you feeling, honey?'

'I'm fine, Mike, thanks. A lot better. Well, coping at least. What's happening?'

'Oh just the usual stuff . . . . you know, wars,

terrorist attacks, hijackings, serial murders, famine, earthquakes, floods. Disasters by the cartload, in other words.' He laughed, but it was a hollow laugh. 'I guess one day the world will blow itself up, but in the meantime, what's happening is what I call the small stuff.' He chuckled again, in that macabre way of his, and asked, 'Know what I mean?'

'I do,' I answered, laughing with him. Mike's black sense of humour appealed to me, as did his penchant for practical jokes. But these things aside, he had always been my strongest ally, a great supporter of mine ever since I'd joined the agency seven years ago. Over the years a close friendship had developed between us. My grandfather had been very taken with him, and Mike had been smitten in much the same way, and the two had remained good friends until the day Grandfather died.

Mike went on, 'I'm not calling to lure you back into the fray, Val. Whenever you want, come on in. But take as much time as you need. It's your call. We all understand how you feel, me most especially.'

'I know that. Maybe in a couple of weeks,' I murmured, and surprised myself with this answer. Two weeks was not so far away; I'd actually planned on taking three months off, and here I was shortening it. I was amazed at my unexpected response to him.

'Well, that's great!' Mike was exclaiming down the wire. 'You're sorely missed around here. But listen, sweetie, the reason I called is because Qemal, the brother of Ajet, got in touch with the agency today.

He asked for *you*, so he was put through to me. He wanted you to know that Ajet's safe. In Macedonia.'

'I'm so glad to hear that!' I cried, genuinely relieved and pleased to have news of the young Kosovar at last. What had happened to him, what his fate had been, had troubled me and Jake for weeks. When we'd attempted to reach his brother there was never any reply at his Paris apartment. 'Jake and I thought Ajet had been killed, Mike,' I explained. 'Where has he been all these weeks? Did his brother say?'

'Yes, he told me Ajet had been wounded the day he was with you outside Peć. Apparently he left the wood where he was waiting for you with the jeep, once the fighting started. He actually went looking for the three of you, but he was shot before he could make contact. He was left for dead in the streets, but later he was rescued by some of the locals. They went out into the countryside a couple of days later and found soldiers from the K.L.A., who were able to get medical help for Ajet. The Kosovar soldiers then took him to Albania, God help him; I've heard the hospital conditions there are primitive. Eventually Ajet got to Macedonia, although his brother didn't say how. You'd written the agency number on a bit of paper and given it to him, and the kid kept it. He asked Qemal to let us know he was safe. He especially wanted you to know that, Val.'

'I'm glad he's safe, and recovered. It was a fluke he made it.'

'I know, I know. Everything's in the lap of the

gods in the long run. That's my belief, at any rate. As Bogie once said, it's a cockeyed world we live in.' Mike half sighed, half coughed, and hurried on, 'I gotta go, honey. Let's talk next week, or when you feel like it. I'm here if you need me, whenever you need me, day or night. Just give me a shout and I'll be there.'

'Thanks, Mike, for everything, and especially for caring about me, and for your friendship . . .' I found myself choking up and left the sentence unfinished.

'Feel better soon,' he murmured into the phone.

We hung up and I lay back against the pillows. Mike Carter was one of the good guys, one of the best, and he'd seen it all. After knocking around the world as a photojournalist, he and several of his colleagues had founded Gemstar, an agency very similar to Magnum which had been started years before, in the late 1940s, by Robert Capa.

When Mike's beloved wife Sarah had been killed in a freak automobile accident outside Paris, he had given himself a desk job at Gemstar in order to stay put so that he could bring up his two young children himself, with the help of a nanny. He was no stranger to sudden death, to unspeakable loss. And grief and sorrow were old companions of his, as I well knew. But he somehow managed to hide his pain behind the gruff heartiness and a genuine warmth. Still, I knew how much he had suffered after Sarah's unexpected and untimely death ten years ago.

Now my thoughts turned to Ajet and that fateful

day near Peć, the memory of it still terribly vivid in my mind. Almost immediately, I pushed the violent images away, smothered them. I closed my eyes, needing desperately to sleep. That was the ultimate refuge from heartache, and now I craved it. Very simply I wanted to blot out everything, everyone, the whole damn world.

II

I must have dozed off and slept for a very long time, because when I awakened with a start the room was no longer filled with the bright sunlight of early afternoon.

Grey shadows lurked everywhere, curled around the bookshelves and the big Provençal armoire, slid across the ceiling and spilled down onto the walls.

The overwhelming greyness gave my normally cheerful bedroom a gloomy look, and involuntarily I shivered. Someone walked over my grave, I thought, as gooseflesh speckled my arms, and then I couldn't help wondering why I'd thought of that particular and rather morbid analogy.

Glancing at the bedside clock, I saw that it was almost six. I couldn't believe I'd been asleep for over four hours. Slipping off the bed I went and looked out of the big bay window.

The beautiful Paris sky of earlier was cloud-filled now and darkening rapidly, the sunny blue entirely obscured. Rain threatened. Perhaps there would be a storm. I turned on the lamp which stood on the *bureau plat*, and sudden bright light flooded across the photograph of Tony in its silver frame. It had been taken by Jake last year when we had been on vacation together in southern France. I stared down at it for a long moment, and then I turned away, filled with sadness.

Sometimes I couldn't bear to look at it. He was so full of life in this particular shot, his hair blowing in the wind, his teeth very white and gleaming in his tanned face, those merry black eyes narrowed against the sunlight as he squinted back at the camera.

Tony stood on the deck of the sloop on which we were sailing that vacation, the white sails above him billowing out in the breeze. How carefree he looked, bare-chested in his white tennis shorts. A man in his prime, obviously loving that he was so virile. You could see this just by looking at the expression on his face, the wide, confident smile on his mouth.

I sighed under my breath and reached out to steady myself against the desk, and then I moved slowly across the floor, retreating from the window area.

His son Rory had taken possession of Tony's body once it had arrived in England, and the boy had taken it on to Ireland. To County Wicklow. There Tony had been buried next to his parents.

Rory would be at the memorial service, wouldn't he?

That question hovered around in my head for a

moment. Of course he would. And so perhaps I would finally get to meet the son Tony had had such pride in and loved so much.

I lay down on the bed again, and curled up in a ball, thoughts of Tony uppermost once more. Absently I twisted his ring on my finger, then glanced down at it. A wide gold band, Grecian in design, set with aquamarines.

'The colour of your eyes,' he'd said the day he'd chosen it, not so long ago. 'They're not blue, not grey, not green, but pale, pale turquoise. You have sea eyes, Val, eyes the colour of the sea.'

Pushing my face in the pillow, I forced back the tears which were welling suddenly.

'Mavourneen mine,' I heard him whisper against my cheek, and I sighed again as I felt his hand touching my face, my neck, and then smoothing down over my breast . . .

Snapping my eyes wide open, I sat up with a jolt, got off the bed and hurried into the bathroom. Pressing my face against the glass wall of the shower stall, I told myself I must pull myself together, must stop thinking about him in *that* way . . . stop thinking about him sexually. I've got to get over him, he's not coming back. He's dead. And buried. Gone from this life. But I knew I couldn't help myself. I knew that his memory would be always loitering in my mind, lingering in my heart. Haunting me.

III

I took off my dressing gown and the rest of my clothes and stepped into the shower, let the hot water sluice down over my body, and then I dumped loads of shampoo on top of my head and thoroughly washed my hair.

After stepping out of the shower and towelling myself dry, I wrapped a smaller towel in a turban around my head. And then I examined my wound. I did this every day. There was a funny puckering around it, but that would go away eventually; that's what my doctor here in Paris had told me.

I'd been very fortunate, he'd explained when I'd first gone to see him, in that the bullet had missed muscle and bone, and gone right through flesh. Where it had exited, it had left a gaping hole originally, and the main problem for the doctors in Belgrade had been picking out the bits of cloth from my clothes which had been blown into the open wound. They had apparently done an excellent job, according to Dr Bitoun, and I had healed well.

There was no question about it in my mind, luck had been running with me that day. Just as it had with Jake. The two of us had somehow been protected.

IV

The storm broke as I finished dressing.

Thunder and lightning rampaged across the sky, and I turned on additional lights in my bedroom before going through into the living room.

A master switch controlled all of the lamps in there, and a second after I'd hit it with my finger the room was bathed in a lambent glow. I glanced around, my eyes taking in everything.

Although I knew this room so well, it always gave me pleasure whenever I looked at it. My grandfather had put it together, had created the decorative scheme, and his choices in furniture, all gifts from him to me, had been superb. Even the lamps and paintings had been his selections, and the room had a cohesion and a quiet beauty that was very special.

Janine, the wonderfully efficient and motherly Frenchwoman who looked after the apartment, and me when I was in it, had been very visible all day yesterday. She had cleaned and polished and fussed around in general, and had even arrived bearing a lovely gift . . . the masses of pink roses which she had arranged in various bowls around the living room.

And tonight the room literally shone from her efforts. The antique wood pieces were warm and mellow in the lamplight, gleamed like dark ripe fruit; how beautifully they stood out against the rose-coloured walls, while the silk-shaded porcelain lamps threw pools of soft light onto their glistening surfaces.

Like the rest of the apartment, the floor in the living room was of a dark, highly polished wood, and left bare as the floors in the other rooms were. The latter were decorated more simply, since I'd done them myself; it was Grandfather's room, as I called it, which looked the best.

After admiring it from the doorway for a moment longer I then stepped inside, went over and straightened a few cushions on the deep rose linen-covered sofa near the fireplace, before bending over to sniff Janine's roses. For once they had a perfume, actually smelled of roses, which was unusual these days. Most bought flowers had no scent at all.

I went into the kitchen, checked that there were bottles of white wine in the refrigerator, and returned to my bedroom. For a minute or two I studied myself in the long mirror on a side wall, thinking that I looked much better than I had for days. Healthy, in fact. But that was merely an illusion, one very cleverly created by my artifice with cosmetics; a golden-tinted foundation camouflaged my deathly pallor, hid the dark smudges under my eyes. The latter I'd enhanced with a touch of eye shadow and mascara; while a hint of pink blush and pink lipstick helped to bring a little additional life to my wan face.

The real truth was that I'd looked quite ill for the past week, haggard, white-faced, and red-eyed from crying, and I hadn't wanted Jake to see me looking that way tonight. He worried enough about me as it was.

I wasn't sure where we were going to dinner, so I'd chosen one of my basic outfits – black gabardine trousers, a white silk shirt and a black blazer. My blonde-streaked hair was pulled back in a pony tail, and, as I regarded myself objectively, I thought: Plain Jane and then some.

Turning around, I went to the desk, opened the drawer and took out a pair of small pearl earrings. I was putting them on when the doorbell rang.

I hurried through into the hall, anxious to see Jake who had been gone for the past week.

'Aren't you a sight for sore eyes,' he drawled when I flung open the door to let him in.

'Likewise,' I answered, and we stood there staring at each other.

Then he reached out eagerly and pulled me into his arms, enveloping me in a tight bear hug. And he held me so close to him I was momentarily startled.

V

When Jake finally let go of me he gave me an odd little smile that seemed a bit self-conscious to me. Then he abruptly swung around and closed the front door.

For a moment I believed that he too was startled by the fervour and length of his embrace, and then I changed my mind. He was my best friend and we had been close for years, so why wouldn't he hug me when he'd just returned from a trip? And especially under the circumstances.

'It's not raining,' I murmured.

'No, it's not,' he answered, turning to look at me. 'The storm seems to have blown away before it got started.'

I nodded and headed for the kitchen to open a bottle of his favourite Pouilly-Fuissé.

Jake followed me.

'I'll do that,' he said when I took the bottle of white wine from the refrigerator. He opened a drawer where he knew I kept the bar utensils and found a corkscrew. While he deftly pulled the cork, I took two wine glasses out of the cupboard and set them on the counter next to him, and a second later he was pouring wine for us.

He handed me a glass, and I said, 'I've got good news, Jake. Mike heard from Ajet's brother. Qemal told him Ajet is safe and well in Macedonia.'

'Hey, that's great!' he exclaimed, and clinked his glass to mine. 'Here's to Ajet. Thank God he made it okay.'

I nodded. 'To Ajet.'

We took our drinks into the living room, where Jake lowered himself into a chair near the fireplace and I sat down in the corner of the sofa, as I always did.

'What's the full story?' Jake asked, peering across at me over the rim of his glass.

'Apparently Ajet went searching for us that day,

when the shelling started, but before he found us he was shot,' I explained. 'He was badly wounded, but fortunately he was found by some local people.'

I went on to tell Jake how Ajet had been passed on to Kosovar soldiers, taken to a hospital in Albania and then moved to Macedonia. I finally finished, 'If you remember, I wrote down my agency number for him. And once he was well enough he asked Qemal to call Gemstar.'

'It's a relief to know he's all right. Ajet was straight with us, and wanted to help any way he could. He's a good kid.'

I settled back, studying Jake, thinking how well he looked after a week's rest in the south. He'd asked me to go with him to St-Jean-Cap Ferrat, but I'd declined, and I suddenly wondered if that might have been a mistake on my part. A vacation would have obviously done me good. His few days in the sun had given him a golden tan, turned his streaky hair more blond than ever, and he was in glowing health. Tonight he was wearing a blue cotton shirt with his grey sports jacket and slacks, and his eyes looked more vividly blue than ever.

'You're staring at me,' he said. 'What's wrong?' That was Jake, who was always questioning me about everything in my life. It had been that way since we'd first met in Beirut.

'Nothing's wrong,' I replied at last. 'It's just that you look in such great shape, I think I ought to have accepted your invitation.'

'Yes, you should have,' he quickly replied. He spoke softly enough, but I detected a certain undertone of vehemence in his voice. He took a long swallow of white wine and then sat nursing his drink, staring down into the glass, his face thoughtful.

When he looked up at me, he said, 'You needed a holiday, and even though you think you look great, you don't really. The make up doesn't deceive *me*. And you've lost weight.'

So much for my efforts with the cosmetic pots, I thought, and said, 'Black makes me look thin.'

'It's me you're talking to,' he answered. 'I know you better than everyone, even better than you know yourself.' He put the glass down on the coffee table and seemed about to get up, but suddenly leaned back against the linen cushions and closed his eyes.

After a couple of minutes, I ventured, 'Are you feeling all right, Jake?'

Opening his eyes, he said, 'Yep. But I'm worried about you, Val.'

'Oh please don't,' I cried. 'I'm fine. I haven't lost a pound,' I lied. '*Nothing. Nada. Zilch.*'

He shook his head. 'Has Mike said anything about your going back to work?'

'He said I was welcome back any time I felt like coming in, but to take my time, that it was my call.'

'The sooner you get back to the agency the better, in my opinion. You need to be busy, occupied, Val, not walking around the streets of Paris every day, and sitting here alone in the apartment afterwards. I know you're suffering. I am too. Tony was my best buddy, but life is for the living. We've got to go on, that's what he would want.'

'I'm trying hard, I really am, Jake. And the walking helps. I'm not sure why, but it does.'

'You're less alone when you're out there in the streets. They make you feel more alive because they're full of life, people, traffic, noise, activity. The streets are the world. Did I ever tell you about John Steinbeck and what he did when he heard that Robert Capa had been killed in Indochina?'

I frowned. I wasn't certain whether he'd told me or not, and yet at the back of my mind I thought that perhaps he had. Or was it Tony who had told me? Certainly we all revered Capa, the greatest war photographer who had ever lived. I said, 'I'm not sure, you might have. But tell me again.'

'Capa was killed in 1954, on May 25th actually, as I'm sure you recall. And of course within hours news of his death spread around the world. Steinbeck, who was a good friend of Capa's, was in Paris when he heard. He was so shaken up he went out and walked the streets for fourteen hours straight. I guess he just couldn't believe it. And he couldn't sit still. He had to be on the move. And you're doing something very similar, but you're doing it every day, Val.'

'No, I'm not, I don't walk the streets for fourteen hours!'

Jake sighed and said nothing, just gave me one of those penetrating looks of his that always made me re-examine everything I said to him. I shrugged, and finally admitted, 'Okay, you're right, I guess I am doing the same thing. And you did tell me the story. It was on one of those days when you were cross with Tony because you thought he was too reckless. You were comparing him to Capa.'

'No, I wasn't.' Jake sat up straighter and gave me a hard stare. 'Capa wasn't reckless in the way that Tony was. Those who knew Capa always said he was very cautious. Don't forget, he was an expert when it came to taking *calculated* risks. When he went to Indochina, it was his fifth war, and only a photojournalist of his great experience would know how to properly calculate when something was truly dangerous or not. From what I know about him, he measured the risks, especially when he had to walk across exposed areas, and he was always cautious, did not take risks unnecessarily. But if he saw the possibility of a great photograph and there was a calculated risk, then he took the risk. Tony just rushed in without –' He cut himself off, and took a swallow of his wine, obviously feeling disloyal.

'Without thinking,' I finished for him, stood up and headed towards the kitchen.

'Where are you going?'

'To get the bottle of wine,' I answered. When I came back, I filled his goblet, and then mine, and put the bottle down on the glass coffee table. 'What about the memorial service?' I said, getting right to the heart of the matter. 'Do you know when it is?'

'Next week. On Tuesday.'

'I see. Where's it being held?'

'At the Brompton Oratory at eleven o'clock.'

I was silent, looked down at the drink in my hands.

Jake said, 'I've booked us in at the Milestone in Kensington. I know you like that hotel.'

I nodded. He had surprised me with the information about the memorial. Events seemed to be moving more quickly than I'd anticipated, and I wasn't prepared at all. Only four days away. And then I'd be sitting there amongst all of his friends and colleagues, many of them *my* colleagues, in fact, and listening to the world talk about the man I was still mourning. I was suddenly appalled at the idea and I sat back jerkily.

Jake was telling me something else, and I blinked and tried to concentrate on his words. He was saying, 'I've spoken to Clee Donovan, and he's definitely going to be there, and I've left messages for the Turnley brothers. I know they'll come too, if they're able.'

I gazed at him blankly. I was feeling overwhelmed and the prospect of going to London frightened me, filled me with tension and anxiety.

'What's wrong?' Jake asked.

I swallowed. 'I'm . . . *dreading* it. There'll be such a lot of people there,' I muttered almost to myself.

Jake made no response for a split second, and then he said, 'I know what you mean, but let's be glad and proud that so many people want to celebrate Tony's life. Because that's what a memorial is, Val, a celebration that the person was ever alive. We are showing our gratitude that Tony was born and was among us for as long as he was.'

'Yes.'

He got up and came and sat next to me on the sofa, took hold of my hand in the most loving way. 'I know it's tough . . . but he's dead, Val, and you've got to accept that because –'

'I do,' I cut in, my voice rising slightly.

'You've got to get yourself busy, start working. You can't just . . . *drift* like this.'

I stared at him. There he was, being bossy again in that particular very macho way of his, and before I could stop myself I exclaimed, 'You've not done very much yourself since we came back from Belgrade.' And I could have bitten my tongue off as soon as these dreadful words left my mouth; I felt the flush of embarrassment rising from my neck to flood my face.

'I wish I *had* been able to work, but my leg's been pretty bad, and it's taken longer to heal than I expected.'

I was furious with myself. 'I'm sorry, Jake, I shouldn't have said that. I know your injuries were more severe than mine. I'm so stupid, thoughtless.'

'No, you're not, and listen: let's make a pact right now. To help each other go forward from where we are tonight, to get ourselves *moving*. Let's get started again, Val, let's pick up our cameras and get on with the job.'

'I don't think I could go back to Kosovo.'

'God, I wasn't meaning that! I don't want to go there either, but there are other things we can cover as well as wars.'

'But we're best known for doing *that*,' I reminded him.

'We can pick and choose our assignments, Val darling.'

'I suppose so,' I muttered, glancing at him.

Jake's eyes changed, turned darker blue, became reflective, and after a moment he adroitly changed the subject, remarked, 'I've booked us on a plane to London on Monday night, okay?'

The whole idea of the memorial was a nightmare to me, and not trusting myself to say anything, I simply nodded. Reaching for my glass, I took a sip of wine, then put the glass down and exclaimed with forced cheerfulness, 'Tell me about your trip to the south of France.'

'It was really great, Val, I wish you'd been with me –' Jake stopped and glanced at the phone as it started to ring.

I extracted my hand from his, got up and went to the small desk on which it stood. 'Hullo?'

VI

To my utter amazement it was my brother Donald calling from New York, and I sat down heavily on the small chair next to the little desk. I was flummoxed on hearing his voice, although after we'd exchanged greetings I quickly pulled myself together and listened alertly to what he had to say. Donald had always been tricky, extremely devious, and dissimulation was second nature to him.

Once he had finished his long speech, I said, 'I just can't get away right now. I have to go to London next week, to a memorial service for a fallen colleague, and I've also got loads of assignments stacking up.'

I listened again as patiently as possible, and once more I said, 'I'm sorry, I cannot make the trip at this time. And listen, I really can't stay on the phone, I have guests and I've got to go. Thanks for calling.' In his typical selfish fashion, determined to get all of his points across, Donald went on blabbering at me, and short of banging the receiver down rudely, I had no option but to hear him out. When he finally paused for breath, I saw my opportunity and jumped in, repeated that I could not leave Europe under any circumstances for the time being. After saying a quick goodbye, I hung up.

Returning to the sofa, I sat down and said, 'What a nerve! I can't believe he called me!'

'*Who*? And what did *he* call you about to get you so het up?'

I turned towards Jake and explained, 'It was my brother Donald calling from New York. To tell me my mother's not well, I should say *his* mother, because she's never been a mother to me. He wanted me to fly to New York. What cheek!'

'What's wrong with her? Is she very sick?'

I saw the frown, the baffled almost confused look in his eyes, and I instantly realized that he'd never truly understood the relationship I'd had with my mother. But then how could he understand, when I couldn't either. From what Jake had told me about himself during the years we'd known each other, he came from a marvellously warm, loving, close-knit Jewish family, and he had been raised with a lot of love, understanding and tremendous support from his parents, grandparents and sisters. Whereas I'd been an orphan within the bosom of the Denning family. If it hadn't been for my father's parents, Grandfather in particular, I would have withered away and died a young death from emotional deprivation. I asked myself then why I even thought in terms of having a relationship with Mother, because there had never been a relationship between us.

Iceberg Aggie, my grandfather had called her, and he had often wondered out loud to me what his son, my father, had ever seen in her. She had been very beautiful, of course. Still was, in all probability, although I hadn't seen her for years, not since my Beirut days.

Cutting into my thoughts, Jake asked me again, 'Is your mother very ill, Val?'

'Donald didn't really explain. All he said was that she wasn't well and that she had told him she wanted to see me. He was relaying the message for her. But it can't be anything serious, or he would have told me. Donald's her pet, Jake, and very much under her thumb. Still, he never fools around with the truth when it comes to her well being, or anything to do with her. He'd definitely have told me if there were real problems, I've no doubts about that.'

'Maybe she wants to make amends,' Jake suggested, and raised a brow as he added, 'A *rapprochement* perhaps?'

I shook my head vehemently. 'No way. She hasn't given a damn about me for thirty-one years. And I'm not going to New York.'

'You could phone her.'

'There's nothing to say, Jake. I told you about her years ago.' I bit my lip and shook my head slowly. 'I can't feel anything for a woman who has never felt anything for me.'

Jake did not respond and a long silence fell between us. But at last he broke it, when he said quietly, and with some compassion, 'Jesus, Val, I've never been able to understand that, come to grips with her attitude towards you. It seems so unnatural for a mother not to love her child. I mean, what could she possibly have had against a new-born baby?'

'Beats me,' I answered, and lifted my shoulders in

a light shrug. 'My Denning grandparents could never fathom it out either, and as far as my mother's mother was concerned, I really didn't know her very well. My grandmother Violet Scott was an enigma to me, and she avoided me.' I laughed harshly. 'I used to think I was illegitimate when I was younger, and that my mother had become pregnant by another man before she married my father. But the dates were all wrong, they didn't gel, because she'd been married to my father for over a year when I was born.'

'Maybe she slept with somebody else *after* she married your father,' Jake suggested.

'I've thought of that as well, but I look too much like my grandmother Cecelia Denning, when she was my age. Grandfather always remarked about it, until the day he died.'

I jumped up and went to the *secretaire*, pulled open the bottom drawer and took out a cardboard box. Carrying it over to the sofa, I handed it to Jake. 'Take a look at these,' I said as I sat down next to him again.

He did so, staring for a few minutes at the old photographs of my grandmother which he had removed from the box. 'Yes, you're a Denning all right, and a dead ringer for Cecelia. If it weren't for her old-fashioned clothes she could be you as you are today.' He shuffled through the other photographs in the box and chuckled. 'I took this one!' he cried, waving a picture at me.

'Hey, let me see that!'

Still laughing, he handed it to me. I couldn't help smiling myself, as I stared back at my own image captured on celluloid. There I was in all my glory, standing outside the Commodore Hotel in Beirut, which is where I'd first set eyes on Jake. I was wearing my safari jacket and pants, and a collection of assorted cameras were slung haphazardly around my neck. It was obvious from my solemn expression that I took myself very seriously indeed. I was looking too self-important for words, and I gave a mock shudder. 'I must have really fancied myself, but God, how awful I looked in those days.'

'No, you were the most gorgeous thing on two legs I'd ever seen!' he exclaimed, and then stopped with suddenness; a startled expression crossed his face, as if he had surprised himself with his words. Clearing his throat, Jake returned to the conversation about my mother, when he said, 'It *is* very odd, Val, the way your mother has always treated you. With all of your accomplishments, she should be proud of you.'

I sighed, and made a small moue with my mouth. 'It's a mystery. And one I have no intention of solving. I just can't be bothered. Now, how about taking me to dinner?'

Chapter Four

I
LONDON, SEPTEMBER

With a great deal of effort, I had managed to put the memorial service out of my mind for the last few days, but now that Jake and I were about to depart for it I was experiencing sudden panic. The service loomed large in my mind, and, very simply, I just didn't want to go. In fact, my reluctance had become so acute it startled me. Later I was to ask myself if I'd had some sixth sense about it, a foreboding of trouble, but I wasn't sure; I can never be certain about that.

In any event, there I stood waiting for Jake in the handsome panelled lobby of the Milestone, wondering how to gracefully wriggle out of going. Naturally I couldn't. It was far too late to pull such a trick as that, and besides, I would never let Jake down.

Turning away from the front door, I spotted Jake coming towards me looking tanned and healthy and very smart in his dark suit, and wearing a shirt and tie for a change. But his expression was as sombre as his dark clothes, and he was limping as badly as he had yesterday when we'd arrived at Heathrow in a thunderstorm.

I didn't dare mention the limp or ask him how he felt, since he'd practically bitten my head off last night when I'd worried out loud about his wounds. Instead I took hold of his arm, leaned into him and kissed his cheek.

He gave me a faint smile and said, 'Sorry I kept you waiting. Now we're running late, so we'd better get going, Val.'

I nodded and walked to the front door with him in silence, thinking how morose he was. He had sounded much more cheerful when we'd spoken earlier on the phone. But then he didn't relish the next few hours any more than I did, I knew that.

The heavens opened up the moment Jake and I started to walk down the front steps of the hotel. The uniformed doorman hurried after us, wielding a large umbrella, and the two of us huddled under it as he led us to the waiting chauffeur-driven car which Jake had ordered last night.

Once we were seated in the car Jake said quietly, 'It'll be all right, Val, try not to worry so much. It'll soon be over.' Reaching out, he took hold of my hand and squeezed it reassuringly.

I glanced at him and gave him what must have been a rather sickly smile, and noticed the tight set of his lips, his drawn face. 'You're dreading the service just as much as I am. We've come to London against our better judgement. It's a terrible mistake.'

'We had no choice, we had to be here, so let's just help each other through this as calmly as possible.'

'Yes,' I answered and turned my head, stared out of the car window, thinking what an awful, dreary day it was, especially for a memorial. Somehow the relentless rain, penetrating damp, and dark English skies emphasized the mournfulness of the occasion.

Being a very private person, especially when it came to my feelings, I'd never worn my emotions on my sleeve. And so I preferred to grieve for Tony in my own way, in the quiet of my home, not in a public place like the Brompton Oratory, although it was apparently a very beautiful Roman Catholic church; the Vatican of London, was the way someone had once described it to me years ago.

After a few minutes of staring out at the rain-sodden streets, as the car ploughed its way through the heavy London traffic, I turned away from the window. Taking a cue from Jake, who was huddled in the corner of the seat with his eyes closed, I did the same thing. And I did not open them until the car slid to a standstill outside the church.

I sat up, smoothed one hand over my hair, which I'd sleaked back into a neat chignon, and straightened the jacket of my black suit. Then I took a deep breath and made up my mind to get through the service with quiet dignity, and as much composure as I could muster.

II

There was such a crowd of people going into the Brompton Oratory it was hard to pick out friends and colleagues, or recognize anyone at a quick glance, for that matter. Everyone was dressed in black or other sombre colours, and faces were etched with solemnity or sorrow, or both.

I had wisely clamped on a pair of sunglasses before leaving the car, and these made me feel as if I were incognito, and also protected, if not actually invisible. Nevertheless, despite the concealing dark glasses, I clutched Jake's arm as we mingled with the others filing into the church sedately and in a very orderly fashion.

We had just entered when I felt someone behind me tap me lightly on the shoulder. I glanced around to find myself staring into the lovely face of Nicky Wells, the Paris bureau chief of A.T.N., the most successful of all the American cable news networks.

She and I had been together in Tiananmen Square in Beijing, when the students had demonstrated against the Chinese government. That had been in 1989, and Nicky had been very helpful to me, since I was a beginner at the time. Fifteen years older than I, she had frequently taken me under her wing when I was such a novice.

We had remained friends ever since those early days,

and would occasionally socialize in Paris. Standing next to Nicky was her husband Cleeland Donovan, another renowned war photographer, who had founded the agency Image some years ago. After the birth of their first child, Nicky had left the field as a war correspondent for her network, deeming it wiser and safer to remain in Paris covering local stories.

Jake and Clee had been good friends for many years, bonded as American expats, war photographers, and also as winners of the Robert Capa Award. This prize had been established in 1955, just after Capa's death, by *Life* magazine and the Overseas Press Club of America, and was awarded for 'the best photographic reporting from abroad requiring exceptional courage and enterprise'.

I knew that both men treasured this particular award as their proudest possession, Capa being a God to them, indeed to all of us in the business of being photojournalists covering wars.

The four of us hung back and spoke for a few moments about Tony and the sadness of the occasion, and then we arranged to make a date for dinner, once we were all in Paris at the same time for more than a couple of days.

As we began to move again it was Clee who said, 'We can't go to the wake afterwards, Jake. Nicky and I have to head back to Paris immediately after the service ends. Are you going?' He looked from Jake to me.

I was so taken aback I couldn't speak.

Jake cleared his throat, rather nervously I thought,

and muttered something I didn't quite catch. Then he added, 'We're in the same situation as you, Clee, we've got to get back too. Commitments to meet. But we might drop in for a few minutes, just to pay our respects.'

Nothing else was said, since the four of us were suddenly being edged forward by the throng pressing in behind us. I held onto Jake's hand, but in the crush we became separated from Nicky and Clee. And a second or two later we found ourselves being ushered down one of the aisles and into a pew by a church official.

Once we were seated I grabbed Jake's arm ferociously, pulled him closer to me and hissed, 'You never told *me* anything about a wake.'

'I thought it better not to, at least not until we got here,' he admitted in a whisper.

'Who's giving the wake?' I demanded, but kept my voice low, trying to curb my anger with him.

'Rory and Moira.' He glanced at me swiftly, and again nervously cleared his throat. 'I have the distinct feeling we won't be going, will we, Val?'

'You bet we won't,' I snapped. I was livid.

III

It was just as well other people came into our pew at this precise moment, because it prevented a continuation of our conversation, which could have easily spiralled out of hand.

I was furious with Jake for not telling me about the wake before now, not to mention irritated with myself for not anticipating that there would be one.

Tony, after all, had been Irish; on the other hand, a wake was usually held after a funeral and not a memorial, wasn't it? But the Irish were the Irish, with their own unique rules and rituals, and apparently a wake today was deemed in order, perhaps because the funeral had been held in Ireland. A wake was an opportunity for family and friends to get together, to comfort each other, to reminisce and remember, and to celebrate the one who had died. I was fully aware I wouldn't be able to face the gathering. Coming on top of the memorial, it would be too much for me to handle. What I couldn't understand was why Jake didn't realize this.

The sound of organ music echoed through the church, and I glanced around surreptitiously. Here and there amongst the crowd I caught glimpses of familiar faces – of those we had worked with over the last couple of years. There were also any number of famous photographers and journalists, as well as a few celebrities, none of whom I knew, but instantly recognized because of their fame.

It was an enormous turnout, and Tony would have been gratified and pleased to know that so many friends and members of his profession had come here to remember him, to do him honour today.

I went on peering about me, hoping to see Rory. I felt quite positive that I would recognize him, since

Tony had shown me so many photographs of his son, and of his daughter, Moira. They were nowhere to be seen, yet they had to be here. It struck me then that they would be sitting in the front pew, facing the altar, and that was out of my line of vision.

I sat back, bowed my head, and tuned myself in to the organ music. It was mournful but oddly soothing. I closed my eyes for a moment, and I was filled with relief that I was keeping my feelings in check. Well, for the moment at least.

When the organ music stopped I opened my eyes and saw a priest standing in front of the altar. He began to pray for Tony's soul, and we all knelt to pray with the priest and then we rose automatically and sat in our seats again. The priest continued to speak, this time about Tony and his life and all that he had done with it, and what he had accomplished.

I took refuge by sinking down into myself, only half listening, absently drifting along with the proceedings, and endeavouring to remain uninvolved. Instinctively, I was scared to be a participant, for fear of making a fool of myself by displaying too much emotion, or weeping. Yet tears had risen to the surface, were rapidly gathering behind my eyes, and I struggled desperately to control myself.

Soon the priest drew to a close and glided over to one side of the altar, and as if from far, far away a lone choirboy's voice rang out. It was an extraordinary voice, a high-pitched soprano which seemed to emanate from the very rafters of the church. The voice was so pure, so thrilling, it sent chills down my spine, and I sat up straighter and listened, enraptured.

'The Minstrel Boy to the war is gone,
In the ranks of death you'll find him.
His father's sword he has girded on,
And his wild harp slung behind him . . .'

Hearing the young choirboy singing so beautifully undid me. My mouth began to tremble uncontrollably, and as my face crumpled I covered it with my hand. I shrank into the corner of the pew and discovered that I wasn't able to quell the tears. They rolled down my cheeks unchecked, slipping out from under my dark glasses and dropping down onto my hand which was clutching the lapel of my jacket.

Jake put his arm around me, drew me closer, wanting to comfort me. Leaning against him gratefully, I swallowed hard, compressed my lips, and finally managed to get my swimming senses under control. The old ballad came to an end at last, and that lilting soprano was finally silent. I hoped there would not be too much of this kind of thing, because I knew it would be unbearable. The emotional impact was already overwhelming.

But of course there was more. First Tony's brother Niall eulogized him; he was followed by Tony's oldest friend in the business, Eddie Marsden, the photo editor at Tony's agency, who spoke at length. And, finally, it was Rory who was standing there in the pulpit, looking for all the world like a young Tony, strong and courageous in his grief. He had inherited his handsome father's Black Irish looks, his mannerisms, and his voice was so similar it was like listening to Tony himself speaking.

Rory's words came truly from the heart, were eloquent and moving. He reminded us of Tony's great charm and his talent as a photographer, of his modesty and his lack of conceit, of his abhorrence of violence, his humanity and his condemnation of the wars he covered. Rory talked of his father's Irish roots, his love of Ireland and of family. He spoke so lovingly about his father I felt the tears rising in my throat once more.

Rory went on, 'He was too young a man to die . . . and yet he died doing what he loved the most, recording history in the making. And perhaps there's no better way to die than doing that, doing what you love the most . . .'

But he could have lived a long life, I thought, as young Rory's voice continued to wash over me. If he hadn't taken such terrible risks none of us would be here today grieving over him. The instant these thoughts formed I hated myself for thinking them. But it *was* the truth.

IV

Rory spotted us as we came slowly up the central aisle. He was waiting to speak to friends of his father's as they left the church, and his eyes lit up as soon as they settled on Jake. Moira was positioned next to him, and on his other side stood a slender, red-haired woman who even from this distance appeared to be quite beautiful. I knew at once it was Fiona, Tony's former wife. I began to shake inside.

Jake had no way of knowing I had been seized by this internal shaking; nevertheless, he took hold of my elbow to steady me, as though he did know.

Fiona was smiling warmly at him, obviously glad to see him, and it was apparent they were old friends. Moving towards her, Jake only let go of me when we came to a standstill in front of her. He wrapped his arms around Fiona and gave her a big bear hug, then hugged Moira and Rory.

Bringing me forward into the group, he introduced me. 'Fiona this is Val – Val Denning.'

'Hello, Val,' she said warmly in a soft voice, and she gave me a small half smile and thrust out her hand.

I took hold of it, and said, 'Fiona', and inclined my head, trying not to stare at her. She had a lovely face, with high cheekbones, a dimpled chin and smooth brow. Her skin was that pale milky white which Irish redheads seem to be blessed with, liberally peppered with freckles across the bridge of her nose and her cheekbones. Her hair, cut short and curly, was flame-coloured and her eyes were dark, black as coal. A true Celt, I thought.

'I'm so glad you were able to come to London,' Fiona was saying to Jake in her lilting brogue that bespoke her heritage. 'To be honest, I'd worried that you might both be off on assignments, that you wouldn't make the memorial service. Thanks for coming.' She looked at me, and then back at Jake and said, 'So you'll be joining us at the house to take a bite with us?'

Jake hesitated uncertainly, gave me a quick glance and said to Fiona, 'Val hasn't been feeling well since we got here last night, have you, Val?'

He had adroitly thrown the ball into my court and I had no option but to go along with him. 'Er, no, I haven't, not really. I think I must be coming down with something.'

Fiona's face dropped. 'Oh, that's such a disappointment, 'tis indeed, Val. And here I was wanting to give you both something of Tony's. As a memento, you know. There's so much at the house, all of his possessions collected over the years. I thought you could choose something, Val, and you Jake, something personal like a camera, or maybe a pair of cufflinks.' She paused and shook her head, and a wry smile touched her mouth. 'Well, as far as Tony's concerned, there would be nothing more personal than a camera I'm thinking, since every camera he ever owned was part of him.'

'We do want you to come, Jake, you worked alongside Dad for so long. And you should come, Miss Denning,' Rory cut in, looking directly at me. 'If you feel up to it. It's not a real wake, you know. It's a sort of . . . well, it's just a gathering of friends remembering my father with his family, in his home –'

'It won't be the same without you,' Fiona interjected. 'Why, Jake, you were so close to him these last few years I thought at times that you were joined at the hip. Please come to the house. It means so much to me and the children.'

Jake said something but I wasn't paying attention. Instead I was staring at Fiona. And I knew with absolute certainty that she was not Tony's ex-wife. Fiona was still his wife. Or rather, his widow.

Chapter Five

I

'Tony came to me at the end of July and said he was divorced. Why didn't you tell me he wasn't?' I asked as evenly as possible, trying to keep my voice level and controlled.

'Because I didn't know he wasn't,' Jake answered, returning my stare with one equally penetrating.

'But *why* didn't you know? You were his best buddy, and you seem very pally with Fiona. You must have known something, known what was going on in their life together!' I exclaimed, my voice rising slightly.

Jake did not answer.

We stood facing each other in my room at the Milestone, where we had returned after leaving the Brompton Oratory. When truth and reality had suddenly hit me in the face at the church, I had hurriedly excused myself to Fiona, hinting in a vague way that I really wasn't well and had to leave. Under pressure from her, Jake had finally agreed to go to her house once he had dropped me off at the hotel. On the way here in the car, he had tried to talk to me, asking me why I had rushed out so abruptly. But I'd hushed him into silence, explaining that we must wait to have our discussion in private.

Now we were having it. He suddenly reached out, as if to take me in his arms. But as he moved towards me, I took a step backwards. 'Don't try to comfort me right now,' I said swiftly. 'I'm not in the mood, Jake, and anyway I want to talk this out with you.' I shook my head. 'I always thought you were my friend, my best friend, actually, but now . . .' I let my sentence trail off.

Instantly I saw that I had annoyed him. His mouth tightened into a thin line and his bright blue eyes, usually so benign, had turned flinty and cold. 'Don't you dare question my friendship and loyalty!' he cried, sounding angry. 'And stop being so damned belligerent, Val. I haven't done anything to hurt you, I'm only an innocent bystander. Now listen to me for a moment.'

'I'm listening. So go ahead, shoot.'

'Okay, okay, and just let's settle down here a mite.' He took a deep breath, and went on in a slightly milder tone, 'Although Tony and I were close, he never confided in me about his private life, only ever hinted at things. I knew there were lots of women –' He cut himself off, looked chagrined, and eyed me carefully before continuing.

I knew Jake would never wilfully hurt me, and

I guessed that he was now worrying he had just caused me a degree of pain. But that wasn't so. 'It's okay, Jake, keep going,' I said in what I hoped was a reassuring voice.

He nodded. 'Val, you have to face up to the fact that you weren't the first, there were others before you. But he never left Fiona. She was always there in the background, his childhood sweetheart, his child bride as he called her, and the mother of his children. She was inviolate, in a sense. At least, that's what *I* believed. As I told you, we never discussed his marriage or his love affairs, just as I didn't talk about my personal life or my divorce from Sue Ellen. We only touched on those things in the most peripheral way. Very casually. Then he got involved with you last year, and eventually I began to think the unthinkable, that he was going to break up with Fiona. Not that he ever said so. Nor did he discuss you. However, when he came to Paris in July he announced, out of the blue, that he was divorced –'

'And you were gobsmacked, as the English say,' I interrupted with some acidity.

Ignoring my sarcasm, Jake continued: 'You're right, in one sense, yes. Because he was such a dyed-in-the-wool Catholic I'd always thought a divorce was out of the question. And then again, he'd done something I'd never expected him to do. Mind you, Val, I understood on another level why he would want to be free. It was for you. Yes, I understood that aspect of it very well.'

'He lied to both of us. He wasn't divorced.'

'We don't really know that,' Jake answered in a reasonable tone.

'Oh yes we do. At least I do.'

'I'd like you to consider a couple of things. Firstly, think about Fiona and her demeanour today. She isn't playing the grieving widow. She seems a bit sad, I'll grant you that, but she's not distraught. And secondly, she's only having a small gathering at the house, just a few friends. In other words, she's not making a big deal out of the memorial.'

'I don't think those are very good arguments.'

'Are you making the assumption they were not divorced just because she talked about Tony's possessions being at the house, and because Rory spoke about Tony as if he lived in the bosom of his family, and very happily so?'

'Perhaps.'

'But those things don't add up to Tony still being married to Fiona when he was killed. Think about it, Val. Even if they were divorced, no one would bring it up *today*, least of all his *son*. It just wouldn't have been appropriate or very nice, and anyway there was no reason to do so. It was a memorial service given by people who loved Tony, and the legal status of their marriage didn't figure into it at all.'

'I guess not,' I admitted. 'On the other hand, there's Fiona's attitude towards me. If there'd been a divorce, why was she so nice to me? So pleasant?'

'Because she didn't know you were involved with Tony, that's why.'

'I see.'

'Please don't make the mistake of using her attitude towards you as a yardstick, Val. That would be very flawed judgement on your part.'

I bit my lip, and thought for a moment, before saying, 'Well, I guess the best way, perhaps the only way, to get to the truth is to ask Fiona if she and Tony were divorced.'

'You wouldn't do that!' He looked at me askance.

'No, I wouldn't. But *you* could ask her, Jake.'

'Oh no, not me. And certainly not today of all days.'

I sat down on a chair and dropped my head into my hands. After a minute or two, I looked up at him intently. 'Jake, I'm going to ask you a question, and I want you to answer it as truthfully as you can. It's this: Do you really believe Tony and Fiona were divorced?'

Jake lowered his long, lean frame into the other chair. 'Yes, I do,' he answered after giving it some thought. And then he slowly shook his head. A doubtful expression flickered in his eyes. He murmured, 'You know, Val, if I'm absolutely honest, I just don't know whether they were divorced or not. On the other hand, why would he announce it to me as well as to you?' Jake lifted his hands in a helpless sort of gesture and shook his head again. 'Why would he invent that? What was his purpose?'

'I don't know. But trust a woman's instincts. The *other woman's* instincts. They weren't divorced.'

II

In the end I went with Jake to Fiona's house in Hampstead.

He wasn't too happy about me going with him, because he was nervous at first, worried that I would verbally accost Fiona. But I promised I wouldn't do that, and he knew I never broke a promise. Also, he understood very well that I would never create an embarrassing scene either.

By the time Jake was leaving my room I knew I had to go with him, there were no two ways about it. Very simply, I had to get to the bottom of the situation, find out everything I could without actually asking any direct questions.

It had occurred to me on the drive up to Hampstead with Jake that their home, whether Tony had vacated it recently or not, would also tell me a great deal about their relationship. And then there were the children, eighteen-year-old Rory, and Moira, who was twenty. In my experience, children frequently said a lot about their parents, and without actually meaning to they invariably revealed a few secrets. I hoped this would be the case today.

III

Where was the monster? Where was the harridan? Where was the disturbed woman Tony had complained about so often?

Certainly not present today, as far as I could ascertain, not unless Fiona was a superb actress or suffering from a split personality. Could she be a Dr Jekyll and Mrs Hyde? I was rather doubtful of that. In fact, she appeared to be a pleasant sort of woman who seemed perfectly normal to me.

I knew she was forty, but she didn't look her age at all. A pretty woman, it was her colouring that was the most striking thing about her; her natural flame-coloured hair and bright, dark eyes gave her a kind of vivid radiance. Of medium height and build, she had an innate gracefulness which was most apparent now as she moved around the room, tending to the needs of her guests. Including Fiona and her children, there were eleven of us altogether, since only Niall, his wife Kate, and several really close friends and colleagues had been invited to the intimate buffet lunch.

I sat on the sofa alone, facing the French windows which led to the garden. Jake was off in a corner, deep in conversation with Rory and Moira, and so I took this opportunity to catch my breath, to relax and review the past few hours. It had been a wild morning. Emotional. Disturbing. And in many ways more dismaying than I'd anticipated.

Outside the windows the scene was pastoral, and I was enjoying sitting here looking at it, enjoying this moment of quietness and solitude in the midst of the gathering. Everyone was engaged in conversation, but this did not bother me; I was part of them yet separate. I might easily have been in the depths of the country, and not in Hampstead, although parts of this area of London were bucolic, I knew that.

From my position on the sofa I could see a number of large trees, including an oak and a sycamore, and a verdant lawn which was held in check by herbaceous borders. There was an ancient fountain spraying arcs of shimmering water up into the air, and beyond this, a high, old stone wall into which had been set a wrought-iron gate with an elaborate scroll design.

This gate led to an apple orchard, so Fiona had told me a moment ago, and she had added, 'Tony's favourite spot. He did love his garden so.'

Nodding, smiling, I had not uttered a word on hearing this. It was something which seemed so unlikely; but I had taken a fast sip of the sherry Rory had poured for me earlier, to be followed by several more sips in quick succession. Her words had startled me. I had no idea how to respond, and then realized that no response was necessary.

When did *he* have time to sit in a garden? I asked myself wonderingly, frowning at her retreating figure, as she flitted away to serve more drinks, and questioning the veracity of her remark. Yet there was no reason for her to make this comment if it were not true. What did she have to gain? Nothing, of course. Anyway, it had been said almost off-handedly, as if no thought had been given to it. Nevertheless, I found it curious.

Almost instantly it struck me that he'd had plenty of time to spend here in the garden, because he had always hot-footed it to London at the end of an assignment, leaving me and Jake to make our way back to France together.

And Tony had usually had plenty of good reasons for rushing off, ready excuses on the tip of his tongue; he had to check in with his news-photo agency, spend time at the agency, see his kids, have lunch with his brother, get a doctor's check-up, go to the dentist, etcetera, etcetera, etcetera. No, he had never been at a loss when it came to explaining away his absence from my life when we were not working.

Tony had been in London through June and most of July, and certainly he could have easily done a lot of garden-sitting then. He had not joined us in Paris until the last few days of July, just before we set off for Kosovo in August to cover the war.

Do we ever really know another person? Until earlier today I had believed I knew everything there was to know about Tony Hampton. Not so, it seemed.

I'd had a bit of a shock in the Brompton Oratory, when it had suddenly hit me, with some force, that I was actually standing next to Tony's widow and not his ex-wife, as I had believed her to be. But the shock had receded somewhat, and I had begun to regain some of my equilibrium.

When I'd rushed out of the church I'd been full of rage; but as the anger had subsided I had accepted the fact that I'd been duped. Not only that, I could also admit to myself that Tony had purposely set out to beguile me last year, and I had been foolishly sucked in, captivated by his Irish charm – if anyone had kissed the Blarney Stone he had. I had been bowled over by his sudden and rather intense interest in me; it had been so unexpected. After all, he had known me for several years and had always treated me as a pal. Suddenly I was the focus of his romantic and sexual interest, and for a while I was baffled. But he was charismatic, and of course I had not been able to resist his looks, his humour, his cleverness, his sexuality. I had been a sitting duck . . .

There was something else. I trusted my gut instinct absolutely, and earlier today it had told me Tony had died a married man. I was convinced I was right about that, even if Jake was wavering on this point.

I was baffled by Tony's behaviour at the end of July. Why had he unexpectedly announced to Jake that he was divorced? And why had he told me exactly the same thing? I'd certainly not been bugging him about marriage. And who could fathom out a blatant lie like that? What was the motivation behind it? What was the reason for the lie? What had he hoped to gain?

All kinds of other questions jostled for prominence

in my mind, as I sat there in his house in Hampstead with his widow playing hostess; I went on sipping her dry sherry and pondering my love affair with him.

Had Tony been playing for time? Had he been intending to marry me, as he had often said he would, and in doing so commit bigamy? Had he merely been stringing me along, hoping that Fiona would leave him? Or that I would tire of waiting? Had he found himself in so deep with me he didn't know how to extricate himself, and therefore had invented the divorce and given me the Grecian ring as . . . *pacifiers*? Had he been hoping that something would happen to solve his problems?

Tony had had a favourite expression, one which he used frequently. 'Life has a way of taking care of itself,' he would say to me and others.

Well, life had indeed taken care of itself in the end. Had he always known he would die covering a war? Had he had a presentiment about this? An icy shiver shot through me at this appalling thought, and I immediately put it out of my head. Otherwise, I might start thinking that his recklessness had in some way been calculated.

A feeling of dismay mingled with frustration now lodged in the pit of my stomach, as I recognized that I would never know what had been in Tony's mind. No one would. The only person who had all the answers was dead and buried.

IV

Not wishing to wrestle any further with the puzzle of Tony's marital status and his terrible game-playing, if that *was* what he had been doing, I focused my eyes on the garden for a short while longer. It was so tranquil, filled with such a calm beauty, I took a measure of peace from it. And again I was thankful that nobody was disturbing me with their idle chatter.

The slashing rain had long since stopped and the day had turned sunny; airy white clouds floated across a soft periwinkle-blue sky, and it had become one of those lovely September afternoons which are so endemic to England.

Suddenly that bright sunlight was pouring into the room. Yellow was the predominant colour and the result was magical; the whole room acquired a shimmer to it, a warm, golden glow that appeared to make everything gleam. My eyes roamed around, taking everything in for the first time since I'd arrived.

There were some attractive modern paintings on the walls, and a number of handsome Georgian antiques were on display. But essentially it was a room which had been furnished rather than decorated, because there was no cohesive decorative theme to it. Beautiful things were dotted here and there, but they looked as if they had been gathered somewhat indiscriminately and then placed around haphazardly. The room did have comfort and there was more than a hint of refined taste at work, but very little of Tony was in evidence here. This setting had been created solely by Fiona, I was sure of that.

Jake moved away from the corner of the room at last, sauntered over to me and looked down. He said, 'You seem a bit pensive. Are you all right?'

'I'm fine. I've just been sitting here, thinking. Thinking things through.'

Jake nodded, gave me a small lopsided smile. 'We'll talk later. In the meantime, how about coming into the dining room, getting a little food? You should try and eat something, Val, before we go to the airport.'

I agreed.

V

In the end it was the study that told the real story.

Jake and I had just finished eating when Fiona came over. Leaning closer to us, she said in a low confidential voice, 'Let's slip away. I want you to choose something of Tony's as a memento.'

I jumped up at this invitation. Jake and I followed her out of the dining room, up the stairs, down the corridor and into the long spacious room which had been Tony's private abode.

The moment I stepped inside I knew that no one else could possibly have occupied it; his own unique imprint was stamped on it everywhere.

The first thing I noticed was the baseball cap, and my stomach lurched.

How could I miss it? I had bought it for him last year, on our vacation in the south of France. There were a number of other hats hanging on the antique mahogany hat-stand near the door, but my baseball cap had been his favourite. The way it hung there now, a bit lopsidedly, made me catch my breath. He might have just flung it onto the peg a moment ago.

Feeling decidedly queasy, I glanced away and moved farther into the room.

Along one wall, a series of built-in cupboards ran down towards the window, and I guessed that this was his filing system; those cabinets more than likely housed hundreds of his photographs and all of his records. And God knows what else. I wished I could get into them, but no hope of that I knew.

Stacks of magazines, piles of books, and a selection of very expensive cameras were carefully arranged on top of the cabinets, and above the long countertop the wall was lined with cork. Onto this Tony had pinned a lot of photographs. Including some of mine, I noticed with a small jolt of surprise.

Walking closer, I looked at them, remembering. Remembering so much.

I instantly closed my mind to those memories. With a rush of irritation I knew he had put them up there as souvenirs of our vacation in France last summer. All of them had been taken near St Tropez, where we had spent a week sailing. Seascapes. Empty beaches.

Sunsets. Shots of the endless sky. Close-ups of flowers, trees, birds, nature in all its forms. Beautiful shots which were a relief for me to take after the horrors of war. They were unidentified, but they were mine all right.

Then my gaze fell on the camera I had given him. A Leica.

Automatically, I reached for it, held it in my hand, thinking of Tony, suddenly angry with him again. I felt betrayed and used by him.

Fiona must have seen me pick it up, because she exclaimed, 'If you want the camera, please take it, Val dear. Rory and Moira have chosen the ones they prefer. I'm so pleased she's taking after Tony, following in his footsteps. I'm sure she's told you all about her plans, Jake, hasn't she?'

I turned around to face the two of them.

Fiona stood near the big partner's desk in the middle of the room, and she was looking up at Jake.

He said, 'Yes, she has been filling me in. She's very excited that she's going to join Tony's agency next year.'

As I continued to look at them it struck me suddenly that Jake looked very tired, as if the day had affected him as deeply as it had me. Also, I couldn't help wondering what Moira and Rory had been talking to him about. Their father, no doubt.

Picking up the camera, I went to join them both. Jake put his arm around me, drew me closer to him, almost protectively, I thought.

'Thanks, Fiona, I'd like the camera,' I murmured, although I didn't want it at all. But I thought it would look churlish, perhaps even odd, if I didn't take something of his, since we had worked together.

Looking pleased, Fiona now picked up a small leather box which was on the desk, and opened it. She showed the contents to us; it held a pair of cufflinks. Glancing at Jake, she said, 'I thought you might like to have these, as a memento of Tony. They're good ones, you know. They're made of eighteen-carat gold, and lapis, as you can see.'

For a split second Jake looked as though he was about to refuse the blue cufflinks but apparently changed his mind. 'Thanks,' he said, taking them from her. He studied them for a moment, closed the box and put it in his jacket pocket without another word.

'Would you like to select one or two of Tony's cameras?' she asked him.

Jake shook his head. 'I've got so many of my own, honey, but thanks for offering.'

Sitting down at the desk, Fiona opened the centre drawer, took out a large, office-sized cheque book andturnedthepages.'Tonymust'veowedyoumoney,Jake. Five hundred pounds, to be exact.' Her expression was questioning, and then she went on, 'He made out this cheque to you, dated and signed it, then forgot to tear it out before he left for Paris at the end of July. I found it the other day, when I'd finally screwed up the courage to go through his desk.'

Jake was obviously not surprised by her words. Nodding, he explained, 'Tony told me he'd left the cheque behind by mistake. I said he should forget it, that it didn't matter.' Jake cleared his throat, and added, 'I'd loaned him some money to buy film when we were in Jordan in March. Look, it's not important, Fiona.'

'No, no, I insist you take it,' she exclaimed, tore out the cheque and handed it to Jake. Since I was standing next to him, I couldn't help noticing that the cheque came from a joint account. An account bearing Fiona's name as well as his.

Well, so much for that, I thought. She had a joint account with him. She has his children. His house. His garden. A whole life with him to remember.

As for me, what did I have?

Chapter Six

I

Jake did not have much to say on the way to the airport. In fact, he was not only silent but rather glum. In contrast, I was brimming with thoughts, theories and comments, and desperately wanted to talk to him. But in the end I remained silent, deeming it wiser to hold my tongue for the moment.

It was obvious to me that he didn't want to talk about Tony and Fiona, or Rory and Moira either, with whom he had spent a lot of time at the lunch. Nor did he want to discuss that lunch, which we had just left, or the memorial service of earlier. I didn't blame him. Everything had become as painful for Jake as it had for me, or so I believed.

Heathrow was as busy as it always was, crowded with people, and as we pushed our way through the bustling throng heading for all corners of the world, I got the distinct feeling Jake couldn't wait to get back to Paris. I hurried along next to him, hauling my one piece of luggage, a fold-over bag which had travelled the world with me.

'Hey, honey, let me help you with your stuff,' he suddenly said, becoming aware of the difficulties I was having with the large hold-all slung over one shoulder.

'I can manage, Jake. Please don't worry, you've enough to carry of your own,' I replied, but I was still struggling, and before I could protest further he grabbed the fold-over bag out of my hands.

'I'm sorry, Val, I should have carried this for you all along. No excuse for me, except that I've been preoccupied.' He gave me a faint smile, and finished, 'I've been very neglectful.'

'Please, it's okay!' I exclaimed. 'I'm a strong, tough girl who can carry her own luggage and take care of herself in any situation.'

Staring down at me, he gave me an odd look, and muttered, 'I'm not so sure about that, Kid.'

I didn't answer. I simply trotted along next to him, trying to keep up with his long strides. After a second or two I remarked, 'Anyway, I know what you mean about being preoccupied. I'm on overload myself at the moment.'

He nodded, gave me a swift glance and said, 'Yes, you are. Emotional overload. The point is, we're *both* top-heavy with a lot of crap, a lot of disturbing and conflicting feelings. I just need to clear my head, Val, so that I can look at . . . things as clearly as possible.'

'I understand,' I answered, 'and I realize now is not

the right time to talk, since we're rushing through an airport like maniacs, trying to make a plane. But we should sit down and chat, Jake. We need to understand about Tony and Fiona. Whenever you want, but we really must do it,' I insisted.

When he made no response whatsoever, I eyed him worriedly, and pressed, 'At the lunch you said we'd talk later, remember? We have to make sense out of Tony's behaviour, you know.'

'I guess we do,' he muttered, and his face became closed, his mouth grimly set. He plunged ahead, making for the gate, deftly handling our luggage.

I sighed under my breath. So much for that illuminating conversation, I muttered to myself, and ran after him to board the plane to Paris.

II

The flight across the English Channel was short, just over an hour, and I spent most of that time wondering why Jake was still so silent, wrapped up in his own thoughts. I'd tried to make small talk with him to no avail. He barely responded, seemed reluctant to say anything at all. And when he did reply to the odd question or comment of mine, his answers were brief and to the point.

If I didn't know better I would have said he was being sulky, but that wasn't his nature. Jake was not a moody man, nor was he temperamental, and like me he was usually on an even keel. Quite aside from that, I always thought of him as being straightforward, honest and dependable. The salt of the earth: and my best friend, the one I relied on.

His quietness, his unexpected reserve, puzzled me a bit, and I wondered if something else was bothering him, other than Tony Hampton. But perhaps not.

Now I stole a look at him. His head was thrown back against the plane seat and his eyes were closed, but even in repose his expression was troubled. His mouth had relaxed, but there was a tautness in his face, a tenseness in his body, even though he dozed. Poor Jake, I thought, I've put him through hell these past few weeks since Tony's death. I suddenly felt very guilty about that. We had both loved Tony in our different ways, and losing him had traumatized us. We had tried to help each other along, commiserating with each other, while continuing to miss him.

But as of today we had a different Tony Hampton to contemplate and contend with, a Tony much less noble, a man without honour, as far as I was concerned.

I asked myself why I had never realized that, never spotted this flaw in him? I prided myself on my integrity, and I found it hard to relate to those who lacked this quality. My grandfather had always held integrity very dear, and he had drilled its importance into me, reminding me about the value of honour, honesty, trustworthiness and decency. I have tried to live by Grandfather's rules and standards and I believe I have succeeded.

Once, long ago, my little slug of a brother Donald had told me that my standards were too high, that I expected too much from people, that no one could live up to my highfalutin expectations, going on to inform me that the world was full of rotten people. 'And most people *are* rotten, whatever *you* think Val Denning,' he had exploded, his rage spilling over. 'They stink. They cheat, they steal, they lie. They commit adultery, and murder, and they're shit! Yes, the whole world is full of shitty people, and the sooner you realize that the better off you'll be.'

I had gaped at him in astonishment at the time, wondering what rock he had crawled out from under, and then I had turned away in disgust. Over the years I had constantly endeavoured to avoid these confrontations with my brother as best I could, but I hadn't always succeeded. Ever since childhood I had loathed getting embroiled with him because he was so opinionated, and he never ever listened. I can't remember now what had set Donald off that particular day, but whenever he started to rant I usually did a disappearing act.

I suddenly remembered that Tony had also once said my standards were too high, and like Donald he had pointed out that very few people could live up to my expectations of them. I wondered now if he'd been thinking of himself that day. Of course I would never know; and the enigma of Tony would puzzle me for the rest of my life.

III

Jake suddenly awakened, stretched and turned to me. 'Well, I've not been much company, have I, Val?' He made a face. 'Sorry about that, honey, but I felt bushed when we got on the plane. I just had to grab a bit of sleep.'

I nodded my understanding. 'Do you feel better?'

Jake grimaced. 'Not really. London's been a tough trip, especially for you, and we *will* talk about Tony and Fiona, I promise. But later, okay? I'm just not up to it tonight.'

'Whenever you can, Jake, because it's important to me.'

'I'm aware of that. It's just as important to me, in more ways than you can imagine.' He reached over, took hold of my hand and squeezed it. 'I'll drop you off at your apartment, and I'll call you tomorrow, Val.'

'All right,' I murmured, feeling disappointed. I'd hoped to have dinner with him tonight, so that I could discuss Tony. But apparently that wasn't to be. Never mind, I could bide my time until he was ready.

Chapter Seven

I
PARIS, SEPTEMBER

The persona Tony Hampton had presented to the world had been dazzling. Intrepid war photographer, one of the most brilliant photojournalists of this decade, courageous, charismatic, a handsome and divine ladies' man, raconteur par excellence, bon vivant, and most generous host.

But there had been another side to him. He had been a liar and a cheat and he had undoubtedly led a double life. This is what I now truly believed even though I had only my own intuition to go on.

Maybe Jake wouldn't entirely agree with me, but I felt quite certain there had been a much darker side to Tony. Being in the bosom of his family at the memorial service earlier today had convinced me of this. And I was now absolutely positive he had never been divorced from Fiona. From his family's behaviour, and all that they had said, I placed him right in their midst until he left London in July. It was then he had come to Paris to pick us up, so that we could head out to Kosovo together. And he had been *happily* ensconced in their midst, from what I deduced.

I was sitting at the desk in my bedroom, and I reached out, picked up the photograph of Tony in its silver frame. I held it in both hands, staring at his face. He stood there on the deck of the sloop anchored off St Tropez last year, squinting in the summer sunshine. So dashing, so debonair . . . so enigmatic . . .

And I couldn't help wondering about him, wondering about his complicated life, and what it had been all about in the end.

He would have been a psychiatrist's dream, I thought. Put him on a couch for analysis and God knows what he would have spilled. Or would he? Psychotics didn't always do that, did they?

Psychotic.

The word hung there. Silently, I repeated it in my head, considered it carefully, asking myself why it had popped into my mind. And yet it did seem appropriate, didn't it? Tony *was* psychotic.

I put the photograph back in its given place on the desk, leaned back in my chair and stared off into space. In the far reaches of my mind, I'd had Tony Hampton under a mental microscope for a good part of the day, and I didn't like what I'd seen; nor did my conclusions about him elate me.

He was not just a liar, telling small white lies – didn't

we all do that at times? – but a pathological liar telling real whoppers, lies that were dangerous because they could conceivably do damage to people, cause them great heartache, change their lives and not always for the best.

That deep-seated lying had probably become a way of life for him. He couldn't stop because he couldn't help himself. Then again, he had needed to lie for his own protection. He had spun a web of deceit he couldn't crawl out of; he had entrapped himself with his complex machinations.

Then there was his adultery. It had been compulsive, excessive, a dominant force in his life, and it had obviously grown out of hand over the years. It became an addiction, I was sure.

I hadn't needed Jake to inform me today about the many women Tony had been involved with before me. I was well aware of his countless affairs; after all, we'd worked together, travelled together on various assignments.

Naturally Tony had tried to keep these women under wraps, and a secret, because his private life was his private life. It was none of my business, in his opinion. Nor was it Jake's business either, and so he had striven for privacy.

However, I could put two and two together, and come up with six, just like everyone else. Tony had always underestimated me and so had Jake. Just because I never discussed Tony's international sexual dalliances didn't mean that I didn't know they existed. I did know, and I didn't care. After all, I wasn't in love with him then, not involved in that way. This knowledge hadn't changed my opinion of him in those days. I thought he was a great guy, a good human being, and naturally I admired his talent as a photojournalist. It was more than that really; I considered it an honour to work alongside him.

But to think Jake believed I hadn't known about Tony's very busy love life . . . how ludicrous that was. I was much smarter than he imagined, than Tony imagined. I suddenly wanted to laugh out loud at the mere idea of it.

All those women . . . and one in particular whom I had known and disliked.

11

It was April 1996, and for once Tony and I were on assignment without Jake. He had gone to New York to deal with his divorce from Sue Ellen Jones, the famous model, and Tony and I had flown out to the Middle East for our respective news-photo agencies. We were in Lebanon to cover the new hostilities which had erupted between the Israelis and Hezbollah.

The long and fierce civil war was over by that time and things were beginning to mend, beginning to get back to normal, and then the skirmishing had unexpectedly started once more.

For the first time in fourteen years the Israelis

had attacked Beirut directly, using laser-homing Hellfire missiles shot from four helicopter gunships off the coast.

The Israelis were not the aggressors, though. They were actually responding to Hezbollah's recent bombing of their country. And that war of attrition had started up again because Hezbollah had then retaliated after the missile attack, sending forty rockets smack into the middle of Israel. And so it went . . .

One lovely spring day – late in the afternoon – Tony and I were sitting in the bar of the Marriott Hotel in the Hamra district of Beirut. I suppose I'll never ever forget that day, because we had had such bad news about a colleague of ours, Bill Fitzgerald of C.N.S., one of the American cable television networks. He had disappeared several days earlier, and none of us knew what had happened to him. We were all a bit nervous and concerned, and afraid for Bill.

Two of his crew, who had been with him out on the streets, had seen him grabbed by three young men, who had hustled him into a waiting Mercedes and then driven off at breakneck speed. The two crew members had been alert, and at once they had jumped into their car and followed in furious pursuit. But the Mercedes had disappeared – into thin air. It was nowhere in sight and they hadn't been able to find it.

Since then there had been no news about Bill, and none of the terrorist organizations had claimed his kidnapping. Who had snatched him, and for what purpose, we did not know.

But as we sat around in the bar that day, drinking with a group of international correspondents, all of us were offering theories and speculation was rampant . . .

III

'Islamic Jihad,' I had said all of a sudden, glancing around the table at my companions. 'They've got him.'

'But why would they have grabbed him?' Tony had asked, 'and if it is them, what have they got to *gain*, Val? Listen, snatching a newsman just doesn't make sense.'

'It might. They've managed to make use of hostages before,' I'd shot back. 'And don't forget, Islamic Jihad is the terrorist arm of Hezbollah. Its members are extremely dangerous, unpredictable, and nuts.'

Tony had given me a strange look, but he had said nothing else.

Frank Petersen, of *Time* magazine, had exclaimed, 'I agree with you, Val, Islamic Jihad *is* full of real wackos. And it's got to be them, in my opinion. They're the ones who took Terry Anderson and William Buckley, and they're not known for their fast releases.'

'Terry Anderson was a hostage for seven years,' I had muttered. 'Jesus, this is just awful. Does anyone know what Bill's network is doing about finding him?'

'There's not a lot they can do, Val.'

I had looked across at Joe Alonzo as he spoke. He had just arrived, and he was Bill Fitzgerald's soundman, had been on the streets with Bill when he was taken. Sitting down at the table with us, Joe went on, 'Bill's photo has been circulated throughout Beirut, throughout Lebanon, in fact. Pressure has been put on the Lebanese and Syrian governments, and on the White House too. But until somebody claims responsibility for the kidnapping there's not much else C.N.S. can do. Our network doesn't know who to deal with, Val.'

At that moment Allan Brent, the Middle East bureau chief for C.N.N., had hurried into the bar, glanced around and made a beeline for our table. His face was extremely grim. 'We've just had a news flash. About Bill. Hezbollah did it. Well, they're *claiming* they've got him.'

'Oh shit,' Tony had said and shaken his head in dismay. 'I still don't get it . . . why would they grab a newsman . . . ?' His voice had trailed off weakly.

The C.N.S. correspondent who was covering for Bill Fitzgerald had also arrived at our table. His name was Mark Lawrence, and it was apparent he was distressed. 'I guess you've heard it from Allan. Islamic Jihad just announced Bill is their captive.' He looked as if he were about to burst into tears.

'That group is so unstable, so fanatical, I think Bill has to be in very grave danger,' I had murmured gloomily. And later, very sadly, I was proven to be correct in this prediction. Bill never did make it out alive.

As the others had gone on talking about Bill's predicament, speculating about his fate in concerned voices, Tony had leaned closer to me and stared into my face in the most peculiar way. He was studying me very intently, almost probingly. For a few seconds I hadn't been able to fathom out the meaning of this close scrutiny, until it struck me he was actually giving me the once-over. It was as if he was suddenly seeing me differently, objectively, and in a new light.

'What's wrong?' I finally asked him, irritated. He had begun to make me feel uncomfortable, nervous even, and I didn't appreciate those feelings. He had never acted like this before and I was puzzled and annoyed with him.

'Nothing's wrong,' he had answered lightly, leaning back, balancing his chair precariously on its two back legs. 'Where do you want to go to dinner tonight, Val? I've invited Anne Curtis to join us. We'll have a good meal, go to a club afterwards, go dancing. If you like, I'll ask Frank to come along. We can make it a foursome, Val.'

I had been thunderstruck, and had stared at him speechlessly, unable to comprehend how he could speak so nonchalantly about having a social evening when we were all so devastated, so worried about Bill's kidnapping. Who the hell cared about dinner, for God's sake, when a man's life was at stake, I had thought furiously, indignantly. But the words hadn't left my mouth; they'd remained stuck in my throat, although more from disgust with him than reticence on my part.

Tony was being insensitive and callous, and I was suddenly very, very angry with him. But before I'd had a chance to reprove him, to chastize him for his heartlessness, Anne Curtis herself came over to join us.

She was English, but so dark of complexion and colouring I'd always thought she must have Mediterranean or Middle Eastern ancestry. She was with the B.B.C. World Service, and was a brilliant radio journalist. On various occasions she'd tried to be friendly, but I'd never warmed to her. There was something about her that struck me as being untrustworthy, although I had nothing specific to go on. It was just an instinctive feeling on my part.

But it was quite obvious she had warmed to Tony.

She had squeezed in between the two of us when Frank had very gallantly pulled up a chair for her, and although Tony had remained cool and detached, the look in her eyes had told me plenty; all I needed to know.

I had guessed at once that they were embroiled in a hot affair; this suspicion was confirmed later that evening, when we did finally go out to dinner, dragging Frank Petersen along with us. Anne had left little to anyone's imagination. The manner in which she had drooled over Tony, in the most disgusting and juvenile way, had telegraphed everything to me. And to Frank, who had appeared to be somewhat embarrassed by her performance. Yet I'd had to hand it to Tony that night. He hadn't batted an eyelash; what's more, he had appeared so completely indifferent to her it was quite amazing. He deserves an Academy Award I'd thought at the time.

The following day I'd run into Anne in the lobby of the Commodore Hotel, and she had attacked me verbally, berating me in the worst way and accusing me of being a spoilsport. 'You don't have to tell me you didn't enjoy the evening,' she had announced, glaring at me. 'It was written all over your face. You made us all suffer, constantly going on about Bill Fitzgerald. Poor Frank didn't know how to cope. He *is* Bill's best friend, you know.'

'Of course Frank knew how to handle it,' I'd exclaimed, glaring back at her. 'Mostly I think he was cringing at your behaviour.'

'You can't have him, my dear,' she had cried heatedly, leaning into me almost threateningly. 'Tony belongs to me. He's mine and I intend to keep him. *Permanently*. So just keep your jealous little paws off him, Valentine. Understand me?'

I remember I had stared at her aghast, told her she'd got it all wrong, and then hurried off mortified. I was furious not only with her, but with Tony as well, for putting me in such an untenable position.

And I had continued to seethe about that evening for quite a while. Anne's accusations didn't particularly bother me in the long run, since they were patently ridiculous, but what did upset me was Tony's callousness, his lack of concern for Bill Fitzgerald.

I began to despise myself for going to that dinner, for being a party to it under the circumstances. I also continued to be disturbed by Tony's behaviour, his thoughtlessness that night. But eventually I let it go, and soon I found myself making excuses for him . . . as war photographers we lived with constant danger, took terrible chances when we hurled ourselves into the fray on the front lines or in disaster areas. And so, in a certain way, we did become inured to tragedy, perhaps because there was so much of it around us. Tragedy was commonplace for journalists like us, human suffering the norm . . .

IV

Reaching for Tony's photograph once more, I gave it a quick glance then opened a drawer in the desk and placed it inside.

I didn't want his face gazing out at me. Sometimes it seemed to me that his brilliant dark eyes followed me as I moved around my bedroom. It was most disconcerting.

Perhaps I ought to take it out of the frame and tear it up. Yes, I would do that, I decided. I would tear up every one of his photographs and destroy those little notes and letters and cards he'd sent me this past year. Tomorrow though, not tonight. I was far too tired, exhausted actually. It had been a very long day, and emotionally draining.

But there was one thing I *could* do now.

I glanced down at my right hand and then I pulled off the Grecian ring with the aqua stones, held it in my hand for a moment, studying it. I was about to throw it in the wastepaper basket and then I changed my mind. Janine was coming to clean the apartment tomorrow; she would undoubtedly find it and put it on my desk, not understanding that I had deliberately thrown it away.

I went through into the kitchen, dropped the ring in the trash can, emptied the used coffee grains on top of it, and then added a lump of wet paper towel to the mess. That way, Janine would never find it, not unless she scrabbled through my kitchen garbage, which I very much doubted.

I went back to the desk in my bedroom and sat down again. My brain still raced. I knew, deep down within myself, that my ultimate conclusions about my dead lover were absolutely accurate. Right on the mark.

Furthermore, I accepted now that I'd been used, abused in a sense, and played for a fool. The first time Tony had taken me out on an actual date, he had confided that he had started divorce proceedings against Fiona. Not true. And he'd never intended to marry me.

A long sigh escaped me. I knew I must pull myself together, start over again, make an effort somehow to get on with my life. But before I could do that I had to unburden myself, get all of this off my chest. I had to talk to Jake; that was imperative. No one else would understand my turbulent feelings, my distress, my terrible hurt inside. And certainly no one else cared in the way that he did. He was my best friend, wasn't he?

Chapter Eight

1

The following morning Jake called me as he had promised he would during our flight back to Paris. We made a date to have lunch.

Several hours later I met him at the Bar des Théâtres on the Avenue Montaigne, a little bit down the street from the Hotel Plaza Athénée. It was one of his favourite haunts, since it was frequented by the gorgeous models who worked at the Balmain haute couture salon on the rue François 1er nearby.

I couldn't help thinking how much better he looked today as he stood up to greet me. The tan he had acquired in the south of France last week gave him a healthy look anyway; but it was his eyes which were different. They were bright and alert again, and he was smiling broadly. It was quite a change from yesterday. In London he had been so gloomy, and introspective on the plane, had appeared weary, worn out, and not a bit like the Jake I'd come to know. He was usually so outgoing, energetic and vital.

After giving me a quick peck on the cheek, he said, 'You look wonderful, Val, the white suit is great on you. Much better than black.'

Well, I'm not in mourning any more, I thought with some acerbity, but I didn't say a word. I simply smiled back at him, and murmured, 'You don't look so bad yourself.'

Once we were seated opposite each other at the table, he asked, 'What would you like to drink?'

'Not sure . . .'

'I'm thinking of having a dry martini. Want to try one?'

I hesitated but only fractionally. 'Why not?' Then quickly, I added, 'But I might get drunk if I do.'

'You don't have to worry, you know I always look after you.'

I shook my head. 'Perhaps I'd better not have a martini, Jake. It's far too strong. A glass of white wine instead, please.'

He grinned at me. 'And I'll have the same. You're right about the martini. It *is* too potent, especially at lunch time.'

Once Jake had ordered the drinks, he turned to me and began, 'I know you need to talk to me about Tony, and I'm ready to listen. Now, or later after lunch, whatever you prefer.'

'Yes . . .' I paused and sighed. 'I've had a sleepless night, running everything through my mind again and again, going over every detail. But whichever way I twist and turn I keep coming up with the same answers, and –' I broke off, shook my head.

'And what?' he prompted.

'I know that certain things are true, without the benefit of anyone giving me information or telling me anything. Tony was a liar, Jake, and he *did* lead a double life, playing other women off against Fiona. Who now has my pity, by the way. He wasn't divorced from her, nor was he intending to be. Tony wanted his cake and he wanted to eat it. I know I'm not wrong.'

'I tend to agree with you. It's a very male characteristic, isn't it, Val?' He looked at me intently and a brow lifted, then he went on, 'Tony wanted a wife and a mistress apparently. And there's nothing new about that, is there? Mistresses have been around for centuries, since the beginning of time. And if you're going to have a wife and a mistress and lead a double life, then you have to be a liar, and a damned good one. Because it seems to me the two go hand in glove.'

'That's true.' I cleared my throat. 'I want you to know something else, Jake.'

'Go ahead, tell me.'

I was silent for a split second; the waiter had arrived with our drinks. But once we were alone again, I continued, 'Just over a year ago, before Tony and I became involved, before he'd even invited me out on a date, he confided in me over lunch one day . . . he said he'd just got a legal separation from Fiona, that he was in the process of divorcing her.'

'I'd no idea he'd said a thing like that,' Jake replied, looking surprised. Picking up his glass, he said, 'Cheers,' and took a sip of the white wine.

'Cheers,' I answered, and tasted the Sancerre. 'I now believe that that was a downright lie, that he invented the story. He knew I would never go out with him because he was a married man. He knew what I felt about married men. They were verboten as far as I was concerned.'

'Yes, he did know that. We both did.'

'In the end it's all a matter of integrity, isn't it?' I shook my head sadly. 'Tony Hampton didn't have any integrity, although until yesterday I thought he did.'

'So did I,' Jake muttered in a low voice. 'Yes, well, he had integrity in his work, of course, but not in his personal life. Obviously.'

'Correct.'

Jake settled back in the chair, his expression reflective.

I sipped my wine, watching him closely. Waiting. He seemed to be mulling something over in his mind.

Finally, after a few more moments of deep reflection, Jake said, 'Your intuition was correct yesterday. In the Brompton Oratory, I mean, when you suddenly *knew* in your bones that Fiona was his widow and not his ex-wife.'

'She told you!' I cried, sounding a bit triumphant, I must admit.

'No,' he said. 'No, she didn't, Val. But I'm certain of it, after talking to Rory and Moira at the lunch. They were both full of Tony, singing his praises, telling me what a good father he'd been to them, and right until the end. Rory explained that Tony had spent a wonderful six-week period with them in June and July, before going off to Kosovo. And Moira became very weepy for a few seconds. She told me how glad they all were they'd been able to have this special time with him. And that he'd taken her to his photo agency, and got her a job and she was starting there next year.'

Although Jake was merely confirming what I already believed to be the truth, I still crumpled a bit, slumped down in my chair. I felt my eyes filling up.

Jake leaned forward, grabbed my hand and said in a concerned tone, 'Don't get upset, Val. Please, darling. You've done enough weeping about him. And he's not worth it.'

'He was a bastard,' I whispered.

II

'Let's look at the menu, and order lunch.' As he spoke Jake motioned to the waiter, who was at his side in an instant.

'What're your specials today, Antoine?'

The waiter told us, and Jake, looking across the table at me, said, 'How about the green salad, entrecôte and French fries? Sounds good to me.'

I wasn't very hungry, but I nodded in agreement, not wanting to argue with him.

After giving the waiter instructions about how he wanted the steaks cooked, Jake added, 'And let's have two more glasses of wine, please Antoine.'

'*Oui*, Monsieur Newberg,' Antoine responded, smiled and hurried off.

'Got to put some flesh on you,' Jake murmured and grinned at me.

I grimaced, and sipped my wine. After a moment, I said, 'You were very quiet on the plane last night. Preoccupied, you said. Was that because of Rory and Moira? And what they'd said to you about Tony?'

Jake sighed. 'Yup, that was it. I suddenly realized your instincts were correct, and I was appalled at what he'd done to you.'

'There's something else, Jake. I think Tony's apartment on the King's Road was just a place for him to develop film and seduce women. I could never reach him there. The answering machine was always on, I was forever leaving messages. He'd call back, of course, but always hours later. Sometimes I tried him on his cell phone, but a lot of the time that was turned off. I know the flat was properly furnished and all that, and he did have clothes and stuff there, but now I think it was just a front. I bet you anything he really lived at the house in Hampstead with Fiona.'

Jake was silent for a minute or two, and then he said, very quietly, 'You're probably right, Val. It's true, he never picked up the phone at his flat. And basically, I have the same problem as you, believing he lived there, I mean. I could hardly ever reach him in London because his cell phone *was* turned off more than it was on. I left countless messages with his photo agency, when I really needed to get him.'

'We were *both* duped by him,' I muttered, giving him a hard stare. 'I'm glad it wasn't just me.'

III

After lunch we went for a walk along the Seine. It was a nice afternoon, quite balmy, and although the sun wasn't shining, the sky was a clear, gentle blue dotted with pale clouds.

We ambled along, heading towards the Pont des Arts, the only metal bridge in Paris, not talking very much, lost in our own thoughts. But Jake and I were comfortable together; we didn't have to keep up a non-stop conversation.

I was the first one to break our companionable silence when I suddenly stopped, turned to Jake and said, 'Do you think Tony was psychotic?'

Also coming to a standstill, he stared at me and exclaimed, 'Val, that's an odd thing to say! And off the top of my head, no, I don't think he was psychotic. From what you and I *think* we know about him, I'll grant you he was a sexual predator and a very clever liar, but not sick in the head. At least, not the way you're suggesting. He always had his wits about him, knew what he was doing, what he was saying. Yes, he was smart, and very devious. But psychotic?' Jake shook his head.

I opened the black satchel bag thrown over my shoulder, took out a piece of paper, and explained, 'Listen to this . . . I looked in the dictionary this morning. *Psychotic*: Of, relating to, or affected by psychosis. *Psychosis*: A severe mental disorder, with or without organic damage, characterized by derangement of personality and loss of contact with reality. Don't you think he'd lost contact with reality, telling us both he was divorced, asking me to marry him?'

'Only if he believed his own lies, Val. *That* would be a loss of contact with reality. I think Tony lived in the real world, I really do. There's nothing more real than war, as you well know, and he was always out there, shooting film, looking for the greatest picture, just as we were. No, I can't say he was psychotic. Just a *sonofabitch*!'

'Yes, he was, and then some. But he had to be off the wall to a certain extent, mentally unbalanced, doing what he did to me. Jesus, Jake, he was nuts thinking he could get away with it.'

'I agree with you. But even so, I can't really explain his behaviour or his reasoning, because he never confided in me. Perhaps he fully intended to lead a double life with you. Many men have got away with that! Fiona in London. You in Paris. Captain's paradise.'

'And a bigamous marriage with me? Is that what you mean?'

'Maybe, Val. I just don't know.'

'We'll never know.'

Jake put his arm around me and we walked on in silence. After a moment, he said softly, 'I didn't sleep much myself last night, turning all this over in my mind. I even thought at one point that I should go back to London to see Fiona, to try and find out the state of their marriage when he was killed. Just so you and I would really know the truth. But I changed my mind. Without actually coming out and asking her if they were divorced, I don't think I'd be able to glean very much having a roundabout conversation with her . . .' He didn't finish, just half shrugged and looked down at me, making a small grimace.

'Oh, just leave it alone, Jake! It's all yesterday's news!' I exclaimed, and I was startled at the shakiness of my voice.

'Hey, Val honey, I didn't mean to upset you.' Jake wrapped both arms around me and hugged me close. 'You're right, it is old news. And I've got a great idea.'

'What?' I whispered against his shoulder, blinking back incipient tears.

'Let's go down to Cap Ferrat this weekend. To Peter Guiseborn's house. I've got the use of it until he comes back from New York.'

'I don't know if I want to go, Jake.'

He held me away from him and looked at me intently. 'It'll do us both good. We can relax, get the sun, have some delicious meals, not that you ever eat, but you won't be able to resist the food there. Simone, Peter's housekeeper, is a great cook. And what are you going to do this weekend anyway, Val? Tramp the streets of Paris, sit alone in your apartment thinking about Tony, getting angry with him. Come on, Val, say you'll come with me. Listen, you've got to move forward now, look to the future.'

'Okay,' I mumbled, giving in, too weary to resist. 'I guess it will help to get away from Paris for a few days.'

Grinning, he hugged me to him again, and then he took hold of my hand, making for the steps near the bridge. These led up to the Quai Malaquais in St Germain-des-Prés, and just beyond the quai was the Rue Bonaparte, where I lived.

As he hurried me along with him I couldn't help noticing again how badly he was limping, and this worried me. But I didn't dare ask him how his wounds were healing; he usually snapped at me when I did so.

And then I thought: But at least he's alive, and I'm alive, and he's right, I have a whole future ahead of me.

And I made up my mind to bury the dead.

Part Two

The Value of Truth

Chapter Nine

I

ST-JEAN-CAP FERRAT, SEPTEMBER

The house hung on a hillside in Cap Ferrat, overlooking gardens filled with an abundance of flowers; beyond, stretching to the horizon, was the glittering deep-blue Mediterranean.

I sat on the terrace of the house, looking out towards the sea, content to drift along with my thoughts, enjoying the perfect stillness, unbroken except for the occasional trilling of the birds, the faint buzzing of a bee. It was a glorious morning, and even though it was sunny and warm a light breeze blew up intermittently. It rippled through the trees, making the leaves dance, and gave the morning air its freshness.

Called Les Roches Fleuries, the villa was aptly named, since so many flowers spilled down over the rocks upon which the house had been built. It was long and rambling, made of a local stone washed pale pink, with a typical Provençal roof of red slate tiles and green-painted shutters at the many windows.

On the plane to Nice on Thursday, Jake had told me all about the villa. Even so, I hadn't expected anything quite like this. And although he had described it well, I'd teased him and said, 'Well, it's true what they say, you know, about a picture being worth a thousand words. Better stick to snapping the old polaroid.'

'Only too true, Val,' he'd laughed as he had taken me on a grand tour. I had at once been captivated by the house, which pleased Jake since he loved it himself; he felt lucky and privileged to be able to use it whenever he wished. It belonged to his old friend Peter Guiseborn, who had moved from Paris to work in New York for a year, and Peter had told Jake to take advantage of his absence. Jake was also flattered and touched because Peter had not extended this invitation to any of his other friends.

The interiors were cool and restful. All of the rooms had white walls, wood-beamed ceilings and terra-cotta tile floors, and they were furnished with wonderful Provençal antiques made of polished dark woods. There was very little clutter in the rooms, which added to the feeling of restfulness.

Colour, bright rafts of it, was introduced in the vibrant paintings hanging on the walls, and in the huge bunches of flowers arranged in large stone pots and placed in almost every room.

'I could move in and live here forever,' I'd enthused.

'And so could I,' he'd agreed.

When we arrived we had received a warm welcome from Simone and Armand Roget, the caretakers, who lived in a small house on the property. It was Simone who kept the place so immaculate and sparkling, and the pantry well stocked with her delicious food.

Her husband Armand was responsible for the upkeep of the property and the gardens, which were filled to overflowing with bougainvillaea, frangipani, honeysuckle, night-blooming jasmine, azaleas, geraniums, and many different species of roses. The flower gardens were set off by velvety green lawns, whilst a long line of twenty-five stately cypress trees stood guard in the background, dark sentinels silhouetted against the azure sky.

Over dinner on our first night here, Jake had told me the story of the house – at least what little he knew about it. Les Roches Fleuries had been built in the 1930s by a French duke for his English mistress, a beautiful opera singer called Adelia Roland. After her retirement from the stage she had made it her permanent home, had lived here until she had died at the age of ninety in 1990. In her will she had left the villa and almost everything else she owned to her great-nephew Peter, Jake's pal from his Oxford days.

I was intrigued by the story of Adelia and the duke, but Jake didn't know much more than he'd already told me. Neither did the Rogets have a great deal to impart to me, when I had quizzed them about her. They had been at Les Roches Fleuries for twenty years; for eight of these they had worked for Peter, once he had inherited the property. The preceding twelve years had been spent in the employment of Adelia Roland, but by that time she was already an old lady, and the duke had long been dead. They said she had been charming, but cool and reserved. And very mysterious.

Earlier this morning, when I'd strolled outside holding a cup of coffee in my hand, I had spotted Armand working in the garden. Walking over, I had started to chat to him about the house and about Adelia. Suddenly, unexpectedly, he had turned garrulous, and he confided that it had been Adelia herself who had been the brains and driving force behind the planning and execution of these most extraordinary gardens.

Apparently she had toiled on them herself, and religiously so, had thought nothing of working alongside the various gardeners who had helped her fulfil her plans over the years. The gardens had been ruined during the German Occupation of France, in the Second World War, but she had restored them later, once the war had ended.

It struck me that she had obviously been as talented a gardener as she was a singer, since the gardens were breathtaking in their beauty. I felt as if I were sitting in the middle of an exotic paradise, surrounded by a riotous mass of colour, breathing in air so fragrant it was heady and intoxicating.

11

I glanced around when I heard footsteps, and I saw Jake walking along the terrace. I waved to him and he waved back, and a moment later he was standing over the chaise where I lay shaded by an umbrella, looking down at me, smiling broadly.

'This is what I like to see!' he exclaimed.

'And what's that?'

'You lying here like this, relaxing, taking it easy, and looking so contented.' He lowered himself onto the edge of the chaise next to mine as he spoke.

'I certainly feel relaxed, Jake. It's just so beautiful here, and the tranquillity's hard to beat, isn't it?'

He merely nodded, and smiled again.

I went on, 'I feel . . . well, I feel really peaceful *inside* . . . for the first time in many weeks.' I genuinely meant every word I said. I *did* feel so much better and after only a couple of days.

There was a moment's silence before he remarked, 'So do I, Val. This house has always had a restorative effect on me in the past . . . it's a benign house, full of love and good vibes. The only other one I've known with exactly the same atmosphere was my grandparents' house in Georgia. I always looked forward to going there as a child. I felt enveloped by love, so safe and secure. I still derive pleasure from going there, in fact.'

How I envied Jake. The truth was I'd never felt safe or secure in my life, except when I was with my grandparents.

'How is your grandmother doing, Jake?' I now asked, knowing how much he loved the old lady. Actually, I think he loved her in much the same way I had loved Andrew Denning.

'Still going strong. You know, Val, she's really quite amazing. Very bright, not a bit senile, and well in health.'

'She's living there alone at the house, then?'

'Oh yes. Well, there's help living there with her. A couple of old retainers who've been devoted to her for forty years or more. It would be hard to get her to leave, practically her whole life has been lived out there. It's an old plantation house, not that big really, but beautiful. An antebellum house, redolent of the Old South that once was. You don't see much of *that* any more, except in a few remote places. Anyway, her place is not too far from Atlanta, and my parents now go there almost every weekend. They worry about her . . . but they shouldn't, in my opinion.'

'Why not?'

'She makes everybody else I know look decrepit!'

I smiled. 'But she's quite old, isn't she?'

'Eighty-eight. Going on thirty-five though! She's independent, opinionated, and very, very feisty. You'd love her.'

Jake started to laugh again and his bright blue eyes sparkled with sudden merriment.

'What is it?'

'I was wondering how to describe her physically, and I can only say this . . . she reminds me of an old movie actress from the 1930s and '40s by the name of Maria Ouspenskaya. Do you know who I mean?' He went on chuckling and then added, 'You're looking mystified, Val.'

'I am. I'm afraid I *don't* know her.'

'Ouspenskaya was petite, fragile-looking, white-haired, and she spoke with the slightest of accents, more than likely Russian with a name like hers. Granmutti Hedy, as we call her, had a bit of a German accent, but it's very slight now. Here's something that might just jog your memory about Ouspenskaya . . . did you ever see an old movie called *Love Affair*?'

I shook my head.

'Well, Ouspenskaya was in it, playing an old lady, of course, and the stars were Charles Boyer and Irene Dunne, and it was about –'

'Wait a minute, I have seen it!' I exclaimed, cutting in as I suddenly recalled the film. 'And I *do* know what Ouspenskaya looked like. Wasn't that the original version of a later movie called *An Affair to Remember* with Cary Grant and Deborah Kerr?'

'Spot on! And so if you think of Ouspenskaya you'll know what my grandmother Hedy looks like. She's an extraordinary woman, and she was so strong and vital when she was younger. A marvel, even though I say so myself. She is also very cultured, well read, full of knowledge about art and music. She was a very, very wonderful grandmother to a little boy and his two sisters.'

III

As Jake had been speaking so lovingly about his grandmother, I'd noticed a change in his voice. It was ever so slight, but it was there, none the less; a soft, southern drawl had crept in to diffuse the transatlantic accent he had acquired from years of living in Paris, and, before that, Oxford.

Now he was saying, 'Don't you think that's a great idea, Val? We'll watch some old movies tonight. Peter has stacks of them, there's quite a wide video selection in his library and there are lots of choices.'

'I wonder if he has *Love Affair*?' I said, thinking out loud.

'He might have. I know he's got *Casablanca*, and many of the other classics from the 1930s, '40s and '50s. He's even got *Gone with the Wind*. I wouldn't mind watching *that* again.'

I started to laugh.

'What's the matter?' he asked, quizzically.

Continuing to laugh, I said, 'Are you feeling homesick for Atlanta, Jake?'

Laughing with me, he nodded. 'I'm always homesick for Georgia in one way or another, but it just happens to be a really fabulous movie. Let's watch it, okay?'

'Anything you want,' I answered. Out of the corner of my eye I could see Simone coming towards us. 'I guess lunch is ready,' I murmured to Jake, and glanced at my watch. I couldn't believe it was already one-thirty. Time seemed to fly here at Les Roches Fleuries with Jake. The last couple of days had gone by in the blink of an eye.

Pushing himself to his feet, Jake stretched out his hand to me. I took it and he pulled me up from the chaise, led me down the terrace.

'We're coming, Simone,' he called out, and she smiled at us, turned on her heels and went back to the arbour at the far end of the terrace. This little shaded area was just a stone's throw away from the kitchen, and it was there she stood waiting for us.

Within seconds Jake and I were seated opposite each other under the vine-covered arbour, and Simone was saying to us, 'Mademoiselle Denning, Monsieur Jake, I found a beautiful *rouget* at the fish market this morning. I've grilled it for you, and I shall bring it now with a dish of vegetables.'

'Thanks, Simone, it sounds delicious,' Jake replied.

She inclined her head, hurried off to fetch the fish, and Jake lifted the bottle of chilled *vin rosé*, which he loved to drink with lunch, and poured it into the large glasses.

'I'm not planning to go back to Paris on Tuesday after all,' he suddenly said, glancing at me across the table. 'It's so restful here, the weather's wonderful, and I'm seriously thinking of spending next week at the house. Won't you stay on, too, Val?'

'Yes, I'd love to,' I answered immediately, without even having to think about it. 'Why not? I don't have anything pressing to do,' I added.

'That's great. I'm glad you'll stay and keep me company.'

'What are best friends for?' I asked, returning his smile.

Chapter Ten

1

And so I stayed on at Les Roches Fleuries with Jake.

It seemed to me that time just sped by, even though we didn't do anything very special. In the first few days we were there together we fell into a routine, a pattern which was built on a number of little rituals and which we both discovered we enjoyed.

I think the reason we found enjoyment in them is because we lived such a helter-skelter life when we were out on assignment, and never knew what was going to happen from one day to the next, or where we might end up.

But at the villa on the hillside our days rarely varied, and neither of us minded this at all. In fact, we thought of it as a blessing.

Every morning Jake and I had breakfast together, sitting at the round table under the vine-covered arbour. The weather was still glorious, and it offered us protection from the early- morning sun. Neither of us ate very much at breakfast, nor were we inclined to talk, so we were, as usual, compatible and at ease with each other.

After breakfast I usually read for a short time, while Jake sunbathed, swam in the pool and occasionally called his photo agency for messages; on other mornings he would spend time writing in his notebook.

Sometimes I would take a swim with Jake, but not always. However, I did go to the basement gym with him at exactly eleven o'clock every day, where I fast-walked on the treadmill. Because of his wounds, Jake avoided the treadmill, but he enjoyed lifting weights.

After about half an hour in the gym, we went off to our rooms to shower and change into cool cottons, then we took the car and drove down into the little town of Beaulieu-sur-Mer.

I knew Beaulieu quite well, since my grandparents had frequently stayed at La Réserve, a lovely pink-and-white hotel in the town. It sat on a wedge of land at the edge of the sea, was renowned for its elegance and its wonderful restaurant. When my grandparents had come to France to see me in the summer, they went down to the south after a week in Paris. I always joined them in Beaulieu, once the Sorbonne was on summer recess.

Because of his frequent sojourns at Peter's villa, Jake was also well acquainted with this charming little town, and we liked to walk around, buying the French and English newspapers and magazines, visiting the antique dealers we liked, and picking up the odd items we needed at the local shops. But our favourite spot was the open-air fruit and vegetable market right in the heart of Beaulieu.

Inevitably our mouths started watering when we stopped to look at the baskets of raspberries, redcurrants, strawberries, blackberries, plums, peaches, and the fragrant melons from Cavaillon, which we both knew from experience were the very best. Everything on the market stalls looked so luscious and tempting; but we never dared buy anything to take back, for fear of offending Simone. She prided herself on her careful selection of produce for the delicious meals she created for us.

There was a small port in Beaulieu, where sailboats and yachts were at anchor in the quiet harbour. It was a charming, picturesque spot, and there were all manner of bistros, cafés and boutiques centred around the port. We loved to linger there, whiling away the time as we meandered along the *quais*.

Just before lunch we went to La Réserve for an aperitif, since the hotel was close to the old port. If we didn't stop there, then we would end up at the Grand Hotel du Cap Ferrat on our way home to thc villa. We had discovered that the outside bar on the tree-shaded terrace of the hotel was a cool place for a *Kir Royale* or a simple *citron pressé*.

This kind of leisurely morning, devoid of the drama, stress and death we were accustomed to coping with, was so unusual for us we got a tremendous kick out of it. 'Being normal, living normal', Jake called it, and he was right. Most of our working days were spent watching people being blown up, maimed or killed while we plied our trade as war photographers.

After our visit to the Grand Hotel, we would then drive on, up the winding hill and through the woods, making it back to Les Roches Fleuries just in time for lunch.

The afternoons were very lazy.

Jake read and slept. I did the same, or listened to music. Neither of us ever thought of turning on the television set and tuning in to C.N.N. We didn't want to hear the bad news, to know about wars, terrorism, earthquakes, hurricanes, floods, fires or famine.

This quiet, uneventful time was rare for us, and therefore seductive . . . we wanted to make it last. And so we were never tempted to venture out in the evening; certainly we had no desire to visit the chic spots in Monte Carlo, Nice and Cannes. For the most part, Jake and I stayed close to the villa, which we were very partial to and enjoyed to the fullest. It seemed to us that there was no reason to go anywhere else. The extraordinary peacefulness was our idea of bliss, and we made the most of it.

11

One morning at the end of my first week at the villa, I woke up and discovered that I felt different.

I lay in bed for a moment, watching the sunlight slither in through the slats of the wooden blinds, wondering *why* I felt this way, and then, in an instant, I *knew*.

It was because I hadn't thought about Tony Hampton for several days. And because I hadn't thought about him, or what he'd done to me, I wasn't angry or hurt.

I was just *me* . . . Valentine Denning. The Val Denning of old again. It was a great feeling.

A second or two later I was standing in front of the bathroom mirror staring at myself. To my astonishment I even looked different. The smudges under my eyes had all but disappeared, and the greyish tinge to my skin had been replaced by a golden glow. Without actually sunbathing, I had somehow managed to catch the sun, had acquired a light tan; even my hair was sun-streaked. I hadn't looked so healthy for a long time, and suddenly I was very pleased.

This miraculous and unexpected change in my appearance gave me a huge boost, a sense of renewed energy, and I threw off my nightgown, stepped into the shower and turned on the water. After lathering myself with shower gel and then shampooing my hair, I rinsed off, stepped out, and towelled myself dry.

Within minutes I was tying my hair in a pony tail, then pulling on a swimsuit; I found a white cotton-voile shirt in the wardrobe, pushed my feet into a pair of flat mules, jammed on my dark glasses and went in search of Jake.

I found him sitting at the edge of the swimming pool with his feet dangling in the water, his ear pressed to his cell phone. He was listening intently. When he saw me coming down the steps to the pool, he merely raised his hand in greeting then beckoned me to join him.

After a moment or two of listening, he said, 'Okay, Jacques. Thanks. Call me back if you think I can be of help.' Listening again, he reached for the notepad next to him. His eyes scanned it quickly, then he said, 'Yup, I got it. See ya, Jacques.'

Once he had clicked off the phone, I walked over and gave him a kiss on the cheek. 'Good morning.'

'And top o' the morning to you.'

I smiled at him. 'In our Irish mode, are we?'

'I guess so. Perhaps because I had a call at the photo agency from Fiona. She's in Dublin. At the Shelbourne Hotel. She wants me to call her.'

I frowned. 'I wonder why?'

'God knows,' Jake murmured, glanced down at his cell phone and then the notepad, and began to dial. A couple of seconds later he was asking for Mrs Fiona Hampton. He waited then said, 'Thanks very much,' and clicked off. Turning to face me, he explained, 'She's checked out. No forwarding address.'

'She's probably gone back to London. To the house in Hampstead.'

'I guess.'

'Did Jacques have anything else to say?'

'He wanted to know if I'd like to go back to Rwanda. To do another story on the gorillas. I said no. He's going to ask Harry Lennox if he wants to do it. I told him I'd help with Harry, if it was necessary. But I don't think it will be. Harry's ambitious, even if he is a bit of an innocent abroad, so to speak. He'll jump at the assignment.'

'Perhaps,' I murmured. I wasn't sure about Jake's assessment of Harry. I thought he was much more worldly than Jake gave him credit for. In my opinion, Harry Lennox was also devious, possibly even treacherous as well. He had always reminded me of my brother, Donald the Great.

'You sound dubious, Valentine. What's your problem?' he asked in his breezy way.

'You are, Jake. I think you underestimate Harry Lennox. He's made dissembling a fine art. And he's a jealous little bugger. Especially jealous of you.'

Jake threw back his head and laughed. 'Oh come on, Val, don't be ridiculous.'

'I'm not being ridiculous, and listen, I know his type. He's like my sneaky little brother . . . I wouldn't trust either of them as far as I could throw them. And that's a fact –' I broke off as I saw Simone hurrying down the steps to the pool. She was as white as bleached bone and obviously distressed.

III

Jake exclaimed, 'Simone, what's wrong?' And as he spoke he pulled his legs out of the pool and scrambled to his feet.

She drew to a standstill in front of us and I saw at once that she was on the verge of tears. I reached out, put my hand on her arm. 'Whatever is it?' I asked.

'It is my daughter, Françoise,' Simone began and then her voice quavered. After a moment she recovered, and continued in a rush of words, 'She had a bad fall this morning. Down the stairs. Olivier, her husband, has taken her to the hospital. They are worried about the baby.'

'My God, that's terrible!' I exclaimed. 'Is there anything we can do?'

Simone shook her head, looking distracted and worried, then brushed her hand across her eyes. 'Olivier, he just phoned,' she added.

Jake said, 'You must go to Marseilles, Simone, with Armand. We can manage here. And you'll only worry if you don't go.'

She nodded. 'That is true, I will. *Merci*, Monsieur Jake. Please come, the breakfast is ready.'

IV

The three of us walked up to the arbour at the far end of the terrace, and Simone disappeared through the door to the kitchen.

Jake and I sat down, staring at each other worriedly. Jake sounded concerned when he said, 'I believe Françoise's about seven or eight months pregnant with her first baby. I hope she hasn't injured herself and the child, that they're going to be all right.'

'So do I . . . but what are they doing in Marseilles? I thought their daughter lived in Cannes?'

'That's Solange, the younger daughter.'

'I see.' I picked up the crystal jug of fresh orange juice which stood on the table and filled our glasses. Before I got a chance to say anything else, Simone was back with a large pot of coffee and a jug of hot milk for the *café au lait* we both preferred.

Returning to the kitchen, she came out a second later carrying a basket of warm *croissants* and *brioches*. She said: 'Armand is telephoning Nice Airport, Monsieur Jake. There's a plane to Marseilles at one o'clock. I will attend to the beds, clean the kitchen –'

Cutting in, Jake exclaimed, 'You'll do no such thing, Simone. I told you, we can manage. Go and get ready, I know how anxious you must be. Once you're packed, I'll drive you to the airport.'

'But Monsieur Jake –'

'No buts,' he interrupted again, holding up his hand, taking charge. 'Go and do as I say, and we'll leave whenever you want.'

'*Merci, Monsieur Jake, c'est gentil de votre part.*'

When we were alone, Jake said, 'How about coming with me to the airport in Nice?' He poured coffee and hot milk into his large cup, then looked across at me.

'Well . . .' I cocked my head on one side, and murmured, 'Maybe it's better I stay here, tidy the kitchen, do a few chores, be domesticated for a change.' I smiled at him. 'And I'll prepare a lovely lunch.'

He nodded. 'Okay, but only if you let me fix dinner.'

'Southern style?' I demanded.

He laughed. 'You're on, Kid.'

V

Once they had left, it didn't take me very long to stack the dishwasher and mop the kitchen floor; I then went to make the beds and tidy up our bathrooms.

When all these jobs were finished, I returned to the kitchen and went directly to the walk-in pantry near the refrigerator. I was amazed when I saw how beautifully kept it was. Everything was arranged so neatly, the glass jars of bottled vegetables, fruits and pickles carefully labelled and dated by Simone.

There were stacks of canned goods on higher shelves, and on the long countertop were most of the ingredients I needed for our lunch. A bowl of large brown eggs, a big wooden board holding different local cheeses, and a straw basket containing tomatoes, lettuce, and cucumbers. I picked this up and took it out to the sink.

After washing and drying the lettuce leaves, I wrapped them in a paper towel and put them back in the pantry. I peeled and sliced half of a long cucumber, then sliced two large tomatoes. Once I had arranged these slices on a platter I covered it with plastic wrap. This, too, went into the pantry.

All I would have to do later was arrange the ingredients in a salad bowl and add Simone's famous vinaigrette dressing, which stood on the shelf right in front of my eyes.

The eggs for the omelette could be beaten later, once Jake had returned from the airport. I would also warm a *baguette* and bring out the cheese board. Everything was on hand, and ready to prepare at the last moment.

Walking to the far end of the kitchen, I pulled open the door leading down to the basement which ran the full length of the house. The first flight of six steps stopped at a wide landing fitted with large stone shelves, and it was here other foodstuffs were stored. A second flight of stone steps continued on to the actual basement where there was a wine cellar, one much appreciated by Jake, since it contained some rare vintage wines. Very generously, Peter had given him the run of this.

It was dark and I switched on a light before descending into the murkiness. I shivered slightly, it was so cold, and glanced around. Simone had arranged things as neatly here as she had in the other pantry. On one of the stone shelves I found small trugs of berries, bowls of fresh figs, several melons, lots of vegetables, and a big basket of apples. Certainly there was plenty to choose from and we weren't going to starve during Simone's absence in Marseilles.

I stood for a moment, my hand resting on the stone shelf, thinking again of Simone's sudden and unexpected departure a short while ago. How white-faced and anxious she had been when she had come to the kitchen to say goodbye to me.

'I'm sure everything's going to be all right, that Françoise is fine,' I'd murmured, wanting to reassure her. I had given her a quick hug, and discovered how tense her body was.

Nodding, Simone had bravely tried to smile, but without much success. '*Ma petite fille*, my little girl . . . I must go to her. She needs me, I know.'

Catching her hand in mine, I'd squeezed it, and agreed. 'Yes, she does need you, Simone, but you'll be with her soon. Try not to worry.'

Again Simone had attempted to give me another smile, but this too had wavered and she had left with Jake and Armand, who had looked as worried as his wife.

I had stood at the kitchen door, waving goodbye to them as Jake backed the car out. A loving mother, a good mother, I had thought, as I'd turned to go back inside. And I hoped that Françoise had not lost the child she was carrying, and that she herself was not in any danger.

CHAPTER ELEVEN

1

Climbing the stairs from the pantry, I went back to the kitchen.

After pouring myself a large glass of water, I went out to the terrace and walked down the steps, making for a favourite spot of mine.

This was in one of the smaller gardens of the villa which was mostly composed of green lawn surrounded by flowering shrubs. The lawn ran to the tip of the property where steep craggy rocks fell precipitously down to the sea.

I felt as though I were on a ship whenever I sat here on the wrought-iron bench which had been placed under an ancient cedar. I leaned back, closing my eyes, enjoying the warmth of the morning air and the early sun filtering through the wide splayed branches of the tree.

When I finally opened my eyes a few minutes later I blinked. Brilliant sunshine was now filling the pale blue sky with incandescent light, and the sea spread out before me glittered like dark-blue glass shot through with golden veins.

A boat came into my line of vision, its white sails billowing out in the morning breeze. What an idyllic scene it was, and so very familiar to me . . . a lone ship etched against the blue horizon where sea and sky merged, sailing along . . . carrying whomever to where? I had often wondered that. It was mysterious, yet oddly intimate in my mind's eye. I'd seen other sailboats just like this so many times before in the past . . .

II

A rush of memories assailed me.

Memories of those days spent here in the south of France with my grandparents, when I was studying at the Sorbonne in Paris. I had always joined them on summer recess from the university. Just a girl I'd been then.

Cecelia and Andrew Denning . . . they had been so good to me. All of my life. Until the day they had died. She had gone first, very sadly, and then him. But thankfully I'd had the comfort of my grandfather for a few years longer.

The three of us a team, three against the world, my Gran used to say with a light, cheery laugh. She was spirited and vivacious, even when she was old, and she had told me so many times that I must always spit in the eye of trouble, keep my back ramrod straight, my head high, and my heart wide open to receive all of the good things which were coming my way.

They had loved me very much, and, more importantly perhaps, they had been able to show that love to me. It had been a shield after they were gone.

How very badly they had wanted to make up for the deficiencies of their son. 'Henpecked', my grandmother had frequently muttered, and a trifle disdainfully at that, her sharp blue eyes glinting like steel, her generous mouth narrowed in disgust at the thought of her weak-kneed son.

What she'd said about him being henpecked was true, I think. My father had never been able to stand up to my mother, who had behaved as if I didn't exist. And therefore so had he.

I would still ponder this from time to time, wonder why my mother had behaved so strangely. There had to be a reason, didn't there? But what could it be?

This question had haunted me most of my life, and I'd never been able to come up with a proper answer for myself. Yet deep inside I was certain I was innocent of any wrongdoing. What *could* I have done to offend her when I was still a small baby?

Why would a mother hate her own child?

Once again, the question hung there in front of my eyes, staring back at me balefully.

I sighed under my breath. Perhaps *hate* was too

strong a word. She had shown no *interest* in me ever, but she hadn't *hated* me, had she?

No, I didn't think she had. Disliked me, perhaps. My mother had certainly never mistreated me, or abused me. At least, not physically. Nor had she abused me verbally, either; that was not her way. Still, in one sense she had been abusive to me, because she had behaved as if I weren't there. No wonder I was insecure, always longing to find a safe harbour for myself.

I wondered, all of a sudden, why I was a war photographer, constantly flinging myself into the face of danger, putting myself in harm's way. I didn't have an answer to that, and I never would. Perhaps only a psychiatrist would be able to provide one.

What a mess I would have been, I thought now, if it hadn't been for my grandparents, especially my grandfather. He had made me what I am, and he was the best part of me. Without him in my life, and with such constancy, without his guidance, love and caring, I would have been nothing; I would have achieved nothing.

He had given me the courage to become who I was today. 'Stand tall, Val, and never be afraid of anybody or anything,' he had said to me often, and I had tried to do that. With all my heart, I had tried.

Unexpectedly, I thought of Tony Hampton. I almost laughed out loud. Here was I, seemingly always seeking a secure place to land, and yet I had become involved with him. Why *him*? He was as likely to offer me security and safety as a violent terrorist holding a gun to my head. So why had I chosen him? Because he had charmed me into a love affair, had truly convinced me he was madly in love with me. And because I hadn't known he was a two-timing, double-dealing lothario who didn't understand the meaning of truth, integrity, fidelity and loyalty.

I pushed the image of him away from me, crushed it under my feet until it no longer existed. And silently I repeated my resolutions like a litany:

I had buried the dead.

I was not about to resurrect the dead.

I had started afresh with a clean slate.

I was only interested in the future.

Lolling back against the bench, I closed my eyes, drifting with my myriad thoughts. Out of the blue, Fiona Hampton came into my mind. Yesterday she had phoned Jake at his photo agency in Paris. Yet again, I couldn't help wondering why. Perhaps just to say hello? To cling to memories? . . . the past? . . . an old friendship? . . . her husband's best friend? I wasn't sure. Nor did it matter. If she really needed to speak to Jake, she'd call again. It had nothing to do with me, nor was it any of my business.

Without knowing, Fiona had enabled me to shake off my searing grief. And she had helped me to bury the dead. Her dead as much as mine, as it so happened.

It was through her that I'd had a moment of the

greatest insight, had seen everything the way it actually was, and not as I imagined it to be.

I had seen the truth, looked it in the face.

And I had suddenly understood the reality of her life. And the reality of mine. She was the wife, I the mistress. Sharing the same man without knowing that we were. Both of us lied to and misled. Sisters under the skin. Linked emotionally without either of us realizing this.

At least, she didn't know it. I did. Now.

Meeting Fiona Hampton had changed my life irrevocably. And I was glad of that. It was she who had given me a future in a certain sense.

The nightmare of the memorial service had fortunately been just that – a very bad dream. And like most bad dreams it had gone away. The burden had been lifted off me.

And now I was truly free.

Opening my eyes, I lifted my face, glanced up at the blue translucent sky. I was as free as that lone bird flying so high up there in the sky . . . higher and higher it seemed to soar . . . until it finally disappeared from sight. Yes, I *was* as free as a bird on the wing. My spirits lifted at this thought.

Rising, I turned away from the glittering sea, slowly made my way back along the flagged path, heading up to the villa. As I walked along I wondered if I would ever fall in love again, have a good relationship with a man, get a chance of lasting happiness with someone, some day, in the not too distant future?

I laughed hollowly to myself at the mere idea. It would take a miracle to make that happen, and I surely didn't believe in miracles. Again, I laughed dismissively, not realizing that I would soon discover how wrong I was.

Especially when it came to miracles.

III

There was no sign of Jake when I got back to the house. I glanced at my watch, saw that it was almost twelve-thirty. He had been gone for several hours now, and it wasn't that far to Nice. Looking up at the kitchen clock on the wall, I checked the time. My watch was five minutes fast, but that was all.

He'll be back soon, I thought, shrugging lightly as I went to the sink where I washed the glass I was carrying, and my hands. I decided I might as well start to prepare lunch.

After retrieving the parcel of lettuce and the plate of cucumber and tomatoes from the pantry, I got out the green cabbage-leaf salad bowl, a glass mixing bowl, and a whisk. I put all of these on the work table near my parcel of lettuce; after opening it up and patting the leaves dry with a paper towel, I tore them into pieces and dropped them into the cabbage-leaf bowl. I then added the slices of cucumber and tomatoes to the lettuce.

I remembered Simone's vinaigrette dressing, and

ran to the pantry to get it. I shook the jar several times before unscrewing the lid and looking at it. The dressing was a little bit thick from being in the cold pantry, and it needed to stand for a while to liquefy a bit more. Taking it over to the table, I left the lid off, and returned to the pantry. I brought out the bowl of eggs and went back for the wooden board holding the selection of cheeses; there was just enough room for all of this stuff on the table.

My first task was to whip up the eggs for the omelette. I broke six into the glass mixing bowl, decided this was not enough, added two more, threw away the shells, picked up the whisk and began to beat them. Once they were smooth and creamy- looking, I reached for the pepper mill and the container of *fines herbes*. I added dashes of both to the eggs, along with several pinches of salt.

Suddenly the door flew open, and I looked up quickly as Jake pushed his way into the kitchen. At least, I assumed it was Jake since his face was largely hidden by the paper bags of groceries he held in his arms. A muffled, 'Hi, Kid,' came from behind the bags.

'Hi to you too,' I replied and went to help him with the bags, grabbed one from him, as he explained, 'Couldn't get everything I needed for my genuine, authentic southern dinner, but enough to give you a sampling tonight, honey.'

'I wondered where you were,' I muttered, peering in the bag which I'd placed on the countertop near the sink. 'Oh Jake!' I cried. 'You went and bought fruit without me, and after all the mouth-waterings we shared!'

He grinned at me and set his bags down on the counter. 'Don't be mad at me. I wasn't going to do it, I know how you've been longing to shop at the open-air market, but I was already there when I remembered that. It saved time, Val, I couldn't really drive back to get you.'

'I know. Anyway, it's almost redundant, the fruit, I mean. There's all sorts of stuff in the second pantry down the steps to the basement.'

'That figures, knowing Simone.'

'They got off all right, I assume.'

'Sure did. Well, I guess the berries'll keep for another meal. I'm certain Simone and Armand won't be back for a couple of days or so. What's that?' He was now staring at my bowl of beaten eggs.

'Your lunch. Soon it will be an omelette *fines herbes*.'

'Great.' He opened the refrigerator door and began to empty the bags into it. I noticed him placing chicken and other items on the shelves, then I turned away and went to get a skillet.

When the bags had been emptied, Jake said, 'I'll bring up some *vin rosé* from the wine cellar,' and headed for the door to the basement. He was back in a couple of minutes carrying two bottles. These he put in the refrigerator. 'Now what can I do?'

'Can you hand me the butter, please?'

'Sure can.' He went over to the refrigerator.

'Thanks,' I said when he gave it to me. I walked to the stone jar which stood on a chest at the far end of the kitchen; it was in this large stone olive jar with its wooden lid that Simone kept her *baguettes*. She purchased these fresh every day at the bakery in Beaulieu. I took one of the long loaves out of the jar but it didn't feel too fresh. And I realized she had not gone to the bakery this morning because of the phone call from Marseilles.

Taking the *baguette* to the sink, I wet it under the tap and put it in the oven. Later, once the omelette was ready, I would turn on the oven, set it at low, and in five or six minutes the bread would be warm, and as fresh as if it had just been made. Simone had shown me this little trick only the other day and now I was pleased she had.

Jake poured himself a glass of water, then sat down on a stool and watched me making lunch, not saying very much but looking thoughtful.

And then quite out of the blue, he said slowly, in a muffled sort of voice, 'I'm worried about Simone.'

I glanced across at him. 'What do you mean?' I quickly turned back to the omelette, not wanting it to spoil.

'She was very strange on the way to the airport, barely spoke at all. Actually, she was sort of rigid with fright in the car. At least, that's what I thought.'

'Well, she *was* worried when she got the news, Jake. A fall like that can be very dangerous to a pregnant woman, especially one who is seven or eight months gone,' I pointed out.

'I realize that. But Simone's worry, her fear, seemed somehow a bit abnormal. Over the top, in a way.'

'What about Armand, how was he?'

'Relatively silent, but then he's not talkative, a quiet sort of guy. Always has been. Simone's much more outgoing.'

Jake sighed so heavily I turned around swiftly, the spatula in my hand, and stared at him. 'You're getting at something, Jake.' I stared at him more intently, saw the genuine worry etched on his face, and then it hit me. 'Oh my God, you don't think Simone's daughter was pushed down the stairs do you?'

He shook his head. 'I kinda think Simone believes that's what happened.'

'What makes *you* think *she* thinks such a thing?' I asked and felt the goose flesh spring up on my neck and arms. 'Did she tell you that?'

'Not in so many words, Val, no.' Jake bit his lip. 'But she said some really odd things. At one point she muttered to Armand about Olivier. I didn't quite catch it completely, but it was something like *I'll kill him if he did that*. And Armand gaped at her. He was startled, and shook his head, as if to warn her not to speak in front of me. Although obviously she knows I speak French. When we got to the ticket counter at the airport, Armand was busy buying the tickets, and I tried to talk to her again. Sort of soothe her, Val. She was so uptight I thought she was going to explode.

In the end I gave up. I didn't want her to think I was prying. I told her to take as long as she wanted; after all, we're just guests here. It's Peter who's her employer.'

I nodded. 'Let's continue our conversation over lunch,' I suggested. 'Everything's ready now.'

Chapter Twelve

1

Between mouthfuls of omelette, Jake said, 'What made you ask me if I thought Françoise could have been pushed down the stairs? I mean, what exactly did I say to convey this to you?'

'It wasn't anything you said, but the expression on your face, Jake. It suddenly struck me that you might possibly be thinking along those lines. Spousal abuse is rampant these days.'

He nodded. 'Don't say *these days* like that, Val, there's nothing new about wife-beating. It's always been with us. We just hear more about it now . . . in the way that we know more about everything, from wars and other disasters, to the infidelities of politicians. Chalk it up to the age we live in, the media age. Instant wars . . . seen on television as they're happening. Instant news. Instant everything on television . . . and on the Internet. Yup, the age of information . . . and misinformation.'

'I guess you're right,' I answered. 'Is Simone going

to call us later today? Let us know how her daughter is doing?'

'She promised she would, once they'd been to the hospital, seen Françoise and talked to the doctors. I heard her say something to Armand about bringing her back here to recuperate. And I must admit, I did think that was odd.' He took a swallow of the *vin rosé*, then added, 'It's as if she wants Françoise to be out of Olivier's way, don't you think?'

'Perhaps . . .' I leaned back in my chair and thought for a moment before continuing. 'Or it could be she just wants to look after her daughter herself. Unless Françoise has a lot of injuries. I mean, you don't fall down a flight of stairs and stand up unscathed, do you? Look, Jake, the doctors might keep her in hospital for a while. Because of her pregnancy.'

'You're right, and if they do let her go home because her injuries are minor, she would still probably need looking after. And Olivier's at work all day.'

'What does he do?'

'He's a cop,' Jake replied and looked at me knowingly.

'Oh,' I muttered. 'Well, that doesn't mean anything. Cops have been known to be wife-beaters you know, and some even think they're above the law.'

'He could be that type,' Jake muttered.

'Oh, have you met him then?'

'Briefly, with Françoise. When I was down here with Peter. They were staying with Simone and Armand for a few days, and Peter introduced us. He's very fond of Simone, and of course Françoise and Solange grew up here at Les Roches Fleuries, so he's known them for years.'

'How old is Françoise?'

'About twenty-six, and Solange is twenty-three, maybe twenty-four. Not sure. But they're both nice girls.' Jake lifted his glass and took another long swallow of the *vin rosé*.

'You know, I never understand spousal abuse, Jake. How can a man be so brutal to the woman he loves and is married to? It just takes my breath away.'

Jake gaped at me, and put his glass down. 'I can't believe that *you* of all people are saying this to me.' He shook his head and his blue eyes were tight on mine. 'You know better than anybody how wicked and cruel human beings are. Just think about the atrocities and brutalities you've witnessed. You know as well as I do that man is evil, Val. In the Balkans alone you've seen men mowing each other down indiscriminately, men who were friends and neighbours once, and doing it without thinking twice. And what about the tortured and maimed we've both photographed?' Bafflement had settled on his face.

I felt a cold chill sweep through me as I stared back at him. And then I glanced away, suddenly not wanting to look into Jake's eyes any longer. Everything he said was true. The problem was I didn't want to remember or contemplate any of it. Not today, at any rate. I did not wish to focus on Kosovo and the other horrific wars I'd covered. I just couldn't bear to do so. I was sickened by it all, weary of war and all the killing. I suddenly wondered if I was burnt out; I frowned and sat up straighter in the chair. I had never thought anything like this before. The idea that I could be burnt out scared the hell out of me. And so I pushed the idea away.

I said slowly, 'Nothing's changed in the world since medieval times, has it? Man hasn't learned anything, has he, Jake?'

'No. Nor will he ever, Val. Human beings will never be any different, not unless some scientist finds a way to give us all a different type of D.N.A., give us new genes. We are what we are because of our genes. James Watson discovered that when he discovered D.N.A. And so over the centuries man has gone on doing the same things over and over again, committing the same acts of cruelty, the same heinous crimes. It's in our genes, it's our nature. I don't think man has altered much since the beginning of time as we know it, since the day he got up on two legs and started to walk upright.'

'Are you saying there's no hope for human beings?'

'That's correct. There isn't.'

'Let me understand this. You are telling me that as humans we are always going to fight wars, kill each other, commit murder and all manner of horrendous crimes, become child- and wife-beaters, adulterers, whatever? Is that what you believe, Jake?'

'Absolutely. History has proven to me time and

again that it *is* cyclical . . . it just keeps repeating itself, and Homo sapiens, modern humans, keep repeating themselves over the centuries . . . endlessly . . . because they *are* humans.'

I studied him intently. Jake was a Rhodes scholar and had read history at Oxford University, and had graduated with very high honours. History was his bailiwick and he took it very seriously. And so I knew he meant every word.

'That's awful . . .' I said eventually and then my voice trailed away. I was at a loss, I didn't know what else to say.

Jake smiled at me. 'It's just the way it is, Val, and the way it's always been. And will always *be*. You can't change it. I can't change it. No one can. We are what we are.'

'What a frightening world we live in, when you think about it.'

'That's true, but there's nowhere else to go. I'm afraid we're stuck with planet Earth. And anyway, living here is better than the alternative.'

'What's that?' I asked.

'Not to be alive at all, Val.'

II

He changed the subject then, and began to tell me about the wonderful dinner he was going to make; later he helped me to clear away the dishes.

We were both stacking the dishwasher in the kitchen when the phone rang. Jake went to answer it, and I knew at once that it was Simone calling.

I stood next to the dishwasher, looking across at Jake as he picked up the phone.

'Hullo?' he said, and listened for a split second, before exclaiming, 'That's great, Simone!' He gave me the thumbs-up sign, and went on, 'We've been concerned. It's a relief to know that Françoise isn't seriously injured.'

I relaxed against the countertop, and it struck me how worried I'd been for Françoise, a girl I'd never even met and didn't know. But I had grown to like her mother in the time I had been at the villa, and I empathized with Simone. And in any case, violence against women disturbed and alarmed me. Not that I knew there *had* been any violence in this particular case, but seemingly Simone had her suspicions.

Jake was still listening, but after a moment he said, 'Yes, I will, Simone, and please, don't rush back. Do what you have to do. Just attend to Françoise and be sure she's all right before you leave. *Au revoir.*'

As soon as he hung up, Jake glanced at me and explained, 'Simone asked me to thank you for being so nice this morning.'

I nodded. 'From what I was hearing Françoise is okay and she didn't lose the baby, thank God.'

'She is, and no, she didn't miscarry. Apparently Françoise is very bruised, and has a sprained ankle, but it wasn't such a bad accident after all. Simone thought she had fallen down the staircase from the second floor, but she'd misunderstood Olivier. Françoise stumbled when she was going down three steps into the pantry. She hit her head against a wall but there was no concussion, just a big bump on her forehead, and some other bruising. But nothing broken, and mother and baby perfectly okay.'

'She was lucky,' I remarked. 'How did Simone sound?'

'Strange, I must admit. Uptight. I felt she was still worried in some way.'

'But that's only natural under the circumstances, Jake. Anyway, it's hard to really know what she feels. I've noticed that her English is very . . . *precise*, I guess that's the best word. But it's also a bit quaint at times. She doesn't always express herself well.'

'She sounds stilted,' Jake said, and laughed. 'She learned English from Adelia Roland all those years ago, and I think that's why she sometimes sounds . . . well, a bit old-fashioned, quaint as you say. But getting back to Françoise, Simone might be overreacting. Perhaps she doesn't like her son-in-law.'

'Did she imply that?'

He shook his head. 'No, she didn't. She just said she'd misunderstood, that the fall hadn't been serious. She said she and Armand would come back tonight, but as you heard, I told her not to rush. She'll be calling us tomorrow.'

III

We finished cleaning up the kitchen, and Jake sat down at the countertop to phone his photo agency in Paris, to check for messages and discuss business. Jacques Foucher was Jake's partner, along with Harvey Robinson in New York and Matt Logan in the Far East. The four photographers had started Photoreal some nine years ago, and Jacques ran the Paris bureau, preferring to be out of the field these days. He and Jake had been close buddies for about twelve years, and Jake relied on Jacques to handle the business end of the photo agency in Paris. They employed four other photographers at the bureau but Jake was the big star.

Whilst he talked on the phone I sat at the kitchen table turning over the pages of the Paris edition of the *New York Herald Tribune*, which Jake had brought back with him from Nice Airport. But I did so half-heartedly, not really interested in the news. Most of it was bad anyway, if the headlines were anything to go by.

I was enjoying being here at Les Roches Fleuries. It was like hiding away in a sense, but at this point I needed the break from the turbulent, dangerous and disturbing world I lived in most of the time. I believe we both did. I was also worried about Jake going out on assignment. His wounds looked as if they had healed, but sometimes he limped badly, and this was cause for concern, I thought. I still had not dared to broach the subject, but I was going to when the opportunity presented itself in the next couple of days.

Eventually Jake hung up and said, 'Nothing very important happening at the agency, Val. So I can relax a bit longer here. Well, I guess I'd better give Fiona a call in London.' As he spoke he was already dialling the number. It rang and rang, and then Jake said, 'Hello, Fiona. Jake here. I'm returning your call. I'm in Cap Ferrat.' He left the number of the villa and signed off with a breezy goodbye.

Looking over at me, he said, 'A machine again. I'm beginning to hate them. Incidentally, have you spoken to Mike Carter?'

'Yes, the other day, when I decided to stay on here with you. I wanted to give him this number. He's still saying I should take my time about going back to work.'

'He's right. Kosovo remains troublesome, but there's not much else for us to cover at the moment, so we might as well take it easy whilst we can.'

I merely nodded.

Chapter Thirteen

I

'I didn't know it was as steep as this,' Jake said, peering down over the craggy rocks that fell into the sea far below. 'It's stupendous here. And what a sheer drop!'

'Don't get so near the edge, it's dangerous!' I exclaimed. 'There should be a railing there, somebody could easily fall over the edge.'

'Yup, you're right about that, Val,' Jake said, swinging around, walking over to join me on the wrought-iron bench in my favourite spot. We had been strolling around the garden following a long drawn-out lunch, and had ended up here.

Now he said, 'But I don't think Peter would come to this part of the gardens, or anyone else, for that matter. Only you, Kid, so nobody's in danger of falling off the edge. I'll say this, it's a fabulous view.'

'Yes, you can see for miles.' I moved slightly on the bench, leaned forward, and went on, 'Tony loved danger, loved being near the vortex of it –' Abruptly, I stopped speaking, wondering why I had brought up his name. I could have bitten off my tongue I was so mad at myself.

Jake simply nodded but said nothing at all, as if he also wondered why I had mentioned Tony. I stared into his lean and expressive face, at a sudden loss for words, and forced a small smile.

Then wanting to change the subject, I found myself blurting out, 'Jake, I'm worried about you. I mean about the way you're limping. Don't you think you ought to see a doctor when we get back to Paris?'

'I saw the doctor before we came down here. He said I'm fine, that it's just a matter of time. It's sort of . . . well, I guess it's a slow healing process . . . inside the leg, I mean. Anyway, I don't always limp. Only occasionally.'

'You limp a lot,' I corrected him, giving him a stern glance.

'Not that much, only when it feels a bit tender.' He took hold of my hand and held it in his. 'Stop being such a Jewish mother.' He was laughing as he said this, and then he added, 'Please stop fussing, Val honey, honestly I'm really okay. Fit and well and on top form.'

I shook my head. 'I can't help worrying. I care about you. You're my best friend, the only family I have.'

'I'm glad I'm important to you. After all, I care about *you* very much.'

There was a tender look in his eyes as he said this

and a lot of love written across his face, and I was both startled and taken aback. All I could do was nod silently.

Finally, he added, 'I hope *you're* on the mend, that you're not . . . dwelling on Tony and his shenanigans any more. He's not worth it, Kid.'

'Of course I'm not dwelling on him, or the past year! I want to forget it, believe me. Anyway, being here has been wonderful, such a treat, and a great rest for me. I've not enjoyed myself so much since we were in Beirut. We've always had a lot of fun together, and it's great being with you, Jake.'

'Likewise, Val, I feel the same way.' He stood up, stretched several times and flexed his arms. Then he announced, 'This kind of indolent life of luxury is very addictive. I could easily become accustomed to it.'

'Not you, my friend,' I immediately shot back, glancing up at him, shaking my head. 'You're a war photographer born and bred. You'd miss the action too much, and if anything is addictive, *action* is.'

'Oh I don't know . . .' He didn't finish his sentence, just shrugged and leaned against the cedar tree.

'Trust me, *I* know.' I studied him, my head on one side. 'Why *did* you become a war photographer, Jake? I'm curious about that.'

'Because I wanted to record history . . . when it was actually happening, when history was being made. I didn't want to learn about it after the event, I guess I wanted to be *part* of it, in one sense. I also wanted to capture the truth on film. I wanted my pictures to do more than merely inform, I needed them to *mean* something as well. It's a funny thing to say, perhaps, but I thought it was important to make people *feel* something about war, to make them conscious of its cruelty and viciousness, and also fully aware of its inhumanity. I hoped people would feel compassion for the dead, when they saw my photographs. What I mean is, I wanted them to feel strongly about dead *strangers*, about people they'd never known. I guess I wanted to make them *care* about those people. Do you understand that, Val?'

'Absolutely, and you wanted to prove that your pictures were meaningful, that they could touch and move people. I hope we both achieve that, Jake, otherwise what we do for a living wouldn't be worth doing, would it?'

'No, it wouldn't. And what about you? I know everything there is to know about you, I think, and yet I don't know why *you* decided to be a war photographer. You never said.'

'I wanted to be where the action was, in the middle of it, actually. I thought it would be exciting, and let's admit it, there *is* always that rush of adrenalin when we're in the thick of the fighting. But when I was a child I just enjoyed being behind a camera. I may have been hiding, you know, pretending to be someone else. It's funny, Jake, but I always thought of my camera as being my third eye. *I am a Camera*, wrote Christopher Isherwood, and I guess I still feel that about myself. I am a camera, and my third eye has always been an accurate eye. It records the truth. I suppose, like you, I'm a seeker of the truth at heart. My grandfather said I was very observant as a child, that I didn't miss a trick when I was growing up, and I'm sure that's true,' I finished, settling back on the bench.

'Being behind a camera, taking pictures of everyone, should have given you a great sense of power as a child,' Jake now said, eyeing me carefully, a thoughtful look in his eyes.

'Do you think so?' I stared back at him, frowning at this idea.

He nodded. 'Sure I do. Haven't you ever thought of it that way? Thought of that aspect of it?'

'No,' I said, shaking my head. 'Never.' And this was true, I hadn't ever thought of photography in terms of power over a person, only as a powerful tool with the public.

'You've always told me your parents, especially your mother, didn't pay attention to you, that they weren't concerned about you, or what you were doing, when you were growing up. I think that must have been a pretty lousy feeling to have, Val.'

He was staring hard at me again, and there was such compassion on his face I was touched by his empathy and concern. He really was a true friend, a good person. I wondered, suddenly, what I would have done without him in my life.

Jake continued, 'Think of how *powerful* it must have been for you, as a child, to have a camera in your hands, recording everyone, having *their* images on *your* reel of film. It gave you an advantage, don't you think, Val?'

'I guess so, yes, I guess you're right, but I never thought of it in that way,' I laughed. 'Still, it's true I was never without my camera, Jake. I shot everything from the dog throwing up to Donald the Great stealing cigarettes from my father's cigarette case –'

I stopped with sudden abruptness, and looked up. A large spot of rain had just hit my arm. I saw that the sky had turned a cold, steely grey and yet there was a curious luminosity behind that greyness. It was an ominous sky which threatened bad weather. I was wondering if a mistral was about to blow up when the rain started to pelt down.

'I have a feeling there's going to be a helluva storm,' I exclaimed, getting to my feet. 'Come on, Jake, we'd better get going.'

Together we hurried up the path through the gardens, and within seconds we were running as fast as we could. The rain was falling in torrents, a heavy, slashing rain that drenched us through to the skin. As we ran past the swimming pool and up the steps to the terrace there was a loud crack of thunder. Flashes of lightning were illuminating the darkening afternoon sky, and I felt the cool touch of the mistral blowing over my body as we stumbled on towards the villa.

11

By the time Jake dragged me into the kitchen we were both sodden to the skin. Water ran off us and pooled around our feet on the terra-cotta tiled floor.

Grabbing hold of the kitchen towel, he dabbed my face with it.

'Hey, stop!' I cried. 'It's a dirty towel, Jake.'

'Sorry, Kid.' He started to laugh as he grasped the roll of paper towel, tore some off and reached for me again.

I backed away, holding up my hands, laughing with him. 'We need proper towels,' I told him, pushing my wet hair out of my face. 'We're both soaked.'

Without a word, Jake dashed through the kitchen door; I struggled out of my dripping voile shirt and threw it on the floor, then stepped out of my ruined sandals.

A second later Jake was back with an armful of towels. After cocooning me in a large bath sheet, he picked up a smaller towel and began to rub my hair. Snatching up a towel myself, I leaned forward to do the same to him. In the process of drying each other off we were becoming a tangle of arms and towels; Jake couldn't stop laughing and neither could I.

III

The laughter died in us both at precisely the same moment.

All of a sudden Jake and I were very sober, gazing at each other intently, motionless and silent in the middle of the kitchen. We might have been struck by the lightning bouncing off the windows outside. Maybe we had been.

After a prolonged moment of total silence, Jake took a jerky step backwards, and he seemed about to say something. Apparently he changed his mind, since he remained mute, but his eyes were very intense and most revealing.

He did not need to say anything to me. What he was thinking was written not only in his eyes but all over his face. Desire and longing were etched there . . . for the first time in our friendship I finally understood how much he cared about me as a woman.

As for me, I had the oddest feeling I was sloughing off a dead skin, shedding forever my old self. Even the events of the past year tumbled away from me, as if they had never happened. I experienced a sense of enormous liberation.

I stood there rooted to the spot, mesmerized by his unblinking blue gaze, and unexpected desire flared in me. This startled me. I realized I was seeing Jake Newberg differently, in a way I had never seen him before, not as my comrade-in-arms nor my best friend, but as a man I desired sexually and with whom I wanted to make the most passionate love.

I took a step towards him, every part of me wanting him now. I was certain he felt the same.

At exactly the same moment, as if he had read my mind, he was moving towards me, reaching out for me.

I stepped into his arms, and I knew as I did so that this was where I belonged, had always belonged. He clung to me, and I held onto him tightly, wondering if he could hear the thundering of my heart.

Eventually he tilted my face to his, looking deeply into my eyes, impaling me with his. Again his expression told me everything I needed to know, and it was confirmation of what I was feeling for him. He brought his mouth down to mine and kissed me gently, tenderly at first. But almost instantly his passion spiralled upward, and he began to kiss me with greater urgency and an eagerness that inflamed me further.

I found myself responding to him with a rush of ardour, my hands pressing on the back of his neck, reaching up into his hair. My body cleaved to his; I felt the light touch of his tongue on mine, seeking, seeking. He ran his hands down my back and onto my buttocks, pulled me tighter to him, pressed me closer. Clinging together in this way, we shared a moment of total and complete intimacy which I had never known before.

It was then I knew that I was his, would always be

his. Perhaps I'd even been his from the first moment we'd met without my knowing it.

There was a sudden stillness about Jake now as he murmured softly against my neck, 'Come on, Val, come with me. Let's be together.'

IV

Arms around each other we moved out of the kitchen, climbed the stairs and went into his bedroom. Outside the huge window the sky was dark, almost as black as night, and the rain slashed down against the glass, driven hard by the wind.

Jake closed the door behind us with one hand, without letting go of me, and led me over to the bed. 'Take this off,' he muttered, touching my wet swimsuit. Stepping away from me, he swiftly shed his soaking trousers and shirt.

He wrapped the bath sheet he had brought upstairs around his waist, picked up the one I'd dropped on the floor and tied it on me toga style. Without a word, we lay down next to each other. Neither of us spoke. My heart was racing.

Suddenly Jake raised himself on one elbow and gazed down at me.

My eyes stayed on his face expectantly.

'I never thought this would happen. I've waited so long for you, Val,' he said in a quiet voice thick with emotion, and his face was congested with desire.

'Oh Jake, I –'

He cut me off. 'Don't say anything. Not now.'

It was apparent he had an overwhelming physical need for me, as I did for him, and we reached out, clutched at each other, devoured each other with our mouths. Our tongues grazed, touched, caressed, and then lay still. Jake pulled away from me, tugged at the towel knotted around me. It fell open, and he brought his mouth to my neck and then my breast. He sucked on my nipple and at the same time he was stroking my inner thigh.

I could feel his mounting excitement. His heart was slamming against mine and I held him tighter, pressing my hands on his back and his shoulder blades. I moved my fingers up onto the nape of his neck and they were strong and supple against his skin.

When we broke away at last we were gasping, out of breath.

'My beautiful Val,' he murmured, and leaned over me, his fingers seeking to know me fully. I stiffened as he touched the core of me, and he whispered, 'Relax, darling, let me love you like this.' And he slid down the bed, rested his head against my thigh, and eventually his mouth joined his fingers in his search for the centre of my womanhood. I opened myself up to him completely. It seemed to me that I floated away on waves of ecstasy of a kind I'd never known before. And then at that moment he pulled himself on top of me and took me to him. 'Mine,' he moaned. 'You're mine now.'

We made love for a long time, absorbed in each other and our bodies. I was reeling from amazement, startled by the passionate and erotic feelings he aroused in me, and revelling in them as well.

Finally spent and exhausted, our desire for each other sated at last, we lay still and unmoving on the bed. Half groaning, half sighing, Jake eventually slid off me and flopped against the pillows. 'Oh God, Val,' he muttered, and then he reached for my hand and held it tightly, before bringing it up to his lips and kissing it with tenderness.

Then suddenly he was half on me again, flinging one leg and part of his body over mine, pulling me closer to him. 'I'm never going to let you go. Not ever, Val.'

V

I lay there next to him, still filled with awe at our amazing lovemaking. I felt euphoric; I was also luxuriating in the sense of wonder and joy he had wrought in me.

'Who would've ever thought we would be so passionate with each other,' I murmured at last.

'I would,' he answered swiftly, and pushed himself up on his arm, looked down at me. 'I knew it from the first; at least, I knew how *I* felt.'

'You did!' I said, surprised.

'Sure. When I met you in Beirut, I thought who

the hell is this chick who's strolled along into my life? Who *is* this tall, long-legged, blue-eyed creature with sun-streaked hair and the face of an angel? I was immediately smitten, instantly undone.' He paused and grinned at me. 'I guess I was gobsmacked, to use your favourite expression.'

'About me?'

'Of course about you. Who else?'

'But you didn't show it, didn't say it!' I exclaimed, staring at him intently.

'How could I? And that's not my way. I was married then, remember? Still struggling with Sue's emotional upset about her miscarriage, fighting off her demands that I go back and live with her in New York, give up being a war photographer, so I could babysit her while she pursued her modelling career and I put mine on hold . . . Val, you *know* what those few years were like. Hell on earth for me. Looking back, I realize she was off the wall in certain ways, and actually not cut out for marriage. Not marriage to me, anyway. It was a big mistake, our being together. Those were bad years for me, and I didn't think I should get involved with you until I had sorted out my mess. And I did eventually sort it out. Suddenly I was free at last – divorced, available. And where were you? Involved with Tony, to my dismay.' He sighed. 'I was out in the cold and there wasn't much I could do about it.'

'Oh Jake, if only I'd known.'

'What difference would it have made?'

'A big difference, I think. If I'd known how you felt before, I'm sure I wouldn't have even looked at Tony. He and I had . . . well, quite a few problems when we were together, and there was a lot to be desired in our relationship. And for lots of reasons . . . some of which we now know.'

'Yep, that's true, I was well aware things weren't always great between the two of you. But I don't go around snatching my best buddy's girl, that's just not me.'

I nodded. 'But I always had a . . . bit of a yen for you, Jake,' I admitted softly, suddenly feeling a little shy with him. 'You were in such a tangled web with Sue, I just tried to be your friend, and sort of disappeared into the woodwork, I guess.'

'I wish you hadn't,' he muttered, sounding regretful.

'So do I.' As I said this, I couldn't help thinking how different my life would've been if Jake and I had been together. What a lot of heartache and pain I would have avoided ultimately; I felt sure I would have found a great deal more happiness with Jake than I had with Tony. He was a much more compassionate and decent man. And unlike Tony he had integrity, and certainly he was honest and straightforward. Basically, what you saw was what you got, as far as Jake was concerned.

Jake was saying, 'Listen, that was then, this is now. *Que sera, sera*, what will be will be . . . it's our time now. Anyway, I hope it is, Valentine Denning.' His bright blue eyes searched my face questioningly. 'It is, isn't it?'

'Oh yes, Jake, it is!' I reached out, put my arms around his neck and pulled him down to kiss me. It was a lingering kiss, and we embraced for a long time, finding pleasure in just holding each other close.

Outside, the storm was raging. The rain sounded like nail heads hitting the windows, sharp and metallic against the glass, and the wind was so fierce I knew that the mistral *had* blown up. But I felt secure here with Jake, safe in his arms. And I, who didn't believe in miracles, knew that one had just happened to me. My miracle was Jake Newberg.

VI

Much later, after we had showered and put on trousers and sweaters, we went down to the kitchen.

Earlier, Jake had put a bottle of Dom Perignon in the refrigerator, and after opening it he poured two glasses and said, 'Here's to you and me, sweetheart.'

We clinked glasses, and as I took a sip of the champagne, Jake added, 'And now I'm about to bowl you over.'

'You just did. And then some. But I'd be happy for you to do it again.'

He laughed, planted a kiss on my forehead and walked over to the refrigerator. 'Now sit down, like a good girl, while I prepare the southern dinner I've been promising you.'

'I'm not going to move an inch,' I answered, parking myself on one of the tall stools. 'In this instance, I don't mind that you're being bossy.'

'Me bossy?' He swung around, raised an eyebrow. 'Never. Just authoritative.'

'We're into semantics again,' I muttered, and chuckled with him.

He was quick and deft, and knew exactly what he was doing, I soon realized, as I watched him moving around the kitchen with speed and grace. 'I couldn't get everything I needed,' he explained at one moment. 'No okra, so I'll have to substitute zucchini in the gumbo. Have you ever eaten gumbo, Val?'

I shook my head. 'No, I'm not even sure what it is.'

'A casserole of rice, tomatoes and okra, but it'll taste just as good with the zucchini, I'm sure. I couldn't find the ingredients for corn bread either, so I can't make us any hush puppies – that's fried round cornbread, Val – and you'd love it. But we'll have that in Georgia, when I take you home to meet my folks,' he finished, and went on expertly working with the food he had spread out on the work table.

I didn't say a word, or acknowledge his comment, just sat there sipping the champagne and watching him, and knowing that I was going to fall hopelessly in love with him. I think I was a little bit already, always had been, actually. How little we know ourselves, I thought, how little we understand our real feelings, our true feelings. We masked so much because we were afraid of looking foolish or of being rejected. At least, I did.

VII

'You can always be a chef if you ever get tired of being a war photographer,' I joked later, as we sat at the dining-room table eating Jake's southern dinner. 'This is all wonderful food, delicious.'

'I'm tired already,' he said, surprising me.

'So you won't be going back to Kosovo then, will you?'

'No, because you won't go there, and I want to be where you are, Val my Val.'

'Likewise,' I murmured and smiled at him.

He smiled back and exclaimed, 'I'm glad you like my southern cooking, and it's great to see you eating properly for once.'

'Well, I've worked up an appetite, don't you know,' I shot back and leered at him.

'So have I,' he replied with a small self-satisfied smile and helped himself to some more of the mashed potatoes and fried green tomatoes.

'You're much too smug, Newberg,' I said, and took a piece of fried chicken. Biting into it, I went on, 'You'll have to teach me how to cook some of these dishes. Your sweet potato pie is heavenly.'

'Wait until you taste the dessert ... my peach

cobbler is as good as my mother makes. But I'll let you be the judge of that.'

I raised a brow and asked, 'Do you mean it? Are you really going to take me to Georgia to meet your parents and your grandmother?'

'You bet,' he responded with a grin, and glanced at the fire. 'I'm glad you decided to light that, Val, we'd be cold without it. The weather's turned lousy tonight. It's the mistral.' Rising, he picked up the bottle of Saint-Émilion, came and poured me a glass, managing to kiss the top of my head as he did. 'You're very special,' he murmured against my hair. 'Don't ever forget that.'

I took hold of his hand resting on my shoulder and squeezed it but I didn't say anything. He lingered close to me, and finally I looked up at him. And I saw such a look of anxiety on his face, I was taken aback. I exclaimed, 'Whatever's wrong, Jake?'

He stood there mute, staring down at me, and then at last he let out a long sigh and said, 'I don't want anything to come between us, least of all the memory of Tony. He's not going to haunt you, is he?'

Pushing back my chair, I got up, put my hands on his shoulders, stood staring deeply into his eyes. I said quietly but in a firm voice, 'He won't haunt me, Jake, I promise you that. As it turns out he was a louse, so how could I let that happen?'

'I don't know, some women might, and the memory of a dashing lover cut down in his prime can be very potent.'

'You don't have to worry about Tony, not after what he did to me!' I reminded him.

'I guess we'll never know what was in his head, Val, why he did what he did to you. He's dead, so he can't tell us. Nobody can.'

I continued to stare at him, saying nothing. But Jake was wrong about this, as we were later to find out. Someone did know about Tony, and that person had all the answers. At least answers that would satisfy me. But this was yet to come. It was in the future.

VIII

After dinner we sat in front of the fire in the living room, sipping a large cognac each and talking endlessly about everything. About ourselves and our childhoods, about the years when we didn't know each other, about our first meeting in Beirut, and about all those missed chances of being together.

'Now *is* the perfect time for us, the right time, Jake, just as you said before. I'm much more grown up and mature, better for you now.'

'You were always better for me, Val, better than anyone else. We were destined to be together. Don't you know that?'

'Yes, I do,' I said, meaning this, and knowing that he had meant every word he had said. I leaned my head against his shoulder, and closed my eyes, but after a moment he took me in his arms, and held me close, stroking my hair. And I knew that at last I had found my safe haven, the place where I was meant to be for the rest of my life. And for the first time in years I was at peace with myself.

Chapter Fourteen

I

Two days after they had left for Marseilles, Simone and Armand returned to Les Roches Fleuries. They arrived in the late morning, as Simone had said they would when she had called the day before, and they came with their daughter Françoise.

I happened to be in the kitchen, making a pot of coffee and wondering what to prepare for Jake's lunch, when Simone appeared in the doorway, very suddenly and unexpectedly, dragging Françoise in her wake.

'*Mademoiselle Denning, bonjour!*' she exclaimed.

'*Bonjour*, Simone. I'm glad you're back, and you arrived just in time to help me.' I grinned at her. 'I was looking around for inspiration – wondering what to prepare for Monsieur Jake's lunch.'

'*Ah, Mademoiselle, c'est pas nécessaire maintenant.* I am here, it is not necessary for you to cook.' She smiled warmly in her usual good-natured way, and then taking hold of her daughter's hand, she brought her forward.

The girl had been hanging back, had positioned herself behind Simone; she appeared to be a little shy, I thought. But I realized, as she came into the sunny, light-filled kitchen, that she was badly bruised on her face; this was probably the reason she was reluctant to show herself to a stranger. She was a lovely-looking young woman, slender and fair of colouring, with blonde hair and light-grey eyes.

'This is my daughter,' Simone said. 'And Françoise, this is Mademoiselle Denning.'

'I am pleased to meet you,' Françoise murmured quietly, in excellent English, shaking my outstretched hand.

I smiled at her, 'And it's nice to meet you, too.'

Françoise endeavoured to smile back, but she was finding this difficult, no doubt because there were bruises around her mouth, as well as on her forehead and cheekbone.

'I'm so glad you're all right, that nothing serious happened to you and the baby when you fell,' I remarked, wanting to put her at ease.

'I was lucky,' she replied in the same low voice.

Sensing that they would both feel better if I left the kitchen, I gestured at the coffee pot and said to Simone, 'I'll be back in a minute or two for the coffee.'

'No, no, rest tranquil. I will bring it to you and Monsieur Jake in a moment. *Avec du lait*.'

'*Merci*, Simone, and I'll tell Monsieur Jake you're

back.' I went outside and walked along the terrace to talk to Jake, who was relaxing on a chaise under an umbrella. 'Simone's here,' I announced, 'and Françoise is with her.' I leaned against the table, stared over at him, and then pulling a chair out, I sat down.

Glancing up at me, looking surprised, Jake put down the book he was reading, and said, 'Odd she didn't mention Françoise would be coming, when she phoned me last night. How does Françoise look?'

'Bruised. On her face. She's a lovely-looking girl though, isn't she?'

'A beauty. Maybe Simone and Armand decided it was wise to bring her back here with them, to keep her safe from Olivier.'

'Or perhaps to recuperate from her fall,' I suggested gently. 'She's not necessarily a battered wife.'

'No. But you did say her face was bruised. And I'm not so sure your face gets bruised when you fall down steps.'

'Yes, I guess she could be battered. Only she knows the truth, and her mother perhaps.'

'Simone would never mention anything to us. But she's a wise woman, from what I know of her, and she'll do everything she can to protect Françoise from Olivier, if that's what is needed,' he said.

'I'm sure you're right –' I began, and then paused when I saw Simone walking towards us carrying a tray. 'Here she is now,' I added sotto voce.

Jake pushed himself up off the chaise just as Simone arrived at our side. She placed the tray of coffee on the table where I was seated and said, '*Bonjour,* Monsieur Jake.'

'Hello, Simone,' he replied, grasped her hand and shook it. 'I hear Françoise is with you.'

'*Oui, Monsieur.* It will be good for her to relax here with us for a few days, to recover from her . . . fall.'

'You're absolutely right. It's the perfect place, and we're glad she's here with you and Armand. Just let me know if there's anything I can do for you, Simone, or for Françoise, and thanks for bringing the coffee.'

With a nod, and a small pleased smile, she disappeared down the terrace.

Jake said to me slowly, thoughtfully, 'She and Armand were so insistent about taking a cab from Nice Airport. They didn't want me to pick them up, maybe because Françoise was with them . . .' He looked at me and made a face, then sitting down at the table, he lifted the coffee pot and poured for both of us, muttered, 'I guess everybody's got to do their own thing.'

'That's true, and *we* can't intrude on them. After all, they've lived here for twenty years, the girls grew up at Les Roches Fleuries, and this is their home. We're just Peter's guests here, Simone and Armand *belong*.'

'Talking of being Peter's guests, when do you want to leave, Val?'

'Never,' I answered, smiling across at him, reaching out, taking his hand in mine. 'This is the best place I've ever been, Jake.'

'And why do you think that is?'

'Because you're here, and because we're together in

the best sense of that word.' I threw him a flirtatious look, and added, 'But anywhere with you would be marvellous. Still, this is such a fabulous house.'

He laughed softly. 'I feel the same way as you do about this house. And I adore *you*, and I don't want to leave either, there's something very special about Les Roches Fleuries . . . it's very romantic, perhaps that's what's so appealing about it.'

'The atmosphere *is* happy,' I remarked. 'And I think that this goes back to Adelia Roland; after all she's the only person who's lived in it, other than Peter. She created a unique villa and extraordinary gardens. And I've always believed that people who inhabit a house give it a certain feeling, either *good* or *bad*. Don't you think that?'

He nodded. 'I do.'

'Anyway, perhaps Peter will let us come back one day.'

'Any time you wish, Val darling.'

'We will have to leave *soon*, I suppose, go back to work, earn our living. So what actually are your plans?' I asked. 'When we leave here?'

'Not sure. Well, that's not exactly true, Val. To be honest, I'm thinking of going to New York for a couple of weeks.'

'Oh.' Flabbergasted to hear this, I gaped at him.

'Don't look so surprised,' he said swiftly. 'Listen, I've been meaning to speak to you about something. About a book I want to do. That's the reason I may be heading to New York. To talk to a publisher.

Harvey Robinson has one in mind, in fact he's already broached the idea to them, and they're very interested. They've told Harvey they want to see me.'

'And you never even told me!' I exclaimed, staring at him somewhat reproachfully.

'I'm telling you now.'

Realizing I had sounded hurt in the most childish way a moment before, I now spoke in a more positive mature voice when I said, 'I think that's terrific, Jake. A wonderful idea.'

'It will be, if you work on the book with me, Val.'

He had surprised me again, and I didn't say anything for a moment, then I asked, 'What will the book be about? And why do you need me?'

'It's about war, to answer the first part of your question. And secondly, I need you as a collaborator, because I need your pictures, plus your help with the text. You're a great reporter, Val, the best, and you write so well. Far better than I do.'

I couldn't help but be pleased with his compliments, and I said, 'That's nice of you to say so, but as far as the book's concerned, I just don't know.' I frowned as I added, 'Anyway, what exactly do you mean when you say, *a book about war*?'

'Not war per se, but rather it would be a book about the children of war. And not the dead children either, but those who managed to survive, who are the future of their countries, the flowers of their countries, the flowers of war, in a sense, who offer hope to the world. You've got loads of dramatic shots of children – before, during and in the aftermath of war. Because that's always been your speciality, not mine, not Tony's.' He leaned closer. 'Come on, honey, say you'll do it.'

Wanting to hedge for a couple of seconds, I said, 'That's a good title.'

'What is?'

'*Flowers of War*.' I put great emphasis on the words.

'Jesus, you're right! You see, I *do* need you.'

'I sincerely hope so,' I murmured, and blew him a kiss.

'Is it a *yes*, Val?' he pressed, his eyes fastened on mine.

I smiled enigmatically. 'It could be . . . it just depends on . . .'

'On what?' he demanded.

'How well you treat me.'

'I'll love you to death,' he promised.

'Then it's a deal.'

Obviously delighted that I had agreed, he exclaimed, 'And it really will be a proper deal, you know, fifty-fifty partners, a split right down the middle on any advance, and on the royalties. How does that sound?'

'Great, Jake.'

'We'll have some fun.' He grinned at me, looking like a little boy who had just won the biggest prize of his life.

11

As usual Simone made a wonderful lunch.

We started with vichyssoise soup, followed by an extraordinary salad Niçoise, served along with finely sliced *charcuterie*, and warm *baguettes*. For dessert, Simone presented us with our favourite Cavaillon melon, topped with redcurrants mixed with raspberries.

All through lunch, as we ate the delicious food and sipped *vin rosé*, Jake talked about what had now become *our* book. His excitement about it was infectious.

I also liked the idea because I felt that working on it would keep Jake away from Kosovo. Although he had said he didn't want to go anywhere without me, I was nevertheless a bit worried that Jacques would pressure him into covering the war again. And if not that particular war in the Balkans, then another one somewhere; there were always wars to cover these days, and after all Jake was a war photographer, as I was. But I had lost my taste for this dark side of journalism, at least for the time being, anyway. I prayed he had too.

And so we talked about the pictures we'd taken, what we had in our files, and which ones would work; we even got down to outlining some of the chapters. With his particular brand of enthusiasm, he made the project sound both exciting and challenging, and by the time we had finished lunch I discovered I was as committed to the book as he was.

III

We went upstairs to take an afternoon nap. But in the privacy of my room resting seemed to be the last thing on Jake's mind. Very slowly, he undressed me, peeling off my shirt, bra, and cotton shorts; and then he shed his own clothes. Leading me over to the bed, he gently pushed me onto it, lay down next to me and took me in his arms.

'Oh Val, my darling Val,' he whispered against my neck, stroking my hair. 'We're so lucky to have found each other . . . we have so much together.'

'Yes, I know we do.'

He brought his face to mine and kissed me softly. I held him tightly, my arms around his neck. Finally, in a low voice, he said, 'I adore you. Val. I have ever since the first day, but much more now.'

'I feel the same way, Jake.'

'Let's not lose this . . . let's try to keep it, keep it as long as we can . . .' His voice tapered off. He looked deeply into my eyes, as if he were seeing into my soul, and his own were very, very blue, reflecting his desire for me, and his love.

'For always. Let's keep it always,' I responded.

'If we possibly can,' he murmured. '*Always* is a

long time . . . but we can aim for it, can't we?' Without waiting for a response, he kissed me again, and then very tenderly and gently he began to make love to me.

Our passion swiftly flared, and we clutched at each other, devoured each other, were unable to get enough of each other. And then afterwards, wrapped in each other's arms, we fell asleep, at ease and content, knowing we belonged together.

Chapter Fifteen

I

Jake went downstairs to call his photo agency as he did every day. He sat at the big, beautiful antique desk in the window area of the room, which overlooked the gardens, and talked at length to Jacques Foucher. As one of the owners of the agency in Paris, Jake liked to know what business they were doing, what assignments were coming in and from which magazines and newspapers.

Knowing he would be occupied for quite a while, I went for a walk in the gardens, as I often did in the late afternoon. The furious storm of two days ago had wreaked havoc, and wrought a vast change in the vegetation and foliage. So many plants and flowers had been damaged by the rain and wind, and I had seen Armand walking around earlier today, looking crestfallen, glum and concerned as he assessed the damage, especially to the azaleas and rose bushes.

The weather had changed as well since the storm. It

was not as sunny as it had been and the air was much cooler. Even the sky had altered in appearance. The vivid blueness had faded away, and this afternoon it was etiolated, a bleached-out sky the colour of celery. In fact, the halcyon days of summer, which we had enjoyed for almost two weeks, had been replaced with a hint of autumn. But I did not mind this change, or the cooling down, since I was happy being with Jake at Les Roches Fleuries.

As I came around the edge of the rose bushes, making for my favourite spot under the cedar tree, I stopped dead in my tracks when I saw Françoise. She was standing so near to the edge of the cliff, looked to be in such a precarious position, I thought she would fall off at any moment. My heart began to pound against my rib cage; I was scared. And I did not know what to do.

I felt panic rising in me, but I managed to push it back, knowing that I must keep a cool head and think very clearly. I dared not move abruptly or with suddenness. If I did I might easily startle her and that could prove fatal.

And so I just stood there, watching her, trying to keep calm, wondering what my next move ought to be. After a couple of minutes, I decided to make a few small noises, light sounds that might catch her attention without frightening her.

One false step on her part, and only one, and she would be tumbling over the edge. I couldn't help asking myself what she was doing there in the first place. I hoped to God she wasn't planning to commit some awful and irreversible act. I wondered again if she was indeed a battered wife, as Jake seemed to believe she was.

Suddenly she moved.

I held my breath, and my eyes closed involuntarily. Immediately I snapped them open. Thankfully Françoise was still there; my heart was racing faster than ever and I felt a terrible fear settling in the pit of my stomach. How could I stop her from jumping, if that was her intention? My mouth went dry.

Taking complete control of myself, I reached out and shook the nearest bush, but the rustling of the leaves did not draw her attention. She seemed oblivious to everything; in fact, she still stood there as unmoving as a statue with her back to me, staring down at the rocks.

Very carefully, and with stealth, I stepped backwards, moved away from the cedar tree, until I was out of sight behind the hedge. Then I turned and hurried down the lawn. I paused in the middle of the grass, took a deep breath and then began to sing. Not too loudly, which would have startled her, but just loud enough for her to hear me, for her to be aware of my presence in the distance, to know it was me and not anyone else. I hoped a distant voice would break into her contemplation of that steep drop to the sea, without scaring her into doing something rash.

'Dance, in the old-fashioned way. Won't you stay in my arms? . . . Come close where you belong.' It

was the only popular song I knew the words to and this old Charles Aznavour classic was my favourite.

As I sang the words over again, I moved forwards more rapidly, going back down the lawn towards her. And as I stepped through the flowering rose bushes I saw to my relief that she had turned around, that she had been alerted to my presence. She was rooted to the same spot on the edge of the cliff, staring at me blankly through troubled eyes.

I stopped and stared back at her, wanting to appear normal, casual, unconcerned.

'Françoise, hello, hello!' I exclaimed in a soft voice. 'I hope I didn't startle you with my awful singing.' I forced laughter onto my lips, went on, 'I don't have a very good voice, I'm afraid.' I laughed once more, hoping to make light of the situation.

But there was no response. She just went on standing there, gaping at me as if she didn't know who I was. But thank God she hadn't taken a false step. Believing that behaving normally with her was my best bet, I began to walk very slowly towards the iron bench under the cedar tree.

In a conversational sort of way, I said, 'You know, this is my favourite spot, Françoise. I love it here. And what a coincidence – I guess it must be your favourite place, too.'

She blinked, and seemed to rouse herself at last from her trance. She said slowly, hesitantly, 'I came here often with Madame Adelia. When I was a child.'

'Please sit down with me, Françoise, talk to me

about her. She fascinates me,' I explained, striving for normalcy.

Françoise hesitated, then she turned her head and looked down at the rocks and the sea far below her, swaying slightly.

Once more, I held my breath, trembling inside. Fear made my throat close. But I said nothing, made no move, simply sat there quietly.

Unexpectedly, she swung around and my stomach lurched, so sudden and swift were her movements, and then to my great relief she actually stepped away from the edge of the precipice and slowly walked towards me. I felt limp as the fear ebbed.

Swallowing, I said, 'Madame Adelia was your friend then?'

Françoise now stood in front of me. She nodded. 'Yes . . . she was a very special woman.'

I rose, took hold of her hand. 'Please sit and talk to me.' And as I led her to the iron bench she did not resist. But she did not say anything further, just sat down next to me, gazing out into space, that preoccupied look continuing to glaze her eyes.

I decided to remain silent.

Eventually she broke the silence when she confided, 'I feel safe here.'

'Do you mean here in this particular part of the gardens?'

'*Oui, oui*. Madame Adelia is here . . . her spirit is here. I am close to her here. She helps me.'

Very gently I asked, 'Do you want to talk to me about your problems, Françoise?'

Looking at me closely, intently, she repeated, 'Problems?' and she frowned, seemed puzzled.

I nodded.

She did not speak.

'Sometimes it's easier to talk to a stranger. An American playwright, Tennessee Williams, once wrote, *I have always depended on the kindness of strangers.* So why don't you?'

A deep sigh escaped her and she looked out into space, and it seemed to me that she saw something I could not see and that she was disturbed by what she saw. At last she muttered, 'I . . . I . . . don't want to go back . . . I am . . . very afraid . . .'

'Of your husband?'

She chose not to answer, turned her head away from me.

'Of Olivier?' I asked very softly.

She inclined her head, but she was still avoiding my eyes.

'Then you must stay here.'

'No, no, I cannot. I must go. Far away.'

'Because he'll come here looking for you, is that it, Françoise? Is that what you mean?'

'Yes.'

'You must talk to your mother. I am sure she must know about Olivier's treatment of you. Or suspect that he abuses you.'

'*C'est possible*,' she agreed. Tears suddenly welled

in her lovely pellucid grey eyes. 'I came here to think. To listen to Madame Adelia's voice. But I became so afraid, I could not hear her voice.'

'We must act very calmly, use our heads,' I said, taking her hand in mine again.

She turned to face me again, and gave me a long sorrowful look. 'That is what she would have said to me.' A sigh escaped again. 'Madame Adelia died here.'

Startled, I asked, 'Do you mean here in this spot?'

'*Oui*. There was a wooden *chaise longue* here, and my father put many cushions on it every morning. Madame Adelia rested here. This was her memory place. That is what she told me. And one day she died. Right here. And then she went to the duke.'

'Her spirit, you mean,' I murmured, and wondered why I myself had been so attracted to this corner of the gardens.

'Yes,' Françoise answered. 'Her spirit. I do not want to return to Marseilles. I am afraid. I would be better off dead. And the baby.'

'No, no, you mustn't say that!' I tightened my grip on her hand. 'And you mustn't make a habit of standing over there at the edge of the cliff. It is a dangerous place. I was so afraid for you a few moments ago. I thought how easy it would be for you to take a false step and fall over the edge. Yes, it's very dangerous to walk around over there.'

'Yes, I know.' She looked into my eyes, searched my face, and there was a plea in hers. 'Mademoiselle Denning, please do not tell *maman* . . . that I was on the edge of the precipice. It will frighten her. And worry her.'

'All right, I won't.'

'Promise?'

'I promise. But you must make a promise to me.'

'What do you wish for me to promise to you?'

'You must promise not to even think of harming yourself or the baby.'

'But I cannot go back to him. He is crazy when he drinks. One day he will kill me. I know. Why should I wait for him to do that? Why should I suffer? It is better I do kill myself. *Maintenant*. And the child. I think it would be less painful. Yes?'

'No, you mustn't even think in that way. We must make a plan. I will come up with an idea, an idea where you can go, where you will be safe.'

Sudden hope flashed across her face, and then it disappeared just as quickly as it had appeared. 'He will find me. He is a *flic* . . . a cop, Mademoiselle Denning.'

'I know. Do you mind if I talk to Monsieur Jake?'

She looked frightened and shook her head. 'No! You must not. He will speak with *maman*. He will tell her.'

'No, he won't, not if I ask him not to, Françoise,' I reassured her. 'He will respect your wishes. He is a man of integrity . . . a man of honour, and he has much compassion, you must trust me on that.'

Folding her hands in her lap, Françoise sat there for a few moments, lost to me, lost to the world, as she tried to come to a decision. 'It is all right,' she murmured finally. 'You can tell Monsieur Jake. Please be kind, ask him not to say one word to my mother.'

'I will. And you can trust him, just as you can trust me. I have an idea already, Françoise. Let me think about it, think it through. Now come, we must go inside. Your mother must be wondering where you are.'

II

When I walked into the library Jake was standing by the desk. He swung around and said, 'Hi, I was just coming out to find you –' Abruptly he broke off, frowning, and asked, 'What's wrong? You're looking mighty strange.'

'You were right about Françoise being an abused wife,' I said, hurrying across the floor, flopping down into a chair near the fireplace. 'She's just admitted to me that she's afraid of Olivier, and that she thinks she'd be better off dead now, rather than waiting to get killed by him at a later date. And suffering until that actually happens.'

Jake sucked in his breath and stared at me. After a beat, he exploded, 'Jesus, Val! How the hell did this all come out so suddenly?' He dropped into the opposite chair, obviously both startled and dismayed.

Leaning forward, I quickly told him what had

occurred in the garden whilst he had been on the phone to his Paris office. He listened attentively, as he always did, and I could see from the expression on his face that he was appalled at what he was hearing.

When I had finished recounting everything in detail, he said nothing, remained absolutely quiet. I became aware of the stillness in him, all around him. It was an internal patience, and I knew it well by now; it was one of the things I'd always loved about him. He had this ability to become very calm and focused in times of trouble or crisis. Jake never panicked or flew off the handle; he was a cool guy who played it cool.

III

I could see that he was deep in thought, and I sat back and waited, trying to be as patient as he was. At last he said slowly, 'Tell Françoise I won't say anything to Simone. Although I'm sure her mother knows she's being battered, beaten up. Simone's nobody's fool, and, anyway, mothers know these things instinctively, don't they?'

'How would I know, I never had a mother.'

I saw him wince, but I couldn't help what I'd said, and I certainly wasn't going to retract it. The words had popped out automatically and they did happen to be the truth.

'Oh God, Val, I forgot! Mike Carter called a few minutes ago, just before you walked in. Your brother's been on the phone to him. This afternoon. He's looking for you. Mike wouldn't give him this number, but he told him he'd try to get a message to you. Apparently your brother wants you to call him. He explained to Mike that it's urgent, important that he speaks to you.'

I really didn't care, and I didn't want to return the call, but I muttered, 'I wonder what that's all about?'

'I guess he didn't give any other explanation to Mike, Val, and I wrote the number on the pad by the phone,' Jake was saying.

'Thanks,' I replied but I made no move to get up.

Pushing himself to his feet, Jake walked over to the French windows, stood looking out at the terrace and the gardens beyond. After a second or two, he remarked, as he turned to face me, 'You said you told Françoise you'd had an idea . . . what is it?'

'It suddenly occurred to me that she would be safe with me in Paris. She could stay at my apartment, there's a daybed in my office, as you know. Besides *I'll* probably be off on an assignment somewhere, or with you. I mean, I could camp out with you at a pinch, couldn't I?'

'I'll have to think about that.'

I smiled, knowing he was teasing me, and continued, 'Olivier doesn't know me. And as long as Simone and Armand keep quiet, he'll never be able to find Françoise, she'll be safe.'

Jake sighed. 'True. But he'll put pressure on them, I reckon.'

'They'll never tell him where she is!' I exclaimed, and rushed on a bit heatedly, 'Simone's strong, and tough, and I'd pit her against anybody any time, even a *flic*.'

He nodded. 'So would I, and Armand's no pushover either. He was in the Resistance during the Second World War, during the German Occupation, he told me once. He was just a kid, of course, but he said it toughened him up, that he learned a lot about life, and about people.' Jake now focused his vivid blue eyes on me steadily, unblinkingly, and asked, 'Why would you take Françoise in, Val? Just like that.' He snapped his thumb and second finger together, and went on, 'It's very nice of you to make the offer, but she's a stranger, you just met her today, and you hardly know her parents.'

'I like Simone a lot,' I replied. 'In fact, I've become rather attached to her. She's so motherly; Mother Earth, the salt of the earth, to me at any rate. This is a terrible predicament for Simone and Armand, and for Françoise, to be in. What a tragedy for them all. And Françoise being pregnant and getting battered is unconscionable. I think I can help them, so why wouldn't I? We see so much suffering and pain, you and I, Jake, and it's suffering we haven't been able to do anything about, at least not much. Look how many times we've rescued kids and their mothers, and pregnant women from bad situations, dangerous situations, and then we've had to leave them to fend for themselves. I just want to rescue her, see something through for once. And I can't bear the thought of that beautiful young woman being battered to death, which is what will happen eventually. If she's not removed from Olivier's grasp, taken out of that hideous marriage.'

'You're right – in everything you say, and it's very admirable of you to want to help Françoise. You know I'll pitch in, do anything I can. Yup, we should go for it.'

'Thanks, Jake, I'm so glad you agree with me.'

'I do . . . and there's something else, something I'm curious about.'

'Tell me.'

'What made you think of making noises, off-stage, so to speak? What gave you the idea to sing? How did you know these antics of yours would work?' An arched brow lifted, and he shook his head. 'I don't think I'd have ever thought of doing that.'

'I honestly don't know why I did what I did. Common sense, I guess. I realized that if I startled her she could easily fall off the edge of the cliff, or that she might just go ahead and jump. I suppose I wanted to distract her, turn her away from her purpose, but in a gentle way. That's why I tried to act so normal. Any other kind of behaviour on my part could have pushed her . . . literally over the edge, so I believe.'

'Is that what you really think? That she was intending to jump?'

I thought about this question for a moment, and then I nodded. 'I do, Jake. She told me she'd gone there to hear Madame Adelia's voice, but that she was so afraid of Olivier she hadn't been able to hear her. I'm pretty sure she would have killed herself this afternoon. If I hadn't come along when I did.'

'Oh Jesus,' he murmured, and came over, sat down on the chair next to me. 'You saved her life.'

'I think so, and I want to save her some more, get her out of Olivier's clutches, get her safely to Paris. She can have the baby there.'

'He's a cop, Val, Simone and Armand will have to be careful about a lot of things, especially phone calls.'

I gaped at him, frowning slightly, not understanding what he was getting at. 'Phone calls?'

'Well, I don't know whether cops can get hold of phone records in France or not, but they sure can in the States. I will have to warn them, they're going to have to use public phones, and mostly Françoise will have to call them. And talking of phone calls, perhaps you ought to get in touch with your brother. Don't you think?'

'I guess,' I reluctantly agreed, and rising I walked over to the desk. I seated myself in the chair, and picked up the piece of paper with Donald's number written on it. And as I read it, I realized how much I really did detest the idea of calling him. For deep within myself I knew it had something to do with Margot Scott Denning. My mother, so called.

IV

It took me ages to pick up the receiver, but finally I did. As I dialled, I hoped Donald the Great would be out and then I would have an easy escape. I could leave a message. No such luck. It was Donald himself who answered, exclaiming, 'Okay, Eliane, shoot.'

'It's Val,' I said.

'Oh gee, hi, Val. I thought it was Eliane, one of my contacts. I just hung up on her and she said she'd call me back right away. So, how're you doing, Sis?'

'I'm fine, Donald. I understand you tried to reach me earlier today. I was told it was urgent, important.'

'It is. You've got to come home. Immediately. Right away. Mom needs to talk to you,' he said in a rush of words.

'I'm not sure I can come, Donald, not at this time, and at your whim. Or hers. And furthermore, New York is not my home, and for another, I've no desire to listen to a woman who's not paid me a blind bit of notice since the day I was born. What could *I* possibly have to say to *her*?' I felt like adding, or you, but I refrained.

'Don't be like that. She's been very ill!' he cried, sounding slightly hysterical.

'Really.' I held the phone a little tighter and pursed my lips.

'Yeah, Sis, she's just had another heart attack, and

you've got to come home. You didn't come when I asked you a few weeks ago, and if you delay again it could be too late.'

'Do you think she might die, Donald?'

'I do, and this is about her *will*. Her Last Will and Testament. It affects me as well as you.'

I sat back in the chair, glanced at Jake.

He frowned at me, and I knew then that he would never truly understand about my family, at least not about my parents and Donald, because his family was so very different.

Donald was blabbering into the phone again, 'I'm telling you the stakes are high, Sis, and I'm going to get screwed if you don't get your ass over here as soon as possible. If she dies and we haven't cleared this mess up, then I'm up shit creek without a paddle.'

'Donald, you're not making a case for yourself, not with your crudeness and vulgarity. And who's *she*? The cat's mother? Or your Mom, as you usually call her. Usually you're the doting son.'

'Aw, come on, don't be such a pain, Val. Relax. What you need is a good f –'

'Donald,' I cut in sharply, thus cutting him off. 'Don't say it or I'll hang up.'

'Okay, okay, so come on, give me a date. This is important. Blood's thicker than water, Sis.'

'*Really*. How come this is the first time I've heard *that* sentiment expressed in the Denning family?'

'The old guy left you *everything*,' he said. 'I got nothing . . . *now* it's my turn.'

'How can you say you got nothing? Grandfather left you a very nice trust.' I knew this statement of mine would be like a red rag to a bull, so I took a deep breath and rushed on before he could respond, 'What this is all about is Margot Denning's will, as far as I can ascertain from your conversation. And I can't imagine why you need *me*. I'm sure you're featured in it and not I. She's barely acknowledged me for thirty-one years. So why would she do so now?'

'Look, Val, I honestly don't understand what it's all about,' Donald said. 'What I do know is that somehow my inheritance is attached to yours, tied up with it. Why won't you just say when you're coming, so I can tell Mom?'

'Donald, I'll have to get back to you.'

'But when? *When*? Come on, don't do this to me!'

'I'll call you at this time tomorrow.'

'Okay, okay. Talk to you then.'

He slammed the phone down and I continued to sit in the chair, still holding the receiver in my hand, staring at it. I slowly replaced it in the cradle, and then I told Jake what had happened. And I must admit, I did so with a sense of sadness for my brother. Like my mother, he had never had much time for me. Until now.

Chapter Sixteen

I
NEW YORK, OCTOBER

If anyone had told me that I would be sitting in the middle of Manhattan a week after this conversation with Donald, I would have laughed in their face.

But here I was at my grandfather's old desk, staring out across the East River at the giant Pepsi-Cola sign anchored in Long Island City, on the other side of the water.

It had been a lovely October day. Now, in the late afternoon, I was whiling away the time, waiting for Jake to come back from a meeting with the publisher. An editor at this well-established house was interested in publishing *Flowers of War*, the tentative title of the coffee-table book. That it would be a joint venture between the two of us was now a foregone conclusion, I would write some of the text as well as provide a selection of my pictures.

Earlier today he had asked me to go to the meeting

with him and Harvey, but I had declined. It had always been Jake's deal, not mine, and he was much more famous than I. Also, I wanted time to catch my breath and relax for a day. I was really praying they would agree on the terms, since I knew the book was dear to his heart. Also, it would anchor Jake in one place, keep him from rushing off to Kosovo or other dangerous parts of the world, and this thought continued to please me no end.

As I sat gazing across the river, which gleamed in the fading afternoon sunlight, I realized how much had happened in the last eight days.

Following my revelations about Françoise to Jake, we had had a long talk with her the following day, during which I had invited her to stay with me in Paris. She was at first rather shy, had been hesitant about this, but when Jake had suggested we take her parents into our confidence, she had instantly agreed, surprising us both. Simone and Armand had been somewhat taken aback by my invitation, then they had quickly seen the wisdom of such a move, and had convinced their daughter to accept. And so the next day we had flown back to Paris, taking Françoise along with us.

Before we left Les Roches Fleuries, Jake had had a serious talk with the Rogets, explaining to them that they must not phone Françoise in Paris, either from their own home or the villa. 'As a cop, Olivier might be able to get the phone records for both places, and trace the number in Paris to an address,' he had pointed out. 'It is much safer and wiser for Françoise to call you.' And they had been in agreement with him, seeing the sense of this. But when we left St-Jean-Cap Ferrat I was suddenly worried about Simone and Armand; Jake had been extremely reassuring, though, reminding me several times how strong they both were, also tough-minded and not easily pushed around.

Jake and I had been back in Paris for only one day when Harvey Robinson had called from New York, to tell him that the editor was anxious to meet with him, to discuss the book. And as soon as possible. Harvey had had another surprise in store for Jake. A well-known Soho art gallery wanted to have an exhibition of his pictures of war, and they wished to talk to him in person as well.

'Let's go, Val. Next week,' he had said to me that evening, obviously excited by these prospects. But I had not been very enthusiastic about flying to New York so unexpectedly, at the drop of a hat. 'Anyway, if I'm there I'll probably feel obligated to see Donald, and I don't want to do that,' I'd muttered, realizing that I'd sounded sullen, which was not like me.

'Why don't you see him? Why don't you see your mother as well?' Jake had suggested. 'Get to the bottom of this Last Will and Testament business. And you should have it out with her, Val. Confront her, find the reason for this attitude of hers, find out why she's treated you the way she has all these years. Get it over with once and for all. You'll probably feel heaps better for it. It would be liberating, I think, Kid.'

I was ambivalent about doing this, and I just

couldn't make my mind up about going to New York. I was also a bit concerned about leaving Françoise alone, and unprotected, so to speak. I mentioned this to Mike Carter the following morning, when I'd gone into Gemstar for the first time since late August, and he had solved the problem for me. Out of the blue, he had volunteered to keep an eye on her, and had convinced me to call her at the apartment and invite her to lunch with us. 'So we can become acquainted,' he had said.

Mike had been his usual warm and easy-going self over lunch, and Françoise had relaxed in his presence. In fact, I was surprised the way the two of them got along so well. She became positively gay in the restaurant, and for once that sad and sorrowful look had left her lovely grey eyes. At least for a short while.

That night, when I saw Jake for dinner, he announced that he had bought our tickets, and that we were leaving in a couple of days. He was taking charge as usual, in that macho way of his. I found myself being swept along by his charm and enthusiasm; I also realized that he was determined to go and make these deals, no matter what, and I wanted to be with him. We had become very close in the south of France, and I didn't want absence and distance to break the euphoric mood which existed between us.

11

Jake and I were staying at my aunt's apartment in midtown Manhattan, a traditional, spacious place just off First Avenue in the Fifties, which I knew well.

Aunt Isobel had inherited it from my grandfather, and one day it would be mine, a stipulation written into his will. If I survived her, that is.

My grandfather had wanted to do the correct thing by his daughter, but he had also wanted me to have a home in New York, even if I rarely used it, and my aunt had concurred with this. Grandfather had called it my safety net, a place of refuge if I ever got tired of wielding my camera on the front lines.

My aunt was my grandparents' only daughter, my father's older sister, although she and he had never been close. Her main home was about two and a half hours away, in the upper reaches of Connecticut, which is where she lived most of the time. She only occasionally stayed at the apartment, about once or twice a month for a night or two, and she had repeatedly told me to make use of it whenever I wished. In the meantime, she paid for its upkeep.

Isobel Denning Cox was a renowned interior designer, with offices in Greenwich and New York, and clients all over the world. Grandfather used to describe her as the Floral Queen, because she favoured so much chintz in many of the interiors she designed. English antiques of the Georgian period were a speciality of hers, and together with the floral fabrics she created the popular cosy, cluttered English country-house look. She had made this her own, as had Mario Buatta, another great designer who had also perfected this style.

But she was an expert on eighteenth-century French furniture and works of art as well, and some of her settings looked as if they had been transported lock, stock and barrel from several *châteaux* in the Loire Valley. I had always admired her for her brilliance and talent, her ability to produce such diverse, beautiful and tasteful homes for her clients.

Her husband, James Mallard Cox, was a retired banker, and something of an invalid these days. Sadly, their only child Johnny, a playboy who had never married, had been tragically killed eight years ago, when the small plane he was piloting himself had crashed in the French Alps in a thunderstorm.

She and I did not see each other very often, unless she came to Paris on a buying trip and I was there, and not shooting photographs of a war somewhere. Then we would get together for lunch or dinner.

We liked each other a lot, and had always been friendly. Aunt Isobel had been forever exasperated with my mother, and had mostly taken Grandfather's side against her.

Opinionated and outspoken, my aunt was the most self-confident person I had ever met. Colourful phrases were never far from her lips, and she had once described my father as 'a spineless twerp who needs his brains washing, preferably in disinfectant, and then hung out to dry in a sharp wind'.

Whenever I thought of Aunt Isobel, I laughed to myself, remembering this description, which had forever endeared her to me; certainly it had made my grandfather chuckle for days on end.

My aunt had had white hair, sleek and thick, for as long as I could recall, and she was a tall, imposing woman, good-looking and elegant, with the finest taste in clothes as well as in antiques and art. She had a marvellous sense of humour and great wit; but she was also down to earth and genuinely kind of heart, all of which made her a very special woman in my eyes. Certainly a woman to look up to and admire, as I did.

Once I had decided to come to New York with Jake, I had telephoned my aunt at her Greenwich office, which is where she worked most of the time.

I had been put through to her secretary, who told me she was in New York, and that I would find her at the Beekman Place apartment. It was there that I had reached her a few minutes later, and she had been thrilled to hear that I wanted to stay at the flat.

'I'm not likely to be here again for several weeks, Val, so do please come and make yourself at home.' She had burst into laughter. 'What am I saying? It *is* your home.' She had gone on to add, 'And if I do have to come in for a night, there's plenty of room for us all. You do have your key, don't you?'

I had assured her that I did. And she had explained

that she would tell Molly, her housekeeper, to come in three times a week instead of twice, for as long as we were staying at the apartment.

When we had arrived last night it was obvious that Molly had been there during the morning. Everything sparkled, cushions were plumped up, and flowers graced the many vases. There was even a fresh supply of milk and other staples in the refrigerator.

Jake had walked around, whistling under his breath, looking impressed. He had said he felt as though he had just strolled into an English country house in the Cotswolds, and then announced that that was all right by him, though.

'It's Aunt Isobel's trademark look,' I had explained, laughing with him, and we had both agreed it was comfortable as well as charming, and a pleasant place to be.

'And certainly much nicer than staying in a hotel,' Jake had murmured as he had lowered himself into an overstuffed sofa covered with a red-rose-green-leaf print, one my aunt often favoured in her decorating schemes.

Leaping up suddenly, he had dashed to the big bay window, exclaiming about the panoramic view, and the life on the river. For at that moment there were a number of barges and boats moving slowly along the waterway. 'It's a very busy thoroughfare,' I told him. 'I remember it well from my childhood.'

III

Naturally, it was full of nostalgic memories for me, and since my grandparents had owned this apartment for over forty years before their deaths, I had spent some very happy childhood times here. They were the only really happy days I could actually recall from those miserable years when I had been growing up in New York.

Once Jake and I had unpacked last night, we had gone out for a walk, needing to breathe some fresh air after being cooped up in the plane. And Jake had remarked about the charm of Beekman Place, a quiet, tree-lined enclave I had always been partial to, and which I knew so well from those long-ago days of my youth.

Later, we had wandered up First Avenue, had gone to Neary's pub on East Fifty-Seventh Street, where Jimmy Neary, the owner and host, had greeted me like a long-lost daughter. Having three of his own, he was a very fatherly type and he welcomed me with a huge smile that was warm, genuine and very sincere.

After his retirement from the architectural firm he had founded, my grandfather had gone to Neary's several times a week for lunch, and he often took my grandmother there for supper. And so Jimmy had known them for many years, and known them quite well. After a drink at the bar, Jimmy had given us a cosy table for two in a corner, where we had had our dinner.

'Just like old home week for you, I reckon,' Jake said as we had walked down First Avenue after a hearty supper of homemade Irish stew and a bottle of good red wine. Arms around each other, we were happy to be together on this balmy night, sheltered by a high-flung, dark-velvet sky littered with stars twinkling like diamond chips. '*Lucy in the sky with diamonds*,' Jake had warbled softly, as we had ambled along, making for Beekman Place. It had been the loveliest return to New York I had ever experienced, and most especially later that night when we climbed into my grandparents' big old four-poster bed and made love . . .

IV

The phone jangled, interrupting my train of thought, and I jumped, startled out of my reverie, as I reached for it swiftly. 'Hello?'

'It's Françoise,' she said in the soft, lilting voice I had come to know.

'Hello, Françoise, hello!' I exclaimed, thinking how close she sounded, 'is everything all right? And how are you feeling?'

'It is all okay, Mademoiselle,' she answered. 'I am feeling well. But it is Olivier, he has been to see my parents at Les Roches Fleuries –'

'Oh my God, are they all right?' I cut in worriedly. 'Has he been pestering them?'

'*Oui* . . . but they are strong. They will not tell him where I am . . .'

Suddenly, abruptly, Françoise stopped speaking, and I heard muttered asides, another voice at her end of the phone. I assumed she was calling from my apartment, since it was now night time in Paris. I couldn't help wondering who was with her.

'Françoise, Françoise,' I said loudly into the receiver. 'Are you there? Are you all right?'

Still she did not respond.

I was about to say her name again, when Mike Carter exclaimed, 'Hi, Val, it's me, honey.'

'Mike, is Françoise upset? Is everything okay with her parents? I'm sure Olivier's being a pest, and I'm being kind when I call him that.'

Mike chuckled. 'You're right, pest *is* too kind a word to describe that son of a bitch. Let's just say he's been pretty difficult with them, but they're holding up okay. All of this blew up yesterday afternoon when her husband showed up at the villa in Cap Ferrat. You were flying over the Atlantic by that time. I think the parents have things pretty much under control. They've assured Françoise they're fine, and I brought her over to stay at my place this afternoon.' He laughed. 'My girls think she's pretty neat and they're good friends already.'

'It's a relief to know she's safe, Mike, thanks so much for being her . . . guardian angel, shall we say?'

'I'm happy to help her, poor kid,' Mike replied. 'I feel sorry for her. She's not had an easy time of it.'

'I know that. Anyway, I feel better knowing she's actually staying with you and the girls. To be honest, I was a bit worried about leaving her alone at my place.'

'I don't blame you, honey. I doubt that her parents would tell him where she is, but even if they did, under duress of some kind, she's no longer there now.' His deep chuckle rumbled down the wire, before he added, 'Gone like a puff of smoke.'

'Do her parents know she's with you? They'll worry if there's no answer to my phone.'

'She's told them she's moving in with a friend, but she didn't say she was coming to my place. We thought it wiser her parents were kept in the dark . . . what they don't know they can't spill.'

'That's smart of you.'

'I thought we'd better phone you though, Val, to let you know where Françoise is, just in case you phoned her and there was no reply.'

'I'm glad you did.'

'And how's little old New York?' he asked, sounding suddenly wistful. New York was his favourite city; he'd told me that so many times.

'Great, just great, and it's wonderful weather . . . Indian summer sort of weather.'

'Enjoy. I'll call you later in the week. Meantime, here's Françoise,' he finished sounding brisk, business-like once more.

'Mademoiselle Denning, please don't worry,' Françoise said.

'I won't. But I told you to call me Val.'

There was a small laugh, and she said, '*Oui* . . . Val. I feel safe with Mike's family. Olivier will never find me here. Because no one knows where I am . . . except you, Mademoiselle, I mean . . . Val.'

'I'm not going to tell anybody.'

'It will be better if you do not telephone *maman*, I think.'

'I understand, Françoise, and I won't. But you can call me any time you wish, I'm going to be in New York for a good week, perhaps even two.'

'Okay. Thank you for everything, and do not worry about me, Mademoiselle Denning.'

'It's VAL,' I half shouted down the phone, and we both laughed.

'*Au revoir*, Val,' she said softly.

'Good night, Françoise, and be well. I'll phone later in the week.'

V

After replacing the receiver, I leaned forward, my elbows on the desk, my head in my hands, thinking. The call from Françoise had brought me back to reality, my reverie about Jake and our lovemaking interrupted by her. My own life was suddenly rather sharply in focus, and I contemplated Jake's advice of earlier.

Before he had left for the meeting, he had suggested that I call my brother Donald. 'Get it over with, once and for all,' he had said, and there had been a stern look in his blue eyes. 'Wipe that slate clean and forget it.'

I knew he was right, and yet I hadn't been able to make the call. At least, not so far; but after all, I had been here for only a day. On the plane I had asked myself if I was *really* coming to see Donald and my mother . . . and not flying to New York simply because I wanted to be with Jake, as I believed.

Examining this thought now, I was able to answer myself; a resounding albeit silent NO reverberated in my head. I *was* here in the city of my birth because of Jake, and that *was* the truth.

VI

Donald and my mother meant very little to me, for all the obvious reasons. Nothing, nada, zilch, I muttered under my breath. They had given me nothing, nada, zilch, and I had no intention of being at their beck and call at this stage of my life.

From this standpoint, Jake was right. I should get rid of all that old baggage, discard it and start afresh without the burden of my past. But to do so I would have to confront them, my mother especially, and I had vowed long ago, and to her face, that I would never speak to her or see her ever again. And I hadn't. And I didn't want to now. I wasn't even remotely curious to know what these sudden overtures were all about.

The truth was, I had come to New York because Jake Newberg was coming, and *he* wanted me with him. And that was where *I* wanted to be, by his side, in his arms, in his bed, in his life, and in his heart. I wanted to be with him when we were working, relaxing, travelling, sleeping. Night and day for as long as I lived.

'I've always loved you, Val my Val,' he had said to me last night. And as we had lain there in each other's arms, resting after our passionate lovemaking, I remembered how he had always run to protect me, pulled me out of harm's way, put himself between me and imminent danger. Always there on the sidelines, looking out for me, keeping me company when I was alone and needy, good old dependable, reliable, steadfast Jake.

And I wondered yet again how I could have been so foolish as to be inveigled into a relationship by Tony Hampton? Because Tony was a clever and adept womanizer who knew how to charm and romance a woman, even against her better judgement. And because I hadn't known how Jake felt. And besides, I had been blind.

Chapter Seventeen

I

When Jake walked in an hour later, I couldn't tell from his expression whether the meeting with the editor had gone well or not. He was poker-faced and his eyes revealed nothing.

After placing his briefcase on a chair, he walked over to me, gave me a bear hug and kissed my cheek. 'Hi, honey,' he said. 'Gotta get a Coke,' and he walked off in the direction of the kitchen.

My eyes followed him. I couldn't help thinking how smart he looked today in the grey pin-stripe suit, pale-blue shirt, and darker-blue polka-dot tie. Everything about him gleams, I thought as he came strolling back with the can of Coke in his hand, from the top of his blond-streaked hair to the tip of his highly polished brown loafers. I felt a little rush of pride in him. He had been gone all day, and ever since we had become involved I was always surprised when I saw him after only a few hours' absence. He was so personable, so good-looking, and so well put together, it was always a bit of a shock when he strolled in nonchalantly, as he was doing now. He was the only man for me, the only man I wanted.

Sitting down next to me on the sofa, Jake said, 'Why don't we go out tonight? I don't think you should cook.'

'Whatever you want,' I answered, and fixing my eyes on him intently, I asked, 'What happened at the publishers? How was the editor?'

His face lit up. 'He's a great guy, Val, you're going to like him. I wish you'd been at the meeting, but I'll get the two of you together real soon. His name's Bill Forrest, and he's very with it, very knowledgeable. Knows what he wants, how the book should look, what it should say, convey in terms of text and photographs. He's very enthusiastic about the project.'

'So we have a contract?'

'Not yet. But that's pretty much a foregone conclusion, I think. Harvey agrees with me. But before we move on to that stage, Bill needs an outline. So what you and I have to do is break the book down into chapters and content, show him some more pictures, and then he'll make the deal, I guess. I told him we'd give him a little presentation next week.'

'Will we have it ready?' I asked.

'Sure. It's a snap as long as I have you helping me.'

'Flattery will get you everywhere,' I said.

'I sincerely hope so. Because I want to get everywhere with you.'

'You have, silly.'

He smiled, said nothing more, took a long swig from the can of Coke. Placing the can on the coffee table, he murmured, 'We can work all weekend, sort the pictures, plan out the book. We'll be fine.'

'I guess so . . .' I paused, gave him a fast glance. '*Jake?*'

He turned to look at me. 'What is it? You sound concerned. And you look it.'

'I am, a bit. About Françoise. She phoned this afternoon, and she's staying at Mike Carter's apartment.'

'Why? What happened? Don't tell me. I can guess! Olivier showed up.'

'Not in Paris, at Les Roches Fleuries.'

'Yes, that's what I meant. I suppose he's been giving her folks a hard time? Is that it, Val?'

'Apparently. But they've been pretty tough with him, from what I can gather. Nevertheless, Mike decided it would be better to move her out of my place.'

'I see. Well, I guess that was shrewd of Mike. A smart cop might well put two and two together and come up with five. We'd been staying down there, he could jump to conclusions, come up with the truth. Why wouldn't you or I provide some sort of help, give her shelter? A sharp *flic* might well figure that out. You and I would be easy to find in Paris, we're so well known. A cop wouldn't have any trouble locating us sooner or later.'

I nodded. 'True. I think Mike likes her . . . what I mean is, I have a feeling he's attracted to her.'

For a moment Jake appeared startled, and then his

expression changed, and he grinned at me. 'And why not? She's a lovely-looking young woman, and she seems very sweet. And Mike's been a widower for . . . what is it, ten years now?'

'Yes, Sarah was killed in that horrible car crash ten years ago, when Lisa was four and Joy was two. They're teenagers now, and quite grown up. Mike told me the girls are very taken with Françoise, he said they'd all become friends.'

'Fast friends fast, heh?' he laughed.

I laughed, too, but made no comment.

'Yup, I guess she's better off with Mike at Mike's. It would be hard for Olivier to track her down there.'

'I hope you're right. You know, I do work for Mike – if Olivier makes the connection, he could show up at Gemstar.'

'Yeah, that's true, but he sure as hell won't get anywhere with Mike Carter.'

'He's a tough guy, I know that. A match for anybody,' I answered.

'What a lousy world we live in,' Jake muttered, swigging the Coke again, then slapping the can down hard on the coffee table.

I saw the flicker of anger in those deep blue eyes and his mouth was drawn in a tight line. He was such a good man, so full of feeling for others.

He went on, 'Wherever you look, people have such problems. Take Françoise – an innocent, loving young woman, beaten and battered about by some tough cop who goes ape when he drinks. Not fair, is it?'

'No, it's not, and I just hope she gets through the birth of the baby okay, that nothing goes wrong. Then once the child is born, she can decide what to do. Personally, I'm praying she stays in Paris. She might have a future with Mike.'

Jake gave me a long, studied look, then leaned back against the sofa, frowning slightly. 'What makes you say that?'

'I don't know . . . well, yes, I do. There was a sort of . . . *connection* between them, the day Mike took us to lunch, and she was so carefree, so *happy*. I couldn't believe it. I know it had something to do with Mike. And he looked . . . well, I guess it was the same for him. He was *happy*, too. I haven't seen that kind of expression on his face for as long as I've known him, and that's seven years now.'

'So they clicked, hit it off, but it doesn't mean there's a future there. Listen, she's married, and married to a maniac, whose child she's expecting . . . better slow down, honey.'

'I know, I know. But it would be nice if they . . .' I stopped, shrugged. 'You know, got together . . . somehow.'

Jake bent forward, kissed the tip of my nose. 'Spoken like a true romantic, Val. And I agree, it would be nice for Françoise. Mike's a good guy.'

II

Since Jake wanted to stay in the neighbourhood but go to a nice restaurant, I led him to Le Périgord on Fifty-Second Street later that evening. I knew he would love it because he preferred French food, after southern soul food, that is. And I was right.

This was another of Grandfather's old haunts, and I'd been brought here for many special occasions in the past, for over twenty years, at that. Georges Briguet, the proprietor, came over to greet us and seat us, and before we could even blink, two glasses of sparkling champagne stood before us on the table. To welcome us, Georges explained, offering us the Perrier-Jouët.

Jake quickly got into the spirit of things, and because I was happy to see *him* so happy and carefree I went along with him. More champagne followed the first glasses. He ordered oysters for us both, and then roast duck, which was accompanied by a bottle of his favourite red wine, Saint-Émilion. We finished the meal with sumptuous floating islands in vanilla sauce.

'I was too thin before, I know that,' I said to Jake at one moment. 'But pretty soon I'm going to be too fat. Far too fat. I've got to go on a diet.'

'You're fine the way you are, fine for me that is,' Jake murmured. 'I don't like sticks.'

I didn't say anything, since I'd just remembered how

anorexically thin his ex-wife, the famous model, had been; a fact that had troubled Jake no end. I focused on her for a moment, wondering how she was, what she was doing. Still a top model, I knew that. They had been divorced for almost two years; God, how time was flashing by me, at the speed of light.

'Did you call Donald?' Jake asked.

Lost in my thoughts as I was, I blinked several times before answering, 'Er, no.'

'You have to, Val.' Jake looked at me closely, intently, and covered my hand with his. He continued, 'Not only for your sake, but ours. I don't want you to have this situation hanging over your head. Your past has always been a terrible burden for you, I realize that as much as you do. I want you to shed it once and for all, get rid of it. You've got to be free, sweetheart.'

'I want to be, Jake, honestly, but –'

'No buts, I won't take buts,' Jake interrupted me sharply. 'Just pick up a phone and make a date to see Donald. Alone. Then see your mother another day. Let's do it whilst we're here in New York, Val, it's such a good opportunity.'

'Oh, Jake, you just don't know . . .'

'I do, and I'll help you. I'm here for you, I'll even go with you to meet him, or we'll have him to the apartment. You can see him alone if you want, but I'll be in another room, a safety net for you. *Please*, Val,' he insisted in a low voice.

'I'll think about it . . .'

'You'll see, it won't be so bad. Call him tomorrow morning, see him tomorrow. The sooner the better.'

'I can't tomorrow. I have lunch with Muffie.'

'Oh that's right, I'd forgotten. But lunch isn't all day, Val. What about the afternoon? Or listen, see him in the evening. Okay?'

'I don't know.'

'Then see him at the weekend,' Jake suggested, determined to settle this.

'I thought we were going to work on the book.'

'We are. And surely you're only going to spend an hour with Donald? It couldn't possibly take longer than that, could it?'

'You never know with Donald the Great.'

'I've often wondered why you call him that.' Jake's blondish brow lifted quizzically, and he fixed his bright blue eyes on me.

'Because my mother thought he was the greatest thing to hit the earth. The greatest thing since sliced bread, my Grandmother used to say. My mother was always saying, "Donald's great at this, Donald's great at that," and I just got fed-up, I guess we all did. And one day I said here comes Donald the Great, and Grandfather was tickled to death, and the name just stuck.'

'I guess nicknames do. But surely it won't take longer than an hour, will it?' he asked again.

'Who the hell knows?' I mumbled, and I shrank down farther on the banquette. I felt as though I were shrivelling up inside. The mere idea of meeting with my sibling was something I could hardly bear to contemplate. I associated Donald with too many painful memories.

Jake said, 'You're really trying to duck it, Val darling, and I don't think you should. Nor should you duck your mother. Face her head-on. You can do it, Val.'

'I can't.'

'Why? You're not afraid, are you?'

'Yes, I think I am,' I whispered.

'Of her? Or of what she has to say?' Jake asked gently, taking my hand in his again, trying to soothe me.

'Of what she has to say,' I admitted. And then I sat up a little straighter, suddenly feeling better now that I'd admitted this to him, and just as importantly, to myself.

'Oh Val, don't be. It's all in her, you know. I bet it's actually nothing to do with you. How could it have anything to do with you? You were only a baby when this started, from what your grandfather told you anyway. Isn't that so?'

I nodded.

'Listen to me . . . you and I have a lot of things going for us. But one of the most important is our shared integrity, that sense of honour, and our love of the truth. The truth in all things. I don't deal in lies, Val, and neither do you. I will always tell you the truth. Just as I know you will tell me the truth. Correct?'

'Yes,' I replied, my eyes glued to his.

'Okay, then. I am telling you the truth now, Val. You've nothing to fear, nothing to be afraid of. Whatever your mother has to tell you, it's nothing to do with anything *you've* ever done. It's all about *her*. Don't you see? *It's to do with her.*'

I let out a long sigh.

'Do you want me to come with you when you go and see your mother?'

'I don't know that she'd like that, she might not open up under those circumstances.'

'Well, it's possible, yes,' he admitted. 'But we won't know that unless we go visit her. Only then will we find out.'

I had to agree with him. 'It's nice of you to offer to come with me, Jake, it really is.'

'I care about you.'

'And I care about you too, and I know you're right in everything you say. I *will* phone Donald tomorrow, I promise, and I'll make a date with him. I think I'd rather hear what *he's* got to say, before I do anything about my mother.'

'Take it slowly, one step at a time,' he said, and leaning closer, he kissed me on the cheek.

III

In the quiet, darkened room, in the vast four-poster that had been my grandparents' bed, Jake made love to me as he never had before. Nor I with him. Slowly, voluptuously, he drew me along the edge of ecstasy, as I did him, tantalizing, teasing, bringing each other to a fine pitch. And then ceasing all touching and kissing suddenly, we rested against each other to catch our breath.

'I want to draw this out, make it last forever,' he whispered against my hair. 'And so do I,' I whispered back, moving my fingers slowly up his stomach to rest on his chest.

Jake raised himself up on one elbow and kissed my eyelids, my cheeks, my lips and my neck. He let his mouth linger on mine, devoured mine, and then kissed each breast. Slowly, he moved his lips down to that final resting place against my thighs, swiftly, surely, brought me up onto another high plateau. My legs were trembling, my whole body quivering under his touch, and I yearned to be part of him. And after a moment, as if he read my mind, he took me to him. We found our rhythm instantly, as we always did, and soared higher and higher together, and as our passion increased he said tensely, 'I love you, Val.' And I said the same to him.

Much later, as we lay together, our arms and legs

wrapped around each other, exhausted and sore, I said to Jake, 'Always . . . it's for always. It's got to be.'

'It will be,' he replied; he held me closer, cradled me in his arms and kissed my hair.

My joy and happiness at being with Jake so filled me with euphoria, it never occurred to me we might well be tempting fate when we spoke of always. But I was to remember this night later, and reflect on our words.

Chapter Eighteen

1

It wasn't such a beautiful day after all. The bright sunshine of early morning had given way to a dull pale sky overladen with whitish clouds, but it wasn't going to rain. At least so I had been assured by Jake, who had been tuned in to C.N.N. for several hours.

And so I decided to walk to the Carlyle Hotel where I was meeting my old friend Muffie Potter Aston for lunch. I said this to Jake as I went into the study to kiss him goodbye.

Jake was seated at the old desk in the window that had been Grandfather's, making notes on a yellow pad, and sipping a Diet Coke from the can.

'I'm off,' I murmured, kissing him on top of his head. 'I'll see you later.'

'You're leaving early.'

'I've decided to walk.'

'All that way?'

'It's only twenty-five blocks,' I said, laughing.

'And across First, Second, Third, Lexington, Park, and Madison,' he pointed out, grinning at me.

'I need the exercise,' I countered. 'I feel like one of those ducks the French fatten for *foie gras*; it's all those meals you've been feeding me, Jake Newberg.'

'Mmmm. Nice and plump and the better for plucking,' he leered.

'*Beast*. And I'm *not* plump.'

He merely smiled in that enigmatic way of his. Or was it a smug smile this morning? I wasn't sure. I said, 'Are you going to the agency later?'

He nodded. 'Gotta get into those files Harvey's been filling up for years. I know there's a batch of my pictures in there, and they could be useful for the book. I'll mosey on over there at about one o'clock, have a bite with Harvey, and then get to work. It's a no-brainer; all I have to do is locate the files. After that it's just a matter of pulling the shots.'

'I'll come back here after lunch,' I said, edging out of the room.

'And you'll call Donald,' he reminded me, giving me a stern look.

'Yes, I will. 'Bye.'

'I'll buy you a Chinese dinner tonight,' he shouted after me.

'I won't be hungry, so thanks but no thanks,' I called back, hurried through the foyer and out of the front door before he could say anything else, smiling inwardly.

11

Since I hadn't gone window shopping in New York for years, I walked down East Fifty-Seventh Street, making for Madison Avenue. As I turned onto this famous fashion street I was amazed to see so many new stores and boutiques. It was a pleasure to stroll along at a leisurely pace, gazing in the windows at the latest clothes, shoes, and bags.

Not that all the styles appealed to me. They didn't. I tended to choose plain, tailored clothes in dark colours, because I knew they suited me. They were also much more practical for the life I led as a war photojournalist. My entire wardrobe was built on black, navy, and grey, a bit sombre, I know, but easy to wear and easy to accessorize. Occasionally I went slightly crazy and bought something in white or cream, but never bright colours because I hated myself in them.

Today I was wearing a lightweight wool jacket in black, cut to resemble a bush jacket, a style I loved, a white silk man-tailored shirt and black gabardine slacks. I wore high-heeled black boots under the slacks, and carried a dark green Kelly bag which Jake had given me for Christmas. As usual, my only pieces of jewellery were pearl earrings and a watch, a lovely old Cartier timepiece. This had been my grandmother's favourite and she had left it to me when she died.

I thought of the unique and very loving Cecelia Denning, whom I so physically resembled, as I walked along. Without her, and Grandpa of course, I would have been a real mess, neurotic and damaged beyond repair, I've no doubt. Together, they managed to counteract the neglect of my parents, by giving me a great deal of love and emotional nourishment. And it was Grandmother who had introduced me to my closest friend, Muffie Potter, who had become my ally and sparring partner fifteen years ago.

Muffie was a couple of years older than me, and she had lived in Washington, D.C. when we were teenagers, but we saw each other whenever she had come to visit her grandparents, who lived in Scarsdale. They were friends of my Denning grandparents, and they also happened to be acquainted with Aunt Isobel, and so our friendship had everyone's stamp of approval.

We had remained friends ever since our teen years, even though our lives had gone in different directions. While I struggled with my camera on the front lines, shooting wars, Muffie had a high-powered job as an executive at Van Cleef & Arpels, the famous French jewellers on Fifth Avenue.

She had recently married Sherrell Aston, the renowned plastic surgeon; unfortunately, much to my disappointment, I hadn't been able to attend their wedding, since I'd been stuck in some hellhole in a misbegotten corner of the world, taking pictures of yet more human suffering.

Over the years we had always stayed in touch with each other by letter, card, fax and telephone, and whenever we were in the same city we met for dinner, lunch or drinks, whatever we could manage. It was nice for me to have such a loyal best friend, and Muffie felt the same, I know.

There was something very special about her. The golden girl I called her, because she *was* golden, inside as well as out, but especially in her nature. She was filled with sunshine and lightheartedness, so it seemed to me anyway.

Muffie was blonde, blue-eyed and very pretty. She had a serious side and was much wiser than most of the other people I knew, had a trenchant way of telling you what she thought about everything. Including your own life, if you were smart enough to ask for her advice.

But only if you sought her opinion. No gratuitous comments from her. She was far too smart for that.

I had called her yesterday to let her know we'd arrived, and to make the date for lunch today. And then last night, when she got home, she had called me, so that we could have a longer chat, catch up with each other's news.

After I'd returned to Paris from Belgrade, I'd called Muffie in New York to tell her about Tony's death. And so she knew all about my grief; and also how I felt later, following the nightmare of the memorial service in London. After listening to my outpourings over the transatlantic wire, she had agreed with me about Tony Hampton's extraordinary behaviour. And then she had told me to put the past behind me, and move on.

When Jake and I had become involved romantically in the south of France, I had phoned Muffie from Les Roches Fleuries to tell her about our budding relationship, and to confide that our friendship had moved to a different plane.

I had wanted her to know that I had done as she had suggested, put the past behind me, buried the dead and moved forward.

She was pleased I had taken her advice, and delighted about Jake and me, because they had hit it off when they'd first met two years ago. She had liked him enormously, and was approving of this new turn of events in my life.

And so for a while last evening we had talked about Jake, my feelings for him, and the future he and I might have together.

III

It was ages since I'd spent time with my best friend, and I was really looking forward to seeing Muffie. As I went into the Carlyle Hotel, and through the lobby to the restaurant, I realized how much I'd missed her.

I was the first, but only by a few minutes.

I had just been shown to my seat when Muffie floated in right behind me on a cloud of perfume, dispensing happy smiles, looking stunning in a suit of soft bluish-grey.

After we had hugged, exchanged loving greetings,

and settled down finally on the banquette, she looked at me intently, her head on one side, her expression appraising.

After a second or two of this close scrutiny of me, she exclaimed, 'You look fantastic, Val! I knew Jake would be good for you.'

'Yes he is. And he always has been, you know, looking back. He was never very far away when we were on assignment, looking out for me, protecting me, keeping me out of harm's way. Apparently he was in love with me then . . .' I left my sentence unfinished, simply gave her a long look.

Muffie laughed. '*Men*,' she said, shaking her head. 'If only he'd told you sooner, you wouldn't have become involved with Tony, and you'd have avoided all that awful heartache about him.'

'Only too true. And listen, you look great yourself.'

'A happy marriage works wonders,' she murmured, smiling at me. Leaning closer across the table, she continued, 'Do you remember what I once told you?'

'You've told me a lot over the years, Muffie. Which thing in particular?'

'That life can turn on a dime, that no one knows what's going to happen. Ever. Sometimes it's the bad stuff, but not always. Sometimes it's the wonderful stuff. Look at *you*. When you got back to Paris from London, after the memorial service, you were miserable, downhearted and angry. Now you're beautiful, blooming, in great spirits, and no longer angry.'

'I am still a *bit* angry, Muffie. Inside.'

'Oh don't be, Val,' she said very softly, getting hold of my hand, squeezing it. 'It's just not worth it. Let it go. Anger's only good when you can express it, get it out. And you certainly can't do that, since you've nobody to express it to . . . Tony's dead.'

'I know. And I think you're right. But –' I stopped when I saw the look on her face. I knew there was no point in continuing; also, she had a knack of making me feel as if I were whining, in the way that Donald whined. I detested whiners, so why should I become one myself? I kept my thoughts to myself for once.

We ordered bottled water and sipped it while we looked at the menus. We decided on our food, choosing the same dishes, as we had so often in the past. We both settled on asparagus vinaigrette, grilled sole and green beans. No potatoes, no bread, and no wine.

'I've got to lose weight,' I said to her, grinning, and continuing to sip the water. 'Jake loves food, and he's been fattening me up. Or so it seems to me. When we're on assignment there's usually nothing very good to eat, and anyway we don't have time to put much in our mouths.'

'You don't look fat, you look . . . divine, darling.'

'Spoken like a true best friend, Muffie.'

We talked for a while about our lives, and how different they were. And then quite unexpectedly, out of the blue, Muffie said, 'It's the oddest thing, Val, but I've been running into your brother lately.'

'Donald!' I exclaimed, staring at her.

She nodded. 'Donald the Great, as you used to call him. He always comes over and says hello, makes a point of it, actually, which is weird, since I know you two aren't exactly close –'

'To say the least!'

Muffie nodded, then laughed. 'But he's turned out to be quite good-looking, and he usually has this beautiful girl on his arm. From what I hear, he's doing well at the magazine.'

I let out a long sigh. 'He's in his element, gossip columnist to the stars. Donald's in pig heaven, what do you bet? Yep, that's one thing I'm certain of, *he's* got the job of his dreams.'

'When did you last see him?'

'When he was in Paris about seven years ago. Actually, that's not correct. I saw him after that, at Grandfather's funeral, and he was positively awful, Muffie. Don't you remember how he was going on about the will, for God's sake?'

'I do remember, and I also remember your mother that day. My mother always said there's less to Margot Denning than meets the eye. But actually, I think she's wrong. There's a lot *more* to Margot Denning, and that's at the root of your problem with her.'

'What do you mean?' I asked, my brows drawing together in a frown, my eyes on her face.

'I've thought a lot about your mother since the day of the funeral, Val, which is when I last saw her. I think she has a past.'

'How could she have a past? She married my father when she was twenty-three, and I was born when she was twenty-five.'

'Well, perhaps *a past* is the wrong phrase. What I really meant is that she has something to hide.' Muffie's expression became thoughtful and her blue eyes narrowed slightly as she said slowly, 'My parents and most other people think your mother's shallow, but I don't believe that's the truth at all. Yes, she *is* concerned about her looks and clothes and jewellery, and all that stuff, but there's a lot of depth there as well.'

I gaped at her. 'I'm sure you're the only person who believes that! My mother, so called, is as shallow as they come, and as cold as ice. You know Grandfather used to call her Iceberg Aggie, the Ice Queen.'

'She's a cold woman, no question about that. But by no means stupid. Margot Scott Denning is nobody's fool. Are you going to see her while you're here?'

'I don't think so.'

'I heard she'd had a stroke, no, a heart attack, that was it. My parents told me.'

'Two heart attacks, according to Donald.'

'But she's not that old.'

'No, she's fifty-six, actually.'

'Is she really ill?'

'Donald thinks she's about to kick the bucket, but perhaps he's being overly dramatic, which is his normal way of behaving, if you recollect.'

'Yes, he was always like that, full of histrionics. How old is he now? About twenty-five?'

'Twenty-six. Going on four. Very infantile.'

She laughed.

And so did I. She always had that effect on me, brought out the lighter side of Valentine Denning, the not-so-serious side. I loved that about Muffie – her uplifting effect on me.

'*Are* you going to see her?' Muffie asked, her head on one side. 'I know how you feel about her, but I just wondered . . .' Her voice petered out, probably because she'd taken note of the dour expression settling on my face.

'Donald says she wants to see me, but I don't know that I will succumb to his blandishments.'

Muffie threw back her head and roared, '*Blandishments*, what a wonderful word, Val, really wonderful!'

I grinned at her. 'I guess it does sound a bit old-fashioned, and the phrase just jumped into my head. *Muffie*?'

'Yes?'

'I want to ask you something . . .'

'Go ahead, you know very well you can ask me anything, and if I can answer you, I will.'

'Were you trying to say that Margot Denning is more *complex* than most people think?'

'*Exactly*. I believe she's a sick woman, as well. Mentally sick. And all of their married life I think your father was an enabler. Whatever it was that troubled her, disturbed her, your father aided and abetted her.

Because he didn't have the strength or the will power to fight her. To *oppose* her, that's what I mean.'

'That could be. My grandmother always thought he was weak-kneed. That was the word she used constantly to describe her son. And Grandfather was disgusted with him all the time; Aunt Isobel, as well. They thought he was under my mother's thumb, and he was. *I* know that for a fact.'

Muffie nodded. 'I saw it too, with my own eyes, Val, you don't have to convince me. And of course he worked for her at Lowell's.' She wrinkled her nose. 'That was a sort of odd situation, come to think about it now. Don't you think so?'

'Yes. But he liked it. My father had a cushy life, in that sense. I don't think he was all that bright when it came to business, and my mother provided him with a great job. Vice President of Lowell's Cosmetics, founded in 1898, a hundred years ago this year. My grandmother, Violet Scott, was the chairman, if you remember. She ran a tight ship, and so does my mother now.'

I took a breath, let out a long sigh, went on, 'When I had that huge row with my mother eight years ago, I told her I'd never speak to her again. But I did, at Grandfather's funeral. However, I barely exchanged a word with her, even though she tried to patch things up. I don't know why she wanted to do that.'

'I witnessed *that* scene,' Muffie exclaimed with acidity.

'There's something else, Muffie. When Aunt Isobel came to Paris about a year and a half ago, she said something about the Scott women being tyrants. And she made a catty remark about Violet Scott.'

'What did she say?'

'That Violet Scott was a hard bitch, and added that my mother took after her. You know how outspoken Isobel is.'

Muffie grinned. 'Don't I just.' After a moment, she became serious. 'Look, Val, you don't have to listen to your brother. If you don't want to see your mother, then *don't*. For heaven's sake, she's never done anything for you. Not to my knowledge.'

'She's given me nothing. Don't you think it would be a bit hypocritical on my part, seeing her I mean?'

Muffie thought for a moment. 'Well, yes, I guess so.' She took a sip of water and asked, 'Why are you even considering it? Because of the heart attacks?'

'Not really. How can I have any feelings for her? A woman who has never shown the slightest interest in me ever. Look, she knew I was shot in Kosovo ... there was a lot in the newspapers about Tony's death, and the fact that Jake and I were both injured at the same time. On television, too. She never once got in touch with me, to see how I was. But that's her. No interest whatsoever. It's Jake, actually, who's after me to see her.'

'*Jake*? But why, Val?' Muffie sounded surprised.

'He thinks I ought to confront her once and for all, ask her why she's treated me the way she has, and most especially when I was a child.'

'You won't find anything out,' Muffie said in an

authoritative voice. 'She'll never confide in you. *If* there's anything to confide.'

'But you said you thought she had a past.'

'Yes, I do think there's something there, something in her background that caused her to behave the way she did, and with your father's acquiescence. But so what? It can't possibly have anything to do with you, can it? It may have made her *behave* peculiarly, but *you're* not the *cause*. How could you be?'

'I don't suppose I could.'

'Don't expose yourself to her, to more pain. She broke your heart when you were a child. And you can be so tender-hearted, I know you.'

'Not about her! I don't have any real feelings for her!' I exclaimed. 'In a sense, she's like a stranger. She made herself a stranger to *me* when I was growing up.'

Muffie nodded, but made no further comment since a waiter was placing a plate of asparagus in front of her. He brought my plate, and we began to eat. Automatically, our conversation turned away from my mother and Donald. As I said to Muffie, we had better fish to fry.

But later, I was to wish I'd encouraged Muffie to rattle on, express her thoughts more fully, because to be forewarned is to be forearmed. I should also have listened to her about not seeing my mother. But I didn't. Regrettably so, as it turned out.

Chapter Nineteen

1

'Who's the Kevin Costner lookalike?' my brother Donald asked as he followed me into the sitting room of the Beekman Place apartment.

Without turning around, I answered, 'That's my best friend Jake Newberg. You'll meet him later. He's a photojournalist. We work a lot together.'

'And sleep a lot together, I bet,' Donald shot back.

I swung around and exclaimed irately, 'You're already irritating me, Donald, and you've only been here a couple of minutes! Let's not forget that you've not come to discuss *my* relationships, but yours with your mother.'

'She's your mother too, Val,' he responded, then continued swiftly, almost apologetically, 'And there's no need to get huffy. I caught a glimpse of him as I walked past the study, and he *does* look like Costner.'

I sighed, sat down in the chair and made no comment.

Donald lowered himself onto the sofa and sat staring at me across the coffee table, not speaking either, just scrutinizing me intently as if he'd never seen me before.

I stared back.

Muffie was right. My brother *had* turned into a very good-looking young man. He took after my mother, had her black hair, the beautifully sculpted looks, the same perfect nose, high cheekbones, and smooth, high brow plus her light-green eyes. But he wasn't tall and willowy as she was; it was I who had inherited those particular characteristics from her. But that was the only physical resemblance we shared. I was a Denning through and through.

It was Donald who was a Scott, her male clone, her spitting image right down to the widow's peak which was such a prominent and striking feature in them both. He was not built like her, though; rather, he resembled my father in physique. Donald was not very tall and he was small-boned, as my father had been.

Donald was studying me so closely I began to feel uncomfortable, and I said, 'What is it? Why are you looking me over in this way? You seem to be memorizing every detail of my face.'

He grinned at me, flashing those perfect pearly white teeth I'd always envied. 'I haven't seen you for a long time . . . but I don't have to memorize your face, I know it well . . .' He let out a long sigh, and said in a low, almost inaudible voice, 'You used to love me once, Val, when I was little.'

Taken aback not only by his words but by his sudden, mild demeanour, I was speechless for a moment; he was usually so combative with me.

'Well, you did, didn't you?' he pressed.

'Yes, you're right, I did,' I admitted. 'I loved you a lot in those days.'

'Why did you stop?'

'I didn't, not really,' I murmured, frowning. 'It was your mother. She got in the way, put herself in between us, so to speak. Your mother took you over, and in so doing she pushed me out.'

'She's also your mother,' Donald remarked.

'This is the second time you've said that in the space of a few minutes! And no, Donald, she isn't my mother. She may have given birth to me, but she has never been a mother nor has she shown me any motherly love.'

'I know that,' he admitted very quietly.

He had startled me again. I couldn't believe that he had actually agreed with me on something to do with our mother. But I didn't say a word. I couldn't help wondering why he had had this change of tune all of a sudden. I was immediately suspicious.

I said, 'What's this all about, Donald?'

He shook his head, but he remained silent.

'Let's get to the point,' I snapped.

Donald sat back and shook his head again. 'I don't understand too much, because she won't tell me. But basically it's to do with the will, her will. Mother won't tell me anything in detail.'

'What do you mean, she won't tell you anything?

You told *me* that your inheritance was somehow tied to mine. I don't get it.'

'Neither do I, because she won't explain. But after she had her first heart attack, she told me to call you, to get you home, to get you to New York. But you refused to come. She wasn't too happy, I can tell you that, and then she had a second heart attack. When she was better, she got really forceful about my persuading you to come to New York. She told me it was *imperative*, she had to see you and that it involved a lot of money. That's all I know.'

'I see. So it's all to do with Margot Scott Denning and her money.'

'True.'

'I'm not interested in her money. You can have my share. All of it, Donald.'

'That's nice, thanks, I accept it,' he said. 'But first you have to talk to her, *see* her. She wants to *see* you, urgently. Come on, Sis, agree to this. Please, for me.'

'Donald, why do you persist in annoying me when you need my help?'

He frowned, looking puzzled.

'You know very well I hate being called Sis,' I reminded him.

'Sorry, *Val*.'

'So, is she at death's door or not?'

'No,' he admitted. 'Not *actually*. Not now. She seems a lot better and the doctor says she can go back to work next week, but only part-time, for a few hours a day. She has to take it easy, and she has to rest a lot.'

'That won't go down well. I used to think she had St Vitus Dance, the way she moved around, rushed hither and yon when we were little. She was never still for a moment, and hardly ever at home, always in her office at Lowell's.'

'That's true. Even when we were just small kids, work came first, I guess. And since Dad died she's been really committed to business, a workaholic.'

'Oh.'

'Well she misses him, Val.'

'He's been dead for ten years, Donald! Has she become keeper of the flame? Is that it?'

He didn't answer, simply looked into the distance, at the space above my head.

The silence became drawn out.

Donald looked so miserable, so perturbed I found myself feeling sorry for him. How I used to bully him. He had looked at me in much the same way when he had been a child. But I had loved him, he was right about that. Until he had been grabbed away by that monstrous woman who'd borne us both.

Taking a deep breath, I broke the silence when I said, 'Muffie told me she keeps running into you these days, and that you always have a beautiful girl with you. Is there anybody special yet?'

'Well, yeah, sort of . . . there's a really great girl and I care about her a lot –' He cut himself off, settled back against the sofa, squinted at me in the sunlight. 'So, you saw Muffie Potter.'

'Yes, for lunch yesterday.'

'Val, listen, I think you really must see her, Mother I mean!' he exclaimed with sudden urgency. 'She won't open up to me until she's talked to you. If she's said that once she's said it two dozen times. I need to know what this *will* stuff is all about, and only you can find out. Val, this is about my future.'

'I hadn't planned on seeing her. Nor had I planned on seeing you, Donald. I came here on business with Jake, and it was he who pushed me into making a date with you. He feels I have to get to the bottom of it. Find out why she was so horrible to me when I was growing up.'

'I guess you do, Sis. I mean Val,' he quickly corrected himself, obviously trying hard to be nicer to me than he normally was, to ingratiate himself. Well, he wanted something, didn't he? But unexpectedly he had such a pleading look on his face, I found myself saying, 'I'm not going to actually promise I'll see her before I leave, Donald, but I will think about it. That I *do* promise.'

This pleased him and he beamed at me. 'Thanks,' he said. 'I'm appreciative. Anyway, we should both know what's on her mind, shouldn't we?'

'That's true,' I acknowledged.

'When do you think you'll see her?'

'I didn't say I'd see her. But, okay, I will *phone* her. Before I leave New York. Now, let's forget it for the time being. Don't nag me, otherwise I might change my mind,' I threatened and instantly realized I'd reverted to my bullying of old.

He laughed, obviously thinking the same thing. 'Fair enough. Now, when do I get to meet Costner's clone?'

'Is somebody talking about me?' Jake asked from the doorway.

I looked across, saw him leaning against the door jamb nonchalantly, looking impossibly handsome, dressed in pristine blue jeans and a white cableknit sweater. And I acknowledged to myself that he did indeed look a bit like the actor.

'Come on in, Jake,' I said, standing up. 'I want you to meet my brother Donald, who's being positively sweet today, and not his usual obnoxious self.'

Donald laughed, also rose.

The two men walked towards each other and shook hands. Jake said, 'Would you like a cup of coffee or a drink, Donald?'

'Not right now, thanks, but maybe later, Jake.'

Jake sat down in the chair next to me, gave me a long, questioning look and asked, 'So tell me, have you solved the problems of the world?'

'No,' I answered quickly. 'But I have promised Donald I'll contact his mother before I leave New York.'

Jake nodded. 'Why not do it now? Make a date to see her as soon as possible? Let's get this family stuff out of the way; you and I have so much work to do on the book.'

'Are you two writing a book?' Donald asked eagerly, his face lighting up. 'What's it about?'

Before I could stop him, Jake was telling Donald all about *Flowers of War*, his excitement and enthusiasm more pronounced than ever. There was no way I could curtail the flow of words, and naturally Donald was eating it all up, his eyes fastened on Jake intently. He was mesmerized.

I stood up and walked across the floor. At the door I said, 'I'm going to get a cold drink. Either of you want anything?'

They both glanced at me and said nothing, simply shook their heads, and immediately went back to their conversation. I shrugged and hurried down the corridor to the kitchen. As I pushed open the swing door and went in I couldn't help thinking that Donald had improved a bit. At least he wasn't as nasty as he usually was. In fact, he was almost civilized. Wonders never cease, I muttered under my breath. And then instinctively I wondered what kind of game Donald was playing.

II

Late that evening, when we were getting ready to go to dinner, Jake turned to me and said, 'Give your mother a call now! Arrange to see her tomorrow.'

'Tomorrow!' I exclaimed, looking horrified. 'It's too *soon*.'

'Too soon for what?'

'To see her, Jake. I need time to prepare myself before I venture into her territory. And I must call her and then go over there at once, otherwise I might . . .' I stopped and stared at him.

'Or you might lose your nerve? Is that what you were going to say?'

I nodded.

Jake came across the room in a few strides, put his arms around me and brought me into his warm and loving embrace.

'Listen, sweetheart, there's nothing she can do to you now. Not any more. You're no longer a little girl at her mercy. You're a grown woman, a war correspondent, a woman who has faced every kind of danger, looked it in the eye, and stared it down. You can see her *any time*, Val, you don't have to prepare yourself. That's silly. Just pick up that phone, dial her number and tell her about Donald's visit today –'

'She'll already know about that!' I exclaimed, cutting him off. 'He'll have told her everything.'

'Okay. Maybe. Just tell her you'd like to see her tomorrow. I'll go with you if you want.'

'I do want,' I said, and immediately felt somewhat foolish about my attitude of a moment ago. What was Margot Scott Denning going to do to me? Nothing, of course. It was just that I had so many bad memories of her and I always felt nervous at the prospect of being in her presence. Not that I'd seen her since my grandfather's funeral.

'All right,' I agreed, 'I'll do it now.'

'Good girl.'

I went over to the phone, picked it up and dialled the number of the apartment on Park Avenue.

When she answered, I said, 'It's Val. Donald says you want to see me.'

'Yes, I do,' she said quietly. 'How are you, Valentine?'

How am I, I thought. What a damned nerve she has. That was the first time she had asked me how I was in my entire life. Instantly my suspicions spiralled into alarm. I said, 'When can we meet? How about tomorrow?'

'Well, I –'

I cut her off coolly. 'We'd better make it tomorrow afternoon. At about four. It's really the only time I have available.'

'Very well,' she said. 'I'll see you at four.'

'Fine,' I answered, and hung up.

Chapter Twenty

1

Although I was nervous about meeting my mother, and had originally wanted Jake to accompany me, at the last moment I suddenly realized I preferred to see her alone.

It had struck me early on Sunday morning that I probably stood a better chance of finding out more if I went to her apartment by myself. And so I explained this to Jake over breakfast, hoping he would understand my motivation.

He seemed a bit uncertain about my decision at first, as always protective of me, and then he quickly came around to my way of thinking.

Nodding, he sounded more positive as he said, 'Okay then, Val, go over there by yourself, if you're more comfortable with that. As long as you stay cool and unemotional you'll be fine. Just be businesslike, and matter-of-fact.'

I promised I would do this, agreeing with him that

it was the best way to handle the situation. My mother had requested the meeting, I had agreed to go, and I would listen to what she had to say.

But, in point of fact, it *was* truly my call, and I could leave whenever I wished. It was as simple as that. And very reassuring.

Later that day, as I walked out onto First Avenue, looking for a cab, I told myself I must make the visit brief and to the point, for my own sake.

Lingering at that apartment where I had grown up so miserably would only exacerbate the deep-seated anger which lay buried inside me. Certainly I didn't want it to erupt, because that would not accomplish anything, other than upsetting me, making me incapable of dealing with my mother.

She had continued to live at the rambling, traditional apartment on Park Avenue after my father's death. Obviously she was attached to the place, which she and my father had moved into when they had married in 1965.

As the taxi turned off East Fifty-Seventh Street and started to go uptown on Park, I suddenly asked the driver to stop and let me off. After paying him, I got out, relieved to be outside in the fresh air. In the cab, I had begun to feel overly warm, even a bit claustrophobic, not to mention anxiety-ridden as well.

Breathing deeply, I walked up Park towards Seventy-Third Street, where the apartment was located, trying to dispel the queasiness which had settled in my stomach.

For a split second, I thought I was going to vomit, then I realized that what I was actually feeling was mounting uneasiness at the prospect of seeing my mother. I had never known what to expect, how she would react to me, or what she would say, and in consequence I dreaded being in her presence.

After walking steadily for ten blocks, the nauseous sensation began to diminish, and I suddenly started to feel much better.

Jake had said yesterday that my mother could no longer hurt me, and this was true. I was not that little girl she had been able to wound so easily, with her cruel neglect and lack of love. I was a grown woman, thirty-one years old, a woman who faced danger in the extreme almost daily in her job. A woman who was self-supporting and independent. A woman fully responsible for herself and her life. I didn't need Mommy anymore, that evasive Mommy I had always longed for as a child and had never had.

My mother had been out of my life for the last fourteen years, so why was I tensing up again about seeing her? Because of the past, of course, I answered myself. As a child all I'd ever wanted was her attention, love and approval. And they had been withheld. I had never understood why. I didn't understand to this day . . . and it was a question that nagged at the back of my mind, one of many.

I sighed. I was about to confront a woman I had never really known. Even though we had lived under the same roof for seventeen years, she had been a stranger to me, chilly, distant and uninvolved in my life.

She had ruined my childhood. I had never forgiven her for that and I don't suppose I ever will.

In spite of my tenseness and vague apprehension, all of a sudden I became unexpectedly more confident about seeing her again. Although I was going to visit my mother for Donald's sake, and because of the pressure he had exerted on me to do so, if I were honest it was also because *I* needed to see her. *For myself.* Jake was correct about that . . . wipe the slate clean, he had said.

By confronting her I hoped I could slay the demons, the demons that had haunted me for as long as I could remember.

II

She looked exactly the same as always.

Margot Scott Denning. Great American beauty.

And she *was* still beautiful. Black hair coming to a dramatic widow's peak on her proud, wide brow; light-green eyes below curving coal-black brows; chiselled features; a perfect nose; the wide mouth, blood-red against the pallor of her flawless white complexion. A face that had bowled men over, probably still did.

Tall. Thin as a rail. Elegant in a perfectly cut, grey flannel skirt, topped with a red cashmere sweater, with a matching cardigan as well, tied round her neck in the way women of her ilk were wearing them these days. The plain pearl studs at her ears, in place as they always were, as was the mandatory string of pearls. Legs sleek and long and shapely, encased in pale-grey, very sheer stockings. Narrow, immaculately shod feet in grey suede pumps.

My mother.

Fourteen years ago I had walked out of this apartment and gone to Beekman Place to my beloved and caring grandparents, who had taken me in eagerly, willingly, and with a great deal of love.

And in all that time, from that day to this, she had not changed. She looked exactly the same. It was not only uncanny, it was unnerving. Nor did she appear to have been ill. She was in blooming health, as far as I could tell.

She let me into the apartment herself, and said hello in that low, cool voice of hers which I remembered so well. But she made no move to embrace me, which didn't surprise me in the least. She had never been affectionate, and certainly not with me. And, of course, I didn't make a move towards her, either. I merely responded to her greeting verbally, in a neutral voice.

I followed her into the sitting room.

It was a spacious, elegant room overlooking Park Avenue, and just like her it had remained unchanged.

For a moment I felt as though time had stood still. My childhood years came rushing back . . . the suffering I had endured, the hurt of her neglect, my loneliness, my terrible sense of rejection. Everything I'd ever felt seemed to tumble all around me, a whirl of emotions in the pale afternoon sunlight that filled this beautiful room.

The decades fell away . . . voices long since stilled, faces long forgotten, all of them were suddenly here with me, echoes and images of the past jostling for prominence amongst the dust motes rising up in the air. For a second I felt dizzy and undone; I thought I would keel over.

Very swiftly, I pulled myself back into the present, blocked out that unhappiness and pain of my early years. I did not want to look behind me ever again. Peering at ghosts in the shadows was a waste. My eyes were fixed ahead, on the future.

III

My mother sat down in her usual place, on a French *bergère* chair covered in oyster satin, positioned near a Louis XV sofa in striped oyster-and-burgundy silk and close to the fireplace.

I did not fall into the trap of taking the chair where I had always been instructed to sit as a child. Instead I remained standing near the fireplace, one hand on the mantel.

She sat looking me over for a moment or two, in much the same way Donald had yesterday.

I stared back at her unblinkingly, my face unreadable.

I knew I looked smart in my black bush jacket, white silk shirt and black gabardine trousers, and this pleased me. I was also much less nervous now that I was actually here. In fact, any nervousness I'd felt before had totally evaporated. I was completely calm, very cool and in control.

'You look well, Val,' she said at last in her well-modulated, upper-crust voice.

I nodded. 'So do you. But I don't think we're here to discuss each other's appearance or state of health. Donald is very agitated. He says you keep alluding to your will and his inheritance ever since you had your first heart attack. But that you won't discuss anything with him. Until you've talked to me, that is. So here I am, on Donald's behalf, so to speak. Shall we get down to business?'

She was absolutely silent.

She simply sat there, gazing at the painting over the fireplace. It had always been there. A fabulous Boudin. And it was filled with the most extraordinary light; I recalled how fascinated by it I had been when I was a youngster. It was the sky that caught and held my attention today, now as then. It was the most perfect blue, a dazzling blue.

Pulling my attention away from the remarkable and very valuable painting, I looked across at my mother and got right to the point.

'I can't imagine how my inheritance is tied up with

Donald's, but I think I ought to tell you now, right at the outset of this conversation, I don't want mine. Leave everything to Donald.'

Rousing herself from her thoughts she sat up straighter and exclaimed, 'That's not possible!'

'Of course it is. I willingly give it up. Rewrite your Last Will and Testament. Make him the sole beneficiary.'

'I cannot do that. And neither can you. *You* must inherit Lowell's. That's a fact that can never be changed.'

'Why can't it be changed?'

'Because you are a female descendant of the founder of Lowell's, and only a woman can inherit Lowell's. This was The Tradition started by your great-great-grandmother, Amy-Anne Lowell. It was she who founded Lowell's in 1898 when she opened a chemist's shop in Greenwich Village. She decreed that only her female descendants could inherit her company. And that's the way it has been since then. Amy-Anne left the company to her daughter Rebecca, who left it to her daughter Violet, who was my mother, your grandmother. And my mother left it to me. I, in turn, must pass it on to you. It is The Tradition in our family.'

I couldn't speak for a moment, I was so thunderstruck. Finally finding my voice, I said, 'And what would have happened if you hadn't had a female child? Only Donald? Or other sons instead of me?'

'In that instance, the wife of the eldest son would inherit the company. She would probably have to be just a titular head. The day-to-day running of the company would be left to others more skilled, those properly trained. But she would be the owner and the chairman. However, that has not come to pass yet, not in one hundred years, since there have always been female descendants of Amy-Anne Lowell.'

I digested her words and asked, 'Have you always known this? Did you know about the Amy-Anne tradition when I was a child?'

'Oh yes.'

'Then why did you treat me so badly when I was growing up?'

She looked at me askance, frowning, the beautifully curved brows pulling together to form a jagged black line that suddenly gave her an ugly look. Leaning forward slightly, she exclaimed, 'I did not treat you badly! How can you say such a terrible thing! You were beautifully dressed, well fed and well cared for in this lovely apartment. You had your own room, and a beautiful one, I might remind you. You went to the best schools, had the most wonderful vacations.' She shook her head denyingly. 'You're absurd. And ungrateful, very ungrateful, and after all I did for you. *Really*, Valentine!'

'Don't *really* me in that tone, or use the word *ungrateful*. What you've just said is perfectly true, about the clothes, this apartment, the food, and the schools. But you did neglect me and shamefully so. You rejected me, you denied me motherly love, treated me with total indifference, and to such an extent, and so blatantly, some people around here at the time construed it as criminal, that indifference of yours.'

'How dare you speak to me in this way. I am your mother. I deserve your respect!'

I threw her a look of condemnation, and said in a cold voice, 'What's so surprising to me now is that all along you knew me to be your heir to Lowell's. I just can't believe it. Nor can I believe your gall . . . how could you ever *think* that I would want Lowell's under the circumstances, and after all you did to me. *You ruined my childhood.* And if it weren't for my Denning grandparents I would probably be in a loony bin today because of you and your treatment of me. That's how wicked you were.'

She sat erect in the chair, imposingly beautiful and as cold as ice. There was something inhuman about her.

I could tell from the coldness in her light-green eyes and the tight set of her mouth that she was angry; also that she had not understood what I was saying. She believed herself to be innocent of any wrongdoing. How appalling, I thought: she has no conscience. And instantly I recalled Muffie's words of the other day. She had said she thought my mother was mentally unbalanced. Perhaps she was right about that. Certainly my mother was seriously disturbed; I knew this deep down within myself. Because only a woman who was not normal could have treated her own child as badly and as unfeelingly as she had treated me.

Staring at her intently, I asked quietly, 'Do you

expect me to give up my career as a war photojournalist? Do you expect me to come back here and start working at Lowell's? Is that what you're getting at?'

She nodded. 'Yes, Val, of course it is. And it is the proper thing for you to do now. I have had two heart attacks already, and I think this is the right time for you to learn about the business, a business that one day will be yours.'

She spoke evenly now, and it struck me once more that my words had meant nothing to her. They had not sunk in. Perhaps she had no conception of just how much she had hurt me when I was growing up.

Taking a deep breath, I explained, 'But I just told you, I don't want Lowell's. Give it to Donald. He was always your favourite anyway.'

'I cannot give it to Donald. I must follow The Tradition. That is the family rule . . . it has always been a . . . a *law* within the family.'

I laughed hollowly, suddenly understanding so much. 'Donald's not married, so there's no female in the immediate family. Other than *moi*, that is. Little old me, I'm the *one*. But you didn't bargain for that, did you?' I shook my head, finished scathingly, 'You fully expected Donald to be married by now, didn't you, Mother?'

A flush crept up from her long neck to invade her face, and I knew my words had hit home. Her expression was one of embarrassment.

'You put all your hopes in Donald. You were always so certain he would marry young, and marry well, and you didn't give a damn about me. But you miscalculated. You never imagined that you'd have two heart attacks in the space of a couple of months at the age of fifty-six. It never occurred to you that you were anything but immortal. But you are indeed mortal, just like the rest of us. And you never expected Donald to still be a bachelor at twenty-six.'

'You are quite wrong about Donald. He has a lovely young woman friend, Alexis Rayne, and I understand the relationship has become serious. I feel quite certain your brother will become engaged momentarily.'

'I expect he will, once he knows the advantages,' I exclaimed. 'He won't be able to resist. He'll lasso her and drag her to the altar if he has to, just to get his hands on the money.'

'How disgusting you are,' she snapped in a shocked voice, giving me an angry look. 'You were always mean to Donald.'

'No, I wasn't. But *you* were *mean* to *me*. And I've never understood *why*, or what prompted your behaviour towards me. So I'm asking you now. WHY?'

'Don't be ridiculous, Valentine. I was never mean to you. Not ever in your life. All of this nonsense is in your very vivid imagination. Furthermore, you have the most extraordinary tendency to exaggerate, especially when it comes to your childhood, which was absolutely normal.'

I ignored her remarks. I thought about pressing her further to explain herself to me, explain her behaviour when I was growing up. But it struck me that this would be useless. At this moment anyway. Instead, I asked, 'How is Donald's inheritance tied up with mine?'

'It isn't. Not in actuality, in reality. When I said that to him, it was just a manner of speaking on my part. I didn't want to explain to Donald about The Tradition, or my will, until I had had an opportunity to explain things to you.'

'So what exactly *is* Donald's inheritance?' I asked, more out of curiosity than anything else.

'Under my will Donald is well provided for,' my mother answered. 'He does receive a large amount of shares in Lowell's. And if he wishes, he can have an executive position there. I am leaving him this apartment, and all of the possessions in it, the art, everything.' She glanced about her, waved her hand around airily.

True to form, I thought, gazing at her thoughtfully. Everything she owned was going to Donald. I was to inherit Lowell's because she had no alternative but to leave it to me under that curious family rule.

Although I knew I was repeating myself, I said, 'I think you should give Lowell's to Donald, as well as everything else. I certainly don't want it, not under any circumstances.'

'No, I cannot do that. I just explained why a moment ago.'

'Listen! I don't want it! And if you do leave it to me, then I'll turn it over to him. Immediately. Lowell's is meaningless to me. You never told me anything about it, or explained about The Tradition, as you call it, when I was growing up. Neither did your mother, my grandmother. And I was next in line, after you. I can't understand why I was never made to understand the importance of Lowell's, as far as I was concerned.'

'You were too young.'

'I see. And what makes you think I could possibly care about the company now? As for this family rule, I personally think it's rather stupid.'

'Amy-Anne Lowell did not think so,' she said slowly. 'And neither would you if you had had her early life.'

IV

I heard the key in the lock and the door slam, and I suspected it must be Donald.

And it was.

'Ah, there you are, Donald,' I said. 'Come on in and listen. I have a big surprise for you. Your mother has explained the famous will. I am supposed to inherit Lowell's. It's an old family tradition, dating back to Amy-Anne Lowell of 1898. Only girls get it, you see. But I don't want it. I therefore give it to you, Donald.'

'You cannot do that!' my mother cried heatedly, half rising from her chair, her face suddenly flushing.

Donald remained standing in the middle of the antique rug, looking from me to his mother, a stunned expression on his very handsome face.

'I don't understand,' he said, speaking directly to her. 'Don't I get any part of the business? Is that what Val's saying?'

'Shares, Donald dear. You will receive shares in Lowell's, and also my other investments will be yours,' she answered in a placating voice. 'This apartment, the art, everything I personally own is coming to you when I die.' She patted the sofa. 'Come and sit here, and I will explain about the will.'

He glanced across at me, then did as she suggested.

Slowly, and very patiently, our mother gave Donald all of the details of her will, and spent quite some time explaining about The Tradition. The way she had pronounced this right from the beginning had made me realize that she was capitalizing it. But then no doubt all of the Lowell women before her had done the same thing. I had meant what I said to her. It *was* a stupid family rule. What if there were no female descendants? No wives or daughters of sons in any given generation? What would happen then?

I thought of asking her that, and then changed my mind. I was itching to escape; there was really no reason for me to stay. I had made my point. And it was obvious she was not going to give me any explanation for her treatment of me when I was little. I could not wipe the slate clean, as Jake had suggested. Nor could I slay the demons after all. So I might as well go.

After hearing his mother out, Donald turned to me.

'You said you didn't want Lowell's. Do you mean that, Val?'

'Of course I do. I don't live in New York, I live in Paris, and I've no intention of moving. Furthermore, I have a *career* – I don't need another one. I certainly have no interest in Lowell's. I wouldn't know what to do with a cosmetics company.'

'You could learn to run it,' Margot Denning said.

'Fat chance of that!' I shot back. Looking across at Donald, I continued, 'You'd better get married quickly. Marry that girl. Then when the time comes for me to inherit Lowell's, I'll just give it to her. It's as simple as that.'

'Is it?' Donald stared at his mother.

'That has never happened in the entire history of Lowell's, but I suppose Val could do that . . . she *would* be passing it to a *female* member of the family . . .' Her voice trailed off.

'But why does a female have to inherit?' Donald asked.

'It was a rule made by the founder of the company, your great-great-grandmother Amy-Anne Lowell. Her early life was terrible. She suffered horrendous physical abuse from her father and her brother. She was a punching bag for them when they were drunk. When she was fourteen she ran away from Boston, where the Lowells lived. She eventually found her way to New York, and worked mostly as a servant girl in the homes of the rich of this city. When she was seventeen she found a position with an old lady, a spinster lady, and she became her personal maid and companion-secretary as well.

'The old lady liked her, was very kind to Amy-Anne, and she left her some money when she passed away three years later. But much more importantly, she left Amy-Anne a handwritten book of recipes for creams, lotions, soaps and candles. Amy-Anne knew they were excellent since they had been made up for the old lady, a Miss Mandelsohn, to her specifications. And Amy-Anne had used them, knew their quality.

'Miss Mandelsohn had brought the book with her from Germany, when she immigrated to America as a girl. It's a long story how Amy-Anne opened her chemist's shop in Greenwich Village, and I won't go into it now. But once she did, she made a vow to herself. She vowed that no man would ever have power over her ever again. Nor over any of her female offspring and her eventual descendants.

'Amy-Anne was most fortunate in her choice of husband, because he was a truly good man, devoted to her and their three daughters. And he was a chemist who helped her to succeed. Nevertheless, that rule remained. It was the law in the family: Only females inherit wealth and power. And it has been passed down from mother to daughter. It is The Tradition.'

Chapter Twenty-One

1

'And there you have the whole story,' I said to Jake, and leaned back against the floral sofa in the sitting room of the Beekman Place apartment.

'It's just amazing – I mean that she denies her behaviour during your childhood,' he murmured, frowning and shaking his head. 'I think you're probably right, Val, she must be seriously disturbed to have treated you the way she did in the first place. And there's something else . . . where was your father when all this was happening?'

'Oh forget him, he was a wimp!' I exclaimed. 'Totally under her thumb. He was besotted with her, gaga about her, actually. I knew that, but Aunt Isobel confirmed it to me a few years ago. She said my mother walked all over him, and he never objected. Aunt Isobel also intimated to me that my mother had affairs with other men, and I'm sure that's true. In a way, I'm sorry you didn't meet her, because she's really something –'

'I'll bet she is,' he cut in.

'Yes, she *is* a piece of work, no doubt about that,' I agreed. 'But what I meant is that she's *very*, *very* beautiful. Glacial, mind you, but still beautiful. And you know what, she doesn't seem to have aged since I was seventeen. She's exactly the same in her appearance. Time passing has not left a trace.'

'I thought she was ill?'

'I guess she made a rapid recovery from the heart attacks. Anyway, all I can say is that on the surface she looks fantastic. There's certainly no sign of illness. And not a line on her face.'

'There's nothing like a sharp knife cleverly wielded by a brilliant surgeon,' he said, and reaching out for the bottle of Beck's he took a quick swig.

'I wouldn't know whether she's had plastic surgery or not, Jake. But I doubt it. I think she has good genes, and, of course, she's taken great care of herself . . . to the point of being obsessed with herself and her appearance.'

He nodded. 'There are a lot of vain women in this world. But, hey Val, you've done your best, tried to get to the bottom of your problem with her and without success. She's in denial, she'll never talk to you about your childhood. So, since you can't wipe the slate clean after all, then I guess you should just sling all that garbage out of the window. Figuratively speaking. Get rid of it. And let's get on with our lives.'

'You're right, as usual, Jake. I'll do just that.'

'One more thing, before we close this subject matter.

What about that rule . . . about only females inheriting the family company . . . it's the weirdest thing I've ever heard. Don't *you* think so?'

'I think it's . . . *daft*, but then the full story of Amy-Anne is quite hair-raising, I'm sure. Being the punching bag for the Lowell men when she was a child must have been soul-destroying as well as brutal on the body. She was probably pushed to the limits of her endurance, so who can blame her for not wanting any man to have power over her ever again? She obviously discovered that money is power, and therefore the best protection ever invented.'

Jake rose, came over and sat down next to me on the sofa. Taking hold of my hand, he gave me a long look that seemed oddly sorrowful, then cleared his throat several times.

'Is there something wrong?' I asked. I knew there was even before he answered. Being sensitive to his moods and his emotions, I could read him like a book. I was convinced he was troubled about something quite separate from my family problems.

Finally, he answered. 'While you were out seeing your mother, you had a call from Mike. He wants you to phone him back. He'll wait up for your call, he said.'

'Something's wrong! What did he tell you?'

Jake sighed and his mouth drooped down at the sides. 'It's about Françoise. She went into labour yesterday. Prematurely. She lost the baby.'

'Oh no! *No, Jake*! That's so terrible for her.' I felt

the sudden pinprick of tears behind my eyes, the rush of emotion in my throat. 'Poor Françoise, oh that poor girl, she's suffered so much. Now she's lost the child . . .'

I shook my head and stared at Jake intently. 'You should have told me when I first got back. This is much more important than my mother and my problems with her.'

'I wanted you to get everything off your chest, it's troubled you for so long.' He leaned into me, kissed my cheek, and finally released my hand. 'There's not much you can do for Françoise from here, you're too far away. And that's why I let you rattle on about Lowell's. But now you'd better go call Mike, honey. He's waiting, and it's late in Paris.'

II

'Jake just told me what happened, Mike,' I said to my boss in Paris, once we had exchanged greetings. 'I'm so very sorry.'

'Yeah, I know . . . it's tough for her, Val, and thanks for calling back, I appreciate it.'

'So where is she? What hospital's she in? And even more importantly, how's she holding up?'

'She's doing fine, she really is . . .'

I waited for him to complete his sentence but he did not. I said, 'Mike, Mike, are you there?'

'Yeah, yeah, sorry,' he answered, sounding down

in the mouth. He sighed, and added in the quietest voice, 'There's something I didn't tell Jake . . . the baby was born dead . . . she'd probably been dead for a few days, maybe even longer . . .'

'Oh my God, Mike! How awful for Françoise, she must be devastated, beside herself with grief.'

'She is pretty heartbroken about it, and she blames herself, because she says she should have left Olivier a long time ago. She's convinced he damaged the baby when he pushed her down the steps in Marseilles. She believes the baby would've been all right if she'd left him. Who knows . . . I told her she shouldn't castigate herself.' He let out another weary sigh. 'Françoise is broken up about the loss of the baby girl.'

'I can imagine. Listen, Mike, can I contact her? What hospital is she in?'

'I put her in a private clinic.'

'That was smart of you. Which one?'

'I'll tell you in a minute. There's something else you should know. I'm pretty damn certain that son of a bitch Olivier has been sniffing around your apartment here. Certainly he came up to the Gemstar office looking for you –'

'You're kidding!' I interrupted peremptorily, taken aback. 'I'm glad I'm not in Paris. What's he like?'

'Good-looking, but I suspect he's one helluva thug. I don't think he'd have any compunction . . . about doing anything. Adam Macklin saw him, I was in a meeting, but I caught a glimpse of him when he was leaving. Anyway, he doesn't know you're in the

States. Adam had instructions from me to say you were in the Bwindi Impenetrable Forest in Uganda. On special assignment. I doubt very much that he'll go looking for you *there*.'

'You think he put two and two together then? Is that what you're getting at, Mike?'

'More than likely. That's why I didn't take Françoise to the American Hospital here. Too obvious. And it would be the first place he'd look, if he had any inkling or suspicion that she'd gone into labour prematurely.'

'Why do you think he seized on me, focused on me?'

'You're a very obvious connection. Françoise told me that her mother had mentioned you when they went to Marseilles. Olivier heard your name that day. He knew you were staying at Les Roches Fleuries with Jake, and were still there when Françoise came back to St-Jean-Cap Ferrat with her parents. It's more than likely he checked the airlines, asked for the manifests when she disappeared. He saw your name and Jake's and, of course, *hers*. I'm sure her parents haven't given anything away. It's all deduction on his part, and let's not forget, he's a homicide cop and he's used to doing complicated investigations, tracking stuff down. And from what she's told me, he's an ace at it.'

'Can I get in touch with Françoise tomorrow, Mike?' I asked, not wanting to hear anything else about Olivier. He scared me.

'Sure. I put her in a private clinic in St Germain-en-Laye, just outside Paris. She's pretty safe there until she's feeling strong enough to come back to the city.'

'What's going to happen to her, Mike? What are her plans now that she's lost the baby?'

'I don't think she has any plans. Not yet. And I honestly don't know what she wants to do in the future. The main thing on her mind had been to carry the baby to full term . . . she'd been having acute pains, other physical problems, and to tell you the truth, I wasn't too surprised when she suddenly went into labour. Nor am I surprised that she lost the baby . . . she's been under such physical and mental stress.'

'She can't go back to Olivier,' I announced. 'She'd be sentencing herself to death if she did.'

'I agree, and she agrees, and let's face it, he's already started tracking her.'

'You and she must be careful, Mike, and I must too . . . because I'm a link to her, in his mind anyway. But she could come and stay here. When she can travel. He thinks I'm in Uganda, and he certainly doesn't know about this apartment. Françoise could stay here and fully recuperate. And at the same time she could do some hard thinking, decide what she wants to do, make some plans for the next few months.'

There was a silence at the other end of the phone.

'Hello, Mike,' I said. '*Hello . . .*'

'Sorry, Val, to go silent on you, I was just thinking that one through. It's not such a bad idea, having her come Stateside. But I was hoping you'd be coming back to work soon. There are all kinds of assignments waiting for you.'

'I plan to, Mike. In fact, Jake and I don't intend to stay here much longer. We've been pulling some of our pictures together this weekend, trying to get the presentation ready for the publisher. And once we've done our stuff, so to speak, we're hightailing it back to France. But Françoise can stay here without me, that's not a problem. It's my grandfather's old apartment, very roomy, comfortable, and there's a maid who comes in several times a week. She'll be fine here. Also, my best friend lives in New York, Muffie Potter Aston, and Muffie will be happy to keep an eye on Françoise. Look, she'll be *safe* here, Mike, I'm sure of that.'

'I believe you, and it may just be the solution she needs. I'll talk to her about it in a few days. She's too troubled right now, honey, and as I told you, heartbroken about losing her baby.'

'Olivier's a bastard . . .'

'That he is . . . You asked about her plans, the future. The thing is, I'd like her to be in *my* future, and so would my girls. They've really taken to her, as I told you before, and I have a strong suspicion Françoise wants that too. But, well . . . listen, she's got that maniac of a husband to shed first, and that ain't gonna be an easy task.'

'You're right. Anyway, let's think about my idea for a couple of days, and if you give me the number of the private clinic, I'll call her.'

'Sure,' he said, and rattled it off.

III

While I was on the phone to Paris, Jake had been busy in the dining room. Earlier, we had spread out the piles of pictures on the table, trying to bring a semblance of order to them. Now he sat making notes on a yellow pad, and when he heard me come in he turned around.

'Mike's pretty upset isn't he?' he said.

Leaning against the door jamb, I nodded and answered, 'Yes, he's very worried about Françoise. I guess he's really become involved with her in the last couple of weeks. I can't say I blame him, she's lovely-looking and sweet-natured. But that husband of hers presents a huge problem.'

'And how,' Jake agreed. 'He's a bully and –'

'Mike called him a thug,' I interjected.

'He more than likely is, and he could prove to be dangerous.'

'I suggested to Mike that Françoise comes to stay here at the apartment when she's up to travelling.'

Jake looked surprised and exclaimed, 'I'm not so sure that was a good idea, Val.'

'We'll be going back to Paris very shortly, and there's

no reason she can't stay here. Aunt Isobel won't mind, and Muffie will keep an eye on her.'

Jake let out a long sigh. 'You seem to have adopted her.'

'Not really, but I do feel so sorry for her. From what she's told me, her life with Olivier Bregone has been a nightmare.'

'And you probably saved her life that day at the villa, so you feel responsible for her now, no?'

'I hadn't thought of it that way,' I said.

'This guy Olivier Bregone is a nasty piece of work from what we've heard about him, Val, and I think if he becomes too frustrated about finding her he'll lash out, and I don't want you to be one of his targets. I don't want you to get hurt.'

I didn't respond, merely stood staring at him from the doorway, and then I explained, 'When Olivier showed up at Gemstar looking for me, they told him I was in Uganda on assignment.'

'He's been to Gemstar!' Jake cried. 'Jesus! That spells trouble to me already. You can't get so involved, Val. But tell me what happened?'

'Mike was in a meeting, but he instructed Adam Macklin to say I was out of the country, and there's no way he could know I'm here in the States.'

'Want to bet?'

'Well, I guess cops can find out things, if they really want to,' I muttered.

'I don't think Françoise should come and stay here, Val, I really don't. Please be sensible about this. She has to work out her problems with her husband, get a protection order, divorce him, do whatever's necessary, and if you think Mike's become emotionally involved, then he should be the one helping her. You hardly know her.'

'You're right, I guess . . .'

Jake jumped up, crossed the floor, grabbed hold of me and pulled me into his arms. 'You're just too good for your own good sometimes, Valentine Denning! I've got to look out for you, and look after you, because you're the most precious thing in my life.'

'Oh, Jake darling,' I said against his shoulder. 'Thank you for that. I feel the same way about you . . . I love you.'

He held me away from him and looked into my eyes. 'And I love you, Val. Very much.'

IV

Leading me into the dining room, he pulled out the chair next to his, and said in a more matter-of-fact voice, 'I've begun to get a theme going here, with the first batch of photos. Look.' As he spoke he began to spread them out a little more neatly.

After a moment of rearranging them, he continued, 'Here are lots of your shots of children . . . children who haven't been injured . . . see, children with little bunches of flowers, with pets, with their siblings. Look at this one, this little boy with a scrap of bread held so close to his chest, as if he's afraid someone will take it away from him. It gets to you . . . in fact they all say so much, and they're very poignant.'

I remembered where and when I had taken most of them; the faces of the children were very touching. They were so sorrowful, so pathetic, heart-rending even, and yet there was something about them that suggested hope . . . hope for the future. They brought a lump to my throat, made me choke up. And if they affected *me* in this way then surely they would move others. I hoped so. I wanted the book to be a success, most especially for Jake.

Chapter Twenty-Two

I

Having confronted my mother and found out nothing, I decided to take Jake's advice and fling the family garbage out of the window.

There was no point in attempting to talk to my mother again. As my grandfather used to say, there's nothing to be gained from flogging a dead horse, and this was true. My mother was in denial about her treatment of me when I was a child, and she probably always would be.

I could think of no way to convince her she had done wrong by me, and so my only course of action was to do nothing. I had to put it out of my mind once and for all, and move on.

This I did by throwing myself wholeheartedly into the book project. Since Jake wanted me to write a great deal of it, I started by working on the captions for the photographs, intended for the presentation to the editor on Friday. 'Practising for the book itself,' I told Jake, as daily I bent my head over my yellow pad and drafted the lines I thought would best convey the feeling behind each picture.

After a couple of days, I discovered how much I enjoyed writing the rather lengthy captions, and I was extremely flattered to hear Jake's words of praise when he read them at the end of each day.

While I wrote, he spent most of his time sorting and cataloguing his pictures, and also mine, which Mike had said we could take from the Gemstar archive in New York. 'As long as you make a copy of each one and send back the original,' he had reminded me on the phone from Paris.

On Wednesday morning we were very busy working on the dining-room table when the phone rang. Since Jake was the nearest to it, he picked it up. 'Hello,' he said, and after listening a moment, he added, 'Oh hi, Marge. Yes, okay. Wait a minute, let me find a pen.'

Automatically I got up, handed him mine, and grabbed the yellow pad, placed it on the side table where the phone stood.

I went back to my chair and stared at the group of pictures I had spread out in front of me. I selected one and studied it for a moment. It was of a ragged-looking little boy, covered in grime, who was hunkered down next to his brother and his mother. They lay dead or dying on a dusty street in a Balkan village. Mounds of rubble surrounded them.

The images I had captured on film told their own story. What I wanted to do was use the back story, the story behind the photo, for the caption. And I needed to do so in a cogent way, but also I had to choose exactly the right words. The whole idea was for the caption to have an emotional impact on the reader, just as much as the images had.

'Okay, right. I'll call now,' Jake was saying, and when he hung up, looked across at me and said, 'You'll *never* guess who's in New York. Who just called me at the agency.' His eyes fastened on mine, and he stood there slightly bemused.

Knowing it had to be someone we didn't expect, or unlikely, I racked my brains. 'Olivier,' I answered, because I couldn't think of any other likely suspect.

'Don't be ghoulish! No, not Olivier, thank God. It's Fiona.'

'Fiona!' I repeated stupidly.

'Yes, Fiona Hampton.'

'I wonder what she's doing here,' I muttered, frowning.

'I'm about to find out,' Jake replied, and before I could say another word he was dialling.

'Hey, wait a minute, let's not be rash here,' I exclaimed, but he was already asking for her.

The next thing I heard was his cheerful, 'Hello, Fiona! How are you? And what are you doing in New York?'

He leaned against the antique mahogany sideboard, the phone pressed to his ear, nodding from time to time, listening intently, apparently interested in every word she had to say.

'Just a second, let me ask Val,' he murmured into the phone, and looked across at me.

I sat up straighter in the chair, and focused my attention on him. 'What does she want?' I mouthed.

'Fiona would like us to have lunch or dinner with her. Which do you prefer, honey?' he asked.

'Are you talking about today?'

'Yep.'

'Then let's make it dinner, since I'm really on a roll here with the captions. I'd like to keep working for a bit.'

Nodding to me, he said into the phone, 'Dinner is much better for us, Fiona. Why don't we meet at, let's see . . .' He stared at me, lifting a brow questioningly.

'Le Périgord on East Fifty-Second. At eight o'clock,' I suggested.

Jake repeated what I had just said to Fiona, adding, 'Yes, it'll be lovely to see you too. Until tonight then.'

II

'So what *is* she doing in New York?' I asked Jake, once he was off the phone.

'She's here on a little holiday, she said. With a friend. Who she is bringing to dinner –'

'Male or female?' I interrupted.

'It's a man.'

'*Oh*. So the grieving widow is no longer grieving.'

'I never thought she really was grieving,' Jake murmured, coming back to the dining-room table, sitting down opposite me. 'She was sad, yes, at the memorial, but looking back now, don't you think she was oddly contained?'

I nodded. 'You're right, Jake, and there weren't too many tears flowing either during the eulogies or the rest of the service. Mmmm. Well, we'll see, won't we?'

'We sure will.' He began to shuffle the photos.

I said, 'By the way, how did she know you were in New York?'

'Don't you remember, she was calling me when we were at Les Roches Fleuries? Calling the Paris office, I mean. I kept trying to reach her, first in Dublin and then London. But she always had a machine on in London. I finally left a message that I was going to New York. I guess she got it, and decided to phone the Photoreal office once she arrived.'

'I think Périgord's the best place to take her, I mean *them*, don't you?' I said.

'Good choice on your part, Val. It's busy and has atmosphere, but there's order there. It's not crazy like some places. I'd better call up about a table.'

'I'll do it if you like,' I replied, glancing at my watch. 'But it's still too early. I'll call a bit nearer lunch time when there's somebody there to take the reservation.'

Once more, I bent my head and began to write, trying to concentrate on the caption I'd been working on before Fiona's call. But she kept intruding, popping into my mind, in the most insistent way.

Tony had brainwashed me into believing she was a harridan and a difficult woman during the year I had been emotionally involved with him. But then I had discovered she was quite the opposite when I finally met her. Ever since that day I had often wondered if she had known about me, but I'd inevitably dismissed this idea. Married men didn't tell their wives about their mistresses. Or did they? Well, certainly not Tony Hampton, because there had been too many women in his life over the years. So many confessions would have surely caused a rift between them.

Gripping my pen I began to slowly write on the pad, but within minutes Fiona was intruding again, and my concentration fled. Damn, I thought, why did *she* of all people have to show up in New York? That's all I need, a reminder of Tony Hampton and his double dealing, his lying, his cheating ways, the pain he caused me. And most probably her.

But as it turned out, Fiona's arrival would prove to be fortuitous, although I didn't recognize that until later.

III

Since black dominated my wardrobe, I wore black for dinner, and in doing so I stayed right in step with New York women who never wore any other colour at night.

But instead of my usual trouser suit, I was actually

wearing a dress, and Jake let out a wolf whistle when I walked into the living room at seven-thirty on the dot.

'Oh boy, don't you look great!' he exclaimed as the whistle faded away. 'With those fabulous legs of yours, you should wear dresses more often.'

'Thanks,' I said, pleased with his reaction. The dress was simple, just a straight wool sheath, but it was stylish; with it I wore sheer black stockings and high-heeled black pumps. The pearl earrings my grandparents had given me, and a gold-and-pearl pin Muffie had rashly bought for my birthday two years ago added just the right touches.

'Do you want a drink before we go?' Jake asked.

'No, thanks. And you look very smart yourself tonight,' I said, looking him up and down, and then leering theatrically.

He began to laugh, and pulled me to him, held me close. 'If you're not careful, we're going to end up in the bedroom not the restaurant,' he muttered against my hair.

Pushing him away gently, I also laughed then I took hold of his hand and said, 'Come on, let's go. It'll take us a few minutes to walk up there to the restaurant, and we ought to arrive before they do.'

'So let's go,' Jake replied.

In the entrance foyer I picked up my black wool shawl and a small black evening bag, flung the shawl over my shoulder as we went out of the apartment, making for the lift.

It was a lovely evening for early October, brisk but not really cold, and after a day inside working on the captions it was refreshing to be outside.

Jake said as much as we walked along, echoing my own thoughts as we crossed Beekman Place heading for First Avenue. Neither of us was used to being as confined as we had been lately, since we were usually out in the field, wielding our cameras.

Linking my arm through Jake's, I asked, 'What do you know about Alexander St Just Stevens, the painter?'

'Not much really. Isn't he supposed to be today's equivalent of Picasso?'

'Yes, that's right, I believe he is.'

'Why do you ask me about him?'

'Mike wants me to go over and see him, take a look at some of his work. Apparently he's halfway through a new series of paintings. He's preparing a big show to open in Paris. Mike has several magazines interested in spreads on him and his new paintings.'

'I didn't realize he lived in New York. I thought he was English.'

'He is, but according to Mike he's got a loft in New York and some sort of fancy estate in Mexico. I don't think he's lived in England for years. Mike said yesterday that he's currently at the loft in New York, painting, and he wants me to go and see him, get a feeling about the art.'

'I can't help you very much, Val. I've seen some of his work, and I remember that it was very strong, that it makes a strong statement. I know several of his war paintings have been likened to Picasso's *Guernica*, which, as you know, Picasso painted during the Spanish Civil War in the 1930s, and which Robert Capa photographed. Anyway, does Mike want you to shoot the art?'

'No, I don't think so. What he wants is for me to make contact with the artist, find out when the series will be finished, and hopefully get some sort of commitment from him. Mike wants us to have first crack at photographing it.'

'*You*, I'm sure he wants *you* to do the spreads, otherwise why doesn't Mike send somebody else from Gemstar in New York to see the paintings?'

I shrugged. 'I don't know . . . I guess he wants my opinion about the art itself.'

'Well I'm sure Alexander St Just Stevens will jump at it. Artists, like everyone else, love publicity; it helps them sell their wares,' he said, chuckling.

We were almost at the restaurant on Fifty-Second Street when I stopped a bit abruptly and looked at Jake. 'I feel funny all of a sudden, about seeing Fiona. Do you think she knows that Tony and I were involved?' I asked worriedly.

'I'm sure she doesn't know, so don't feel awkward, Val. And she was very pleasant with you at the memorial. Fiona's a lovely woman, take it from me, and very straightforward,' he answered in a reassuring voice. 'You always know where you stand with her, so please relax, Val.'

'I'll try to, but it suddenly hit me this afternoon . . . the thought that she might know something. But you're right, she is very straight, that was one of the first things that struck me about her.' I took a deep breath. 'Okay, come on then, let's go inside.' I laughed as I slipped my arm through his and added, 'She'd hardly be wanting to see us if she suspected anything about me.'

'True,' Jake agreed as we arrived at the door of the restaurant.

As always, Georges, the owner, was there to greet us, and he showed us to a lovely table for four in a quiet corner. Jake and I had just settled ourselves when Fiona arrived, escorted by an attractive-looking man with premature silver hair and a fairly ruddy complexion.

Jake and I both stood up, hugged Fiona and then were introduced to David Ingham, an Englishman.

Once we were all settled, and drinks had been ordered, Fiona said, 'It's lovely that you were able to have dinner with us tonight. We arrived yesterday and today's our only free time in New York. Yes, it's lucky for us you were free.'

Jake smiled, then asked, 'And where are you going?'

'Connecticut,' Fiona answered, and explained, 'David's daughter is married to an American and they live in Greenwich. We'll be driving up there tomorrow evening.'

David said, 'Pamela, my daughter, and her husband Frank have a lovely house on the water. I know Fiona's going to enjoy the weekend.'

'It's a pretty town,' I murmured, glanced at Fiona and asked, 'How're Moira and Rory?'

'Oh, thanks for asking, Val, they're both getting along fine, very fine indeed. They've adjusted now to . . . er . . . to Tony's death.'

Jake said, 'I did try to get hold of you in Dublin, you know, Fiona, but you'd checked out of the hotel by the time I called.'

'Oh don't be worrying about it, Jake, I was only phoning to say hello, to see how you were. And you both look wonderful, 'tis the truth. And what are you doing in New York, the two of you?'

'I had business here with a publisher,' Jake began, looked at me, and took hold of my hand lying on top of the table. 'And I insisted Val come along . . . she and I –'

'Oh don't tell me, Jake, you and she . . . oh that's so lovely . . . you're an item then, are you?'

'I guess you could say that,' Jake replied, laughing, motioning to the waiter, ordering a second round of drinks.

'I suppose you could say Fiona and I are an item too,' David volunteered, glancing at us and then turning a loving smile on Fiona.

I thought she looked uncomfortable for a moment, but perhaps it was my imagination because she instantly beamed at Jake and me, and confided, 'David's a very old friend, and he's been wonderful to me these last few years, what with Tony travelling so much an' all. Anyway, he's proposed to me, and I've accepted, but we won't be getting married until next year. 'Tis a bit too soon right now, and we decided to wait. We thought that was the decent thing to do, although Moira doesn't agree, under the circumstances.'

Jake stared at her. A puzzled look crossed his face. 'What does that mean?'

Fiona gave a little shrug of her shoulders, and a faint smile flitted across her pretty mouth before instantly disappearing. 'Well, Jake, surely you know Tony and I were married in name only for the last few years . . .' Leaning across the table, she said sotto voce, 'I couldn't compete with all of his other women. I didn't want to, if the truth be known.'

I sat back in my chair, and my hand crept towards Jake's knee. I felt uncomfortable, awkward again. Jake took my hand in his and squeezed it. I knew he was trying to reassure me, but the moment Fiona had mentioned *other women* I had gone cold inside. Did she count me in amongst them? Surely not, I told myself, eyeing her surreptitiously. Her expression was warm and loving; I decided there was nothing devious about this very charming and pretty woman with her halo of burnished red hair and beautiful eyes. Jake's assessment of her was accurate, I felt.

Jake had given his entire attention to Fiona, and now he was saying to her, 'To tell you the truth, I didn't pay too much attention to Tony's private life,

I'd enough problems of my own to contend with. And I'd no idea, none at all, Fiona, that your marriage was in name only. He never told me.'

'Oh no, he wouldn't, that was Tony,' Fiona responded quietly. 'He loved to play games with everybody. He always maintained they were harmless, but they weren't. They were most dangerous games indeed.'

Thankfully, at this moment the waiter arrived at our table, and handed around the menus. It was with a degree of relief that I opened mine and hid behind it, not wishing to be drawn into this particular conversation. I was worried about where it was drifting, what Fiona would announce next.

IV

Fortunately the conversation about Tony's women died a natural death as everyone studied their menus. Jake pushed his leg against mine under the table, and when I looked up at him he smiled and sent me a reassuring message with his eyes. It was as if he were saying he would protect me, take care of things, and I knew he would.

There was a bit of discussion about some of the dishes, and since I knew the restaurant better than anyone else at the table, I made a few recommendations. I myself settled for oysters and grilled sole, as did Fiona; Jake and David both ordered smoked salmon to be followed by the beef stew country style.

With the orders given, Jake studied the wine list, ordered a bottle of Pouilly-Fuissé and his favourite Saint-Émilion, and then, turning to Fiona, he said, 'I'm sorry it's such a short trip for you.'

''Tis very short, I'm afraid. David's got to get back to England. We'll be leaving on Tuesday, so it'll have been less than a week. We're staying with Pamela until Monday night, flying out the next morning. Directly to Manchester.'

'*Manchester*,' Jake repeated. 'Whatever for?'

Fiona burst out laughing, since he had said the name of this northern city in the most disparaging way. 'Manchester's not so bad. It rains a lot in Lancashire, mind you. And we're flying to the north because I've bought a house in Yorkshire and I'm in the process of furnishing it.'

'Are you moving from London?' Jake asked; he sounded surprised, and looked it. 'You're not selling the beautiful house in Hampstead, are you?'

'Oh no, not at all. I'd never sell that. It's too special, and part of me. But I will be living in Yorkshire in the summer, when the weather's always better. I bought a business there, as well, you see.'

'My goodness, Fiona, you're full of surprises,' I exclaimed, staring at her intently across the table. 'What kind of business?' Fiona fascinated me; Tony had never done her justice when he had spoken about her. More fool he.

'A restaurant and bar,' she said. 'David's in the wine and food business, always has been, and when he retires he'll be running it with me. In the meantime, his son Noel will be working alongside me . . . Noel's a superb chef.'

'Where's the house? *And* the restaurant?' Jake asked.

'The house is in Middleham, so's the restaurant, actually. It's a lovely place, Jake, 'tis indeed. You and Val have to come and stay with me, and sample the food at Pig on the Roof . . . that's its name. Noel's a cordon bleu chef, you know –'

'And a *great* chef,' David interjected, 'even though I do say so myself. He's made good, old-fashioned English fare his speciality. You know, steak-and-kidney pudding, roast leg of lamb, lamb stew, roast beef and Yorkshire pudding, game pies, meat pies, fish pies, bangers and mash, all the dishes that are so very tasty when properly made. I think Fiona's going to have a great success.'

'So do I! I love that kind of food,' I confessed. 'It's really my favourite. It's a good thing I don't live in England, I'd be as fat as a pig! And where's Middleham exactly?'

'North Yorkshire, just outside Ripon,' David told me. 'That's a lovely cathedral town in the Dales. Middleham has a very famous ruined castle, which used to be called the Windsor of the North, and it was exactly that. It was the stronghold of the great magnate Richard Neville, the Earl of Warwick, who brought up Richard III, and who put the Plantagenets back on the throne of England.'

'It sounds like a beautiful place,' I remarked.

'Oh it is.' He laughed and added, 'Well, it *is* if you like uninhabited rolling moors strewn with heather and gorse, endless empty skies, flocks of sheep, and quaint old stone cottages. I'm afraid there's really not much there –'

'Except lots of horses,' Fiona interjected. 'There are a number of very famous stables around Middleham, and some of England's greatest racehorses have been, and are, trained there. You see, Yorkshire is truly horse country, Val, and in case you hadn't guessed, David's a Yorkshireman through and through.'

'And you come from Middleham,' I asserted, smiling across at him.

'No, actually, I don't,' David answered. 'I know it very well indeed, but I hail from Harrogate, which isn't very far away, of course. I'm taking early retirement next year, and moving to Middleham. I'll be working with Fiona in the restaurant.'

'He's my business partner in it,' Fiona suddenly thought to point out. 'As well as my life partner.'

V

Our first course arrived and everyone fell silent as the plates were put in front of us and the white wine poured.

I demolished my six oysters so rapidly I felt slightly embarrassed, then realized that Fiona, too, had finished quickly, and I was relieved.

The conversation turned to all manner of subjects during the main course. Fiona asked lots of questions about the book, and Jake and I told her what we were doing. Then she and I talked about the best shops in Manhattan, while the two men fell into a discussion about sports.

Suddenly it was time to look at the dessert menus, which we did. Fiona and I both ordered camomile tea only; Jake went for a floating island again, as he always did here at Le Périgord, and so did David.

It was when we were sitting waiting for the desserts that Fiona dropped her first bombshell.

Quite out of the blue, she brought up Tony again, when she said to Jake, 'Tony was a charmer, a bit of a rogue, as we all know, but a very loveable one. Wouldn't you agree?'

She was looking at Jake and me. I nodded, afraid to say a word, and Jake said, 'You're right, Fiona, I always said Tony had kissed the Blarney Stone . . . I don't think I ever met anyone more charming than he was. And he was my best buddy, I loved him.'

'And he loved you too,' she said. 'But he was also very jealous of you, Jake. He always wanted what you *had*, or what he thought you *wanted*. He couldn't stand for you to get there first.'

My eyes were on Jake and I saw how startled he was. He sat there staring back at Fiona, saying nothing.

Seemingly without a second thought, she hurried on, 'Take the Robert Capa award . . . you won it, he didn't, and he never got over that. He always felt that you and Clee Donovan had one up on him.'

Finding his voice at last, Jake murmured softly, 'But Tony did win other awards, lots of them; he was a world-famous war photographer, Fiona.'

'Oh, I know, but he had set himself up in competition with you, so naturally he was jealous, because some of your awards were more important than his.'

Obviously at a loss, not knowing what to say, Jake simply shook his head, leaned back in his chair and sipped the last of his red wine. Although I knew him well, knew his moods and feelings, I couldn't define the expression in those bright-blue eyes. It was unreadable.

Fiona said, 'I'm not telling you this to run Tony down, to denigrate him in your eyes, but I do want you to know the truth.' She was speaking very softly, and then she glanced at me and said in that same quiet voice, 'It was the same with you, Val. He was awfully jealous of you . . . professionally.'

'Oh,' I said in a low voice. I was relieved she had added the word professionally. I went on, 'I can't imagine why. He was a much better photographer than I was.' My heart was pounding against my rib cage; I wondered what was coming next.

'In some areas, yes,' she replied. 'Action. Wars. But your pictures of children are very moving, and your still lifes are superb. Didn't you recognize some of them in Tony's study that day . . . the day of the memorial?'

'Yes, I knew they were mine,' was all I could muster, and I settled back in the chair, just as Jake had, and sipped the water.

It was at this moment that David pushed back his chair and excused himself, went off to the men's room.

Once we three were alone, Fiona dropped her second bombshell.

Looking from me to Jake, she said, 'When your divorce was coming through from Sue Ellen, and you were about to be a free man, Tony moved in on Val.'

I tried to stifle a gasp without much success.

Jake, totally unperturbed, nodded, and said, 'I've figured that out for myself.'

Turning her attention to me, Fiona went on, very quietly, in a subdued tone, 'I knew all about you and Tony, Val, and I just want to say this . . . I'm not upset or angry, I never was. I just felt sorry for you, because I knew he was playing his usual games with you. As he had with so many other women before. He just couldn't help himself, it's the truth, Val.'

Chapter Twenty-Three

1

'Why did you invite them back for a nightcap?' I asked, giving Jake a hard stare.

Frowning slightly, he said, 'Does it bother you, Val?'

I shook my head. 'No, not at all. Fiona's been perfectly sweet to me, ever since she dropped her second bombshell an hour ago. And I believe her . . . I know she's not angry or upset with me, quite the opposite. I just wondered why you wanted to prolong the evening. It's already ten-thirty.'

'Because Fiona obviously wants to unburden herself some more. Also, I'd like to ask her a few pertinent questions,' he answered as he opened the refrigerator and took out a large bottle of carbonated water.

'There's quite a few *I'd* like to ask her myself, come to think of it,' I remarked and emptied the contents of two ice trays into the small silver bucket standing on the countertop.

'Then why don't you, Val? She'll certainly tell you the

truth, honey. I told you before, Fiona's always been as straight as a die.'

'I'll think about it,' I replied noncommittally as the two of us left the kitchen together and went down the corridor to the sitting room.

Fiona and David were standing at the big window, looking out across the East River, and they turned as we came into the room.

'We were just admiring the view,' she said. 'And we can't get over the beautiful metal bridges, and the way they're strung with emerald-green lights. How lovely they look at night.'

'When you're actually on the bridges, the lights are white, just like any other electric light bulb. It's the atmosphere that makes them appear green from a distance,' I explained. 'The emerald green is just an illusion.'

'Like so many other things in life, eh, Val?' Fiona remarked pithily. 'We're surrounded by illusions, aren't we?'

'Nothing's truer,' I agreed, and I carried the ice bucket over to the console table, where glasses, bottles of liquor and liqueurs were arranged.

Jake was already hovering at this end of the room, and I gave him the ice bucket, then went and sat down on the floral sofa.

Looking across at Fiona, Jake asked, 'Now, what would you like?'

'I think I'll have a Bonnie Prince Charlie, please Jake.'

He frowned at her, looking baffled. 'I don't think we have *that* . . .'

'Oh silly me,' she said, laughing lightly, shaking her auburn curls as if chastizing herself. 'That's just a nickname. What I'm referring to is Drambuie. It's a marvellous liqueur from Scotland; you should try it sometime, it has a lovely spicy flavour.'

Jake searched amongst the bottles, looked up a second later, smiling triumphantly and holding the Drambuie in his hand. 'You're in luck! There's a bottle here after all, Fiona.'

'Oh good. I'd like a wee drop over a couple of ice cubes, please Jake. In a straight tumbler, not a liqueur glass.'

I was curious about the drink, and asked, 'Why did you call it a Bonnie Prince Charlie?'

'Bonnie Prince Charlie was the great grandson of Charles I, who was beheaded, and legend has it that when the prince was a fugitive in Scotland he was aided by a member of the MacKinnon clan of Skye,' Fiona told me. 'As a reward for the man's help, Prince Charlie gave him his own recipe for his personal liqueur, and that recipe has been passed down over the generations. Actually, it's been kept a secret for three hundred years or more, and only the MacKinnons know what goes into Drambuie. But whatever the ingredients are, the drink *is* delicious.' She smiled at me, and finished, 'Have one, Val, you'll enjoy it.'

'All right, I will.' I looked at Jake, and said, 'I'd

love a glass of water as well, please. Shall I come and help you?'

'No, no. Thanks anyway, but I can manage. And David, what can I get you?'

'Thanks, Jake, I'd like a cognac.'

II

Jake not only insisted on being the bartender, he was the waiter as well, taking Fiona and David their drinks, and bringing mine over to me.

I observed him surreptitiously as he moved with an easy grace around the long room. I noticed that his limp was barely perceptible. His leg had been steadily improving over the past few weeks, until it had suddenly acted up again the other day, worrying me. I was relieved to see that he was walking with such ease tonight.

As I watched him, I couldn't help thinking how good he looked in the dark-blue suit, white shirt and blue-and-grey striped tie. I rather liked Jake's sudden sartorial elegance, which had come into being in New York. It suited him.

Once he had poured himself a small cognac, he joined me on the sofa. Lifting his glass he glanced around and said, 'Cheers, everyone.'

'Cheers,' we all echoed, and sipped our drinks.

I liked the taste of the Bonnie Prince Charlie at once. It was thick and sweet with a tangy taste, almost spicy, as Fiona had said. I took another sip, decided I could easily become addicted to it, and put the glass down on the coffee table. A wise move.

After a moment or two, Jake focused on Fiona, who still stood near the window with David. 'Apropos of what you said in the restaurant earlier, about Moira thinking you and David shouldn't wait to get married . . . I'm inclined to vote along with her, Fiona, for what it's worth. I just wanted you to know that.'

'You're absolutely right, old chap,' David agreed. 'I think it's ridiculous to wait . . . silly really.'

Fiona smiled, then looking over at Jake she said, 'Tony's only been dead for a few months, and –'

Jake interrupted her. 'But your *marriage* has been dead for years. At least, that's the impression you gave, when you were talking to us about it earlier in the restaurant. Actually Fiona, you made me think your marriage had been a sham since Rory was born, or thereabouts, anyway.'

Fiona moved away from the window, came and joined us; she took a chair next to the sofa. David followed suit, sitting down in another chair.

There was a brief silence as Fiona settled down, composed herself, and took a sip of the Drambuie. Finally she volunteered, 'Things started to go wrong about three years after Rory was born, when Moira was five. By then we'd been married about seven years. I used to think it was the seven-year itch, as they called it in those days, but it wasn't . . . it was just *an itch*. And it had always been there.

I know that now, and it grew worse as he got older.

'You know, Jake, 'tis a terrible hard thing to be married to a man who can't keep his hands off other women. I suppose as long as you don't know, it doesn't matter . . . but, oh dear, when you do know, how painful it is. Dreadful, I am thinking. And hard to live with, trust me on that, both of you. Well, David himself knows what I went through, don't you, darlin'?'

'I do indeed,' David said with a quiet vehemence. He looked across at Jake and me. 'I've been comforting Fiona for ten years now, and wishing she would leave him, and marry me.' He paused, then rushed on, 'I've been widowed for fifteen years, and ready, willing and able to marry *her*, to take her out of her misery. Needing to do so very badly, in fact. Because I love her. But Fiona wanted Rory to be a bit older before she took that final step.'

Fiona nodded, and exclaimed, 'David's been a saint, waiting for me for all these years the way he has. I don't know how I'd have managed without him.'

Jake inclined his head, but he didn't comment and neither did I. There were all kinds of questions on the tip of my tongue, but I was afraid to ask them. I suppose because I didn't want to upset Fiona; also, perhaps I was afraid to hear her answers. Sometimes it was better to remain ignorant. What was that line? *Where ignorance is bliss, 'tis folly to be wise.* I wasn't sure who wrote it, but it was very apt.

I leaned back against the floral pillows and tried to keep my mind very still. I didn't want to get upset tonight, especially in front of Fiona and David. And talking about Tony might exacerbate my anger, which still ran deep, ran to my core.

More than ever, I felt as though I had been lied to, used and abused, as had Fiona. We're a gang of two, she and I, I suddenly thought, and smiled inwardly. It was a cynical smile, at that. A gang of two hundred was more like it. Who *were* all those women he had had? And where were they now? As if I cared!

The others were talking quietly about Tony, and their words washed over me for a moment or two, and they truly didn't register because I was lost in my own troubled thoughts. But eventually I sat up straighter, and began to listen more attentively.

'Is that really why you didn't divorce Tony in those days? Because you had two small children and wanted them to be in their teens before you separated? Or were there other considerations?' Jake probed.

'Other considerations as well,' Fiona admitted softly, in her lovely lilting Irish brogue. She let out a small sigh. 'And why wouldn't there be, Jake? Firstly, I'm a Roman Catholic, and with me, divorce goes against the grain. I've always believed in the sanctity of marriage, and once you're married it's for life, as far as I'm concerned. So there was my belief in marriage and my religion to contend with. But secondly, I was still very much in love with Tony, if I'm absolutely honest with you. But 'tis awfully hard to love a man who comes home with the smell of other women on him all the time. So humiliating. And that's only *one* of the things that erodes love, yes, it's the truth, Val.'

Swallowing hard, I nodded my understanding, unable to say a word. I looked at this beautiful woman and I hated Tony Hampton with a vengeance, even though he *was* dead.

What a fool she'd been, and more fool I. At this moment I hated myself as much as I hated Tony. And I suppose that's why I hadn't wanted Fiona and David to come back for a drink. I had sensed she was determined to talk about him, and I didn't want to be cast in the role of his last mistress. But of course I was, and anyway it *was* the truth. Might as well admit it.

Suddenly, Fiona was addressing herself directly to me. 'There were always a lot of women, Val, I just want you to know that. I'm not trying to upset you, please believe me, I just want to make you understand that by the time you came along I was well and truly out of love with Tony. Because of all the other women that had gone before you. I was beyond hurt, beyond humiliation, beyond caring. It just didn't matter any more.'

'I know you're not trying to hurt me, Fiona,' I reassured her.

A deep sigh trickled out of her and for a moment she looked weary; finally, she straightened in the chair, and hurried on, 'I was biding my time, waiting for Rory to go to university, and planning to leave Tony. I'd been with David for six years by then. And we'd been best friends for four years before that . . . after ten years of knowing this lovely man, I knew I could have a good life with him, a happy life, and not one fraught with jealousy and lies, betrayals and humiliations. We were right for each other.'

I nodded.

Jake said, 'All the more reason to get married as soon as you can, in my opinion.'

David looked very pleased to hear this statement uttered so forcefully once more, and although he refrained from making a comment, he nevertheless beamed at Jake.

Finally summoning all of my courage, I said, 'Fiona, I would like to tell you my side of the story, tell you about my relationship with Tony . . .' My voice trailed off weakly, and I wondered if I'd made a mistake, embarking on this saga. It was after the fact, now. And perhaps she didn't want to hear it, and I wouldn't blame her.

Immediately, she said, 'I have a good idea what it was about, but why don't you tell me anyway, Val. I am thinking it will make you feel better, my dear.'

Jake reached out and took hold of my hand, held it lovingly in his, and smiled his encouragement. 'Talk to Fiona,' he said quietly. 'It'll be cathartic for you, honey.'

After swallowing some water, I began, 'It was like this, Fiona . . . When we met I wasn't interested in Tony, because he was a married man. I thought he was a great photographer and a good friend, but that's all, a comrade-in-arms, as he always said about Jake and me and him. What you don't know is that I was really attracted to Jake when we first met, but he was trying to solve his divorce problems with Sue Ellen. You know the outcome of all that, so I won't belabour it. Anyway, about a year before he was killed, Tony let it drop to me that he was in the middle of a divorce from you, and he asked me out.' Staring at her, I took a deep breath, released it and said, 'But he wasn't, was he? It was a lie.'

'Yes, it was a lie, Val,' she replied gently. 'We were never divorced, I *am* Tony's widow. But I would have given him one. However, he never asked me for a divorce in all the years we were married.'

'*I've* got something to tell you, Fiona,' Jake said, leaning forward slightly. 'I was always somewhat emotionally involved with Val, from the first day we met. She didn't know this, because I'd never told her, which was foolish of me now that I look back. When Tony got entangled with Val I was thrown for a loop, upset, and disapproving of his liaison with her. I told him so, and he immediately said he was on the level, serious about her, and that he was now separated from you.' Jake took a sip of my water, and continued, 'And then later, this past summer, he was obviously in a sticky situation with Val, even though neither she nor I understood this.'

'Yes, he was, Jake, I can see that . . . and it was because he'd led her on,' Fiona murmured, nodding her head. 'He'd told her so many lies.'

'Yup, he was hoist on his own petard. Then, when he came to Paris in late July, just before we went to Kosovo, he told me he was divorced from you,' Jake finished.

'My God, he didn't do that, did he?' Fiona looked at us askance.

'Oh yes, he did,' I said quickly. 'And he told *me* exactly the same thing. He also said we – he and I – would be married by the end of the year.'

There was a total silence, and I wondered if I had said too much.

Fiona was very pale all of a sudden. Her freckles stood out starkly. She looked from me to David to Jake, and then she leaned back in the chair and closed her eyes. It occurred to me that she seemed wiped out, weary. And shocked. But a moment later she pulled herself together. She sat up, and said, 'I don't know why I'm so appalled, because he was capable of anything. But I must admit to you both, I am horrified he told you such terrible lies. It was unconscionable. How awful for you, Val, and you too, Jake. But mostly I am hurt for Val, who was the victim here, I'm thinking.'

In a whispery voice, I asked her, 'And how did you find out about me?'

For a split second she was startled, and then she answered, 'But I didn't find out, Val. He told me . . . he told me he was having an affair with you, and that's why he was away so much between assignments . . . he said he was with you in Paris, because you needed him to be there.'

'But he wasn't!' I cried. 'He was hardly ever in Paris with me. He always came home to London. *To you.*'

'No, no, he didn't, Val! Oh, of course he spent some time with us, he loved the kids and his garden and the house in Hampstead, but he was away an awful lot between his jobs.'

Jake said, 'Well, he certainly wasn't in Paris, that I *can* attest to.'

Fiona murmured, 'It was odd really, our life together. We sort of muddled along when he came home; certainly there was nothing between us any longer. He knew that David and I were close, and he didn't seem to mind, but I think he thought it would never come to anything. He thought I'd always be there.'

David said, 'Very simply, Val, Tony didn't want a divorce. He wanted to stay married to Fiona and have all of his other women as well. That lifestyle suited him.'

Jake said, 'But he made such a point to me about having to be in London, Fiona. I can't believe he even lied about that.'

'If he wasn't with you, Fiona, and if he wasn't in Paris with Val, then where was he?' David asked, sounding mystified.

'*I* certainly don't know,' I said. 'I've no idea where he went.'

'I think I know . . .' Fiona began, and instantly broke off. A look of comprehension had crossed her face, and she now said in a sudden rush of words,

'It's just come to me . . . how involved he was with Anne Curtis –'

'Oh my God!' I practically shouted, cutting across Fiona's words, and I brought a hand to my mouth. '*She* was in Beirut when I was there with Tony. You were in the States, Jake, and I wasn't involved with Tony then, but I remember at the time I thought she had designs on him. Yes, yes, and now I remember . . . it was when Bill Fitzgerald was captured by the Islamic Jihad.'

Fiona looked so stricken that I thought she was about to burst into tears.

I said, 'Oh Fiona, do you think he was having an affair with me, and with her too . . . at the same time? You do, don't you? That's it, isn't it?'

For a moment all she could do was nod. But after a few minutes she spoke. 'I'm so sorry, Val, but I'm afraid I am thinking that. And if it wasn't Anne, then it was certainly *someone* else . . . *somewhere* else . . . because he was hardly ever at home between jobs.'

'What made him think he could get away with any of it?' Jake asked heatedly.

Shrugging, Fiona replied, 'I've no idea . . .'

'I suppose you have to be a little bit mad, a bit off the wall to think you can deceive the entire world . . .' I stopped, wishing that I hadn't volunteered this comment. I no longer wanted to talk about Tony Hampton. I was sickened by this whole mess.

Jake said: 'Tell me something, Fiona, do you think

Tony *would* have committed bigamy and married Val?'

'I don't know, Jake. Perhaps he would. Other men have done it, 'tis a well-known fact that they have. And they got away with it, too. At least, for a long time – until they were eventually caught.'

'Or he could have found an excuse to break it off,' I remarked. 'Other men have also done *that*.'

Jake raised a brow. 'The mind of a man,' he began and stopped abruptly, looked away; he was uncomfortable.

David ventured, 'All kinds of excuses would've worked. Such as: My wife is seriously ill, I can't leave her now . . . that's just one of them that comes to mind.'

'And if the mistress throws a tantrum, or protests unduly, she looks like a bitch,' I muttered.

David glanced at Fiona and murmured, 'You may not agree, love, but I think Tony would have broken the law and married Val.'

'And why not Anne Curtis, if she was the other one?' I asked.

Ignoring my comment, Fiona answered David when she said, 'Maybe he would have committed bigamy with Val. He was impulsive and unpredictable. On the other hand, the "*my wife is desperately ill*" excuse would've appealed to Tony. He might have used it . . .'

'Listen, all of you! He duped me!' I cried, my voice an octave higher. 'Because I'm a grown-up, a mature woman, I *can* accept that. But what I want to know is WHY did he do it?'

'Do you mean why did he do it to you? Or why was he the way he was?' Fiona asked me. 'Do you mean why did he have so many women and tell so many lies?'

'*Absolutely*. I mean all of that, yes. You've hit it on the head exactly,' I answered tensely. I sat bolt upright on the sofa, filled with fury all of a sudden. I tried to relax, to ease the anger away.

She took a deep breath, allowed the air to trickle out of her, and then slumped against the chair-back. After a small silence, she said slowly, but with total assurance, 'He picked you, Val, because he knew Jake wanted you. I told you that in the restaurant. But it was also because you were fair game, gorgeous, and a challenge to him. But Tony was a born womanizer . . . through and through. And through again. I always suspected he was unfaithful to me on our honeymoon, you know, but I had no way of ever proving it. He was also very selfish, with an infantile need for instant gratification. If he wanted something, he wanted it *now*. Just like a child.'

Fiona looked from me to David to Jake, and she shook her head sadly. For a split second I thought she was going to burst into tears. But she didn't, she just sat there staring at us wordlessly. I felt so sorry for her because of the life he had inflicted on her.

No one said a word.

What was there to say?

But eventually Fiona spoke, explaining in a low, almost inaudible voice, 'Yes, he was extremely selfish but he was also a very sick man. In his head. But not a bad man, no, not that . . . he was mentally disturbed, in certain ways. I am also thinking he was addicted to sex. I believe he needed different women all the time in order to . . .'

'Get it up,' I said, unable to curb myself. 'To get an erection.'

'That's right,' she responded, her eyes meeting mine.

'He was rotten to the core, in my opinion,' David announced. 'And you know it, Fiona. We all know it.'

I was really surprised at David's courage. This quiet, laid-back man was impressing me more and more. He certainly knew who he was, what he believed, and he wasn't afraid to say what he thought, even at the risk of upsetting Fiona. He had earned my respect in just a few hours, and he was certainly much more worthy of Fiona than Tony had ever been.

'There's something else,' David went on, addressing Fiona. 'I know you won't misunderstand . . . and it's this. Basically, Tony didn't give a damn about your feelings, or the children's feelings either. Or Jake's or Val's. Or mine, for that matter, not that *I* really count in this domestic drama.'

'But you do, David! You do!' Fiona protested, her voice rising sharply. 'And he knew that. Tony knew I cared for you, and that you cared for me and his children.'

'*Your* children,' David announced very quietly. 'He never had much to do with their upbringing. He was always away.'

'But I got the impression from Moira and Rory that he spent a lot of time with them this past summer,' Jake said, puzzled, looking at Fiona and David.

'He was at home for a couple of weeks . . .' Fiona replied. 'Well, you know, Jake, they do tend to exaggerate a bit and fantasize. They wished he'd been there for months on end, but that was not actually the way it was. Even though they told you that perhaps.'

David downed his cognac, and got up. 'Mind if I help myself, Jake?'

'No, go ahead, David.'

David walked across the floor, and then turned around when he was almost at the console table. 'Tony did what he wanted, took what he wanted, and to hell with the consequences. That was his attitude. Nobody else mattered. Oh, yes, he was a charmer, and lovely to us all. And talented. And he could spin the best yarns, take the best photographs, prepare the greatest meals, make us all laugh. And cry. We all loved him at one time or another. But he was a bastard, nevertheless.'

Fiona sighed. 'He's the father of my children . . . and I did love him once, but 'tis true, what David's just said.'

III

Jake's bright-blue eyes settled on Fiona as he asked in a warm voice, 'Why did you bring this up tonight, Fiona? Had you been planning it?'

Emphatically she shook her head from side to side. 'Oh no, no, Jake, I hadn't been planning it at all. But when I saw you and Val together at the dinner table, saw the way you were . . . so very much together, so in love, I thought you should know the truth, know about the real Tony. I knew him better than anybody, and I suppose you could say I knew what made him tick, what went on in his mind. He was so complex . . .' She sighed and shook her head again. 'Well, there's nothing worse than having a tantalizing ghost hanging around, and I wanted you to know about him.'

'There's a lot to be said for that, getting rid of ghosts,' I exclaimed. 'And I for one am glad we've had this chance to talk. I knew you were Tony's widow, not his ex-wife, the day of the memorial service. When I stood next to you in the Brompton Oratory, I just knew, Fiona.'

'I didn't want you to suffer needlessly, grieve needlessly, ruin your life yearning for such a man. I felt you should understand about him, know the truth about him. I have always put great value on truth.'

IV

I had believed for the last few weeks that I had exorcized the ghost of Tony Hampton. And that Jake had too. But only after this very honest discussion with Fiona did I really feel truly liberated.

It struck me that Jake felt the same way. We didn't mention it or discuss it after they finally left just after midnight. We simply turned out the lights and went into the bedroom. But there was a carefreeness in him, a lightness that had not been present before. It was as if a weight had been lifted, and I certainly felt as though my shoulders were lighter, a terrible burden finally sloughed away.

Yes, Tony Hampton was gone from my life, and from Jake's, as well. And also from my memory, and I hoped from his. I didn't want to bring this up, and I prayed he wouldn't either. All I wanted now, tonight, was to lie next to him, make love to him, have him make love to me. I wanted to be with the man who truly loved me, and whom I loved with all my heart.

V

The past became dust. The present was passion.

Jake pulled down the strap of my nightgown and began to kiss my breast very tenderly. After a moment, he looked deeply into my eyes, and I saw that his were full of his love for me.

He gently stroked my cheek with his fingertips and kissed my eyelids, and then he tugged lightly at my nightgown again, and murmured, 'Take this off, Val, please darling. Take it off.'

I did as he asked, and eagerly so.

He slipped off the bed and shed his pyjama bottoms, and as he stood there naked, looking down at me in my nakedness, I shivered slightly.

The room was dim except for the moonlight filtering in through the windows. And he looked so masculine in that pale light, my breath caught in my throat. Tall, lithe, broad of chest, his face finely etched, and those eyes such a vivid, startling blue. He was all man; and his manhood proclaimed his desire and longing for me.

He lay down on the bed again and pulled me into his arms, murmuring my name. He began to kiss my breast, sucking on the nipple until it hardened, became erect. And he entwined his legs around mine, and held me close, and I could feel his hardness against me. And I wanted him.

The heat of passion and an urgent desire raced through me, burned me up, and I cleaved to him, holding onto him tightly. 'Oh Jake, oh Jake, I want you so much,' I whispered against his shoulder. 'Now.'

He pushed himself up on one elbow and looked down at me, and said softly, 'Oh look, look. Just look at you . . . you're so beautiful, Val.'

All of his attention became centred on that mound of blondeish-brown hair between my thighs, and he bent over me, lavishing me with kisses and tender touching until I opened up to him fully. And as always he brought me to the edge of climax, then stopped, took me to him with infinite tenderness and care, fitting the length of himself into me with expertise.

Swiftly and with precision we rose and fell together, lost ourselves in each other, gave ourselves to each other. And as deep shuddering began to overcome me, and I found myself spiralling into ecstasy, he let himself go. He rushed headlong into me, calling my name over and over again, as we came together, were fused together as one.

After our passion was spent, and we lay wrapped in each other's arms, I looked deeply into those clear blue eyes, and I saw that he was at peace with himself and with me. Just as I was.

Jake had said we were destined to be together. And he was right. It had always been so, from the beginning. We had simply missed our way for a short while. But I *was* his . . . his woman, his passion, his love.

And he was the only man for me, the only man I wanted. And that was the absolute truth.

Chapter Twenty-Four

I

A week after our remarkable dinner with Fiona and David, my new-found inner peace and contentment was suddenly shattered, blown to smithereens by several unexpected and unwelcome phone calls.

The bad news came filtering into the Beekman Place apartment on a cold but sunny Wednesday morning, thereafter etched in my mind as Bad Day at Black Rock, to remind me that the good things didn't last very long for little old Val.

The first call came from Mike Carter in Paris. My boss began by telling me that I had missed the boat with the famous artist, who'd retreated to his compound in Mexico to wield his magic brush in a more congenial environment than a Soho loft. And then he had added in a dour voice that there was serious trouble developing with Olivier, the abusive husband. He had somehow discovered that Françoise was staying with Mike, and was apparently on the warpath, violent, threatening and out to make mayhem.

Before I got into what I knew would be a difficult discussion about Françoise, I apologized for missing the great Alexander St Just Stevens, who had never even had the courtesy to return my innumerable phone calls to him. Which was the reason why I had never had a peek at his paintings before he had flown the coop for more exotic climes.

I then addressed the problem of Olivier, cop on the rampage.

'You've got to send Françoise here,' I pushed, only to be told by Mike that she did not want to come Stateside, as he called it.

'New York is too far away, Val, and she says she won't like it. Especially since you're not going to be there. And you're not, are you? You *are* coming back to work next week, aren't you?'

After reassuring him that I was indeed returning to Paris and work, I decided to offer him a bit of good advice. 'If you haven't done it already, get her a lawyer. And make sure he's not only tough but has vast power within the French legal system – you know, the right *connections*. That's the only kind of legal eagle who'll be able to handle Olivier. That *flic* obviously has pull somewhere. And tell me, how the hell did he find out she's staying with you and the girls?'

'No idea. As for the lawyer, I *have* hired somebody, a powerhouse, a real shit I'm told, and just the kind of guy she needs. Françoise is seeing him tomorrow.

But I wish I knew where I could send her for a while . . . out of the country would be preferable. London would be great, but I don't know anybody –'

'Pig on the Roof!' I practically shouted down the phone, clutching the receiver tighter as an amazing brainstorm hit me.

'What the hell does that mean, Val?' Mike bellowed from Paris.

I had to laugh, even though I knew this wasn't a laughing matter, and also that my laughter would annoy him. Taking a deep breath, adopting a more sober tone, I explained, 'It's a restaurant, Pig on the Roof is . . . and it is being opened imminently by Fiona Hampton, Tony's widow. She also bought a house close by, both in Middleham. That's in Yorkshire. She told me she was looking for an assistant to help her pull both places together, especially the decoration of the restaurant. It just occurred to me that Françoise might be ideal, since she works for a decorator in Marseilles, or at least used to work for one.'

'I don't know,' Mike mumbled uncertainly.

'She would be safe there, I'm sure, Mike, and listen, Yorkshire's not that far from Paris. Fiona invited Jake and me to go and stay with her for Christmas if we want, and she said we could fly from Paris to Leeds-Bradford Airport. Or fly into Manchester Airport and drive to Yorkshire from there. Françoise would be in easy reach if you wanted to see her, Mike.'

'It's a possibility, yes,' Mike responded, suddenly

sounding a bit brighter. 'And could she live with Fiona Hampton?'

'I don't know, but under the circumstances I would think so, yes. Fiona's one of the most understanding women I've ever met. Do you want me to call her? She went back to London yesterday.'

'I'd better talk to Françoise about it first.'

'It sounds to me as if you're heavily involved there,' I ventured, and then stopped abruptly, deeming it wiser not to pry. Besides, as Jake kept telling me, the less we knew about that particular mess, the better off we were.

Mike was saying, 'Well, yes, I am very involved. I'm in love with her and she with me . . . I want to marry her.' There was a pause before he added, 'She's the only woman I've loved since Sarah's death.'

I wasn't a bit surprised to hear this declaration, but the mere idea of this union made me excessively nervous, not least because Olivier was definitely not someone to tangle with by choice.

Taking a deep breath, I forced a cheerfulness I suddenly did not feel when I said, 'I'm going to be bridesmaid, I hope. Or should I say maid of honour?'

Mike chuckled, promised to call Françoise immediately, and get back to me pronto.

After cautioning him to be careful about Olivier, I hung up.

II

I had no sooner put the phone down when it rang again.

'Hullo?' I said and was startled when my brother answered.

'I've got to come and see you, Val,' Donald said in a rush of words, and with no preamble whatsoever. 'As soon as possible.'

'But it's only seven-thirty in the morning! I haven't even had coffee yet,' I protested, and wondered what had happened to Jake who had gone out to the supermarket to buy milk.

'I don't mean this minute,' Donald explained. 'But later this morning. Please, Val, we've got to talk.'

'What about?'

'The will.'

'Oh, come on, Donald! We talked about that the other Sunday. You know how I feel. You can have everything, Lowell's included. I don't want her stuff or her business, and I explained that to you. And to her.'

'But she says you *have* to inherit the business, she won't listen to me. I thought perhaps you could give it one more shot. Maybe work something out with her.'

'Oh Donald,' I groaned and sighed heavily. 'She won't listen to *me*. You're her favourite. You used to be able to twist her around your little finger so why don't you try doing that again?'

'She's stuck on this family thing, The Tradition, as she calls it, with two capital Ts.'

'Do you think that's a binding legal document? Or is it simply a tradition within the family, something started by Amy-Anne Lowell a hundred years ago?'

'I just don't know,' Donald answered, his voice glum.

'It didn't occur to me to ask her the other day, but I wonder if it's written into the articles of incorporation? Try to find that out, if you can.'

'I will, but why do you want to know?'

The dumbness of this question took my breath away, but then you didn't have to be a genius to be duplicitous, which was Donald's main claim to fame in the family. 'Because if it's written into the articles of incorporation of Lowell's then it has to be treated as a legal matter,' I replied patiently. 'But if it's just a wish, a suggestion, a desire put forward by Amy-Anne, then I guess it would be simple to break. Because it's not *legal*.'

'She'd never let us break The Tradition.'

'What's the matter with you this morning, Donald? Get with it! If there's no legal document, then I can simply decline to accept Lowell's. Or better still, I suppose I should accept it, then give it to you by drawing up the appropriate papers.'

'You keep saying you'll do that. But *will* you give it to me?'

'Don't you trust me?'

'Sure I do,' he muttered, sounding doubtful, I thought.

'Call up your mother, find out what you can, and meet me here at one o'clock,' I ordered tersely, resorting to my bullying of old. 'I'll take you to lunch at a local joint, and we can settle this damn thing once and for all. Okay?'

'Okay, Sis.'

'Donald!' I shouted. 'Don't call me –'

He hung up on me.

Ungrateful little pig, I thought, and wondered why I bothered with him. Well, I *had* cared about him once, when we were small. Anyway, I didn't want Lowell's, that was the absolute truth, and he should have it as our mother's son. There was no one else, except for those distant Lowell cousins who received annual cheques for doing nothing.

Desperate now for a blast of caffeine, I padded into the kitchen and filled a mug with coffee, adding sweetener. I didn't particularly like it black, but Jake hadn't returned from his errand to buy milk.

I stood standing at the kitchen window, looking out, thinking that it appeared to be one of those clear, crisp autumn days. The sky was a blameless blue and the sun was already edging out from behind foamy white clouds. I always enjoyed the change of seasons, which is why I had never wanted to live permanently in a hot climate . . .

The sudden shrilling of the wall phone made me jump, and I grabbed the receiver and said hello, wondering who it was this time.

'Is that you, Valentine?'

I didn't recognize the woman's voice, and said, 'Yes, it is, who's this?'

'Good morning, Val, it's Lauren, Jacques Foucher's wife.'

'Hello, Lauren! How're you?'

'I'm fine, but I'm afraid Jacques has had a terrible accident. I was looking for Jake to tell him about it. Is he there?'

'No, he's out on an errand. He'll be back any minute, but please, tell me what happened, Lauren.'

'Jacques is badly injured, but he *will* recover. Eventually. He's in hospital, obviously, and he's lucky to be alive. He was on his way home last night when he had a heart attack. In the car. He was driving, Val, and he hit a parked van, empty, thank God! And then he careened across the street and slammed into a brick wall head-on.'

'Oh my God!' I cried. 'You're right, he is lucky to be alive. How bad are his injuries?'

'He broke his nose and his collarbone, and an arm and a leg, and of course he has a lot of contusions, bruises. Some minor internal injuries. But that's about the extent of it.'

'It could have been worse, let's face it.'

'Yes, he could be *dead*,' Lauren said. 'Anyway, will you tell Jake I'm at the office now, and I'll come in every day until you get back to Paris. When do you think that'll be?'

'Next week, of that I'm absolutely sure. But Jake might want to leave earlier now.'

'It's not necessary,' she replied. 'Everything's under control, and fortunately Jacques is in the best medical hands. Please tell Jake I can cope with the agency, not too much is going on at the moment anyway.'

'I know you can cope,' I said, remembering just how efficient Lauren Crane was. English born, brought up and trained, she was a successful agent running the Paris office of a well-known American talent agency. Like me, she had lived in Paris for a number of years and was a dyed-in-the-wool Francophile. She was Jacques Foucher's second wife, and he adored her and their four-year-old daughter Jasmine.

'But how are you going to run your own office?' I now asked Lauren.

'I'm going to spend the mornings here at Photoreal,' she explained, 'and the afternoons at my own office. Since I'm dealing with New York and Los Angeles, the time differences work in my favour.'

'I see,' I responded. 'And I'll have Jake call you the minute he gets back. It won't be long. And give Jacques my love, and tell him I hope he's feeling better soon.'

'I will, Val, and thanks.'

III

After we had both hung up, I stood drinking my coffee, continuing to gaze out across the East River, though a little absently now, I must admit. I was thinking of Jacques and trying to remember his age. I knew he was older than Jake, by about fourteen years I thought, which would make him around fifty-two. Still, that was relatively young to have a heart attack, wasn't it? Luck was running with him, I thought, just as it was with me and Jake in Kosovo. Our time wasn't up then, and neither was Jacques's last night. It's all to do with destiny.

When the phone began to ring again, I cursed under my breath, and reached for the receiver once more. 'Yes,' I said somewhat sharply. This unexpected early-morning activity was suddenly getting to me.

'Val, 'ello, it is me, Françoise.'

'Françoise, hello, how are you?' I asked, my voice softening. 'You must be glad to be out of the clinic, and back with Mike.'

'*Oui*. Yes, I am very 'appy with him. He is wonderful. But Val, it is Olivier, he will grab me any minute, and take me back to Marseilles, I feel this.'

'Listen to me, Françoise,' I instructed, 'and listen carefully. You must get out of Paris, after you have seen that lawyer tomorrow. And I think I can arrange for you to stay with a friend in England. How do you feel about that?'

'I will go. Mike explained it to me. About the Pig on the Roof lady. I am so frightened of Olivier. And so are my parents now. He is going to see them at Les Roches Fleuries. All the time.'

'I'll bet he is! And I also bet he's got the phone tapped and the mail monitored. Stay away from them, Françoise, if you want to be safe.'

'*Oui*, *oui*. I know this must be the way. They are worried about *me*.'

'Things will turn out all right,' I reassured her. 'I'm going to phone my friend in London, and I'll get back to you. Or rather, I'll call Mike. That would be better. Just be careful, Françoise, and don't take any chances.'

'I understand. *Merci*, Val. *Au revoir*.'

''Bye, Françoise, keep your chin up.' As I put the phone back in the cradle I wondered if she knew what that phrase meant. Too late to explain.

I walked out of the kitchen, now more baffled than ever by Jake's prolonged absence; I was heading down the corridor to the living room when I heard the key in the lock. Then the door slammed.

As I hurried into the entrance foyer, I saw Jake struggling with three large brown paper bags from the supermarket. He was dressed in a heavy white fisherman's sweater, blue jeans and a baseball cap worn backwards. He looked a little flushed, or perhaps it was windburn.

'Hi, Kid,' he said, grinning at me over the top of the bags. 'It's bitchy out there, cold all of a sudden. Sorry I took so long, but I bought stuff for dinner tonight, to save time. I thought we could –'

'There's bad news, Jake,' I interrupted, going forward to help him with the overflowing supermarket bags.

'What bad news? What's wrong?'

I told him.

IV

Jake went immediately into the study to call Lauren in Paris.

I retreated to the kitchen to make fresh coffee and toast the bagels Jake had bought.

While the coffee perked and the bagels browned, I set up a tray with milk, sweetener, butter and apricot jam. I added mugs, plates, spoons, knives and napkins, and then stood watching the bagels, not wanting them to burn.

Earlier, I had planned a cosy little domestic scene. A blissful breakfast with Jake, since our sojourn in New York was soon coming to an end. I craved intimacy with him. All kinds of intimacy, and most especially the domestic kind. I asked myself why I needed this; then it had occurred to me the other day that domesticity with Jake made me feel safe, secure, and nurtured. Things I'd never really known.

But today unfortunately life had intruded.

Once the coffee was ready, I put the pot on the tray, then peered into the toaster oven to evaluate the bagels. They looked perfect, and I lifted them out with a clean kitchen towel and dropped them on one of the plates.

As I carried the tray into the study and put it down on the big coffee table, Jake hung up the phone after saying goodbye to Lauren.

'What a lousy thing to happen to Jacques,' he said, walking over, sitting down on the sofa and pouring coffee for us both. 'The funny thing is, there's no history of heart trouble. Lauren says he had a check-up only two weeks ago and he was fine.'

'Thank God he's alive,' I said, flopping down next to Jake. 'He could have so easily been killed. He had a narrow escape, you know he had.'

Jake nodded, buttered a bagel and spread it with apricot jam. He bit into it and nodded his approval.

While he munched on it, I relayed the news about Françoise and the rampaging husband out to get her and Mike and his two daughters. And whomever else got in his way. Like little old Val, perhaps.

'Shit!' he exploded, almost choking on the bagel. 'I knew that situation spelled trouble right from the beginning!'

'And then some,' I muttered and told him about my idea of asking Fiona to take Françoise under her wing for a few weeks.

'But you're doing it again, Val!' he exclaimed.

'Doing what?' I asked, feigning innocence.

'Meddling, for God's sake!' he almost shouted.

'Having meddled once, and created a problem called Love with a capital L, certainly not anticipated by me, I feel I have to help them overcome the newer problem. The problem which that love has brought upon them. In short, the fury of Olivier.'

'Mike's a big boy,' Jake snapped. 'He can take care of Françoise, and I don't want you getting mixed up in this any more than you already are. A guy like Olivier can easily go berserk, and if you get in his way, he'll think nothing about exterminating *you.*'

'What you say is true, but calm down, Jake, please. All I want to do is put a call in to Fiona, explain the situation, and ask her if Françoise can go and stay with her for a while. Surely there's no harm in that?'

Jake let out a long, exasperated sigh, took off his baseball cap, flung it to the other side of the room, grabbed me, and pulled me into his arms. 'You're . . . you're just . . . *incorrigible*, Valentine Denning, the most impossible, stubborn, interfering, meddling, beautiful, sexy –'

I stopped this flow of words by planting my lips on his. I gave him a long, soulful, passionate kiss; which was a big mistake on my part, because it only inflamed him, gave him all the wrong ideas.

Except that they were not so wrong, I decided, as he slowly but deliberately and very sensually began to make love to me on the sofa.

What a lovely intimate breakfast it turned out to be after all, I thought, smiling.

Chapter Twenty-Five

I

When Donald turned up on my doorstep at exactly one o'clock, carrying a large bunch of expensive-looking flowers wrapped in cellophane and tied with pink ribbon, I was immediately suspicious. I had to curb the impulse to snarl at him.

Did he think I was a fool? Didn't he realize I saw through this ruse, this sudden loving gesture, the first one in years? *Flowers, indeed.*

He underestimated me if he thought I hadn't twigged that he was cosying up to me, being sweet and ever so friendly because I had suddenly become vital to his future.

But somehow I managed to swallow the acerbic words that had leapt to my tongue. I might as well be pleasant; I had nothing to lose. I laughed inside. Sex with Jake for breakfast was infinitely more satisfying than coffee with bagels for breakfast; our unexpected and wonderfully fulfilling lovemaking on the study sofa had put me in a generous mood. And so I allowed Donald to get off unscathed.

Smiling sweetly, I offered him my cheek to kiss, thanked him for the flowers and told him to throw his coat on the bench in the entrance foyer. After putting the flowers on the kitchen counter, I led him into the panelled study overlooking the East River.

'Where's the Costner clone?' he asked, glancing around.

'Having lunch with Gwyneth Paltrow,' I lied in a snippy voice, knowing that this would make him crazy. Donald the Great had always grovelled at the feet of female movie stars.

'Is he really?' my brother asked, impressed, his eyes widening.

'Donald, come on! Don't be daft. I was kidding. Jake's gone to have lunch with the publisher. At the Four Seasons.'

'You've got a publisher?'

I nodded. 'Sure do. He apparently gave a great presentation, and the deal's made. They're drawing up the contracts now.'

'Congratulations, Sis.'

'*Donald*,' I said threateningly, glaring at him.

'Sorry, *Val*.'

I pointed to the sofa where earlier Jake and I had enjoyed our delicious sexy romp, and said, 'Sit there, and start talking. What did she tell you?'

He did as I said as I stood hovering over him, my eyes on his face.

'She didn't tell me much –'

'What!' I exclaimed, cutting across his sentence. 'You come here with no information, expecting me to welcome you with open arms. Is that why you brought the flowers? As a peace offering?'

'No, no. And you didn't let me finish!' he whined.

'Okay, shoot.'

'Listen, Val, you don't let me get the words out. You've certainly reverted to your old self. You're so fucking bossy and bullying again, I can't stand it.' He started to get up. 'I think I'm going to leave and you –'

'You're not leaving, Donald,' I snapped. 'So put that idea out of your head. And please refrain from using bad language, you know it irritates me.'

'Okay, okay. Let's get back to Mom. She didn't say much when I first got there. Just sat like Elizabeth I on her throne, looking regal and imposing. Then she eased up after I'd stroked her ego and yabbered at her for half an hour. I finally managed to establish that there's no legal document. About The Tradition thing.' He sat back, looking pleased with himself.

'That's good to know,' I exclaimed, and beamed at him, hoping to encourage him to keep talking. 'What else did she say?'

'She explained about The Tradition. And that's all it is, Val, a tradition started by Amy-Anne, who wanted to give the women in the family the power, not the men. But even though there was, *is*, nothing in writing per se, Mom says the Lowell women have taken it very seriously for a hundred years. It's kinda . . . like . . . well, I guess it's like their bible.' Leaning forward slightly, Donald looked up at me, and confided, 'Mom says that the women descendants of Amy-Anne believed that it would bring bad luck to the family if a woman stopped being the head of Lowell's. Maybe she believes it too?'

'Goodness me, Donald, where does that leave you?' I asked sweetly, and walked across the room, stood leaning against the fireplace, trying to hide the amused smile that had sprung to my lips.

'I'm getting engaged. To Alexis. She accepted my proposal.'

'How fortuitous for you, Donald,' I purred sarcastically, thinking what an opportunist he was. He wasn't wasting any time or taking any chances. But what did I care? It suited my purpose to give him the family business. I certainly didn't want anything to do with it. Nor did I want anything from her.

He said, 'I think Mom wants to see you again, Val.'

'What for?' I demanded, turning frosty with him.

'I don't know, she didn't say.'

'God, Donald, you are dim at times! Why didn't you ask her?'

'I did. And stop being a *bitch*!'

I ignored this and said, 'And how did she answer you?'

'She didn't, at least she wouldn't tell me her reason, except that she said something about owing you an explanation.'

'No kidding,' I murmured, wondering what had prompted this sudden need for truth-telling on my mother's part.

Donald nodded, and sat back against the pillows.

I softened my attitude towards him, and said in a pleasant tone, 'Well, Donald, this is really good news for you. About there not being a legal document. That makes it so much easier for me to give you the company.'

'I told her you wanted to do that, and she says she won't let you.'

'I don't inherit Lowell's until she dies, Donald, and when she's dead she won't be able to stop me handing the business over to you. Now will she?'

'Mmmm. Yes, that's true, I guess.'

'No guessing. It *is* true.'

'You're going to have to see Mom again, Val.'

'No way, brother mine.'

'I'll go with you.'

'I bet you would, under the circumstances,' I said.

'Please, Val. Be nice. You used to love me, and when you stopped I was really hurt. You damaged me when I was a child because you dumped me, withdrew your love.'

'Cut the crap, Donald, you know she took you away from me the moment it suited her.'

'Bad language, Val, *really*!'

'Donald, tell me something. Why the hell do you want Lowell's anyway?' I asked, truly perplexed by this, and genuinely wanting to know.

'Because you don't want it, and it should stay in the family.'

'But would you work there?'

'Sure as hell I would.'

'But you've got your dream job on the magazine. You always wanted to be a gossip columnist – after all you cut your teeth on gossip in the family.'

'There you go again, being a bitch.'

'Oh stop using that word. You're getting monotonous. So tell me, why would you want to give up your column (which, I hear from Muffie, is very influential), to go and work in an office every day, making and selling cosmetics that nobody's ever heard of or really cares about?'

Donald looked at me alertly, his eyes narrowing slightly, and after a split second he said, 'You don't know, do you?'

'Know what?' I asked swiftly, noting the sudden change in his demeanour, and wondering what bombshell he was about to drop.

'About Lowell's, and what's happened to the company?'

I shook my head. 'How would I know? I spend most of my life shooting pictures of the dead and dying on the battlefronts of the world.'

Donald stood up. 'Let's go to lunch,' he said, suddenly becoming authoritative, 'and I'll tell you all about it.'

11

He had intrigued me with his comment about Lowell's and I tried to pump him as we walked across Beekman Place and out onto First Avenue. But he wouldn't be drawn, and insisted on telling me about his fiancée Alexis, whom he wanted me to meet before I returned to Paris.

To shut him up I finally agreed to this, and hoped Jake wouldn't mind that I'd invited them to have dinner with us on Friday.

By the time we arrived at Billy's, a place I liked for its fish and chips and great hamburgers, Donald was all over me like chickenpox, being sweet because of the dinner invitation, no doubt. And everything else I was doing for him.

After hanging up our coats, we were shown to a table in the second room, which I preferred. The restaurant had a warm, attractive pub-like atmosphere, with bare wood floors and tables covered in red-and-white checked cloths. Its informality and good food made it a favourite of mine, especially when I was in a hurry and wanted to eat well without a lot of fuss.

Donald said, 'Let's have a glass of white wine to celebrate.'

Frowning, I asked, 'Celebrate what?'

'My engagement to Alexis,' he answered, staring at me. 'What did you think I meant?'

'Er, er, I didn't,' I said, although it had just struck me that perhaps he was counting his chicks before the hatching, *if* he was now celebrating his entry into the business world.

When the waitress showed up at our table with the menus, Donald ordered two glasses of dry white wine, and took the menu from her, as did I.

Once she had departed to fill the drinks order, he leaned across the table and said, 'A lot of siblings wouldn't tell you this, Val, they'd let you go back to Paris in ignorance. But I'm not like that, and whatever you think, I've always loved you. I may not have always liked you, but loved you – yes.'

I stared at him, but made no comment. Let him hang himself, I thought, and sat back in the chair, wondering why he was suddenly making these protestations of love for me.

He said, 'Don't look so suspicious. And *doubting*. I know you think I'm like Mom, but I'm not.'

'Let me go back to Paris in ignorance of *what*?' I demanded.

'Lowell's amazing success. The company's become a gold mine.'

'*Lowell's*?'

He started to laugh. 'Yes, Lowell's. They've had an amazing success in the last ten years, thanks to Mom. The products are in all of the best stores in New York, and across the –'

'What stores?' I asked, leaning closer, now riddled with curiosity.

'The *best* . . . like Bergdorf's, Saks, Barneys in New York, Neiman Marcus – in fact, Lowell's products are distributed across the country. The line has become very popular with women in every city in America. Going to take Europe soon.'

'Those little dinky bottles, the homespun creams and lotions,' I exclaimed, totally taken aback by this news.

'Oh yes, Val, and you shouldn't sound so disparaging about those dinky bottles and homespun creams, as you call them. That's part of the success, according to our mother.'

'What do you mean?' I asked, frowning.

At this moment, the wine materialized, and the waitress asked if we wanted to order. I selected a hamburger medium-rare with French fries, and so did Donald. With the lunch order out of the way, he lifted his glass. 'Cheers,' he said.

'Cheers,' I answered, touching my glass to his. 'So, Donald, tell me more.'

'I was just saying that the dinky bottles, as you call them, are not really so dinky. And they haven't changed much since Amy-Anne started Lowell's. They're actually a modern version of the apothecary jar, in miniature of course, with the glass stopper and the plain printed label. And that's where the homespun bit comes into play. Did you know the labels on the Lowell products haven't really changed in a hundred years, Val?'

'How could I possibly know that?'

'I guess you couldn't, and I didn't either until quite recently.'

'Been doing your research already then, have you?' I asked, trying to curb the sarcasm which frequently crept into my conversation when talking to my brother. But he missed it, as he so often did; or maybe he merely chose to ignore it.

He replied, 'No, I haven't. But Mom sometimes talks to me about business when I go over to dinner, and she was telling me about a Japanese company recently who want to import the products to Japan. And the president of this company told her that Japanese women love the plain old-fashioned apothecary bottles and simple printed labels that merely state the product, its purpose, and give the ingredients.'

'You're kidding me!'

'No, I'm not. It's funny about the Japanese. Do you know, hundreds of thousands of them love Early American furniture?'

'What's that got to do with Lowell's cosmetics, Donald?'

'Nothing, I was merely making an analogy. But it's the old-fashioned apothecary bottle and the old-fashioned label that appeal to millions of women here too. Call it nostalgia, confidence in something that looks homemade, whatever . . . it's part of the secret, Mom says. The old-fashioned packaging apparently works better than ever, and by keeping to the simple bottles and simple labels, she's managed to keep her costs down. It's the same with the products . . . by limiting them she's kept production costs down too.'

'What do you mean when you say *limiting* them? I'm not actually following you,' I said.

'Mom told me that when Dad was alive he wanted her to make a lot of other products . . . lipsticks, eye makeup, nail polish, that sort of stuff. But she wouldn't, she remained faithful to the line created by Amy-Anne. You know, the face, hand and body creams, shampoos and bath products. That decision has played into the success of Lowell's today, because her costs have remained fairly reasonable. Also, she hasn't had to cater to fashion and its changes.' Donald paused, took a big swig of his wine, and finished, 'Where she has spent money is on marketing.'

'How the hell did she suddenly turn this company around?' I exclaimed, and shook my head, totally baffled. 'When we were little there were always money problems, as I recall.'

'Things weren't that bad, were they?' Donald muttered and looked at me questioningly over the rim of his glass.

'I think money *was* very tight at times,' I responded. 'But the only really nasty problem I can remember was when they wanted to let Annie go, and we both became so hysterical that in the end she wasn't fired. But I have a feeling our grandfather paid her salary for a while.'

'Annie loved us, didn't she, Val? She was the best nanny.'

'Yes, she was . . .' I let my sentence trail away,

thinking that without Annie Patterson looking after me from birth I would have probably never survived in that household.

'Anyway, Val, to give you a final definitive answer about Lowell's success today, let's say it's all been in the marketing. Apparently Mom sent it to every top model, every Broadway actress, every movie actress, and every female celebrity she could think of. She had an old-fashioned carpetbag made, filled it with products, and enclosed a handwritten letter on Victorian-style notepaper. It worked, everybody fell for ... the carpetbag, the *dinky* bottle and the *homespun* products, as you just called them.'

'So she's making millions?' I said, grinning at him. 'Is that what you're trying to tell me?'

He nodded. 'She sure is. She has a mail-order catalogue. She's on the Internet. And she has her own Website, and Lowell's has one, too. In about eighteen months, after she's launched the product in Europe and Japan, I think she'll go to Wall Street and do an I.P.O.'

'My God, Donald, our mother's a veritable tycoon, and I never knew it!' I hoped he'd get my sarcasm, but I could tell he hadn't.

'I had no idea either. I've picked up stuff from her from time to time, but Alexis is a financial journalist and she's the one who's filled me in with a lot of information lately.'

'Do you mean in the last week, Donald?' I asked, eyeing him speculatively.

He shook his head, 'No, I don't. I mean ever since Mom got sick, you know, had the first heart attack.'

'Well, congratulations, Donald darling, I think you're going to inherit a great company and be very rich.'

'You really mean that, don't you, Val? I can see you're not leading me on.'

I stared at him and frowned. 'Of course I'm not, why would I?'

He took a deep breath. 'When Mom does the I.P.O. next year, or in the year 2000, Lowell's could bring in between five hundred million to a billion dollars, give or take few hundred thou.'

I gaped at Donald, unable to speak. Taking a deep breath, I said at last, 'I'm gobsmacked, Donald, utterly and completely gobsmacked!'

He laughed, but I think more from the expression on my face than the words that left my mouth. When he stopped laughing, he said, 'But I don't know what gobsmacked means, Val.'

'Smacked in the mouth, in the parlance of the British,' I explained.

III

It was after lunch that Donald broached the subject of seeing our mother. 'Please, Val, let's go and visit her now. Get this worked out properly, before you go back to Paris.'

'Donald, I'll give you the company when I inherit it,

I've already told you that half a dozen times. I don't wish to see her.'

'She said she wanted to see *you* again, to explain something, to come clean with you, I guess. So let's go up to the apartment. And at the same time, maybe you can reiterate your feelings about Lowell's. And me, I mean.'

I looked across the table at him, and saw him very objectively for a split second. He really was a handsome young man, twenty-six and very virile-looking. He has movie-star good looks, I thought, just like our mother. He wasn't so hard to take. If I were honest with myself, I guess I'd always been jealous of him, because she had favoured him above me, and spoiled and petted him. He was a bit devious and gossipy, but not a bad young man, just human, really, like all of us.

I sighed and shook my head, and then I said slowly, 'Donald, you can't imagine what a hardship it is for me to go and see her, really you can't.'

'I guess I can,' he answered swiftly. 'I admit she wasn't always . . . *loving* with you, Val.'

'So, at long last you're *finally* admitting that, Donald.'

'I've always known it,' he said, sounding defensive. 'But we haven't really had a heart-to-heart conversation since we've been grown up, have we?'

'Only too true.'

'Look, I realize what a pain in the ass she can be,' he said, 'and how painful it is for you to see her, but surely it'll help if I come with you.'

'Actually, Donald, what do you want me to say to your mother when we get there?'

'Our mother,' he corrected. 'And I want you to ask her to have some sort of paper drawn up. A paper that says if you want you can give the company to me and that I, a man, can inherit it.'

'You mean a legal document, is that it?'

He nodded. 'Yeah.'

'Don't you trust me?' I asked, swallowing a smile. I was playing with him now, and that wasn't really fair.

'Yeah, sure I do, that's one thing about you, Val, you've always been straight. But don't you think there ought to be a document? Look, God forbid something happens to you in your job, then what? I mean who gets the company?'

'You have a point there,' I said, leaning back in the chair, sipping my coffee. If I got killed covering a war somewhere my mother would *have* to leave the company to Donald. 'You,' I said at last. '*You* would Donald, or rather, your wife.' I paused and looked into the distance, then muttered, 'Gee, I wonder how they work that out when there's a divorce?'

Donald said, 'I guess there's never been one. Maybe we should ask Mom.'

'No,' I said, coming to a decision. 'Let's not ask her anything. Let's go up there to see her, present a united front and explain that we think there should be something in writing about me wanting you to have the company. Just in case I die in the line of duty as a war photographer.'

'Okay,' he said, and looked at me curiously. 'I wonder what it is she wants to explain to you.'

'I don't really need to hear what she has to say, Donald. I'm just going up there to make sure she does right by you.'

'Why? Why do you care about me, Val?' he asked, looking at me intently, frowning.

'Because you're my little brother and I loved you a lot when you were a small boy; and besides, it's your *right*. We're almost in the year 2000 and we've got to move on from a rule made in 1898. It was a good rule, I'm certainly on the side of women, but it needs . . .'

'Updating,' Donald volunteered.

IV

Donald took out his cell phone and called our mother, asked if we could come over, made a date for three-thirty, and then clicked off.

'That's all set,' he said, slipping the phone into his jacket pocket. 'Let's have another coffee.'

'Okay.' I glanced at my watch. 'We do have a little time to waste. So tell me some more about Lowell's.'

'Such as what?'

'Well, you've talked about the packaging and the marketing, but what about the products? I guess they're good, that people do like them.'

He nodded. 'According to Mom, they do, and I guess the success of the company proves that. Alexis loves them; she says the creams are very rich and very effective.'

'You said Lowell's will be launched in Europe. Where exactly?'

'London and Paris to begin with. Mom hasn't really said. Listen, I don't know as much as you think I do. She's never said anything about Lowell's to me in the past, I've only just found things out since she had the heart attack, I told you that. Plus Alexis has filled me in a bit, since she's studied the financial side of all the cosmetic companies for her job.'

'I realize all that, Donald. When we get there I want to get straight to the point with our mother. You know, let's talk about the legal document for you right away. I don't want to start discussing other stuff.'

'I understand. We'll go in and out. And there'll be no discussions, no explanations from her.'

'Correct. I don't want to hear anything at all. And if she starts yammering at me, I won't listen.'

But how wrong I was about that.

V

My mother was still under doctor's orders to take it easy, so she wasn't spending as much time at her office as she usually did.

When we arrived at the Park Avenue apartment the door was opened by a maid in uniform.

'Hi, Florina,' Donald said, nodding to her as he struggled out of his overcoat. 'This is my sister, Miss Valentine Denning.'

The young woman stared at me with interest, smiled, took my coat and said, 'Pleased to meet you, Miss Denning.'

'I'm glad to meet you, Florina.'

A moment later my mother was walking into the foyer, looking staggeringly beautiful in a black wool jumpsuit trimmed with velvet with a large pearl pin on one shoulder. She was wearing very high heels which made her even taller, but then so was I today and I matched her in height.

Her jet-black hair was pulled back in a chignon, and her face looked all cheekbones and eyes, and I wondered unexpectedly how she had ever coped with this amazing beauty. Had it been a burden? Had it ruined her life? I had no idea. It suddenly struck me that I knew so little about this woman who had given birth to me.

Chapter Twenty-Six

1

'Hello, Val . . . Donald . . .' Margot Denning said, and with an airy wave of her hand towards the sitting room, she added, 'Shall we go in there and have tea?' Without waiting for our responses she glided into the room.

I followed her, saying, 'I don't want anything thanks. Donald and I just finished lunch.'

'Nothing for me either, thanks, Mom,' Donald muttered as he trailed after me.

Naturally she went and sat in her usual chair, because she had been sitting there for years. She obviously knew she looked her best in that particular area of the room; certainly the lighting near the fireplace was flattering to her.

I went and took up a position near the fireplace, standing as I generally did, and Donald came and joined me. He was apparently my ally now since we were presumably presenting a united front.

'I'm happy you came, Val,' she murmured, looking directly at me, smiling faintly. 'I told Donald I wanted to explain something –'

'Oh, but I don't want any explanations . . . about anything. I haven't come for that reason. I've come to do the talking not the listening. And I'm going to talk sense about Lowell's and your will.'

She stared at me, frowning. 'We've had that discussion already.'

'But it was not to my satisfaction.'

'There's nothing more to say.'

'There's a lot to say. Donald has told me about Lowell's as it stands today, and the success you've made of it. You're obviously a very clever businesswoman. That's why I can't understand why you cling to some antiquated tradition started a hundred years ago. Donald tells me there's no legal document backing up this tradition, so you can very easily leave the company to him.'

'I can't. A female descendant of Amy-Anne Lowell has to inherit.'

All of a sudden it hit me why she was being so stubborn, and I exclaimed, 'Don't tell me you believe all that crap about bad luck for Lowell's if a woman's not holding the power.' I began to laugh. 'Oh my God, you do!' I went on laughing.

Donald gaped at me. Our mother was poker-faced. I noticed a vein pulsing on her temple. She remained totally silent.

I said, 'Lowell's is no longer the same company

it was. Its structure has changed radically. You're going into worldwide distribution imminently, from what Donald tells me, and next year you're apparently going to do an I.P.O. on Wall Street. You've pushed this dinky little old-fashioned company into the twenty-first century, yet you yourself are still lingering in the past, clinging to an antiquated idea started by the founder.'

'No I'm not!' she protested, her voice rising shrilly.

'Yes, you are. Please get it through your head once and for all. *I don't want your company when you die*. Leave it to Donald, who would love to be involved with it. And he's entitled, as your only son. He should be your heir. And he was always your favourite anyway. Forget about this tradition nonsense, act like the smart businesswoman you apparently are.'

'Is that why you don't want Lowell's?' she asked.

'I'm not following you,' I murmured, but I was. I just wanted to hear what she would have to say.

'I mean because you believe, mistakenly, that I mistreated you as a child?'

'No,' I replied, but I was telling a lie.

'The company is going to be worth millions,' she said suddenly, obviously believing this would influence my decision.

'*Billions*, more than likely, Mother. But I'm still not interested. Thanks, but no thanks.'

'Please, Val, reconsider.'

'I can't.'

'You mean you *won't*,' she snapped in her snooty voice.

'Look, I have a life of my own. I don't want a life you're trying to create for me, suddenly out of the blue, after years of indifference and neglect.'

'You're bearing a grudge . . . how ridiculous when there's so much money involved.'

'I couldn't care less about the money.'

'More fool you!'

I sighed. 'If I said *okay*, I'll take Lowell's, leave it to me, what would it entail? Just out of curiosity, what would you expect of me now? What would you want me to do?'

I felt Donald tense, he was standing so close to me at the fireplace.

My mother sat up straighter in her chair, and studied me for a moment.

I hated this close scrutiny of hers; almost frantically I wished I could escape, get out of her presence. I disliked her intensely, and I now regretted that I had come. I had done so because I wanted to help Donald, who wasn't such a bad guy after all. I thought he was getting the short end of the stick.

My mother said carefully, in that well-modulated, upper-class voice of hers, 'I would expect you to come home, Val, to live in New York. And of course I would want you to work at Lowell's alongside me. I would train you, teach you the business, teach you everything I know. It would give me great pleasure, Val.'

'You've had two heart attacks, unexpected because

you've always been so healthy, and you're young. And so now you feel a bit . . . vulnerable, and it occurs to you that you need . . . a daughter. Is that what all this is about?'

'Don't be ridiculous! I want you to come home because this is where you belong. With me. In the business.'

'This is certainly NOT where I belong,' I almost yelled. Taking a deep breath and clinging to my control, I added, 'We're not getting anywhere. If you won't change your will, I must certainly go and see my lawyer, have some legal document drawn up that protects Donald if something happens to me. After all, I'm a war photojournalist, I could easily be killed when I'm working. I will leave Lowell's to him.'

Donald said, 'Thanks, Val.'

Our mother was silent.

II

Florina came hurrying in with a large tea tray, which certainly curtailed the conversation for a moment or two. She placed it on the mahogany coffee table in front of the sofa and said to my mother, 'Shall I pour, Mrs Denning?'

'No, no, we can manage, Florina. Thank you.'

Florina hurried out.

'No tea for me,' I said. 'I'm leaving.' I walked towards the door.

Donald called, 'Wait for me, Val.'

'I'm in a hurry,' I responded, but I paused in the doorway and turned. 'Goodbye, Mother. So long, Donald. I'll see you around.'

'No, wait, Val. I'll only be a second.' Donald went to our mother, pecked her on the cheek. 'I'll talk to you later, Mom.'

I was halfway across the entrance foyer, heading for the front door, when she said, 'But I want to explain!'

'I don't need an explanation. Not any more,' I replied without turning around.

'Don't you want to know why . . . I was never able to love you?' my mother asked.

This stopped me in my tracks. And of course her words were irresistible.

Very slowly, I walked back to the sitting room, stood in the doorway, leaning against the door jamb. My eyes did not leave her face.

III

'Come in and sit down, Val. And I think you, Donald, should leave. This is private.'

'Donald stays,' I snapped.

'Yes, I'm staying,' my brother said, surprising me, since he'd never argued with her in the past, or defied her.

'I'll stand, if you don't mind,' I said. 'I'm sure this isn't going to take long.'

Donald joined me by the fireplace. He stood close to me and reached out, took hold of my hand, as he had when we were small.

How often we had been brought to task for something or other in this very room. We had always stood in this exact spot and our mother had always seated herself in that antique French chair.

But today I was not afraid of her. And I was certain that Donald wasn't either.

Together, showing our united front, we waited for her to speak.

IV

'This really doesn't have anything to do with Donald,' she said, addressing me directly. 'I *do* think it would be better if we were alone, Val. This is very private.'

'No way Donald leaves. He stays.'

Donald said, 'I sure do, Mom,' and squeezed my hand.

Margot Denning didn't say anything for a very long moment. She simply sat bolt upright in the chair, her posture superb, her head held high, remote, her regality intact.

Finally, she said, 'It all began a long time ago, when I was very young, just a girl . . .' She stopped and for a moment I thought she was going to burst into tears, but she steadied herself, gripped the arms of the French chair.

If I hadn't known better, I would have said she was suddenly emotional. But this wasn't possible; she had ice water in her veins.

Because I so disliked her, I said, 'A very short story indeed. Well, so long, I'm off.' I began to move towards the door.

'No, no, I was just . . . trying to formulate the words . . . to get things in order in my mind, Val. I was a girl, just seventeen, when I met a young man. His name was Vincent Landau and I fell in love with him, and he with me. Unfortunately, my mother did not approve of him, and his parents did not approve of me. We were from different worlds you see. And I –'

'Why didn't your mother approve?' I asked, curiosity getting the better of me.

'Because he was Jewish.'

'And his parents disapproved because you were a gentile? Is that it?'

'Yes, but it was more than that. The Landaus were extremely rich, they owned a private bank, and they were aiming high for Vincent. They thought he should marry someone of his own ilk, someone in society. I was a nobody, as far as they were concerned.'

She paused again and Donald said, 'So what happened, Mom?'

'Vincent was sent away to Europe; he was a few years older than me, and his father sent him to work in the Berlin branch of the family bank. Eventually – Two years later Vincent came back to New York, and sought me out immediately. We began to see each other in secret, and not long after we had resumed our relationship I discovered I was pregnant. I was nineteen. I knew if I told my mother she would push me into having an abortion, and so I didn't tell her I was pregnant until it was too late to do anything. Vincent was worried about his parents' reaction, but at the same time he was pleased. He hoped that once they met me and knew I was having his child, they would relent, accept me, allow him to marry me.'

She paused, took a deep breath and smoothed her hand over her hair.

I said, 'But they didn't.'

'That is correct. In fact, they were more furious with him than ever, and did everything to break us up.'

'Did they succeed?' Donald asked.

'Oh yes, they did.'

'And you miscarried,' I said.

'No, I didn't,' she answered with a small frown.

'The baby was born dead then?' I asked.

'No, the baby wasn't born dead,' she replied. 'She was a beautiful little girl. Perfect in every way. But my mother was beside herself, bitter about Vincent's behaviour, because she thought he should have defied his parents and married me. She didn't know how to cope, and she was also angry and frustrated. Here was I, not quite twenty, and the mother of an illegitimate child.'

I began to feel cold inside and I became fearful. I didn't want to hear any more, but I knew I couldn't stop the flow of words from her mouth. I was frozen to the spot, unable to leave.

Donald was saying, 'So what happened, what did you do?'

We stood there together, he and I, holding hands, united for a short while, protective of each other, and I sensed that Donald was as apprehensive as I was. I realized I didn't want to hear the rest because I knew I wasn't going to like it.

She said, 'I settled down to being a mother. Vincent came to see me all the time. He loved us both so much, he loved little Anjelica. She was such a beautiful baby. So perfect. His presence kept my mother calm for a while, and she began to believe we would ultimately marry, and then out of the blue Vincent was sent to the Paris branch of the Landau bank. Soon after he left New York his engagement to the socialite Marguerite Shiff was announced in *The New York Times*. I called him up in Paris and he admitted he'd been forced into the engagement.

'My mother made me put Anjelica up for adoption, and I had to do as she said, I had no alternative. I never saw my baby again. It broke my heart. Vincent came back to New York, and we did meet a few times, but we knew it was an impossible situation, quite untenable. So we said our goodbyes. He killed himself a week before his marriage. He drove to his family's country estate, into the garage, turned on the ignition, and died of carbon-monoxide poisoning.'

'So you never saw your baby again, Mother, and

your lover killed himself. But what does all this have to do with me?' I asked. I was icy inside now, very fearful.

'Please let me finish.'

'All right,' I responded, looking across at her. I thought she seemed pale all of a sudden and her expression was stark, her mouth taut. It was apparent she was having difficulty with this.

'I met your father several years later, and we were married. He was very kind to me, good to me, but I could never love him. At least, not in the way he wanted to be loved, not with the same passion I had loved Vincent Landau.'

'And you couldn't love me either, is that it?' I exclaimed in a cold and angry voice. 'Is that what you're leading up to?'

'I tried, Val, I really did try to love you. But whenever I looked at you, I thought of little Anjelica and my guilt overwhelmed me. I couldn't bear to think of her being out there without me, living with another family, being brought up by another woman. Losing Anjelica and Vincent shattered me completely, my heart was broken and I knew it would always be broken. I lived in a kind of netherworld for years. I was like a zombie in some ways, I suppose. I thought of Anjelica every day. She was never far from my thoughts. When Donald was born it was different, because he was a boy.'

I was gaping at her, stunned, and so was Donald. Neither of us spoke.

'I'm sorry,' she said at last. 'So sorry . . .'

'SORRY,' I screamed at her, losing it completely. 'Is that all you can say after thirty-one years of torture? *SORRY*. Well, thanks a lot, *Mother*. Thanks for the indifference, the injustice, the neglect, and that monumental lack of love and caring. I had a miserable, tormented childhood because of you! Oh, how you made me suffer, and all because of your selfishness, and your ridiculous self-involvement.' I was shaking with rage, and it took all of my self-control not to rush at her and strike her. 'You talk about your broken heart, but what about mine? You broke my heart, Mother, you punished me because of your mistakes. My God, you're monstrous, wicked! No, more than wicked, it goes beyond that . . . you are evil!'

V

Margot Denning was gaping at me, as stunned and devastated as I was. Her face was white, stricken, but I did not care. I had no sympathy for her. How could I? She had ruined my childhood and almost ruined my life, and if it had not been for Annie Patterson, our nanny, and my Denning grandparents, God knows how I would have ended up. In a straitjacket, perhaps. Or worse, a coffin.

To deny maternal love to your own child, an innocent child, was cruel, inhuman, and unconscionable, and that was what she had done to me. I felt the tears rising in my throat, pricking behind my eyes, but I pushed them back. I was damned if I was going to let *her* see me cry.

Drawing myself up, I said, 'And somehow, now, because you need me, you think you can lure me back into your orbit, into your world. Well, tough luck, Margot. I'm not buying your brand of shit today. As for Lowell's, if you don't want Donald to have it, who *is* entitled by the way, I suggest you give it to that daughter you gave away so long ago. Little Anjelica. If you can find her after all these years.'

VI

Donald's face was crumpled up, as if he were going to cry, and he reached for me protectively, and said, 'Val, please let me –'

'No, I don't need help, I'm fine,' I cried, and shook free of him, stepped away, stepped to one side.

Margot Denning was frozen in place like a marble statue in the chair, her face as white as bleached bone, so stark-looking her cheekbones appeared more prominent than ever, as though they were protruding from her face. She cried, 'Val, I –'

'Don't say a word to me!' I screamed. 'You've said and done enough these past thirty-one years.' I was shaking all over and my heart was hammering in my chest I was so outraged. I knew I was in danger of doing something violent if I didn't escape this room.

'You are a reprehensible and destructive woman,' I shrieked at her. 'And when I think of my painful childhood, of the cruelty you inflicted on me by refusing to love me, to acknowledge my existence, I only have this to say to you: I hope you rot in hell, Margot Denning.'

I stumbled out of the room blindly, my body wracked by the terrible pain and anguish I'd bottled up for years.

Donald came rushing after me, and got into the lift with me. As we rode down together he endeavoured to comfort me, to calm me, without any success. I just couldn't stop shaking and I felt nauseous, ready to vomit.

Donald must have retrieved our coats when he ran out of the apartment, and he wrapped mine around me when we got out onto Park Avenue. As he shrugged into his, he hailed a cab and bundled me into it, gave the Beekman Place address.

Riding across town, edging through the rush-hour traffic, I clung to him, buried my face against his shoulder, praying this awful shaking and feeling of sickness would go away.

But it didn't, and it took all of my self-control not to throw up all over my brother. Donald kept trying to talk to me, to sympathize, to soothe me, but I just couldn't speak, and I refused to cry, although hot tears were very near the surface.

Once we arrived at the apartment building in Beekman Place Donald helped me out, paid off the cab, and put an arm around me as he manoeuvred me across the lobby and into the lift.

At the front door of the apartment I began to fumble in my bag for the keys, but I wasn't doing too well, and Donald took the bag away from me, found my keys, and opened the front door.

With Donald still helping me, both his arms around me, we went into the apartment together.

Jake must have heard us, and came out of the study, exclaiming, 'Hi, where've you been –' But the words died on his lips when he saw me half crumpled over, clinging to Donald as if my life depended on it.

'My God! Val, what's wrong? Are you sick, darling?' he cried, rushing into the entrance foyer.

Letting go of Donald at last, I moved forward and stumbled into Jake's arms, filling with relief as I did. He looked into my stricken face, and cried again, 'You're as white as a sheet, what is it?'

I stared back at him, struck dumb, unable to utter a word.

Looking over my head, he asked my brother, 'Donald, what the hell's wrong? What happened to Val?'

'Let's get her inside, let's sit down,' Donald muttered and at once Jake did as he asked, half leading, half carrying me into the study. I collapsed on the sofa and Jake sat down next to me, after pulling off my coat and throwing it to one side. He wrapped his arms around me again.

'Come on, let's have it, Donald! Why is Val in this terrible state?'

Donald sat down in the chair opposite and began to tell him.

And I began to weep, finally letting go, now that I was safe with Jake.

VII

I wept all through Donald's excruciating narrative, desperately holding onto Jake, clinging to him. As he listened to Donald he stroked my hair, tightened his grip on me, but did not interrupt my brother with questions. He simply listened and digested everything.

When Donald finished, Jake exclaimed in an angry voice, 'I've never heard anything so disgusting, so despicable in my entire life. It's monstrous, and your mother must be a monster. Or mentally ill.'

'A monster,' I mumbled through my tears.

'And mentally ill in certain ways,' Donald ventured.

Unexpectedly I began to sob brokenly, and I couldn't control myself. I cried for a very long time, sobbing out the tears that had been filling me up for years. Ever since the day I had been born, in fact. That's how long she had punished me for not being Anjelica.

Part Three

A Question of Trust

Chapter Twenty-Seven

I

PARIS, NOVEMBER

'I'm glad Françoise has settled in so well with Fiona,' I said to Mike Carter, leaning back in the chair, crossing my legs.

'I am too, and there's absolutely no way Olivier can find her, I'm convinced of that,' Mike responded, looking at me intently across his desk.

'I agree, I'm sure she's safe. It was a good idea of yours, to charter a private plane.'

'It was Fiona's idea, not mine, and she arranged everything with a local charter company. Her point was, private plane, no manifest, no way Françoise could be traced through the airlines. And it was a point well taken, Val. And much appreciated by me. Thanks for introducing Fiona.'

Mike rose, walked across his office at Gemstar and closed the door, then returned to his desk. He was a big burly man with a barrel chest and thick dark hair tinged with grey at the sides. His craggy, masculine face was open, honest and kind, reflecting his character, and his dark eyes were full of humour and wisdom. Intelligent, hard-working and supremely loyal, he was the best boss I'd ever had, and a truly good friend.

He said, 'As I told you on the phone, I flew over with her –'

'Was that wise?' I interjected, frowning. 'What if Olivier has a PI tracking your movements?'

Mike let out a belly laugh. 'You think of everything, Val. And I do too, I must confess. I took a circuitous route to Le Bourget, and travelled alone. So did Françoise, also alone. I doubt anyone could have followed us.'

'And Fiona welcomed you with open arms, from what you and Françoise have told me.'

He nodded. 'She's a terrific gal, and we got on well; more importantly, she took Françoise under her wing, and I think it's all working out very well. Françoise loves decorating and designing, and she's really been able to make inroads on the restaurant, it's going to be finished in record time. Fiona wants to open it before the Christmas holidays.'

'That's great, and I'm so relieved Françoise is okay. Listen, I hate to bring Olivier up, but what's happening with *him*? Any information?'

'A bit, yes. Apparently he's working on a big murder case in Marseilles, to do with drug dealers and the worst bunch of criminals around, the scum of the earth, in fact. So that's keeping him busy, since he *is* the crack homicide cop down there. The lawyer I hired for Françoise has been in touch with him, and so Olivier knows she's taken out a restraining order, filed for divorce and moved out of Paris. I think he'd like to get his hands on her if he could, and if he knew where to look. But as I said, he's really caught up in that case, and he's vital to the investigation, seemingly. Therefore his bosses are not going to let him off the hook all that easily, so that he can go searching the world for his estranged wife. I've been in touch with Armand and Simone, and they haven't heard a peep out of him or seen him lately. They know nothing about him, other than that he's working on the murder case. There's been a helluva lot of press coverage about the case, and he's always mentioned, and in glowing terms, I might add.'

'I'm presuming Armand and Simone have no idea where Françoise is staying.'

He grinned. 'In a pig's eye they don't! What do you think I am, honey, stooopid?'

I started to laugh. 'Oh, Mike, you're a card! Anyway, let's keep our fingers crossed, let's hope he stays tied up with the murder case, that he's far too preoccupied with it to hunt down Françoise.'

'From your mouth to God's ears, honey,' Mike replied, and shuffled the papers on his desk, glanced down at them, then looked up, squinting in the sunlight.

'No wars,' he said, 'nothing dangerous, that's what

you told me when you got back two weeks ago. This rule still holding, Val?'

'Absolutely, Mike. Very honestly, I'm burnt out. And I don't want to risk my life for a picture any more, nor do I want to go out of town on a job.'

'Unless it's with Jake, right?'

'That's correct. I do want to go back to work now, Mike, take on some assignments, providing they're interesting, and local.' I gave him a long look and went on, 'I'm tired of all the junk that's flung around in war, Michael. Tired of all the lies, all the deceit, all the nonsense that goes on with the military and the politicians. And on both sides. I've seen too much. Too much death, too much destruction.' I sighed heavily, shook my head wearily. 'Frankly, I don't think I could take it any more. And I *know* I don't want to experience that awful fear, the panic inside, that sick feeling when I have to look at the dead, the dying, and the mutilated. Or deal with those who are alive but frightened out of their wits, so terrified they're incapable of saving themselves.

'You know, Mike, there's nothing glorious about seeing the dead in their Sunday clothes, killed by surprise, after a special lunch or a religious service, or a day's outing with the family. And I'm weary of picking my way through rubble and broken glass, mud and blood and . . . dead bodies. I suppose what I'm trying to say is that the devastation of war has devastated me.'

Mike was silent for a moment, and then he said

quietly, in a serious voice, 'I know exactly what you mean, Val. And you *are* burnt out. That doesn't surprise me, either. You've covered too many wars already in your young life, and it's time for a change. So –' He paused, shuffled through the papers on his desk once more, and said, 'I think this story might appeal to you . . .'

'What is it?'

'It's a fashion shoot, and no, don't pull a face like that. This could be interesting. Behind the scenes of Paris haute couture, mainly three houses . . . Balmain, Lacroix and Givenchy. The designing and preparation of the Summer Collection for 1999. It's got glamour, beauty, and intriguing people. You could make it into something interesting, Val, and very easily. It has potential, and it can be a lot more than just a few pretty pictures.'

'I'll think about it. Anything else?'

'Well, I am hoping that the famous painter will let us shoot his big canvases in Mexico, but that's a few months off.'

'Alexander St Just Stevens? Who never returned my calls. I don't think so, and what kind of a name is that anyway?'

'It doesn't matter what the guy's called, Val, he's a genius,' Mike said, and laughed at my expression. He went on, 'I have a movie shoot which you could do with your eyes closed. And incidentally, before I forget to ask, how's the book coming along?'

'Wonderfully, Mike!' I exclaimed. 'Jake and I put

quite a lot of effort into the selection of the pictures in New York, and he's been working on it in Paris for the last few weeks. He's had time, actually, because he's not been out in the field.'

'Oh hell, that's right! Jacques is still in hospital. How's he doing?'

'Really great, thanks. His broken limbs are mending, thank God, and the doctors at the hospital have been treating him for his heart. He's going to be fine, but he's going to have to take it easy. He'll never go out in the field again, and he was hankering after that. It's an office job, and *permanently*, for Jacques Foucher, I'm afraid.'

'So Jake's been running the agency, has he?' Mike asked, and chuckled. 'I bet that's not pleased him too much.'

'Not really. On the other hand, he has had time to work on the book.'

I got up. 'I won't keep you, Mike, I know what kind of day you have, and listen, I'll do the haute couture shoot. Why not? Anyway, I've got to earn a living, you know.'

'Don't we all, Val.'

I grinned at him, went to the door, paused. 'Listen, let me know when you want to come to dinner, and I'll cook up a storm for the three of us.'

His face lit up, and he asked eagerly, like a kid: 'Would you make a pot roast? A real American pot roast, Val?'

'Sure I would, just name the night, and we're all

set.' I stepped into the corridor, then turned, stuck my head through the door, and added, 'And for dessert it'll be homemade apple pie and ice cream. How about that?'

He grinned and gave me the thumbs-up sign.

II

After the meeting at Gemstar with Mike, I went home to my apartment on the Left Bank.

By the time I got back to the Rue Bonaparte, Janine had gone for the day, but she had left the place as immaculate as always, gleaming brightly and filled with fresh flowers.

The whole apartment smelled faintly of beeswax, lemons, potpourri overlaid with the scent of cinnamon, and pine cones, a mingling of fragrances that evoked autumn to me.

I had done the shopping earlier, and I went immediately into the kitchen to start dinner. I had always liked clay-pot cooking, and since it was such a cold, damp day I had decided earlier to make my version of *poulet grandmère*, using a clay pot called a Römertopf. My chicken casserole was based on a whole chicken, along with a melange of winter vegetables such as carrots, parsnips, turnips, onions, leeks, mushrooms, and a handful of chopped celery. All of these went into the pot with the chicken, which I had left in the refrigerator marinating in chicken stock, tomato juice and a mixture of herbs when I had gone to Gemstar.

As I prepared the vegetables for the casserole I thought of the last couple of weeks since our return to Paris. Once again, Jake and I had fallen into a pleasant routine, which worked for us, since we were both addicted to order. Every day we worked on *Flowers of War* because we had to meet a December deadline for the publisher. My dining room had always doubled as an office, with a big English partner's desk in the bay window, and my filing boxes hidden inside an antique armoire set against an end wall.

And so when Jake went off to his photo agency every morning, I settled down to complete the captions and edit the main body of text. Jake struggled with this every day at the office, or at night at the apartment, and he was making excellent progress. Once he was relatively satisfied with the pages he had written, he passed them to me for editing and polishing.

When Jake had been a Rhodes scholar at Oxford he had majored in European history, and he was much better educated than I was, and certainly better equipped to write the book since he was a historian. But this aside, the book was his idea and I felt he should be ultimately responsible for the text, that it should reflect his point of view.

The good thing was that we were working well together on this project, just as we did out in the field when we covered wars. We were making great progress, beginning to see the light of day; the book would be finished sooner than expected, and we now hoped to accept Fiona's invitation to go to Yorkshire for Christmas.

Jake was living at my apartment with me, although he made frequent trips to his own place, to check things out, collect his mail and bring back fresh clothes.

In the beginning, when we first returned from New York, he had been concerned that Olivier might be loitering about, lurking near my place looking for Françoise. And even though Janine had assured us things had been quiet in my absence, he insisted on moving in. I was glad he had; I certainly didn't argue. His presence pleased me, and we quickly settled into that pattern of normalcy, of domesticity which I craved, needed to share with him.

With all of the vegetables now ready, I placed the chicken in the clay pot, added the thick, herb-flavoured stock and the vegetables, then put the pot in the cold oven, a necessity for clay-pot cooking. I turned the oven on and went into the dining room to set the table. Once this chore was finished, I hurried into the living room; after turning on the lamps, I found a box of matches and lit the fire which Janine had left ready, the grate filled with paper, wood chips and logs. It was already growing dark outside and it had started to rain. To my way of thinking there was nothing more welcoming and cheerful than a roaring fire on a night like this. Jake would appreciate it, I knew that.

How nice everything looks, I thought, as I sat down on the sofa, enjoying my surroundings which had been so lovingly created by my grandfather. And in this moment of quietness in my busy day it was not long before my thoughts turned to Margot Denning.

III

After the revealing confrontation with my mother, I had bottled it all up again – the rage, the hurt, the anguish. I had done so in order to survive.

But there were times when a pall hung over me, and I continued to be haunted by my disturbed past, by the terrible injustice meted out to me by that woman who called herself my mother.

My childhood had been a tragedy, that was the only word for it. How sick she had been and probably still was . . . unable to love me because of her love for the illegitimate daughter she had given away, had abandoned to her own fate. She had been saddled with a guilt that burdened her down, a guilt that ultimately must have ruined her life. Because it became a morbid and obsessive guilt which dominated her and submerged all rational thought. I had come to believe that Margot Denning *was* irrational, amongst other things.

I wondered if she had ever tried to find that abandoned child, Anjelica. And I also wondered about *her*, wondered what had happened to her, and where she was today. Somewhere out there I had a half-sister, a sister who had probably had as bad a childhood as I, given the terrors of this lousy world we lived in.

I had discussed some of these thoughts with Jake but I really tried hard not to burden him with my pain. Anyway, there really was nothing anyone could say to give me comfort, or help alleviate the agony I experienced at times.

Nor could I simply stick a band-aid on my psychic wounds and hope they would eventually heal. They wouldn't, at least not all that easily, and not for a long time. But now that I had a grasp of the truth at long last perhaps I could do something to heal myself. I hoped I could.

The only thing I had not asked my mother during our confrontation in New York had to do with my father. And it was actually a two-fold question – had he known about her involvement with Vincent Landau and her illegitimate child? And why had he condoned her cruel behaviour towards me when I was a child?

Troubled and perplexed, I had finally called her up before leaving New York, and she had immediately come to the phone to speak to me. No doubt she thought I had changed my mind about Lowell's.

When I launched into the questions about my father she had obviously been taken aback momentarily. There was a silence before she had finally answered in a clipped tone, 'No, I never told your father about Vincent and Anjelica. What was the point? That part of my life was over, finished.'

I had then posed the most pertinent question of all. Why had my father followed her lead, and virtually ignored me all of my life until the day he had died?

Her answer had flowed so easily down the wire, she hadn't even had to think about it. 'Peter didn't want children, he believed they would get in the way of our relationship. He wanted me all to himself, you see. I suppose he resented you, and Donald too, even though you were both fathered by him. He thought you were a nuisance. And I know for an absolute certainty that he was jealous of you.'

'Jealous!' I had retorted. 'That's a laugh under the circumstances. And tell me, why did you bother to have kids at all?' I knew the answer before she spoke.

'For Lowell's, of course. I needed an heir. Or perhaps I should say an *heiress*.'

I had hung up.

Who could deal with a woman like that? Later that morning, when I had related everything to Muffie over our farewell lunch at Le Cirque, she had been as upset and as angry as I was myself.

But there were moments when I dwelt on Margot Denning, as I was doing now, trying to fathom her out, to understand her, as I struggled to slay the demons of my blighted childhood. And in the process I hoped I could help myself and my mental health.

On the surface I was calm, controlled, and functioning very well on a daily basis. But I was aware that I was needy in a variety of ways. I was still insecure about Jake, afraid of losing him, and I craved his nurturing. And sometimes I was assaulted by a terrible panic that something awful would happen to him and I would be left alone. And on those days I asked myself if I should visit a psychiatrist. But I kept changing my mind about that, strangely ambivalent about taking this step. On the whole, I did manage to cope, and so I never did go to a doctor for help.

IV

My brother and I had talked about Peter Denning before I had left for Paris, and Donald had said right from the outset that he had not been a normal father. 'No Little League for me, or any of that other stuff!' Donald exclaimed. 'Have you forgotten? We didn't do anything together, none of those typical father-son activities. Oh, no siree. And listen, don't you remember, they even left us to our own devices with Annie when we went on holiday. She used to call them "the lovebirds" and we'd laugh about them.'

'You're right, I'd forgotten. But your mother fussed about you, Donald. She was always singing your praises and listing your virtues.'

He was quiet for a moment, looking somewhat abashed, and then he had agreed. 'That's true, Val, she did do that,' he had answered in a quiet voice.

Donald and I had grown closer during my visit to New York, and he was pleased that Jake and I had taken to his fiancée, Alexis. She was a nice young woman and very pretty, but most importantly, she was clever and street-smart. Jake and I both agreed on that, and we believed that Donald had made a good choice for himself.

Ever since my return to Paris, my brother had stayed in touch with me, and I was beginning to realize this was not merely out of self-interest on his part. In fact, Donald had more than proved that he cared for me. I would never forget how well he had looked after me when I had fled our mother's apartment the day of the row. This *rapprochement* pleased me, and I was glad we had a normal relationship at long last.

Chapter Twenty-Eight

I

YORKSHIRE, DECEMBER

'We get quite a lot of tourists in the summer and autumn, and even in the winter,' David Ingham told me as we walked together down a narrow cobbled street, doing some last-minute Christmas shopping together.

'I can well imagine why,' I answered, smiling at him. 'This is magnificent country. I don't think I've ever seen anywhere like it.' As I spoke I lifted my eyes to the higher moors which rose up above the quaint little town of Middleham in a grand and majestic sweep. 'I went for a walk with Françoise yesterday and I couldn't get over it . . . the country is so beautiful in its starkness, in its emptiness.'

'Aye, by gum, it is, lass!' David responded and then immediately began to laugh.

'What is it?'

'I can see you eyeing me again, Val, wondering

about my accent. But it always happens to me when I get back here. I sort of lapse into Yorkshire talk.'

I laughed with him, and remarked, 'But at least I can understand *you*. When Fiona and I were out shopping I needed a translator in some of the food shops, especially the butcher's. Yorkshire dialect is a bit odd, isn't it?'

He nodded. 'Aye, it is, and even those who have been brought up here, like me, can't always make out what some of the dalesmen are saying. And you're correct about the countryside. Coverdale is probably the most beautiful of all the Yorkshire dales. Did you get some nice pictures yesterday?'

'I did, especially of Middleham Low Moor and those steep, bare hills beyond. It's very bleak country indeed, but breathtaking. I also got some great shots of the castle ruins.'

'I'm hoping it snows,' David said. 'You'll be amazed how the moors look then, like a giant white patchwork quilt because of the higgledy-piggledy drystone walls. Their distinct patterns look like seams on a quilt. And the castle ruins are eerily beautiful.'

'I can't wait for Jake to get here, to see this place. He's going to fall in love with Yorkshire, just as I have, and with Fiona's house.' Glancing at David, I squinted in the bright morning sunlight, and murmured, 'That's a strange name, isn't it . . . *Ure* House?'

'It does sound a bit peculiar, I'll grant you that, although not to the locals. You see, the river Ure runs through here, which is obviously how it got its name in the first place. It was built at the turn of the century, and it's always been called Ure House, and I think Fiona felt a little funny about changing the name. Superstitious, I suspect.'

'She's done a fabulous job with the decoration, David.'

'Hasn't she just!' he agreed, sounding proud. 'And Françoise has really helped to pull the restaurant together. Pig on the Roof has acquired a bit of Continental charm, I must admit, but we all love her touches, Frenchified though they might be.'

'So do I. And listen, thanks for all you've done, David. You and Fiona. She's so much calmer than when she stayed with me in Paris.'

'She's doing fine, although I have a feeling she gets nervous from time to time about that husband of hers.'

'Jake might have some news when he gets here tomorrow. He was planning on calling her parents. He's always been quite close to Simone.'

'Not from his office, I hope!' David exclaimed sharply, glancing at me.

'No, from a pay phone. I just hope that Olivier hasn't got a private investigator watching Mike, or me and Jake for that matter.'

'That gets to be very expensive, so I doubt it,' David reassured me. 'And from what she's told us about him, he sounds like a conceited bugger. He more than likely thinks he can do better than anybody else, when the time is right. I understand he's still caught up in that murder investigation.'

'He is, according to the French newspapers.'

'Anyway, don't worry about investigators. I doubt there are any on your tail, as I just said, and there's been no one snooping around here. Also, Jake and Mike are coming by private plane to Yeadon, which is the best way, the safest, in my opinion.'

'I guess I sort of took a chance,' I muttered, frowning to myself. 'But at least I didn't fly. Thank God for the train.'

'Now, shall we go in here?' David suggested, and explained, 'I want to get a couple of extra gifts.' As he was speaking he pushed open the door of a shop that had a collection of carved wooden sheep in the window. 'Best place for slippers,' he added as he bundled me inside.

He was right about that, I soon realized, as I browsed around the shop. It was a boutique really, and it specialized in a variety of items made from sheep's wool. Most of all I liked the slippers David had mentioned. Each pair had been handmade and hand sewn from sheep shearings, the hide turned on the outside, the fluffy white wool on the inside.

I immediately bought a pair for Jake and Mike's two daughters, who were flying in tomorrow with their father and Jake. I knew that Lisa and Joy would love them, and that the Fair Isle sweaters which were on display would also appeal to the girls. After a short discussion with the sales lady, I settled on medium-size sweaters for the two teenagers, who were fourteen and twelve. Not sure of what else I might need at the last moment, I finally took a couple of lovely hand-knitted scarves, two more pairs of slippers, a knitted vest which I suddenly spotted for Jake, and a heavy cream-coloured fisherman's knit sweater for Mike. I had brought gifts for Françoise, Fiona, David and his son Noel from Paris; perfume and silk scarves for the women, Hermès ties for the men, Jake and Mike included.

II

Armed with our shopping bags full of gifts, we walked back to Ure House at a steady pace, chatting in a desultory fashion as we walked.

David, who was full of folklore, local legend and genuine history, kept me well entertained as he spoke about Middleham and its historic and illustrious past, when the castle had been the stronghold of that great feudal baron Richard Neville, the Earl of Warwick.

'And what a man he was,' David told me. 'Handsome, persuasive, rich, charming, brave and courageous. And powerful. At one moment in his life, and in the history of England, he was the most powerful man in the land. The cousin of Edward IV, who was Edward Plantagenet of the House of York. The prized White Rose of York, a true prince of the blood and one of England's greatest kings. Thanks to Richard Neville, who put him on the throne of England and brought an end to the Wars of the

Roses, and ruled the land, the real power behind the throne.

'And here he lived at Middleham Castle, known in those days as the Windsor of the north, and it was at the castle that he raised Richard of York, who married Neville's daughter, and also became, for a short while, Richard III of England.'

'Jake will love all this historical stuff,' I exclaimed. 'I find it fascinating myself, and Jake will just eat it up.'

David said, 'I shall be eternally grateful to Jake, you know, Val.'

'Oh, why?' I asked, raising a brow, glancing at him.

'Because he spoke the truth and was very straightforward with Fiona in New York. It did her good, I'll tell you that. We're going to get married in the New Year. I wanted to do it immediately after we got back from New York, but she was a bit reluctant. We even talked about tying the knot at Christmas, but changed our minds because we knew we would open Pig on the Roof on December fifteenth. I've taken a couple of weeks off from my job in order to help out, and it's going very smoothly so far. Much to our delight we've done record business.'

'So Fiona told me, and listen, congratulations . . . about getting married I mean.'

'Thanks, Val.' He came to a halt and stood looking at me.

I also stopped walking and stared back at him. 'What is it, David?'

'What about you and Jake? When are you two going to get married?'

I shook my head. 'I don't know. Jake hasn't asked me.'

'More fool he! Such a grand lass like you, he'd better not leave you hanging around too long, somebody else'll snatch you up.'

'That's not likely, David,' I answered swiftly, and laughed as we set off walking again.

'What, a gorgeous lass like you! Don't be daft, Val!'

III

Ure House stood a little up the hill from the centre of the picturesque little town, nestled in the fold of the lower moors. The higher undulating moorland swept around it like a giant Elizabethan ruff, just touching the edge of the sky which was a lucid blue this morning and scattered with wispy clouds.

But how easily these Northern skies could change, I had discovered after only being here for two days. When the thunderheads blew in from the sea coast of East Yorkshire the sky turned black as night and looked eerily lit as if from behind. And the fierce and icy winds brought sleet and rain from the North Sea and a decided change in the temperature.

Ure House was set back from the road on a patch of green grass, with a semi-circle of trees growing behind it. The house was surrounded by a low wall made of local grey stone, and a paved stone path, cut through a neat front lawn, stopped at the front door.

Beautifully proportioned, the house was built of a different grey stone, which Fiona had explained came from the ruins of Middleham Castle. At least the stones on the front façade of the house. Low and rambling, it had a sloping slate roof, many windows, tall chimneys and a door made of heavy oak painted white and trimmed with black wrought-iron hinges.

When I first saw it two days before I had thought at once of my grandfather. He would have loved Ure House because it was ideally suited to the moorland landscape, designed to blend into those bleak implacable moors, and yet able to stand on its own without being humbled by the breathtaking scenery. The architecture was somewhat similar to the stone houses of the Cotswolds which my grandparents had both loved, as did I.

As we walked up the path together, the door suddenly sprang open and Fiona stood there, smiling at us cheerfully, her fiery halo of red hair brought even more into focus by the emerald-green twinset she was wearing with her tailored grey slacks.

'You two look as if you've bought up the whole town!' she cried, eyeing our packages and then coming forward to help us.

'Val raided the sheep boutique,' David told her, grinning.

'And so did you, it seems, my lad,' Fiona shot back. 'But I'm glad to see you've both been supporting the local industry.' She glanced at me and added, 'The one thing they've got in Yorkshire is a lot of sheep. Now, you both look as if you could do with a wee drop of something. Soup or a drink, which will it be?' she asked as we trooped into the front entrance hall. It was warm, welcoming with its stone floor, terra-cotta-coloured walls and moss-green velvet draperies at the windows.

Although I didn't like to drink much at lunch time, I said, 'I wouldn't mind one of those Bloody Marys you make, David. They're so delicious. And you can't even taste the vodka.'

He laughed good-naturedly and said, 'Am I being accused of stinginess with the vodka, Val? Oh dear, that's not good.'

I began to laugh too, and explained, 'No, not at all. I'm not a big vodka drinker and what I meant was that you put in all those wonderful spices, and I don't notice the taste of the alcohol.'

After hanging up my coat and his own, he and I followed Fiona who had walked on into the living room. This was a long room with four windows which looked out onto the moors, and a huge stone fireplace was built at one end. A highly polished wood floor was covered with a large cream rug patterned with green-and-black scrolls, and this picked up the colour of the green-and-black striped silk draperies at the windows.

Thc walls had been painted a funny green, which Françoise had informed me was called *Eau de Nil*, literally Water of the Nile, created by putting a lot of grey into the pale-green paint. I had discovered that Françoise was a fund of information about design and decoration, and had quickly come to understand how useful she must have been to Fiona with the decor of Pig on the Roof.

The room was comfortable yet it had elegance without being overly pretentious. Two overstuffed cream sofas faced each other near the fireplace, and antique tables, brass lamps and several good paintings completed the setting.

David went out to the small bar that opened off one end of the living room to mix Bloody Marys for us all, and Fiona and I moved towards the fireplace. I sat down in one of the armchairs, and she went and stood with her back to the fireplace.

After a moment, she said, 'We can have dinner alone tonight, Val, if you like. David's going down to Pig on the Roof, to play "mine host", and Françoise wants to help Noel in the kitchen, you know how she loves cooking. Anyway, when you got here on Monday you said you needed to talk to me, and tonight is as good a time as any. Before the others arrive tomorrow.'

'That's great, Fiona, thanks,' I responded and then I thought to add: 'It's nothing to do with Tony, I just want you to know that.'

She gave me a funny little smile and murmured, 'I think it would be fair to say that we've exhausted the subject of Tony Hampton, don't you agree? Is it Jake you want to be discussing, Val?'

'No, it's not, actually. I wanted to talk to you about my mother, about something that happened between us in New York. I've struggled hard with the problem, tried to understand her, and I've hit a blank wall. I thought if I told you a few things you might be able to give me some insight . . . I don't know what makes her tick. You're so wise, Fiona, and understanding, and I'm sure you can help me.'

'I'll certainly try, Val. 'Tis my pleasure.'

'Oh there you are, Fiona . . . Val!' Françoise cried from the doorway, and came hurrying into the room. She was now fully recovered from the loss of the baby and the spousal abuse, at least physically. I did not know how she was coping with the psychological damage because she had not talked to me on that level as yet.

But she looked wonderfully fit and healthy, and seemed more relaxed. Her entire demeanour was different than it had been in Paris. There was no question in my mind that this was because she was so far away from the dreaded Olivier, cop with an agenda.

She came across the room, kissed me on both cheeks, French-style, and then kissed Fiona, whom she obviously adored. I had spotted that on Monday afternoon when I had arrived from London and walked into this warm and friendly house.

Fiona said, 'Did you and Noel get the tree finished, Françoise? I can help this afternoon, if you haven't, I am thinking.'

'No, no, it is not necessary, Fiona. Noel finished it an

hour ago. I helped him . . .' She began to giggle. 'I have never seen a tree like it. Oh *Mon Dieu*!'

'It's full of little pigs, isn't it?' Fiona said.

Françoise nodded. 'But what funny pigs!'

'Don't tell us any more, you'll spoil it for us.' Fiona glanced around as David came back into the room carrying a tray of drinks. She said to him, 'Moira phoned when you were out shopping with Val. She's coming for Christmas after all. She'll take the train to Harrogate with Rory on Thursday morning.'

'Is she bringing the boyfriend?' David asked as he placed the tray of drinks on the coffee table.

'No, and seemingly that's the whole problem, David. They've broken up, and so she now has nowhere to go, since they were intending to spend Christmas Day with his parents. I gather she had really wanted to come up here to us, and that's when the rift started. They quarrelled about it.'

'I'm sorry it blew up,' David murmured to Fiona as he handed me a Bloody Mary. 'He seemed like such a nice boy. But I must say, I am pleased she's going to be with us. I feel we should all be together as a family at Christmas.' He gave Françoise a glass of white wine, handed a Bloody Mary to Fiona, and took the last one for himself.

'Cheers, one and all!' he said.

'Cheers.'

'And to our extended family, Françoise, and Val,' Fiona graciously added.

IV

After lunch, which consisted of hot tomato soup with croutons, Quiche Lorraine, green salad and Stilton cheese, followed by coffee spiced with cinnamon, I helped Françoise to clear the table.

As we were carrying the dishes through into the spacious kitchen, Françoise said, 'Shall we go to the ruins . . . it is such a nice walk, Val.'

I nodded, smiling at her. I had noticed that she had a funny way of saying my name, as if she still wanted to call me Mademoiselle Denning. 'That's a terrific idea, and perhaps it'll help to get some of the calories off, although I doubt that.'

'You will have to go on a *régime* after Christmas. So will I,' Françoise added.

Once the dishwasher was stacked, we put on our heavy coats, wrapped scarves around our necks, and set out to walk to the ruins of Middleham Castle, close to the town.

Françoise didn't say much on the way to the castle, and I remained silent myself. I hadn't realized Rory and Moira were coming, since Fiona had not mentioned it before today; and I had not bought presents for them in Paris. It was a good thing I picked up some extra items at the sheep boutique, I thought, as I shoved my hands farther into my pockets and increased my pace to keep up with Françoise.

'I miss *Maman* and *Papa*,' Françoise eventually volunteered, staring straight ahead as we walked at a brisk pace down the hill.

'Yes, I know you must. But it is wise to play it cool at the moment, Françoise. They know you are safe and well, and being looked after by friends of ours. And that's all they care about. They don't need to know exactly where you are.'

'*Oui*.' She sighed and glanced at me out of the corner of her eye. 'The day I met you at Les Roches Fleuries I wanted to die. Now I want to live. I hope Olivier doesn't find me. If he does, he will kill me. I know he will.'

I did not respond immediately.

Françoise said, 'Val, you must believe me . . . that is the truth.'

'Yes, I think you're right. But you must trust me when I tell you that Olivier will never find you. How can he? Your parents don't know where you are. You came here on a private plane. Mike and Jake are coming on a private plane tomorrow. Please, Françoise, try to relax.'

'I am trying but –' She broke off, shook her head. 'I worry . . . I worry so much. What if he has an investigator looking?'

'Did Olivier have a lot of money? Spare cash?'

'*Non*,' she said swiftly, shaking her head emphatically. 'He had no spare money. Only the money he earned as a *flic*.'

'Believe me, there's no investigator looking for you.

Olivier can't afford one. And please, trust me, trust my judgement.'

'*Oui, oui*, I do, Val.'

V

As I wandered with Françoise through the roofless chambers of the once-glorious Middleham Castle I stared up at its shattered battlements, and wondered about those who had lived here long ago. The great magnate Richard Neville, his wife, his daughters, and the young princes of the blood. And I thought of the splendour of old that was gone, lost forever in the dust of time passing. Weeds and tufts of grass pushed up through the broken walls, and birds built their nests in ancient crevices and sheltered corners of the massive ruins.

Centuries ago great nobles and their ladies, dressed in rich and elegant clothes, had walked amidst these splendid halls, where banquets and sumptuous entertainments had been held. And here had lived the most powerful in the land . . . here they had worked and played and plotted together. Made love, given birth, quarrelled, fought and made up. And died.

How hard to imagine as I glanced about me. Frost covered the hardened winter ground, bits of grey stone lay all around me, remnants of those walls that had crumbled long ago. It was a stronghold no more, had not been for eons.

Dead, all of them, and buried. Their lives forgotten

by most. And what had their lives been all about in the long run? And why did those lives matter now? They didn't, did they? *Ashes to ashes, dust to dust* . . . one day Françoise would be dust, and so would I, and why did her life and mine matter? One day we would be gone and nobody would care. Yet whilst we lived we fought so hard to have what we thought we should have . . . what mattered to us . . . what we conceived as being ours . . .

What had they been like, all those who had inhabited this place? So many ghosts here, flitting through the ruined chambers . . .

'Val, Val, is something wrong?'

I stopped in my tracks and turned to her. 'No, I'm fine. Why?'

She said quietly, 'Are you weeping? There are tears on your face.'

I touched my cheeks with my fingers and realized they were wet. She was right, and I was surprised. I shook my head. 'I was thinking about the people who once lived here. All of them dead these hundreds of years, and I was contemplating their lives. All that they suffered, enjoyed, lost and regretted, longed for and attained. And all the things they never had. Lives lived, then snuffed out. Just like that. Gone in a flash. We are here for such a short time. And then we are dead and nobody cares . . . why does *any* of it matter? Why do we bother? Why do we struggle?'

She stared at me thoughtfully and then after a

moment she answered slowly, 'I think . . . because we are human.'

'Yes,' I agreed. 'And perhaps we always see . . . *hope*. Hope for ourselves and our lives. Hope for something better.'

Chapter Twenty-Nine

I

The night had turned icy cold and it had begun to snow. I stood at the living-room window looking out at the moors, watching the flakes float down, delicate and crystalline in the moonlight. The high-flung sky was like the inside of a bowl turned upside down, jet-black, hung with bright stars and a clear silver orb of a full moon.

Fiona had built up the fire and turned on the central heating, and now as she hurried in with the coffee on a tray she exclaimed, 'Thank God we had the foresight to put in a heating system. These old houses are impregnable, built like fortresses, but they can be cold. On a night like this the extra heat is very welcome. Come, Val, have a cup of coffee and let's settle down for our chat.'

'It was a lovely dinner, Fiona, thank you,' I said as I walked across to join her near the fireplace.

'You're welcome, but it *was* only cottage pie,' she

laughed and poured our coffee.

I sat down on one sofa and she took a seat on the other, so that we were facing each other. It was warm and cosy in the room, with the fire hissing and crackling in the hearth, and the lights turned low. The soft mood was conducive to intimacy and sharing; not that we were shy with each other after our conversations about Tony in New York in October.

'You don't know anything much about my life,' I began, looking across at her. 'So let me tell you about those years before I came to live in Paris.'

She nodded. 'That's a good idea, I'd like a bit of background, Val. I'll be able to comprehend things much better.'

And so, trying to be as succinct as possible, endeavouring to avoid embellishments, I told her the story of my childhood growing up in New York. I gave her enough details for her to fully understand how I had been brought up, and told her about those people who had been part of my life: my mother and father, Annie Patterson, the nanny, Donald, and my grandparents.

When I had finally finished I sat back, gazing at her intently, waiting for her to say something.

Fiona looked ineffably sorrowful, and her eyes were moist, as though she was on the verge of tears. After a long, long moment of silence, she said in a low voice, 'How tragic, what a sad childhood you had, Val. And how dreadfully sad for your mother. She missed so much, missed all the joy of you, of your early years when you were a little girl, and then those wonderful teen years.' She shook her head. 'And how terribly hard for you, heartbreaking really. How you must have suffered.'

I exclaimed, 'It's a wonder I'm as sane as I am, when you think about it, Fiona! I know my troubled past has done all sorts of things to me, but somehow I've managed to cope, and lead a relatively sane life, although I also accept that I am damaged in certain ways . . . psychologically damaged.'

'I supposed that's true, but you did have that lovely Scottish nanny, Annie. And your grandparents were wonderful to you, and of course you had a little brother to love until your mother stepped in, broke the two of you up, so to speak. 'Tis a shame she did that.'

'Yes, it is, and I foolishly blamed Donald for it when it wasn't his fault. And I realize now that I must have been very jealous of him in those days. After all, she was forever petting and spoiling him. It was like a knife in my side, although Annie did try to assuage my hurt, dry my tears, make me feel wanted.'

'You're lucky to have had her, you know. Those early months and years are so important in a child's development. The child must know it's loved, feel that love, have that nurturing, that cuddling and caring. Thankfully Annie gave it to you, was there for you, to love you, make you feel safe.'

'Yes. And yet I do still crave nurturing, you know . . .' My voice trailed off; I didn't want to mention Tony or Jake at this point in my story.

I told Fiona everything. I told her about my mother's

love affair with Vincent Landau, about her illegitimate daughter Anjelica, the child whom she gave away, and about Vincent's suicide a week before his marriage to the society heiress Marguerite Shiff. Finally I finished: 'My mother said she couldn't love me because of her guilt about Anjelica, about giving her away.'

Fiona sat there staring at me, her shock and disbelief written all over her face. Eventually she roused herself, shook her head from side to side, and exclaimed, 'I'm appalled! Absolutely *appalled*. What that woman did to you is unconscionable . . . that she could treat her own daughter in such a cruel way, it's just beyond understanding, beyond belief. She has to be bonkers, off the wall.'

'Yes, I think she was, is, more than likely mentally ill, disturbed. In New York that day, I told her she was wicked, and added she was beyond wicked, that she was evil. And, in a way, I think she is evil . . . but there's also something else, something very odd about her. She's so very beautiful, Fiona, movie-star beautiful, but oh God is she cold. Icy cold. My grandfather called her the Ice Queen.' I let out a long sigh. 'When I asked her why my father had followed her lead, and behaved towards me in exactly the same way she had, she told me he didn't want children, that he abhorred them. She said he was jealous of me, and of Donald as well, because he didn't want to share *her*. We were a nuisance, totally unwanted, as far as he was concerned, so she said anyway. I guess we were in the way. But he was a wimp, and she walked all over him.' I paused and looked into the fire for a second or two, and then I said to Fiona, with a small frown, 'Yet she was able to love Donald, you know. She took him away from me when I was eleven and he was six . . .' I left my sentence unfinished, stared at her helplessly.

'Because he was probably rather cute by then, and he was perhaps a useful accessory for a woman like her; and then again, she knew it would hurt you if she split you up.'

'But why would she want to hurt me?'

'I just don't know, Val. I think it would take a psychiatrist years to get to the bottom of your mother's troubled psyche, to find out what motivated her, what made her tick. And what makes her tick today. I will say this though: among other things I think she's probably rather stupid.'

I frowned on hearing this. 'But she's not, she's become a very good businesswoman, something of a tycoon, in fact.'

Fiona raised an auburn brow and exclaimed, 'Really!'

I told Fiona about Lowell's, how it had been started in 1898 by Amy-Anne, and about her rule, commonly known in the family as The Tradition. 'So you see, she has to leave it to me. There's no legal document apparently, but that's the family rule. The company's now worth millions, and its value will only increase next year if Lowell's makes a public offering. But I don't want it. I refused my inheritance. I told her to leave it to Donald.'

Fiona looked startled momentarily, and then broke into delighted laughter. 'Good for you, Val. But you wouldn't do anything else but that. You have far too much integrity. Anyway, getting back to my remark about your mother being stupid, I really do think she might have been both stupid and a little weak when she was a younger woman. And that has nothing to do with being clever in business.'

'Stupid and weak in what sense?'

'Look, she had an illegitimate child, and her mother had allowed her to keep the baby for months. Why not simply adopt the title of Mrs and pretend to be a young widow? Your mother wasn't well known, so who would know the difference? She behaved in a very stupid way, and she was weak in her handling of her mother, your grandmother Violet Scott. They could have worked something out between them. Then there's Vincent Landau, what kind of jackass was he? He was just as stupid and weak as your mother, in my opinion. He should have either defied his parents and married her, if he loved Margot so much, and to hell with the consequences. Or he should have married his society fiancée and kept your mother on the side as his mistress, and supported her and Anjelica. Or, if she didn't want that, he could have simply provided for them financially. And why did he commit suicide? None of it really makes sense. I don't understand . . . like you, I'm baffled, Val.'

'I've wondered lately . . . if it's all a bunch of lies.'

…y would she lie to you?' Fiona looked at …y, her eyes widening.

…pose she felt she had to try to explain to me …he couldn't love me, and maybe she thought it would be a much more sympathetic story . . . an innocent young woman forced to give up her illegitimate child, etcetera, etcetera, and becoming guilt-ridden thereafter.'

'You could have a point, but no, I don't think she lied. There's something about the story that has the ring of truth. But you know, Val me darlin', you shouldn't be trying to fathom out your mother, her mental state, her personality disorder, and what was at the root of her behaviour towards you when you were a child. It's basically of no consequence, because knowing *why* she did what she did won't change anything. That's all water under the bridge now. And anyway, knowing won't help you, now will it?'

'No, I don't suppose it will,' I replied.

'You must forget all about your mother and worry about yourself, Val darlin'. Get yourself truly well inside, so that you can move forward the way Jake said you should.'

'But how . . . I don't know *how* to do that, Fiona,' I said.

'By forgiving your mother. You must have the courage and strength to do that, to empty your heart of your hatred for her, your condemnation of her. It will be your forgiveness of her that will set you free.'

I didn't speak. I merely gazed at Fiona, digesting her words, trying to heed her wisdom.

Rising, she came over, sat next to me on the sofa; she put her arms around me, held me close, as a mother holds a child in distress. 'She did terrible things to you in your childhood, Val, but you must let them go . . . they're simply not worth holding onto. They're of no value now.'

Unexpectedly, I began to weep, the tears spurting out of my eyes and falling down my cheeks unchecked. I hadn't known I was going to become so emotional, and I tried hard to take hold of my swimming senses. But I didn't do very well, and soon I was sobbing uncontrollably, as though my heart would break.

But slowly the weeping did eventually subside under Fiona's calming influence. Finally I extricated myself from her arms and sat back. I offered her a weak smile. 'I'm sorry,' I said. 'I didn't know the floodgates were going to open like that.'

'I know you didn't, but perhaps it's just as well they did. There's nothing like a good cry to make you feel better.'

I nodded and groped for a tissue in the pocket of my jacket.

She said, 'It's not going to be easy, because you've struggled with the problem of your mother's behaviour towards you for your entire life, but now it is time to expunge it. And always remember this, Val: forgiveness, like the truth, *does* set you free. Trust me on that.'

11

The moors were covered with a giant quilt of white by the following day. Jake and Mike, along with Mike's two daughters, Lisa and Joy, arrived at Ure House in time for tea on Thursday. It was Christmas Eve, and there was already a festive feeling in the air. Fiona and Françoise had decorated most of the downstairs rooms with holly; and a large sprig of mistletoe dangled from the brass chandelier in the entrance hall.

The tree stood there at the back of the hall, tall and stately, a dark-green fir which awaited its yuletide decorations. The dressing of the tree was planned for later that evening, and I told Jake about Fiona's plans as the two of us went upstairs to our bedroom.

The moment Jake walked into our room he exclaimed with pleasure, 'This is great, Val! And just look at that bed! I've never seen one so inviting.'

I laughed and agreed with him. The four-poster dominated the room, was piled high with fresh white linen pillows and a plump duvet in an antique linen cover. 'It's very cosy,' I pointed out, 'I've been sleeping in it for the last couple of nights. And isn't it great to have a fire in the bedroom.'

He nodded, strode across the room, and looked out of the mullioned windows which offered a panoramic view of the windswept, snow-covered moors. He shivered slightly. 'Oh boy, I bet it's kind of cold up there.'

'But beautiful, Jake. You're going to love this place, and it's so full of history. David's been filling me in. It's fascinating.'

'So he told you about the Kingmaker, did he?' Jake asked, joining me by the fire, putting an arm around my shoulders.

I frowned. 'I'm not sure who you mean? He did tell me about the Earl of Warwick –'

'That's him,' Jake said, interrupting me. 'He's one of my favourite characters in British history. Quite a guy, he was.' Jake tightened his grip on me, and added, 'I'm glad we're here, Val, and Fiona's wonderful, the way she's planned this old-fashioned family Christmas for all of us.'

'She's been very loving to me, Jake,' I confided, and then I told him about our heart-to-heart talk of the night before.

Jake listened carefully, as he always did, forever attentive and concerned about my problems. When I'd finished, he asked, 'And do you think you *can* forgive your mother, Val?'

'Yes, I do. Because there is nothing else *to do*. Anyway, I believe that everything Fiona said is true. If I can see it in my heart to forgive my mother, then I myself can go forward into the future, putting the past behind me.'

III

Christmas Eve at Ure House was only a foretaste of what was to come for the next few days . . . a typical Yorkshire Christmas.

Fiona and David gathered us all in the big living room later that evening and served eggnog, chilled white wine and champagne, along with hot sausage rolls and bite-sized cheese tartlets. After our first drink, we all trooped out into the entrance hall and started to dress the tree.

'Everything's silver and gold,' Fiona explained, showing us the stacks of boxes in one corner, 'so no one can make a mistake. Just hang *something* anywhere you want.'

There was a lot of banter and laughter and everyone enjoyed the traditional activity of hanging the ornaments. And as she said, it was impossible to make an error.

The smells emanating from the kitchen were delicious. I breathed in the aroma of chestnut stuffing and goose roasting in the oven, and my mouth began to water. A bit later Noel appeared. David's son was a younger, taller version of his father, and he came out dressed in his white chef's uniform and toque. Waving his wooden spoon, he announced, 'Your goose is cooked! Well, almost.'

'My goose was cooked the moment I met Fiona,'

David quipped, and we all laughed.

'Back to the kitchen to finish up,' Noel said, and disappeared, but not before he'd admonished us to hurry up with the dressing of the Christmas tree.

I was hanging a silver pear when I paused to listen. In the distance I heard the church bells ringing out, and how beautiful they sounded on the still night air.

Fiona explained, 'There's a service at the church tonight and it's lovely. But there's also one tomorrow for those who'd like to attend.'

Almost immediately after this the carollers were at the front door of Ure House, and the strains of 'Silent Night' rang out. This time we all stopped what we were doing and listened, marvelling at the beautiful young voices.

Fiona and David went to the front door when the carol was finished, and invited the young people in for eggnog and titbits and a chance to warm up by the fire. And after their little respite from the cold, they sang 'The Twelve Days of Christmas' before leaving to wend their way through the neighbourhood.

I stood to one side watching everyone, pleased to see the happiness on their faces. Mike was relaxed, joking with Jake, who couldn't stop smiling tonight. Mike's girls, besotted with Françoise, were laughing and helping her to hang golden cherries and apples on a high branch. Rory was draping tinsel with Fiona, and Moira was talking to them with great animation; and David, like me, was standing on the sidelines, the quiet observer. But I could see from the expression on his face how happy he was, and contented. His eyes never left Fiona.

I realized as I stood there that I had never had a Christmas like this in my entire life . . . so family-based, old-fashioned and full of love.

IV

The dinner was superb.

It had been chiefly cooked by Noel, since Pig on the Roof was closed for the Christmas holidays. But Fiona, Françoise and Moira had helped out during the day. I had been shooed away, but at least I'd volunteered to pitch in.

Once the meal was ready, Noel went off to change out of his uniform, and when he came back he, Rory and Moira hurried into the kitchen and brought out the first course: smoked salmon, *foie gras*, and potted shrimps. 'Something for everyone's taste,' Fiona said, glancing around the dining-room table. She had dressed it herself that afternoon, and the beautiful china, crystal and silver gleamed on the antique lace cloth. White winter roses arranged in a silver bowl sat in the centre of the table between silver candlesticks with white candles. A perfect setting for the dinner.

After the salmon from Scotland, the potted shrimps from Morecambe Bay, and the French *pâté de foie gras*, the roast goose was served with its chestnut stuffing, roast potatoes, steamed vegetables, gravy and apple sauce.

We all kept telling Noel how delicious it was, and he just beamed and beamed, looking pleased. It was true, he was a great chef; a pleasant young man with an easy-going, carefree manner: he was interested in everyone.

Halfway through dinner, David startled me when he looked across at me, Mike, and Jake and remarked, 'I hope you'll find time to go into Leeds in the next few days, to look at the wonderful new art at the museum there.'

Mike asked, 'The paintings are that good, are they?'

David nodded. 'Absolutely, and if you do wish to go I'll drive you into the city. It's about an hour and a half from here. You'll get a wonderful surprise when you see what's hanging there.'

'Who's the artist?' Jake asked.

'A local lad, a kid from Leeds who is immensely talented. Well, he's no kid any more. He's a man. But he originally hails from Leeds, and his name's Bill Smith. But the rest of the world knows him as Alexander St Just Stevens.'

'He's from Leeds!' I cried, staring at David, and then Mike and I exchanged glances.

Mike said, 'I didn't know that, David. Is it common knowledge?'

David shrugged. 'I'm not sure, to tell you the truth. We all know in Yorkshire, of course, because he's from these parts and something of a character. He was born in a poor neighbourhood of Leeds, studied at Leeds College of Art before going to London, where he was a student at the Royal College of Art. It was around that time that he changed his name, adopted a posh, upper-class accent and became a bit of a fancy, rather eccentric dresser. Reinvented himself when he was a student, and never looked back from that moment on. But he's a genius, no two ways about it, and the paintings he has given to his hometown are mind-boggling. Yes, he's been extremely generous to the city where he was born. And everyone appreciates him and his art.'

'We'll be gobsmacked, will we?' I asked.

'You certainly will, as will I, Val, yet again. His paintings have that effect on everyone,' David responded.

Mike said slowly, 'It's an odd coincidence, David, but I wanted Val to go and see him when he was in New York. Unfortunately he'd left, gone back to his place in Mexico before she could visit his loft. I have several magazines wanting photographs of his new series, which he's painting for the Millennium Art Show to be held in Paris in 2000.'

Looking from Mike to me with great interest, David exclaimed, 'Then you should see the paintings in Leeds, Mike, and you too, Val, if you're going to be photographing the new series.'

'I'm not sure that I am,' I said, frowning at Mike, and then I added, 'But Alexander St Just Stevens does sound like an intriguing character.'

'Oh he is,' Moira volunteered. 'Very colourful, isn't he, Mum?'

Fiona nodded. 'Let's try to go to Leeds on Saturday,' she suggested.

We agreed to try and Alexander St Just Stevens became the topic of conversation for the rest of the meal.

V

'What a lovely evening,' I said later to Jake, as we headed upstairs and went into our bedroom.

'Yes, it was, and especially because we were together, Val.' Pulling me into his arms, he kissed me on the cheek, and then reached into his pocket. Slowly turning me around, so that my back was to him, he hung a string of pearls around my neck, and said, 'Happy Christmas, honey.'

I looked at him in surprise, touched the pearls and ran to the mirror to look at them. Swinging to face him, I exclaimed, 'Jake, they're beautiful! And you shouldn't have. But thank you, I love them.'

He grinned at me. 'They're not the best, not South Sea pearls, but they are good ones.'

'As if I care about that. They're gorgeous,' I responded and went to hug him. 'Your gifts are downstairs, in that pile near the tree,' I explained. 'Shall I creep down and get them?'

'They can wait until morning,' he laughed.

I nodded, then touched the pearls again, and turned once more to regard myself in the mirror. As I admired them I promised, 'I'll wear them always, Jake.'

'Not on the front lines, I hope.'

'I'm not going to be on the front lines and neither are you,' I replied. I did not realize I was tempting fate again.

CHAPTER THIRTY

I

PARIS, MARCH 1999

We went back to Paris after the New Year's celebrations, but Jake waited for over two months before dropping his bombshell.

One afternoon, at the beginning of March, I was minding my own business, feeling happy and contented as I worked at home, sorting through a batch of polaroids of paintings by Alexander St Just Stevens. Mike was still on my back about the British artist, urging me to go to Mexico to do the shoot. As I sat there studying the shots I wondered how to talk Jake into coming with me, *if* I did accept the assignment, when suddenly he was standing there.

He must have entered the apartment quietly, because I didn't hear him come in and then there he was, as large as life, leaning nonchalantly against the door jamb.

'Hi!' I exclaimed, grinning at him. 'I was just

thinking about you.'

'And what were you thinking?' he asked with a faint smile.

I took a deep breath and decided to plunge. 'Mike's still after me to do the shoot in Mexico, you know, of the paintings by St Just Stevens, and I was wondering how to talk you into coming with me. *If* I accept the job.'

'Do you want to do it, Val?' he asked, scrutinizing me intently, and shifting slightly against the door frame.

'To be honest, I'm not sure. It could be interesting, certainly the art is just . . . *mind-boggling* as David said, and as we saw for ourselves in Leeds. But I don't know, it's such a long trek to Mexico.'

'But nice weather at this time of year.'

'True. Anyway, what are you doing home so early? I thought you had an important meeting at the agency with Jacques Foucher and the guy from *Life* magazine.'

'Yeah, I did, and we had the meeting.'

'Did it go well?'

He nodded, then walked into the dining room, which served as my office, and came to a stop just before he reached my desk.

I stared at him, a brow lifting quizzically. 'What is it?'

'Val, there's something I want to talk to you about.'

'What? Why do you look so serious all of a sudden?'

There was an almost imperceptible hesitation on his part, before he said, 'I'm thinking of going back to Kosovo.'

For a split second I thought I'd misheard. But I knew I hadn't really. I was so stunned I couldn't speak for a second, and I just sat there gaping at him like a fool. When I could finally speak, I said in a faltering voice, 'But you promised you wouldn't go back there.'

'I didn't actually *promise*, Val, I merely said I *thought* I wouldn't go back to Kosovo.'

'Jake, it's me you're talking to, and you're splitting hairs!'

'No, I'm not. I said I didn't *want* to go back, that I *thought* I wouldn't, but I never made you a promise.'

'And now you're saying you do want to go, is that it?'

'Yes. Because I have to, Val.'

'No you don't, there's no earthly reason why you should go back to that lousy war.' My voice rose slightly, as I added a bit shrilly, 'You'll get killed.'

'I won't. I'm not like Tony Hampton, I don't take risks.'

'No, I guess you think you're like Robert Capa, who didn't take risks either according to you, and made sound judgements before he rushed into the fray. But even so, Capa got himself killed in Indochina, by stepping on a land mine. So much for sound judgements.'

'I must go Val, really, it's important to me that I do –'

'Why?' I cut in peremptorily, and in a harsh voice.

'Because I'm a Jew, that's why. I can no longer ignore what's happening in Kosovo, what Slobodan Milosevic's up to, in all good conscience I can't. I have to go and take photographs of the atrocities . . . of the killing and murder, torture and mayhem that's occurring there right now. This war is escalating, and before you can blink, NATO will intercede, they have to, because Milosevic is perpetrating genocide.'

I couldn't move or speak for a moment, and I knew then that whatever I said I had probably already lost the battle to stop him going. I finally managed, in a low voice, 'But, Jake, genocide has been committed in other countries in the world. And you didn't –'

'This is different. This is happening in Europe, and I'm of European stock, and I feel compelled, impelled to go. I was born of German Jews, and this is a repetition of what happened in Nazi Germany in the 1930s, and I just can't stand by and let it happen without lifting a finger. I should say lifting a camera.'

'I bet if you talked to your mother she'd tell you not to go.'

'I'm not a little boy needing his mother's permission,' he said in a suddenly snappish tone. 'And no, she wouldn't tell me not to go, she'd tell me, yes Jake, go, get over there and take the pictures. Prove that this monstrous man is a criminal, that he should be brought to trial as a criminal.'

'I didn't mean you needed permission,' I said weakly. 'You misunderstood me.'

'Listen to me,' he said, leaning forward slightly, resting his hands on the edge of my desk. 'My grandmother, Granmutti Hedy, and my grandfather Erich Neuberg fled Nazi Germany in 1937, because they knew only too well what was going to happen to them if they stayed. My mother's parents Ernst and Anna Mayer were just as smart, and left Germany in 1935, also fleeing racial persecution. Hitler was already on the rampage. And frankly, Milosevic is of the same ilk. He is waging an ethnic war against the Kosovar people, and it is a criminal war.'

'Oh Jake, I understand what this means to you!' I exclaimed. 'Intellectually, I do. Truly, I do. But emotionally, I don't want you to go, I'm so afraid you'll be . . . *hurt*.'

'It's just seeping through to the world that Milosevic is prepared to act like Hitler, and Stalin . . . he's going to fight a war against a *whole people*. Jesus, Val, he's already doing it!'

'I realize it's about ethnic cleansing, and that it's wrong –' My voice wavered, came to a stop, because I saw the look on his face. His expression was obdurate; his blue eyes blazed with passionate intensity.

Jake said, 'I can't help but think the Nazi era is being repeated in Kosovo. That this terrible, primitive kind of fascism is making a comeback, and I don't believe the world can accept that. I just have to stand up against genocide, Val. *I do*! Almost all of my grandparents' relatives were murdered in the Holocaust, on both sides, Neubergs and Mayers, and Steiners in Munich, on Granmutti Hedy's side.'

'Please don't go to Kosovo,' I whispered, leaning back against the chair. I felt sick inside and I was terrified, because I suddenly had a terrible premonition that something unspeakable was going to happen to him. I loved him so much and I had to try and stop him going, and I had to do it now, before it was too late. 'I'm begging you not to go, Jake. For my sake, for our sake. For our future's sake.'

'Oh Val, darling,' he said quietly, 'you know I have to do this. I couldn't live with myself if I ignored my conscience. You've seen the newspapers every day, watched television . . . it's growing by the minute. And you'll see, by the end of March, before this month is out, NATO will have to go in and bomb. We have to intervene. And I want to be there, Val, taking the pictures that might help to change somebody's perception of this war. That's one of the reasons I became a war photographer, I wanted to make people really *see* violence and terror and wholesale slaughter. It's a sea of sorrow and blood over there.'

'If you go, it's over between us,' I threatened, using the only weapon I had left.

He ignored what I said. 'Come with me, Val.'

'No, I just can't Jake, I'm totally burnt out. I can't go. I don't belong there on the front lines any more.'

Nodding his understanding, he walked around the desk, bent over me and kissed me, hugged me tightly.

I choked up, yet somehow managed to push back the tears. But my voice wavered as I said, 'Oh Jake, please, please stay . . .'

Releasing me, he looked down into my face, and gave me a small boyish smile. 'I'm going to be fine, Val. Really I am, you must trust me.'

II

And so he left for Belgrade.

I was all alone in the apartment, suddenly lost and helpless without him, after seven months of emotional and physical closeness and involvement.

I kept shaking my head, wondering to myself how this had happened. It had all been so sudden, so fast; he had told me what he was going to do, and then he had gone. Toting his cameras and his big bag, in which he had packed his combat boots and flak jacket.

He had gone back to Kosovo, where Tony Hampton had been killed and where my life had changed forever, and because of this I was superstitious. I knew that this place did not bode well for me, and I knew he would be killed. And it was something I could not bear to contemplate.

There *was* one thing in his favour. I knew he was not rash or foolhardy, as Tony had been, and I hoped and prayed that he would use his good judgement and wisdom, once he was in harm's way.

Yes, I wished him well, because I loved him with all my heart. But deep within myself, at my core, I was hurt, because he had chosen his cause over me. And that was hard for me to accept.

III

It was Mike who convinced me to take the assignment in Mexico. Although I was at first reluctant, I finally decided my boss had a good point. I would be far away, busy working, and so less inclined to sit and worry about Jake. Of course, I *would* worry, I knew that only too well. But he was right, inasmuch as Acapulco was at the other side of the world. C.N.N. was broadcast there too, but I didn't have to turn it on.

The project was quite complex, and since we had finally received Alexander St Just Stevens's permission to fly out to his compound, fairly elaborate arrangements had to be made. 'You'll need a couple of assistants,' Mike had said a few days before, and had suggested two of the junior photographers at Gemstar in New York. They were nice kids and competent, but I turned them down.

'I'd like to take my brother Donald and his fiancée, Alexis Rayne,' I said to Mike, explaining, 'She's an excellent journalist and so is Donald. I need somebody to make notes, keep a written record for me, and in general act like journalists who would be writing the story. Also, they can both help me set up the lighting, assist with that kind of thing. And they wouldn't be all that expensive,' I'd thought to add.

Mike had agreed, I suppose because he realized how much I was hurting about Jake. Also, I think he wanted to make me feel better. He was aware I'd patched up my rift with Donald, and I knew he was in the mood to encourage family affection these days.

In the first few days that Jake had been gone I had cried myself to sleep at night, but eventually I had managed to pull myself together. I had to be grown up about the situation, act like the mature woman I believed myself to be. I was thirty-one years old and responsible for myself, and I had to earn a living. I had bills to pay, commitments to meet, and floating around like some mad Ophelia wasn't going to get me anywhere.

And so I packed suitable clothes for working in a hot climate, a few outfits for relaxation time, and all of my best cameras. I also loaded up on film, enough to last me for the two weeks I would be taking photographs of the amazing works of art by the eccentric Alexander St Just Stevens, born Bill Smith in Leeds. It was quite a story really, an amazing success story about talent and genius propelling a poor boy, born in the slums of Leeds, to great heights. Fame and Fortune. Success and Wealth. The public would eat it up, Mike was right about that. They loved anything stamped money, success, power.

Janine had been working today and she had helped

me to get my packing finished, and put everything in order in the apartment. She had promised she would come in several times a week, as she usually did, to keep the place as immaculate as always until my return.

I wasn't very hungry that night, but since she'd made me a veal stew with vegetables, I decided to eat a little of it while watching television. I sighed to myself as I reheated the stew. I knew that as long as I was in Europe I would be tuning in, looking for the war coverage from Kosovo.

I stood stirring the pot, my thoughts miles away with Jake. He was somewhere in Kosovo, probably Priština, which is where Jacques Foucher said he had gone. When the phone on the wall began to ring loudly, I jumped out of my skin, startled.

Hoping against hope it was Jake, I grabbed it. 'Hello?'

'*Il est mort, il est mort*,' a strangely hoarse woman's voice whispered down the wire. I did not recognize the voice.

My heart missed a beat, and I clenched the phone tightly, swallowing hard. 'Who is dead?' I demanded. 'Who is this? Who's speaking?'

'*Il est mort, Mademoiselle* Denning. Olivier Bregone is dead!'

'Oh my God, it's you, Simone!' I shrieked, filling with relief. 'I thought it was somebody calling me from Kosovo to tell me Monsieur Jake was dead.'

'I am sorry, mademoiselle, if I gave you the fright.'

'You certainly did! Now, please start again. Is it really true? Is Olivier really dead?'

'*Ah oui, mademoiselle, oui*. I do not wish anybody dead . . . but I am relieved he cannot any longer make the life of my Françoise difficult. She is free.'

'But how do you know this?' I asked swiftly, the journalist in me taking over. Rumours, suppositions, they did not work for me.

'It was on the television. Tonight. He was shot to death by one of the criminals in Marseilles. One of the drug lords,' Simone explained in her excellent but stilted English.

'I'll turn on the television later, Simone, but thanks for letting me know. It's a relief that he can't bother Françoise any more.'

'*Oui*. Mademoiselle, please make the phone call for me, to Françoise. I want her to know. Better, give me her number so I can speak to her wherever she is.'

'Simone, I'll call her and ask her to get in touch with you. I think that's best.'

She chuckled down the phone, and said, 'Ah, you do not trust me, Miss Denning. You are perhaps not sure I am I.'

'Oh I am, Simone, honestly I am sure it's you. I recognize your voice.' This was the truth, I did, but I also wanted to be absolutely certain Olivier was really dead before I handed out phone numbers that might fall into the wrong hands.

'Very well, I wait to hear from my daughter. Her father and I are here at Les Roches Fleuries.'

After she had hung up I called Mike at home. Joy answered and immediately passed the phone to her father, when I said it was urgent.

'What's up, what's wrong, Val?' Mike asked as he came on immediately. 'Is there a problem?'

'I just had a phone call from Simone. She says Olivier Bregone is dead, that he was killed in Marseilles, shot to death by one of the drug lords down there.'

'Jesus Christ!' Mike exclaimed. 'How does she know?'

'She saw it on television. Can you check it out? Let's be positive it's true, before we tell Françoise.'

But he didn't get right back to me. In fact Mike didn't call me for over an hour, and then when he did he was not entirely sure that Olivier Bregone was dead.

'Listen, Val, I talked to a contact of mine at Interpol, who knows everyone there is to know in the police and justice systems throughout France, and he's made a couple of phone calls for me. Now he's waiting for his contacts to get back to him. But his first reaction was that it's more than likely true. He said he was sure the television network wouldn't run a phony story, which is what you're getting at, isn't it?'

'Yes, it is.'

'Okay, we won't call Françoise in Middleham for the moment. Let's hang in there, play it cool, Val, and as soon as my guy gets back to me, I'll call you pronto.'

We said our goodbyes, and I went back to the kitchen where I washed the pan, the plate and the cutlery, and made myself a cup of tea. I then sat down in front of the television and made myself miserable watching C.N.N., which had a great deal of coverage on the war in Kosovo. And I worried about Jake.

It was almost ten-thirty when Mike did finally phone me again, and he was triumphant. 'Absolutely true, he's dead all right, Val. Shot to death by one of the crooks, just as Simone told you. The Marseilles homicide department confirmed it to my guy from Interpol. Shall I tell Françoise?'

'Oh Mike, yes, you make the call. It's better coming from you,' I exclaimed, hearing the relief mingled with eagerness in his voice. 'Tell her to call her mother, please, Mike, and let her know I'll phone tomorrow before I fly off to Mexico.'

'I will. Thanks for everything. And Val?'

'Yes, Mike?'

'Please try not to worry about Jake. He's going to be all right, he'll make it.'

'I hope so,' I answered. 'I'll be in touch later this week.'

'Okay, no sweat. And I have your phone and fax numbers at the hacienda in case I need to get in touch with you.'

IV
ACAPULCO

The Hacienda Rosita had to be seen to be believed. It was undoubtedly the most beautiful property in the area, a compound composed of a series of villas, guest cottages, a huge studio where Alexander St Just Stevens painted, a building where kitchens were housed, and a house where the domestic help lived.

All of the buildings were of white stucco, very Spanish in feeling, and beautifully designed and built. Inside the main villa, where the artist lived, the floors were of white marble, as were some of the walls; the rooms were filled with distinctive antique pieces, of Mexican origin, many of his own paintings, and eye-catching accessories and lamps.

These buildings were perched high on a cliff, just outside the town, and the view from any part of the grounds was spectacular. Far below, the brilliant azure sea glittered, and the gardens were filled with a riotous profusion of flowers, plants, flowering shrubs and trees.

The entire compound was surrounded by a very high wall, guarded at the main gate and the back service gate by armed guards.

I have to admit that I was startled when I first saw the gun-toting guards when we drove into the property the day I arrived, over a week ago now. I had been picked up at the airport in Acapulco by Len Wilkinson, the painter's personal assistant, and it was the genial and courteous Len who had explained: 'The guards are necessary, Val, because there's so much of value here, quite aside from Alexander's paintings. So why make the place a temptation to thieves? The guards keep the unwanted at bay, believe me they do.'

I had taken to Len at once. He was from Leeds, and as he had volunteered himself, 'I'm part of the Yorkshire mafia that surrounds our hero.' He'd had a twinkle in his eye when he'd used the word *hero*, and I knew at once we would get on, that there was no pomposity or pretension in him.

Donald and Alexis had arrived two days before I did, and they had brought with them the lights and other equipment I needed for the shoot. As it turned out, nothing I'd requested had been superfluous, and I soon realized the two of them worked well together. I liked Donald's fiancée; she was charming, willing, energetic, and sure of herself, the kind of young woman who was reliable, and who was going places. She was also pretty and stylish, and obviously well brought up.

On the afternoon I arrived, Len Wilkinson had taken me straight to the large sun-filled villa I was sharing with Donald and Alexis. 'See you later for dinner. At nine o'clock,' Len had said, before disappearing through the front door.

Donald had greeted me warmly, obviously pleased to see me, and Alexis had immediately volunteered to help me unpack. I was grateful that she had, since I'd travelled from Paris to New York by Concorde, spent the night in the Beekman Place apartment and then flown out to Acapulco on Mexicana Airlines that morning. I was used to travel, but I felt bushed the first day I arrived; all I had wanted to do was lie down and go to sleep.

'How on earth will I stay awake 'til dinner at nine?' I asked Donald, who had laughed and said, 'Have a nap once you've unpacked and we'll get you up later.'

'If you say so,' I agreed, and set about emptying the big bag I'd brought, while Alexis put my clothes on hangers.

Once this had been accomplished and everything had been hung up, Donald, Alexis and I went out and sat in the garden for a while, drinking iced tea.

They couldn't wait to fill me in, and I had listened in amazement as Donald had explained the setup at Hacienda Rosita.

'It's quite a place,' Donald had confided, 'and you're going to like Alexander. He's kinda neat, very eccentric though, and a flashy dresser.'

'But he's very handsome,' Alexis had volunteered.

'And a womanizer,' Donald had added, winking at me.

I had nodded. 'Yes, I do know a few things about him. I did a bit of research before I left Paris. He's had several wives, several mistresses, and there are innumerable children.'

'And they all live here,' Donald had told me with a huge grin.

'The first wife can't possibly live here, Donald,' I had answered, laughing. 'She died long ago.'

'True, but you know what I mean. They're all here. But there's no one special that I know of at the moment. They're all exes. You know, ex-wives, ex-mistresses. Better watch out, Valentine, he's got an eye for a pretty face.'

'You don't have to worry about protecting me, brother mine,' I had retorted. 'Just keep an eye on Alexis.'

'Oh, he's not interested in her,' Donald had muttered, and had broken into amused laughter again. 'He's looked her up and down already, and turned away.'

'Well, thanks a lot for those few kind words,' Alexis had exclaimed and punched my brother on his arm.

V

That discussion was now a week old. I had quickly settled in at the Hacienda Rosita, so much so I wondered if I could ever bear to leave. It was the most beautiful spot and so calm and tranquil. The weather was temperate, warm and balmy during the day, cooler in the evenings. The sky was always blue, the sun was always shining, and I felt rejuvenated here.

I knew everyone now. The Yorkshire mafia was made up of several old friends of Alexander's from his student days, and that was one of the things I liked about the artist. He seemed to have a strong streak of loyalty in him. Len Wilkinson was the *capo di tutti capi*, as Alexander liked to call him jokingly. And Len was indeed the boss of all bosses, in charge of everything to do with the painter's business transactions, his art exhibitions, and the sale of his paintings.

Len was of medium height, fresh-faced and silver-haired, an attractive man with an attractive wife. Jennifer Wilkinson was also an old friend from the painter's earliest days in Leeds; then there were two former fellow students who hadn't made it themselves in the world of art, and who helped Alexander move canvases, prepare them, frame the giant-sized paintings in plain wood, mix paints and assist him any way they could. They all enjoyed working with Alexander and it was easy to understand why. He was kind, respectful of them, and always courteous.

For all his eccentricity, flamboyance and womanizing he was at heart a good man; dedicated to his work, a devoted father, and nurturing of the women who had once occupied a place of importance in his life.

As for the art, it was extraordinary. The new series of paintings was overwhelming. Each one had strength, energy, power, and brilliant colour. They really were mesmerizing, and took my breath away. They would take the art world by storm, of that I was absolutely certain.

For a whole week I had been photographing these marvellous paintings, which I considered to be masterpieces and in a class of their own. They were huge, dominating, and dramatic, and I knew my photographs would do them justice.

But today I was going to start taking pictures of Alexander St Just Stevens . . . at work in his studio, in his white marble villa with his small children, and out in the grounds of the compound with his friends from Yorkshire. All of these settings could not be covered in one day, as I had explained to him, and he had agreed to spend the next few days with me, posing for the camera.

VI

I brushed my hair back in a pony tail, tied a piece of ribbon around it, slipped on a pale-blue T-shirt, then stepped into a pair of white cotton shorts. I decided to wear a pair of comfortable tennis shoes, old but clean, since I would be scrambling around all over the place, and on my feet all day.

'I'm leaving, Donald,' I called to my brother, who was still in his room.

The door flew open and he exclaimed, 'Oh, that's right, you're having breakfast with the maestro this morning. Be careful, Val. This guy definitely has the hots for you.'

'I'm sure he doesn't,' I said evenly, aware that Donald enjoyed teasing me.

'But he does, Val,' Alexis remarked, coming out of the room.

I frowned. 'Honestly, you two, you've got sex on the brain.'

'No, he does,' Donald quipped. 'His eyes are lascivious.'

I burst out laughing. 'Donald, what an expression! You *must* use that in your column.'

Alexis said to Donald, 'Let's have breakfast now, and then we can go and meet Val at ten, as she said we should last night. Is that still all right, Val?'

I nodded. 'That's about right. Alexander invited me to the studio for coffee, not the villa, so meet me over there at ten.'

'Okay.' Alexis bit her lip, hesitated slightly before saying, 'Look, are you going to photograph any of his women or not?'

'I'm not sure he'll sit still for it. Why, Alexis?'

'I just think it adds a bit of . . . colour, spice, if you like, to the story.'

'But this is about the art, *great art*, as a matter of fact, and about the painter. It's not about his love life, his women and his four kids.'

'Six altogether,' Donald interjected. 'Two are away at university.'

'Thanks a lot, Donald, for reminding me but I hadn't forgotten, honey.'

'I just thought he might like to be photographed with his . . . extended family. It sort of makes him more . . . *human*,' Alexis said.

'You have a point,' I answered. 'I'll think about it and decide later.'

Picking up my cameras, I added, 'Don't forget to bring all the equipment, Donald. Even though that studio is so well lighted, I want to create the same feeling we had the other day.'

Donald nodded. 'No problem, Sis.'

I smiled at him. 'Thanks, Donald.'

My brother began to laugh.

'What's wrong?'

'I've been calling you *Sis* all week, and you haven't screamed at me once.'

'It doesn't bother me any more,' I said, meaning every word.

Chapter Thirty-One

I

I thought of Jake as I walked through the garden of the guest villa, heading in the direction of Alexander's studio. He was never far from my mind, and I fretted about him, worried about his safety. Often I turned on the television at night, for news of the war in Kosovo, but switched off almost immediately. Chaos and mayhem reigned over there.

Mike, good friend that he was, stayed in daily contact with Jacques Foucher at Jake's photo agency, and sent me updates by fax. For the moment, Jake was alive and covering the war from Priština. Knowing he was still there continued to trouble me. But of course he wouldn't leave; his conscience wouldn't let him.

And so I held my breath, got on with my work at the villa, and prayed for his safety.

I had liked the subject of my photo shoot right from the beginning. At forty-five, Alexander St Just Stevens was considered to be the world's greatest living artist, often called the Picasso of the Millennium. But to me his paintings were much more exciting, had more visual impact; they were so full of life and vibrant colour they took my breath away time and again.

Alexander was an extremely good-looking man, with a strong well-defined face. His dark hair was tinged with white prematurely, and these silver wings at his temples seemed to make his green eyes all that more piercing as they gazed out at the world from beneath thick black brows. Tall, well built with a wonderful physique, he was tanned and fit, and something of an athlete, enjoying tennis, swimming and deep-sea fishing.

I knew full well he was a womanizer. I hadn't needed my brother to inform me of that. His passion for women, and his many involvements with them over the years, were well documented in the newspaper and magazine articles I'd read for my research before coming here. And in a sense his passion for the female sex reflected somewhat his passion for his art, his work.

Len Wilkinson had told me that Alexander often painted for days on end without cease. And I had noticed myself that the artist had an unusual energy and strength, visible in everything he did.

Although I had pooh-poohed the idea that Alexander was eyeing me speculatively, Donald had, in fact, been accurate. My brother didn't miss a trick. His lively, observant eyes were everywhere, and since he was working alongside me on a daily basis he saw everything.

But I deemed it wiser to claim ignorance, pretend I was unaware of Alexander's interest in me, and so keep a lid on the situation. But it did worry me at times because I knew he was more than merely attracted to me. I felt he was actually becoming involved with me, even though I had not encouraged this.

On the other hand, in the past nine days we had spent an enormous amount of time together, in the same environment, working, eating and relaxing. We had come to know each other extremely well, without there being any sexual intimacy, of course. And we had discovered we were compatible, understood each other, and enjoyed being in each other's company.

There had been a lot of socializing in our free time. Alexander had invited us all to dinner at the villa every night; we also took lunch together during the photography sessions. But even though two ex-wives and two ex-mistresses lived within the compound, in their own villas, they had not been included in these social occasions. Len and his wife Jennifer were always present, as were Neal Lomax and Kevin Giles, Alexander's devoted assistants who worked with him in the studio. Marcia Dermot, Alexander's secretary, was often there as well, but not always since she had a three-year-old daughter.

Alexander lived alone at the main house, the white marble villa. It was here that he did his lavish entertaining, although I knew he often worked in the studio long after we had all gone to bed. He was obsessed with his art; it was his life, he told me.

It was Jennifer Wilkinson who had explained that there was no one special in Alexander's life at the moment. However, this had been an off-hand remark, not pointed in any way. And I had merely nodded, made no comment whatsoever.

When I arrived at the studio I paused for a moment and looked up at it. Poised as it was close to the edge of the cliff, but within the encircling outside wall, it looked grand and imposing in the early-morning sunlight.

Walking on, I pushed open the heavy oak door and went inside, and, as I usually did, I remained standing in the doorway, admiring this extraordinary interior.

The studio itself was one vast room, with a wall of glass that soared to the ceiling and overlooked the sea. This glass wall moved up onto the ceiling to form a wide skylight, which cut through the roof at one end, to allow more light to enter the space.

At another end, a raised platform, a kind of stage, was used to display the finished paintings, some of which were huge. Behind this stage there was a fully equipped kitchen, a bathroom, and a bedroom where Alexander frequently slept when he was working at night.

A second platform was built at the opposite side of the studio. Here light flooded in through the skylight as well as the wall of glass; Alexander painted both day and night on this platform, and overhead ceiling spots flooded the area with artificial light after dark.

I hesitated in the doorway. There was no sign of Alexander and the studio was quiet. 'Hello! Hello!' I called and walked into the room, glancing around.

'Is that you, Val?' Alexander's voice boomed out, and he suddenly appeared from behind the stage. His face was covered in shaving soap and he was holding a razor. Bare-chested, he wore a pair of white cotton slacks, badly smeared with paint, and tennis shoes which were equally as messy.

'Who else?' I said, laughing. 'Good morning, Alexander, I hope I'm not too early.'

He glanced at his watch and shook his head. 'No. Anyway, *you* could never be too early for me. Give me a minute and I'll be right with you. They've already brought breakfast over from the kitchens.'

'I'll wait for you on the terrace,' I said, as he disappeared.

I went outside; the terrace was on the far side of the studio, quiet, secluded and hidden from the rest of the buildings in the compound. It overlooked the sea, and there was a table with a sun umbrella attached, as well as four chairs. I sat down at the table to wait, and within a couple of minutes Alexander came out carrying a large wooden tray. He was now properly dressed in fresh white cotton slacks, pristine tennis shoes and a white Mexican shirt.

11

'I've been working,' he said, putting the tray down on the table.

'All night?' I asked, looking up at him.

He shook his head. 'No, since dawn. I wanted to finish something – something special I think. I'll show it to you later.'

He served the coffee and motioned to the basket filled with thick slices of home-baked bread and pound cake, and slices of toast.

I shook my head. 'I'm not hungry,' I murmured, and sipped my coffee.

Alexander also drank his coffee, then buttered a piece of toast and munched on it. And we sat together in a companionable silence for a short while.

Finally I said, 'Would it be all right if we started shooting in the studio this morning? I mean, could I do the first shots of you with the finished paintings?'

'Yes, if you wish, Val.' His green eyes rested on me for a moment before he said, 'I'd like to keep the pictures of me to a minimum, Val, if that's all right with you?'

I nodded. 'Okay, but I would like to get a couple of shots of you painting, as well as standing next to the ones you've completed. And also . . .' I stopped, hesitating, suddenly wary of continuing.

'You're not going to ask me to pose with my former wives and mistresses, are you?'

I was silent.

'I know my ex-wives are somewhat reluctant to be photographed, and certainly Danielle and Carole are extremely shy. They too prefer *not* to be featured in the story.'

'Well . . .' I began and stopped.

'Well, what?' he asked softly.

'I guess I can understand that, but –' I paused again and stared at him. 'I guess I thought it would add a human touch to the story.'

He smiled at me. 'Listen, Val, I've led, still lead, a somewhat unconventional life. Many people think I'm crazy to have everyone living here at the compound, but it's none of their business, and I consider it best for the ladies and my small children. They are all safe, protected, well looked after and taken care of all the time. They can come to no harm here. But I am not too certain about advertising my lifestyle to the world.'

'I realize that, Alexander, but I thought that perhaps a photo of you with the children?'

He shook his head. 'Oh no, I don't think so. The world is full of crazies, you know that, and I don't want to expose my children to the possibility of kidnapping.'

'But they live here with you in this highly protected compound.'

'True.' He sighed. 'Let me think about it.'

A silence fell between us and I did not want to

break it. I needed a moment to collect my thoughts and rethink some of the photographs I'd planned on taking. I glanced away, stared up at the sky. And then I stretched slightly, turned my face to the sun, and closed my eyes for a few minutes.

At last I sat up straighter in the chair, and turned to Alexander. 'I'm sorry if I've asked too much, but the photographs are so important, and the feature is going to be appearing worldwide.'

'Oh I know, and I want you to do the pictures, Val, but I prefer to keep my private life out of this shoot.'

'I understand,' I responded, realizing I was not going to win this one, and I didn't want to antagonize him by pressing further.

Alexander suddenly said, 'I've enjoyed having you here. You like Hacienda Rosita, don't you?'

'I certainly do!' I exclaimed, my enthusiasm apparent. 'It's beautiful, peaceful . . . a paradise. And there aren't many of those left in this world.'

'Why don't you stay on a bit longer?'

'I wish I could, but I've got to leave at the end of the week. Got to get the pictures back to Paris.'

'If that's the only reason you have to go, I can easily send Neal. He'd love a trip to Paris.'

I stared at him speechlessly.

He said, 'I like you, Val. When I first set eyes on you I knew you'd do me good.'

Still I didn't say anything. I just looked at him, and I wondered what he would say next.

'We've had some good talks, you and I this past week, Val,' Alexander said in his mellifluous voice. 'I've never opened up to anyone the way I have with you, at least not since I was an art student in Leeds.' He offered me a warm smile. 'And you know all about those days now, about my whole life, about me and what makes me tick. And I know *you*, and what you're all about, and that's quite unique.'

'I feel the same way, Alexander. You're a wonderful listener . . .' I began to laugh. 'You're the possessor of all my secrets. I think I've really bent your ear, talking so much.'

'I did my share of talking too, and I'm glad you stayed up late with me, sharing so many things. It's not often that happens to me these days.'

'I think we've become truly good friends, don't you?'

'I hope we have.' He leaned forward and pinned his eyes on me. 'Stay a bit longer, Val. You've brought something special here.'

'I'll think about it,' I replied, not knowing how to answer him. It was true, we had confided a great deal in each other. We'd talked about our childhoods, our lives, and those we had loved. We had become exceptionally close, although that wasn't so surprising under the circumstances. We had been thrown together, and we had clicked.

III

In the end it was a long day.

I shot endless film of Alexander in the studio, and with his two assistants. We worked well together, and it was a smooth shoot, with Donald and Alexis backing me up. They were efficient yet relaxed about things, made no fuss.

We all had lunch together on the terrace, and then went on working until early evening. Finally we packed it in at seven. I was tired but Alexander was still full of energy and vitality. He insisted on cocktails on his terrace at the villa, a swim in the pool before supper, and after we had eaten we sat and watched a movie in his screening room, eating popcorn and laughing at the comedy he had chosen.

At midnight, I said, 'I'm on my last legs, I've got to go to bed.' I got up, and started to leave the screening room with the others.

He nodded, and I knew he wanted to walk me back to the villa. But Donald and Alexis sidled up to me, and that was that.

When we got back to the guest villa there was a fax from Mike. In it he told me that Françoise was finally back in Paris, and that all was well. He had not mentioned Jake, and so I assumed that he was still alive and in Kosovo.

Later I fell asleep easily, because I was so exhausted.

And I had a dreamless sleep for once, awakened refreshed and rested the next morning.

IV

Towards the end of the week, Alexander asked me to meet him in the studio for a drink. He said I should come alone, because he wanted to show me something.

I'd had a good day with him, taking some marvellous pictures of him with the Yorkshire mafia, and I looked forward to our drink as I now walked down the path to the studio.

The main room was empty when I went in, and as I always did I called out, 'Alexander, I'm here!'

He appeared instantly, coming out from behind the platform where the large paintings were displayed. He had a bottle of champagne in one hand, two glasses in the other.

'There you are, Val!' he exclaimed, hurrying forward, smiling hugely. 'A drop of the old bubbly first, and then the unveiling.'

'*Unveiling*,' I repeated, looking at him alertly. 'Don't tell me there's a picture I haven't yet seen?'

'Yes, there is. And it's just finished, that's why I haven't shown it to you before.'

Placing the glasses on one of the tables, he poured the champagne, gave me a glass and took one himself. Lifting his flute, he touched it to mine and said, 'Here's to you, Val, may you live a long and happy life.'

'And to you, Alexander, may you enjoy the same.'

Putting his arm around me, he led me over to the far side of the studio, to the platform where he painted. We went up the steps, walked towards an easel that was covered with a large white cloth. He positioned me where he wanted me to stand, then walked over to the easel and pulled off the cloth.

I stared at the painting. I was stunned. Alexander had painted a portrait of me, in his own very special style, but it was very obviously me. I stood against a seascape, and I looked extraordinary.

'Alexander, it's just beautiful! I don't know what to say . . . I'm so flattered. But how could you paint me? I mean, I didn't sit for this.'

'From my memory of you, Val. After all, you've been with me practically night and day for two weeks now. Your face is engraved on my mind.'

'I am so flattered,' I said again. 'It's . . . wonderful. What an honour to be painted by you.'

'I'm happy you like it.' He took hold of my hand, led me down the steps, and out onto the terrace overlooking the sea.

After we were seated on a long rattan sofa, he said, 'Stay here, Val. Let Neal take the pictures back to Paris.'

'You know I can't do that. Anyway, I want to see the feature through to the end, and I've still got work to do on preparing it.'

'I was thinking the other day . . . how you can know someone all your life and yet never know them. And then meet another person and know them *instantly*, know all about them. I feel that way about you, Val.'

I stared at him but I didn't respond. I had no words.

'Did you know that King Hussein of Jordan met, fell in love with and became engaged to Queen Noor within twenty days?'

I shook my head. 'No, I didn't.'

'So can you understand it when I say this . . . I've fallen in love with you.'

'*Oh, Alexander.*'

'Please stay here with me,' he repeated.

'You know, I don't think I'm cut out to be your mistress, or anybody's mistress,' I said softly, and sat there frowning at him speechlessly.

He laughed. 'I've always said that when you marry your mistress you create a job vacancy and –'

'That's not an original line, somebody else said that before you.'

'Yes, and I knew him.'

'Oh, Alexander,' I said again, and simply shook my head, totally at a loss.

'But it would be different with you. I would be faithful. I wouldn't be looking for someone to fill the job vacancy.'

When I still remained silent, he moved closer to me on the sofa and took me in his arms. He kissed me tenderly and I found myself responding, returning his kisses, and my arms went around him.

Pulling away, he looked deeply into my eyes. 'Stay here with me.'

I was incapable of speech.

'We don't have to sleep together tonight; I'll be patient . . . if that makes you feel more secure about this old devil.'

'You're not old,' I said, finding my voice at long last.

'You need a lot of loving, Val, to heal those hurts of yours. I can heal them with my love, you know. *And you're so good for me.* Say you'll stay here at the hacienda.'

I didn't answer him, and so he folded me in his arms and held me close, and we sat there for a long time on the terrace.

I knew he was sincere, and I did find him attractive and compelling. Yes, I could easily become involved with him, even fall in love with him, and be happy at the hacienda. We could probably have the best life together.

The problem was, I loved another man. Truly loved him. I was committed to him, and he was my destiny. And that was why I would have to leave.

Chapter Thirty-Two

I
KOSOVO, APRIL

It was a cold day even though spring had come to this blood-soaked land, and the sun shone, rode high in a pale-blue sky filled with white puffball clouds. And despite the bitter wind it was a pretty day. But few people noticed that.

Jake had been right about NATO intervening in the war. The air strike was on and bombs had begun to fall on March 24th. NATO was still in the fray, and I suspected the battle would last a long time.

I was in Priština, the capital of Kosovo, looking for Jake, which is where he had been a few days ago. Jacques Foucher had given me all of the information when I had arrived in Paris, having flown from Acapulco to New York, and from there to Paris on the French Concorde.

After a night at my apartment on the Left Bank I had filled a small backpack with film, put in an extra camera, a few toiletries and a change of underwear, plus two clean T-shirts. When I left for Belgrade I was wearing my combat boots and flak jacket, and thus was able to minimize my luggage, travel light, be mobile at all times.

The streets of Priština were filled with masses of rubble; people were hurrying through the streets, dodging Serbian bombs and gunfire, trying to find somewhere safe to hide.

So many had apparently left, were moving on foot and cart and tractor towards the borders of Albania and Macedonia, hoping against hope to be allowed to enter these countries. But luck was running out now for all these refugees who were fleeing Milosevic's terror.

It was a hellhole here.

The barrage of gunfire was deafening, and dust rose up from the rubble to choke me. I had a camera slung around my neck and the backpack was on my shoulder. Travelling light worked, I decided as I hustled along, dodging the crowds as best I could.

There were so many people moving through the streets it was hard to spot anyone, although I'd kept my eyes peeled for Jake ever since I'd arrived.

Suddenly and unexpectedly I spotted Hank Jardine, an American war correspondent with one of the cable networks.

'Hank!' I screamed and began to run towards him. 'Hank, wait! It's me, Val Denning!'

He was hurrying down the street ahead of me with

his cameraman, and it was the cameraman who heard my voice, and grabbed Hank's arm. The two men swung around, and Hank waved when he saw me, looking surprised.

I caught up with them and exclaimed, 'Hi, guys.'

'Hi, Val,' Hank said.

The cameraman smiled at me, and said, 'John Grove.'

'Val Denning.' We shook hands and then I addressed Hank. 'I'm looking for Jake. Have you seen him?'

'Sure did, about two hours ago. He was with Clee Donovan, and they were down by the Red Cross tents. About ten minutes down this road. The tents are set up at the edge of a field.'

'Were they wounded?'

'I don't think so. But I'm not sure.'

'Thanks, Hank. Are you heading that way?'

'No, I'm going over to talk to some of the Kosovars who have been wounded. I want to do a couple of interviews.'

'Thanks,' I said again, and hurried off on my own. It worried me that Jake and Clee were at the Red Cross tents. It didn't bode well, I thought.

I began to fill with anxiety, and as apprehension got the better of me I started to run, pushing myself forward, dodging people, intent on getting to the tents as fast as I could.

I was panting and out of breath by the time I came to the field where the Red Cross tents had been set up. In the distance I could see several K.L.A. soldiers talking in a group, and a couple of Red Cross doctors close by. *And Clee Donovan.*

I came to a standstill for a moment, and my heart stopped. Oh my God, something had happened to Jake. I just knew it. This place was unlucky for me. It stank of death.

I took a deep breath and began to run again, and as I continued sprinting hell for leather down the road I spotted Jake.

'Jake! Jake!' I screamed, rushing forward, my feet flying along the road, my heart racing.

He heard me and swung around.

'Val!' he shouted, raising an arm, and then he began to run towards me.

We met in the middle of the dusty road.

I stumbled into his outstretched arms.

We clung to each other, and I began to sob with relief.

'Oh, thank God you're all right, that nothing's happened to you,' I cried, my voice cracking.

'I told you I'd be all right, that you should trust me,' he said, holding me away, looking into my face. An amused smile made his mouth twitch, and he said, laughing, 'Your face is dirty, Val.'

I gaped at him, uncomprehending for a second, and then I yelled, 'What the hell do you expect it to be in this muck hole!' But I started to laugh myself.

He held me close again, saying, 'Val, oh, Val, it's so wonderful to see you. This has just been the worst few weeks. I sure am glad you weren't here, it's been very rough, pretty damned lousy, Kid.'

I drew away from him, stared into those very bright-blue eyes of his, and murmured, 'But I'm here now, Jake, with you. Where I belong. Here in your arms. On the front lines. Or wherever you want me to be. Just as long as we're together.'

Staring at me, he said, 'And I want you with me, Val. But not here, not here any more. I've sent out enough pictures, done what I set out to do when I came. I was planning to get out just before you arrived.'

'You mean you want to leave Kosovo?' I asked, looking at him intently.

'Yes, I do. Let's go and say goodbye to Clee.' He put an arm around me and we headed on down the road towards the field.

Abruptly, Jake stopped, looked down at me, and said, 'There's just one more thing, Val.'

'What's that?'

'You just said you belong with me . . . does that mean you'll marry me?'

'Yes, I will,' I said, looking up into his face, smiling at him.

'I'm glad,' he said as he smiled back.

He took hold of my hand and held it tightly as we set out across the muddy field, and I knew that at last I was safe from harm.

Her Own Rules

To Bob, with love

Contents

PROLOGUE

Time Past

Prologue

The child sat on a rock perched high up on the river's bank. Elbows on knees, chin cupped in hands, she sat perfectly still, her eyes trained on the family of ducks circling around on the surface of the dark water.

Her eyes were large, set wide apart, greyish green in colour and solemn, and her small face was serious. But from time to time a smile would tug at her mouth as she watched the antics of the ducklings.

It was a bright day in August.

The sky was a piercingly blue arc unblemished by cloud, the golden sun a perfect sphere, and on this balmy summer's afternoon nothing stirred. Not a blade of grass nor a leaf moved; the only sounds were the faint buzzing of a bee hovering above roses rambling along a crumbling brick wall, the splash of water rushing down over the dappled stones of the river's bed.

The child remained fascinated by the wildlife on the river, and so intent was she in her concentration that she barely moved. It was only when she heard her name being called that she bestirred herself and glanced quickly over her shoulder.

Instantly she scrambled to her feet, waving at the

young woman who stood near the door of the cottage set back from the river.

'Mari! Come on! Come in!' the woman called, beckoning to the child as she spoke.

It took Mari only a moment to open the iron gate in the brick wall, and then she was racing along the dirt path, her plump little legs running as fast as they could.

'Mam! Mam! You're back!' she cried, rushing straight into the woman's outstretched arms, almost staggering in her haste to get to her.

The young woman caught her daughter, held her close, and nuzzled her neck. She murmured, 'I've a special treat for tea,' and then she looked down into the child's bright young face, her own suddenly serious. 'I thought I told you not to go down to the river alone, Mari, it's dangerous,' she chastised, but she did so softly and her expression was as loving as it always was.

'I only sit on the rock, Mam, I don't go near the edge,' Mari answered, lifting her eyes to her mother's. 'Eunice said I could go and watch the baby ducks.'

The woman sighed under her breath. Straightening, she took hold of the child's hand and led her into the cottage. Once they were inside, she addressed the girl who was sitting in a chair at the far end of the kitchen, reading a book.

'Eunice, I don't want Mari going to the river alone, she might easily slip and fall in, and then where would you be? Why, you wouldn't even know it had happened. I've told you this so often. Eunice, are you *listening* to me?'

'Yes, Mrs Sanderson. And I'm sorry, I won't let her go there by herself again.'

'You'd better not,' Kate Sanderson said evenly, but despite her neutral tone there was no doubt from the look in her eyes that she was annoyed.

Turning away abruptly, Kate went and filled the tea kettle, put it on the gas stove and struck a match.

The girl slapped her book shut and rose. 'I'll get off then, Mrs Sanderson, now that you're home.'

Kate nodded. 'Thanks for baby-sitting.'

'Shall I come tomorrow?' the teenager asked in a surly voice as she crossed the kitchen floor. 'Or can you manage?'

'I think so. But please come on Friday morning for a few hours. That would help me.'

'I'll be here. Is nine all right?'

'That's fine,' Kate responded, and forced a smile despite her lingering irritation with the teenager.

'Ta'rar, Mari,' Eunice said, grinning at the child.

'Ta'rar, Eunice,' Mari answered and fluttered her small, chubby fingers in a wave.

When they were alone, Kate said to her five-year-old daughter, 'Go and wash your hands, Mari, that's a good girl, and then we'll have our tea.'

The child did as she was bidden, and went upstairs to the bathroom, where she washed her hands and dried them. A few seconds later, she returned to the kitchen; this was the hub of the house and the room they used the most. It was good-sized and rustic. There was a big stone fireplace with an old-fashioned oven built next to it, lattice windows over the sink, wooden beams on the ceiling and brightly-coloured rag rugs covered the stone floor.

As well as being warm and welcoming, even cosy, it was a neat and tidy room. Everything was in its proper place; pots and pans gleamed, and the two windows behind the freshly laundered lace curtains sparkled in the late-afternoon sunshine. Kate took pride in her home, and this showed in the care and attention she gave it.

Mari ran across to the table which her mother had covered with a white tablecloth and set for tea, and scrambled up onto one of the straight wooden chairs.

She sat waiting patiently, watching Kate moving with swiftness, bringing plates of sandwiches and scones to the table, turning off the whistling kettle, pouring hot water onto the tea leaves in the brown teapot, which Kate always said made the tea taste all that much better.

The child loved her mother and this adoration shone on her face as her eyes followed Kate everywhere. She was content now that her mother had come home. Kate had been out for most of the day. Mari missed her when she was gone, even if it was for only a short while. Her mother was her entire world. To the five-year-old, Kate was the perfect being, with her gentle face, her shimmering red-gold hair, clear blue eyes and loving nature. They were always together, inseparable, for the feeling was mutual. Kate loved her child to the exclusion of all else.

Kate moved between the gas oven and the counter-top next to the sink, bringing things to the table, and when finally she sat down opposite Mari she said, 'I bought your favourite sausage rolls at the bakery in town, Mari. Eat one now, lovey, while it's still warm from the oven.'

Mari beamed at her. 'Oooh, Mam, I do love 'em.'

'Them,' Kate corrected softly. 'Always say *them*, Mari, not 'em.'

The child nodded her understanding and reached for a sausage roll, eating it slowly but with great relish. Once she had finished, she eyed the plates of sandwiches hungrily. There were various kinds – cucumber, polony, tomato and egg salad. Mari's mouth watered, but because her mother had taught her manners, had told her never to grab for food greedily, she waited for a second or two, sipped the glass of milk her mother had placed next to her plate.

Presently, when she thought enough time had elapsed, she reached for a cucumber sandwich and bit into it, savouring its moist crispness.

Mother and child exchanged a few desultory words as they munched on the small tea sandwiches Kate had made, but mostly they ate in silence, enjoying the food thoroughly. Both of them were ravenous.

Mari had not had a proper lunch today because Eunice had ruined the cottage pie her mother had left for them, and which had only needed to be reheated. The baby-sitter had left it in the oven far too long, and it had burned to a crisp. They had had to make do with bread and jam and an apple each.

Kate was starving because she had skipped lunch altogether. She had been tramping the streets of the nearby town, trying to find a job, and she had not had the time or the inclination to stop at one of the local cafés for a snack.

Kate's hopes had been raised at her last interview earlier that afternoon just before she had returned home. There was a strong possibility that she would get a job at the town's most fashionable dress shop, Paris Modes. There was a vacancy for a sales person and the manager had seemed to like her, had told her to come back on Friday morning to meet the owner of the shop. This she fully intended to do. Until then she was keeping her fingers crossed, praying that her luck was finally about to change for the better.

Once Kate had assuaged her hunger, she got up and went to the pantry. The thought of the job filled her with new-found hope and her step was lighter than usual as she brought out the bowl of strawberries and jug of cream.

Carrying them back to the table, she smiled with pleasure when she saw the look of delight on her child's face.

'Oh Mam, *strawberries*,' Mari said and her eyes shone.

'I told you I had a treat for you!' Kate exclaimed, giving Mari a generous portion of the berries, adding a dollop of cream and then serving herself.

'But we only have treats on special days, Mam. Is today special?' the child asked.

'It might turn out to be,' Kate said enigmatically. And then seeing the look of puzzlement on Mari's face, she added, 'Anyway, it's nice to have a treat on days which aren't particularly special. That way, the treat's a bigger surprise, isn't it?'

Mari laughed and nodded.

As so often happens in England, the warm August afternoon turned into a chilly evening.

A fine rain had been falling steadily since six o'clock and there was a dank mist on the river; this had slowly crept across the low-lying meadows and fields surrounding the cottage, obscuring almost everything. Trees and bushes had taken on strange new shapes, looked like inchoate monsters and illusory beings out there beyond the windows of the cottage.

For once Mari was glad to be tucked up in her bed. 'Tell me a story, Mam,' she begged, slipping further down under the warm covers.

Kate sat on the bed and straightened the top of the sheet, saying as she did, 'What about a poem instead? You're always telling me you like poetry.'

'Tell me the one about the magic wizard.'

Kate smoothed a strand of light brown hair away from Mari's face. 'You mean *The Miraculous Stall*, don't you, angel?'

'That's it,' the child answered eagerly, her glowing eyes riveted on her mother's pretty face.

Slowly Kate began to recite the poem in her soft, mellifluous voice.

'A wizard sells magical things at this stall,
Astonishing gifts you can see if you call.
He can give you a river's bend
And moonbeam light,
Every kind of let's pretend,
A piece of night.

Half a mile,
A leaf's quiver,
An elephant's smile,
A snake's slither.
A forgotten dream,
A frog's croaks,
Firefly gleam,
A stone that floats,
Crystal snowflakes,
Dew from flowers,
Lamb's tail shakes,
The clock's hours.
But – surprise!
Not needle eyes.
Those he does not sell at all,
At his most miraculous stall.'

Kate smiled at her daughter when she finished, loving her so much. Yet again, she smoothed the tumbling hair away from Mari's face and kissed the tip of her nose.

Mari said, 'It's my best favourite, Mam.'

'Mmmmm, I know it is, and you've had a lot of your favourite things today, little girl. But now it's time for you to go to sleep. It's getting late, so come on, snuggle down in bed . . . have you said your prayers?'

The child shook her head.

'You must always remember to say them, Mari. I do. Every night. And I have since I was small like you are now.'

Mari clasped her hands together and closed her eyes.

Carefully she said: 'Matthew, Mark, Luke and John, bless this bed that I lay on. Four corners to my bed, four angels round my head. One to watch and one to pray and two to keep me safe all day. May the grace of Our Lord Jesus Christ, the love of God and the fellowship of the Holy Spirit be with us all now and forever more. Amen. God bless Mam and keep her safe. God bless me and keep me safe. And make me a good girl.'

Opening her eyes, Mari looked at Kate intently. 'I *am* a good girl, aren't I, Mam?'

'Of course you are, darling,' Kate answered. 'The best girl I know. My girl.' Leaning forward, Kate put her arms around her small daughter and hugged her close.

Mari's arms went around Kate's neck and the two of them clung together. But after a moment or two of this intimacy and closeness, Kate released her grip and settled Mari down against the pillows.

Bending over the child, she kissed her cheek and murmured, 'God bless. Sweet dreams. I love you, Mari.'

'I love you, Mam.'

Wide rafts of sunlight slanted through the window, filling the small bedroom with radiance. The constant sunshine flooding across Mari's face awakened her. Opening her eyes, blinking and adjusting herself to the morning light, she sat up.

Mari had recently learned to tell the time and so she glanced over at the clock on the bedside table. It was nearly nine. This surprised the child; her mother was usually up and about long before this time every morning, calling her to come down for breakfast well before eight o'clock.

Slipping out of bed, thinking that her mother had overslept, Mari trotted across the upstairs hall to her mother's bedroom. The bed was empty. Holding onto the banister, the way she had been taught, she went down the stairs carefully.

Much to Mari's surprise, her mother was nowhere to be seen in the kitchen either. At least, not at first glance. But as she peered around the table she suddenly saw her mother on the floor near the gas stove.

'Mam! Mam!' she shouted, ran around the table and came to a standstill in front of her mother. Kate was lying in a crumpled heap; her eyes were closed and her face was deathly white.

Mari saw that there was blood on her mother's nightgown and she was so frightened she could not move for a moment. Then she crouched down and took hold of her mother's hand. It was cold. Cold as ice.

'Mam, Mam,' she wailed in a tremulous voice, the fear intensifying. 'What's the matter, Mam?'

Kate did not answer; she simply lay there.

Mari touched her cheek. It was as cold as her hand.

The child remained with her mother for a few minutes, patting her hand, touching her face, endeavouring to rouse her, but to no avail. Tears welled in Mari's eyes and rolled down her cheeks. A mixture of panic and worry assailed her; she did not know what to do.

Eventually it came to her. She remembered what her mother had always told her: 'If there's ever anything wrong, an emergency, and I'm not here, go and find Constable O'Shea. He'll know what's to be done. He'll help you.'

Reluctant though she was to leave her mother, Mari now realized that this was exactly what she must do. She must go to the police box on the main road, where Constable O'Shea could be found when he was on his beat.

Letting go of her mother's hand, Mari headed upstairs. She went to the bathroom, washed her face and hands, cleaned her teeth, and got dressed in the cotton shorts and top she had worn yesterday. After buckling on her sandals, she returned to the kitchen.

Mari stood over Kate, staring down at her for a moment or two, her alarm and concern flaring up in her more than ever. And then turning on her heels decisively, she hurried outside into the sunny morning air.

Mari raced down the garden path and out onto the tree-lined lane, her feet flying as she ran all the way to the main road. It was here that the police box was located. Painted dark blue and large enough to accommodate two policemen if necessary, the box was a great convenience for the bobby on the beat. Fitted out with a telephone, running water and a gas burner, it was here that a policeman could make a cup of tea, eat a sandwich, write up a report and phone the main police station when he had to report in or request help. These police boxes were strategically placed in cities and towns all over England, and were indispensable to the bobbies on the beat, especially when they were on night duty and when the weather was bad.

By the time Mari reached the police box she was panting and out of breath. But much to her relief Constable O'Shea was there. He'll help me, I know he will, she thought, as she came to a stop in front of him.

The policeman was standing in the doorway of the box, smoking a cigarette. He threw it down and stubbed it out when he saw Mari.

Taking a closer look at the panting child, Patrick O'Shea immediately detected the fear in her eyes and saw that she was in a state of great agitation. Recognizing at once something was terribly wrong, he bent over her, took hold of her hand and looked into her small, tear-stained face. 'What's the matter, Mari love?' he asked gently.

'It's me mam,' Mari cried, her voice rising shrilly. 'She's lying on the kitchen floor. I can't make her wake up.' Mari began to cry even though she was trying hard to be brave. 'There's blood. On her nightgown.'

Constable O'Shea had known Mari all of her young life, and he was well aware that she was a good little girl, well brought up and certainly not one for playing tricks or prone to exaggeration. And in any case her spiralling anxiety was enough to convince him that something *had* gone wrong at Hawthorne Cottage.

'Just give me a minute, Mari,' he said, stepping inside the police box. 'Then we'll go home and see what's to be done.' He phoned the police station, asked for an ambulance to be sent to Hawthorne Cottage at once, closed the door and locked it behind him.

Reaching down, he swung the child up into his arms, making soothing noises and hushing sounds as he did so.

'Now then, love, let's be on our way back to your house to see how your mam is, and I'm sure we can soon put everything right.'

'But she's dead,' Mari sobbed. 'Me mam's dead.'

PART ONE

Time Present

One

Meredith Stratton stood at the large, plate-glass window in her private office which looked downtown, marvelling at the gleaming spires rising up in front of her. The panoramic vista of the Manhattan skyline was always eye-catching, but tonight it looked more spectacular than ever.

It was a January evening at the beginning of 1995, and the sky was ink-black and clear, littered with stars. There was even a full moon. Not even a Hollywood set-designer could have done it better, Meredith thought: there's no improving on nature. And then she had to admit that it was the soaring skyscrapers and the overall architecture of the city that stunned the eye.

The Empire State building still wore its gaudy Christmas colours of vivid red and green; to one side of it, slightly to the left, was the more sedate Chrysler building with its slender art deco spire illuminated with pure white lights.

Those two famous landmarks dominated the scene, as they always did, but this evening the entire skyline seemed to have acquired more glittering aspects than ever, seemed more pristinely etched against the dark night sky.

'There's nowhere in the world quite like New York,' Meredith said out loud.

'I agree.'

Meredith swung around to see her assistant Amy Brandt standing in the doorway of her office.

'You gave me a start, creeping in on me like that,' Meredith exclaimed with a grin, and then turned back to the window. 'Amy, come and look. It takes my breath away.'

Amy closed the door behind her and walked across the room. She was petite and dark-haired, a contrast to Meredith, who was tall and blonde. Amy felt slightly dwarfed by her boss, who stood five feet seven in her stocking-feet. But since Meredith always wore high heels she generally towered over most people, and this gave Amy some consolation, made her feel less like an elf.

Gazing out of the window, Amy said, 'You're right, Meredith, Manhattan's looking sensational, almost unreal.'

'There's a certain clarity about the sky tonight, even though it's dark,' Meredith pointed out. 'There're no clouds at all, and the lights of the city are creating a wonderful glow . . .'

The two women stood looking out of the window for a few seconds longer, and then, turning away, moving towards her desk, Meredith said, 'I just need to go over a couple of things with you, Amy, and then you can get off.' She glanced at her watch. 'It's seven already. Sorry to have kept you so late.'

'It's not a problem. You'll be away for a week, so I'll be able to take it easy while you're gone.'

Meredith laughed. 'You taking it easy would be the miracle of the century. You're a workaholic.'

'Oh no, not me, that's *you*! You take first prize in that category.'

Meredith's deep green eyes crinkled at the corners as she laughed again, and then pulling a pile of manila files towards her she opened the top one, glanced down at the sheet of figures and studied them.

Finally, she looked up and said, 'I'll be gone for longer than a week, Amy. I think it will be two at least. I've quite a lot to do in London and Paris. Agnes is very set on buying that old manor house in Montfort-L'Amaury, and you know she's like a dog with a bone when she gets her teeth into something. However, I'm going to have to work very closely with her on this one.'

'From the photographs she sent it looks like a beautiful property, and it's perfect for us,' Amy volunteered, and then asked, 'You're not suddenly off it, are you?'

'No, I'm not. And what you say is true, it *is* ideal for Havens. My only worry is how much do we have to spend, in order to turn that old house into a comfortable inn, with all the modern conveniences required by the seasoned, indeed pampered, traveller? That's the key question. Agnes gets rather vague when it comes to money, you know that. The cost of new plumbing is not something that concerns her particularly, or even interests her. I'm afraid practicalities have always eluded Agnes.'

'She's very creative though, especially when it comes to marketing the inns.'

'True. And I'm usually stuck with the plumbing.'

'And the decorating. Let's not forget that, Meredith. You know you love designing the inns, putting your own personal stamp on them, not to mention everything in them.'

'I do enjoy that part of it, yes. On the other hand, I must consider the costs, and more than ever this time around. Agnes can't put up any more of her own money, so she won't be involved in the purchase of the manor or the cost of its remodelling. And the same applies to Patsy in England: she can't offer any financial help either. I have to raise the money myself. And I will. Agnes and Patsy are somewhat relieved that I'll be taking care of the financing, but more than ever I'll have to keep a tight rein on the two of them when it comes to the remodelling.'

'Are you sure you want to go ahead with the new inns in Europe?' Amy asked. Until this moment she had not realized that Meredith would be doing all of the financing, and she detected a degree of worry in her voice.

'Oh yes, I do want to buy them. We have to acquire additional inns in order to expand properly. Not that I want the company to become too big. I think six hotels is enough, Amy – certainly that number's just about right for me, easy to manage, as long as Agnes is running the French end and Patsy the English.'

'Six,' Amy repeated, eyeing Meredith quizzically. 'Are you trying to tell me something?'

Meredith looked baffled. 'I'm not following you.'

'You said six inns are easy to manage, but with the

two new ones in Europe you'll actually own *seven*, if you count the three here. Are you thinking of selling off one of the American hotels?'

'I *have* been toying with the idea,' Meredith admitted.

'Silver Lake Inn would bring in the most money,' Amy remarked. 'After all, it's the most successful of the three.'

Meredith stared at Amy.

Suddenly she felt the same tight pain in her chest that she had last week, when Henry Raphaelson, her friendly private banker, had uttered the same words over lunch at '21'.

'I could never sell Silver Lake,' Meredith answered at last, repeating what she had said to Henry.

'I know what you mean.'

No, you don't, Meredith thought, but she remained silent. She simply inclined her head, dropped her eyes, stared at the financial breakdown, the costs of remodelling the manor in Montfort-L'Amaury, but not really concentrating on the figures.

She was thinking of Silver Lake Inn. No one really knew what it meant to her, not even her daughter and her son, who had both been born there. Silver Lake had always been her haven, the first safe haven she had known, and the first real home she had ever had. And Jack and Amelia Silver, the owners, had been the first people who had ever shown her any kindness in her entire life. They had loved and cherished her like a younger sister, nurtured her, brought out her potential – encouraged her talent, helped her to hone her business acumen, applauded her style. And from them she had learned about decency and kindness, dignity and courage.

Jack and Amelia. The only family she had ever had. For a moment she saw them both very clearly in her mind's eye. They were the first human beings she had ever loved. There had been no one to love before them. Except Spin, the little dog, and even she had been taken away from her just when they had become attached to each other.

Silver Lake was part of her very being, part of her soul. She knew she could never, would never, sell it whatever the circumstances.

Meredith took a deep breath and eventually the pain in her chest began to subside. Lifting her eyes, she remarked almost casually, 'I might have a buyer for Hilltops. That's why I've decided to go up to Connecticut tonight.'

Amy was surprised, but she merely nodded. 'What about Fern Spindle? Don't you think you'd get more for the Vermont inn than for Hilltops?'

'It's certainly a much more valuable property, Amy, that's true, valued in the many millions. But someone has to want it, has to want to buy, only then does it become viable to me.'

Amy nodded.

Meredith went on, 'Blanche knows I'm coming up tonight. I'm staying at Silver Lake, there's no point in having her open up the house for one night. Jonas will stay over and drive me up to Sharon tomorrow morning, to meet the potential buyers. After the meeting at Hilltops I'll come straight back to the city, and I'll leave for London on Saturday as planned.'

Picking up a manila folder, Meredith handed it to Amy. 'Here're my letters, all signed, and a bunch of cheques for Lois.' Leaning back in her chair, she finished, 'Well, I guess that's it.'

'No . . . you have e-mail, Meredith.'

Meredith swung around to face her computer on the narrow table behind her chair, peered at the screen.

Thurs. Jan 5 1995

Hi Mom:

Thanks for cheque. Helps.
Have a fab trip. Go get 'em.
Bring back the bacon.
Luv ya loads.

JON.

'Well, well, doesn't he have a way with words,' Meredith said, shaking her head. But she was smiling, thinking of her twenty-one-year-old son Jonathan, who had always had the ability to amuse her. He had turned out well. Just as his sister had. She was lucky in that respect.

Left alone in her office, Meredith studied the figures from her French partner. She thought they seemed a bit on the high side, and reminded herself that Agnes was not always as practical as she should be, when it came to refurbishing: with her long scarves and trailing skirts she was bohemian but stylish.

Agnes D'Auberville and she had been involved

in business together for the past eight years, and their partnership had been a successful one. They got on well and balanced each other, and Agnes's flair for marketing had helped to put the inns on the map.

Agnes ran the Paris office of Havens Incorporated and oversaw the management of the château-hotel they jointly owned in the Loire Valley. But she was unable to participate financially in the acquisition of the manor house in Montfort-L'Amaury, although she was keen that they buy it. 'You won't regret it, Meredith, it's a good investment for the company,' Agnes had said to her during their phone conversation earlier that day.

Meredith knew that this was true. She also knew that a charming inn, situated only forty-eight kilometres from Paris, and within easy striking distance of Versailles and the forest of Rambouillet, was bound to be a money-maker, especially if it had a good restaurant.

According to Agnes, she had already lined up a well-known chef, as well as a distinguished architect who would properly redesign the manor house, help to turn it into a comfortable inn.

As for Patsy Canton, her English partner who had come on board ten years ago, the story was a little different in one respect. Patsy had fallen upon two existing inns for sale quite by accident. She believed them to be real finds.

One was in Keswick, the famous beauty spot in the Lake District; the other was in the Yorkshire dales near the cathedral towns of York and Ripon. Both were popular places with foreign visitors. Again, such an inn, with its good reputation already established, would more than earn its keep.

Unfortunately, Patsy had the same dilemma as Agnes. She was unable to put up any more money. She had already invested everything she had in Havens Incorporated; her inheritance from her parents had gone into Haddon Fields, the country inn Havens owned in the Cotswolds.

In much the same way Agnes did in Paris, Patsy oversaw the management of Haddon Fields, and ran the small London office of Havens. Her strong suits were management and public relations.

Meredith let out a small sigh, thinking about the problems she was facing. On the other hand, they weren't really insurmountable problems, and, in the long run, the two new inns in Europe were going to be extremely beneficial to the company.

Expansion had been her idea, and hers alone, and she was determined to see it through; after all, she was the majority stockholder of Havens and the Chief Executive Officer. In essence it was her company, and she was responsible for all of its operations.

Henry Raphaelson had told her at the beginning of the week that the bank would lend her the money she needed for her new acquisitions. The inns Havens already owned would be used as collateral for the loan. But Silver Lake Inn was not included. Henry had agreed to this stipulation of hers, if somewhat reluctantly, because she had convinced him Hilltops would be sold quickly. She hoped she was right. With a little luck Elizabeth and Philip Morrison would commit to it tomorrow. Of course they will, she told herself, the eternal optimist.

Pushing back her chair, Meredith rose and crossed to the lacquered console against the long wall, where she had put her briefcase earlier.

Tall though she was, she had a shapely, feminine figure and long legs. She moved with lithesome grace and swiftness; she was generally quick in everything she did, full of drive and energy.

At forty-four Meredith Stratton looked younger than her years. This had a great deal to do with her vitality and effervescent personality, as well as her youthful face and pale blonde hair worn in a girlish pageboy. This framed her rather angular, well-defined features and arresting green eyes.

Good-looking though she was, it was her pleasant demeanour and winning, natural charm that captivated most people. She had a way with her that was unique, and she left a lasting impression on all who met her.

Carrying her briefcase back to the desk, a glass table top mounted on steel sawhorses, Meredith filled it with the manila folders and other papers she had been working on all day. After closing it and placing it on the floor, she picked up the phone and dialled her daughter's number.

'It's me,' Meredith said when Catherine answered.

'Hi, Mom!' Catherine exclaimed, sounding genuinely pleased to hear her mother's voice. 'How're things?'

'Pretty good. I'm off to London and Paris on Saturday.'

'Lucky thing! Can I come with you?'

'Of course! I'd love it. You know that, darling.'

'I can't, Mom, much as I'd enjoy playing hookey in Paris with you, having a good time. I have to finish the illustrations for Madeleine McGrath's new children's book, and I've several book jackets lined up. Oh, but I can dream, can't I?'

'Yes, you can, and I'm so glad things are going well for you with your work. But if you suddenly decide you can get away, call Amy. She'll book your flight and get you a ticket before you can even say Jack Robinson.'

Catherine began to laugh. 'I haven't heard you use that expression for years, not since I was a kid. You told me once where it came from, but now I can't remember. It's such an odd expression.'

'Yes, it is. It's something I learnt when I was growing up in Australia. I think it originated in England and was brought over by the pommies. Australians started to use it, and I guess it became part of our idiomatic speech. Sort of slang, really.'

'Now I remember, and you told us that it meant *in a jiffy*.'

'Less than a jiffy, actually,' Meredith said, laughing with her daughter. 'Anyway, think about coming to Paris or London. You know how much I enjoy travelling with you. How's Keith?'

Catherine let out a long sigh. 'He's fantastic ... yummy.'

'You sound happy, Cat.'

'Oh I am, Mom, I am. I'm crazy about him.'

'Is it getting serious?'

'*Very.*' Catherine cleared her throat. 'Mom, I think he's going to propose soon.'

For a split second Meredith was taken aback and she was silent at the other end of the phone.

'Mom, are you still there?'

'Yes, darling.'

'You do approve . . . don't you?'

'Of course I do. I like Keith a lot. I was just surprised for a moment, that's all. It seems to have progressed very quickly . . . what I mean is, you haven't known him all that long.'

'Six months. That's enough time, isn't it?'

'I suppose so.'

Catherine said, 'Actually, Keith and I fell in love with each other the moment we met. It was a *coup de foudre*, as the French are wont to say.'

Meredith smiled. 'Ah yes, struck by lightning . . . I know what you mean.'

'Is that how it was with my father?'

Meredith hesitated. 'Not really, Cat . . . Well, in a way, yes. Except we didn't admit that to each other for a long time.'

'Well, you couldn't, could you? I mean, given the peculiar circumstances. It must've been hell for you.'

'No, it wasn't, strangely enough. Anyway, that's an old, *old* story, and now's not the time to start going into it again.'

'Was it a *coup de foudre* when you met David?'

'No,' Meredith said, and thought of Jonathan's father for the first time in several years. 'We loved each other, but it wasn't a . . . crazy love.'

'I always knew that, I guess. It's a crazy love between me and Keith, and when he asks me I'm obviously going to say yes. You really *do* approve, don't you, Mom?' she asked again.

'Very much so, darling, and if he pops the question while I'm in London or Paris, you will let me know at once, won't you?'

'I sure will. And I bet we make you a grandmother before you can say . . . Jack Robinson.' Catherine giggled.

Meredith said, 'You're not pregnant, are you?'

'Don't be silly, Mom, of course I'm not. But I can't wait to have a baby. Before I get too old.'

Meredith burst out laughing. 'Don't be so ridiculous, you're only twenty-five.'

'I know, but I want to have children while I'm young, like you did.'

'You always were a regular old mother hen, even when you were little. But listen, honey, I'm going to have to go. Jonas is driving me up to Silver Lake Inn tonight. I have a meeting at Hilltops tomorrow. I'll be back in New York tomorrow evening, if you need me. Good night Cat. I love you.'

'I love you too, Mom. Say hello to Blanche and Pete, give them my love. And listen, take care.'

'I will. Talk to you tomorrow, and God bless.'

After hanging up the phone, Meredith sat at her desk for a moment or two, her thoughts with her daughter. Of course Keith Pearson would propose, and very soon, Meredith was quite certain of that. There was going to be a wedding this year. Her face lit up at the thought of it. Catherine was going to be a beautiful bride, and she would give her daughter a memorable wedding.

Rising, Meredith walked over to the window and stood staring out at the Manhattan skyline. New York City, she murmured to herself, the place I've made my home. Such a long way from Sydney, Australia . . . how far I've come . . . I took my terrible life and turned it around. I made a new life for myself. I took the pain and heartbreak and I built on them . . . I used them as foundations upon which to built *my* strong citadel, in much the same way the Venetians built theirs on pilings driven into the sandbanks. And I did it all by myself . . . no, not entirely by myself. Jack and Amelia helped me.

Swinging around, Meredith stood gazing at her office.

Her eyes swept around the elegant room decorated in various shades of pale grey, lavender and amethyst. They took in the expensive silks and velvets used to upholster the sofas and chairs, the sleek grey lacquer finishes on the modern furniture, the French and American modern impressionist paintings by Taurelle, Epko and Guy Wiggins.

She saw it as if for the first time, through newly objective eyes, and she could not help wondering what Jack and Amelia would think of it . . . what they would think of all that she had accomplished.

Her throat tightened with a rush of sudden emotion, and she stepped back up to the desk and sat down, her eyes now lingering on the two photographs in their silver frames which she always kept there in front of her.

One photograph was of Catherine and Jonathan taken when they were children; Cat had been twelve, Jon eight, and what beauties they had been. Free spirits and so finely wrought.

The other picture was of her with Amelia and Jack. How young she looked. Tanned and blonde and so unsophisticated. She had been just twenty-one years old when the picture was taken at Silver Lake.

Jack and Amelia would be proud of me, she thought. After all, they helped to make me what I am, and in a sense I am their creation. And they are the best part of me.

Two

Whenever she came back to Silver Lake, Meredith experienced a feeling of excitement. No matter how long she had been absent, be it months on end, a week, or merely a few days, she returned with a sense of joyousness welling inside, the knowledge that she was coming home.

Tonight was no exception.

Her anticipation started the moment Jonas pulled off Route 45 North near Cornwall, and nosed the car through the big iron gates that marked the entrance to the vast Silver Lake property.

Jonas drove slowly down the road that led to the lake, the inn and the small compound of buildings on its shores. It was a good road, well illuminated by the old-fashioned street lamps Meredith had installed some years before.

Peering out of the car windows, she could see that Pete had had some of the workers busy with the bulldozer earlier in the day. The road was clear, the snow banked high like giant white hedges, and in the woods that traversed the road on either side there were huge drifts blown by the wind into weird sand-dune shapes.

The branches of the trees were heavy with snow, many of them dripping icicles, and in the moonlight the white landscape appeared to shimmer as if sprinkled with a fine coating of silver dust.

Meredith could not help thinking how beautiful the woods were in their winter garb. But then this land was always glorious, no matter what the season of the year; it was so special to her that no other place in the world could compare to it.

The first time she had set eyes on Silver Lake she had been awed by its majestic beauty – the great lake shining in the spring sunlight, a smooth sheet of glass, surrounded by lush meadows and orchards, the whole set in a natural basin created by the soaring wooded hills which rose up to encircle the entire property.

She had fallen in love with it instantly, and had gone on loving it, with a glowing passion, ever since.

Twenty-six years ago this year, she thought, I was only eighteen. So long ago, more than half her life ago. And yet it might have been only yesterday, so clear and fresh was the memory in her mind tonight.

She had come to Silver Lake Inn to apply for the job of receptionist, which she had seen advertised in the local paper. The Paulsons, the American family who had brought her with them from Australia as an *au pair*, were moving to South Africa because of Mr Paulson's job. She did not want to go there. Nor did she wish to return to her native Australia. Instead, she preferred to stay in America, in Connecticut, to be precise.

It had been the middle of May, not long after her birthday, and she had arrived on a borrowed bicycle, looking a bit windswept, to say the least.

Casting her mind back now, she pictured herself as

she had been then – tall, skinny, all arms and legs like a young colt. Yet pretty enough in a fresh young way. She had been full of life and vitality, eager to be helpful, eager to please. That was her basic nature: she was a born peacemaker.

Jack and Amelia Silver had taken to her at once, as she had to them. But they had been concerned about her staying on in America without the Paulsons, had inquired about her family in Sydney, and what they would think. Once she explained that her parents were dead they had been sympathetic, sorry that she had lost them so young. And they had understood then that she had no real reason to go back to the Antipodes.

After they had talked on the phone to Mrs Paulson they had hired her on the spot.

And so it had begun, an extraordinary relationship which had changed her life.

Meredith straightened in her seat as the inn came into view. Lights blazed in many of the windows, a welcoming sight. She could hardly wait to be inside, to be with Blanche and Pete, surrounded by so many familiar things in that well-loved place.

Within seconds Jonas was pulling up in front of the inn. He had barely braked when the front door flew open and bright light flooded out onto the wide porch.

A moment later Blanche and Pete O'Brien were at the top of the steps, and as Meredith opened the car door Pete was already halfway down, exclaiming, 'Welcome, Meredith, you've certainly made it in good time, despite the snow.'

'Hello, Pete,' she said as he enveloped her in a hug.

She added, as they drew apart, 'There's nobody like Jonas when it comes to driving. He's the best.'

'That he is. Hi Jonas, good to see you,' Pete said, nodding to the driver, smiling at him. 'I'll help you with Mrs Stratton's bags.'

'Evening, Mr O'Brien, but I can manage. There's nothing much to carry.'

Meredith left the two men to deal with the bags, and ran up the steps.

'It's good to be back here, Blanche!'

The two women embraced and then Blanche, smiling up at Meredith, led her inside. 'And it's good to have you back, Meredith, if only for one night.'

'I wish I could stay longer, but as I explained on the phone, I've got to get back to the city after the meeting at Hilltops tomorrow.'

Blanche nodded. 'I think you're going to make a deal with the Morrisons. They're awfully keen to buy an inn, get away from New York, lead a different kind of life.'

'I'm keeping my fingers crossed,' Meredith said, shrugging out of her heavy grey wool cape, throwing it down on a bench.

'I know you'll like them. They're a lovely couple, very sincere, straight as a die. and quite aside from wanting to start a new business they love this part of Connecticut.'

'And why not, it's God's own country,' Meredith murmured. She glanced around the entrance hall. 'Everything looks wonderful, Blanche, so warm, welcoming.'

Blanche beamed at her. 'Thanks, Meredith, you

know I love this old place as much as you do. Anyway, you must be starving. I didn't think you'd want a proper dinner at this late hour, so I made some smoked-salmon sandwiches, and there's fruit and cheese. Oh, and I have a hunter's soup bubbling on the stove.'

'The soup sounds great. You make the best, and they're usually a meal in themselves. I'm sure Jonas is hungry after the long drive, so perhaps you'd offer him the soup too, and some sandwiches.'

'I will.'

Pete came in with Meredith's overnight bag and briefcase. 'Jonas has gone to park the car,' he explained. 'I'll take these upstairs.'

'Thanks, Pete,' Meredith said.

'I've put you in the *toile de Jouy* suite,' Blanche told her, 'because I know how much you like it. Now, do you want a tray up there? Or shall I bring it to the bar parlour?'

'I'll have it down here in the parlour, thanks, Blanche,' Meredith said, peering into the room that opened off the inn's large entrance hall. 'I see you have a fire going . . . that's nice. I think I'll make myself a drink. Would you like one, Blanche?'

'Why not? I'll join you in a vodka and tonic. But first let me go and fix a tray for Jonas. I'll be back in a few minutes.' She hurried off in the direction of the kitchen.

Meredith went into the parlour, glancing around as she strolled over to the huge stone hearth at the far end of the room. The fire burning brightly, the red carpet, the red velvet sofas and tub chairs covered in red-and-cream linen gave the parlour a warm, rosy feeling. This was further enhanced by the red brocade curtains at the leaded windows, the polished mahogany panelled walls, and the red shades on the wall sconces. It was a slightly masculine room in feeling, rather English in overtone, but there was a mellowness about it that Meredith had always liked.

The carved mahogany bar was to the left of the fireplace, facing the leaded windows, and Meredith now went behind it, took two glasses, added ice and poured a good measure of Stolichnaya Cristal into each one. She smiled to herself when she noticed the small plate of lime wedges next to the ice bucket. Blanche had second-guessed her very accurately. Her old friend had known she would have her drink in here. The bar parlour had always been a favourite spot of hers in the inn, as it was with everyone, because it was so intimate and cosy. And conducive to drinking. Jack had been smart when he had created it.

Once she had made the drinks, Meredith went over to the fireplace. She stood with her back to it, enjoying the warmth, sipping her vodka, relaxing as she waited for Blanche, whom she thought had never looked better. If there was a tiny fleck of silver in her bright red hair, she was, nonetheless, as slim as she had been as a girl, and the merry dark brown eyes were as lively as ever. She's wearing well, Meredith thought, very well indeed.

The two women, who were the same age, had been friends for twenty-four years. Blanche had come to Silver Lake Inn two years after Meredith had taken the job as receptionist. She had started as a pastry chef in the kitchens, had soon been promoted to chef, since she was an inspired cook. Blanche had enjoyed working in the kitchens until she married Pete, who had always managed the estate for the Silvers, and became pregnant with Billy.

By then Meredith was running the inn, and she offered Blanche the job of assistant manager. Blanche had been delighted to accept the offer at once, glad to be out of the heat, relieved not to lift heavy pots and pans, and thrilled to be able to continue working at the inn.

These days she and Pete ran Silver Lake Inn together and were responsible for its overall management as well as the upkeep of the entire estate. She's been good for this place, Meredith mused, her thoughts centred on Blanche for a moment. She's as passionate about it as I am, and it shows everywhere, in everything she does.

Blanche interrupted her musings, walking rapidly into the bar parlour, saying, 'By the way, you're not going to believe this, but we're rather busy this coming weekend. All the rooms are taken. And several suites. Unusual for January, I must say, but I'm not complaining.'

'I'm delighted. In some ways it's not that surprising. A lot of people do like being in the country in the snowy weather, and this place has such a great reputation. Thanks, in no uncertain terms, to you and Pete. I do appreciate all you both do, Blanche.'

'We love the inn, you know that.'

'By the way, Catherine sends her love to you and Pete.'

Blanche smiled. 'And give her ours. How is she, Meredith?'

'As wonderful as always, and doing so well with her work; she's turned out to be a fine illustrator. And of course she's madly in love.'

'With Keith Pearson?'

Meredith nodded. 'She told you?'

'Yes, when you were all here at Thanksgiving.'

'I think it's become rather serious.'

'Are we looking forward to a wedding?' Blanche asked, staring at Meredith quizzically.

'I think so . . . I'm pretty sure.'

'You will have it here, won't you?'

'Where else, Blanche? Cat was born here, grew up here, and so I'm certain she'll want to be married here. And it is the perfect setting.'

'Oh, I can't wait to start planning it!' Blanche cried, taking a sip of her drink. 'Cheers. And here's to Cat and the wedding.'

'The wedding,' Meredith said and lifted her glass as Blanche was doing. She wondered if it was bad luck to drink to something so prematurely.

'*Marquees*. We'll have to have marquees,' Blanche said, gazing into space, obviously already envisioning the reception.

'But they'll no doubt get married in the summer,' Meredith pointed out.

'Yes, I know. June probably, every girl wants to be a June bride. But it *can* rain up here at that time of year, you know that as well as I do, and it's best to be safe. Oh it'll be great, though. We'll do wonderful flowers and table settings. And a special menu.

Oh, it's going to be fabulous. Leave it all to me.'

Meredith laughed. 'I'm happy to, my darling Blanche.'

'Good.' Blanche sipped her drink, and then suddenly she looked across at Meredith and said, 'Do you ever hear from David?'

'David Layton?' Meredith asked, slightly surprised.

'Yes.'

'Rarely. Why do you ask?'

'I thought of him just now ... have you forgotten that you married him here and that I did the entire wedding?'

'No, I haven't,' Meredith said slowly, and began to shake her head. 'Funny, isn't it ... how someone's name is rarely, if ever, mentioned, and then it comes up twice in one day.'

'Who else mentioned David?'

'Catherine. When we were talking on the phone earlier this evening. She asked me if I'd been crazy in love with him, or words to that effect.'

'And what did you say?'

'I told her the truth. I said that I hadn't.'

'Of course not. You were only crazily in love once, and that was with her father.'

Meredith was silent.

'Have you ever wondered what your life would have been like if he hadn't –'

'I really don't want to discuss it,' Meredith snapped, cutting in peremptorily. Then she bit her lip, looking chagrined. 'I'm sorry, Blanche, I didn't mean to bite your head off like that, it's just that I prefer to leave that particular subject matter alone tonight. It's been a long day and I don't really feel like delving into the tragedies of the past.'

Blanche smiled gently. 'It's my fault. I brought it up and I shouldn't have . . . now you're looking sad . . . I've upset you.'

'No, you haven't, I promise you, Blanche.'

Deeming it wiser to change the subject, Blanche put down her drink and said, 'By the way, we're going to have to order new carpet for the *toile de Jouy* suite, and the blue room. There's been some leaks this winter, and the carpets are damaged. I hate to tell you this, but there's also been a leak in your bedroom in the house. I'll show you tomorrow. I'm afraid you'll have to replace the carpet there as well.'

'These things happen, Blanche. We know that from years of experience. And even after we put in new roofs last year. I'll call Gary at Stark tomorrow, before I go to London. He's got everything on the computer, so it won't be a problem.' Meredith frowned. 'The carpets were from the standard lines, weren't they?'

'Yes, I'm sure,' Blanche said, and then began to walk towards the door. 'It's getting late. I'm going to the kitchen to bring you that bowl of soup.'

Meredith put down her glass and followed her. 'I'll eat in the kitchen, Blanche, it's much easier.'

Three

Hilltops, the inn Meredith owned near Sharon, was built on top of a hill, as its name suggested. The site was the highest point above Lake Wononpakook, and the views from the inn's windows were spectacular: endless miles of lake and sky and wooded hills, with hardly another structure in evidence on the expansive land.

The inn started out as a mansion, the summer retreat of one of America's great tycoons, who built it in the late 1930s, sparing no expense. He and his family spent summers there until his death in the mid-1960s, when it was sold.

When Meredith bought it in 1981 it had been an inn for almost twenty years, and it was already well established. But it was her stylish refurbishing and the two new restaurants she created which gave it a certain *cachet*, and put it on the map.

Hilltops evoked images of Switzerland in her mind, and turning to Paul Ince, who was the manager of the inn, she said, 'I feel as if I'm looking down on Lake Geneva this morning, Paul.'

He laughed and answered, 'I know what you mean. I always get the sensation of being in the Swiss Alps myself, especially in winter.'

Meredith had arrived at Hilltops fifteen minutes earlier, and the two of them stood together in the inn's lovely old pine-panelled library, waiting for the Morrisons to arrive for the meeting.

Glancing out of the window again, Meredith murmured, 'All this snow. It really came down this year, but it doesn't seem to have affected business, does it?'

'No, not at all, Meredith. Well, I shouldn't say that. As you know, we did have a few problems last week, and had to close the restaurants for a few days. But we soon got rid of the snow, once the bulldozer was up on the main road here. When it was shifted we were fine.' He paused, turned to her. 'And we are fine,' he reassured.

'What are your bookings like for the weekend?' she asked.

'Pretty good, twelve out of the fifteen rooms are taken. And both restaurants are almost full. Local trade as well as the hotel guests.'

Paul cleared his throat, briefly hesitating, and then said, 'I know you'll be able to sell this place, Meredith. Whether it's to the Morrisons or someone else, because it's such a good buy. And I just wanted to say this now . . . I'm really going to miss working with you. You've always been great, such a wonderful boss.'

'That's nice of you to say so, Paul, thank you. And I've enjoyed working with *you* all these years. I couldn't have done it without you. You're definitely a big part of the inn's success, you've put so much of yourself into it, built up the business so well. And as I told you earlier, if the Morrisons do end up taking it over, I'm sure they'll want you to stay on. If *you* want to, that is.'

'I do, and when they were over here last weekend they indicated they felt the same way.'

'What're your feelings about them? About their intentions, Paul?'

'They're more than interested, Meredith. I'd say they're extremely keen to get their hands on Hilltops, as I told Blanche the other day. It's apparently what they've wanted for the last few years . . . a country inn in Connecticut, far away from the hectic pace of New York City and the rat race of Wall Street and Madison Avenue. New careers for them both. New life styles for them and their kids.'

'I didn't know they had children,' Meredith said, frowning. 'Does that mean they'd want to live in the cottage? Your cottage?'

Paul shook his head. 'No, Mrs Morrison's indicated that they're going to keep their house in Lakeville. But if they did want the cottage, Anne and I could always move into the inn until that apartment over the garage was made habitable.'

Meredith nodded her understanding; she walked over to the fireplace, where she sat down, poured herself another cup of coffee. 'Do you want a second cup, Paul?'

'Yes, please.' Paul joined her by the fireside.

They sat in silence for a few minutes, drinking their coffee, lost in their own thoughts. It was Meredith who spoke first, when she said, 'As you know, the asking price for the inn is four million dollars, and so far I've not budged from that figure. Between us, I would come down a bit, just to make the sale. What's your assessment of them, regarding the price?'

'It's hard to say,' Paul replied, looking thoughtful. After a moment or two's reflection, he went on, 'I'd stick to your guns for a bit and see what happens. But just be mentally prepared to accept three million.'

She shook her head. 'No way, Paul, I've got to get three and a half million, at least. Anyway, the inn's worth that . . . in fact, it's worth four. My real-estate people actually valued it at four and a half.'

'But you've always said to me that someone's got to want to buy a property to make it a viable holding, an asset.'

'I know, I know, but I really do need three and a half million dollars for my expansion programme,' Meredith said, putting her cup down with a clatter. 'The two inns in Europe are going to cost money, and I'd like to have something left over from this sale for operating costs and to plough back into Havens.'

'Look, Meredith, I'm sure the Morrisons are quite well placed. He's worked on Wall Street for years, and she's been one of the partners in an ad agency on Madison Avenue. In any case, when you meet them, talk to them, you'll be able to judge for yourself what the freight can bear.'

'Too true . . . why try to second-guess?'

There was a knock on the door, and as Paul called, 'Come in!' it opened.

The receptionist looked in and said, 'Mr and Mrs Morrison have arrived.'

Paul nodded. 'Show them in, Doris, please.'

Several seconds later Paul was introducing

Elizabeth and Philip Morrison to Meredith. Once the handshakes were over they all sat down in the chairs near the fire.

Meredith said, 'Can I offer you something? Coffee, tea, mineral water, perhaps?'

'No, thank you,' Mrs Morrison said.

Her husband shook his head and murmured something about just having had breakfast. Then he began to speak to Paul about the weather, the snow on the roads, and the drive over from Lakeville, where they owned a weekend home.

Mrs Morrison looked across at Meredith and said, 'I love the way you've decorated Hilltops . . . it's so charming and intimate. It reminds me of an English country house.'

'Thank you,' Meredith said, smiling at the other woman. 'I like decorating, creating a look, an ambience. And lots of comfort for the guests, of course. I think an inn should be a haven; that's why I called my company Havens Incorporated.'

Elizabeth Morrison nodded. 'Very apt, very apt indeed. And I think all your little touches are wonderful. The hotwater bottles in silk cases, the special reading lights by the bed, the cashmere blankets on the chaises, little luxuries like that make all the difference.'

'That's what I believe,' Meredith murmured, 'and that's my policy in all of the inns we own.'

'We've always wanted to run an inn like this,' Mrs Morrison confided. 'And now's the time to do it, when we're both still young. Also, we want to get out of the city, bring up our three children in the country. The city's become so violent, hard to take.'

'I understand. I raised two children in Connecticut, and I've always felt lucky that I was able to do so. As you know, since you've been residents up here for a few years, there are plenty of good schools. Yes, it's a great spot for a family.'

Elizabeth Morrison was about to say something else when she caught her husband's warning look; she simply cleared her throat and sat back in her chair, having suddenly become a mere spectator at this meeting.

Meredith, who missed nothing, noticed this infinitesimal exchange. She understood immediately that Philip Morrison did not want his wife saying any more. Nor did he wish her to sound too enthusiastic about the inn. He wanted her to play it cool. As he had been doing all along. He was obviously ready to deal.

Not giving him an opportunity to start the ball rolling, Meredith jumped in with both feet.

Staring directly at him, fixing him with an appraising eye, she said, 'I know you've been back to look at Hilltops many times now, and that you both like it. The question is, do you really want to buy it?'

'Yes,' Philip Morrison said. 'At the right price. For us, that is.'

'The price is four million dollars, Mr Morrison. I think my real-estate lawyer in the city has already told you that.'

'He did. But as I told Mr Melinger, it's a bit steep for me.'

'Actually, the inn *is* worth four million dollars, even

more if the truth be known,' Meredith pointed out. 'As a matter of fact, its true value is four and a half million dollars. You can check that with the real-estate people, both here and in the city. It just so happens that I'm willing to take less because I'm expanding my company. Otherwise, I'd hold out for the *proper* price, I can assure you.'

'I'll give you three million,' Philip Morrison said, glanced at his wife, and added, 'That's all we can pay, isn't it, Liz?'

Momentarily startled to be drawn into this exchange, she looked nonplussed. Then she said quickly, emphatically, 'We're selling our Manhattan co-op and hoping to get a mortgage on the Lakeville house, and by cashing in some of our other assets we can raise three million. But that's it.'

Meredith gave her a long and thoughtful look but made no comment. Leaning forward, she picked up her cup of coffee and took a sip.

Morrison said, 'What do you say, Mrs Stratton? Will you accept three million?'

'No,' Meredith said, looking him right in the eye. 'I can't. As I told you, when I first decided to sell Hilltops my original price was four and a half million dollars, because that *is* its true value. It's in perfect condition. New roof, new plumbing and new wiring in the last few years, among many other major improvements. And there's a great deal of land attached to the inn. I only came down in price because it was suggested I do so by my advisers, in order to sell now. But I must stick at four million.'

'Three million and a quarter,' Morrison countered.

Meredith pursed her lips and shook her head. 'Four.'

'Three and a quarter,' he offered again.

Meredith let out a small sigh and gave the Morrisons a slow, resigned smile, glancing from one to the other. 'I tell you what, I'll take three million, seven hundred and fifty thousand.'

'I just can't do it,' Philip Morrison said.

'But it's a bargain,' Meredith stated quietly. 'If you consider that the proper price is really four and a half million, I've just come down by three-quarters of a million dollars.'

Philip Morrison smiled wryly. 'But we've always been talking *four* million, not *four and a half*, Mrs Stratton, let's not forget that, shall we?'

Meredith made no response.

She rose and walked across to the bank of windows overlooking the lake, and stood there staring out at the view for a few moments.

Finally, when she swung around, she said, 'You want the inn. I want to sell it. So I'll tell you what I'll do, *I'll* compromise. I'll sell it to you for three point five million.'

The Morrisons exchanged pointed glances.

At last he said, 'I'd like to do it, but I just don't think I can. I can't raise any more.'

'You could go to your bank,' Meredith suggested, 'and get a loan – or better still, a mortgage on the inn.'

Philip Morrison stared at her. But he remained silent.

'I can introduce you to the right bank,' Meredith volunteered, wanting to conclude the deal.

'Do you think they would give me a mortgage on the inn?' he asked, taking the bait.

'I'm pretty certain, yes. There's something else I'll do. I'll have my real-estate lawyer structure a reasonable payment schedule, one that won't cripple you.'

Elizabeth Morrison said, 'That's very decent of you.'

Meredith answered, 'I want to make the deal and I don't want to take advantage of you. You want to make the deal and I'm sure you don't want to cheat me.'

'Never! We're not people like that!' the other woman exclaimed indignantly.

'I must say, you're making it very tempting,' Morrison muttered, directing his gaze at Meredith. 'Making it hard to resist.'

'Then don't resist, Mr Morrison,' Meredith said.

He got to his feet when she drew to a stop next to his chair.

Meredith thrust out her hand. 'Come on, let's not haggle. Let's make the deal. It's good for us both, beneficial to us both.'

He hesitated only fractionally. Then he took her hand and shook it. 'All right, Mrs Stratton, you've got a deal. Three and a half million dollars it is.'

Meredith nodded and smiled at him.

He returned her smile.

Elizabeth Morrison came over and shook Meredith's hand.

Paul Ince, who had been on tenterhooks throughout this negotiation, congratulated everyone, then said, 'I think this calls for a toast. Let's go to the bar and I'll open a bottle of Dom Pérignon.'

'What a great idea, Paul,' Meredith said, leading the way out of the library.

On the drive back to New York City, Meredith gave only fleeting thought to Hilltops. She had accomplished what she had set out to do; she had sold the inn for the amount she wanted, and she was well satisfied. Three and a half million dollars would meet her expansion needs more than adequately.

Before leaving the inn, she had settled everything. Arrangements had been made for the Morrisons to meet with her real-estate lawyer, who would draw up the necessary documents next week. She had also set up an appointment for them to see Henry Raphaelson. The banker had sounded amenable during the phone call, had assured her he would endeavour to work things out with the Morrisons.

And so she turned her thoughts to other matters as Jonas drove back to Manhattan. Mostly she focused her attention on her trip to England, and on the purchase of an inn there. She was confident she would like one of the two Patsy Canton had found. With luck, she would be able to bring that bit of business to a conclusion fairly quickly, so that she could go to Paris to see Agnes D'Auberville.

Patsy had invited her to lunch on Sunday, so that they could go over business matters and map out a plan, and in so doing save time. The general idea was that they would travel to the North of England on Monday, going first to Cumbria. After looking at the inn located in the Lake District they would drive down to Yorkshire to see the one in the dales.

When she had asked Patsy which of the two inns she preferred, her partner had been somewhat evasive. 'The one in Keswick needs much less done to it,' she had said and then clammed up.

When Meredith had pressed her further, Patsy had refused to make any more comments. 'I want this to be your decision and yours alone,' Patsy had murmured. 'If I give you my opinion now, before you've seen either hotel, I'll be influencing you, setting you up in advance. So don't press me.'

It had been Patsy's suggestion that, if she had no reason to return to London, she should fly to Paris from the Leeds–Bradford Airport. 'There're lots of flights to Paris from there and also from Manchester.' Meredith had agreed that this was a great idea, since it would save so much time.

Leaning back against the car seat, she closed her eyes, thinking of the packing she still had to do, trying to decide what clothes to take. Unexpectedly, she thought of Reed Jamison and the dinner date she had made with him. The mere idea of seeing him filled her with dismay. But she knew she must keep the appointment if she was to break off with him.

It was never on, she thought, sitting up, glancing out of the window. Their relationship had never really lifted off the ground, although lately he seemed to believe otherwise. In an effort to make herself feel better, she adopted a positive attitude, assured herself that it was going to be easy. He would understand. After all, he was a grown man.

But deep down Meredith felt she was wrong. Instinctively, she knew he was going to be difficult. Her dismay turned into apprehension.

Four

'I know you thought I was being stubborn the other day,' Patsy Canton said. 'When I wouldn't discuss the inns with you, but –'

'More like evasive,' Meredith interrupted.

'Not evasive, not stubborn, either. Just cautious. I didn't want you to get any preconceived ideas, especially from me, before you saw the inns. But now I can give you a sort of – *preview*, shall we say. The owner of the inn near Lake Windermere sent us a batch of photographs. They arrived yesterday. Let me get them for you.'

Patsy pushed herself out of the chair, walked across the small red sitting room of her house in Belgravia, where she and Meredith were having a drink before lunch on Sunday.

In her late thirties, she was an attractive woman, more handsome than pretty, almost as tall as Meredith and well built. Her hair was blonde, cut short, and it curled all over her head; her grey eyes were large and full of intelligence. But it was her flawless English complexion that everyone commented on.

Pausing at the small Georgian desk, Patsy picked up a large envelope and walked back to the sofa, where she sat down next to Meredith.

'Ian Grainger, the owner of Heronside, is rather proud of the pictures. He took them himself, last spring and summer.' So saying she handed the envelope to Meredith, who pulled out the photographs eagerly.

After a few seconds spent looking at them, she turned to Patsy and said, 'I'm not surprised he's proud of them. The pictures are beautiful. So is Heronside, if these are anything to go by.'

'Very much so, Meredith. In a way, the photographs don't really do the inn and the grounds justice. There's such a sense of luxury in the rooms, you feel pampered just walking into one of them. The whole inn is very well done, lovely antiques and fabrics, and I know you'll like the decorative schemes, the overall ambience. As for the grounds, they're breathtaking, don't you think?'

Meredith nodded, shuffled through the pictures again and picked one of them out. It was a woodland setting. The ground was carpeted with irises and rafts of sunlight slanted down through the leafy green canopies of the trees. Just beyond were brilliant yellow daffodils growing on a slope, and, far beyond this, a stretch of the lake could be seen – vast, placid, silvery, glistening in the sun.

'Look, Patsy,' Meredith said, and handed it to her partner. 'Isn't this gorgeous?'

'Yes, especially the slope covered in daffodils. Doesn't it remind you of Wordsworth's poem?'

Meredith stared at her.

'The one about the daffodils. Don't you know it?'

Meredith shook her head.

Patsy confided, 'It's one of my favourites.' Almost involuntarily, she began to recite it.

'I wandered lonely as a cloud
That floats on high o'er vales and hills,
When all at once I saw a crowd,
A host, of golden daffodils;
Beside the lake, beneath the trees,
Fluttering and dancing in the breeze.'

'It's lovely,' Meredith said.

'Didn't you learn it at school?'

'No,' Meredith murmured.

Patsy went on, 'I like the last verse best of all. Would you care to hear it?'

'Please,' Meredith replied. 'You recite poetry extremely well.'

Once more Patsy launched into the poem:

'For oft, when on my couch I lie
In vacant or in pensive mood,
They flash upon that inward eye
Which is the bliss of solitude;
And then my heart with pleasure fills,
And dances with the daffodils.'

'It's really beautiful,' Meredith said, smiling at her. 'It's very peaceful . . . serene.'

'That's how I feel about it.'

'I think I've heard that last verse before. *Somewhere.* But I'm not sure where,' Meredith murmured. 'Not at school, though.' For a moment or two she racked her brain, but try though she did, she could not remember. And yet the poem had struck a chord in her memory . . . The fleeting memory remained elusive.

Patsy remarked, 'Unfortunately, I don't have any pictures of the inn near Ripon. The Millers, who own it, did have a few photos, and they were very good, too. Yet somehow they didn't quite capture the spirit of the place, its soul. You'll have to judge it cold, when we get there.'

'That's no problem.' Meredith looked at her closely. 'But you *do* like Skell Garth don't you?'

'Oh yes, Meredith, very much, otherwise I wouldn't be dragging you there,' Patsy quickly reassured her partner. 'The setting is superb, the landscape awe-inspiring, picturesque, actually. And from the inn there's a most fabulous view of Fountains Abbey, one of the most beautiful ruins in all of England. Yes, Skell Garth is a unique place.'

'Skell Garth,' Meredith repeated. 'You know, when you first mentioned it, I thought it was such an odd name.'

'I suppose it is. Let me explain. The Skell is a river which flows through Ripon and through the land on which both the inn and the abbey stand. Garth is the ancient Yorkshire word for field, and many of the local farmers still refer to their fields as garths.'

'So the name actually means *the field of the River Skell*. Am I correct?'

Patsy laughed, delighted with Meredith's astuteness. 'You're absolutely correct! I'll make a Yorkshirewoman of you yet.'

The two friends and partners sat talking about the

inns for a while, as they sipped their white wine, and then they moved on, became involved in a long and involved discussion about their business in general.

It was Patsy who brought this to a sudden halt when she jumped up, exclaiming, 'Oh my God! I smell something awful. I hope that's not our lunch getting burnt to a cinder.'

She flew out of the sitting room and ran downstairs to the kitchen.

Meredith charged after her.

Patsy was crouching in front of the oven, looking at the roast, poking around in the pan with a long-handled spoon.

'Is it spoiled?' Meredith asked in concern as she walked in.

'Fortunately not,' Patsy said, straightening. She closed the oven door and swung to face Meredith, grinning. 'A couple of potatoes are singed around the edges, but the lamb's okay. It's the onions that are a bit scorched. They're *black*, actually. Anyway, everything's ready, well, *almost*. I hope you're hungry . . .'

'I'm starving. But you didn't have to go to all this trouble, you know. I was quite happy to take you out to lunch. Or have you to the hotel.'

'I enjoy doing this occasionally,' Patsy assured her. 'It reminds me of my childhood growing up in Yorkshire. And anyway, Meredith, it's not often you get a traditional English Sunday lunch, now is it?'

Meredith chuckled. 'No, and I'm looking forward to it.'

Five

It was a windy afternoon.

A few stray leaves danced around her feet, and her full-length cream tweed cape billowed occasionally as she walked briskly through Green Park.

Meredith did not mind the wind. It was sunny and this counteracted the sudden gusts, the nip in the air, and she was glad to stretch her legs after sitting so long over lunch with Patsy.

It had been fun to visit her old friend and partner, and to catch up with everything, both business and personal. Also, Meredith always enjoyed going to Patsy's little doll's house, which is the way she thought of it. Situated in a mews in Belgravia, the house had four floors; it was charmingly decorated, very much in the style they used in the inns. This was a lush country look, which was built around good antique wood pieces, a mélange of interesting fabrics skilfully mixed and matched, vibrant colours carefully co-ordinated to each other plus a selection of unusual accessories.

As Meredith walked on, her thoughts settled on Patsy, of whom she was extremely fond. It was her New York banker, Henry Raphaelson, who had introduced them in 1984. Henry had known Patsy from her teenage days, since he had been for many years a close friend and business associate of her father, until his death a merchant banker in the City.

Patsy and she had taken to each other at once, and, after several constructive meetings they had decided to go into business together, opening a London office of Havens Incorporated.

In the ensuing years, Patsy had been good for the company, a great asset. She was as solid as a rock, hardworking, dependable, devoted and loyal. While she was not as visionary or as imaginative as Agnes D'Auberville, Patsy more than made up for these minor shortcomings because she was loaded with common sense. Also, her talent for public relations had worked well for Havens. There wasn't a hotel in England that received as much publicity and press attention as Haddon Fields in the Cotswolds, and all of it was positive. In fact, they had never had a negative write-up in the entire ten years the inn had been open.

When Meredith had expressed an interest in opening an hotel in France, Patsy had taken her to Paris to meet Agnes D'Auberville. The two young women had attended the Sorbonne at the same time, and they had been good friends since those youthful days in Paris.

Agnes, like Patsy two years earlier, had been looking to invest inherited money in a business she could be involved in on a full-time basis. And so she had jumped at the chance to open a Paris branch of Havens Incorporated, and had plunged enthusiastically into the creation of the inn situated in the Loire Valley.

Meredith and Agnes had found the Château de Cormeron, which stood on the banks of the beautiful

Indre river in the centre of the Loire Valley. After purchasing the château, they had spent almost a year getting it into proper shape and turning it into an inn. Many of the rooms had needed new floors, some new ceilings; they had had to install central heating and air conditioning; almost all of the plumbing had to be replaced, as had the wiring. Once this had been done, they had set about decorating it in the appropriate style, mostly using French country furniture, wonderful old tapestries, luxurious traditional fabrics and unique accessories culled from local antique shops.

They had put a tremendous amount of energy, effort, talent and money into its remodelling and redecoration, but the transformation was so stunning they both knew it had been well worth it.

And much to their gratification, it had proved to be a tremendous success as a small hotel. Château de Cormeron was close to many of the great châteaux of the Loire, such as Chinon, Chenonceaux, Azay-le-Rideau, Loches and Montpoupon, all open to the public and especially popular with foreign visitors.

Well-heeled tourists gravitated to their charming little Château de Cormeron, seeking its luxury, comfort and superlative service, which was becoming renowned, its bucolic surroundings and its proximity to so many famous châteaux. And the fact that the hotel boasted one of the finest restaurants in the Loire region did it no harm.

Agnes D'Auberville had become as good a friend as Patsy, as well as a most dependable business partner, and all three women enjoyed a good relationship.

Like Meredith, Patsy was divorced with two

children, twin boys of ten who were away at boarding school. Agnes, who was thirty-eight, the same age as Patsy, was married to Alain D'Auberville, the well-known stage actor, and they had a small daughter, Chloe, who was six.

I've been lucky with them, Meredith thought, as she completed her circle around Green Park and went out into Piccadilly. We all balance each other very well, and they've both done a great deal to make Havens work in Europe, been instrumental in its success.

Coming to the Ritz Hotel, she stood at the kerb, waiting for the lights to change. Once they did, she crossed Piccadilly and headed back to Claridge's on Brook Street.

Meredith had always liked walking around London, and she was thoroughly enjoying her stroll, feeling invigorated by the brisk air and the exercise. Turning down Hay Hill, she went up into Berkeley Square. But as she crossed it, she couldn't help thinking that the little park in the centre looked a bit bleak today, with its bare trees and patches of dirty snow on the shrivelled brown grass.

On the other hand, she took great pleasure in looking at the lovely old buildings in Mayfair, which was the area of London she knew best. She had been coming here for twenty-one years, ever since her marriage to David Layton in 1974. Twenty-three she had been at the time, and so young in so many ways; yet in others she had been rather grown up.

England had made a lasting impression on her. She felt comfortable on its shores, and she enjoyed the British people, their idiosyncrasies as well as their good manners and civility, not to mention their great sense of humour.

David Layton had been a transplanted Englishman, living and working in Connecticut when she met him. After their wedding at Silver Lake, he had brought her to London to meet his sister Claire, her husband and children.

Meredith had liked David; she had loved him well enough to marry him, and she had felt regretful that their marriage had floundered. Their genuine attempts to make it work had come to nothing, and in the end divorce had seemed to be the best, the only, solution.

The one good thing that had come out of this rather dubious and tenuous union was their son Jonathan. The sad thing was, David never saw his son these days. He had moved to California in the 1980s and had never made any effort to come East to see Jonathan. Nor had he ever invited Jonathan to visit him on the West Coast.

David's loss, Meredith muttered under her breath: she couldn't help wishing that things were different, for her son's sake at least. But Jon didn't seem to care that he was so neglected by David and he never mentioned his father.

Being a single parent all those years had been a strain on her at times, Meredith was the first to admit it. But Jon had turned out well, and so had her darling Cat. And so it had been worth it in the end . . . the hard work, the sacrifices, the endless compromises, the cajoling, the bullying and the unconditional loving. Being a good mother had taken its toll on her life, but she was proud of them. And of herself in a funny way.

Those years of bringing up Cat and Jon alone, plus creating and developing her business, had left her little time to meet another man, let alone become involved with him. There *had* been a few boyfriends over the years, but somehow her children and her work had intruded, got in the way. Deep down, she had never really minded. Her children had been her whole world, still were.

Circumstances had been right when she had met Brandon Leonard four years ago. But he had been a married man. In no time at all, she had come to understand that not only was he *not* separated, as he claimed, but that he had no intention of ever leaving his wife, or getting a divorce. Simply put, Brandon wanted his wife. He also wanted a mistress. Since she was not a candidate for the latter role, she had terminated their friendship, and in no uncertain terms.

Then this past September, on a trip to London, Patsy had taken her to the fancy opening of an exhibition of sculpture at the posh Lardner Gallery in Bond Street.

And there, lurking amongst the Arps and the Brancusis, the Moores, the Hepworths and the Giacomettis, had been Reed Jamison. The owner of the gallery.

Tall, dark, good-looking, charismatic. The most attractive man she had met in a long time. And seemingly very available. 'Beware,' Patsy had warned. When she had asked her what she meant, Patsy had said, 'Watch it. He's brilliant but difficult.' Again she had pressed Patsy, asked her to elucidate. Patsy then answered her enigmatically, 'Save us all from the brooding Byronic hero. Oh dear, shades of Heathcliff.'

Meredith had only partially understood, and then, before she could blink, Reed Jamison, having taken one look at her, was in hot pursuit.

Drawn to him initially, she had fallen under his spell; but gradually, over the following months, she had begun to feel unexpectedly ill at ease with him. And she had begun to pull away from the relationship within herself.

On his last visit to New York, in late November, she had been turned off. He had been morose, argumentative, and possessive. Furthermore, she had detected a bullying attitude in him and this had alarmed her.

Tonight she was going to tell him that she could not see him again, that their relationship, such as it was, had come to an end. She wasn't looking forward to it, but she knew it must be done.

'Why bother?' Patsy had said over lunch earlier. 'Have dinner with him tonight. Say nothing. Tomorrow we're going to the Lake District and Yorkshire. And then you're off to Paris. Don't make yourself sick over this. Avoid a troublesome confrontation.'

'I have to tell him it's over,' Meredith had answered. 'Don't you see, he'll be in my life, pestering me, circling me, until I make it clear I don't want him anywhere near me.'

'What went wrong?' Patsy had asked curiously.

'Reed went wrong. He's just too complex a man for me.'

'I hate to say I told you so,' Patsy had murmured.

'It's all right, you can say it, Patsy. Because you did warn me, and you were right about him all along.'

They had then gone on to talk about other things,

but now Meredith could not help wondering if maybe Patsy was right. Might it not be infinitely easier to have dinner with Reed and say nothing?

Maybe I should do that, she thought as she turned into Brook Street.

'Good afternoon, madame,' the uniformed doorman outside Claridge's said as she went up the steps.

'Good afternoon,' she responded, smiling pleasantly, and pushed through the door which led into the hotel.

Martin, one of the concierges, greeted her as she crossed the lobby, making for the lift.

'Meredith!'

She stopped in her tracks, freezing as she recognized the cultivated masculine voice.

Slowly turning, she pasted a smile on her face as she moved towards the man who had called her name. 'Reed! Hello! But you're a bit early aren't you?'

He smiled and leaned into her, put his arm around her waist, drawing her closer. He kissed her cheek. 'I'm here having tea with friends.' He jerked his head in the direction of the salon, which opened off the lobby, and indicated a group of people at one of the tables. Afternoon tea was being served and a string quartet played.

'Darling, it's lovely to see you,' he went on, staring deeply into her eyes. 'I've missed you, but then I told you that on the phone this morning. I was actually just coming out to ring you up in your room, to invite you to come down and join us, when I saw you heading for the lift.' He took hold of her arm firmly, and drew her towards the salon.

Meredith resisted and held her ground, shaking her head. 'Reed, I can't. It's so nice of you to invite me, and thank you, but there are a number of things I must do before dinner.' Peeking at her watch, she added, 'It's almost five. We're still meeting at six-thirty, aren't we?'

'Of course. Unless you want to make it earlier. Look, do join us now,' he pressed, and once more tried to draw her into the salon.

Meredith said softly, 'Please, Reed, don't make a scene here. I just can't have tea. I've some phone calls, and I must change for dinner.'

He let go of her arm abruptly and stepped away from her. 'Very well,' he said, sounding suddenly grudging. 'Don't get frightfully dressed up. I'm taking you slumming tonight.'

Giving him a fraudulent smile, she murmured, 'I'll see you in a short while, Reed.' Not giving him a chance to say another word, Meredith spun around on her heels and walked rapidly to the lift.

Once she was inside her suite, she threw off her cape and unbuttoned the jacket of her cream trouser suit, then went through into the bedroom. Pulling open the wardrobe door, she looked at her clothes hanging there, settled on a black trouser suit for dinner, wishing deep down inside herself that she had never met Reed Jamison.

Six

At precisely six-thirty there was a knock on the door of the suite, and Meredith knew it was Reed Jamison.

Walking out of the bedroom into the sitting room, buttoning her jacket, she arranged a pleasant smile on her face before opening the door.

'Not too early, I hope,' Reed said, kissing her on the cheek.

'Exactly on time,' Meredith murmured, and stood back in order to let him walk into the suite. 'I'll just get my bag and coat and we can be off.'

'Oh, but it's far too early for the restaurant, darling. Why don't we have a drink here first?' He put his overcoat on a chair and sauntered into the middle of the sitting room. After giving it a sweeping glance, he went to the fireplace where he draped himself against the mantel, striking an elegant pose.

'All right,' Meredith said, trying to be gracious, although she couldn't help wishing he had not come up to the suite. She had fully expected him to phone her from the lobby. Pressing the bell for the floor waiter, clearing her throat, she asked, 'What would you like?'

'Scotch and soda, please, my dear.'

'Where are we going for dinner?' she asked, making small talk.

'Aha, that's a surprise!' he exclaimed.

'You said we were going slumming.'

'I'm taking you to a wonderful Chinese restaurant, rather off the beaten track. But you'll enjoy it. The place has tremendous local colour, and the food is the best Chinese in London. Genuine, too, not the bastardized stuff served in fancy West End restaurants.'

'I'm looking forward to it,' she murmured and then moved out into the hall of the suite as the waiter knocked and then let himself in. After ordering their drinks, she returned to the fireside and sat down.

Looking at her intently, shifting his stance slightly and leaning forward, Reed said, 'I'm really rather put out with you, darling.'

'*Oh.*' Meredith stared at him questioningly. 'Because I didn't want to come down to tea and meet your friends?'

'No, no, of course not. That didn't matter. But I am somewhat surprised that you went to lunch with Patsy when I had invited you to come over to the house.'

Meredith was taken aback. 'But Reed, Patsy and I had a lot of business to discuss. I told you last week, when I was still in New York, that I had many things to attend to on this trip, and –'

'Oh *really*!' he cut in with a sardonic laugh. 'You could have dealt with Patsy on the phone, surely.'

'No, I couldn't!' she shot back, her voice rising in exasperation. She was irritated with him; she realized, yet again, that he did not really take her work seriously. Suppressing a rush of impatience, she went on more calmly, 'We had business to discuss, and I was anxious to see her.'

'But not anxious to see me.'

'Reed, don't be –'

There was a loud knock and the waiter entered with the tray of drinks. Meredith got up, thanked him, and handed him some of the coins she kept in the ash tray for tips. After giving Reed his drink, she picked up her own, and sat on the sofa.

'Cheers,' Reed said and took a swallow of his scotch and soda.

'Cheers.' Meredith merely touched the glass to her lips, then put it on the coffee table. She had no desire to drink tonight.

Once again Reed looked at her; this time he was smiling.

She was relieved the awkward moment had passed. It struck her that he seemed less morose tonight, and certainly he was in a better mood than he had been earlier, when she had run into him in the lobby.

'Have you told Patsy you're planning to move to London within the next few months?' he asked.

Meredith gaped at him. 'What makes you say that, Reed? I'm not moving anywhere.'

'When I was in New York in November you certainly indicated that you intended to live in London.'

'No, I didn't.'

'Oh Meredith, how can you say such a thing! I practically proposed to you, and I told you it was hard for me to go on like this any longer, that we couldn't continue our affair if we were separated by the Atlantic Ocean. I made it quite clear I wanted you here with me. Very much so. And you certainly acquiesced.'

'Reed, that's not true, I didn't!'

'You did!'

'You imagined it, Reed. Never in a million years would I lead you to believe such a thing.'

He stared at her incredulously, sudden anger flaring in his dark eyes. 'I distinctly remember telling you that I needed you here with me in London. And you agreed to come.'

Meredith had no recollection of this at all and was about to say so when he came and sat down next to her on the sofa.

'What's wrong with you, darling? Why are you behaving like this?' he asked, moving closer, draping his arm along the back of the sofa. 'Don't be difficult, my dear, you know how I feel about you. I need you, Meredith, and I need you *here*. Not in New York, but living with me in London. I told you when I was in the States, and I assumed you would get rid of the business and move as soon as you could. Settle here permanently with me.'

'Reed, you've truly misunderstood. I don't know how that happened . . . but it did, somehow. And I've no intention of giving up my business.'

'Then don't, darling. If you want to work you can, although it's really not necessary. I can support us extremely well, you know that. Forget the gallery, that's not important, merely my hobby. Just remember that I do have a very large private income from my trust. Monty might be inheriting the old man's title when he dies – after all he's the eldest son – but I've got Mummy's money.'

Meredith sat gazing at him mutely. She was at a complete loss for words, and filled with acute dismay.

Suddenly, unexpectedly, Reed pulled her into his arms. He was a tall man, well built and strong, and he caught hold of her hard, held her in a vice-like grip, pressing his mouth on hers.

She struggled, managed partially to push him away, and pulled herself up on the sofa, straining to extricate herself from his arms.

Unexpectedly, Reed let go of her as abruptly as he had grabbed her. Giving her an odd look, he said in a quiet, icy voice, 'Why did you pull away from me as if I'm suddenly a leper? What's wrong?'

Meredith bit her lip, said nothing. Then she sprang to her feet, hurried over to the window and stood looking out.

A cold silence filled the room.

Meredith was shaking inside. She wanted to get this over. Be done with him. End the whole thing as gracefully as she could. But he was being difficult – and worse, imagining things which hadn't happened.

After a moment or two, when she was calmer, she turned to face him and said slowly, in her kindest voice, 'Reed, listen to me . . . things are . . . well, not right between us any more. They haven't been for weeks.'

'How on earth can you say that! We had a wonderful time in New York. Only a month ago, unless I'm sadly mistaken.'

Meredith shook her head, her dismay intensifying. She wanted to be considerate, to let him down lightly, yet she knew within herself that she must make her feelings absolutely clear to him. 'It wasn't wonderful, Reed, at least not for me. I realized you and I were completely incompatible, not suited to each other at all. I began to feel ill at ease with you, and I certainly knew our relationship was on the skids, that it couldn't possibly work.'

'That's not so, and you know it. If you lived here and we weren't conducting our relationship long-distance, everything would be entirely different. Please move to London to be with me, Meredith.'

'Reed, I've just told you, as far as I'm concerned we don't have a future together. And anyway I have such a huge commitment to my business.'

'Oh don't go on so, Meredith. I can't believe for one moment that you're such a dyed-in-the-wool career woman as you claim to be. I couldn't love that kind of woman, and I do love you.'

Meredith was silent.

He repeated, 'I love you.'

'Oh Reed, I'm so sorry . . . but I just don't feel the same way.'

'That's not what you led me to believe,' he said softly, his eyes narrowing.

'I admit I was infatuated with you last fall, that's true. But it *was* an *infatuation*, nothing stronger or more lasting. I can't make a commitment to you, I just can't.'

'It's been so good between us, Meredith. Why are you saying these things?'

Taking a deep breath, Meredith plunged in. 'I've come to understand that you don't take my life seriously. Not my personal family life with my children, and certainly not my work. I will not deny my children's existence for you, or anyone else for that matter, and I will never give up my work. It's far too important to me. I've put too many years and too much effort into my business.'

'You're not living up to my expectations of you, Meredith,' he said, his voice suddenly grown cold and disparaging. 'Not at all. I thought you were different. I thought you were an old-fashioned woman with old-fashioned values. What a miscalculation on my part. I can't believe my judgement was so flawed. Or perhaps you simply deceived me.' He raised a dark brow.

Slowly, and in a cold tone, Meredith answered, 'You know, you've just put a finger on something of vital importance, Reed. I *feel* the weight of your expectations, and I just can't handle that. I began to realize in November that you believe you come first in my life. I'm afraid you don't. The reason I wanted to see you tonight was to explain this, to tell you about my feelings and to bring our relationship to an end.'

Reed Jamison was speechless. In all of his forty-one years he had never been discarded by a woman. He had always been the one to end affairs or start them, controlling, manipulating, pulling the puppet's strings and getting his own way.

He continued to stare at Meredith. She was the only woman who had ever bested him, and a terrible rage began to fulminate in him. He leapt to his feet, glaring at her. He shouted, 'I'm glad I found out what kind of woman you really are! Before I made the terrible mistake of marrying you!'

Without another word Reed strode across the room, picked up his coat and left, banging the door behind him with such ferocity that the chandelier rattled and swayed on its chain.

Meredith ran to the door and locked it; she leaned against it for a few seconds. She was shaking. Calming herself, she walked over to the desk, sat down and dialled Patsy's number. It rang and rang. She was just about to hang up when she heard Patsy saying, 'Hello?'

'Patsy, it's me. Reed was here, and I told him it was over between us. He's gone . . . he marched out in a fury.'

'Well, that's a relief. That you told him, I mean. And naturally he left in high dudgeon. He's not used to getting dumped unceremoniously. That's part of his problem, you know. He's always been spoilt by women, and he thinks he's God's gift to everything that walks in skirts.'

'Yes, I know what you mean. He's also a male chauvinist pig, to use a very out-dated phrase. However, it is appropriate. That's something I guess I detected when he was last in New York. He doesn't take my business seriously, or my life. He's self-involved, and he just can't imagine why I'm not rushing over here to set up house with him. He said he wanted me to marry him.'

'He proposed! Good God! Well, I must say, you must've really got to him, Meredith, my girl. Ever since his divorce from Tina Longdon he's been a hit-and-run man.'

'I'm not sure what that means.'

'You know, the kind of chap who has an attitude . . . *love me on my terms, darling. Thanks for everything.*

Farewell. Hit-and-run chaps, that's what we call them over here. I know several women who've suffered at Reed's hands.'

'Why didn't you tell me?'

'I did, Meredith – at least I tried to warn you as best I could. I did say he was a difficult man.'

'Actually, you said he was a brooding Byronic hero, or words to that effect, and I never did *really* understand what you meant by that.'

'Oh that's only the role he's adopted for years. In essence, it's a pose. But I suppose it has been rather effective, got him a long way with women. Not that he needs a pose, actually. His looks aside, he's charming most of the time, despite that smouldering manner of his.'

'All too true. But do you think women fall for that . . . for that brooding thing?'

'Oh yes, I think so. Let's face it, *many* do. The smouldering eyes, the soulful expression, the moody demeanour can be appealing. There are a lot of women who go for the suffering, anguished Heathcliffs of this world. They want to change them, make them happy.' Patsy paused, then said, 'Wasn't that one of the things about him that attracted you?'

'No,' Meredith answered quickly. 'To tell you the truth, it was only this past November, in New York, that he turned morose and moody. It irritated me more than anything else.'

Patsy laughed. 'I bet it did! Anyway, the main thing is you don't sound any the worse for giving him the boot.'

Meredith also laughed. 'I'm not. Naturally, I'm not

thrilled about hurting someone's feelings. But it had to be done; Reed had to be told. I needed that closure.'

'I realize you did.'

'I thought it only fair that Reed knew exactly how I felt. And immediately. It was much better to clear the air, cut it off before it dragged on any longer. These kinds of situations can end in such bitterness.'

'Don't I know it!' Patsy exclaimed. 'Tony's been bitter about our divorce for years. Blames me, of course. Listen, do you want to come over for supper? Or we could go out if you like, if you don't want to be alone . . .' Patsy's voice trailed off.

'That's sweet of you, but I want to stay in tonight. I'll order room service and pack. You did say you were picking me up at six tomorrow morning, didn't you?'

'Yes. Sorry about that, but we do have to leave early. We'll be about four hours on the road, three and a half if the traffic's light. We'll spend a couple of hours in Keswick and then head down to Ripon. We've a great deal to do in one day. In fact, we might have to spend the night in Ripon.'

'No problem. And Patsy?'

'Yes?'

'I don't think I hurt his feelings too much, do you?'

'You may have. Don't underestimate the effect you had on him.'

'I've probably damaged his ego, that's all.'

'Oh definitely, Meredith, I'm certain of that. But I also believe that our Reed, the glamorous playboy, fell rather heavily for you. That's *always* been my opinion. Oh well, what can one do ... He finally met his Waterloo.'

Seven

Meredith found it hard to fall asleep.

For a long time she tossed and turned until finally, in exasperation, she got out of bed. After putting on a warm woollen dressing gown, she went and sat on the sofa in the sitting room. Her mind was racing.

She had not drawn the heavy velvet draperies earlier and moonlight was filtering in through the muslin curtains which hung against the window panes. Everything had a silvery sheen from this natural light, and the room was peaceful.

Meredith leaned back against the silk cushions of the sofa, thinking of Reed. How unpleasant their parting had been, and how foolish she had been to get involved with him in the first place. She was forty-four years old; she ought to have known better.

How unlucky she was with men. Always.

No, that was not quite true.

There had been one man. *Once.* A man who had been exactly right for her. He was dead. He had died too young. Such an untimely death . . . that's what they had all said. And how truthfully they had spoken.

To die at the age of thirty-six was some terrible trick of God's, wasn't it?

Meredith had asked herself this question a thousand times. And she had striven hard to find some special meaning in that awful, untimely death. She had found nothing. There was no meaning in it. None at all.

And all she had been left with was a void.

Of course there had been Cat, just a toddler, and Amelia, poor Amelia, and they had shared that void with her, and the grief. How they had mourned him . . . endlessly . . . she and Amelia. His women. The women who had loved him.

I'll always mourn him, Meredith thought, the old familiar sadness rising in her, filling her throat. Oh Jack, why did you die? How many times had she asked herself that in the silence of her mind? There was no answer. There had never been an answer. Not ever in twenty-two years.

And how many times had she asked herself when she would meet another man like Jack? She never would, she knew that now, because men like him were amongst the very few. And they were already spoken for. Jack had been spoken for early on in his life, when he was only twenty-two. He had married that youthful love of his. *Amelia*. Then one terrible day she had been thrown by her horse. When she was only twenty-five and pregnant. She had lost the baby and been crippled for life, a paraplegic trapped in a wheelchair. But he loved her; he would always love and cherish Amelia and she would always be his wife; he had told Meredith that and she had understood. And she had loved Amelia and Amelia had loved her and Jack; and Cat – she had loved her, too. Amelia had given them her blessing in her own silent, smiling way, full of approval, and gratitude for their love and kindness and loyalty.

Jack.

Blond, blue-eyed, tanned. So quick and sprightly and energetic. Full of good humour, tall tales, laughter and life. No wonder she had fallen in love with him instantly, the first day she had set eyes on him. A *coup de foudre*.

So long ago now.

May of 1969.

She had been just eighteen.

Meredith closed her eyes. Behind her lids she could see his face. She remembered what had gone through her mind that day as she had stared back at him, held in the grip of his mesmeric gaze.

Such a beautiful face for a man, she had thought, such a sensitive mouth and those extraordinary eyes. Such a lovely blue. Bits of sky, she had thought then. His eyes are like bits of a summer sky.

Now tonight, so many years later, Meredith saw herself as she had been on that May afternoon . . . the images of the three of them floated before her. They were all so clear . . . so very vivid and alive . . . she and Jack and Amelia.

The decades fell away.

She tumbled backwards in time . . . tumbled back into the past.

'Can I help you?' the young man asked politely, getting up off the steps where he had been sitting, pulling off his tortoise-shell sunglasses, peering intently at her.

Meredith stared back at him. 'I'm looking for a Mr

Silver,' she answered, jumping off her bike, almost falling in her haste and sudden confusion. Unexpectedly she was feeling self-conscious in front of this handsome man, so well groomed and well dressed, wearing grey trousers and a dark blue cashmere sweater over his lighter blue shirt.

The man walked over to her, thrusting out his hand. 'Well, you've found him,' he announced, 'I'm Mr Silver.'

'Mr *Jack* Silver?' she asked, shaking his hand.

He nodded. 'That's right. And the only Mr Silver who's alive and kicking. That I know of, anyway. The rest are over there.' He indicated a plot of land behind him.

She followed the direction of his gaze and saw a small walled cemetery to the right of a copse of trees. 'You have your own graveyard?' she asked, sounding awed.

He nodded, and there was a questioning expression on his face as he asked, 'How can I help you?'

'I've come about the advertisement in the newspaper . . . for a receptionist.'

'Oh yes, of course. And whom might I be speaking to?'

'I'm Meredith Stratton.'

'Well hello, Meredith Stratton. Pleased to meet you!' he exclaimed, thrusting out his hand once more. 'Pleased to meet you indeed, Meredith Stratton!'

She took his hand and shook it for a second time. He did not let go of it. Then he smiled at her, a wide warm smile that showed his beautiful teeth. They were very white in his tanned face.

She smiled back at him, liking him.

He started to laugh, for no apparent reason.

She laughed with him, instantly captivated by this man whom she had never seen before.

Still holding onto her hand, he led her and the bike she was clinging to over to the front steps where he had been sitting. 'Come inside. But I do think you'll have to leave your transportation out here,' he said, and grinned.

Meredith nodded, her eyes dancing, and then she removed her hand from his and propped her bike against the porch railings.

'Nice bike you have.'

'It's not mine. I borrowed it. That was the only way I could get here.'

'Where did you come from?'

'New Preston. We've been living up above Lake Waramaug.' She glanced away, her eyes on the lake at the bottom of the rolling lawns and flower gardens. 'You've got a nice lake,' she murmured.

'Silver Lake,' he told her. 'It used to have a Native American name a few years ago, a few *hundred* years ago that is. Lake Wappaconaca. But an ancestor of mine bought this land and the local folk got into the habit of calling it Silver Lake, after him, and that name stuck. And this, of course, is Silver Lake Inn, built in 1832 by that same ancestor . . . 137 years ago this year.'

Meredith stood looking up at the inn. 'It's a lovely old building.'

'Come on, let's go inside. I want you to meet Amelia.'

The moment she stepped through the doorway of the inn Meredith knew that it was a very special place. The walls were painted a cloudy mottled pink and they gave the entrance the warmest of rosy feelings. The floor was so highly polished it gleamed like a dark mirror; an old carved chest, two high-backed chairs and a small desk were obviously vintage antiques, and looked valuable even to her untrained eye.

Everywhere there were fresh flowers in tall crystal vases and bulbs growing in Chinese porcelain bowls; their mixed fragrances assailed her . . . the scent of mimosa, hyacinth, narcissi mingled with the smell of beeswax, lemons and dried roses, ripe apples cooking on a stove somewhere.

As she took all of this in, looking around her wide-eyed, Meredith was awed. Yet she was filled with a curious kind of excitement and pleasure, such as she had never known before. She crossed her fingers, praying she would get the job. Glancing at the small antique desk, with its silk-shaded porcelain lamp and telephone, she could not help thinking how nice it would be to sit in this entrance hall, being a receptionist, greeting guests. It was certainly more appealing to her than working as an *au pair*, looking after children all day long, even though she loved children.

Jack ushered her down a short corridor and opened the door at the end. A woman sat behind a desk with her back to the door; she was gazing out of the window.

'Amelia,' Jack said. 'We have an applicant at last. For the job of receptionist.'

The woman slowly turned, and Meredith realized immediately that she was sitting in a wheelchair. Her breath caught in her throat as she returned the woman's steady gaze. Meredith was startled by her beauty. Dark hair, parted in the middle, tumbled around a pale heart-shaped face. Wonderful high cheekbones, a dimpled chin and a sensual mouth were nothing in comparison to the amazing vivid green eyes below perfectly arched black brows. It's the woman from *Gone with the Wind*, she thought.

Amelia said, 'You're looking rather strange. Are you feeling all right?'

Meredith realized she was staring and exclaimed, 'Oh yes, I'm fine. *Sorry*. I'm so sorry to stare at you, it's very rude.' The words tumbled out, and then, because of her youth and ingenuousness, she rushed on unthinkingly, 'You're so beautiful. You look like Vivien Leigh in *Gone with the Wind*. Doesn't everybody tell you that?'

'Not everyone. But thank you for your lovely compliment,' Amelia answered with a smile and exchanged an amused look with Jack.

Jack cleared his throat and took charge. 'Amelia, darling, may I introduce Miss Meredith Stratton. Miss Stratton, this is my wife, Mrs Amelia Silver.'

Meredith walked across the polished wood floor and took the woman's slender hand in hers, then stepped back, still moved by such perfect beauty.

'Please, do sit down, Miss Stratton,' Amelia murmured. 'Make yourself comfortable.'

'Thank you.' Meredith lowered herself into a chair, straightening her cotton skirt as she did. 'I'd feel better if you called me Meredith, Mrs Silver. I'm not used to *Miss Stratton.*'

Again a small smile fluttered briefly on Amelia's pretty mouth. 'I'd be happy to call you by your first name.'

Jack, who was now sitting on the window seat to the right of his wife, remarked, 'Meredith comes from New Preston. At least, that's where she bicycled from this afternoon.' He now directed his words to Meredith and went on, 'But you originally hail from Australia, don't you?'

She nodded. 'Sydney. But how did you know? Oh, my awful voice, that's how, isn't it?'

'It's not awful,' Amelia said. 'But you do have a slight twang, one that's distinctly Australian. Tell me, when did you come to live in Connecticut?'

'Last year. I'll have been living here just a year this July. I came with the Paulsons. They're an American family I met when they were living in Sydney. Mr Paulson's with an advertising agency. I worked for them in Sydney as an *au pair*.'

'And now you wish to leave them. May we inquire why?' Jack probed.

'I want to change jobs, Mr Silver. But it's a bit more complicated than that. Mr Paulson has been transferred again, this time to South Africa. The family are about to leave for Johannesburg. They asked me to go too, but I don't want to. I want to live in America. I never want to leave Connecticut. It's the most beautiful place I've ever seen.'

'But what about your family? Your parents back in Australia? How do they feel about this?' Amelia seemed slightly puzzled. 'Surely they want you to go home?'

'Oh no, they don't . . . what I mean is . . . well, you see . . . they're . . . dead. They died, yes, they did. In a . . . car crash. When I was ten.' Meredith nodded to herself. 'When I was ten,' she repeated.

'Oh you poor girl,' Amelia exclaimed, her face filling with sympathy. 'How terribly sad, heartbreaking for you. And do you not have other family out there? Relatives?'

'No, I don't. There's no one.'

'But how awful for you to be so alone in this world.' Amelia turned her chair to face Jack. 'Isn't it sad, darling?'

'Yes, it is.'

'How old are you?' Amelia asked, giving her a warm encouraging smile.

'Eighteen. I was just eighteen at the beginning of May.'

Jack said, 'Have you ever worked as a receptionist? Had any experience in a hotel?'

'No, but I'm good with people. At least, Mrs Paulson says so, and I've been helping her with her paperwork for two years. You know, her chequebook, household accounts, things like that. She's even taught me a bit about bookkeeping. She says I have the right skills for this job, Mr Silver. And you can phone her any time. She's also going to give me a written reference. It'll be ready later this afternoon. I can bring it back to you tonight if you want.'

'That won't be necessary,' Amelia said briskly, then addressed Jack. 'I think you should speak to Mrs

Paulson about Meredith right away. Now. You don't mind if we call her whilst you're still here, do you, Meredith?'

'Oh no. She's at home, packing. I think she's sort of expecting you to give her a ring.'

'What's the number, Meredith?' Jack asked, crossing to the desk, picking up the phone.

She gave it to him; he dialled. And a moment later he was engaged in a conversation with Mrs Paulson, or rather he was listening, saying very little, hardly able to get a word in edgewise.

Amelia sat quietly, waiting for the conversation to come to an end.

Meredith clasped her hands tightly in her lap, suddenly anxious and tense. Even though she knew Mrs Paulson would say all the right things, she couldn't help worrying a little. This job was important to her.

When Jack finally hung up he said to Meredith, 'She's full of praise for you, says you're a clever girl, diligent, honest and hardworking, and she told me you looked after her children very well.'

Meredith beamed, and relaxed, then looked at Amelia expectantly.

Amelia said, 'It's good to know that Mrs Paulson thinks so highly of you.'

'Yes. And she did say she'll come to see you,' Meredith volunteered. 'She'd like to meet you.'

Jack walked over to the window seat, sat down, then said to Amelia, 'To continue. Mrs Paulson's sorry to lose Meredith, but she understands her reasons for wanting to stay in Connecticut. In any case, she thinks Meredith's cut out for better things.' Then to Meredith, he remarked, 'She says you were very good with her children. Apparently they love you.'

'I love them,' Meredith replied. 'I'm going to miss them, Mr Silver, but I don't want to go to South Africa.'

'I can't say I blame you for wanting to stay on in Connecticut,' Amelia murmured. 'The Litchfield Hills, in particular, are very lovely. Now, when would you be able to start?'

'Next week.' Meredith sat up straighter and glanced from Amelia to Jack. 'Do I have the job then?'

'Yes,' Amelia said. 'Mrs Paulson's recommendation sounds wonderful, and it's good enough for us. I don't think we'll find anyone better than you, Meredith. Isn't that so, Jack?'

'Yes, I agree. However, there's a slight problem, you know.'

'What's that, Jack darling?'

'Where is Meredith going to live?'

Taken by surprise on hearing this, Meredith gaped at the Silvers. 'Here at the inn!' she cried. 'The advertisement said *food and lodging provided if required.* I wouldn't have applied otherwise. That was the thing that pleased Mrs Paulson . . . that I would be living here at the inn with you. That I wouldn't be out on my own.'

'We do have a room, but it's up in the attic,' Jack explained. 'And it's not very nice. The assistant housekeeper occupies the one good staff bedroom. We're a bit short of staff quarters, if truth be known.'

'I don't mind the attic,' Meredith said, suddenly afraid the job would slip through her fingers. 'Honest, I don't.'

'We were hoping we'd find a receptionist who lived nearby and could come in daily,' Amelia murmured. 'But no one applied, even though the advertisement's been in for a few weeks. Until you came today, of course.' Amelia gave Jack a long, searching look. 'Perhaps we could make the attic more presentable, get it painted and wallpapered. We could put in a few pieces of really nice furniture, spruce it up. And let's not forget that it is fairly spacious.'

'I don't know . . .' Jack began and stopped when he noticed the crestfallen look on Meredith's face. Making a sudden decision, he jumped up. 'Let me show you the room.' Turning to his wife, he explained, 'I think we should let Meredith be the judge of the room. Let's hear what she thinks of it.'

'You're quite right. Run along with Jack, Meredith. He'll take you to the top floor.'

A few minutes later Meredith and Jack were standing in the attic under the eaves. Meredith was relieved to see there were two dormer windows and that the room *was* quite large, as Amelia had indicated. She walked around, then said to Jack Silver, 'But I love it; it's quaint, cute. I'll soon make it look nice. Don't worry, I'll be fine up here.'

Jack merely nodded and they went back downstairs.

'Well, what do you think, my dear?' Amelia asked, raising a brow quizzically as they walked in.

'It's unusual, Mrs Silver, but it'll work nicely for me. I'll make it comfortable. Do you want me to start next week?'

'If you can. I'm really looking forward to your arrival, Meredith.'

'So am I. And I'll bring the written reference with me.'

'If you wish. Goodbye for now,' Amelia said, and wheeled herself behind the desk. 'I must get back to all this tedious paperwork which has recently landed in my lap.'

Jack and Meredith went out to the front porch and he walked with her down the steps. 'The inn's not busy at the moment,' he confided, 'but it will be in another week or so. What day do you think you can come?'

'Monday. That's only four days from now. Will that be all right, Mr Silver?'

'It certainly will. You're going to take a huge burden off me, and I'll be able to tackle some of the other chores that Pete O'Brien has been doing. He's the estate manager and he's badly overworked. Amelia will feel more at ease too, once you're installed. She gets so tired at times, but try though I have, I've not been able to find anyone to assist her.'

Meredith nodded her understanding, full of empathy for the Silvers. 'It must be difficult, but don't worry, Mr Silver, I'll help her with that paperwork. I'd really like to do so, in my spare time.' She glanced across at him, hesitated, and then said softly, 'What exactly happened to Mrs Silver? Why is she in a wheelchair?'

'Amelia had a riding accident eleven years ago. Her spine was damaged. She's been paralysed from the waist down ever since.'

'How dreadful, I'm so sorry . . . she's so beautiful.'

'Yes, she is . . . inside as well as out. She's a truly

good person, Meredith, the best I've ever known. So brave, so patient . . .'

There was a small silence, and then Meredith said, 'Thank you for giving me the job. I won't let you down. And I'll work very hard.'

'I'm sure you will.'

Meredith walked over to her bike, then suddenly, swinging around, she stood looking across at the lake. She could see it through the trees, glistening in the late-afternoon sunlight. 'Do you get much wildlife on the lake?' she asked at last in a strangely wistful voice.

'All year round, I'm happy to say. There're probably flocks of birds down there now. Ducks, Canada geese especially. Shall we walk over and have a look?'

Meredith nodded, reached for her bicycle and wheeled it along between them.

Jack said, 'Do you like biking?'

'Sometimes. Why?'

'I have a bike, and I often ride it around the property. I can't claim to have covered the whole hundred and fifty acres, but I've done my best to see as much as I can. And there's a lot to see, most of it interesting.'

'It's a big place, isn't it?'

'Yes, but not as big as some of the spreads in the outback, I bet.'

She laughed. 'The only part of Australia I know is Sydney.'

He shrugged. 'But it *is* a big country.'

'Yes, it is. And is this all your land, Mr Silver?'

'It is. My great-great-great grandfather, Adam Silver, and his wife Angharad, bought it in 1832, as I told you. They built the inn, the house next to it which is the one where Amelia and I now live, and various other small buildings on the property. And, of course, the family's been running the inn since those days.'

'An unbroken chain,' she said, the awe creeping into her voice again.

Jack simply nodded.

The two of them walked on, taking the wide path. This cut down through the green lawns and flower gardens, which were just starting to bloom; it stopped at the edge of the lake.

'I know it's called Silver Lake because of your name, but the lake *is* silver in colour. And it's so calm,' Meredith said.

She leaned against the handlebars of the bike and shaded her eyes with one hand. 'I've always liked being near water, for as long as I can remember. I don't know why, but it makes me feel . . .' She paused, unable to finish her sentence, at a loss for the right word to describe her emotions.

'*What* does it make you feel, Meredith?'

'I'm not sure . . . I can never really put my finger on the feeling.'

'Happy? Content? Secure? It's surely a *good* feeling you experience, or you wouldn't like being near the water at all.'

'That's true. I suppose it makes me feel . . . well, all of those things you've just mentioned. But sometimes I feel sad, as if I've lost something . . . something precious. The water reminds me of it.'

He made no response, merely looked at her closely before focusing on the lake. Suddenly he pointed and cried excitedly, 'Oh look! Over there! That's the blue heron that comes every spring. It flies away after a few days and rarely comes back to the lake until the next year. But it's marvellous and I'm certain it's the same bird.'

'How strange. I can't imagine why it does that. If I were a bird I would never want to leave Silver Lake. I would want to live here forever and ever, it's so beautiful.'

Jack Silver stared at her, taken by her words so softly spoken.

Meredith met his eyes. She was quite startled by their intensity. They did not leave her face and there was an expression in them she could not fathom. And she discovered that she could not look away . . .

It was Jack who broke the spell between them. He said suddenly, gruffly, 'I'm glad you're coming to work at Silver Lake Inn, Meredith. I have a feeling things will go well. Amelia likes you. I like you. I sincerely hope you like us.'

'I do, Mr Silver, and *I'm* glad I'm coming here, too.'

They walked back to the inn in silence, both lost for a few moments in their own thoughts.

'See you on Monday, Mr Silver,' Meredith said, climbing onto her bike, riding away.

'Call me Jack,' he shouted after her.

'All right, I will,' she answered, half turning, waving before disappearing down the long drive.

He stood watching her until she was out of sight, and he was amazed at himself when he suddenly realized he did not want her to leave. There was something most appealing about this girl; she was fresh and sweet and very beautiful, although he knew *she* did not realize just how beautiful she truly was. Nor did she understand the impact she made with her long legs, sun-streaked brown hair and smoky green eyes. He discovered he missed her already and he had only known her for a couple of hours; and he was further amazed at himself.

The insistent ringing of the telephone awakened Meredith with a sudden start. As she jumped up and went to answer it she realized she had fallen asleep on the sofa earlier.

'Hello?'

'Good morning, Mrs Stratton. This is your wake-up call. It's five o'clock,' the hotel operator informed her.

'Thank you,' she answered, putting the phone back in the cradle and turning on a lamp. Glancing at her watch she saw that it *was* five; it surprised her that she had spent the entire night on the sofa without waking up once. She must have been extremely tired. On the other hand, the big overstuffed sofa was as comfortable as the bed.

Patsy will soon be here, she thought, hurrying into the bedroom, slipping out of her dressing gown, then heading for the shower. She was filled with relief that she had packed the night before.

An hour later she was standing in the lobby of Claridge's waiting for her partner who was going to drive them to the North of England.

Eight

It was a dull morning, grey and overcast, when Patsy and Meredith drove away from Claridge's. Leaden skies threatened rain and by the time Patsy was pulling onto the motorway, pointing the Aston Martin in the direction of the North, it was already pouring.

Meredith leaned back against the car seat, only half listening to the radio, her mind preoccupied with business. But at one moment she closed her eyes, and then, almost against her own volition, she began to doze, lulled by the warmth in the car and the music on the radio.

'Go to sleep if you feel like it,' Patsy said, glancing at her quickly, before focusing on the road ahead again. 'I don't mind, and we don't have to talk if you're tired.'

'I'm fine,' Meredith replied, opening her eyes, sitting up straighter. 'Even though I spent the night on the sofa I did in fact have a good rest.'

'Why did you sleep on the sofa?'

'I was still wide awake at one in the morning, too much on my mind, I guess. So I decided to get up, then I must have dozed off a bit later on.'

'I hope you weren't up in the middle of the night fretting about Reed Jamison.' Patsy frowned, throwing her a concerned look.

'No, of course not.'

'Good, because he's certainly not worth worrying about.'

'I agree, and I'm relieved I told him how I felt, Patsy.' Meredith laughed dryly. 'It's probably the only time I've had his full attention.'

'What do you mean?'

'I always thought Reed wasn't really listening to anything I had to say. It seemed to me that he was very busy formulating his reply, preoccupied with what he was going to say rather than with the meaning of my words.'

'A lot of people suffer from *that* particular ailment,' Patsy muttered. 'It's a kind of self-involvement, I suppose. Then again, nobody seems to *really* listen any more. Except you. You're the best listener I've ever known.'

'I learned that from Amelia. She taught me how important it is to listen. She was always saying that you didn't learn anything if you were the one doing all the talking. How right she was, but she was generally right about most things; she taught me such a lot.' There was a small pause, and then Meredith added, 'She was quite the most remarkable person I've ever known.'

'I'm sorry I never knew her,' Patsy said. 'And it's funny you should mention her this morning, because I was thinking about her only last night, thinking what an influence she's been on both our lives, although indirectly on mine, of course. Just think, if John Raphaelson hadn't been her lawyer and then yours, you would never have met his brother, who was one of my father's best friends, and therefore *we* would never have met, would we?'

Meredith smiled. 'That's true, and *I* wish you'd known Amelia. She was so special.' Meredith let out a little sigh. 'You know, if she'd lived she'd only be sixty-two this year. Not that old at all.'

'And Jack? How old would he have been?'

'He was four years younger than Amelia, so he would have been fifty-eight . . . at the end of this month, actually.'

'How sad for you that they died so young.'

'Yes . . . Amelia struggled to keep going after Jack's death, but the light had gone out for her. She just gave up in the end. I've always thought she died of a broken heart, if that's possible.'

'Oh *I* think it is, Meredith. I believe my mother did . . . she went so quickly after my father passed away. I've always thought she just lost all interest in living once he was gone. In fact, I found out from my aunt, after Mummy had died, that she was always saying, "I want to go to Winston," and she stopped eating – well, she ate very little. It was as if she lost her appetite . . . for everything, including life. I do think she'd made up her mind to die.'

'Amelia was a bit like that too, although she did live for a year after Jack's death. Not surprising really, when you think about it. People who have been together for a long time are so dependent on each other, and when one of them is suddenly alone it's traumatic.'

'They're lonely, and loneliness is a pretty unbearable state to be in.'

'Amelia once said the same thing. Actually, she said loneliness was another kind of death. She loved me and she loved Cat, but Jack was the light of her life. Without him she seemed to lose her purpose, her *raison d'être*. Did I ever tell you that they'd known each other since their childhood?'

'No, you never did. Did they grow up together?'

'Part of the time, yes. Her parents had a summer home in Cornwall Bridge, not far from Silver Lake, and they were friends of the Silvers. Jack and Amelia met when they were children. Amelia was fourteen and Jack ten. They became best friends. They were both only children, you see, only children of only children, so there were no brothers and sisters or cousins. "I'm going to marry you when I grow up," Jack was forever telling her, and she'd laugh and say she couldn't possibly marry a younger man. But they did marry when they were in their twenties. And then Amelia had the riding accident . . . how different their lives would have been if she hadn't been thrown by her horse. But that was her destiny . . . at least, that's what she used to say to me.'

'What did she mean?'

'Exactly that, Patsy. She said that none of us could tamper with fate. Or avert it. *Qué será será* she would say, *what will be will be*. She said it was fate that brought me to Silver Lake that day in May of 1969. She said I was simply living out my destiny, just as she was doing, and Jack too. "I'm meant to be in this chair, Meri, I don't know why, but I am," she would tell me over and over again.' Meredith paused, looked at Patsy through the corner of her eye. 'According to

Amelia, fate brought me to them. And as I've told you many times before, they changed my life, just as I changed theirs, in so many different ways. For the better . . . for all of us. They gave me love and warmth and understanding, and the only real home I'd ever known until then. And I gave them something they'd always wanted, always missed . . .'

'You were like a sister to them, the sister neither of them ever had.'

'Yes, I *was* a sibling, in a sense. But what I meant was that I gave them Cat. My baby was like their child as well as mine. And how much they loved her.'

'I know, and just think how happy they'd be if they could see her today. She's really grown up to be such a fine young woman. Do you think she *will* get engaged to Keith?'

'I do, and it'll be soon. Catherine has very good instincts, and she wouldn't have said anything to me the other night if she hadn't felt Keith was on the verge of proposing.'

'I hope I get an invitation to the wedding.'

'Don't be so silly, of course you will. Cat loves you, and she's never forgotten how marvellous you were to her the year she lived with you in London. And neither have I, for that matter. Because of you I was able to sleep every night. I didn't have to worry about my daughter being alone in a foreign country.'

'I was happy to look after her, be a big sister. Will you have the reception at Silver Lake?'

'Oh, yes, I'm sure of that. Cat wouldn't want it anywhere else. She loves that place the way I do. And it's the perfect setting for a wedding. Blanche is all excited, planning it already in her mind. The other evening she was talking about marquees and the menu and no doubt she's got everything planned by now, from the flowers to the parking arrangements. Anyway, you're going to come, and you'll stay with me at the house.'

'How lovely, thank you. Oh gosh, Meredith, being in love is wonderful! I'm thrilled for Cat, thrilled that she's found the right man. I wish I could.'

'When you're looking there's never one around.' Meredith leaned her head against the back of the seat, closed her eyes. 'And a man isn't always the answer, you know.'

'Only too true!' Patsy peered ahead, cursing under her breath. The heavy rain was slashing against the windscreen, so that everything looked blurred despite the wipers. 'I hope this awful weather is going to let up soon. It's just miserable.'

'Do you want me to drive?'

'No, no, I'm okay. And I know this road like the back of my hand. Don't forget, it leads to the North of England.'

'Your favourite place.'

'One of them anyway,' Patsy said, smiling to herself.

Meredith fell silent, her thoughts taking over.

Patsy concentrated on her driving. There was a strong wind blowing, and she suspected it was bitterly cold outside; the road had recently grown slick, icy, suddenly slippery because of the freezing rain and sleet.

As she drove on, her eyes fixed ahead, she thought of Meredith and how she had gone to Silver Lake all those years ago, how her life had been transformed overnight. What an extraordinary story it was. She knew that Meredith had become indispensable to Amelia very quickly; the two women had developed a symbiotic relationship. Meredith had once told her how Jack had come to rely on her as well, teaching her so much about the management of the hotel, teaching her everything he knew about business. Yes, Meredith had confided a great deal about her years with the Silvers, but not much else about herself. She never talked about her earlier life in Australia. In fact, everything before the Silver Lake years seemed to be clouded in mystery. It was as if there were another part of her life, a secret part, which Meredith did not want anyone to know about. Patsy had no inclination to pry, ask questions; that was not her way. She respected Meredith's desire for privacy.

Meredith interrupted Patsy's thoughts when she turned to her and said, 'This may sound funny to you, but I have a feeling you prefer the inn in Ripon. Skell Garth is your favourite of the two, isn't it?'

Taken aback, Patsy exclaimed, 'Why do you say *that*?'

'I just know. I've put two and two together from the few things you've said. Anyway, you love Yorkshire so much, it's where you grew up.'

'As I've been telling you all along, I want you to be the judge, Meredith, I really do. I don't want to influence you, set you up in advance.'

'What's wrong with the one in the Lake District?'

'Nothing. You've seen the pictures.'

'Yes, and it does look gorgeous, and so do the gardens and the view. You've said it's luxurious, beautifully done, and yet there's a *but* in your mind; I know you.'

'Too many cushions,' Patsy muttered.

Meredith began to laugh. 'I'll never live that down, will I?' she said, remembering a comment she had made about another inn they had considered six months ago. 'So what you're saying really is that it's *overstuffed, over-decorated.*'

'Sort of . . . lots of luxury and comfort, and I think the place does make you feel terribly pampered. But despite all the lovely fabrics and rugs and nice antiques there's nothing unique or different about Heronside. There's nothing there that's gone awry. You've always told me that it's important for a room to be slightly askew, a bit "off". You said it makes a place interesting.'

'Oddities add character, and that's something we have always taken into consideration.' Meredith looked at her partner and friend, and nodded to herself. 'I *feel* you don't like Heronside.'

'I don't *dislike* it,' Patsy answered, speaking the truth.

'Look, why are we going there? Why not go directly to Ripon?'

'Because it is a wonderful inn, and I want you to see it for yourself. It doesn't need much money spent on it, since it was redone two years ago, and the views are magnificent. Also, I'm not sure I'm right about it. Truly, Meredith, I want *you* to make the decision.'

'All right, I will. But you're not often wrong, Patsy. We have very similar tastes.'

Nine

The morning was clear, cold, the kind of crisp bright day that Meredith liked. The sky was a dazzling blue without cloud and the sun was shining; whilst this offered little warmth it added radiance to the day.

It was just turning nine o'clock on Tuesday morning. Meredith was bundled up in boots and a sheepskin coat, walking through Studley Park. The stately avenue of lime trees down which she hurried led to Studley Church, just visible on top of the hill at the end of the avenue. She knew, from Mrs Miller's directions, that within a few minutes she would be at the abbey.

Yesterday afternoon, when she and Patsy had arrived in Ripon, they had gone directly to Skell Garth House. It was situated between the tiny villages of Studley Royal and Aldfield, and stood on the banks of the little River Skell, as did Fountains Abbey on the opposite bank.

After the Millers had been introduced to her, Patsy had explained to the couple that they would like to stay the night at Skell Garth. Since it was midweek in winter, this had not presented a problem. There were plenty of available rooms and Claudia Miller had given them a choice.

'I think we'd like those two that adjoin each other on the top floor,' Patsy had said, as they followed the owners up the wide main staircase. 'You know, the two that face Fountains.'

The minute they had walked into the first of the rooms, Patsy had dragged Meredith to the window. 'Now isn't that the most spectacular sight!' she had cried. 'Behold Fountains Abbey! One of the two most beautiful ruined abbeys in the whole of England.'

Meredith had stared out across the sloping lawns and gardens of Skell Garth House, now obliterated by a covering of snow, her eyes fastening on the abbey. It rose up out of glistening white fields, huge, dark, monolithic, silhouetted against the fading greenish sky like some ancient tribute to God. She caught her breath, struck by its beauty. She agreed that it *was* magnificent; that was the only word to describe it, she thought.

'It's one of the best-preserved abbeys in the country,' Bill Miller had pointed out. 'There are stone masons working on it all the time, trying to keep it from crumbling away. It's a national treasure, you know.'

At that moment, and for a reason she could not fathom, Meredith had made up her mind to take a closer look, feeling oddly drawn to those ruins.

After they had taken tea with the Millers, the rest of the afternoon had been devoted to a complete guided tour of Skell Garth House, which dated back to the nineteenth century. By the time they had finished talking with the owners, going over all aspects of the inn and the pros and cons, it had grown dark outside. I'll go tomorrow, before we leave, Meredith had resolved, filled with determination to visit the ruins, a determination she did not quite understand.

This morning, when she was finishing her breakfast, Claudia Miller had come into the dining room to see if she needed anything else. Meredith had seized the moment and had asked her how to get to the abbey from the inn.

'You'll have to approach it on foot, that's the best way. Wear a pair of wellies, if you've got them with you, or boots. There's still a bit of snow out there by Studley way.' Claudia had then given her directions.

And I'm almost there, Meredith told herself, as she finally reached the top of the hill at the end of the avenue of limes. She glanced over at Studley Church, so picturesque in the snow, and at the obelisk nearby; she then directed her gaze to the lake below, glittering in the sunlight. The River Skell flowed beyond it, and there, just a short distance upstream, was the abbey.

Meredith stood for a moment longer on top of the hill, shading her eyes against the sun with one hand, thinking that Fountains looked more imposing than it had yesterday afternoon. But of course it would, she told herself. She was, after all, much closer to it now, viewing it with the naked eye, not through a glass window from a distant house.

Unexpectedly Meredith shivered. She felt as though a cold wind had blown around her, through her. But there was no wind this morning. Someone walked over my grave, she muttered under her breath, and then wondered why she had thought this, wondered how she knew such an odd phrase. She had never used it in her life before.

A strange sensation came over her. She stood very still, all of her senses alert. Instantly, she knew what it was . . . a curious feeling that she had been here before, that she had stood on this very spot, on this very hill, gazing down at those medieval ruins. It seemed to her that the landscape below her was familiar, known to her. She shivered again. *Déjà vu*, the French call it, *already seen*, she reminded herself. But she had not been here before; she had never even been to Yorkshire.

Yet this ancient place stirred something in her. The ruins beckoned, seemed to pull her forward urgently; she set off, began to hurry down the hill, her boots crunching on the frozen snow. She was almost running, slipping and sliding in her haste to get there. Several times she almost fell but managed to recover her balance and go on running.

At last, somewhat out of breath, she was hurrying into the centre of the ruined Cistercian monastery.

It was roofless, open to the vast arc of sky floating above it like a great canopy of blue, and the glassless windows were giant arches flung against that empty sky. Meredith stood there, turning slowly, her head thrown back as she gazed up at the soaring stone walls, jagged and broken off at the top . . . the immense columns only partially intact . . . the cracked flagstones covered today in pure white snow. A sense of timelessness enveloped her.

As she looked around, absorbing everything, her heart clenched, and she felt a strange sense of loss. So acute, so strong, so overwhelming was this feeling, that tears came into her eyes. Her throat closed with such a rush of emotion she was further startled at herself.

Something was taken from me here ... something of immense value to me. *I have been here before*. I know this ancient place ... somehow it's part of me. What was it I lost here? Oh God, what was it? Something dearer than life. Part of my soul ... part of my heart. Why do I feel this way? What do these ruins mean to me?

Meredith stood perfectly still in the middle of the ruined abbey. Unexpected tears ran down her face, warm against her cold cheeks. She closed her eyes, not understanding what was happening to her; it was as though her heart were breaking. Something had been taken from her. *Or someone*. Someone she loved. Was that it? She was not sure. The only thing she really knew at this moment was that she was experiencing an immense sense of deprivation.

Opening her eyes, moving slowly, she went and stood near one of the walls of the monastery, resting her head against its time-worn stones. There was a stillness here, a quietness that was infinite; it calmed her.

Far away, in the distance, she heard the call of a lone bird high on the wing. There was a sudden rush of wind through the ruins, a moaning, sighing wind, and then everything was still, silent again.

She began to walk towards the cloisters, moving like a somnambulist. She knew the way. Once inside she was protected from the wind. And there was no sound here at all. Just perfect silence in these great vaulted halls of the cloisters.

Pain, she thought. Why do I feel pain and hurt and despair? What is it about this place that makes me feel like this? What does Fountains mean to me? She did not know. It was a mystery.

When Meredith returned to Skell Garth House an hour later, Patsy was waiting for her in the sitting room.

'My God, you look frozen to death!' her partner cried as she walked in. 'Come and sit by the fire and have a hot drink before we leave for the airport.'

'I'm all right.' Meredith took off her coat and walked across to the fireplace, warming her hands in front of the flames for a moment.

'I couldn't believe it when Claudia told me you'd gone to Fountains Abbey. And in this weather. If you'd waited for me to come down for breakfast I would have driven you there. At least, I would have driven you as close to the abbey as I could get.'

'I enjoyed the walk.' Meredith sat down on a chair, turned her head, gazed into the flames burning so fiercely.

'I'll go and order a pot of tea,' Patsy said, jumping up. 'Would you like something to eat? Pikelets, maybe? I know you enjoy them as much as I do.'

'No thanks, not now. The tea would be nice, though.'

When Patsy came back she threw Meredith a curious glance. 'This may be a strange thing to say, but you look quite white, as if you've seen a ghost.' Then she grinned and added, 'A couple of Cistercian monks perhaps, walking around the abbey's ruins with you?'

When Meredith did not respond with a gale of laughter, as she usually did, but looked at her oddly and remained silent, Patsy stared at her harder.

'*Is* there something the matter, Meredith?' she probed.

At first Meredith was silent, then said, 'No, there's nothing wrong. But I did have a funny experience at Fountains.'

'What happened?'

'I was drawn to the ruins. It was as though a *magnet* was pulling me forward. I practically ran there from Studley Church. I almost fell a couple of times. The thing was, Patsy, I couldn't wait to get there, to be in the middle of those ruins. And once I was standing in the centre of them I felt as if I knew that place so well. It was curiously familiar. And then something happened to me . . . I had this immense sense of loss. It was so overwhelming, I was shaken. I can't explain it, I really can't.' Meredith stared at Patsy. 'You probably think I'm crazy . . . Anyway, Fountains Abbey *does* mean something to me, of that I'm sure. Something special. And yet I can't tell you why that is so. I'd never heard of it until the other day. And I've never been there in my life.'

For a moment there was no response from Patsy, then she said, 'No, you never have. Not in this life, at any rate. However, maybe you were there in another. In the past . . . in a past life. Do you believe in reincarnation?'

'I don't know.' Meredith shook her head. 'To say I don't believe sounds so arrogant . . .' She shrugged, looking suddenly baffled. 'Who knows anything really about this strange world we live in?'

'Perhaps you saw a movie – a documentary about Yorkshire that featured the abbey. Perhaps that's why it's so familiar to you,' Patsy suggested.

'I don't think so. And how do you explain that peculiar sense of loss I experienced?'

Patsy said, 'I can't.'

A young waitress came in with the tray of tea; the two women fell silent.

Once they were alone again, Patsy remarked quietly, staring closely at Meredith, 'You were pretty excited last night . . . I mean about buying Skell Garth House. I hope your odd experience this morning hasn't made you change your mind.'

'No, it hasn't, Patsy. Quite the contrary. It's obvious that Fountains Abbey means something, although I don't quite understand what. Still, I see that as a good omen for the future. Anyway, I like the inn. You were right about it.' She gave her partner a warm smile. 'It's a little gem in its own way, and certainly it's got a lot more going for it than Heronside. Too many cushions *indeed*. Skell Garth is charming, and it has a great atmosphere, is loaded with comfort. Of course, it's a bit shabby, but it doesn't need any big money spent on it.'

'All Skell Garth House needs, in my opinion, is a good decorating job. And you're the best person to do it, Meredith.'

Meredith nodded, but made no comment.

Patsy lifted her cup of tea. 'Here's to our new inn, then. May it be ever prosperous.'

'To Skell Garth House.'

Ten

Luc de Montboucher looked from Agnes D'Auberville to Meredith and said, 'You must allow six months at least for the remodelling. To cut the time down to four months will only mean disaster.'

Agnes said, 'We'd hoped to have the inn open by the summer –'

'That is not possible!' he exclaimed, cutting in swiftly. 'There's too much to do, and some of the work is major, such as the architectural changes you want. And which are necessary, I might add. Then there's new wiring, plumbing, windows, and floors. Most of the walls have to be re-plastered and sanded.' He lifted his hands in a typically Gallic gesture, and finished, 'To be honest, Agnes . . . Meredith . . . six months is going to be a tough schedule for the contractor, please let me alert you to that fact right now. I sincerely hope he can keep to it.'

'But the Manoir de la Closière is not such a large house,' Agnes remarked, and turned to Meredith. 'You've now been there twice this week. What's your opinion?'

It was Friday. The three of them were having lunch in the Relais Plaza of the Plaza Athénée Hotel in Paris, having spent the morning going over ideas for the transformation of the old house.

Now Meredith put down her fork and returned her French partner's look. 'You're right, Agnes, inasmuch as it's not a huge house, but it *is* in terrible disrepair, in much worse shape than the château was. I happen to think Luc is correct. And I doubt very much that we can get the remodelling finished in less time than he suggests. In fact, I believe it's a bit foolhardy to allow only six months.' Glancing at Luc, she asked, 'Don't you think it would be wiser to settle for eight?'

Before he had a chance to answer, Agnes exclaimed, somewhat heatedly, 'But we remodelled and redecorated Château de Cormeron in a year! And that's a much bigger place.'

'I know. However, the manor house at Montfort-L'Amaury hasn't been so well cared for,' Meredith pointed out. 'I think it's unfair of us to expect Luc to work with unrealistic time schedules. He's right, we're only going to end up with a disaster.'

Agnes was silent.

Luc nodded, gave Meredith the benefit of a warm smile. 'Thank you for understanding my problems.'

Meredith liked him. He was an attractive man, with a great deal of continental charm, yet sincere.

'When *would* we open the inn then?' Agnes asked.

'I think it will have to be next spring . . . the spring of 1996. I don't believe we have any other alternative. Luc's pretty clear in his mind about what we want, and he will soon know what's feasible. I suppose he could start the work in a month from now. Am I correct, Luc?'

'You are. I will complete my plans for your approval as quickly as possible. If you like them and give me the go ahead, I can have the contractor in there by the end of the month. He can start demolition of some of the interiors. And if there are no unforeseen problems we should be able to finish by June. I will try to complete the job in six months, not eight, as you suggested. Thank you for offering those extra two months; however, I don't think we'll be needing them.'

Meredith said, 'That's good to know.' Addressing Agnes, she continued, 'As soon as the contractor is finished we can bring in the other trades . . . the painters, paperhangers, etcetera, and they will be finished in four months quite easily. Starting next week, you and I can begin to create the decorative schemes.'

'Well, all right,' Agnes murmured. 'If you think it's going to take a whole year then it will.' She laughed, suddenly relaxing, and shrugged. 'I must admit, you're rarely wrong when it comes to a remodelling job.' Digging her fork into a piece of fish, she finished, 'The problem with me is that I'm over-anxious. I can't wait to get the new inn running properly and open to the public.'

'There's nothing wrong with that,' Meredith responded. 'But if we try to do it at breakneck speed it's asking for trouble.'

'I'm glad we're all agreed,' Luc said. 'And let me just add that the manor is charming, and has endless possibilities, especially since the grounds are also so pleasant. I think you've made a good choice.'

'Thanks to you, Agnes,' Meredith said. 'You spotted the house.'

Looking pleased, her nervousness about the schedule now abating, Agnes took a long swallow of white wine. 'Then it's settled. Luc will get the plans done quickly and once they're ready he can send them on an overnight to New York. Now . . .' She paused, reached out and squeezed Meredith's arm. 'What are *your* plans for the weekend?'

'Nothing special, really. I thought I'd take it easy, do a little shopping, and maybe go to the *Marché aux Puces* on Sunday. But please don't worry about me, Agnes, I know you've got your hands full.'

Agnes grimaced. 'I'm afraid I do, with Alain and Chloe both down with the flu. Thank God I haven't caught it from them.'

'I'm sorry they're not well, and you mustn't fuss about me, I'll be all right on my own this weekend.'

Luc lifted his glass, drank a little of his wine, and sat back in his chair, scrutinizing Meredith across the luncheon table. Eventually he said, 'If you really don't have anything special to do this weekend, I would like to invite you to my house in the country. I'm leaving tomorrow morning; we could drive there together, and I would bring you back to Paris early on Monday.'

'That's so nice of you, Luc,' Meredith murmured and hesitated. 'I don't know . . . I don't want to impose . . .'

'But you're not imposing, I invited you. And I would *like* you to come. It's not going to be a very fancy weekend with lots of guests, if that's what is worrying you. In fact, I must warn you, we will be there alone and you might find that boring. Although the countryside is beautiful, and perhaps you would enjoy it.'

'Well, thank you . . .' Meredith began and stopped, still uncertain.

Agnes looked from one to the other and jumped in, saying swiftly, 'Luc has the most charming old house. In the Loire. It's really unique, Meredith, you'll love it. You *must* go for the weekend.'

'Yes, do please come, Meredith,' Luc insisted.

'All right then, I will,' Meredith said, suddenly making up her mind. 'And again, thank you very much for inviting me.'

After lunch Agnes and Meredith walked back to the Havens offices, which were located in a narrow street off the Rue de Rivoli.

'I've been collecting fabrics and wallpapers for the past few weeks,' Agnes explained, once they were ensconced in her cluttered private domain.

Flopping down onto a sofa, she dragged two large shopping bags towards her and said, 'Come on, Meredith, sit here next to me and we'll go through some of these. I thought it would be a good idea to have something on hand, so we can start formulating our decorative schemes well in advance.'

'You must have scoured the whole of Paris,' Meredith laughed, joining her, plunging her hands into one of the shopping bags. 'I've never seen so many samples.' She took out a blue-and-red fabric and stared at it. 'I like this . . . it looks like a Manuel Canovas . . . oh yes, so it is.'

'He's very eligible, you know,' Agnes said, also delving into one of the bags.

'Who? Manuel Canovas? I thought he was married.'

'No, not Manuel Canovas. *Luc de Montboucher*. That's who I'm talking about.'

'Oh.'

'Why do you say *oh* like that? In that surprised tone?'

'Are you trying to be a matchmaker, Agnes?'

'Not really,' Agnes laughed. 'It hadn't really crossed my mind until he invited you for the weekend. Then it suddenly hit me . . . he's attractive, successful and, most important, single.'

'Divorced?'

'No, I don't think he's been married.' Agnes frowned and bit her lip. 'No, wait a moment . . . perhaps he *was* married and she died. I can't remember. He's a friend of Alain's, I'll have to double check that.'

'How old do you think he is? About forty?'

'I think he's a bit older than that, if I remember correctly. About forty-three perhaps. I'll ask Alain when I get home tonight and I'll call you at the hotel.'

Meredith laughed, shook her head. 'He's only asked me to go to his house for the weekend, he hasn't proposed marriage.'

'I know. On the other hand, my dear Meredith, I believe he's rather taken with you. I've noticed him looking at you over the past few days, and looking at you with great interest, I might add. In that certain way.'

'What do you mean by *certain way*?'

'With curiosity. It's perfectly obvious he wants to get to know you better. Do you like him?'

'Of course, otherwise I wouldn't have accepted his invitation to go to the Loire with him.'

'He's a very talented architect. But you know that from the examples of his work he showed you at his office yesterday. We've been lucky to get him for this job. And as I said, he's very eligible, which is most important.'

'The way you spoke, you must know his house,' Meredith murmured, changing the subject.

'Yes, Alain and I have been there a couple of times. In the summer . . . never at this time of year. But it's a lovely old place. Between Talcy and Menars.'

'Where's that in relation to our inn?'

'It's higher up, just up beyond Blois, closer to Orléans than Cormeron. Do you remember that time Alain and I took you to Chambord?'

Meredith nodded.

'Well Chambord is in a direct line to Talcy across the River Loire.'

'I think I know where you mean. What kind of house is it?'

'Big . . . Clos-Talcy has been in his family for hundreds of years. It's been well looked after, kept in good repair. I think Luc goes there most weekends; it's only a few hours' drive, closer to Paris than Cormeron.'

'I'm glad I brought some country clothes,' Meredith said, now suddenly wondering what she had let herself in for this weekend.

'Oh, you don't have to worry, I think he lives quite casually,' Agnes remarked and handed her a swatch of fabric. 'Do you like this?'

Meredith examined it and nodded. 'You know I love

red *toile de Jouy*. It would work well with black furniture or black accessories.'

'Luc really was looking at you in that certain way, *chérie*,' Agnes remarked, eyeing Meredith. 'I'm not inventing that.'

'I believe you,' Meredith answered, and began to laugh, amused by Agnes and her romantic notions.

Eleven

Her first sight of Clos-Talcy was of a double image – the house itself and its reflection in the large ornamental lake in front of it.

'Oh how beautiful!' Meredith cried when Luc de Montboucher walked her around the bend in the driveway and directed her attention across the lake, pointing out the house in the distance.

'I wanted you to see it from here, not from the car,' he said. 'This view surprises everyone, and I must explain to you that it's one of my own special favourites . . . it's the reflection, of course, that intrigues me.'

'What a perfect house in a perfect setting,' Meredith murmured, almost to herself. She stood next to Luc surveying the great château with interest. It was built of pink brick and pale stone, topped with a roof of dark grey slate. There were a number of tall, slender chimneys rising up from the roof and she counted thirty-eight windows and five dormers.

The many tall trees surrounding the château were reflected in the lake, along with the façade of the house itself, and to Meredith there was a marvellous symmetry to the two in combination. Certainly it was the loveliest initial view of any house she had ever seen.

Turning to Luc, she asked, 'How old is the château?'

'It was built in the early seventeenth century, and the gardens were designed about fifty years later by Le Nôtre, the famous landscape artist.'

Taking hold of her arm, he continued, 'But come, let us go back to the car. Later, after lunch, I'll drive you around the park, and we can go for a walk in the gardens, if you would like. I must warn you, though, they are rather bereft-looking at this time of year.'

'Oh I don't mind that; in fact, I like gardens in winter. Very often they're interesting, different naturally, but still eye-catching.' She gave a wry little laugh. 'Well, some of them, anyway.'

'I happen to like winter gardens myself,' Luc remarked, opening the car door, helping her in, then going around to the other side.

Starting the car, he drove up the majestic avenue lined with plane trees, continuing, 'Fortunately, we haven't had much snow here this year, so we'll be able to have a pleasant stroll later in the day.'

Meredith nodded and turned her head, glancing out of the car window. She saw another lake, this one smaller than the first, and it prompted her suddenly to confide, 'I've always been drawn to houses that are on water, or very near it, although I've no idea why.'

'Oh, I understand that feeling well,' Luc replied, giving her a swift look, then immediately swinging his eyes back to the road. 'I have the same attraction myself. There's something truly wonderful about water in the middle of a land mass; it enhances natural surroundings as well as any buildings that might be nearby. We have a lot of water here in Talcy. Apart from the ornamental lake, there's the smaller one you just noticed, plus a fish pond near the orchard, a stream that runs through the woods, a waterfall, and innumerable fountains.' He began to chuckle. 'I had an ancestor who was obviously extremely fond of those . . . we've got over a dozen of them in the park, and some are quite magnificent, even though I do say so myself. You'll find you're never very far from running water at Talcy.'

Meredith smiled. 'That's nice . . . You know, Luc, all of my inns are near water too, except for Montfort-L'Amaury. That's the only thing I wasn't happy about when I first saw the manor earlier this week.'

'If you wish, I could create a lake or a pond at the new inn,' Luc volunteered. 'It's not so difficult to do, and there is a fair amount of land attached to the manor house. What do you think?'

'That might be rather nice. I'll talk to Agnes, and perhaps you could give me some idea of the cost.'

'*Mais certainement* . . . of course. Ah, here we are, Meredith, we've arrived at the house at last.'

Luc had driven into a large cobbled courtyard and parked; it was apparently the front entrance to the château. Wide steps led up to a huge double door made of dark wood embellished with iron ornamentation. Before they had even alighted, a middle-aged man in his shirt sleeves, wearing a black waistcoat and a green-striped apron, had come out of the house. He ran down the steps, a broad smile creasing his cheerful face.

'*Bonjour*, Vincent!' Luc called as he climbed out of the car and hurried to assist Meredith.

'*Bonjour, Monsieur,*' the man responded.

Luc and Meredith walked towards him. He shook Luc's hand.

Luc said, 'Meredith, this is Vincent Marchand, who, with his good lady Mathilde, runs this place. Vincent, this is Mrs Stratton.'

'*Madame,*' the man said, inclining his head reverentially.

Meredith smiled at him. 'I'm pleased to meet you, Vincent,' she said, stretching out her hand.

Shaking it vigorously, he responded, '*Grand plaisir, Madame.*' With a nod he hurried to the boot of the car and took out the luggage. Grasping several bags, he followed them up the front steps.

Luc led her into a vast entrance hall which was almost cavernous, with soaring stone walls and a stone-flagged floor. The pale-coloured limestone walls were hung with two Gobelin tapestries and a bronze-and-crystal chandelier floated down on chains from the high ceiling. The only piece of furniture was a long ornately carved and gilded console upon which stood two large stone urns filled with dried flowers; a huge gilded mirror hung above the console and there was a stone statue of a knight in armour in one corner.

Luc said, 'Let me take your coat,' and after she had shrugged out of it he carried the sheepskin over to a cupboard built into one of the walls.

A split second later, a door at the end of the hall flew open and a tall, plumpish woman came hurrying towards them on fast-moving, nimble feet.

'*Monsieur!*' she exclaimed, beaming at Luc before

flashing Meredith a glance filled with undisguised curiosity.

Luc kissed her on both cheeks. '*Bonjour, Mathilde.* I would like to introduce Mrs Stratton. As I told you on the phone, she's my guest for the weekend.'

Nodding, smiling, Mathilde stepped forward. The two women shook hands, and Mathilde said, 'I will show you to your room, *Madame.*' Glancing at Luc, she continued quickly, 'As you suggested, *Monsieur*, I have given Mrs Stratton the room of your grandmother.'

Luc guided Meredith towards the staircase, saying, 'I do hope you like your room, it was my grandmother's favourite. I'm sure you will . . . it overlooks water . . . the ornamental lake, actually, which was your first glimpse of Talcy. It was a lucky choice on my part, I think.'

'Yes, it was, and I'm sure I'll love it.'

Mathilde led the way upstairs, followed by Meredith and Luc, with Vincent bringing up the rear, carrying Meredith's two suitcases.

Mathilde marched them down a long corridor, thickly carpeted and lined with windows; the walls were hung with many paintings. Meredith sneaked a look at them as they hurried by, realized they were family portraits, probably of minor members of the family, since they were relegated to this corridor.

'*Voilà!*' Mathilde suddenly cried, flinging open a door. 'Here is the room of *Grand-mère* Rose de Montboucher. Whom everybody loved.'

'And feared,' Luc added, winking at Meredith. 'She

was quite a terror at times. But also very, very beautiful.'

Noticing her glancing around, Luc explained: 'This is the sitting room, the bedroom and bathroom are through that door over there. But to continue, my grandmother fell in love with this suite of rooms when my grandfather brought her to Talcy for the first time. And she made them hers. That's a portrait of her, by the way. The one hanging over the mantelpiece.'

Meredith followed his gaze.

Her eyes settled on the painting of an extraordinarily lovely young woman. Red-gold curls framed a piquant face set on a long white neck. Her eyes were bright blue under arched auburn eyebrows and her wide mouth had a generosity about it.

Walking over to the fire, Meredith gazed up at the portrait with great interest. The artist had captured something of the woman's personality . . . there was an inherent warmth in the smile, and happiness dwelt in that face as well. Rose de Montboucher wore a dress of palest pink chiffon with a softly draped collar and a string of pearls. Meredith decided the portrait had been painted in the 1920s.

'Your grandmother was absolutely gorgeous, no two ways about it,' she said, looking over her shoulder at him. 'I think she was probably a bit mischievous: there's a certain glint in those rather remarkable eyes and in her smile.'

Luc nodded. 'Quite an accurate assessment of her. *I* believe she had a lot of mischief in her, as well as a special kind of *joie de vivre*. It was a true gaiety that people found irresistible. I knew her as a much older woman than she is in that portrait. But even then I felt she was up to something all the time. Up to no good, my father always said. He was her firstborn and the favourite of her four children. I recall that she had a good sense of humour and was a marvellous ranconteur. I think she must have kissed the Blarney Stone.'

'Was she Irish?'

'She was. My grandfather met her in Dublin. At a ball. He had gone there to shoot.'

Mathilde bustled in from the bedroom with Vincent in her wake. 'Would you like to have help with your unpacking, *Madame*? I will send Jasmine to assist you.'

Meredith shook her head. 'Thank you, Mathilde, but I can manage.'

The housekeeper nodded, gave her a quick smile, then flew out of the room. Vincent hurried after her, endeavouring to keep pace.

'He's her shadow,' Luc murmured in a low voice, once they were alone. 'They're both the salt of the earth, and have worked at Talcy all of their lives, and their parents before them. They have two daughters, Jasmine and Philippine, and a son Jean-Pierre, who all work here at the château. I'll leave you now, Meredith, so that you can freshen up. Are you quite sure you wouldn't like Jasmine to come upstairs and help you with your clothes?'

'No, really, I'm fine, thanks.'

Luc looked at his watch. 'Ah, it's only just a little after twelve. Let us meet, then, in the library, in an hour, shall we say? Does that give you enough time?'

'Of course.'

He half smiled, turned on his heel and headed towards the door.

Meredith said, 'Luc, where *is* the library?'

He swung around, grinning, and answered apologetically, 'So sorry, I forgot you don't know the house. The library is the middle room of the *enfilade* . . . that's the series of rooms which adjoin each other, off the entrance hall on the right-hand side. We'll have a drink in there before lunch.'

'Yes, that'll be nice.'

The door closed softly behind him. Meredith turned back to the portrait of his grandmother; she studied it again for a moment or two.

'Irish eyes are smiling,' Meredith murmured aloud, thinking of the famous old ballad. And indeed Rose de Montboucher's eyes *were* full of laughter; and it was very much an Irish face, of course. It couldn't be anything else. Stepping back, Meredith stared at the portrait for a second longer, her head held on one side. Her eyes narrowed slightly; Rose de Montboucher reminds me of someone, she thought, but she had no idea who that was. Rose's grandson perhaps. No, not Luc. He was dark-haired with dark brown eyes. A woman with a red-gold hair and clear blue eyes . . . this image and a tiny fragment of a memory leapt into her mind. But it was fleeting, disappearing before she could grasp it properly. Shaking her head, she gave the portrait a last glance and went through into the adjoining bedroom.

The minute she entered it a smile settled on Meredith's face. It was charming, welcoming, with a fire burning brightly in the grate and the silk-shaded lamps turned on. The room was decorated in a mélange of greys and soft greyish blues. The walls were covered with silver-grey moire silk, the flowing, bouffant draperies at the three tall windows were of silver-grey taffeta, and the large four-poster bed was hung with the same taffeta that looked as if it had been hand-embroidered. On closer inspection, Meredith realized that the pink, red and yellow roses and trailing green vines had been hand-painted on the grey silk. There were several chairs and a loveseat covered in pearl-grey cut velvet arranged around the fire, and in a corner stood an unusual antique dressing table made entirely of Venetian mirror.

Fascinated, Meredith walked slowly around the bedroom, looking at everything closely, admiring its style and elegance, nodding to herself as her glance lighted on a particular painting or an *objet d'art*. Certain things in the room were worn, even a little shabby, but the overall ambience was one of old-world elegance, luxury and a bygone age. It also had a restful feeling, as did the adjoining sitting room which was decorated in a mixture of greyish pinks, smoky blues and greens, all taken from the colours of the Aubusson rug on the floor.

Moving across the bedroom, Meredith finally came to a standstill in front of the Venetian dressing table. Silver brushes with Rose de Montboucher's initials were lined up on the mirrored surface, and there was a collection of crystal perfume bottles, silver-topped powder bowls and rouge pots grouped together.

To one side of them stood a silver-framed photograph of a darkly handsome man in evening dress.

Meredith bent down, stared at it, and for a split second she thought it was a picture of Luc. Then she realized it was not he; the evening suit bespoke the 1920s. It was obviously his grandfather, Rose's husband. That's who Luc must resemble, she decided. His grandfather . . . he's the spitting image of him.

After unpacking her two suitcases, Meredith picked up her toilet bag and went through into the bathroom. Immediately she came to standstill, taken aback by its size and by the fire burning merrily in the white-marble hearth.

The bathroom was enormous, with a soaring window draped with white lace curtains, an old-fashioned tub on feet and bell pulls dangling over it to ring for the maids. She wondered whether they still worked but refrained from pulling one, just in case they did.

Twelve

Downstairs in his office at the rear of the château, Luc de Montboucher sat at his drawing table, a series of blueprints spread out in front of him.

The plans had been done by a colleague in his architectural firm, and Luc had fully intended to go over them before lunch, hoping to give his approval. But so far he had paid scant attention to the blueprints.

His mind was not on work. It was on Meredith Stratton.

From the moment he had met her on Wednesday morning, out at the manor house in Montfort-L'Amaury, he had been intrigued by her; he was very taken with her, in point of fact. Being an architect and a designer he was an extremely visual man, and so it was her looks which had initially attracted him to her. He liked her height, her blondeness and fair skin, those smoky green eyes which told him so much about her.

She was a good-looking woman with a great deal of personal style, and he experienced a jolt of genuine pleasure whenever his eyes rested on her. He also appreciated her self-confidence and composure, found them reassuring. Skittishness in women invariably made him nervous.

Luc had realized within the first couple of hours of being in her company that she was businesslike, practical, professional, organized, and decisive, and, not unnaturally, these traits appealed to his love of order.

He couldn't abide chaotic women who dragged trouble in their wake, who lived in perpetual mess and created mess in other lives. Also, he found Meredith's energy and effervescent personality most appealing; they buoyed him up, gave him a sense of *élan*, the like of which he had not experienced in a long time.

What a pity she lives so far away in New York, he thought, tapping his pencil on the drawing table. But it was not so far away that it made a relationship impossible. There was, after all, a supersonic flight. He could be in Manhattan in three and a half hours, four at the most, on Concorde. He had made the trip from Paris to New York only three weeks ago, to visit a client. It had been easy.

Luc wanted, had the *need*, to know Meredith Stratton better. Much better. *Intimately*. He found her sexually attractive, more so than any woman he had met in some years. He realized on Wednesday night, after their first business meeting, that he desired her. If a man didn't know that after the first encounter, then when would he ever know? Luc suddenly wondered. And he felt certain it was the same way for a woman.

Almost against his own volition, he had confided in Agnes, but only to a degree. He had merely told her of his interest in Meredith, his wish to know her better. These confidences had been passed on

Thursday evening, when he had called her at home. He had not been able to help himself. Then he had invited the D'Aubervilles and Meredith to Talcy for the weekend, but Agnes had been obliged to decline because Alain and Chloe were ill with the flu.

Agnes had said he should issue the invitation to Meredith anyway. 'Don't worry,' Agnes had promised, 'I'll suggest we all have lunch after our Friday-morning meeting, and you'll find a way to invite her to the château. I'll lead you into it quite naturally.'

When he had demurred, Agnes had exclaimed, with a laugh, 'Don't be so faint-hearted, such a coward, Luc. Meredith has absolutely nothing to do this weekend, and she has no friends in Paris, other than us. I happen to know she likes you, so she'll accept the invitation. And you're going to enjoy being with her. She's wonderful. Everyone loves her.'

Love, he murmured to himself. Will I ever find love again? He wanted to, very seriously. He liked women, admired and respected them, and he wanted a wife. Certainly he did not relish the idea of living alone for the rest of his life.

So far love had proved elusive. After Annick his life had stopped. He had been numb. But eventually he had tried to start over, God knows he had, to start life anew, to have a worthwhile relationship. But there had been no success. Only abundant failure.

It was true he had known a couple of women in the last few years, and they had been perfectly nice human beings, but neither of them had ignited a spark in him. He had begun to wonder if the spark had left him forever, had quite recently decided that it had, convinced himself of it, really. Until Meredith. But she had so enthralled him, without even trying, that he had actually been startled at himself. So rare was this feeling, so strong this desire, this need to become part of another person, part of her life, that he felt bound to pursue her.

How often did a man feel like that? Once in a lifetime perhaps. Instantly he corrected himself. It was twice in his case; he had felt the same way about Annick.

Meredith Stratton, he said under his breath, and wrote her name on the notepad in front of him, stared down at it.

Who are you, Meredith Stratton? And why are you so troubled? Where does that deep well of sadness inside you spring from? Who was it that hurt you so badly they've scarred your soul? Who broke your heart? Instinctively, Luc knew Meredith had experienced great unhappiness. He saw pain mirrored in those smoky eyes, saw infinite sadness dwelling there. He wanted to ease the pain, chase away the sadness, if he could; he was sure he could, given the chance.

Luc had not wished to ask Agnes questions about Meredith, although he longed to do so. He had felt awkward about prying, which went against the grain. In certain ways, he felt that he did *know* Meredith, knew what she was truly like, the kind of person she was inside. A good woman.

What was that phrase his lovely Irish grandmother had always used? 'True blue,' Rosie de Montboucher would say to him, 'your grandfather is true blue, Luc.'

And so was Meredith.

The small black clock on the drawing table told him it was almost twelve-thirty. Throwing down the pencil, suddenly impatient, he stood up, stretching his long legs. He was tired of sitting, and he felt cramped after the drive from Paris this morning.

Leaving the office, he ran up the back staircase and down the corridor to his bedroom. Shrugging out of his blazer, he went through into the bathroom, where he splashed his face with cold water, dried it, and combed his hair.

Luc peered at himself in the mirror. There were a few silver strands in his black hair these days; he stared harder, thinking he seemed drawn, fatigued. There were lines around his eyes. He decided he looked older than forty-three.

Meredith was also in her early forties, he was certain of that. It was something Agnes had said about her age, before Meredith had arrived from London. He wondered if that was too old to have a child, then supposed it depended on the woman. He had always wanted a child. To carry on the line. But if he didn't have one, it wouldn't matter in the long run. Life was such a struggle, and Luc suddenly understood that he wanted to reach out, grab life, grab happiness. Loving someone was not about progeny.

Meredith. She could make me happy. I know it in my bones. Bones don't lie, Luc, Grandma Rosie used to tell him when he was a boy growing up. You can tell a lot by the bones, child, she would add. Breeding's in the bone, Luc. Look at horses. Even when the stamina's there, it's not enough. Got to have breeding in a racehorse. I know my horseflesh, Luc, I'm a good judge. *Oui, Grand-mère,* he'd answer dutifully. Luc, please speak English today. Yes, Grandmother. Always trust your bones, she would repeat. They never lie, Luc, never. Oh Grandma Rosie, he thought, smiling inwardly at this lovely memory of her, you were a genuine original.

Turning away from the mirror, Luc hurried into his bedroom, took a grey tweed jacket out of the armoire, put it on over his black sweater and dark grey slacks, and left the room.

He ran down the front stairs at a rapid pace, crossed the front entrance hall and strode into the library, glancing around as he did.

The fire crackled in the hearth, the drinks tray was well stocked and there was a bottle of Dom in the silver ice bucket, just as he had instructed Vincent. There was nothing to do but wait for Meredith to appear.

Walking over to one of the French windows, he stood looking out at the garden, thinking how arresting the parterres looked: the clipped, dark green hedges were covered with a light frosting of snow that highlighted their intricate geometric shapes. His thoughts moved on, turned to his sisters. How lucky it was they had decided not to come to Talcy this weekend. He loved them dearly and liked their husbands, but he was relieved, and glad to have the house to himself. He had no great seduction plans, that was not his style; he liked everything to happen naturally. But he did want Meredith to feel relaxed, at ease, not on display for his family.

There was a slight noise, the sound of a step.

Swinging away from the window, he looked towards the adjoining living room expectantly. Meredith was walking towards him and he felt that same jolt of pleasure at the sight of her, the rush of excitement inside.

Moving forward, he exclaimed, 'There you are! Come in, Meredith, come to the fire where it's warmer. Now, would you care for a glass of champagne?'

'That would be lovely, Luc,' she answered, gliding across the floor.

He went to open the bottle of Dom Pérignon, but could not resist looking at her surreptitiously out of the corner of his eye. She was wearing a beige check jacket over a cream cashmere sweater and trousers, and he thought she looked stunning. He bit back a smile. Of course she did. There was no question in his mind that he was quite prejudiced when it came to Meredith Stratton.

After bringing their flutes of champagne to the fireside, Luc sat down on the sofa opposite Meredith and said, 'I hope you have everything you need, that you're comfortable in Grandma Rosie's rooms?'

'Oh yes, I am, thank you very much. I love them, and that bathroom. My goodness, a fireplace, no less.' She laughed and added, 'What a luxury. I feel thoroughly spoiled.'

He laughed with her. 'All of the bedroom suites on that floor have fireplaces in the bathrooms, but we don't often use them, only for guests really, and only when it's cold weather. It's such a lot of work, keeping all the fires going. In my great-grandfather's day, even

Grandfather's, they had armies of servants to do that, to look after everything. Nowadays it's hard to get staff, and expensive, so I keep such things as fires down to a minimum.'

'I can't say I blame you.' She looked across at him, smiled warmly. She liked him a lot, wanted to know more about him. 'Did you grow up here?' she asked, filled with curiosity.

'Yes, I did. With my sisters Isabelle and Natalie. They're younger than I, but we had great times together, and an estate such as this is a wonderful place for young children.'

'It must have been an idyllic childhood.'

'I suppose it was, although it didn't always seem so at the time. My father was rather strict. And rightly so.'

He observed her over the rim of the flute for a brief moment. 'You're looking rather wistful. Is something wrong?'

'Oh no, not at all,' she replied swiftly. 'I was just thinking how different my childhood was – ' Meredith stopped abruptly, wondering what had induced her to say this. She rarely confided details about her childhood to anyone.

Although he had no way of knowing her thoughts, Luc suspected that Meredith had said more than she had intended. He could tell from the startled expression on her face. Quickly he said, 'But you grew up in the country, too, didn't you? In Connecticut?'

She shook her head. 'No, I didn't. I suppose Agnes told you I come from Connecticut, that I have a family home there and an inn, and that's true, I do. But I grew up in Australia. My childhood was spent in Sydney.'

'You're an Australian?'

'Yes. At least, I was born there, and that's my original nationality, but I became an American citizen when I was twenty-two.' Leaning back against the tapestry cushions, she gave him a direct look and finished, 'That was exactly twenty-three years ago.'

'You're forty-five? But that doesn't seem possible. You certainly don't look it.' Luc was genuinely surprised.

'Thank you, I'm still forty-four, actually, Luc. I'll be forty-five at the beginning of May.'

'And I'm forty-three ... I'll be forty-four on June third.' There was a small pause, and then he said carefully, not wanting to stir up bad memories, 'From the tone of your voice, I rather got the impression you didn't have a very good childhood.'

'I didn't. It was terrible. Horrible, really. No child should have to go through that,' she blurted out, and then bit her lip, averted her face, stared into the fire.

So that's the source of the pain, he thought, at least some of it. There's much more that she is concealing. He remained silent for a few moments, allowing her the space and time to compose herself.

Eventually, Luc said, 'I'm sorry to hear that you were unhappy, Meredith. What happened to you?'

'I was orphaned when I was young. Ten years old. My parents were killed in a car crash. I got pushed around a lot after that ... it was rough, hard –' She cut herself off again, forced a smile, met his direct gaze. Hers was equally as candid, as she finished. 'But that's such a long time ago. I've forgotten about it really.'

Not true, he thought to himself, and asked, 'When did you go to America?'

'When I was seventeen. I went to Connecticut as an *au pair* with an American family who'd been living in Sydney. Later I worked for Jack and Amelia Silver. They sort of . . . turned my life around.' A lovely smile spread across her face. 'What I mean is, I was like a younger sister to them. You see, Luc, they weren't much older than me, in their early thirties. Anyway, they treated me like a member of the family. Amelia and Jack made up for . . . well, for all those bad years.'

Luc nodded, refrained from commenting. He sat staring into her smoky green eyes. The sadness of a moment ago had lifted, but he knew it still lurked at the core of her. He wondered if he could make it go away entirely; he was not sure. All he knew was that he wanted to try.

Meredith said, 'You're staring at me, Luc. Do I have a smudge on my nose or something?'

'No, you don't.' His dark brown eyes suddenly twinkled. 'I was just admiring you, if you want the truth. You're a beautiful woman, Meredith.'

She felt the colour rising up from her neck to flood her face and was mortified at herself. Men had paid her compliments before; why was she blushing because Luc had? 'Th-thank you,' she managed to stammer, and was relieved when the telephone began to shrill.

Luc rose, went to answer it. 'Clos-Talcy. *Bonjour.*'

After listening for a second, he said: 'Hold on for a moment, please,' and looked across at her. 'It's your daughter Catherine.'

Meredith's face lit up and she jumped to her feet. She stepped over to the desk, took the receiver from him, thanking him as she did.

Luc merely nodded, walked over to the window, stood gazing out, his head full of this woman. He felt he knew her intuitively, and yet she baffled him. There was an air of mystery about her. He found her irresistible.

'Hello, Catherine, how are you, darling?' Meredith asked, then listened attentively as her daughter's voice floated to her across the transatlantic wire from New York. Her smile widened. 'Yes, I'm happy for you, darling, I'm thrilled, actually.' She clutched the phone tightly, continued to listen, then said into the mouthpiece, 'Yes, I'll be back in Paris on Monday, and no, I won't be home for at least another week.' There was a pause at Meredith's end, before she answered, 'Yes, all right, I'll call you on Wednesday. Give Keith my love. Don't forget to tell Jon. Have a great weekend. I love you, Cat. 'Bye now.'

She replaced the receiver and smiled at Luc when he turned around to face her, an expectant look in his eyes.

'My daughter just got engaged. Last night. She's floating on cloud nine.' Meredith blinked and looked away, pushing back sudden tears. She was so happy for Catherine that her emotions got the better of her for a moment.

'What wonderful news! It calls for a toast and

another glass of bubbly, as Grandma Rosie used to call it.'

After filling their crystal flutes, Luc raised his and clinked it against hers. 'Here's to love . . . and happy endings,' he murmured, staring at her closely, his dark eyes on hers.

Meredith stared back, felt the warmth rising to fill her face again. 'Love and happy endings, Luc,' she repeated and took a sip of champagne. Then she went over to the sofa, where she sat down. She was very conscious of Luc de Montboucher all of a sudden.

Luc followed her, but remained standing, his back against the fire. 'How old is your daughter?' he asked.

'Twenty-five. And I have a son, Jonathan, who's twenty-one. He's studying law at Yale.'

A smile flashed across his face, and he exclaimed, 'I studied architecture there. Graduate school after the Sorbonne. What a coincidence! Does he like it?'

'Yes, he does.'

'I'm glad. I did, too. Best years of my life.' He chuckled.

'Were they really?'

'Up to a point. I had some other good years. Before. After.' He took a swallow of his drink, a reflective look washing over his face.

'Luc?'

'Yes?'

'Have you ever been married?'

'Oh yes. Didn't Agnes tell you about me?' He raised a brow questioningly.

'No.' She frowned. 'What makes you think she would?'

'Oh no special reason,' he answered and shrugged. 'I thought she might have, that's all. And yes, I was married. My wife died six years ago. Annick was in good health one day, dying of cancer the next. It was virulent; she went very quickly. Just six months after being diagnosed. She was only thirty-seven.' He paused, cleared his throat. 'We were married eight years.'

'Luc, I'm so sorry. How tragic. What a terrible loss for you.' Meredith looked up at him worriedly, hoping she had not upset him. How stupid she had been, thoughtless, to bring up his wife.

'We didn't have children,' Luc volunteered.

Meredith said nothing, gazed across the room, lost in thought.

Luc put down his drink on the coffee table between the two sofas; he threw a couple of logs onto the fire, straightened up. Lifting his drink, he took a sip.

The room had gone very quiet. The only sounds were the crackling logs, the ticking clock.

At last Meredith said, 'Nobody's life is ever easy, whatever we might think. There's always pain and heartache, trouble, problems, ill health. Loss . . . of one kind or another.'

'That is so . . . yes, it's very true what you say. My Irish grandmother was not only beautiful but also very wise. She was forever telling us, when we were growing up, that life had always been hard, was meant to be hard, and that it would never be anything else but hard. That is the earthly lot of us poor mortals, she would say, and therefore we should grab what bit of happiness we could whenever we could. And if we found the right person we must hang onto them for dear life. Forever. That's what she said, and I strongly suspect that Grandma Rosie spoke the truth.'

'I've never met the right person,' Meredith said, surprising herself, instantly regretting these words.

'I did. But she died.' Luc stared off into the distance for a moment, as if he could see something visible only to himself. Then he said, 'I've never met anyone else. But I haven't given up hope . . .' He looked at her pointedly, but Meredith did not appear to notice.

'Catherine's father died,' she suddenly said, 'but he was a married man anyway . . . I would never have been able to marry him. I divorced Jon's father . . . that was all wrong . . . we weren't right for each other at all . . .' She let her sentence float in mid-air, unfinished.

'Was that a long time ago? Your divorce?'

'Sixteen years.' Confessions, she thought. And more confessions. What's suddenly got into me? Why am I telling him all these private things about myself? This man is a stranger.

Luc said, 'You will meet the right person, Meredith. I know you will.' He wanted to add that perhaps she already had, but he refrained.

Mathilde appeared in the doorway at the far end of the library. She cleared her throat.

Luc glanced at her. 'Ah, Mathilde. Is lunch ready?'

'Oui, Monsieur.'

'Merci.' Turning to Meredith, he said, 'I don't know about you, but I'm ravenous.'

'Yes, I am too.'

As he led her across the library in the direction of the dining room, Luc explained, 'I asked Mathilde to make a fairly simple lunch. Vegetable soup, plain omelette, green salad, cheese and fruit. I hope that's to your taste.'

'It sounds perfect,' Meredith answered, looking at him.

Luc smiled at her warmly, and took hold of her arm, led her into the dining room where Mathilde was waiting to serve lunch.

Suddenly Meredith did not care what she had told him about herself. She knew he would not judge her; she trusted him.

She felt safe with Luc de Montboucher.

Thirteen

After lunch Luc took Meredith on a tour of the park in which Clos-Talcy stood. As they walked they talked about a variety of things, but eventually the conversation came back to his grandmother. Luc told her several amusing stories about Rose de Montboucher, keeping her thoroughly entertained.

At one moment, she said, 'The way in which you speak about *Grand-mère* Rose really brings her to life for me. I wish I'd known her.'

'You would have enjoyed her,' Luc answered, glancing at Meredith. 'She was a true original. Strong of character, spirited and courageous, and she truly ran our family. Ruled it with an iron hand. In a velvet glove, of course.' He chuckled, continued, 'My father loved to tease her, and when her birthday came around he always used to lift his glass and say, "Here's to that great man whose name is Rosie," borrowing the line from Voltaire.'

'Who said those very words to Catherine the Great, when he met her in Russia for the first time,' Meredith remarked. 'She's one of my favourite characters in history. I've read a number of biographies about her. *She* was strong and courageous, too. And she made her own rules.'

'That's true, she did, but then most strong women do that, don't you think?'

'Yes, they do ... sometimes they have to, because they have no other choice.'

Luc took hold of her arm and led her down a side path, heading for the orchard ahead of them. 'In 1871, when my great-great-grandfather acquired Talcy from the Delorme family, he built the fish pond over there. It's actually fed by the stream that flows through the wood. It was a marvellous bit of engineering on his part.'

They came to a stop by the edge of the pond, and Meredith peered down into its murky depths. 'There really are fish in it,' she said, sounding surprised.

'Of course. When I was a little boy, I used to fish here. My sisters and I all had rods and lines, and sometimes Grandma Rosie joined us. She was rather good at fishing.'

'I can just imagine.' There was a silence between them as they walked around the pond, turned, and headed towards the woods. After a moment, Meredith murmured, 'Your grandmother was a great influence on you, wasn't she?'

'Oh yes. She brought us up, you see. My mother died in childbirth, giving birth to our little brother Albert, who was premature. He also died that same week. It will be thirty-three years ago this summer, to be exact.'

'How sad for you and your sisters ... for your whole family.'

'Everyone took it very hard, especially my father.

He never remarried, and I believe he mourned my mother until the day he died.'

'When was that, Luc?'

'Almost two years ago. He wasn't very old, only seventy-one, which is no age at all these days. He dropped dead suddenly of a stroke. He was in the stables, didn't know what hit him, thankfully. It would have been terrible if he had been an invalid; he was a very active man, a great sportsman.'

'And your grandmother? When did she die?'

'In 1990 at the age of ninety. She was wonderful right to the end, not a bit senile or decrepit, and she was very active, had all of her faculties. Oh yes, *she* was still the boss around here. One night she went to bed and never awakened, just died in her sleep, very peacefully. I was glad of that, glad she didn't suffer. Neither did my father, for that matter.'

'I think that's the best way to go, with your boots on, so to speak,' Meredith said, thinking out loud. 'Or when you're asleep, as your grandmother was. Dying of old age is the most natural thing.' Meredith turned to Luc, smiled at him. 'That painting of her in my sitting room is very lovely, isn't it? I was trying to figure out how old she was when it was painted.'

Luc's brow furrowed as he said, 'I'm not exactly sure. However, she'd just married Arnaud de Montboucher, my grandfather, and come to live at Talcy when she sat for the portrait. So she must have been in her early twenties.'

'That's what I thought. She reminds me of somebody, I'm not sure who.'

'My sister Natalie favours her, but you've never met Natalie. Or have you?'

Meredith laughed, shook her head. 'No, I haven't.'

'Natalie resembles Grandmother physically, she's really rather beautiful, but she's not like her in character. Neither is Isabelle. I'm the one who inherited Rose's basic character,' Luc confided.

'She really put her imprint on you, didn't she?'

'*Absolutely*. I have come to realize that I think like her, and I have a tendency to do things the way she did. When someone really influences you in childhood, you carry their imprint. Always, I think. It's like an indelible stamp. And who was it who put their imprint on you, Meredith?'

'No one did,' she answered almost fiercely, and bit her lip, suddenly aware that she had sounded angry. Speaking in a softer tone, she went on, 'I just muddled through on my own, doing the best I could, teaching myself. Nobody influenced me. There was no one in my life to do that, no one at all, I was completely alone.'

They had stopped walking a few seconds before, had paused near one of the fountains, now stood face to face as they spoke. The sadness invading her face touched Luc; he wanted to reach out, pull her into his arms. But he did not dare. He was about to say something comforting to her when she suddenly smiled. The bereftness vanished instantly.

Meredith said, 'But there was someone later, when I was a bit older ... eighteen. Amelia Silver. She showed me how to do certain things, taught me about antiques and art. She had wonderful taste and was very artistic. Her husband Jack influenced me in certain ways, too.'

'Are the Silvers still living in Connecticut?'

'Oh no, they're both dead. They died years ago, over twenty years ago. Sadly, neither of them was very old.'

'I'm sorry. They were like family, weren't they?'

She nodded, half turned away from him. 'I was twenty-two when Jack died, twenty-three when Amelia followed him to the grave. I only had them in my life for a few years.'

Aware that the sadness had surfaced again, Luc took hold of her hand. 'Come on, let's walk down to the ornamental lake. It's so picturesque, one of the prettiest parts of the park.'

By the time they reached the lake, at the far side of the house, Meredith was beginning to feel unwell. A wave of nausea passed through her and a peculiar kind of exhaustion seemed to settle in her bones. Unexpectedly, she thought she was going to collapse, and she grabbed hold of Luc's arm, said in a faint voice, 'I don't know what's wrong with me, but I feel awful. Nauseous, and suddenly very tired.'

Luc looked at her in concern. 'I do hope you're not getting the flu, that Agnes hasn't passed on any germs.'

'I doubt it, and Agnes wasn't ill.'

'No, but her family were. Do you think it was the wine at lunch? Could that have upset you?'

She shook her head. 'I didn't drink very much. Anyway, I remember now that I felt a bit queasy when I arrived in Paris on Tuesday night. I'd spent the morning wandering around an old ruined abbey in

Yorkshire, and it was bitterly cold. That night I thought that I'd probably caught a chill. But I was all right the next morning, so perhaps I'm just tired in general, run down.'

'Perhaps. Let us return to the house. You must rest for the remainder of the afternoon.' So saying, he put his arm around her and together they walked back to the château.

Luc accompanied her upstairs to her rooms and fussed around her. He made her take off her boots and forced her to lie down on the sofa. After adding more logs to the fire, he brought her a thick cashmere wrap and laid it over her.

'Don't go away,' he said, smiling down at her. 'I'll be back in a few minutes with a pot of hot lemon tea laced with honey. It'll do you the world of good . . . one of Grandma Rosie's cures.' He left the room, closing the door quietly behind him.

Meredith leaned her head back against the pile of soft velvet cushions and closed her eyes; she was so sleepy she could barely keep her eyes open.

She must have dozed off, for she awakened with a start when Luc bent over her and moved a strand of hair away from her face. This intimate gesture on his part startled her for a moment, and then she realized that she did not mind. It suddenly seemed perfectly natural to her.

'I put the tea here on the ottoman,' he said, his voice low, concerned still. 'Drink some of it whilst it's hot. Now I shall go and let you rest.' He squeezed her shoulder.

'Thank you, Luc, you're so kind. I'm sorry I cut short our walk, but I –'

'Think nothing of it,' he said swiftly. 'It's not important.'

'Would you turn off the lamp, please?'

'Of course. Now rest.' He left the room.

Meredith turned on her side, lay curled in a ball under the cashmere wrap, staring into the fire's bright flames. The logs hissed and crackled and sparks flew up the chimney. She raised her eyes at one moment and gazed for a long time at the portrait of Rose de Montboucher.

The afternoon light was fading rapidly, the room filling with shadows, but the roaring fire and its dancing flames introduced a rosy glow. In the soft incandescent light it seemed to Meredith that the painting of Rose came alive. Her face was full of life, her delphinium-blue eyes brilliant, sparkling with joy, and the red-gold curls framed the sublime face like a halo of burnished copper. How beautiful she was ... so radiant.

Meredith's eyelids drooped. She drifted on a wave of warmth. Her mind was filled with that face ... memories jostled for prominence ... fragmented into infinitesimal pieces. She fell into a deep sleep. And she dreamed.

The landscape was vast and it stretched away endlessly, as far as the eye could see, miles and miles of desolation. There was something oddly sinister about this place where there were no trees and nothing bloomed on the parched, cracked earth.

She had been walking and walking for as long as she could remember. It seemed like forever. She felt tired. But some inner determination pushed her forward. She knew they were here somewhere. The children. She had followed them here. But where could they be? Her eyes darted around. The land was empty; there was nowhere for them to hide.

Help me to find them, please. Oh God, help me to find them, she pleaded. And immediately she understood that her prayers fell on arid ground. There was no God here. Not in this empty void. It was Godless, this netherworld.

And then unexpectedly she saw something moving near the pale rim of the far horizon. She began to run. The cracked dry earth suddenly gave way to mud flats and her shoes squelched and sank into the mud and sometimes stuck and her progress was slowed. She persisted. Soon the land was dry again. She ran and ran.

The specks on the horizon grew closer and closer, loomed up in front of her as if they had jumped backwards. She saw a young boy holding a girl's hand. Just as they had drawn closer to her, now they withdrew, moved forwards again, rapidly. She ran, almost caught up to them once more. They walked on slowly, the two of them, still hand in hand, perfectly in step. She called out to them, called for them to wait for her. But they did not. They went on walking as if they had not heard her. The sky changed, turned a strange greyish-green and a high wind began to blow, buffeting her forwards. Suddenly the boy flew up in the air, as if blown upward by a gust of wind. He disappeared into the sky.

The little girl was alone now. She suddenly turned around and began to walk towards her. Meredith hurried forwards to greet the girl, so wan, so pathetic, with her pale pinched face and big sad eyes. She wore black stockings and shoes, and a heavy winter coat. There was a small black beret on her head and a long striped scarf was wrapped around her neck. The label pinned to the lapel of her coat was huge. The girl pointed to it. Meredith peered at it, trying to decipher the girl's name written there, but she could not.

Suddenly, taking her by surprise, the girl began to run away. Meredith tried to run after her but her feet were stuck, encased in the mud. She cried to the girl to come back but she did not stop, just went on running and running and running until she was gone out of the landscape.

There was a cracking sound and then a terrible noise like shell fire and everything exploded around her . . .

Meredith sat up with a jolt. Her face and neck were bathed in sweat. She was disoriented, and it took her a moment to get her bearings. Then she realized she was in Grandma Rosie's sitting room at Talcy.

Outside a storm was raging, lightning streaking through the darkening sky, thunderbolts rattling the windows. She shivered and huddled under the wrap that Luc had put around her earlier, stared at the fire, grown low in the grate. And the fear was there inside, ravaging her.

Closing her eyes, she tried to push the fear away, not understanding why she was so frightened. She was here at the château, perfectly safe from the violent storm raging outside.

And then it came to her. She knew why she was so fearful. It was the dream. The dream that had recurred so many times in her life. She had not dreamed it for years now. Suddenly, the old, familiar dream had come back to haunt her, to frighten her again, as it always had in the past.

Fourteen

Once she had returned to Paris, Meredith's thoughts frequently focused on her weekend at Clos-Talcy. And most particularly, Luc de Montboucher was at the centre of her reflections.

She liked him, more than liked him, in fact, and his kindness to her had left a lasting impression.

Kindness had always been important to Meredith, perhaps because she had experienced so little of it in her life. None at all when she had been a child, and growing up without kindness had made her acquire a carapace of iron. Only Mrs Paulson had been able to break through this tough protective shell; and then, of course, the Silvers, when she had gone to work for them at Silver Lake.

And just as kindness was important to a child, so it was to a grown woman, and especially a woman over forty. But this characteristic aside, she found him extremely attractive as a man.

Luc was very good-looking, darkly handsome and fine of feature, but that was not his most important asset, as far as she was concerned. Just a pretty face had long ago ceased to hold her interest.

She admired his intelligence and talent, and his integrity, which instinctively she knew was unassailable. He also had a good sense of humour, and she discovered they liked so many of the same things – good books, classical music, a glass of icy champagne in front of a blazing fire on a wintry night, not to mention houses built on water, stained-glass windows and the delicate paintings of Marie Laurencin. All in all, Luc was an impressive man and she was glad she had met him, glad she had accepted his invitation to go to the château in the Loire.

They had driven back to Paris early on Monday morning, and she had spent most of the afternoon with him and Agnes out at the Manoir de la Closière in Montfort-L'Amaury, going over the changes they wanted to make. That evening Luc had taken her to dinner at the Relais Plaza, and last night they had eaten at Grand Vefour.

They had laughed a lot over the past few days, and she had begun to realize what an enormous impression he was making on her, and just how much she really did care about him.

Meredith had known Luc only a week, but he was already under her skin, and she knew she was going to miss him when she returned to New York. In her mind she was already planning her next trip to Paris. There was business to attend to in Manhattan; also, she had to sign the initial documents for the sale of Hilltops Inn to the Morrisons. And she couldn't wait to see Cat, to hug her, fuss over her, and celebrate her engagement to Keith.

But all of this would take only ten days at the most, she had calculated, and then she would fly back on Concorde. In any case, she was needed in Paris because of the remodelling and renovation of the old manor house. The three of them had agreed on Monday that it must be modern and up-to-date in every way, whilst still retaining its basic character and charm. And of course it required her decorative imprint, the look and the stylishness which proclaimed it to be a creation of Havens Incorporated.

In the quietness of her hotel suite last night she had wondered what would happen after the inn was finished; she had an immediate answer for herself. The inn would take a whole year to complete, therefore she would be spending a great deal of time in this city. Paris. The City of Light. And of lovers.

Things will work themselves out, she had reassured herself in the early hours of the morning. A long time ago Meredith had come to understand that life had a way of taking care of itself.

Day by day, step by step, she had decided, as she had prepared for bed. It's the only thing I can do, and we'll see what happens. Everything must take its normal course.

Meredith knew only too well that a relationship which looked promising could quite easily come to nought, fizzle out in a flurry of recriminations and bad feeling. After all, that had happened with Reed Jamison. Her face had changed at the thought of him. What an unpleasant encounter that had turned out to be in the end. But then Reed and Luc were as different as any two men could be, poles apart.

Luc was so straightforward, so honest, she believed she would always know exactly where she stood with him. No game-playing there. He was a thoughtful, responsible, mature man whom she knew respected her; certainly she respected him.

Meredith had spent most of Tuesday with Agnes, and had been surprised that her French partner had not probed too deeply about the weekend; Agnes had asked only a few cursory questions. But then again, they had been very preoccupied with their plans for the inn and busy rushing around Paris. They had visited innumerable antique shops and fabric houses, taking polaroids of furniture and collecting samples of fabric and wallpaper. Since they had similar tastes and the same ideas about the decoration and furnishing of the inn, there were no problems in this respect.

It was on Wednesday afternoon, when they were sitting in Agnes's office at Havens, that Meredith mentioned Luc. The two of them were selecting fabric swatches and lining them up on a flat board, trying to create viable colour schemes.

Quite suddenly, Meredith said, 'Last night Luc invited me to the château again. For a long weekend.'

Agnes glanced up. 'I'm not surprised, he likes you a lot.'

'And I like him.'

Agnes laughed. 'Most women do. He's irresistible. I've always wondered why he's never remarried.'

'Perhaps it's taking him a long time to get over his grief for his wife.'

'Oh, so he told you about her?'

'Yes, which is more than you did, after you'd promised. I sort of blundered in on that one, and I was afraid I'd upset him.'

'I'm sorry I didn't phone you, as I promised, but Chloe was so sick I had my hands full. Anyway, Alain and I only had a chance to talk on Sunday afternoon, and I certainly didn't want to call you at Talcy to gossip about your host.'

'No, I understand that, and I'm glad you didn't. I would have been embarrassed.'

'Alain has known Luc off and on for many years, Meredith, but not really well. We only became a bit closer to him in the last year, mainly because he was designing a house for Alain's sister. And even so, he never discussed Annick ... his past was sort of ... well ... *vague* to us, and we're not the kind to pry ...' She did not finish her sentence, merely looked across at Meredith and shrugged.

Meredith said, 'I understand. You can know people, be very friendly, and yet not know too much about their private life at all.' She leaned back in the chair and crossed her long legs. 'There's so much I like about Luc, Agnes. He's very straight, honest. Also, he really listens, pays attention. That's a rarity these days.'

'I believe him to be the kind of man who's worth taking seriously. I know for a fact he's not a playboy. Not at all, not one bit the philanderer.' Agnes eyed Meredith, and probed, 'Could you become involved with him? On a serious level?'

There was a brief hesitation on Meredith's part and then she said, 'Yes, I could, Agnes. He's the type of man I like, the kind I thought I'd never meet again. Men like Luc are usually well and truly spoken for.'

'You are indeed correct, *ma chérie*, but I think Luc has chosen not to be spoken for. Until now. He did tell me he liked you, wanted to get to know you better.'

Meredith stared at Agnes. '*Oh*. And when was that?'

'Last week, just after he met you.'

'And you never told me. Thanks a lot, friend!'

Agnes burst out laughing. Shaking her head, her grey eyes full of merriment, she said, 'He didn't tell me not to say anything, but I thought discretion was the better part of valour, and all that. In any case, I didn't want to frighten you off him. I thought you'd probably bite my head off and tell me I was a romantic fool. Consider them, Meredith, the various men I've introduced you to in the past eight years. They were attractive, eligible, but you never seemed interested in them. Not one little bit.'

'I wasn't.'

'But you *are* interested in Luc?'

Meredith nodded.

'*Mmmm*, I can't say I blame you. He is very sexy-looking. Sensual, I think, no?'

Fifteen

They worked together in Luc's office from the moment they arrived at Talcy until seven on Thursday night. And then they started again at nine the next morning.

Once more it was a long day, broken only by lunch. Late on Friday afternoon Luc put his pencil down and looked across the room at Meredith. She was seated at a small desk, pasting fabric, carpet and paint samples onto boards, creating her first schemes for the inn.

'I shouldn't have done this to you,' he said, leaning back in his chair, his eyes lingering on her.

'What do you mean?' she asked, looking up.

'I've kept you cooped up in this office since yesterday morning, and all because I wanted to work and wanted you near me whilst I did so.'

She said nothing, merely stared back at him.

He went on, 'I've been rushing, trying so hard to finish the plans for the pond, and complete this drawing of it. I feel guilty though, about you. I should have sent you walking or riding, or at least let you rest –'

'Luc, I enjoyed being here with you,' she interrupted, 'working alongside you. And I would have been doing the same thing in Paris anyway, sorting through the swatches, making my boards. Truly, it's been wonderful sharing this time here with you.'

'Has it?'

'Oh yes.'

'Meredith?'

'Yes, Luc?'

He opened his mouth to say something, changed his mind, and stood up, walked over to her. He placed the sheet of paper he was carrying in front of her on the desk. 'This is the drawing of the pond, as it will look when it's finished.'

'Oh Luc, how marvellous! It's like the fish pond here!'

'I positioned the pond near the small wood behind the manor in Montfort-L'Amaury, in the same way the pond is next to the orchard at Talcy. I think it is picturesque, don't you?' As he spoke he bent over her, his finger tracing the drawing of the pond, the copse, and the manor house in the background.

She could feel his warm breath against her neck and she held herself perfectly still, hardly daring to breathe. Her cheeks flamed and she felt an unexpected warmth spreading through her, desire flooding her.

He said, 'I wanted to please you, Meredith.'

Meredith half turned to look at him, tilted her face up to his. 'I love it, Luc, it's perfect.'

She smiled.

He was dazzled.

He said nothing. He was unable to speak. *I want you*. Those were the words on the tip of his tongue. It was the only thing he could think of at this moment. He had been thinking of it for days. He was about to tell her so, but instead he leaned closer to her and before he could stop himself he kissed her on the lips, lightly at first, and then as she responded ardently his kisses became more intense.

He paused after a moment, but only briefly, in order to pull her to her feet. She was in his arms instantly. He held her close; her arms went around his neck. They were clinging to each other, their passions rising.

Meredith thought: Oh Luc, my darling, I've longed for this, longed to hold you in my arms. But her thoughts were unspoken; his hungry kisses stopped her words.

And then he stopped abruptly and said, in a voice thickened by emotion, 'I want you, Meredith, I've desired you since the day we met.'

'Oh Luc –'

He was kissing her again, greedily, as if he were about to leave her forever. He pulled her closer to him, fitting himself to her body, and he thought how perfectly they blended together.

She knew this was how it should always be between a man and a woman. He was kissing her cheeks, her eyes, her brow, her neck, her ears. His mouth went back to her mouth, and then he whispered against her neck, 'I've thought about you so much, I feel as if we've already made love. Do you understand what I mean, how I feel?'

'Yes.'

'I'm serious about you, Meredith. Say no to me now if you don't feel the same way. Because once we start this, there's no going back. Not for me.'

'I want *you*, Luc, I feel as you do.'

He held her away from him, his hands firm on her shoulders, and looked deeply into her eyes. Smoky green eyes, always mirroring her thoughts, her feelings, mirroring her soul. He had seen intelligence shining there, and reflectiveness and merriment, but also a deep-rooted sadness. Now he saw only desire and longing, and it was for him.

He took hold of her hand, and led her across the room, and still gripping her tightly he hurried her up the back stairs and down the corridor.

Once inside his bedroom, he locked the door with one hand, drew her into his arms, kissing her over and over as he walked her in the direction of the bed. Releasing her at last, he pulled down the quilt, threw his jacket on a chair, struggled out of his sweater and jeans. Slowly she undressed.

Luc reached for her, pulled her to him, repeating her name as they fell onto the bed. They lay together, still half dressed, their bodies entwined. He ran his hands up into her thick golden hair, caught hold of it, wrapped his fingers around it, brought his face down to hers, his mouth, his tongue grazing her lips, touching her tongue lightly, tantalizingly.

Meredith responded to him eagerly; she knew this was right, that it was meant to be. She harboured no qualms about this man. The desire in his voice, the yearning in his dark eyes had told her everything she needed to know.

Her heart lifted. She wanted him, wanted to feel his hands all over her like this, taste his kisses, savour his passion. She wanted to be with him, joined to him.

Luc was fully aware of her desire for him, her growing ardour, and this further inflamed him. The most sensual sensations rolled over him; he wanted to give himself up to them entirely.

Somehow they hastily shed the rest of their clothes, came back into each other's arms. He looked down into her face for a long moment, took pleasure from seeing her pleasure reflected there, now just visible in the fading afternoon light. He brought his hand to her face, traced a line down her cheek and across her mouth and he did so with tenderness.

Arms entwined, legs entwined, mouth on mouth, hands smoothing and stroking, caressing and exploring, each of them hungry for the other. It had been too long for them both.

Luc gave himself up to the pure joy of her touch, of her kisses falling on him. On his mouth, his face, his eyelids. He rolled on top of her, aligning his body to hers.

Silken arms, silken legs wove themselves around him, bound him to her, the most welcome and softest of ropes. He moved into her deeper, harder, heard the soft moans escaping her throat. Deeper and deeper he sank, revelling in the sheer pleasure of her, knowing he had found the right woman. At last. The woman he had known would one day come to him . . . to fill the darkness, fill the void in him, and as he buried himself yet deeper in her there was, miraculously, the total cessation of pain. She had liberated him, set him free. He soared. Higher and higher.

Meredith was moving against him, matching his

rhythm; they were joined, became one entity. A perfect mating, he thought, and it was exactly as he had imagined, had known it would be.

And as she had known, too. Luc was touching the core of her, reaching to her heart, filling her as she had never been filled, not since she was a young girl ... so long ago ... time past. He slipped his hands under her buttocks, brought her closer to him. I want you closer still, she cried out silently, all of you, Luc, I want all of you. And she willingly abandoned herself to him.

Luc could feel his heart pounding as he moved against her, almost violently now, caught up in the rhythm of their moving bodies; their joy was mounting.

Oh God, he thought, there is only this. Only this woman. Only me and her and this joining. She is all I will ever want. For the rest of my life, until the day I die. With her I am made whole again. And then he stopped thinking as they moved together in a sudden frenzy, flying higher and higher until they reached that peak of pure sensation. He wanted it to last forever, this ecstasy.

And Meredith understood that she had found her true mate at last, after all these years. He carried her upwards with him.

He was shuddering, wracked by spasms, shouting her name as he lost himself in her. And she answered him, calling out, 'Luc, oh Luc.'

Later, when their frenzy had ceased, he held her in his arms, stroking her hair. She moved closer to him, draping her leg over his, and he tightened his hold on her.

Her face was against his chest. She kissed it, then he felt her smile.

'What is it?' he asked.

'What do you mean?'

'Why are you smiling?'

'Because I'm happy, Luc.'

'This is only the beginning,' he answered and bent over her, kissed the top of her head. 'I thought I would never find you.'

'Were you looking for me?' Her voice was light, filled with happiness.

'Oh yes, *ma chérie*, ever since . . . for a long time.'

'And I've been looking for you, although perhaps I didn't realize it. I was beginning to think I'd never find the right man.'

'Am I?'

'Are you what?' she teased, knowing what he meant.

'The right man, Meredith?'

'Oh yes, Luc, very much so, in every way.'

'We're good together, Meredith, very good. I enjoy every minute we are together, and just now, well, you gave me such pleasure I'm still reeling. And you? Did I please you?'

'Of course. You must know that.'

'Yes, I suppose I do, but it's nice to hear it from your lips, Meri.'

He felt her stiffen against him. 'What's wrong? Don't you like me to call you Meri?'

'I don't mind,' she replied quickly, catching the note

of concern in his voice. 'It's just that few people do.'

Pulling her around and up into his arms, he touched her face lightly, gazed into her bright eyes, and said in the softest of voices, 'I don't want to see that terrible sadness in your eyes ever again. There's been too much hurt and pain in your life, too much sorrow.'

She did not respond.

'I'm here for you, Meri, if ever you want to talk about it. Sometimes it is helpful to unburden oneself.'

'One day, perhaps.'

He nodded, leaned forward and kissed her on the lips. 'I've fallen in love with you, Meri.'

Meredith stared at him. Unexpectedly, tears welled up in her eyes. She swallowed hard, trying to push them back, but she could not. Slowly they rolled down her cheeks.

'Oh, *ma chérie*, don't weep, there's nothing to weep about.' Luc lifted his hand, wiped away her tears with his fingertips. 'Do you think you could fall in love with me?'

'I already have,' she whispered and began to cry again.

'Thank God!' Luc exclaimed, and kissed her on the lips. And as he kissed her cheeks and her eyes he tasted the salt of her tears. 'No more sorrow. I'm going to make sure of that,' he said against her damp face. 'Only happiness from now on, Meri.'

But he was wrong.

PART TWO

Time Present, Time Past

Sixteen

Meredith stood at the far end of the drawing room, leaning against a Sheraton cabinet. The interior of the antique piece was illuminated, its shelves filled with priceless Meissen figurines.

A few minutes before she had wandered over to look at this unique collection and had suddenly felt weak. Reluctant to manoeuvre through the crowded room looking for somewhere to sit down, she had stayed where she was, nursing a glass of champagne.

She took a deep breath, hoping she was not going to have one of her attacks, which was what she had begun to call them. There had been two in January when she was in France, then three last month; she wondered how many she would have in April.

They passed as quickly as they occurred, and she was never the worse afterwards; nonetheless, they made her nervous. She never knew when one would strike her.

The other day, in the office, she had told Amy about them, had explained how they had started in Paris and had continued off and on.

Amy had said at once, 'They're becoming too frequent. I think you should get medical advice. Let me make an appointment for you with Jennifer Pollard.'

Meredith had shaken her head, told Amy not to call the doctor. Now she asked herself if she had been foolish. Perhaps she should have listened to her assistant. At this moment her legs were weak, she could feel the fatigue slowly creeping through her entire body, and she could not help wondering whether she would be able to last through the evening.

She must do that, no matter how she felt. Tonight was a very special occasion in her daughter's life, and in hers. It was Cat's engagement party and she had been looking forward to it.

Meredith believed that by rights *she* should have been giving the party, but Keith's sister Margery, and her husband Eric, had insisted on hosting it at their Park Avenue penthouse; she had had no alternative but to acquiesce.

But she fully intended to plan a celebration dinner for Cat and Keith, which she would give in the next few weeks, and she hoped Luc would be able to attend. He had spent the past week in New York with her, and had planned to stay on for the engagement party tonight. Then at the last minute he had been called back to France. A problem had developed with one of his larger architectural jobs, a shopping complex in Lyons, and his presence on the site had been imperative.

They were both disappointed he had been forced to leave. But he was coming back to New York in ten days, to spend a long weekend with her at Silver Lake; she could hardly wait for his return. They were very much in love, and in the past two months had grown extremely close. They were rarely apart when they were in the same city, and when separated by the Atlantic they spoke every day by phone. He's everything I want in a man, she thought now, missing him. How she wished he were here with her tonight.

Meredith constantly marvelled at her luck in meeting Luc, and at their extraordinary compatibility. Her children knew him now and liked him, and he was very taken by them. He and Jon got on extremely well; apart from having Yale in common, they were both sports fans and especially addicted to football. And Cat was equally at ease with Luc, since they both had artistic natures. He was impressed with Cat's talent as an illustrator, thought her an accomplished artist. She had been very proud when he had congratulated her on her fine children, noting the admiration in his voice.

Meredith now peered into the milling crowd filling the drawing room, wishing Cat or Jon would reappear. There were about sixty people present and she hardly knew any of them, only the immediate members of the Pearson family: Anne and Paul, Keith's parents, his sisters Margery, Susan, Rosemarie, Jill and Wendy, and his two brothers Will and Dominick. And Eric Clarke, Margery's husband, one of her hosts this evening.

The Pearson family was a large and boisterous American-Irish clan. As big as the Kennedy tribe, Cat had told her recently. However, the Pearsons did not hail from Boston; they were dyed-in-the-wool Yankees from the heart of Connecticut. It struck Meredith that the Pearsons were out in full force this evening, since there were innumerable aunts, uncles, cousins and their offspring present.

And we are only three, such a small family, she thought. Not much of a match for a crew like the Pearsons. Meredith felt unexpectedly overwhelmed, and then she experienced such a sudden sense of loss that she was startled. It was a feeling she could not rightly explain to herself.

Blanche and Pete O'Brien had come in from Silver Lake to attend the party, and they were extended family. But even so . . . Meredith snapped her eyes shut, endeavouring to shake off that awful feeling.

Opening her eyes a moment later, she scanned the room wondering where Blanche and Pete were. Somehow she had lost track of them in the last hour. Perhaps they were in the crowded dining room, where a buffet table groaned with all manner of fancy hors-d'oeuvre.

Meredith felt strangely isolated, standing there alone, propped up against the cabinet. I must sit down, she thought, and decided to head for a chair near the fireplace. It was then that she spotted her daughter.

Catherine was glancing around, obviously looking for her.

Meredith raised her hand, waved.

Instantly Cat saw her, smiled, waved back and hurried across the drawing room.

'Mom, there you are, I've been looking all over for you,' Catherine said, rushing up to Meredith. 'Isn't this a wonderful party? I'm so excited tonight. I can't stand it.' She looked down at her left hand, gazed at her sapphire ring admiringly, then flashed it at Meredith. 'It's gorgeous, isn't it, Mom?'

'Beautiful, darling,' Meredith answered, and caught hold of Cat's arm to steady herself.

Catherine gave her a quick look, and exclaimed, 'Mom, are you all right?'

'Yes.'

'But you're very pale. Not only that, you look taut, tense. Are you sure nothing's wrong? Look, if you're not ill, is there something else the matter? You're not angry are you? I mean because Margery and Eric insisted on throwing the party?'

'Don't be silly, you know I'm not like that. I feel a bit tired, that's all. I've probably been overdoing it at the office.'

'Let's go and sit on the sofa over there, Mother. My feet are killing me anyway. These shoes are fab, but gosh, they're agony.'

Meredith allowed her daughter to guide her to a sofa near the fireplace, and she sat down gratefully. A moment ago she felt as though all of her strength was ebbing away. The last thing she wanted was to pass out here. She would be humiliated in front of all these people.

Turning to Catherine she said, 'Perhaps a glass of water would help. Could you get me one, please?'

'Of course, Mom. I won't be a minute.' Catherine threw her mother a reassuring smile and glided across the floor towards the large entrance foyer, where a bar had been set up.

No one would know her feet are killing her,

Meredith thought, watching her daughter float through the room as if she were walking on air.

How beautiful Catherine looked tonight, so elegant in her short, midnight-blue taffeta cocktail suit and Amelia's pearls. Her brown hair was cut in a sleek shape and her lovely, open face looked so young and fresh, her wide-set eyes very blue. Cat was tall, like she was, with long shapely legs. I can't imagine why she wants to wear five-inch heels, Meredith thought in bafflement, then leaned back against the sofa, trying to relax.

Suddenly, there was her son, pushing forward through the throng. She watched him walking rapidly towards her, tall, slender, as blond as she, with her green eyes. Cat resembled her father, whilst Jon took after her.

As he drew closer, she saw that he wore a worried expression on his lean face. 'Mom, what's the matter?' he asked, drawing to a standstill by her side. 'I just saw Cat getting you a glass of water, and she thinks you're not well. Are you ill?'

'No, Jon, I'm not,' she answered evenly, in a firm voice. 'Truly, darling. I felt a bit queasy earlier. Perhaps I'm tired.'

'You work too hard,' he said, bending his lanky frame over her, resting his hand on the sofa's arm. Bringing his face closer to hers, he dropped his voice. 'If you want to leave, I'll go with you. I wouldn't mind splitting this scene myself.'

'I'm fine,' she replied swiftly. 'And I don't think we can leave. It wouldn't be polite, and anyway we can't abandon Cat to all these Pearsons.'

'She's got Keith to protect her, and anyway she'll be a Pearson herself soon.'

Meredith frowned, searched his face. 'Aren't you having a good time, Jon?'

'Sure, it's okay, but . . .' He shrugged. 'I'm just here for Cat and you, Mom. I don't have a lot in common with this group.'

'*Oh.*' She drew back, looked at him closely. 'Are you trying to tell me something?'

Jonathan shook his head and grinned. 'No, not at all. And don't get me wrong, I like Keith. I think he's a pretty nifty guy, and he's great for Cat. But I'm not particularly close to their friends, my group's different, that's all.' He looked directly at his mother, grimaced, and finished, 'The Pearsons are a nice family, just a bit too social for me.'

'I know,' Meredith murmured. 'And I'm glad you came . . . for my sake and Cat's.'

'You can always depend on me, Mom. I wish Luc were here, he'd liven things up a bit.'

Meredith laughed. 'Here's Cat now.'

'With Keith hot on her heels,' Jon said, straightening up, glancing over his shoulder at his sister, who was heading their way.

'Here's your water, Mom.' Cat handed her the glass and sat down on the sofa next to her.

'Thanks, darling.'

'I'm sorry you're under the weather, Meredith,' Keith said, bending over her as Jon had done a moment before. 'Is there anything else I can get you?'

Meredith looked up into his freckled face, as always thinking how honest his light grey eyes were, and shook her head. 'Thank you Keith dear, but I'm feeling much better.' She smiled at him warmly, liking him, knowing he would make her daughter a good husband, just as Jon knew. Cat would be safe with Keith Pearson; he was devoted, loyal and loving.

Clearing her throat, Meredith said, 'The three of you are beginning to make me feel like an invalid.'

Keith grinned at her. 'We don't mean to, we just care about you, that's all.'

'You're very sweet, Keith,' she answered.

'You *will* come to dinner later, as planned, won't you?' Keith went on, fixing her with his serious grey eyes. 'I don't want to pressure you, but we'll all be disappointed if you don't. It won't be the same without you.'

Meredith answered, 'I wouldn't miss it,' and patted his hand reassuringly. 'Jon is my escort, he'll look after me.'

'Keith's right, Mother, the evening would certainly fizzle out for me without *you* at the engagement dinner,' Catherine said.

'I'll be there.' Meredith smiled at her daughter, loving her.

Catherine smiled back, lifted her left hand, tightened a loose pearl earring. The sapphire engagement ring flashed in the bright lamplight.

It's the colour of her eyes, Meredith thought. Jack's eyes.

'You're a good sport, Mother,' Jonathan said several hours later, as he helped Meredith out of her coat and hung it in the hall closet.

'It was a lovely dinner in many respects, and generous of the Pearsons to have it in the private room at La Grenouille. But they're a bit – '

'Overwhelming,' Jonathan interrupted and shook his head. 'My God, all those Pearsons, Mom! My sister's pretty brave, taking on that clan. I wouldn't want to, I can tell you that.'

'I know what you mean, but individually they're very nice really, and Keith's parents are lovely, Jon.'

'True, but Keith's sisters are a pretty rowdy bunch.'

'The problem is, darling, we're used to a whole different kind of family life, so much quieter. After all, there's only been the three of us all these years.'

'And thank God for that,' he answered, hanging up his overcoat. 'In my opinion you deserve a medal, sitting through the dinner the way you did, all those toasts. *Mind-boggling.*'

Meredith laughed. 'Yes, it was a bit much. But I began to feel better once we left the apartment, and I got some fresh air. And I do like the food at La Grenouille.'

'You didn't eat very much.'

She smiled at her son. 'I'd like a cup of tea, Jon, how about you?'

'Great idea.'

He followed his mother into the kitchen and glanced out of the window. The lights of the Fifty-Ninth Street Bridge twinkled brightly against the dark night sky; beyond he could see another bridge glowing in the distance. Beautiful glittering city. He had always loved Manhattan. Jonathan stared down at the East River flowing far below and then across at Roosevelt Island. Funny how his mother always wanted to live near water, needed to, really. This was the second apartment she had owned on Sutton Place. He liked this one the best; they lived in the penthouse and the views of Manhattan were spectacular.

Meredith said, 'When are you going back to New Haven?' and put two cups and saucers on a tray as she spoke.

'Tomorrow morning. Early. I'll do it in under two hours. It's not that bad a drive. By the way, has Cat indicated when she wants to get married?'

Meredith nodded. 'This year, certainly. They don't want to wait too long, she told me. I've suggested September. It's very lovely at Silver Lake at that time of year.'

'Early October's better, Mom, when the leaves are turning. I think an autumn wedding would be picturesque.'

'You're right, and I did suggest that only the other day. Cat's going to let me know sometime next week, so we can get the invitations engraved and sent out, make proper plans.'

'Aunt Blanche is all worked up about the reception,' Jon said, laughing. 'She's been planning it for weeks. In her head that is . . . she told me tonight that she wants to top your wedding reception, which she was apparently involved in.'

'Very much so. In fact, she really designed and planned the entire thing by herself. She has such a talent for that kind of occasion. Make the tea, Jon, the kettle's screeching its head off.'

'Okay. Why don't you go and sit in the library. I'll bring the tea.'

'Thanks, darling,' she said, and did as he suggested, walking out of the kitchen, across the entrance foyer and into the library, which overlooked the water. She went to one of the windows, stood staring out. A great barge was floating down, loaded with cargo, heading for the docks, no doubt.

Meredith never got tired of looking at the East River. There was a great deal of traffic on this waterway and something was always moving on it, going up or down.

Her thoughts turned to Catherine as she swung away from the window and went and sat down near the fireplace. She was going to give her the best wedding any girl had ever had, make sure that she –

Jon interrupted her thoughts when he said, 'Where do you want the tray, Mom? Over there by you, I guess.'

'Yes, that's fine, put it here on this coffee table.' Meredith moved a pile of large art books to make a space.

Meredith poured, and they sipped their tea in silence for a few minutes, and then Jon suddenly said, 'Are you going to make it permanent with Luc?'

Startled, Meredith gaped at him.

Jon said, 'What I mean is, are you going to marry him, Mom?'

'He hasn't asked me,' Meredith replied.

'But would you, if he did?' Jon pressed.

'I honestly don't know.'

'*Why?*'

'Why don't I know? Is that what you mean?'

'Yes.'

Meredith lifted her shoulders in a small shrug. 'I just don't, that's all. It would be a big step for me to take, it would mean rearranging my life completely.'

'So what? I think you *should* marry him.'

'You do, do you?'

'Sure. You're in love with him, he's in love with you. I bet if you gave him half a chance, he'd ask you.'

Meredith said nothing.

'You've been used to having *us* with you always, Mother. The Three Musketeers, remember? That's what you used to call us. Cat's getting married, starting a whole new life soon, her own family. And I expect I'll get married when I meet the right woman. I just don't want you to be all alone one day.'

Meredith stared at her son, touched by his words, then her brows drew together in a furrow. 'You're worrying about my old age, is that it, Jon?'

Laughing, he shook his head. 'You'll never be old, Mother. You'll be beautiful forever. You're the greatest-looking forty-four-year-old I've ever seen.'

'And you've lived such a long time,' she shot back, laughing with him. 'Known so many women.'

Jonathan's face sobered when he continued, 'I just don't want you to be by yourself, lonely later in your life.' He cleared his throat, and gave her a piercing look. 'When I was little I used to hear you . . . *crying*, Mother. Sobbing as if your heart were breaking, at night in your bedroom. I used to stand outside the door and listen, hurting for you inside. But I didn't dare come in, even though I wanted to comfort you.'

'You could have,' she said softly, touched by his words.

'I was afraid. You could be very fierce you know in those days. Do you remember, I once asked you why you cried at night, when I was a bit older?'

'Yes, vaguely.'

'Do you recall what you said?'

Meredith shook her head.

'You told me you cried because you'd lost someone when you were a child. When I asked you who, you wouldn't answer me, you just turned away.'

Meredith stared at her son, speechlessly.

'Mom, who was it that you lost? I've always wondered.'

'I don't know,' she replied after a long and thoughtful pause. 'If I did I would tell you, Jon. Truly, I would.'

Her son rose and came and sat next to her. He took hold of her hand, looked into her face. His own had a loving expression on it. Slowly, he said, 'It broke my heart to hear you crying. I wanted to help you and I didn't know how. It's always worried me that you cried in that way.'

'Oh Jon.'

'That's why Luc is so important to me . . . I want him for you, Mom, he's such a great guy, and he loves you. Maybe he can make up for . . . everyone that hurt you.'

During the night Meredith awakened.

Immediately she slipped out of bed, put on a dressing gown and went into the library. There was a tray of drinks on a console table and she poured herself a small brandy in a tall glass, added soda water, then carried it over to a chair. She sat down, made herself comfortable, took a sip of the drink.

Lately she had discovered that it was far better to get up when she awakened in this way. It was easier to think through what was troubling her when she was sitting in a chair, rather than lying down in bed.

Now placing the glass on the coffee table, she sat back, relaxing, thinking of her son's words of earlier.

Jon had taken her by surprise, but she had also been moved by his words, his loving concern. Although she did not want him to worry about her, it was gratifying, in some ways, that he did. Her son cared about her wellbeing, and that was important to her.

She had tried to bring her children up properly, had always striven to do the right thing for them, and she believed she had succeeded. Catherine and Jonathan had turned out to be good human beings, with all of the right values. They functioned, were well adjusted, very normal young people, and thank God they had never been tempted by their peers to experiment with drugs, nor did they drink much. She had been lucky with her children.

It was startling to her that Jonathan remembered how she used to weep at night, when she thought her children were fast asleep. The odd thing was, she had no recollection of ever telling him she cried for someone she had lost when she was a child. Yet she knew he was not lying. Why would he? She must have forgotten what she had said to him, all those years ago.

And who had she meant? She had no idea; she was truly baffled.

Sighing to herself, finishing the drink, Meredith got up, walked back to her bedroom. Perhaps now she would be able to fall asleep. Certainly she must try. She had a busy day ahead of her. She took off her dressing gown and got into bed. Almost immediately she began to doze, drifting off into a deep sleep.

There were many children. Boys and girls. Some of them were very young. Three and four years old. Others were older, perhaps seven and eight. They were all walking across the vast landscape. Some were hand in hand, boys and girls, and girls together. Many walked alone. Too many children, she thought, filling with fear. I'll never find that little girl again. Or the boy. They are lost to me. Where are they? They must be among these children. I must find them.

She was frantic, running in amongst the children as they walked, perfectly in step, towards the distant horizon. She peered into their faces. She did not know them. They marched across the parched, cracked mud flats like automatons, staring straight ahead, paying no attention to her. Their faces were glazed, empty of expression, their eyes dull, lifeless.

Where are you going? she cried. Where are you heading? None of them answered her. Have you seen them? she cried. The girl with the long striped scarf? The boy with the cap? Please tell me if you've seen them.

The children turned en masse, veered to the right, began to walk towards the sea. She had never seen the sea before. The water was black, the colour of oil. She shuddered and called to the children to come back.

They did not heed her. She was afraid, shivering with fright. The children marched on. No! she cried. Stop! Still they paid no attention. They marched on and on, marched right into the sea. Slowly they sank, disappeared from sight. Oh God, no! she cried. Nobody heard her.

The landscape was empty. She was the only one left. And then she saw them. They were skipping towards her holding hands. The little girl with the scarf and the boy in his school cap. She waved. They waved back. She began to run. She was getting closer and closer. The labels pinned to their coats were huge, bigger than before. They fluttered in the wind, blew against their necks, obscuring their faces. Suddenly they turned around, veered to the right and began to walk towards the sea. No! she shouted. No! Stop! Don't go there! They did not listen. She ran and ran. Parts of the arid landscape opened up, cracking in half. She jumped over the cracks. Went on running. Her breathing was laboured. Finally she caught up with the children. She reached out, grabbed the boy's shoulder. He resisted. Then slowly he swung around. She screamed. He had no face. She grabbed the girl's arm. The girl turned. Meredith screamed again.

'Mother, what's wrong, what is it?' Jon exclaimed, bursting into her room, snapping on the light as he did. He hurried over to the bed.

Meredith was sitting up, her eyes wide with fright, her face and neck damp with perspiration. She shook her head.

Her son sat down on the bed. He stared at her closely, took hold of her hand, wanting to comfort her. Again he asked, 'What is it, Mom?'

Meredith took a deep breath. 'I had a strange dream, a nightmare.'

'It must've frightened you. I heard you screaming.'

'Yes, it must have. I'm sorry I woke you, Jon.'

'That's okay.' He frowned. 'What was the nightmare about?'

'It doesn't make sense, it was very muddled.' She forced a smile onto her face, hoped it reassured him. 'Let's forget it. I'm all right, really. Go back to bed, honey.'

Jonathan leaned forward, kissed her lightly on the cheek. 'I'm just across the hall if you need me.'

'I'm fine,' she replied.

Long after Jonathan had returned to his own room, Meredith lay awake, remembering every detail of the dream, pondering on it.

It was a dream she had first dreamed many years ago, when she was young and still lived in Sydney. It had recurred off and on over the years; and then it had stopped all of a sudden when she was in her thirties. Unexpectedly, she was having the dream again – twice in the space of two months.

The details were always the same. The barren landscape, sinister and Godforsaken. The children marching to their doom in the sea. Her desperation as she tried to find the little girl and boy.

She always woke up in a cold sweat. And she was always fearful when she awakened. Why? What did the dream mean?

Seventeen

'How many of these attacks have you had?' Dr Jennifer Pollard asked, scrutinizing Meredith across her desk.

'I had two in January, two in February, three in March, and two this month . . . last Thursday at Catherine's engagement party and again on Sunday. The last was the worst one yet. It lasted most of the day, and I felt more debilitated than usual. So much so, I didn't go to the office yesterday. When I went to work this morning I was still feeling very tired. I thought I'd better come and see you.'

'I'm glad you did,' the doctor answered. 'Earlier, on the phone, you told me the symptoms are always the same – nausea and a feeling of total exhaustion. Are there no other symptoms, Meredith?'

'None at all.'

'No vomiting, fever, pains in your stomach, diarrhoea, high temperatures, headaches, migraines?'

Meredith shook her head. 'No, nothing like that. I just feel sort of queasy, but mostly very tired, exhausted really.'

'I see.' Jennifer brought her hand up to her chin, looking thoughtful.

Meredith leaned forward intently. 'Jennifer, what do you think is wrong with me?'

'Frankly, I'm not sure. First we must give you a very thorough examination, then I'll be able to make a proper diagnosis.' As she was speaking the doctor opened the folder in front of her and scanned the top page. 'I looked at your records just before you arrived, and you had a check-up three months ago, at the end of December. You were in perfect health then, Meredith.'

'Yes, I know, that's why I'm so baffled.'

'We'll get to the bottom of it, don't worry.' Closing the folder, the doctor went on briskly, 'All right then, let's start by getting the tests done.'

She stood up, walked around the desk.

Meredith also rose.

Jennifer Pollard put her arm around Meredith's shoulder. 'Don't look so apprehensive. We'll get to the bottom of the problem.'

'What do you think it *could* be?'

Jennifer hesitated, then said, 'Any number of things, but I don't want to make guesses. Also, I'm not going to pretend it's nothing, Meredith, I've too much respect for your intelligence, and in any case, you know that's not my way. I believe in being very honest with my patients. The kind of exhaustion you've described can mean any number of things. It could be caused by anaemia, a hormonal disorder or a chronic infection of some kind. Then again, it might be tiredness due to burn-out.'

'Not burn-out, no!' Meredith exclaimed. 'Most of the time I'm full of energy and vitality.'

'Let's go through to Angela,' Jennifer said, leading the way out of her office and down the corridor. 'You know the routine after all these years. Angela will take blood samples, do the EKG and a chest X-ray. We'll also need a urine sample from you. Once these tests are completed, I'll give you a thorough physical examination.'

Opening the door of the small examination room, Jennifer said, 'I'll send Angela in with a gown, so you can get undressed.'

'Thank you,' Meredith murmured.

Exactly one hour later Meredith was dressed again and sitting in her doctor's office, once more staring at Jennifer Pollard. Her expression was worried and there was a questioning look in her eyes. 'What did you find?'

'Nothing.' Jennifer smiled at her confidently. 'As far as I can tell, there's nothing physically wrong with you. No lumps, no swelling anywhere, and you didn't flinch when I put pressure on your abdomen. And your reflexes and blood pressure are normal. Of course, I don't know what the blood and urine tests are going to reveal, and I won't have the results for a couple of days. But frankly I'm pretty sure they're going to be normal, too. It seems to me that you're as physically fit as you were three months ago.'

'Then how do you explain the attacks?'

'Not sure.' Jennifer leaned back in her chair, focused her eyes on Meredith. 'Nerves, maybe? Stress? You push yourself very hard. For as long as I've known you, which is a good ten years now, you've been a workaholic, to use a nasty word. And stress can play havoc with a person's nervous system.'

'I realize that, but I don't feel stressed out, not at all. Honestly, Jennifer, I've been taking it a lot easier lately, especially when I'm in France. I'm remodelling an inn there, but I have a very good French partner, who takes a load off my shoulders. And I spend long weekends with my boyfriend in the Loire. He has a country house there.' Meredith leaned forward and finished, 'I've never been happier on a personal level. Business is good, the kids are great.'

'I'm glad to hear it,' Jennifer answered. A reflective expression flickered in her eyes, and after a moment she asked, 'Is there anything at all worrying you?'

'No. As I just said, my life has never been better.'

Jennifer nodded. 'Let's see what the blood tests tell us. I'll call you as soon as they come in. Probably by Thursday, Friday at the latest.'

Meredith was signing a batch of letters late on Thursday afternoon when the private line in her office rang. Picking up the phone, she said, 'Hello?'

'*C'est moi, chérie.*'

'Luc!' she exclaimed. 'How are you, darling?'

'Not so good, I am afraid.'

'What's wrong?' she asked, her voice rising slightly, her concern apparent.

Luc sighed over the transatlantic line and explained, 'I am so terribly sorry about this, Meredith, but I cannot now come to New York this weekend. I am afraid I am stuck here in Lyons. Because of the job, I am needed here.'

'Oh Luc, what a shame, I was so looking forward to it,' Meredith said. 'I'm very disappointed, darling, but I understand. Work has to come first.' She too sighed resignedly.

'I have to be on the spot,' he continued. 'There is an unanticipated condition in the foundation that is going to require major redesign. I can't just delegate this particular part of the job. We have run into subsurface ledgerock which requires redesigning the foundation in the first of the buildings. It is vital that I am here. I'm meeting with the contractor and structural engineer tomorrow. We'll complete the design on Saturday and bring in the crew next week.' There was a fractional pause before he laughed quietly and said, 'I don't suppose you could come to Lyons, could you?'

'I'd love to but I can't. I told you, I have the closing on the inn tomorrow. And I have to be in New York on Tuesday for a meeting with the bank. Henry Raphaelson is going to the Far East the following day, so I can't change that appointment. Next week is a bit tough for me, Luc. I'm due in Paris soon, in case you've forgotten.'

'I hadn't, *ma chérie*, I was just hoping to see you before.'

Meredith glanced at the calendar on her desk. 'I was planning on being there at the end of April, and I will be staying the whole month of May, you know.'

'Well, that is wonderful! I am happy. But I shall miss you, Meri.'

'And I will miss you too,' she said. They went on talking for another ten minutes. At one moment, Meredith almost confided in him, almost told him about her visit to the doctor, and then changed her mind.

She did not want to worry him. He had enough problems with the shopping centre in Lyons.

'There's absolutely nothing physically wrong with you, Meredith,' Jennifer Pollard said, reclining in her chair, smiling at her. 'I'm happy to tell you the blood and urine tests are normal.'

Meredith smiled back, filled with relief, and then she frowned and asked, 'But this morning when you called the office you told Amy you wanted to see me, talk to me.'

The doctor nodded. 'I do.' Jennifer cleared her throat, and went on, 'There's still something wrong. Those attacks. Now, in my experience, people who suffer from the kind of exhaustion you described to me earlier this week usually do so all the time. In other words, it's chronic. And permanent. It doesn't come and go, the way you have described *your* attacks.'

'Meaning what?'

'Meaning that your attacks could easily become increasingly frequent, until, in the end, you too have the exhaustion on a permanent basis, rather than only occasionally.'

Meredith was silent; she sat staring at the doctor.

'Let me explain something to you, Meredith,' Jennifer said. 'Very often this kind of exhaustion is due to psychological causes.'

'Do you think that's the case with me?'

'Possibly. You could be suffering from psychogenic fatigue.'

'What does that mean?'

'That the cause of your tiredness is an emotional

problem. Or alternatively, you could be depressed, without knowing it.'

'I'm definitely not depressed!' Meredith answered with a dry laugh. 'When I was here on Tuesday, I told you my life was on an even keel, and rather wonderful these days. I'm in love with a fabulous man, he with me.'

'I believe you, and I'm happy for you. However, let's not dismiss the idea of psychogenic fatigue due to an emotional problem, or an upset mental state. What's causing it, the thing that's bothering you, doesn't necessarily have to be of this moment. It could go back in time.'

'How do you treat something like that?' Meredith asked nervously, eyeing her doctor warily.

'We have to determine the nature of the actual problem, get to the root of it, then treat it.'

'*Psychiatry*. Is that what you're getting at, Jennifer?'

'Yes, it is. If you are suffering from psychogenic fatigue, I recommend that you see someone immediately. The illness, and it *is* an illness, is not going to go away on its own. Furthermore, it could become chronic.'

'Who . . . who would you recommend?' Meredith asked quietly.

'Dr Hilary Benson. She's very sympathetic, you'll like her. And she's a brilliant psychiatrist. Her office is just around the corner from me on Park and Sixty-Ninth.'

Meredith leaned back in the chair, looking worried.

'There's nobody saner than you, Meredith,' Jennifer said swiftly, responding to the look in Meredith's eyes.

'I can testify to that. Listen to me, you might not have psychogenic fatigue at all. It could be stress . . . I said that to you earlier in the week.'

'I don't think so.'

'Then you will go and see Hilary Benson?'

Meredith nodded.

Eighteen

Meredith was nothing if not decisive, and once she had agreed to see the psychiatrist she told Amy to make an appointment for the following week.

After that she tried to put the matter out of her mind; she had always had the ability to pigeon-hole problems until it was the appropriate time to deal with them. And so she managed to get through the next few days without dwelling too much on her health or mental state, and fortunately there were no more attacks.

On Tuesday afternoon, when she walked into Dr Hilary Benson's private office, her first impression was of a good-looking but stern woman. The doctor had a rather lovely face with high cheekbones, and the palest blue eyes that appeared almost transparent. But her mouth had a severe set to it and her dark brown hair was pulled back in a plain chignon that was singularly schoolmarmish.

There was a no-nonsense, businesslike air about her, and for a split second Meredith was put off, thinking that she might be a cold fish. Then she recalled her physician's words. Jennifer had told her that Hilary Benson was a sympathetic person as well as a brilliant psychiatrist.

I must give her a chance, give this a chance, Meredith decided. She needed to understand what was wrong, why she was having these attacks. According to Jennifer, only a psychiatrist could help her get to the root of the problem.

After greeting Meredith pleasantly, and shaking hands, Dr Benson said, 'Come and sit down, Mrs Stratton.'

'Thank you,' Meredith answered and followed the doctor over to the desk, where they sat facing each other.

Meredith, studying the doctor, decided that she was probably the same age as Jennifer and herself: in her early forties.

The psychiatrist said, 'Dr Pollard and I have spoken at length. She has filled me in, given me your medical history in general. Apparently you're a very healthy woman.'

'Yes, I am, thank goodness,' Meredith replied, smiling faintly.

Dr Benson nodded, and sat back in her chair, taking stock of Meredith for a moment. Beautiful woman. Puts up a good front, she thought. But there's pain in her, hurt. I can see it in her eyes. Getting straight to the point, she said, 'Jennifer believes you could be suffering from psychogenic fatigue.'

'So she told me.'

'Let's talk about that fatigue, the attacks you've been having. When did the first one occur, Mrs Stratton?'

'Early in January. I was in Paris on business. I'd been travelling part of the day, and that night, after

I'd checked in to my hotel, I felt quite ill. Exhausted, a bit queasy . . . nauseous.'

'Where had you travelled from?'

'England. Not a long trip by any means, and travelling doesn't affect me usually. I have a lot of stamina and tremendous energy, Dr Benson.'

'So, feeling ill was unusual for you. I understand.' There was a moment's pause, then Hilary went on, 'Had anything happened to upset you that day?' She put her elbows on the desk, steepled her fingers, and looked over them at Meredith.

'No, it hadn't. To tell you the truth, I thought I was probably coming down with the flu. That morning I'd been outside for a long time in the cold, in the snow. I'd been wandering around a ruined abbey. I thought that –' Meredith stopped short, abruptly cutting herself off.

'You thought what, Mrs Stratton?' Dr Benson asked, giving Meredith a quiet, encouraging smile.

'I was going to say that I thought I'd caught a chill when I was lingering at the abbey. But come to think of it, something odd *did* occur that morning, something quite strange, really.'

'And what was that?'

'I had a peculiar sense that I'd been there before. It was a feeling of *déjà vu*.'

'But you had *not* been there before. Is that what you're saying?'

'Yes, it is.'

'Can you recall how you actually felt?'

Meredith nodded.

'Will you tell me about it, Mrs Stratton?'

'Yes. But let me explain something, Dr Benson. I saw the abbey for the first time the day before . . . I was looking at it from the window of an inn, viewing it across snow-covered fields. It was beautiful. And I realized I was curiously drawn to it. The next morning I had a little time to spare, I was waiting for my English partner to get up, come down to breakfast. Well, anyway, not to digress . . . I had a little free time, so I went to look at the abbey close up. As I approached the ruins I felt that I was literally being pulled towards them, and that even if I'd wanted to, I couldn't have turned back. A short while later, when I finally walked into the actual ruins, I had the queerest feeling that I'd been there before. It was strong, rather overwhelming.'

'And you *are* positive you didn't know this place?'

'Oh yes. I had never been to Fountains Abbey before; I was visiting Yorkshire for the first time in my life.'

'I see. Did you experience anything else? Did you have any other emotions that morning?'

'Yes, I did, as a matter of fact. I felt a great sense of loss. And sadness . . .' Meredith paused. There was a reflective look on her face when she added quietly, 'I experienced a feeling of true sorrow.'

'Have you any idea why?'

'Not really, although I do recall that I had a sudden flash of clarity at that moment. I was sure that I had lost someone there, someone very dear to me. Or rather, that someone had been *taken* from me. It seemed to me that I *knew* those ruins, and I sensed a tragic thing had happened there. Yet it didn't feel like a bad place. Quite the opposite. I had a sense of belonging, and I was at ease.'

'Do you know England well, Mrs Stratton?'

'Not really, although I've been going there for over twenty years. However, as I just said, I had never been to Yorkshire.' Meredith leaned forward, gave the psychiatrist a piercing look. 'How do you explain what happened to me that morning?'

'I don't think I can. At least, not at this moment.'

'Do you think my experience at Fountains Abbey triggered the first attack?'

'I don't know.' Hilary Benson shook her head. 'The human mind is a strange and complex piece of machinery. It takes a lot of understanding. Let's leave your experience at the abbey alone for the moment, and go in another direction. I understand from Dr Pollard that you're an Australian. Please tell me a little about yourself, about your background.'

'I'm from Sydney. I grew up there. My parents were killed. In a car crash. When I was ten years old. Relatives brought me up.' Meredith sat back in the chair, crossed her legs and gave the psychiatrist a cool, very direct look.

Hilary Benson returned this glance and thought: Her expression is candid but she's lying. I know it. What she's just said has been well learned. She's repeating it by rote to me, just as she's done before, to countless others.

After a short pause, Hilary said, 'How sad for you to be orphaned so very young. Who was it that brought you up?'

'Relatives. I just told you.'

'But *who* exactly?'

'An aunt.'

'I see. Did you have any siblings?'

'No, I didn't. There was just me. I was always on my own.'

'Is that actually how you felt, that you were on your own, even though you had an aunt?'

'Oh yes, I always felt that way.'

'Tell me how you came to this country, Mrs Stratton.'

'I'll be happy to,' Meredith replied, and then added, 'I'd like you to call me Meredith, Dr Benson.'

The doctor nodded. 'Of course. Please give me a little background about your arrival in America.'

'I came with an American family who'd been living in Sydney. The Paulsons. I'd been working as an *au pair* for them since I was fifteen. Mr Paulson was transferred back to the States two years later, when I was seventeen, and they asked me to go with them. So I did.'

'And your aunt didn't object?'

'Oh no. She didn't care. She had four daughters of her own. She wasn't interested in me.'

'And so she gave her permission for you to travel to America with the Paulson family? Am I understanding this correctly?'

Meredith nodded. 'She helped me get my passport.' Meredith made a small grimace. 'She was glad to be rid of me.'

Hilary Benson frowned. 'You were not very close then?'

'Not at all.'

'And what about your parents? Were you close to them?'

'Not really.'

'But you were an only child. Only children are usually very close to their parents.'

'*I* wasn't, Dr Benson.'

The psychiatrist was silent. She looked down at the pad in front of her, made a few notes on it. She was more convinced than ever that Meredith was lying about her background. It seemed to her that everything was too well rehearsed, and Meredith spoke in monosyllables, as if she was afraid to elaborate in case she made a mistake. Or revealed something she was trying to hide.

Hilary put down her pen, and looked up, smiling at Meredith. 'You came to New York with the Paulson family. Did you ever go back to Australia?'

'No, I didn't. I stayed here. In Connecticut. That's where we lived, near New Preston. Up above Lake Waramaug. I was with the Paulsons for another year, and then Mr Paulson was transferred to South Africa. He was a trouble-shooter for an international advertising agency, and he was always moving around.'

'And did you go there with them?'

'No, I didn't want to go to Johannesburg. I stayed in Connecticut.'

'*Alone?* You were only eighteen.'

'Well, Mrs Paulson agreed I could stay on, because I had found myself a job. At the Silver Lake Inn. She came to meet the Silvers and liked them. They were providing room and board, as well as a wage, and she approved. The Silvers were from an old family and well known, very respected in the area.'

'So at the age of eighteen you were on your own, working at an inn. How did you feel about this? About being so . . . so independent.'

'I was pleased, but I wasn't really on my own, Dr Benson. The Silvers treated me like family right from the beginning, and they made me extremely welcome. I felt at home, as I'd never felt before in my life, actually.'

'If I am understanding you correctly, they treated you like a daughter. Am I right, Meredith?'

'Not a daughter, no, they weren't that much older than I was. More like a sibling, a younger sister.'

'How old were the Silvers?'

'Amelia was thirty-six when I went to work there, and Jack was thirty-two.'

Hilary Benson nodded. 'And what was your job at the inn?'

'I started as a receptionist, but it was always understood, right from the beginning, that I would help Amelia with the office work. She was very overloaded, and since she was paralysed, things weren't easy for her. I became her assistant, as well as the receptionist. And I helped Jack a lot with the management of the inn.'

'What had happened to Amelia Silver? Why was she paralysed?'

'She'd had a riding accident when she was twenty-five, just after they were married. She injured her spine and she lost the baby she was carrying. It was a great tragedy. But she coped very well.'

'Tell me more about her. She was obviously someone you cared about.'

'Oh yes, I did. She was remarkable, and she taught me so much. Not only that, Amelia was the most beautiful woman I've ever known, ever seen. She was like Vivien Leigh in *Gone with the Wind*. That was the first thing I said to Amelia . . . that she resembled Vivien Leigh.'

'Then she must have indeed been beautiful. You say she taught you many things. Would you explain this to me, please?'

'She loved art, antiques, and decorating, and I learned about those things from her. But I also learned about courage . . . she was so courageous herself. And I learned about dignity and decency from Amelia Silver. Those were some of her other qualities.'

'What you're saying is that she gave you certain values.'

'Yes. And so did Jack. I learned about true kindness from him, and he encouraged me, helped me to understand business. He taught me a great deal about running an inn, almost everything I know, in fact. He was a very smart man.'

'Was it a busy hotel?'

'Only at weekends. It was quiet during the week. Silver Lake Inn was and is very much a weekend retreat, all the year round. But more people came in the good weather, in the spring and summer, than they did in winter. And we were always full in the autumn, of course, when the leaves changed colour. People loved to come and see the foliage. They still do.'

'You describe the inn in a very loving voice, Meredith.'

'I do love Silver Lake. I always have, from the very first moment I saw it. And it was the first real home I ever knew. My first safe haven –' Meredith stopped. She had said too much. She shifted slightly in the chair and focused her eyes on the painting above Hilary Benson's head.

Hilary said, '*Safe* haven . . . had you not felt safe before then, Meredith?'

'It's just an expression,' Meredith hedged.

'You speak so beautifully about the Silvers, I know you must have loved them, obviously still do. How are they –'

'They're both dead!' Meredith exclaimed, interrupting the psychiatrist.

'I'm sorry to hear that. Their passing must have been a great loss to you.'

'It was. I was heartbroken.'

'When did they die?'

'Jack died in 1973. He was only thirty-six. And Amelia about a year later, just a bit longer than a year, actually, late in 1974. She was young too, only forty-one.'

'How truly sad for you to lose two people you cared about so close together. They must have loved you very much.'

'Oh, yes, they did,' Meredith said softly, remembering them, cherishing them inside. 'That's why it was so hard for me when they died. Jack was the first person to ever show me any affection in my life, put his arms around me, comfort me.'

There was a brief silence before Hilary Benson asked softly, 'Are you saying that there was a sexual relationship between you and Jack Silver?'

'I'm not suggesting anything of the sort!' Meredith shot back, her voice rising. 'Amelia also loved me as much as Jack did. She showed me a great deal of affection too, but it was verbal. The poor woman was in a wheelchair. *She* couldn't very well put *her* arms around me.'

'I understand,' the psychiatrist replied quietly, noting Meredith's anger, her over-reaction, realizing that there had indeed been a sexual relationship between Meredith and Jack. But it was far too early to probe this. Meredith Stratton was not ready.

Meredith looked at her watch; it was four o'clock. She had been here almost an hour. 'I have an appointment at my office at four-thirty, Dr Benson, and in any case I think our first session is finished, is it not?'

'Yes, you are correct,' Hilary answered, glancing at the clock on her desk. 'I believe we have another appointment on Thursday of this week.'

'Yes, we do,' Meredith replied, standing up. As she shook the doctor's hand and then left the private office she wondered if she would keep it.

Nineteen

Despite her misgivings, Meredith did keep her Thursday appointment with Dr Hilary Benson. And she agreed to three more sessions the following week. So far, the psychiatrist had not pinpointed the cause of her attacks of fatigue.

It was at her fifth appointment, at the end of the second week, that Meredith finally decided to make it their last meeting.

'I don't think we're getting anywhere at all, Dr Benson,' she said slowly. 'I've talked endlessly and you've listened, and we've not really progressed, or come up with anything of real value. We don't even know if I'm suffering from psychogenic fatigue.'

'*I* think you are,' the psychiatrist said firmly.

'But I haven't had any more attacks.'

'I know. But that doesn't mean very much.'

'Let's make this our last session.'

'I think that would be foolish of you,' Hilary answered quietly, observing her closely. 'Something is troubling you. I am certain of that. We just haven't uncovered it yet.'

'I can't come again for several weeks. I'm going to London and Paris for a month.'

'When are you leaving?'

'On Wednesday or Thursday of next week.'

'Shall we see how we do today, Meredith?'

'All right,' she agreed. She did so because she had grown to like Hilary Benson, felt at ease with her and she trusted her. Even though they had not discovered the root of her problem, she knew that she was at fault. For years she had lived with half-truths, had hidden so much, that it was difficult to unearth it all now.

Hilary said, 'I'm not going to mince my words today, Meredith, I'm going to be brutally honest with you. I know you are lying to me. I know you had a sexual relationship with Jack Silver. I want you to tell me about it.'

Meredith was so taken aback, she blurted out, 'It wasn't just sexual. We loved each other – ' Breaking off, she swiftly averted her face, regretting the words.

'You mustn't be embarrassed,' Hilary murmured in an understanding tone. 'I'm not here to judge you, I'm only trying to help you . . . Talk to me, tell me about Jack, tell me what happened all those years ago at Silver Lake Inn. I *know* you'll feel better if you do, and having more information about your past will help me to trace the cause of your illness.'

There was a very long silence. Meredith did not answer. Instead she rose, walked over to the window, stood looking down onto Park Avenue, thinking about Jack and Amelia and herself, and all that had happened between them so long ago. It had shaped her life, changed her life. She had had so much from them. She did not want Hilary to think badly of Jack. Or of her.

Turning around, she walked back to the chair and sat down opposite Hilary, who was behind the desk. 'Yes, it's true. We did have a sexual relationship, but we also loved each other very much. I haven't wanted to talk about it to you because I don't want you to misunderstand. Words can sound so cold when they're said. Perhaps you could never understand the love, the emotions, the feelings there were between us, because you were not a witness to them. No one could understand.' Meredith gave her a long hard stare.

Hilary nodded. 'I appreciate everything you're saying. I know exactly what you mean. But as I just told you a moment ago, I'm not a judge or juror, just your doctor. And if I am to help you I must understand your past.'

'Do you think that's troubling me? Our love affair? Jack's and mine?'

'I'm not sure, Meredith. I have to hear everything first before I can make an assessment.'

'Because *I'm* sure it isn't. However, I will tell you about Jack, and what happened between us when I went to work at the inn in 1969.'

'Are you comfortable? Would you prefer to sit over there on the sofa?'

Meredith shook her head. 'No, I'm fine here. I just want to preface what I have to say about Jack with something else. A couple of weeks ago, my son Jon told me he used to listen to me crying at night when he was very young. And I did, I wept endless tears until I thought I had none left in me, but I always had. I cried for a lot of things in those days, but especially for Amelia and Jack. I missed them so much.'

Meredith paused, cleared her throat, then she went on softly, 'Jack Silver was my true love. I loved him from the first day I met him. He had fallen in love with me too that day. He called it a *coup de foudre*. I'd never heard that phrase before. He told me what it meant . . . struck by lightning. But we kept our love at bay for weeks, never disclosed our feelings for each other. Then Amelia had to go away. She had to visit her mother in Manhattan. The old lady was very ill, probably dying, and Jack drove Amelia into the city. When he returned on that July night he came looking for me. He found me down by Silver Lake, lying in the grass, trying to cool off. It was extremely hot that month, blistering. He said he needed to talk to me about Amelia; he was worried because he had left her alone with her sick mother, and with only two young maids in attendance. He wondered out loud if he ought to drive me into the city the next day, so that I could stay with Amelia, look after her. I told him I would be happy to go, that I'd do anything for him.

'And then suddenly, without either of us understanding exactly how it happened, we were in each other's arms, kissing each other. I'd never experienced anything like it before, the surging passion, the desire, and the love I felt for him. I hadn't had any previous sexual encounters, Dr Benson, and Jack was upset when he discovered I was a virgin, scolded me for not telling him. But by then it was too late. We had already made love.'

Meredith fell silent for a second.

Hilary Benson said nothing; she knew it was wiser

to wait until Meredith was ready to continue her story.

After a few moments, Meredith said softly, 'And we went on making love to each other even after Amelia returned to Silver Lake. We just couldn't help ourselves, we were so crazily in love. Jack had been terribly deprived for years, before my advent on the scene. He told me that he had once gone to a call girl in New York, but that it had been a failure, a waste of time because he had no feelings for her. But Jack loved me, and he loved Amelia, and we were scrupulous. We never displayed our intense feelings for each other in front of her. Jack always said that Amelia must never know about us, that we must not hurt her in any way whatsoever, and we never did.'

'She never knew?' Hilary asked.

Meredith did not answer. Instead, she went on, 'Then one day I missed my period. I knew I must be pregnant. I was terrified, convinced Amelia would guess the baby was Jack's child. But he reassured me, told me Amelia would never suspect. I believed him, why wouldn't I? I loved him beyond all reason. When I asked him what I would say to Amelia, how I would explain my pregnancy, he said I must invent a boyfriend, say that my new young man was the father. Later I could explain to her that my boyfriend had let me down, gone away and left me in the lurch, left me to fend for myself. And this is what I did tell Amelia, and she believed me.

'Actually, Dr Benson, Amelia was so thrilled I was pregnant she was in seventh heaven. When I became really heavy, six months into my pregnancy, she insisted I move into the apartment over the garage adjoining their house. I had been living in the attic of the inn, and Amelia just decided one day that the stairs were too much for me, and this was true. And so we all settled down in the house together. Naturally, Jack and I were as careful as we'd always been in front of Amelia.

'One afternoon, when I was eight months into my pregnancy, Amelia asked me if I intended to go away once the baby was born. I told her I didn't want to leave, that I hoped I could stay at Silver Lake, continue working for them. She was very happy to hear this, and I remember how she placed her small hand on my stomach and smiled and said, "Our baby, Meri. It'll be our baby. We'll all bring it up, and we're going to be so happy here together." And we were, that's the truth. Sometimes, I wondered out loud to Jack whether Amelia suspected the baby was his and he assured me she did not.

'Finally, our daughter Catherine was born. The most perfect baby any of us had ever seen. Beautiful, with Jack's bright blue eyes. And then three years later tragedy came to Silver Lake. Jack died, just like that, in the flick of an eyelash. He had a heart attack when he was talking to Pete O'Brien on the front lawn. And he never knew he had a heart problem, none of us did.' Meredith sat back in her chair, stared off into space, lost again in that faraway time.

'And then what happened?' Hilary asked after a few seconds had elapsed. 'Please continue.'

'What happened? We *grieved*, Amelia and I. We were so sorrowful. But I had the baby to look after and the inn to run for Amelia . . . so much work in those days, but I was young, strong . . . I had my hands full but I coped. And poor Amelia was in such a bad way, I had to take care of her as well. You see, she did not really want to live after Jack's death, and by the following spring she was fading. I knew she was not long for this world. At least, I felt that, felt that she was literally willing herself to die. My heart grew heavier and heavier as the months passed. I couldn't bear the thought of losing her so soon after Jack . . . the very idea of it filled me with dread.

'One day, a Friday it was, Amelia and I were sitting together in the flower room of the hotel, arranging daffodils for the restaurant tables. Cat was playing on the steps in the spring sunshine. Suddenly Amelia looked at me in the most peculiar way, and she told me she had made a will. "It's all for you and Cat, Meri. I've no one else to leave all this to, and besides, Catherine is a Silver. The last of the Silvers, until she grows up and has a Silver of her own. So all this belongs to the child, Jack's child. *You* must keep it safe for her. I trust you to do the right thing; you're smart, Meri. If you ever have to sell the inn for any reason, then do so. Or rent it out, if running it gets to be too much for you. But keep the land, keep the Silver Lake property, no matter what. It is already worth millions, and can only increase in value. That's what Jack would want you to do, Meri, he'd want you to keep the land. It's belonged to the Silvers for almost two hundred years." As you can probably imagine, I was stunned, Dr Benson. Aghast that she knew Catherine was Jack's child.

'Once I'd recovered from my surprise, I asked

Amelia how she had guessed about the baby, and she gave me that weird look again and said, "But I've always known, Meri, since the day you became pregnant." I suppose I must have looked extremely baffled, and so she went on to explain. "Jack told me, Meri dear," she said, and then took hold of my hand, held it tightly in hers. "He loved me from childhood, but he loved you, too, and he needed you desperately, Meri. He was a virile young man, full of passion. I was of no use to him as a woman any more, not after my accident. He never looked at another woman and for years he was celibate, until you came here. He fell for you, Meri. And once you were pregnant he wanted the child, oh how he wanted it, my darling. And I've never begrudged the relationship he had with you. I knew he would never hurt me or leave me. And I also knew you would always be loyal to me. I loved Jack so much, Meri, and I love you and the baby, too. She's like my child." And she meant every word, Dr Benson, Amelia always spoke the truth.'

Meredith fell silent again. Remembering that particular day with Amelia, so long ago now, still affected her deeply. Her eyes were bright with tears when she eventually focused her gaze on the psychiatrist. 'Amelia died later that year – 1974 – and she made me a wealthy woman and Cat an heiress. She did leave us everything, and there was so much more than the Silver Lake Inn and the land. There was her own estate, which she had inherited from her mother. She made a few bequests – to Pete O'Brien, who had run the property for years, and his wife Blanche, and other people who worked at the inn. But the bulk of the

Silver estate and her own inheritance came to us. And yet I would have given it all up just to have Amelia back. I longed for her, grieved for her for years. And I also grieved for Jack.'

'It's a most unusual story, very moving,' Hilary said, her voice low, compassionate. She had noted Meredith's emotions a moment before, and she fully understood how much Meredith had cared for the couple. It was on the tip of her tongue to ask Meredith if she thought the Silvers had used her as a surrogate, and then she instantly changed her mind. In her heart of hearts, Hilary knew this was not the case. She believed that Meredith had told her the story of her life with the Silvers exactly the way it had happened. Her words had the ring of truth to them. She might well be lying about other parts of her life, but not about these particular years.

There was a carafe of water on a console table nearby, and Meredith rose, went to pour herself a glass. Turning to look at Hilary, she murmured, 'I am convinced my attacks of fatigue have nothing to do with my early years in Connecticut. I was very happy with the Silvers, they were very good to me.'

'I know,' Hilary replied. 'And I think you are right. The attacks are not related to that time at all. So we must dig deeper, go further back. But I don't know when we can do this. Unless you come in for another session before you leave for London and Paris. That would give us a start, at least.'

Meredith hesitated momentarily, and then she made a decision. 'All right,' she said, 'I'll come tomorrow afternoon, if you can fit me in.'

'Let me check my other appointments with my secretary,' Hilary responded, pressing the button of the intercom.

That night Meredith dreamed the dream of her childhood again.

After a light supper she had gone to bed early.

She had a number of important appointments the next morning, and she also wanted to clear her desk before her afternoon session with Hilary Benson.

Almost immediately she fell into a sound sleep, and it was a dreamless sleep for most of the night. Then just as dawn was breaking she awakened with a start and sat bolt-upright in bed. Her face, neck and chest were covered with beads of sweat and she was filled with apprehension.

Snapping on the light, she glanced around the room, and then she lay back against the pillows. After a moment, she reached for a tissue on the bedside table, wiped her neck and face, and then crumpled the damp tissue in a ball in her hand.

She had just had that awful dream again, and as always it alarmed her. She focused on it, remembering.

She was alone in the vast, parched landscape. She was looking for the little girl and boy. But she could not find them. They had disappeared, had fallen through a giant crack in the earth's surface. She had seen them dropping away, and she was afraid for them. Now she must find them again. They knew. They knew the answer to the secret.

She walked and walked, her eyes scanning the landscape. Just as she gave up hope of ever finding them again they appeared at the edge of the dried mud flats. She was so happy she had found them. The boy took off his school cap and waved it in the air. Suddenly they were all together, the three of them holding hands, walking across the vast and arid landscape towards the far horizon. Now she was dressed like the little girl. She wore a dark coat, a long striped scarf around her neck and a beret on her head. They all had giant labels on their coats. Luggage labels. She peered at the little girl's label. The writing was smudged from the rain. She could not read the name. Or the name of the boy. She looked down at her own luggage label. This too was indistinct. What was her name? She did not know.

Ahead of them was the great ship. It was so huge it loomed up high on the docks. The little girl was afraid. She did not want to go on the ship. She began to cry. The boy cried and so did she. None of them wanted to go on board. Tears rolled down their cheeks. It was so cold the tears froze on their skin. It began to snow.

The sea was like black oil. They were afraid, terrified. They clung to each other, weeping. They were led off the ship. They had reached their destination. It was the grey cracked landscape where nothing grew. The sky was very blue; the sun blistering. They walked and walked. There were many, many children, all walking until they came to the black sea once more. And they all walked into the sea. She pulled back; she would not move. She tried to stop the little girl from walking into the sea, walking to her doom. But she could not. The girl moved away from her, and so did the boy. Together the two of them walked into the sea. She tried to shout at them to stop. But no words came out of her mouth. She was alone again on the mud flats. And she was afraid. They knew the answer to the secret. She did not. Now they had gone. Forever. She would never know.

This time the dream had been different, Meredith realized that as she examined every detail of it. She wondered what it meant; she had no idea. But she now resolved to tell Hilary Benson about it. Perhaps the psychiatrist would have an explanation for her.

'There's something I haven't told you,' Meredith said to Dr Benson later that afternoon.

Hilary looked at her alertly. 'Oh, and what is that, Meredith?'

'It's something to do with my attacks. At least, I think that's so. Certainly it started again after my second attack.'

'What started again?'

'The dream. A nightmare, in fact. I've had it on and off for years.'

'How many years?' Hilary asked, leaning forward over the desk, scrutinizing her patient intently.

'For as long as I can remember. Since I was about twelve, thirteen, perhaps even a few years younger. The dream stopped when I first came to Connecticut. In fact, I only had it once in the early years there, when I first started working for Jack and Amelia at the inn. Then it occurred a couple of times in my twenties, again in my thirties. But I hadn't had it since then until January of this year.'

'And the dream occurred after you had an attack of fatigue?'

'Yes. I was in the Loire Valley, staying with a friend. I suddenly felt ill that afternoon and I went upstairs to rest in my room. I fell asleep, I was so tired. And I had the dream. When I awakened I was startled that it had come back after so many years, and also that I felt the same way.'

'How did you feel?'

'Frightened, alarmed.'

'Try to recount the dream for me, please, Meredith.'

Meredith nodded and did as the psychiatrist asked. Then she explained that the dream had differed slightly each time she had had it in the last few months.

'So last night in the dream you were finally reunited with the boy and the girl in the arid landscape,' Hilary said. 'Was there anything else? Anything different?'

'Yes. There was the ship in the dream . . .' Meredith left her sentence unfinished, snapped her eyes shut.

'Are you all right?' Hilary asked.

'Yes, I'm fine,' she answered, instantly opening her eyes. 'Dr Benson?'

'Yes?'

'What do dreams mean?'

'I think they are usually manifestations of impressions we store in our subconscious. Then again, sometimes what truly frightens a person can come to the fore in sleep, when the unconscious rises. I personally think that we dream our memories, and also dream our terrors, Meredith.'

'So what do you think my recurring nightmare means?'

'I'm not certain. Only by talking, exploring a little more can we eventually come to some interpretation of it.'

Meredith took a deep breath. Unexpectedly and inexplicably she felt as if she were choking. Agitation took hold of her. She had to get out of here; she needed air. She stood up, then sat down again abruptly. She thought she was going to open her mouth and start screaming. She compressed her lips, striving for control.

Hilary Benson frowned, stared at her. She realized that Meredith, who had always appeared the calmest of women, was suffering from acute agitation. She was twisting her hands together anxiously, and her eyes had opened wide.

'You're suddenly extremely upset. What is it, Meredith?'

Meredith said nothing; she began to shake visibly, and she wrapped her arms around her body, hugged herself.

Hilary Benson jumped up, went to her, put a hand on her shoulder comfortingly.

Meredith gaped at Hilary. Her eyes filled with tears. 'I've not told you the truth . . . not told anyone . . . not ever . . .'

Hilary hurried to her desk, picked up the phone and spoke to her secretary. 'I can't see any other patients at the moment, Janice. Please reschedule them for another day. I have an emergency with Mrs Stratton.'

Walking back to Meredith, who was bent double in

the chair, rocking back and forth, the psychiatrist took hold of her arm, forced her upright.

'Come to the sofa, Meredith, sit with me. You're going to tell me everything. Slowly, in your own time. There's no hurry.' She had spoken softly, sympathetically, and Meredith allowed herself to be led to the sofa.

The two women sat down.

There was a long silence.

Finally, Meredith began to speak in a low voice. 'I don't know who I am. Or where I come from. I don't know who my parents were. Or my real name. I have no identity. I invented myself. I made my own rules and I lived by them. I had no one to teach me. No one to love me. I was completely alone. Until I met the Silvers. For seventeen years I was a lost soul. I'm still a lost soul in some ways. Help me . . . Oh God. *Who am I?* Where do I come from? Who gave birth to me?'

Meredith was weeping, the tears gushing out of her eyes and falling down onto her hands. She was in an agony of despair, and she started to rock back and forth again.

Hilary Benson let Meredith weep. She said nothing, did nothing, and presently the tears stopped. She handed Meredith a box of tissues in silence. Then she walked over to the console, poured a glass of water and brought it to her patient.

Meredith took it from her, sipped the water, and said, after a moment, 'I'm sorry for my outburst.'

'I'm not, and you shouldn't be either. You should be glad. It's done you good, I'm sure of that. And it is the first step towards your recovery. Whenever you are ready to start talking again, I am here to listen. Don't rush . . . the rest of the day is for you. The evening too, if that is necessary, Meredith.'

'Thank you. Yes . . . yes . . . I must tell you . . .' Meredith now took a deep breath and began:

'I grew up in an orphanage in Sydney. I was eight years old when Gerald and Merle Stratton adopted me. She didn't like my name, so she called me Meredith. They weren't very nice. Cold, hard-hearted people. They treated me like a maid. I did all the housework early in the morning and after school at night. I was only eight. They didn't really mistreat me, but he thought nothing of hitting me. She was mean, too, and stingy – with food especially. I grew to hate them. I wanted to go back to the orphanage. Then they were killed in a car crash when I was ten. His sister Mercedes didn't want me. She sent me back to the orphanage. I was there until I was fifteen. I only saw Mercedes once again, when she helped me get my passport. She was glad I was leaving with the Paulsons.'

Meredith stopped, leaned against the sofa cushions and closed her eyes. She took several deep breaths to steady herself. After a short time she opened her eyes and looked directly at Hilary. She began to tremble.

The psychiatrist took hold of her hand, asked softly in a gentle voice, 'Was there any sexual abuse when you were living with the Strattons? Did either of them abuse you?'

'No, there was never anything like that. They didn't sexually molest me. There was just this awful coldness and indifference, as if I wasn't there. I was only there to be their maid, that's what I thought then. I still think it. I was relieved when they were killed. They never showed me one iota of affection. I had always thought that when I got adopted somebody was going to love me at last. But no one did.'

A bleak look crossed her face, hurt shadowed her eyes, and when she spoke pain echoed in her voice. 'I can never begin to explain to you the horror of being in an orphanage. Nobody cares a thing about you . . . never to be touched, or held, or shown any love. I never knew why I was there. I worried a lot about that. I thought I'd been put there by my parents because I'd been bad. I didn't understand. All I wanted was to find out who my parents were. I never did. Nobody told me anything, they never answered my questions . . .'

'What is your earliest memory, Meredith? Close your eyes, relax, try to go back in time, try to focus on your youngest years. What do you see? What do you remember?'

After a while Meredith spoke. She said in a quiet voice, 'I see a river. But that's all.' She opened her eyes. 'Perhaps that's why I like living near water.'

'How old were you when you went to the orphanage?'

'I don't know, Dr Benson, I was always there.'

'From being a baby?'

'Yes. No. No, I don't think so. In my nightmare last night there was the ship. When I was a very little girl I used to remember being on a ship.'

'Do you mean a ship or a boat? There's a difference.'

Meredith closed her eyes again, pushing her

memory back to her childhood. She saw herself in her mind's eye; she saw boys and girls going up a gangplank. She was one of them. She saw sailors, seamen, docks. She saw a flagpole. The Union Jack flying atop it.

Meredith sat up straighter, opened her eyes and looked at Hilary intently. 'I do mean a ship and not a boat. And an ocean-going ship, too. A British ship, flying a British flag. I *must* have been on a ship, perhaps with other children. Maybe that explains the children who are always in the dream.'

'It's possible. Please try and think harder, think back. Could you have been born in England and taken to Australia when very young?'

'Maybe I was. But why don't I remember anything about it? Why don't I remember those years?'

'It's called repressed memory, Meredith. I believe something terrible happened to you when you were a small child, causing deep trauma which resulted in repressed memory. In fact, I'm pretty positive that's what you're suffering from, and I believe it's the reason for your attacks of fatigue. Psychogenic fatigue.'

'But why now? Why haven't I had the attacks in the past? Why not years ago?'

'Because the memory stayed deeply buried. That was the way you wanted it. So that you could function. Now something has triggered it. The repressed memory is trying to surface.'

'What do you think triggered it?'

'I can't be absolutely certain, but I believe it was your visit to Fountains Abbey.'

'You *do* think I was there before?'

'Possibly. Most probably. It would certainly explain a great deal.'

'Is there any other way you can trigger my repressed memory, Dr Benson?'

'Only you can do it really, by endeavouring to go back in time to your earliest childhood years. You're going to England next week. Something else might give your memory a good jolt whilst you are there. In the meantime, let us talk a little longer about your years in the orphanage.'

Meredith shivered violently and threw Hilary a look of horror. 'No child should ever have to live like that,' she exclaimed, anger surfacing. 'But I'll tell you more about it if you want me to.'

'I do. I realize how painful it is for you, but it may well give me more clues, something else to go on, Meredith.'

Later that night she rang Luc. She could no longer bear to keep the secret of her past from him. Also, she felt the need to confide, share, and in turn receive comfort from him.

Twenty

Catherine Stratton sat back and studied the illustration on her drawing board, her head held on one side, her eyes narrowed slightly as she assessed her work.

The watercolour in front of her was of a small boy curled up in a crib sleeping, with one hand tucked under his cheek. She smiled to herself, liking its innocence, its charm. It was perfect for the last poem in the children's book of verse she had been illustrating for the past few weeks. Now, at last, it was finished and ready to go to the publishers.

Work well done, she thought, taking up a fine-nibbed pen, signing *Cat* with a flourish. She had always used her diminutive on her work, and it was a signature that was becoming well-known these days.

Sliding down off the tall stool, she lifted her arms above her head, did a few stretching exercises, and then walked across her studio and out into the main loft space, heading for the kitchen.

This was a good size, decorated in a crisp blue-and-white colour scheme, and it was equipped with all the latest appliances. It was the perfect kitchen for a dedicated chef, which Catherine was. She had loved cooking since childhood, had been encouraged and taught by her mother and Blanche O'Brien, at Silver Lake, who had always been like a favourite cuddly aunt.

Catherine stood washing her hands at the sink under the window which looked uptown. It offered a unique view of the Chrysler and Empire State buildings. This afternoon those towering skyscrapers sparkled against the blue April sky, and she thought they had never looked better than on this lovely spring day. Except perhaps at night when they were fully illuminated, their glittering spires etched against the dark sky. To Catherine they would always typify Manhattan.

Reaching for the kettle, she filled it and put it on to boil. Then she busied herself with cups and saucers, took out various items from the refrigerator, and started to make a selection of small tea sandwiches.

Catherine and her mother had designed her SoHo loft. Her studio was at one end, with big windows and a skylight in the sloping roof; the dining area flowed off the kitchen, and beyond there was a large living room decorated like a library. Two bedrooms were situated to the right of the living room, and each had its own bathroom.

It was a vast loft, cleverly divided to maximize the space and the light and it had a pristine, airy feeling. This was not only due to its grand size and many windows, but the pale colour schemes used throughout.

The loft had been Catherine's twenty-first-birthday present four years ago. 'But it's not from me, you know,' her mother had told her. 'It's from Jack and

Amelia in a sense, even though they're dead. I bought it for you with money from their estate.'

It was then that Meredith had fully explained about Amelia's will, the vast inheritance that was now hers along with Silver Lake Inn, the house she had grown up in, and all of the Silver land: 150 acres. All of this had been held in trust for her by her mother ever since Amelia's death; Meredith had effectively increased its value through clever investing of the money Amelia had left. Catherine had suddenly understood that day four years ago that she was an heiress, and a very lucky young woman.

Catherine had always known that Jack Silver was her father. Her mother had told her the truth when she was old enough to understand. She barely remembered him and even Amelia was a shadowy figure in her mind. Her mother had always been the dominant person in her life, and she adored Meredith.

Catherine had never judged Meredith and Jack. She was far too intelligent to do that, and mature enough to realize that no one else ever knew exactly what went on between two people. Three in this case, for obviously Amelia had acquiesced, or had perhaps turned a blind eye to their relationship.

Once, when she had questioned Blanche O'Brien, Blanche had said that she shouldn't waste time dwelling on that old situation. 'Nobody got hurt, everybody was happy, they all three loved each other, and you were the crowning point in their lives. They adored you, and Amelia behaved like a second mother to you.'

Sometimes she wondered about her mother's past; she understood many things about it, even though

Meredith had always been somewhat secretive about her early years in Australia. It seemed to her that her mother only started to live her life when she came to Connecticut.

From odd things her mother had said over the years, Catherine knew that her childhood had been terrible – bleak, without love, or even the merest hint of affection.

Meredith had loved Jon and her with a sort of terrible fury, single-mindedly, with total devotion, to the exclusion of anyone else.

Perhaps this was because of the deprivation Meredith had endured as a child. Certainly it had always seemed to Catherine that her mother had set out to give them all of the things she herself had never had, and much, much more.

Meredith had always been the most wonderful mother, probably to the detriment of her relationship with David Layton, Jon's father. She and her brother had always come first with Meredith, and perhaps he had grown tired and resentful of taking second place in her life and her affections.

That marriage had floundered after four years, and within no time at all, David, the country lawyer, had moved to the West Coast. Much to their amazement he had turned himself into a hot-shot show-business lawyer with a string of famous movie-star clients. They had never seen him again, heard only infrequently, and not at all after the first year or so. Not that her brother or she cared. Jon had always loved his mother the most, and anyway, David Layton had not been much of a father, or stepfather, for that matter.

Meredith was her best friend. She had not only given her a great deal of love and been supportive, she had encouraged her to chase her dreams and fulfil her ambitions. In fact, she had been instrumental in helping her to do this. And she had been exactly the same with Jon, always there for him, advising him when he asked, rooting for him, cheering him on. Meredith had been mother and father to them both.

She and her brother were delighted that their mother had met Luc de Montboucher. They had taken to him immediately, and had encouraged their mother in this relationship.

They thought he was the perfect man for her, and Jon was convinced they would get married. She hoped her brother was correct in this conviction. Nothing would please her more than to see Meredith in a happy relationship, especially now that she herself was getting married. She hated to think of her mother alone. It was about time she had some personal happiness in her life.

Luc had been to New York a number of times, and her mother was virtually commuting to Paris, and this seemed to bode well for the future. Also, she had put the Vermont inn up for sale, and had confided, only the other day, that she was not looking to make a big profit. 'I just want to get out unscathed financially,' Meredith had said. 'Fortunately, I've several potential buyers.'

When Catherine had told Jon about this conversation he had grinned and said, 'See, I told you so! Mom's going to marry Luc and move to France, or at least spend most of her time there. Just you wait and see, Cat.'

Her mother was leaving for Europe tonight, first stop London. She had business with Patsy, but she was planning to spend time in France.

Catherine covered the plate of tea sandwiches with a dampened linen napkin, the way Blanche had taught her as a child, and pushed the plate to a corner of the countertop; then she rinsed the strawberries and hulled them.

Her mind was still on her mother. She had been seeing a psychiatrist for the past few weeks, trying to discover why she had these peculiar attacks of fatigue. Over the weekend they had talked on the phone, and Meredith had said that Dr Benson was helping her to unearth repressed memories of her childhood. Finally she believed she was getting somewhere, making headway.

Catherine hoped so. All she wanted was for her mother to come to terms with her past, gain peace of mind, as well as a bit of happiness for once. After all, she was going to be forty-five years old next month.

'Everything looks beautiful, darling,' Meredith said an hour later, as she walked into the loft, glancing around. 'You've added a few things since I was here last. That painting over there, the lamp, the sculpture in the corner.' Meredith nodded approvingly. 'You've given it a wonderful look. It really works.'

'Thanks, Mom. Like mother like daughter, I guess. I take after you, you know, always fiddling with rooms, adding accessories and stuff. I'm a real "nester", just as you are.'

'Am I really?' Meredith said, sounding surprised, giving her daughter a quick glance. 'I hadn't realized.'

Bursting into laughter, Catherine exclaimed, 'Oh Mom, honestly, how can you say that! You can walk into the dreariest room, anywhere in the world, and transform it in a couple of hours, just by adding flowers, a bowl of fruit, a few cushions and photographs, magazines and books. Other bits and pieces. You've got a real talent that way. To coin a phrase, you make wonderful *havens*, Mom.'

Meredith had the good grace to laugh.

'Your company is aptly named, I've always thought.'

'I suppose it is.' Meredith sat down on the sofa, and continued, 'I'm glad I can spend a couple of hours with you before I catch the night flight to London; we don't see enough of each other these days. And perhaps we can talk about the wedding a little, come to a few decisions.'

'Yes, we can, Mom. Keith and I batted a few dates around this past weekend, and I think we'd like to have the wedding in the autumn, as you suggested.'

Meredith's face lit up. 'That's wonderful, Cat, the perfect time. I suppose you're thinking of early October, just as the leaves begin to turn?'

Catherine nodded. 'The second Saturday in October, that would be the fourteenth. Originally, Keith and I toyed with the first Saturday in the month, the seventh. But we weren't sure whether the foliage would have changed by then. What do you think?'

'Better go for the second Saturday, Catherine. The leaves will be in full colour, and they don't drop that quickly, remember. I'm assuming you're going to have the ceremony at Silver Lake?'

'Yes. Briefly, and only briefly, Keith and I had talked about the little church in Cornwall, but in the end we came to the conclusion that it's too small.' Catherine grinned at her mother. 'All those Pearsons, you know.'

Meredith smiled. 'From the sound of it, I'm going to be giving you a very big wedding.'

'Do you mind, Mom?'

'Oh darling, of course not! I'm thrilled. That's what I've always wanted for you, a big white wedding with all the trimmings. Anyway, getting back to the details, I think you'd better call the minister of the church in Cornwall, to make sure he will be able to officiate at the marriage, that he's available that day.'

'Yes, I'll do it tomorrow.' Catherine rose. 'Mom, I want to show you the sketches of my wedding gown. Let me get them, they're in the studio.'

A moment later she was back, sitting down next to Meredith on the sofa. The two of them pored over the series of drawings Cat had done; all were beautifully rendered and showed the gown from different angles.

'What do you think, Mom?' Catherine asked, eyeing her mother worriedly. 'You're not saying anything. Don't you like it?'

'It's absolutely beautiful, Cat. Very ... *medieval*, wouldn't you say?'

'In a way. But perhaps a bit more Tudor in feeling, Elizabethan. I've spent a lot of time on the design, Mother, and on the details in particular.'

'I can see it's quite elaborate.' Meredith stared at the sketch she was holding, which was a front view of the dress, and nodded her head. 'Yes, I see what you mean about it being Elizabethan . . . the squared-off neck, cut very near the edge of the shoulders, the long puffed-up sleeves, tight bodice and bouffant skirt. Very stylish, Cat; all you need is a white ruff.'

'Don't think I hadn't thought of it,' Cat laughed. 'Because I have, but I decided that might be going a bit too far. The veil will be held by a Tudor-style headdress, and this will fall into a train. I've yet to design the headdress. So, what do you think? Can I get away with it?'

'Of course you can, Cat, you will carry it off very well. I think you'll look stunning. Have you decided who's going to make it?'

'I thought I'd go to Edetta; she's created some lovely evening gowns for us in the past few years.'

'Yes, she has, and I'm sure she'll be able to find the right kind of white silk for you. Now, to move on to a few other details, do you know what time of day you want to have the marriage ceremony?'

'Keith and I thought it would be nice to have it at noon. Drinks first, then the ceremony, and a luncheon afterwards. With dancing.' Cat lifted a dark brow. 'Would that be all right?'

'Yes, I think that's a lovely idea, Cat. If I'm going to give you a big wedding we might as well do it in style. Do you know how many guests you'll be inviting?'

'I think the total will be around a hundred and thirty, or thereabouts. Keith and I counted about eighty, maybe ninety, from the Pearson side, and I figured around fifty from our side.'

Meredith laughed. 'I'm not sure that we can even rustle up that number, honey.'

'Oh we can, Mom, really we can. There are all my girlfriends and their husbands or boyfriends. Blanche and Pete. Some of the new friends I've made in the publishing world, the people from Havens, and Patsy will come from London, I'm certain of that.'

'She's already said she's coming. And there will be Agnes and Alain D'Auberville from Paris. Yes, I think you're right, we probably will be about fifty.'

'Luc will come, won't he, Mother?'

'I hope so.'

'Keith and I like him. So does Jon.'

'Oh I know. Your brother's made that only too clear.'

'Mom?'

'Yes, darling?'

'Luc loves you.'

'I know.'

'Do you love him?'

'Yes, Cat, I do.'

'So what's going to happen?'

'Are you and your brother in collusion?'

'What do you mean?'

'He was asking me the same thing, after your engagement party a few weeks ago. And to answer your question, I don't know what's going to happen. Being in love is one thing, getting married another. And there's so much to consider in my case.'

'I know, but you will work it out. You're both smart.' Catherine jumped up. 'I'm glad you came to see me at this time of day. I've made us a lovely tea . . . like you used to do when we were little. A nursery tea you called it. I've prepared all sorts of tiny tea sandwiches, cakes, the works, actually. I'll just go and boil the water again. Be back in a jiffy . . .' Cat winked at her mother, laughed, and added, 'Before you can say Jack Robinson,' and hurried off in the direction of the kitchen.

Meredith smiled and leaned back against the sofa, thinking about Luc. She would be seeing him soon, once she had completed her business in England. There were certain matters at the London office of Havens to attend to, and she and Patsy had to make a trip to Ripon. The refurbishing of Skell Garth House was almost finished, and they had various things to do before the inn reopened in May. She would then fly to Paris and base herself there, since she had much work to complete on the manor in Montfort-L'Amaury. Good progress was being made there, thanks to Luc and Agnes. Once she was in France she would spend weekends at Talcy with Luc, and they were both looking forward to this.

She wondered what she would do, if he did ask her to marry him. Jon and Cat thought it was all so simple, but in reality her life was rather complicated. She lived in America, he lived in France, and they both had businesses, commitments, responsibilities. She couldn't very well walk away from Havens Incorporated, and certainly Luc would never give up his architectural practice in Paris. Nor did she expect him to. So how could they ever work it out . . .

'Mom, let's have tea in here,' Catherine called from

the archway leading into the dining area. 'It's so much easier.'

'I'll be right there,' Meredith said, pushed herself up off the sofa, and went to join her daughter. 'How nice it looks,' she said a moment later as she surveyed Catherine's handiwork.

'Thanks. Sit here, Mom.' Cat indicated a chair, took the one opposite, picked up the teapot, and poured. 'Now, here's this lovely cup of tea, Mother, just the way you like it, and help yourself to some sandwiches. There's cucumber, tomato, egg salad, and ham. Tiny ones but tasty.'

'I remember our nursery teas,' Meredith said, taking a minuscule cucumber sandwich. 'They *were* fun, weren't they?'

Catherine nodded as she munched on a sandwich. After a moment she said, 'I tried to get scones today, but no luck. My local bakery sometimes has them. I was hoping to give you warm scones with clotted cream and strawberry jam.'

'Thoughtful of you, darling, but this is fine. Not too fattening,' Meredith replied with a dry laugh.

Catherine eyed her mother. '*You* don't have to worry, Mom, you look wonderful.'

'Thank you.'

Catherine stood up. 'I won't be a minute, I've got to get something from the kitchen.'

When she returned to the table Catherine was carrying a glass bowl and a jug. She stood there, smiling at her mother, her bright blue eyes full of love.

'I have a treat for you, Mom. *Strawberries*. Your favourite.'

Meredith stared at Cat.

She felt herself go cold all over.

And then she heard a voice echoing in her head, faintly, as if it came from a very long distance. *'Mari . . . Mari.'*

A moment later the same voice was calling, once again echoing in Meredith's head. *'Mari . . . Come on. Come in.'*

A scene flashed.

In her mind's eye she saw a young woman with sparkling blue eyes and red-gold hair bending over a small child, her expression loving. *'Strawberries, Mari. A special treat.'* The child beamed at the mother. It was such a happy scene; there was such love on the mother's face. Then she heard the child crying. *'Mam, Mam, what's wrong?'*

The scene faded.

Meredith felt icy cold. She stared at Catherine. For a moment she was unable to say anything.

Catherine, who had been looking at her mother intently, now asked in a concerned voice, 'What's the matter? Don't you feel well? You've gone awfully white, Mom.'

'I'm fine,' Meredith managed to say. She shook her head. 'I think I've just had what Dr Benson would call a flashback. My first.'

'What exactly is it?'

'It's a memory, really, usually a repressed memory coming to the surface. I believe I just had one from my childhood. I saw a young woman of about your age, with bright blue eyes like you, and a small child. Maybe a five-year-old. At first the scene was happy, then suddenly the child was crying. It faded away.'

Meredith took several deep breaths. 'I think I had a memory of my mother and me. My biological mother, Cat.'

'Why do you think you had this flashback all of a sudden?' Catherine asked curiously, sitting down in the chair, her eyes pinned on Meredith's face.

'I believe you triggered it. It was the way you said *strawberries*, then mentioned *special treat*. And it was your eyes, Cat, so blue, so full of love.'

Meredith paused, shook her head. 'Jack had very blue eyes, and I always thought you had inherited yours from your father. But perhaps they're my mother's eyes.'

Catherine reached out, took hold of Meredith's hand resting on the table. 'Oh Mom, this is wonderful.' She felt her throat tighten, and she said in an emotional voice, 'Maybe you'll keep remembering more and more until you know everything about your past.'

'I hope so, darling.' Meredith bit her lip. 'Perhaps I ought to call Hilary Benson, tell her about this. She would want to know.' Glancing at her watch, she went on, 'It's just turned six o'clock. I'm sure she's still at the office.'

'Yes, call her,' Catherine exclaimed, getting up. 'The phone in the kitchen is the nearest.'

Meredith nodded and followed her daughter, then quickly dialled the psychiatrist's number from the wall phone. 'May I speak to Dr Benson please, Janice?' she said when the secretary came on the line.

'Who's calling?'

'It's Mrs Stratton.'

'Oh, hello, Mrs Stratton. I'll put you through right away.'

'Good evening, Meredith,' Hilary Benson greeted her a split second later. 'How are you?'

'I'm good. As you know, I'm going to London tonight. I stopped off to have tea with my daughter this afternoon, and she said something that triggered a memory. I think I've just had my first real flashback.'

'This is very good news, Meredith. Very good indeed. What exactly did you remember?'

Meredith recounted the flashback in every detail.

When she had finished, the psychiatrist exclaimed, 'This is your first significant memory, a true breakthrough, and I think it's just the beginning. You may find you have more in the next few days. That frequently happens. Try to focus on some of the details you've just mentioned to me, they might lead you into a whole series of significant memories.'

'I hope so. I'd really love to unearth the mystery of my early years.'

'You will, Meredith, I'm quite certain of that. If you have the need to call me, don't hesitate to do so. And I'll see you in a few weeks.'

'Yes, and thank you, Dr Benson. Goodbye.' Meredith hung up the receiver, turned around to face Catherine, who was standing in the doorway, an expectant look on her face.

'What did she say?' Catherine asked.

'That it was a significant memory, and that I'll probably have more now.'

'Oh Mom!' Catherine hurried into the kitchen, wrapped her arms around Meredith and held her close. 'I love you so much, Mother, I just want you to have peace of mind. And some happiness in your life finally.'

Twenty-one

Patsy Canton had been listening attentively to Meredith for the past hour.

Now she said in a low, thoughtful voice, 'So what you're saying to me, in essence, is that you believe you were born in England and then taken to Australia as a child.'

Meredith nodded. 'Exactly. I think I must've been about six years old.'

'And you went alone? That can't be so. You must've been with your parents.'

'I'm pretty sure I went alone, Patsy. I'm convinced my mother was dead by then.'

'No father?'

'I don't remember him.'

'But why would you go *alone*? That seems awfully strange to me. And who sent you?'

'I don't know.' Meredith gave a light shrug of her shoulders. 'I truly don't have the slightest idea.'

'In your recurring dream, there are children . . . could you have been sent with other children, perhaps? You know, the way evacuees were sent in groups to safe places during the Second World War.'

'Maybe. But *why*? There wasn't a war on in 1957,

when I was six years old, so why was I sent away? Exiled from England?'

Patsy shook her head. 'I haven't a clue, my darling. I want to help you, but I don't know how I possibly can. I'm as baffled as you.'

Meredith sighed and took a sip of water. She leaned back in the chair, glancing around the restaurant in Claridge's, and continued quietly, 'Last night on the plane, I couldn't sleep. I suppose I dozed off and on, but mostly my mind was racing, trying to remember things.'

'And did you?'

'A couple of things came back to me. The first has to do with my name. I was called Mary Anderson in the orphanage in Sydney. It was Merle Stratton who changed my name to Meredith. And of course I took their surname when they adopted me. But I was never Mary – what I mean is, that wasn't *my* name, even though they called me Mary at the orphanage. My real name is Mari, and my last name is Sanderson.'

'I see. So how did it get changed?' Patsy shook her head and exclaimed in a dismayed voice, 'Oh God, bureaucracy! Do save me from it. Your name probably got muddled up by some idiot at the orphanage.'

'That's exactly what happened, I think. I had this memory on the plane last night. It was of a woman, a rather stern one, who told me that my name wasn't Mari with an *i*, but Mary with a *y*. I kept telling her that I was called Marigold, but she wouldn't believe me. She scoffed and said that it wasn't a child's name, but the name of a flower.'

'There are some bloody awful people running these

institutions. It's just terrible what goes on in this world. Despicable.' Patsy sighed heavily, and gave Meredith a sympathetic look. 'So Marigold was your first name, and I suppose they also managed to get Anderson and Sanderson confused.'

'Yes,' Meredith replied. 'And this confusion about my name might well explain the luggage labels in the dream.'

'Absolutely,' Patsy cried. '*Brilliant*, darling.'

There was a small silence between them. Eventually, Meredith looked at Patsy earnestly, and said, 'My mother's name was Kate – I've remembered that. And I know she's dead, so there's no possibility of my meeting her. But now I've remembered her at last, after all these years, I need to do something. For myself. I need closure. And so I would like to visit her grave, at least. See it, take flowers, be with her there. That would truly help me. And perhaps I'll start feeling better, and maybe – hopefully – the attacks of psychogenic fatigue will go away.'

'I'm sure you *would* feel much better, Meredith. And I really understand your need . . . visiting her grave will give you solace, in a way.'

'At least I'd finally know she really did exist, and that she isn't a figment of my imagination. The only thing is, I don't know where she's buried. I've remembered her name, but I can't remember where we lived.'

'Yorkshire,' Patsy announced after only a moment's thought. 'I'm positive. And certainly it would explain the experience you had at Fountains Abbey. That's always seemed rather significant to me. I haven't forgotten the way you explained it that day: you had a very strong reaction to the abbey. You must have gone there as a child.'

'I agree. But I have a feeling I didn't grow up in that area. I remembered something else . . . being taken into a city. On a bus. It was a very big city, bustling, with lots of people milling around. There was a large square in the centre, with black statues. My mother used to take me to this city to go to a market. It was huge, covered with a domed glass roof.'

'And they sold everything at stalls. Am I correct?'

'Yes, you are.'

Patsy nodded. 'Vegetables and fruit stalls, fish, meat, cakes, bread, clothes, furniture, crystal and china stalls. Men calling out to passersby to come and look, sample their wares. All of them doing a very loud verbal selling job. Do you remember that?'

'Oh yes, I do, Patsy! We used to stand and listen to them. They all had . . . different pitches for their goods.'

Patsy nodded. 'Leeds Market. It's very famous, and in Leeds City Square there are black statues of nymphs holding torches. There is also a statue of Edward, the Black Prince, on a horse. Both are lifesized. Does that ring a bell?'

'It does. Let's assume I do come from Leeds . . . how can I find out where my mother is buried? Who would know anything about Kate Sanderson thirty-eight years later?'

'*Somerset House*. Actually, it's no longer called that, they changed its name. Now it's St Catherine's House, but it's the right place for us to begin. It's the general register office of births, marriages and deaths, for the whole of Great Britain. It's a place of records, a mine of information, in fact.'

'Where is it?'

'Here in London, in Kingsway. It's a quick cab ride from here.'

'I must go there this afternoon.'

'Yes, you must, and I'll come with you, Meredith.'

An hour later Meredith and Patsy were at St Catherine's House in Kingsway. They walked through the glass doors and found themselves immediately in the actual records office itself. On all sides were stacks and stacks of ledgers lined up on shelves.

'It looks like a library,' Meredith said as she and Patsy walked up to the security desk.

After the security officer had checked their handbags, Patsy said to him, 'How do we go about finding the record of a death?'

The officer directed them to an inquiry desk at the far end of one of the long aisles of ledgers on the left. Five clerks were standing behind the inquiry desk, ready to be of assistance. Patsy and Meredith approached one of them, and Patsy repeated her question.

The young woman clerk handed Patsy a pamphlet. 'This tells you how to use the Public Search Room. It's simple enough. Records of deaths are bound in the black ledgers, stacked on the left. Births are bound in red, and they are on the right. Look for the year of death. You'll find there are four books for the four quarters in each year. And there are three volumes per quarter. These are alphabetical. A to F, G to O, and P to Z.'

Patsy thanked her and she and Meredith retraced their steps. Once they were back in the Public Search Room they headed for the black ledgers and found the year they wanted. Meredith took hold of the handle on the spine of the first ledger inscribed March 1957, P to Z, pulled it off the shelf and placed it on the book stand which ran the length of the aisle in front of the shelves. Opening it, she saw that it covered January to March.

'To save time, why don't you look at the quarter that follows on,' Meredith suggested. 'That would be April May, June.'

'Good idea,' Patsy said, and went to look for the appropriate ledger.

Meredith ran her finger slowly down the lists of Sandersons deceased through the first quarter of the year 1957. The name of Katharine Sanderson was not amongst them. Glancing at Patsy, she said, 'She's not listed in this book. How about yours?'

'Give me a minute or two, I haven't quite finished.'

Meredith returned the ledger to its shelf, pulled out the one covering July, August and September of 1957. Once again her mother's death was not shown; nor was her death recorded in the two volumes Patsy perused in quick succession.

'We've covered the whole year,' Patsy murmured to Meredith. 'Are you absolutely certain your mother died in 1957?'

'Yes. Well, I think so.'

'But how do you know this, Meredith? You said you had so little information about yourself. Do you actually remember her dying?'

'Not really. But I do know I went to the orphanage in Sydney when I was six years old.'

'You remember that, do you? Are you really sure? How do you know?'

'Because Merle Stratton told me. She once said to me that I'd been at the orphanage since I was six but they hadn't taught me much in two years.'

'All right, so you went there when you were six years old in 1957. But that doesn't mean your mother died that year. Maybe it was 1956, when you were five.'

'I don't think so . . . I know I was six. But let's look at the ledgers for 1956.'

'Good idea.' Patsy agreed.

An hour later Meredith and Patsy had searched the entire set of ledgers for the year 1956 and turned up nothing. Meredith looked at her friend and said quietly, 'This is a wild goose chase. Her death is just not listed.'

'Do you want to try some other years?'

'No, there's no point,' Meredith answered. 'Maybe I have made a mistake about the date, but we can't stay here all day, searching through endless ledgers. Come on, let's go.'

'No, wait a minute,' Patsy said. 'What if she died abroad?'

'My mother was never abroad.'

'Humour me, let's go and talk to one of the clerks. Just for a minute. Please, Meredith.'

'All right.'

When they got back to the inquiry desk, Patsy zeroed in on the young woman who had helped them earlier. 'We're looking for the record of a death, and we haven't been able to find it. Now, what if the person died abroad, that would mean it isn't listed, correct?'

The young woman shook her head. 'No, it would be listed. Wherever a British subject dies, the death is eventually recorded here. The information comes through all of the British embassies and consulates around the world.'

'I see.'

'It's really quite simple,' the clerk went on, looking from Patsy to Meredith. 'If a person's name is not in one of the registers, then that person is not dead. He or she is still alive.'

Meredith gaped at the clerk.

Patsy said, 'Thank you very much for your help,' and with a slight nod she turned away. She took hold of Meredith's arm, led her down the short flight of steps and along one of the aisles.

They stood in front of the glass doors opening onto the street, staring at each other.

Meredith looked stunned and she was slightly trembling.

Patsy, who was nobody's fool, understood all of the implications inherent in this unexpected knowledge, and she murmured, 'I know what you're thinking, darling.'

'I'm sure you do,' Meredith answered, her voice so low it was almost inaudible. 'If my mother's not dead, which according to those ledgers she isn't, then she's alive. Somewhere. In England probably.' Meredith paused, took a deep breath and clutched Patsy's arm. 'Why did she send me away when I was a little girl? Why in God's name was I sent to an orphanage in *Sydney*, of all places? The other side of the world. Why? *Why*, Patsy?'

Meredith's eyes were filled with misery and her face was so bleak Patsy's heart went out to her friend. For a moment she was speechless. She swallowed hard, and replied in a gentle voice, 'I don't know, Meredith, it doesn't make any sense to me.'

'She sent me away because she didn't want me.' After she had said these words Meredith was so shaken she went and leaned against the wall, biting her lip. For a moment she was floundering; her senses were swimming.

Patsy took charge. 'Listen to me, if your mother's alive, which she must be since there's no death certificate, then we are going to *find* her. Whatever it takes, we're going to do it. Come on, let's go back and look for your birth certificate.'

'Why?' Meredith asked miserably. 'What for?'

'We're going to get a copy of your birth certificate. If you *were* born in this country, as you think you were, and not Australia, then your birth will be registered in one of those red books.'

'How will my birth certificate help us to find my mother?'

'There's a lot of information given on a birth certificate, Meredith. I know from my own and my children's. The name of the father, his occupation. The married name of the mother, and her maiden name.

Place of birth of the child, residence of the parents, date and year of birth, obviously. We'll have enough to start with. Besides, I would have thought you'd like to have a copy of it . . . just for yourself, your own edification. And peace of mind.'

Meredith nodded but said nothing. She was reluctant to start a search for her birth certificate. What if it wasn't there? She would feel even worse than she already did.

Patsy coaxed her a little more, drew her slowly back to the aisles of ledgers. This time they went down the one on the right-hand side, where all of the red-bound books were stored. Fifteen minutes later she discovered that she *had* been born in Great Britain. Her birth *was* registered.

'You see, I knew you'd find your name in one of those lovely red books,' Patsy exclaimed, smiling at her, wanting to cheer her up. 'Now let's order a copy of the birth certificate. Maybe they will be able to have it ready for us later today.' Patsy pulled an order form out of the lucite pocket attached to the end of the reading stand, handed it to Meredith and said, 'Fill this in, and then we'll take it over there, to one of those windows, to order the copy.'

Meredith nodded and pulled out a pen. After completing the form they went to a window. She was able to get priority service for twenty pounds. The copy of her birth certificate would be ready at the same time the following day.

On Friday afternoon, promptly at four, Meredith and Patsy returned to St Catherine's House. Within minutes she was holding a copy of her birth certificate in her hands.

The two women went out into the street, got into the waiting taxi and headed back to Claridge's Hotel.

Settling back against the seat, they pored over the certificate. Meredith saw that her mother's full name was Katharine Spence Sanderson. Her father's name was Daniel Sanderson and his occupation was listed as accountant. Was it from him that she got her head for figures? she wondered. The address given for her place of birth was Three, Green Hill Road, Armley. Her parents' residence was listed as Hawthorne Cottage, Beck Lane, Armley, Leeds. Her date of birth was shown as the ninth of May, 1951, and her birth had been registered on the nineteenth of June by her mother. Her name *was* Marigold Sanderson.

'You know quite a lot about yourself now,' Patsy said, turning to Meredith, squeezing her arm affectionately.

'More than I've ever known, Patsy.' Meredith cleared her throat, and went on, 'I never had any sense of identity when I was young. Not knowing who you are and where you come from is very frightening. It's almost like being a non-person. Since I didn't have an identity, I invented myself.'

'Getting your birth certificate must mean a great deal to you.'

'It does. It's . . . well, it's a kind of validation of who I really am.' Meredith forced a small smile. 'At least I've been celebrating my birthday on the correct date. The orphanage did get that part right.'

'What are you going to do next? Oh, stupid, stupid

question, Patsy Canton.' Patsy looked at her intently. 'You're going to Leeds, of course.'

'Tomorrow, Patsy. We were going to Ripon on Sunday anyway, so I'm going to make it a day earlier.'

'I'll drive you.'

'But – '

'No buts,' Patsy exclaimed. 'For one thing, you need my help, my expertise. I know Leeds very well, and the rest of Yorkshire, and you're going to need a guide. Besides that, I care about you, Meredith. I wouldn't let you embark on a search like this alone. The whole situation is too emotionally fraught. You're going to look for a long-lost mother, and who knows what you're going to unearth in the process. You really do need a friend with you.'

'Especially a good and dear friend like you, Patsy. Thank you. Thank you for helping me.'

'We'll set off at the crack of dawn tomorrow, and get to Leeds in about two and a half hours. Maybe three. I think our first stop should be Hawthorne Cottage in Armley.'

'Do you know this place?'

'Oddly enough, I do. I had an uncle who owned a woollen mill there, and he lived in Farnley, which is nearby. Farnley Lee House, lovely old manor it was. Well, anyway, I used to go there with my parents, and we usually drove through Upper Armley to get to Farnley. Do you have any recollection of Hawthorne Cottage?'

'Vaguely. The cottage was near a river. There was wildlife on it . . . ducks, I think.'

'The more we talk, the more you'll remember, I'm

sure of that,' Patsy said. 'Isn't this what your psychiatrist said?'

'Yes, it is.'

As they got out of the cab in front of Claridge's, Patsy linked her arm in Meredith's. 'Let's go and have a drink. Celebrate.'

'Celebrate what?'

Patsy laughed. 'I always said I'd make a Yorkshirewoman of you. Now I don't even have to try, because you actually are one by birth. I'd like to drink a toast to that.'

The phone was ringing as Meredith came into her suite at Claridge's. As she picked it up and said, 'Hello?' she heard Luc's voice saying, *'Chérie, comment vas tu?'*

'I'm fine, darling. I was just going to call you in Paris. Guess what happened today? I found out that my mother is alive.'

'Mon Dieu.' There was a moment's silence and then he asked, 'But how did you find out?'

She proceeded to tell him in great detail, then added, 'We're leaving for Yorkshire tomorrow instead of on Sunday as planned . . . to begin the search.'

'Do you want me to fly over and go with you?'

'No, no, that's not necessary. I'd love to see you, darling, but I've got Patsy to help me. She knows Yorkshire like the back of her hand.'

'All right, I understand. You want to concentrate. But I will be thinking about you. Call me tomorrow, *chérie*, I'll be anxious. I love you.'

Twenty-two

They left for Yorkshire very early on Saturday morning, and arrived in Leeds in record time. Patsy circumvented the busy city centre and took Stanningley Road to Armley. After asking directions a few times, she soon found Beck Lane.

As she pointed the Aston Martin down the lane, she glanced at Meredith and asked, 'Does anything seem familiar to you?'

'Not really, not even Beck Lane. It looks so short, so ordinary. But then again, when you're a small child things always appear to be so much bigger, more impressive. And also more frightening, of course.'

'That's quite true,' Patsy agreed. 'We're almost at the bottom of the lane, and it looks to me as if it ends in a cul-de-sac.'

Meredith peered out of the car window, her eyes scanning the scenery. 'What I don't understand is why we're not seeing the river.'

'I'm sure we will in a minute. When I looked up this area on a map of Leeds last night, I noticed that the River Aire and the Leeds and Liverpool Canal are adjacent to each other, run parallel. We learned that at school but I'd forgotten. Those two waterways *are* ahead of us, Meredith, you'll see.'

Beck Lane came to an abrupt end at a partially demolished brick wall, which cut the lane off from a large field beyond. It was here that Patsy stopped, turned off the ignition and parked.

'Let's go and investigate,' she said, opening the car door, getting out.

Meredith followed suit.

The two women glanced around. They were standing in a deserted area; there were no houses, no buildings of any kind in sight. But back down the lane a few yards there was an old gate set in a ramshackle wooden fence, and Meredith suddenly noticed this.

'I didn't see that gate as we drove past,' she said, 'and it must lead somewhere.' As she was speaking she began to walk down the lane towards it.

Patsy followed her.

The gate was open, hanging off its rusted hinges; Meredith went through it and realized that there had once been a pathway here. Now it was overgrown with weeds and grass, barely visible. The partially obscured path led towards a tumble-down building, in reality several large piles of bricks, stones, wood and other rubble.

'Could *that* be Hawthorne Cottage?' Patsy asked, catching up with her.

'Possibly,' Meredith replied quietly. Suddenly, she felt deflated, sad. During the drive from London she had begun to believe that Hawthorne Cottage was still standing, that her mother still lived there. But this had been wishful thinking on her part, she accepted that now. How foolish I am, she thought, expecting things to be the way they were almost forty years ago. Everything changes.

Arriving at the demolished building, Meredith circled it several times, then she turned to face the River Aire which was visible from this vantage point. She could see it gleaming in the pale spring sunshine, and, just behind it, flowed the canal. She wondered why she had never noticed the two waterways running parallel when she was a child.

Turning to Patsy, she voiced this thought.

Patsy said, 'But you were so little, darling, only five or six. You wouldn't have paid any attention to something like that. Or maybe you've simply forgotten.'

'I guess you're right.' Meredith half smiled. 'Also, I was much shorter then, I might not have been able to see that far.'

Patsy laughed. 'True enough.'

Meredith remained standing in front of the mounds of stone and rubble, still gazing thoughtfully towards the River Aire. She was trying to move backwards in time, concentrating hard on the past, in the way Hilary Benson had told her to do.

Unexpectedly, in her mind's eye, she saw a neat little lawn and flower beds, and, beyond the garden, a white gate set in an old brick wall, rambling roses growing all over it.

Hurrying forward, she walked through the desolate garden, heading for the river, and as she approached the bank she saw, behind a clump of overgrown bushes, the wall and the remnants of the gate. The wall had been reduced to a crumbling pile of brick but the rambling rose bushes still spread themselves over it, and she supposed that in summer the roses would be in full bloom.

Her heart gave a small leap. She recognized this place, knew it well. Then she saw the rock and she stood perfectly still. A memory came rushing back, almost knocking the breath out of her with its clarity and vividness.

She saw herself as she had been as a small girl, sitting on that rock, always sitting there daydreaming. It was her favourite place, that rock high up on the river's bank. It was her view of the world.

She went and sat down on the rock; her eyes were moist as she gazed out at the water flowing past, splashing and tinkling as it fell down over the dappled stones of the river's bed. There was wildlife on this river, and she remembered how she had loved to watch the antics of the ducks, the moorhens and the other birds on the water.

Hugging her knees with her arms, she rested her head on them and closed her eyes . . . memories . . . memories . . . they were coming back.

The mother was there. The mother with the red-gold curls and very blue eyes. Eyes so supernaturally blue they were almost blinding. The mother loved the child on the rock, loved her to distraction. The child was the mother's whole world.

Then why did she send me so far away from her. *Why?*

Meredith had no answer for herself. Only Kate Sanderson could answer that question. If she and Patsy ever found her, which was most unlikely in her view.

The pain came back all of a sudden, the pain of her childhood, the constant she had lived with as a little girl. 'Mam, Mam, where are you?' she heard the small girl cry, and Meredith's heart tightened. How she had dreamed of that face, the mother's pretty face. How she had longed for her, longed for those soft arms around her, longed for the warmth of her love, the soothing voice, the comfort of her presence. Meredith's heart held the memories intact, held them inviolate . . . the pretty face, the sparkling eyes of blue, the love, the tenderness, the scent of her . . . the mother she had never stopped loving or longing for . . . *her* mother. Kate Sanderson.

Meredith squeezed the tears back and swallowed. Her throat ached.

'Are you all right?' Patsy asked softly.

Unable to speak for a moment, Meredith did not answer. She sat up straighter and flicked the tears away from her eyes with her fingertips.

'I just don't know why she did it,' she said to Patsy at last. 'A moment ago I thought we'd never find her, but now I know we *must*. Just to ask her that question. *Why?*'

Patsy was silent; she simply nodded, affected by Meredith's emotion, the pain reflected on her face.

Finally, Meredith got up and looked at her friend, met her steady gaze. 'You see, Patsy, my mother loved me very much. The way I love Cat and Jon . . . and that's why I can't fathom out why she did what she did. It's a mystery.'

Patsy put her arm around Meredith's shoulder. 'We'll find her, I promise you that.'

Together they walked back through the weed-filled garden, heading for the car. As they passed the mounds of rubble, Patsy asked, 'Do you think that is Hawthorne Cottage?'

For a moment Meredith did not answer. She stood staring at the mass of old stones, but she did not really see them. Instead she saw Hawthorne Cottage as it had been thirty-eight years ago. She saw the sparkling windows, the fresh, white lace curtains, the copper pots gleaming in the kitchen. She saw her neat little bedroom with the rose-patterned quilt. And she heard that mellifluous voice. '*A wizard sells magical things at this stall, astonishing gifts you can see if you call* . . .' The voice faded away.

'Yes,' Meredith said softly, 'that's Hawthorne Cottage. What's left of it.'

'This is number Three, Green Hill Road,' Patsy said, slowing the car, indicating the big Victorian building set behind wrought-iron gates. 'You were born there, Meredith. For years it was a maternity hospital. Now that I see it, I remember coming here with my aunt, when my cousin Jane had her first child. They used to live at Hill Top. I'll show you where on our way into town.'

Meredith stared at the building with interest, and then asked, 'You said *used* to be a maternity hospital. Isn't it any more?'

'I don't think so,' Patsy replied. 'I vaguely remember that it became a general hospital, or perhaps a home for the elderly, I'm not quite sure.' Glancing at

Meredith, she finished, 'Do you want to get out, go over there and have a closer look?'

Meredith shook her head. 'No, no, that's fine. But I can't help wondering where I was christened though.'

Turning on the ignition, driving on, Patsy said, 'Probably at Christ Church in Armley. Do you want me to take you there?'

'I don't think so, I'm sure I won't remember anything. But thanks, honey.'

'What about Leeds Market? Would you like to stop off, see whether or not it triggers any other memories? It was rebuilt in the seventies, after it burned down in a fire. But fortunately it was rebuilt in the same Victorian style it had always been. So it's the same now as it was when you were five or six.'

'I doubt I'll have any significant recollections there, Patsy. I think that we ought to go to Ripon. We've quite a lot of things to review, and to discuss with the Millers. By the way, that was good news that they're going to stay on as the managers.'

'Isn't it just,' Patsy exclaimed, a smile flashing on her face. 'I was thrilled when they first told me last week. I hope you're not angry that I didn't pass it on then, but I wanted it to be a lovely surprise for you when you arrived.'

'No, I wasn't angry, and it was a *marvellous* surprise. Now we don't have to search for a good management team or interview anyone.'

'True, but we do have to interview the various chefs. The Millers have done a lot of weeding out, as I told you, and we're down to three.'

'That's not too bad, but hiring a chef is always

a tricky business; you know that, Patsy. They usually do a lovely meal to impress, but invariably that happens only once ... disaster frequently follows.'

'The Millers have tried out these three off and on for a couple of weeks. One's a man, Lloyd Bricker. The other two are women, a Mrs Morgan and a Mrs Jones. So we'll be eating well this weekend, that's a certainty. However, I tend to agree with you: hiring a chef is dicey.'

'We should be able to open the inn in May,' Meredith remarked. 'You don't foresee any problems, do you?'

'No, I told you that when you arrived. It's just this chef business that nags at me. It's going to be fine, let's not worry.' Patsy threw her a quick glance, then focused on the road again. 'By the way, when are you planning to leave for Paris?'

'I had hoped to go next Wednesday. Now I'm not so sure. Agnes and I are supposed to visit Montfort-L'Amaury on Thursday, so that I can see the progress they've made with the remodelling. And then I was going to Talcy with Luc. For the weekend. However, now that we're looking for my mother, I don't know what to tell you.'

'Let's just take it day by day,' Patsy suggested.

That afternoon, after they had eaten a delicious lunch prepared by the chef, Lloyd Bricker, Meredith and Patsy did a tour of Skell Garth House.

Each of them made copious notes, and once they had reviewed every room in the inn they found a corner in the empty dining room and went over their punch lists together.

'There're still a lot of things missing in many of the rooms,' Patsy said. 'Claudia's only partially understood me, I think. I explained to her several times that we're upgrading the inn, creating much higher standards, both in accommodation and service. She seems to have missed the point that real comfort and luxury are absolutely mandatory.' She glanced at her pad, and added, 'I'm sure you've listed the same things as I, Meredith. Hot-water bottles in covers, oodles of towels in every room, bowls of potpourri and scented candles, hairdryers, etcetera, etcetera, etcetera.'

'Yes, I've noted all those things, Patsy, and they're easy items to add. We just have to ship them up from London.'

'They've already been shipped,' Patsy replied, making a moue with her mouth. 'Well, perhaps she just didn't put them out yet. I'll talk to her about it. What do you think about the refurbishment in general?'

'It's good, Patsy, we picked some lovely fabrics and carpets. I noticed the draperies and bedcovers have been extremely well made, and the sofas and chairs beautifully reupholstered. Thanks to you. And the wallpapering and painting is excellent. But I am going to have to rearrange all of the furniture – and in most of the rooms.'

'I knew you'd say that. When I came up two weeks ago to oversee the installation of the carpets and the draperies, I gave them your floor plans for the furniture arrangements. They seem to have ignored them completely.'

Meredith nodded. 'They certainly did.' A faint smile flickered. 'The Millers simply put everything back where it was before, and those old groupings were not the best. Or the most comfortable.'

'I hope we haven't made a mistake, keeping them on,' Patsy murmured, throwing her an apprehensive glance. 'Do you think they're too set in their ways?'

'Perhaps. But I'm sure we can overcome that. I'll have a long talk with them over the weekend. They've simply got to understand that we're raising our prices. Therefore our standards have to be higher, too. They're both bright, so I'm sure we can re-educate them, help them to operate the inn the Havens way.'

Patsy grinned. 'I'm glad you're such an optimist, Meredith. I was getting really concerned about them when we were upstairs.'

'If I hadn't been an optimist, I don't think I would have survived that orphanage in Sydney.'

'No, you wouldn't.' Patsy glanced down at her pad, and went on, 'The rest of the stuff on the hit list is all minor, to do with electrical outlets, the wattage of the light bulbs, and such; so we don't have to worry now. It can wait.'

'I don't have a lot of other things either,' Meredith said, and pushing back her chair she stood up. 'I'm going to take that walk, Patsy.'

'Are you sure you don't want me to drive you to Fountains Abbey?'

'No, thanks anyway for offering. I really do want

to walk, I need the exercise and the fresh air. See you later.'

Patsy smiled at her and nodded.

Returning the smile, Meredith left the dining room, crossed the foyer and headed out of Skell Garth House.

It was a fine afternoon, not too cold even though it was still April. The sky was clear, a soft pale blue filled with scudding white clouds. Wherever she looked, Meredith saw that spring was truly here. The trees were in bud, the grass already thick and verdant, and, here and there, patches of wild flowers grew in the hedges. She noticed primroses and irises, and then, as she came to the avenue of limes leading to Studley Church, she caught her breath. Daffodils were blooming everywhere, on the banks by the side of the road and under the limes.

As she walked past them, the Wordsworth poem Patsy had recited to her in January ran through her mind. It had seemed familiar then and now she realized that she knew the last verse: For oft when on my couch I lie/ in vacant or in pensive mood,/ they flash upon that inward eye/ which is the bliss of solitude;/ And then my heart with pleasure fills,/ and dances with the daffodils.

She knew it by heart because her mother had taught it to her all those years ago. And it had stayed in her mind, dormant perhaps, but nevertheless there.

Her mind focused on Kate Sanderson. The shock of discovering that her mother was not dead had partially receded, but she was still upset, troubled that Kate had apparently abandoned her, and so callously, when she was a little girl.

Meredith knew herself extremely well, and she had begun to realize earlier in the day, as they had driven from Leeds to Ripon, that anger and resentment were beginning to simmer deep down inside her. As she walked on, heading up to the church on the hill, she resolved yet again to find Kate, no matter what it took.

Upon reaching the top of the hill she stood looking down at Fountains Abbey, and just as it had in January, it seemed to beckon to her, pull her forward.

A magnet, she thought, it's like a magnet for me. She hurried down the steep path, almost running, and within a few minutes she was entering the ancient ruins.

On this clear bright April day she was more stunned than before by the dramatic beauty of the soaring ruined monolith.

Dark and imposing, it was silhouetted against the pale sky as if flung there by a mighty hand. But the blackened stones were softened by the greenness of the trees surrounding them. Just a few feet away from where she stood the Skell flowed towards Ripon. Yet another river, Meredith thought; no wonder I love to live near water. I grew up with it.

Seating herself on a piece of ruined wall, she cast her mind back in time, trying to envision herself visiting this place with Kate Sanderson, but no memory came to her, even though she sat there for half an hour. Her mind was totally blank. Still, again she had the strongest sense that she knew Fountains, had been here before, and that something momentous, and tragic, had happened to her here in this ancient spot. But what?

Only her mother had the answer.

Always, in the past, Meredith had used work to subjugate heartache, bring it to heel. Working hard until she dropped had enabled her to keep her mind off her troubles, to function properly.

And so for the rest of the weekend she threw herself wholeheartedly into creating a new look, her look, in most of the rooms in the hotel. It kept worry about her mother at bay.

With the help of Patsy, Bill and Claudia Miller and three handymen, she had furniture moved around until every arrangement pleased her, and each room had the look she was striving for. Beds, chairs, sofas, antique tables and chests were repositioned under her direction; once this had been accomplished, she set about rearranging lamps and accessories and rehanging pictures.

The Millers were astounded by her. As Bill put it to Patsy: 'We couldn't believe it when she took off her jacket, rolled up her sleeves and got down to it herself.'

Claudia Miller was particularly impressed with Meredith's energy, stamina and sheer doggedness. At one point, late on Sunday afternoon, a weary and exhausted Claudia said to Patsy, 'I've never seen anyone work like this before. She doesn't stop, she's a whirlwind.'

'I know. Meredith's never ceased to amaze *me*. She's a real workhorse. And also very talented,' Patsy pointed out. 'She has terrific style.'

Claudia merely nodded.

Patsy added, 'Meredith has really fine taste in decorating. She was born with it. And she has a great eye.'

'So I've noticed. The rooms do look better the way she has arranged everything. I suppose Bill and I were a bit slow on the uptake. We really should have followed the plans you gave us more precisely.' Claudia's expression was suddenly worried, as she asked, 'Are you and Meredith upset with us?'

'No, of course not. It's all right, don't worry,' Patsy reassured her. 'But do try and follow our instructions *exactly* in future, Claudia, please. It'll save a lot of heartache for everyone. Tomorrow I'll help you to unpack all of the items I shipped from London last week, and Meredith will finish the public rooms down here. She expects to be done by lunchtime.'

'You will interview the chefs tomorrow, won't you?' Claudia said. 'Monday *is* the deadline.'

'That doesn't present a problem. By the way, I enjoyed lunch today. Mrs Morgan cooked it, didn't she?'

'Yes. She's also going to make dinner tonight.'

'Not Mrs Jones?'

'I'm afraid not. She burned her hand cooking dinner for us last night and she begged off today.'

'I see. Do you have a favourite, Claudia?'

'Yes. Mrs Morgan. She's the best in my opinion, and besides, she's the most adaptable, more easy-going in a way, not quite so temperamental as Lloyd.'

'And Mrs Jones? Aren't you impressed with her?'

'She's a good cook, but I don't think she's right for

the inn . . . at least, not the way it's going to be in the future.'

'Do you mean she's not sophisticated enough?'

'No, I don't mean that, not really. You and Meredith said you wanted high-style English cooking, and country-type cooking to a certain extent. In my opinion Mrs Morgan's the winner. She's the most all-round cook of the three of them.'

Mrs Morgan turned out to be a woman in her middle fifties, with rosy cheeks, bright brown eyes and a cheerful smile.

Meredith noticed at once that she had a pleasant manner, and within moments of being in her company she felt quite at ease. The woman exuded calm self-confidence, and Meredith could tell from Patsy's expression that her partner had also taken an immediate liking to the chef.

'I understand from Claudia Miller that you are used to cooking for relatively large numbers of people, Mrs Morgan,' Meredith began.

'Oh yes, I am. Until a few months ago I was chef at a hotel in the Scottish border country. It was an old house turned into an inn like this, but a bit bigger. And we also got a lot of local trade in the restaurant. So numbers don't faze me, oh no, they don't at all, Mrs Stratton. Of course I'm used to having a couple of sous chefs.'

'Yes, I understand, Mrs Morgan. That's not a problem,' Patsy interjected.

'I gave Mrs Miller all of my references, so I expect you've seen them.' She looked from Patsy to Meredith.

'We have indeed.' Meredith smiled at her. 'And they're excellent. We also enjoyed the meals you've cooked this weekend.'

'Thank you very much, Mrs Stratton, and please call me Eunice. I prefer it. Much friendlier, isn't it?'

Meredith said, 'Yes, it is, Eunice.' She paused for a moment, shook her head, then said, 'I've only known one other person called Eunice. And that was my baby-sitter when I was a child.'

Eunice laughed. 'What a coincidence. You had a baby-sitter called Eunice in America, and I was a baby-sitter here in Yorkshire.'

Meredith stared at her. After a split second, she said, 'Where in Yorkshire?'

'Leeds. That's where I come from originally. My husband's from Ripon, and he's been nagging me to come back here for years.'

'Who did you baby-sit for?' Meredith said, continuing to stare at the chef.

'A lovely little girl. Her name was Mari.'

'What was her last name?' Meredith asked in a strangled voice.

'Sanderson,' Eunice answered, and threw Meredith a swift glance. 'Are you all right, Mrs Stratton? You look a bit odd.'

'I'm the little girl, Eunice. I'm Mari Sanderson.'

'Get away with you then, you can't be Mari!' Eunice exclaimed, her astonishment only too apparent.

'But I am.'

'Well, I'll be blowed, this is one for the books, I can tell you that.' Eunice chuckled. 'Can you imagine me, of all people, being a chef, Mari? Do you remember how I always used to burn your lunch? I drove your poor mother crazy.'

'I'd like to talk to you about my mother,' Meredith said, quietly.

Twenty-three

'My mother and I got separated when I was little,' Meredith explained. 'I don't know how this happened, but it did.'

'She was poorly. In hospital, I do know that,' Eunice told her.

'Who was looking after me?'

Eunice brought her hand up to her mouth, frowning slightly, looking thoughtful. Finally, pursing her lips, shaking her head, she murmured, 'I don't know, to be right truthful with you. I suppose at the time I thought you'd been taken in by relatives.'

'*Relatives,*' Meredith said slowly, 'I don't ever remember relatives, Eunice. There was only my mother and me. Just the two of us.'

'Yes . . .' Eunice sat back in the chair, her face troubled. Hesitatingly, she asked in a quiet voice, 'So what exactly happened to you?'

'I don't exactly know. But I did eventually go to live abroad.'

Patsy glanced from Meredith to Eunice, and addressed the chef: 'When did you last see Mrs Sanderson? Can you remember that?'

'Let me think . . . Well, it must've been the summer she got ill. I've got to think back . . . yes . . . yes, it was then. The summer of 1956. I went to Hawthorne Cottage to baby-sit one day and there was no one there. So I went back home. We lived in the Greenocks, just off Town Street, in those days. Anyway, a few days later I ran into Constable O'Shea, he lived near us in the Greenocks. He told me Mrs Sanderson was in hospital. When I asked about Mari he said she was fine, being taken care of very well. And that was that. A few weeks after that we moved away from Armley. My mother found a house near her sister in Wortley, so off we all went.'

Meredith had listened carefully; leaning forward intently, she said to Eunice, 'The name Constable O'Shea rings a bell, but I can't quite place him in my mind.'

'Can't you? Well, he was very fond of *you*, Mari. Very fond. He was the local bobby, walking the beat in Armley. He used to be stationed at that police box on Canal Road. Are you sure you don't remember him?'

'No, I don't.'

Patsy said, 'Constable O'Shea might be able to throw some light on what happened to you.'

'Yes, that's true,' Meredith agreed and turned to Eunice again. 'Do you think he still lives in Armley?'

'Oh, I don't know, I mean I lost touch donkey's years ago. And he'll be retired. He was about thirty in those days; so he'd be sixty-eight, thereabouts, by now. Mmmm. Now who do I know who still lives in the Greenocks? Let me just think.'

Patsy stood up. 'I'll go and get the Leeds telephone directory from the office.' She hurried across the dining room and out into the small foyer.

Left alone, Meredith and Eunice looked at each other carefully without speaking. It was Eunice who finally said at last, 'You've grown up to be a wonderful-looking woman, and you've certainly made a go of it, you really have. Living in America, owning all these inns.'

Meredith half smiled, made no comment. She was looking back into the past again, trying to remember Constable O'Shea, but she was having no success at all. She couldn't even picture his face.

Eunice went on, 'Are you married then?'

'I was. I'm divorced now. I have two children. And what about you, Eunice, do you have children?'

'Two, like you. Malcolm and Dawn. They're both married, and I have five grandchildren. Are your children married?'

'My daughter's engaged. My son's still at college; he's only twenty-one.'

Patsy came back into the dining room carrying the Leeds telephone book. Placing it on the table in front of Eunice, she sat down next to her and said, 'Now let's look at all the O'Sheas who live in Armley. There can't be that many. Perhaps we'll find one living in the Greenocks. What was Constable O'Shea's first name, Eunice?'

'Peter. No, wait a minute, it wasn't Peter. It was an Irish name. Let me see ... *Patrick*! Yes, it was Patrick O'Shea.'

Patsy was running her finger down the O'Sheas listed and she looked up and said, 'There are two living in Armley and one in Bramley with the initial

P. But none in the Greenocks. Well, I might as well go and phone all three numbers, that's the only way we'll find out anything. I'll use the phone over there.' Carrying the directory, she hurried over to the phone on the table at the entrance to the dining room.

Meredith got up and walked over to the window, stood looking out at the garden, her mind on her mother. Turning around, she asked, 'Did you ever run into my mother afterwards?'

'No, I didn't.' The chef's eyebrows drew together in a frown. 'She didn't die, then?'

'I don't think so, Eunice. We're trying to find her.'

'Oh.'

A moment later Patsy rushed across the dining room, still clutching the telephone book in her arms. She was beaming. 'I've found him! He now lives at Hill Top. That's near St Mary's Hospital, Meredith. He's out at the moment, I didn't actually speak to him in person. But I talked with his wife, and he's definitely the right Patrick O'Shea. He's a retired police sergeant, she told me, and she vaguely remembers Mari and her mother. Anyway, she said he would be home around two o'clock this afternoon. I asked if we could go and see him then, and she said we could.'

Meredith sat facing Patrick O'Shea in the sitting room of his house at Hill Top in Armley. She did not remember him at all; she realized that she had probably so blocked him out it was almost impossible to recover the memory. He was a tall man, well built, with greying dark hair and a pleasant manner.

'You were such a bonny little girl,' he said to her,

smiling. 'Marigold. I always thought it was such a lovely name for a child. Anyway, to continue, that morning you came looking for me you were so upset. Crying. You thought your mother was dead –'

'But she wasn't was she?' Meredith cut in swiftly.

'No, but she wasn't well. You'd come to the police box on Canal Road. I carried you home, it was quicker. And anyway you were weeping, so upset you were. We found your mother sitting in a chair in the kitchen. She was white, white as a sheet, and obviously very sick. At least that's what I thought. She said she'd fainted earlier that morning. I'd put in a call for an ambulance, and it came within fifteen minutes. They took her to Leeds Infirmary.'

'And what happened to me?' Meredith's eyes were riveted on Patrick O'Shea.

'The last thing she said to me, as the ambulance doors closed was, "Look after my Mari for me, Constable O'Shea." And I did. I spoke to my sergeant at the station, and we decided the best thing to do was take you to Dr Barnardo's in Leeds, the children's home, until your mother was well.'

'And what happened when my mother got better?'

'You went back to live with her at Hawthorne Cottage, as I recall. But I don't believe things were good with her, she was struggling, you know, trying to find a job.'

'What happened to . . . my father?'

'I don't rightly know. At least, I don't have a lot of details. Kate told me once that he'd left her, gone off to Canada. That's all I knew. I suppose he didn't come back.'

'I don't remember him. He must have left when I was very little.'

Patrick O'Shea nodded. 'I believe he did.'

'Do you think my mother became ill again, Mr O'Shea?'

'She did indeed. She was in the Infirmary a second time . . . oh, it must have been the following year . . . about 1957, if my memory serves me well.'

'Do you think I was put back into the children's home?'

'Possibly. Yes, that's very likely. There was no one to look after you. And I sort of lost track of your mother after that. In fact, I never really knew what happened to you both. Suddenly you'd left Hawthorne Cottage, another family was living there. I never saw you or your mother again, Mari. I mean, Mrs Stratton. A few years later I did hear she was working in Leeds.'

'Do you know where?'

'Yes, just let me think for a moment . . . it was a dress shop, I do know that. A posh one too, in Commercial Street . . . Paris Modes, that was the name of it.'

'Is it still there?'

'Oh yes, I think so.'

'As I explained, Constable O'Shea, my mother and I got separated. I was sent abroad. I thought she was dead. But I've just discovered she's probably still alive. I must find her.'

'I understand. She's not listed in the phone book then?'

'No, she's not.'

'Perhaps there's someone at Paris Modes who can help you, give you more information about her whereabouts.'

'Well, he was certainly nice enough,' Patsy said, as she and Meredith drove away from Constable O'Shea's house at Hill Top, heading for the city. 'But you don't remember him, do you?'

'Not really, Patsy. I wish I did.' Meredith sighed. 'I suppose I truly blocked everything out. If only I could recall those early days more fully, but I can't. I have flashes of memory like an amnesiac sometimes does, but that's it.'

'Try not to worry, I'm sure we'll get more information at the dress shop.'

'I'm not sure at all. Frankly, Patsy, we're on a wild-goose chase, in my opinion. All of this happened thirty-eight years ago, and my mother's not going to be *still* working at Paris Modes. And I'm certain there's no one there who will remember her.'

'You don't know that for sure, Meredith. So let's just go to the shop, ask a few questions. Somebody might remember Kate Sanderson, and give us a lead.'

'Yes, we can go, but hasn't it occurred to you that my mother might not live in Yorkshire any more? She could have moved away. Moved anywhere. There's a very big world out there.'

'I know what you're saying, darling, but I think you're wrong. I have this feeling inside, call it intuition if you like, that your mother is very close by. You'll see, we're going to find her.'

When Meredith was silent, Patsy sneaked a look at

her. Her heart sank. Meredith's face was bleak.

Patsy drove on in silence for a short while, but then she said, 'I'm not too sure about parking in Leeds. I think the best thing to do is to go to the Queens Hotel and park the car there, near the railway station. It's only a few minutes' walk to Commercial Street from City Square.'

'Whatever you say. I don't remember Commercial Street. Only Leeds Market.'

But twenty minutes later as they walked down that particular street Meredith suddenly stopped and clutched Patsy's arm. 'Marks & Spencers is somewhere near here. I remember that now. My mother liked to go there; she bought my underwear at Marks.' Meredith had an instant vision of herself walking down this street clinging to her mother's hand. She said to Patsy, 'Almost always my mother bought me an ice cream. Once I tripped and dropped my cone. I was so upset, I started to cry. And I remember how she comforted me . . . and gave me her ice cream . . .'

'You see, more and more memories are coming back,' Patsy exclaimed, looking pleased. 'And here we are at Paris Modes.'

Patsy pushed open the door and the two of them walked into the elegant dress shop. Immediately a young woman in a neat black dress came gliding forward.

'Can I help you?' she asked politely, smiling at them. 'We have some wonderful new lines in from Paris.'

'Oh, yes,' Patsy said, 'we know you have lovely clothes, very smart indeed. But we don't want to buy anything. Actually, we came to see the manager.'

'We don't have a manager,' the young woman replied. 'Mrs Cohen owns the business, and she runs it herself.'

'I see. Is she here? Can we see her?' Meredith asked.

The young woman nodded. 'I'll go and get her, she's in the office.'

A few seconds later a woman of about fifty, elegantly dressed and well put together, walked out into the shop from the office behind a Coromandel screen.

'I'm Gilda Cohen,' she said, extending her hand to Patsy.

'Pleased to meet you, Mrs Cohen. I'm Patsy Canton, and this is my friend, Mrs Stratton.'

'A pleasure, Mrs Stratton,' Gilda Cohen said, shaking her hand.

Meredith smiled at her. 'I'm looking for someone, Mrs Cohen. A woman who used to work here. But many years ago. I'm afraid it was long before your time.'

'Who are you looking for?' Gilda Cohen asked curiously.

'My mother. She worked here in the late fifties, or perhaps the early sixties. Her name was, or rather is, Kate Sanderson. We were separated when I was small and I always believed she had died when I was a child. But lately I've been given reason to believe she's still alive. I want to find my mother.'

'I'm sure you do, Mrs Stratton, that's quite understandable; and you're correct, Kate did work here, when my mother was running the shop. I inherited it from her. I was at college in those days, but I knew

Kate slightly. A lovely woman. My mother was very fond of her indeed, and sorry to see her leave.'

'When was that, Mrs Cohen?' Meredith asked.

'I think it must've been in the middle or late sixties. But don't let's stand here in the middle of the shop. Come into my office and sit down. Can I offer you a cup of tea?'

'No, but thank you anyway,' Meredith said.

Patsy also declined, and the two of them followed Gilda Cohen into her office. They sat down together on the sofa, and looked at Gilda, who had positioned herself behind her desk. 'As I said, my mother was rather fond of Kate, took her under her wing a bit, and she stayed in touch with her after she left.'

'Do you know where she went to work?'

'Yes, she returned to the town she came from, Harrogate, and took a job with Jaeger. My mother once told me Kate hadn't been happy in Leeds, and she always referred to her as "my wounded bird", although I'm not certain why. I married young and had a child, so I wasn't working in the shop in those days. I didn't know her all that well. But she certainly made an impression on my mother, and on other people, too. Everyone spoke nicely about Kate.'

Meredith sighed. 'I don't suppose she could still be working at Jaeger. What do you think, Mrs Cohen?'

'Oh I know she's not, Mrs Stratton. She didn't stay at Jaeger for longer than a couple of years, then she moved on. The last time I heard about her from my mother Kate was running Place Vendôme in Harrogate, a really fine boutique selling couture clothes.' Gilda Cohen leaned back in her chair. 'If only my mother were still alive, she would be able to tell you so much more about Kate.'

Meredith gave Mrs Cohen a sympathetic look. 'I'm sorry you lost your mother.'

'Yes, it was sad for us all. However, she had a really grand life and lived to be ninety. Never had a day's ill health as long as she lived.'

There was a small silence, and then Patsy said, 'Is Kate Sanderson working at Place Vendôme now?'

'I don't believe she is, Mrs Canton. The last I heard she had left there. She'd moved away from Harrogate, actually.'

'Another dead end,' Meredith said in a miserable voice.

Gilda Cohen said, 'I can ring Annette Alexander, the owner of the boutique. She just might have an address for Kate.'

'Oh, would you? Are you sure you don't mind?' Meredith asked. 'Otherwise, we can just drive over to Harrogate.' She glanced at her watch. 'It's only four-thirty.'

'Yes,' Patsy said. 'We can pop in to see her on our way to Ripon. We have to pass through Harrogate.'

'No, no, that's all right, I'll call her for you right away. I don't mind at all.' So saying Gilda Cohen picked up the phone and dialled the boutique.

'Hello, this is Gilda Cohen, is Mrs Alexander there?'

There was a small silence, as Mrs Cohen listened. Then she covered the mouthpiece, and explained: 'They've gone to get her, she's just saying goodbye to a client. Hello, oh there you are, Annette, how are you?'

Gilda listened once more, and then said, 'I have two ladies here who are looking for Kate Sanderson. I know she left you a few years ago, but you wouldn't happen to have an address or a telephone number for her, would you?' The next short silence was followed by an exclamation. 'Oh really!' Gilda cried. 'Just a minute, let me ask.'

Again covering the mouthpiece with her hand, Mrs Cohen said, 'According to Mrs Alexander, your mother left to marry someone. But she can't remember his name. She wants to know where she can contact you, if she does remember?'

'Skell Garth House in Ripon, Mrs Cohen,' Patsy said. 'The number is Ripon 42900.'

Gilda Cohen repeated this to Annette Alexander and after thanking her, saying goodbye, she hung up. Looking directly at Meredith, she said, 'If my mother were alive she'd be very pleased to know Kate got married finally. Mother always thought Kate was so sad, and she used to tell me Kate had had a tragic life.'

'You've been very helpful, Mrs Cohen,' Meredith murmured softly, standing up. 'Thank you so much.'

'Yes, thank you,' Patsy added, also standing.

'It's been my pleasure, I just wish I could have done more to reunite you with your mother, Mrs Stratton. Annette is very dependable, and I can guarantee she'll ring you up if she remembers who it was your mother married.'

'I hope so.'

Gilda Cohen escorted them to the door, shook their hands. As they stepped out into Commercial Street she said, 'I'd love to know if you do find Kate, Mrs Stratton, she was such a favourite of my mother's.'

'I'll be in touch,' Meredith promised.

'Why didn't we think of that,' Patsy muttered as they walked along Commercial Street. 'It's the most obvious thing. She was a young woman, and pretty, you said.'

'*Very* pretty. Beautiful really.' Meredith linked her arm in Patsy's, continued, 'We'll never find her. This is yet another dead end, you know.'

'No, it isn't!' Patsy cried. 'Quite the contrary. I'll call Valerie at the office first thing in the morning and she can go to St Catherine's House. They keep marriage certificates there. I'm quite sure they do. We'll find out who your mother married.'

Meredith instantly brightened. 'What a great idea! Let's call her now.'

'She's not in the office today. Don't you remember, she went to Milan for the weekend. She won't be back until late tonight.'

'Are you certain they keep marriage records?' Meredith asked in a quiet voice as they walked down into City Square.

'I'm positive. It's a general register office of births, deaths and marriages.' Patsy paused before adding: 'I've been thinking . . . perhaps we ought to go to Dr Barnardo's Home, make inquiries there. They may be able to throw some light on what happened to you. And to your mother.'

Meredith looked at her askance. 'No way. I know those places. They never tell you anything, they're cloaked in secrecy. I'd only go to see them as a last resort.' Her mouth settled in a grim line.

Glancing at her, Patsy decided to say no more for the moment. On the drive back to Ripon she talked about a variety of other things, wanting to take Meredith's mind off her mother. And orphanages.

Laughing suddenly, at one moment, she said, 'You know, Meredith, we're really quite awful.'

'What do you mean?'

'Once we'd discovered who Eunice Morgan was, we put her through an interrogation and then fled, raced off to find your mother. The poor woman must think we're crazy. We didn't even finish our interview with her.'

'I realized that myself a short while ago. Anyway, how do you feel about hiring Eunice?'

'I'm all for it. I think she's the best of the lot. I found Lloyd Bricker a bit of a snob and too arrogant by far, and Mrs Jones didn't really impress me that much.'

'In my opinion she's a shirker,' Meredith said. 'I agree with you about Lloyd. So let's hire Eunice, shall we? She's certainly a good chef. We've sampled her fare.' Meredith gave Patsy a small smile. 'And obviously she no longer burns the food as she did when I was a child.'

Patsy laughed, glad to see a flash of Meredith's good humour.

The telephone call came the next morning.

Meredith and Patsy were sitting in the dining room, having breakfast and going over their notes about the inn, when Claudia Miller came hurrying over to their table.

'Excuse me. You have a phone call, Meredith. It's a Mrs Alexander.'

Meredith and Patsy exchanged startled glances, and Meredith immediately got up. 'Thanks, Claudia. I'll take it over there on the phone by the door.'

'All right. I'll just go and put it through.'

A few second later Meredith was saying, 'Hello, this is Mrs Stratton.'

'Mrs Stratton, good morning. Annette Alexander here, I hope I haven't called too early.'

'No, not at all, Mrs Alexander.'

'I thought I'd better ring you immediately. I just received a bit of information that might help you. Do you know, I wracked my brains last night, trying to remember the name of the man Kate married, but to no avail. And then it occurred to me that my sister might know who he was. She used to work for me at Place Vendôme, at the same time as Kate Sanderson. In any case, I rang her up last night, but she was out. She just got my message and phoned me ten minutes ago. Apparently Kate married a man called Nigel. My sister thinks his last name was Grange or Grainger, and that he was a veterinarian. In Middleham. I know it's a trifle sketchy, but I do hope it helps.'

'It does, thank you very much Mrs Alexander. Whilst I have you on the phone, perhaps you can tell me something else. Do you recall when Kate Sanderson left Place Vendôme?'

'She left my employ in the early seventies.'

'I see. Well, thanks again, Mrs Alexander.'

'I was happy to be of help, and give Kate my best, if you find her.'

'I will. Goodbye, Mrs Alexander.' Meredith hung up and returned to the table.

Patsy looked at her questioningly, raising a brow. 'Well?'

Meredith took a deep breath, exhaled, then said, 'According to Annette Alexander, my mother married a man called Nigel, and his last name was either Grange or Grainger. He is, or was, a vet. And in the early seventies, when my mother left her employment, he was living in Middleham. Or rather, *they* were.'

'Middleham! Good heavens, Meredith, that's right next door practically. It's a small village on the moors, about half an hour from Ripon. You see, I told you I had a sense that your mother was close by.'

'We don't know that she is. We don't know what happened really. And they could have divorced, or moved away.'

'I'll soon find out if he's still around,' Patsy cried assertively and jumped to her feet. 'I'm going to look him up in the local telephone directory. He's bound to be listed if he's the vet in Middleham.'

Meredith sat back in her chair and watched Patsy walking across the floor with great determination. Whatever it took, her friend was hell-bent on finding Kate Sanderson. And what a *good* friend Patsy had turned out to be. Meredith knew that she would have been lost without her in the last few days.

Patsy was suddenly back at the table, looking pleased with herself. She sat down, glanced at the paper she was holding, and said, 'His name's Grainger, not Grange, and he lives in Middleham. At Tan Beck House. And there's the phone number.'

Meredith took the paper and glanced at it, then raised her eyes to meet Patsy's. 'Thank you,' she said, and looked down at the paper again. 'Now that I know she could only be a few miles away I feel rather strange.'

'Do you mean about seeing her?' Patsy asked, her brows furrowing.

'Yes.'

'Perhaps you're afraid.'

'Do you know, I think I am.'

'I'll go with you to Tan Beck House.'

'Thank you, but perhaps I should go alone, Patsy.'

'Shouldn't you phone her first?'

'I'm not sure. In a way I prefer to see her face to face before she knows anything about me. If I phone first I'll have to start explaining myself.'

'You're right. So do it your way.'

Twenty-four

It was with some trepidation that Meredith walked up the path to the front door of Tan Beck House.

For the last thirty minutes she had been sitting in Patsy's Aston Martin, trying to gather her courage to go there in search of Kate Sanderson.

Since her apprehension had only seemed to increase the longer she sat, she had, in the end, turned on the ignition and driven back down the road.

As she had alighted from her car a moment ago she had seen that the lovely old stone house was substantial but not overly large, the kind of house a vet or a doctor or lawyer would live in. It was well kept, with a freshly painted white door, sparkling windows and pretty lace curtains; an array of spring flowers brought colour and life to the beds in the garden on either side of the flagged path.

Now she stood at the front door, her hand on the brass knocker. Her nerves almost failed her. Taking a deep breath she banged it hard several times and then stood back to wait.

The door was opened almost instantly by a youngish woman with dark hair, who was dressed in a grey sweater and matching slacks under a green striped pinafore.

'Yes, can I help you?' she asked.

'I'm looking for Mrs Grainger. Mrs Nigel Grainger. Is she at home?'

The young woman nodded. 'Is she expecting you?'

'No, she's not.'

'Who shall I say is calling?'

'I'm Mrs Stratton. Meredith Stratton. She doesn't know me. I'm a friend of a friend. I was hoping she could help me with something.'

'Just a minute,' the young woman said and leaving the door ajar she hurried across the highly polished floor of the small entrance foyer.

She returned within seconds, opened the door wider, and said, 'Mrs Grainger would like you to come in. She won't be a minute, she's on the phone. She told me to take you to the sitting room.'

'Thank you,' Meredith said, stepping into the foyer, following the young woman, at the same time glancing around quickly, wanting to see everything.

She noticed a handsome grandfather clock standing in a corner and a collection of blue-and-white porcelain effectively arranged on an oak console table.

Showing her into the sitting room, the young woman said, 'Make yourself at home,' and disappeared.

Meredith stood in the middle of the room, thinking how welcoming it was, struck by its warmth and charm. It was of medium size, tastefully decorated, the walls painted red, with bookshelves running floor to ceiling on two of them. The woodwork was a dark cream, handpainted to resemble *faux* marble, and there was a dark red-and-blue oriental rug in front of the stone fireplace. Between two tall windows an antique desk faced out towards the back garden and a small lawn. Beyond were rolling moors and an endless expanse of blue sky filled with scudding white clouds.

Meredith turned away from the window at the sound of footsteps. She held her breath as she waited for Mrs Nigel Grainger to open the door.

At the first sight of her Meredith's heart dropped. This was not the beautiful young mother of the red-gold curls and bright blue eyes whom she had worshipped in her childhood dreams.

Mrs Grainger was a woman in her early sixties, Meredith guessed. She wore beige corduroy trousers and a white shirt with a navy-blue blazer; she looked like a typical country matron.

The woman hesitated in the doorway, looking at Meredith questioningly. 'Mrs Stratton?'

'Yes. And hello, Mrs Grainger . . . hello. I hope you'll forgive this intrusion, but I came to see you because I'm hoping you can help me.'

'I'm not sure how, but I'll try,' Mrs Grainger said, still poised in the doorway. 'You're American, aren't you?'

Meredith nodded. 'Mrs Grainger, I'll come straight to the point. I'm looking for a woman called Kate Sanderson. Annette Alexander of Place Vendôme in Harrogate gave me reason to believe that you and she are the same person. Is that so?'

'Why yes, it is. I'm Katharine Sanderson Grainger, and I used to work at Place Vendôme, years ago, before I was married.' Kate frowned, the quizzical expression reflected in her eyes again. 'But why are you looking for me?'

Meredith was extremely nervous. She had no idea how to tell Kate who she was and, momentarily, she was at a loss for the right words. Finally, she said in a tremulous voice, 'It's about . . . about . . . it's about Mari.'

Kate Grainger looked as if she had been slapped in the face, and slapped hard. She recoiled, gaped at Meredith, and took hold of the door to steady herself.

Then recovering her equilibrium to some extent, she asked in a tense voice, 'What about Mari? What is it you want with me? What do you want to tell me about Mari?'

'I . . . I knew her, Mrs Grainger.'

'You knew my Mari?' Kate cried eagerly, sounding breathless. She took a step forward.

Meredith could see her better now. She noted the vividness of the blue eyes, suddenly filled with tears, the reddish-gold hair, paler than it once was and shot through with silver; recognized that well-loved, familiar face, touched by time but still quite lovely. And she knew with absolute certainty that this *was* her mother. Her heart tightened imperceptibly, and she was seized by an internal shaking. She wanted to go to Kate, put her arms around her, but she did not dare. She was afraid . . . of rejection . . . of not being wanted.

'You knew my Mari,' Kate said again. 'Tell me about her, oh please tell me . . .'

Choked up, unable to speak, Meredith simply inclined her head.

'Where? Where did you know my little Mari? Oh please, please tell me, Mrs Stratton. *Please,*' Kate pleaded.

'In Australia,' Meredith answered at last in a strangled voice.

'*Australia.*' Kate sounded outraged, and she drew back, her eyes wide.

'Sydney.' Meredith's eyes were riveted on Kate, who was shocked and also puzzled.

'She loved you so much,' Meredith said, her voice a whisper.

Kate reached out, grabbed the back of a wing chair. She gripped it tightly to support herself. 'You speak of her as if she's . . . you speak of her in the past tense. She's not . . . *dead*, is she?'

'No, she's not.'

'Oh thank God for that,' Kate exclaimed. 'I've prayed for her every day for years and years. Prayed that she was all right, that she was safe. Please, Mrs Stratton, tell me something. Did she send you to me? Send you to find me?'

'Yes.'

'Where is my Mari? Oh do please tell me.' Kate's emotions were very near the surface, her feelings visible on her strained face. Who was this woman bringing news of Mari? News of her beloved child, lost to her for so many years? She began to tremble.

Meredith took a step forward, drew closer to Kate. Kate's heartache was written on her face, and Meredith realized how distraught she was. And also how sincere.

Groping around in her mind, she sought appropriate words to explain to Kate who she was.

Stepping closer to Kate, she looked into her face, and before she could stop herself she said, 'Mam . . . it's me . . . Mari . . .'

Kate could not speak for a moment, and then she exclaimed, 'Oh my God! Oh my God, Mari, is it really you?' Kate took hold of Meredith's hand and drew her to the window. 'Let me look at you. Is it you, Mari, after all these years?' Reaching out, she touched Meredith's face tenderly, with one hand. 'Is it really you, love?'

Tears were spilling out of Kate's eyes, trickling down her face. 'Oh Mari, Mari, you've come back to me at last. My prayers have been answered.'

Meredith was also crying. And the two women, separated for almost forty years, automatically moved into each other's arms, held onto each other tightly.

Kate was sobbing as if her heart would break. 'I've waited for this day for over thirty-eight years, prayed for it, begged God for it. I'd given up hope of ever seeing you again.'

Mother and daughter stood holding one another for a long time, drawing comfort from each other as they shed their tears of sorrow and joy . . . sorrow for the past, for all those years they had missed together . . . joy that they had been reunited at last, before it was too late.

They sat together on the small sofa in the sitting room, a tray of tea and sandwiches on the coffee table in front of them. But neither of them had touched the sandwiches which the young housekeeper, Nellie, had prepared.

They held hands, kept staring at each other, searching for similarities. And there was a kind of wonderment on their faces. It was the special wonder a mother feels when she sees her newly-born child. And in a way, Mari was newly-born for Kate today.

'I never came to terms with my loss,' Kate said, her voice soft, echoing with sadness as she remembered all those grim years she had endured without her only child by her side. 'I thought of you every day, Mari, wondered about you, yearned for you, longed to hold you in my arms.'

Meredith stared deeply into those marvellous eyes. 'I know, Mam, I know. It was the same for me always, and when I was very little, especially. I was always wondering about you, wondering why you'd sent me away from you, why you didn't want me. I never did understand that.' Meredith brushed the tears away from her eyes. 'How did you . . . lose me? How did we get separated?'

'It was a terrible thing and it really started with Dr Barnardo's home . . . do you remember that day when you were five, when you found me passed out on the kitchen floor?'

'Oh yes, I went to fetch Constable O'Shea.'

'He'd arranged for an ambulance. I was put in Leeds Infirmary and he took you to the children's home. I never blamed him, he didn't know what else to do, since I didn't have any family. Anyway, I was in hospital for about six weeks. As soon as I was on my feet again, I went and got you, and we were together at

Hawthorne Cottage, the way we'd always been. But about a year later, in the spring of 1957, I became ill once more. I took you to Dr Barnardo's myself this time. I'd nowhere else to put you. Dr Robertson was worried about me, he wanted me to go into the Infirmary for some tests. It was there that they discovered I had tuberculosis. Seemingly it had been dormant for several years. Suddenly it had flared up, fanned no doubt by undernourishment, worry, stress, and a run-down condition in general. Tuberculosis is very contagious, it's air-borne, and I couldn't be near you, Mari, for your own sake. The doctors at Leeds Infirmary sent me to Seacroft Hospital, near Killingbeck, where I was treated. I was in quarantine for six months.' Kate paused, took hold of Meredith's hand, held it tightly, and looked into her eyes. 'I sent you messages all the time, Mari. Didn't you get any of them?'

'No.' Meredith returned her mother's intense look. 'Why didn't you come and get me when you were better?' she asked, a hint of resentment flaring. She pushed it down inside her.

'But I did! As soon as I was released from Seacroft Hospital. I was on the mend, no longer contagious, taking antibiotics. But you weren't there any more. The people at Dr Barnardo's told me you had been adopted. I was in shock. Distraught and angry. And heartbroken. I didn't know how to find you. I had no one to help me, no family, not much money. It was like battering my head against a brick wall. They just wouldn't tell me anything and there was no way I could get you back.'

Kate shook her head sorrowfully, found her handkerchief and wiped her streaming eyes. 'I was utterly powerless, helpless, Mari, and so frustrated. I've never really dispelled my anger, it's still there inside. It's gnawed at me for years. What happened ruined my life. I have never recovered from the loss of you, never really been happy, or had any peace of mind. I've always been haunted, worried about you. My only hope was that one day, when you were grown up, you might want to meet your biological mother, and that *you'd* try to find *me*.'

Meredith, who had again been moved to tears by Kate's words, exclaimed, 'But no one adopted me! They lied to you at Dr Barnardo's. They put me on a boat with a lot of other children and shipped us all to Australia. I was in an orphanage in Sydney.'

'An orphanage!' Kate was stunned. She stared at Meredith in horror as the terrible truth dawned on her. 'What kind of thinking is that? It was stupidity to send you from an orphanage in England to another one at the far side of the world. And why?' She closed her eyes for a moment, then snapped them open. 'They said you'd been adopted by a nice family, that you were living in another city in Britain. It was my only consolation . . . that you were growing up with people who cared about you, loved you, and were good to you. Now you're telling me you were never adopted.'

Kate was shaking.

Meredith soothed her, tried to calm her, then explained. 'Well, I was adopted, but in Sydney of course, not in England. When I was eight. But it was only for two years. The Strattons were killed in a car crash when I was ten. They weren't very nice people. His sister put me back in the orphanage.'

Stiffening on the sofa, grasping Meredith's hand tighter, Kate said in a fearful voice, 'The Strattons didn't hurt you in any way, did they? Abuse you?'

'No, they didn't. But they weren't very loving or kind.' Now staring at Kate in bafflement, Meredith went on, 'If you didn't give them permission to send me to Australia, then how could Dr Barnardo's do that? I mean, they did it without your consent.'

'Yes, they did.' Kate drew away slightly. 'All of a sudden, you sound as if you think I'm not telling you the truth. But I am, Mari. You must believe that.'

'It's not that I doubt you. I just don't understand this whole thing.'

'Neither do I. I've never been able to understand it. All these years it's been like living a nightmare.' Kate extricated her hand from Meredith's and stood up.

Slowly, she walked across to the desk, opened a drawer and took out a large envelope. Tapping it, she said, 'A few years ago in the late eighties, I read some articles in the *Observer*. And what I read truly frightened me, filled me with horror, not to mention sorrow. The articles were about child migrants being sent alone to Australia and put in homes and institutions. At the time I prayed that you hadn't been one of those children. I suppose I clung to the belief you were living somewhere in England with your adoptive family. Now my worst nightmare has come true.' Kate's voice faltered and she was close to tears again. 'You *were* one of those children, Mari.'

Fighting her tears, Kate paused, and then after a

moment she asked in a low voice, 'You are telling me the truth, aren't you, Mari? You weren't abused, were you?'

'I promise you I wasn't . . . I *wasn't*, Mam. I was in mental anguish, and I cried myself to sleep for years, missing you so much. It was such a loveless upbringing. And, of course, I had to work hard, we all did, scrubbing floors, doing mountains of washing. And we weren't very well fed. But no, I wasn't physically or sexually abused.'

'Just mentally and emotionally,' Kate said, anger surfacing again. 'Imagine, sending you and other little children 12,000 miles all the way across the world just to put you in another institution. It was wicked.'

Kate walked back to the sofa, sat down, still clutching the envelope. Finally she gave it to Meredith. 'The articles were called *Lost Children of the Empire*. I kept them. You can read them later. They'll make your hair stand on end.' She shook her head. 'No, of course they won't . . . you lived through it . . . lived what the journalist wrote about.'

'Why did you keep the articles?'

'I don't know. Later Granada Television made a documentary about the child migrants. I watched it with growing horror. It left its terrible imprint on me, I've never been free of it.'

'So Dr Barnardo's sent a lot of children to Australia. Hundreds. Is that what you're saying?'

'No, Mari, thousands. Over a hundred and fifty thousand, actually. Probably even more, but it wasn't just Dr Barnardo's. Many other worthy charities were involved in the child migration schemes.'

'Such as?' Meredith asked, staring at Kate questioningly.

'The Salvation Army, the National Children's Home, the Children's Society, the Fairbridge Society, and a variety of other social and welfare agencies operating under the aegis of the Catholic Church, the Church of England, the Presbyterian Church and the Church of Scotland.'

'Good God!' Meredith exclaimed, aghast. 'It was enormous.'

'I'm afraid so,' Kate answered. 'And a lot of those children, especially the boys, were made to work outside in the blistering sun, doing all manner of chores, bricklaying, building dormitories. And they were often horribly abused – sodomized by the priests. It was an horrendous life for them.'

'But *how* could it happen? I mean why didn't the government intervene?'

'The British Government weren't going to do that. They were part of it. What *they* did to us, to mothers and fathers and children, was unconscionable.'

'It was also illegal,' Meredith pointed out. 'Hasn't anyone thought of suing the British Government? I certainly feel like it . . . all those wasted years, all those years of grief.'

'I don't know whether anybody sued or not. There was a huge public outcry after the documentary was aired. It revealed an horrendous scandal. People were outraged. The government tried to deny their complicity, but everyone understood there had been collusion.'

'But why did the government do it?'

Kate said in a voice of scorn, 'What an easy way it was to populate the colonies, sending children to the far-flung corners of the empire. It's been going on for hundreds of years, and small children were still being shipped off as late as 1967.'

'How appalling. It's contemptible.'

Kate nodded and said, 'You'll see a clipping from the *TV Times* in the envelope, announcing the documentary. The magazine listed telephone numbers, help lines. I rang them up, Mari. I was so worried you might be one of those children. I wanted to know how a mother could find a child that had been sent as a migrant. The help-line people told me that wasn't possible, that a mother couldn't find a child. Apparently a parent and child could only be reunited if the child set out to find the long-lost mother or father.'

Kate leaned back against the sofa, closed her eyes for a moment. Then, looking at Meredith at last, she said, 'You grew up to be a beautiful woman, Mari. You look like my mother. You have her face, her eyes.'

Meredith was thrilled to hear this, and a vivid smile flooded her face with radiance. 'I don't remember having a grandmother.'

'She was already dead when you were born. She was killed in a bombing raid in the Second World War. It was my father who brought me up after he got out of the army. He died when I was seventeen.'

'What about my father? Where is he?'

'He's dead too, Mari. He left us when you were about eighteen months old. He went off to Canada with another woman, deserted us. I finally divorced him when Nigel wanted me to marry him.'

'Has he made you happy?'

'He's tried very hard, very hard indeed, Mari. But I haven't been easy to live with over the years. My grief for you has always consumed me to a certain extent . . . it's so hard to lose a child, especially the way I lost you. It's not as if you died. I knew you were out there somewhere. I yearned for you . . . yearned to see you, to touch you. My heart was broken. Poor Nigel, he's had a lot to contend with. But, he's patient. Long-suffering. He's a good man.'

'And you never had another child?'

'Oh no. I was thirty-eight when I married Nigel. Perhaps I should have, maybe it would have helped me, I don't know . . . Nigel was a widower, his wife had been a friend of mine. Veronica. A lovely woman. She died of a brain tumour, and I helped Nigel through that very bad period in his life. Comforted him as best I could. Five years after her death he proposed. I brought up his two sons, Michael and Andrew. And it's been a good marriage in so many ways.'

'I'm glad you've had someone nice like Nigel. I've wondered . . . how old were you when I was born?'

'Nineteen. I'll be sixty-three this summer, Mari.' Kate let out a deep sigh. 'All those years without you. How did you find me? Did it take you a long time?'

'No, not really, once I'd started looking. Before I tell you how I *did* locate you, I have another question for you.'

'Anything, Mari, ask me anything.'

'Did you ever take me to Fountains Abbey?'

'Yes, several times. It's a favourite spot of mine, always has been. Coming from Harrogate as I do, I've spent a lot of time in Ripon over the years. But why do you ask?'

'Did anything terrible or upsetting ever happen to me or to us at Fountains?'

'Yes. I started to feel unwell there in the spring of 1957. I'd taken you on a picnic, and I passed out for a while. I know you were very frightened because we were alone. Eventually I came around, and somehow we made it into Ripon and caught the bus back to Harrogate, then another one to Leeds. It was a Sunday. Later that week I was diagnosed as having TB, and I was packed off to Seacroft.'

'I never saw you again, did I?'

'No, you didn't.'

'That explains it.' Meredith recounted her experiences at Fountains, told her about her sense of *déjà vu*. 'No wonder I felt a tragic thing had happened there, had such a sense of loss. Anyway, what that experience did was create something called psychogenic fatigue in me. My physician sent me to a psychiatrist and she and I began to dig into my past. She was convinced I was suffering from repressed memory.'

'You mean you repressed your memories of me?'

'No, not exactly. I did remember certain things. But being torn away from you so cruelly, wrenched away from your love and care as a child was so painful to me I'd blocked everything out. Doctor Benson managed to get me on the right track, but it was my daughter Catherine who triggered the most important memory, at least so *I* think.'

'You have a daughter and you named her for me?' Kate exclaimed, her face lighting up.

'She's twenty-five and beautiful. She has your eyes. And I think your disposition. I didn't actually know I was naming her after you . . . I spelled her name with a C. But obviously I'd remembered your name was Kate . . . Katharine. It was buried in my subconscious.'

'What was the memory she triggered?'

'Just before I left for London last week I went to see her, to discuss plans for her marriage. She made tea, later brought out a dish of strawberries, and she said something to me that brought a memory rushing back. I saw your face very clearly, that face I'd loved all of my life and longed for. And I just knew it was my mother's face I was seeing in my mind.' Meredith had begun to weep; she searched for her handkerchief, blew her nose.

Kate's eyes were moist when she asked, 'What was it Catherine said?'

'Just a few simple words actually . . . "I have a treat for you, Mom. *Strawberries.*" Instantly your face was before my eyes and *you* were serving me strawberries. At that moment a variety of other memories came back to me, and I had many more on the plane coming over to London that same night.'

Meredith paused, blew her nose again, and continued, 'There's something I should explain to you. I'd always believed you were dead. That's what they told me at Dr Barnardo's. So when the memory of you had fully returned, I confided in my English partner, Patsy Canton. She took me to the General Register Office in London to look for your death certificate. You see, I wanted, *needed*, to visit your grave. I wanted closure for myself at long last. But of course there was no certificate; we knew you must be alive. It was Patsy's idea to look for my birth certificate, since we were seeking as much information as we could. My birth certificate led us to Armley and Hawthorne Cottage. Although it's now a pile of rubble, I did discover how well I knew that spot, and more lovely recollections of you surfaced.'

'I'm glad you found me before it was too late,' Kate murmured.

'So am I.'

Now Kate glanced at Meredith curiously and said softly, 'You don't wear a wedding ring. Are you divorced?'

'Yes, I am. You have a grandson, by the way. His name is Jon and he's twenty-one. He's studying at Yale. I can't wait for you to meet him and Catherine.'

'*Grandchildren*,' Kate said wonderingly. 'I have grandchildren. How wonderful.'

'I'm very proud of them. They've turned out well.'

'The one thing you haven't told me is how you got from Australia to America.'

'That's a very long story,' Meredith responded. 'I'll explain everything later. After all, we've got the rest of our lives.'

There was the sound of footsteps in the hall, and Meredith swung her head. She saw a tall, distinguished-looking man standing in the doorway observing them.

Kate had also turned around. She jumped up, exclaiming, 'Nigel, she's found me. Like I always prayed she would. My Mari's found me. She's home to me at last.'

'Thank God,' he said, walking into the sitting room to join them, a look of immense relief spreading across his face.

Meredith rose, stretched out her hand to him.

He took it. And without any kind of preamble he pulled her into his arms and embraced her. 'Now, at last, Kate will have peace of mind,' he said.

As they drew apart Meredith found herself looking into one of the kindest faces she had ever seen.

Nigel Grainger's smile was warm as he gazed at her.

'Thank you,' she said. 'Thank you for keeping my mother safe for me.'

EPILOGUE

Time Future

Twenty-five

'Now ladies, look right at me and smile,' Jon said, picking up his camera, peering into the lens. 'Not quite right,' he muttered. 'Mom, move in closer to Grandma. And Cat, you do the same thing. I want to get a really tight shot.'

'Oh do hurry up, Jon, I want to go and find my lovely new husband!' Cat exclaimed.

After a few minor adjustments, Jon finally began to shoot the roll of film. Within minutes he was exclaiming, 'There, all finished, and it wasn't so bad, Cat, was it? Now I have a lovely set of shots for Grandma's album, and for you if you want them. *Three generations of women.* I never dreamed I'd see that day.'

Cat offered him a loving smile. 'I just know I'm going to like yours better than the professional photographer's pictures.'

Grinning, he said, 'Go on, scoot. Find that new husband of yours. In a few minutes there's going to be chaos here, once the Pearson clan start swarming all over like locusts.'

'Hey, watch what you say,' Cat cried, waving her hand at him, displaying her wedding ring. '*I* just became a Pearson, remember.' Walking over, she kissed him on the cheek and said affectionately, 'Thank you for giving me away, Jon.'

'Did I do okay, Sis?'

'You were terrific.' She laughed again and floated off on a cloud of white silk and tulle, heading towards Keith, who stood talking to his father in the entrance hall of the inn.

Jon strolled over to Kate and Meredith. He said, 'It was a great ceremony, Mom, and the old barn was really effective as a church. I guess it was the way you decorated it with all that white silk and the banks of white flowers.'

'Thanks, darling. I was pleased myself with the way it turned out.'

Kate murmured, 'I found the ceremony very moving.' She smiled at her daughter and grandson. 'I must admit, I cried.'

'Most women do cry at weddings, Grandma.' Jon squeezed her arm. 'And you're the icing on the cake. I'm so glad Mom found you.'

'Oh, so am I,' Kate answered.

'Well, I'm off to have a drink with the guys,' Jon announced, edging away.

'Guys?' Meredith repeated, raising a brow. 'Who do you mean?'

'Luc and Nigel. They just came in.'

He strolled off, leaving Meredith and Kate near the entrance to the inn's dining room.

Both women looked elegant; Kate was dressed in a dark rose-pink wool suit and Meredith in a smoky blue dress and coat; standing close together as they were, it was easy to see they were mother and daughter. They bore a strong resemblance to each other, although Meredith was taller.

It was the second Saturday in October, a lovely Indian-summer day. The sky was cerulean blue, clear and cloudless, filled with brilliant sunshine, and the foliage at Silver Lake was spectacular. The trees had just turned, were a riotous mass of reds and pinks, russets and golds.

'We couldn't have asked for a better day,' Kate said, glancing out of the window, looking down towards the lake. 'It's perfect for the wedding.'

'We've been lucky, although Connecticut usually is lovely in October.' Taking hold of Kate's arm, Meredith ushered her into the dining room, recently enlarged to accommodate the many guests attending the wedding today. 'Just come in here for a moment, Mother, I want to say something to you.'

Kate threw Meredith a concerned look. 'Is there something wrong? You sound so serious.'

Meredith shook her head. 'No, I just wanted to thank you for being here with me these past two weeks, and for doing so much to help with Cat's wedding. You've been wonderful.'

'I should be thanking you, Mari,' Kate replied and smiled. 'I'll never be able to call you anything else but Mari, you know.'

'That's all right . . . I understand.'

'I never thought this would happen,' Kate suddenly volunteered. 'That I'd be able to spend this precious time with you. You'll never know what it's meant to me.'

'Oh but I think I *do* . . .'

'You've spoilt me, Mari, and Nigel. The trips to Paris and the Loire, as well as New York. All this wonderful travelling – why we'd hardly been out of Yorkshire until you came back into my life.'

Meredith made no comment, she simply touched her mother's arm affectionately. There were moments when she couldn't quite believe that she had found her mother after all these years.

Kate glanced out of the window again, her face thoughtful when she finally turned back to Meredith. 'I'm glad you found your way here to Silver Lake those many years ago. It's such a beautiful spot, so like Yorkshire. You must have had a guardian angel watching over you.'

'Perhaps I did.'

'Yes, you were lucky to find Amelia and Jack, to have them in your life, if only for those few brief years. They made up for your earlier heartbreak, Mari, that loveless upbringing at the orphanage in Australia. You had love and kindness and caring from them, and I will be forever thankful for that. They helped to make you what you are today.'

'Who knows what I would have been like, if I hadn't met them. A terrible mess, probably.'

'Maybe not, we'll never know. But I think there's something special in *you* . . . a will to endure, to succeed, no matter what.'

Meredith leaned into Kate, kissed her on the cheek. 'I love you, Mother.'

'And I love you too, Mari.'

The two women walked back through the dining room, their arms linked. Just before they reached the door, Kate said, 'It's going to be wrenching, leaving you. I wish I didn't live so far away.'

Meredith was silent.

Kate looked at her swiftly, and added, 'I know you said I can visit any time. But I can't very well keep leaving Nigel alone. And he can't always come with me, Mari, because of his practice.'

Meredith said, 'As it turns out, I'm not going to be so far away after all.'

'Oh.'

Meredith peered across the entrance hall of the inn, now crowded with people. The reception was in full swing. A small smile flitted across her mouth.

Kate noticed this, followed the direction of her daughter's gaze, then looked back to Meredith.

'I'm going to marry him, Mother,' Meredith said, her gaze still resting on Luc. 'And so I'll be living in Paris. Only a couple of hours from Yorkshire.'

'Oh darling, I'm so happy for you. Congratulations!' Kate exclaimed. There was a brief pause before she said worriedly, 'But what about your business here? It means so much to you.'

'There's only Silver Lake Inn left, now that I've sold the one in Vermont. Blanche and Pete have been running this place for years, and doing such a good job of it. They'll continue. I've enough to keep me busy with the inns in England and France.'

'It's good that you've been able to work it out. Luc's such a wonderful man.'

'He's had his share of heartbreak, too. I think we both deserve a bit of happiness . . .' Meredith broke off as Luc walked over to join them.

Putting his arm around Kate, he looked down at her and said, 'Ever since we met in June I had a feeling I knew you, Kate. Suddenly, a moment ago, I realized why. You remind me of the woman who brought me up, my grandmother.'

Grandma Rose, of course, Meredith thought, recalling the painting at Talcy. They had the same colouring, the same blue eyes, the same heart-shaped face.

'How lovely,' Kate murmured. 'I understand congratulations are in order. I'm so happy the two of you are getting married.'

Luc beamed at her. 'Ah, so Meredith told you the good news.'

Kate nodded, excused herself, wanting to leave them alone. She walked across the room lightly, as if floating on air, went in search of her husband. She was so happy, so proud. Who would have thought that her little Mari would turn out to be such a remarkable woman?

Luc took hold of Meredith's hand, stared deeply into her smoky green eyes. 'You know, *chérie*, you look so very serene today. It lifts my heart to see you so happy. From the moment I met you, I wanted to erase the sadness from your eyes, dispel the pain I knew lurked deep within you. But now I don't have to . . . I believe finding your mother has done that.'

Meredith did not answer for a moment or two. She simply returned his penetrating gaze; then finally she said, 'It was finding *both* of you, Luc. You and she make me feel complete, whole.'

Luc smiled at her. 'That's because we love you.'

He tucked her arm through his, and together they moved forward into the throng of wedding guests.